I0772333

I

SHADOW BOUND SERIES
BOUND *by* FAITH

MOONS AND SHADOWS

M.D. PETROCCO

Moons and Shadows

Shadow Bound Series
Book 1

M. D. Petrocco

Weaver of Worlds Publishing, LLC

Illustrations and graphics by pbj creative studios, Kelly Pernell

Editing by Brandi Crowe

First print edition July 2025

First eBook edition July 2025

Revised edition November 2025

www.theshadowboundseries.com

Sign up for updates with M.D. Petrocco

Join the Discord: Click Here

 Formatted with Vellum

To My Dearest Reader,

This could change your life if you allow it to do so. The gifts provided within these pages offer something priceless: time.

Time to breathe, time to think, and time to sit within a circle of those who love you dearly and want the best for every bit of your life.

What I can tell you is this: when life happens, it doesn't come with trigger warnings or a manual on how to respond and function effectively. That is what time is for. That is what this story will give you: time.

I promise you, if you choose to join me on this path, it will change your life. Time did that for me, and I pray it does the same for you.

As you turn these pages, remember—what you choose to do with this story—my story, your story, our story—is entirely up to you. Picking up this book was the first step. The next belongs to you. How these words settle in you will be different from anyone else. What they stir, what they shift—that's yours alone. And whatever they become will shape the path ahead.

So take your time. Pause. Breathe. Reread if you need to. This is a path you've chosen. And it will become yours with every step.

If you need me, my dearest reader, know that I am here. You do not have to feel alone in this world any longer; you never were alone.

Pull up a chair or plop down on our couch, and join me as I share my path with you—the good, the bad, and a bit of the ugly. It's simply about my life, and I only pray you will stick with me till the end.

All my love forever more,

Runa

Join the Moonlighters Discord!

Hosted by author M.D. Petrocco's amazing Moonlighters team.

◇ Spoiler-safe chapter-by-chapter discussion
◇ Behind-the-scenes content
◇ Links to live chats and exclusive sneak peeks
◇ A place to return to—again and again

Step through the moongate.
We've been waiting for you.

https://discord.gg/jKcD7uqfB3

Contents

The Lands
Valley of Visions
Sanctuary
Starlight Beach
Shadow City
Training Center & Base
The Dark Forest
Treefall Lagoon
Shadow City

Prologue

Present Day

Izayah leaned against the balcony's edge, forearms draped over the banister, drink of choice in hand—whiskey on the rocks. Simple in appearance, complex in depth.

Look at her go.

His eyes glinted as he watched Runa dart through the forest clearing, her laughter mingling with the delighted shouts of Zane's children. He hadn't seen her in what felt like eons. Despite that, she still stole the very breath from his lungs. His fingers tensed against the cool glass in his grip, something tightening deep in his chest.

He had left. Abruptly. Choosing duty, choosing the Shadow Guard. A swift climb through the ranks, landing him an Elite standing in the Guard. If he was being honest, leaving had been worth it. *Zane had been right. He always was.*

And yet, when he saw her like this, the certainty of his choices wavered. His gaze drifted, distant, as he swirled the amber liquid, sinking into quiet reflection. The weariness in his features spoke volumes—a silent testament to relentless trials. Grueling days spent pushing past his limits. Nights wrestling with unseen battles that carved themselves deep into his soul.

Pressing the glass to his temple, he savored the slow, rhythmic glide of its cool surface, easing the tension in his furrowed brow.

And yet, the tempered burdens remained, ever present beneath his stoic facade. He exhaled—a quiet surrender—but regret still clung to him, a weight neither dulled nor diminished—unyielding, unwavering, unforgiving.

In all transparency, she softened him in ways he never thought possible—turning something untamed into something wholly his own. The man, not just the beast. A truth only sharpened by distance, time, and reflection.

With a slow breath, he let his face sink into the butt of his palm, chasing a moment of relief, however brief.

He stood in this space, stronger and more resilient than ever.

Basic training and countless deployments had tried to break him, to strip him of everything he was. The guard had been brutal, but no more than his upbringing. He had long since learned to endure—his father's constant disapproval, relentless criticism, and punishments that left more than just bruises.

At least in the Shadow Units, he'd carved his own path—proving to himself that he was more than capable. Rising through the ranks to the Elite Guard, he had done it by his own merit, on his own authority.

Lord Brannon, his father, the iron-fisted leader of Shadow City, had made it clear from the start: "The Shadow Guard will make you formidable." He spoke it like gospel; it was a commandment from the man who believed he knew best. Every hardship was a test, every bruise a lesson, every drop of sweat a step toward the greatness he insisted they achieve.

The rigorous trials had been countless, replacing the carefree joys of youth, designed to mold them into Elite fighters. As Izayah reminisced, he recalled Lord Brannon's unyielding belief in this harsh training—it wasn't exactly the kind of life meant for younglings.

Yet now, as he stood, perched on the sturdy wooden planks of the balcony, he wrestled with the confusion.

The disapproval had always been there. No matter how much he achieved, Izayah was the one who could never seem to get it right.

I've faced every challenge—from basic training to the Elite Guard's trials.

Now, I'm even being considered for General of the Shadow Guard Guild. So why is he still unhappy with the path I've chosen?

His father's words echoed in his mind, laced with the same disapproval, mingling with the bitterness of feeling undervalued despite surpassing expectations.

Isn't this what he wanted? Izayah questioned silently.

He carried the weight of a respected family name—if you could even call it that. *Feared* was far more accurate. Lord Brannon wasn't someone you crossed without repercussions.

The truth was, he could have ridden his father's coattails to achieve his current rank. But he refused. He built his own foundation. Held ground on his own merit. Earned it by his own hand.

One day, he would walk the halls as General of the Elite Guild, head held high. The Guild commanded both the Shadow Guard and the Shadow Elite. Without doubt, he had earned that rank through sheer skill and unwavering discipline.

So he endured. The rigorous conditioning, the grueling tests, the endless hours. He had earned his place through relentless effort and iron will—not privilege.

Upon his elevation into the Shadow Elite, he cemented his resolve to live at the heart of battle strategy, protecting the citizens of Shadow City and its outlying territories.

Everything up to this point had left its mark, the weight of it settling deep. *Every step, every decision—* all of it had led him to one goal: to become General. *The one thing I can control.*

Starting from scratch. No shortcuts, no favors. I earned my stripes in the Shadow Guard. Clawed my way into the Elite. The title isn't the goal; it's proving I deserve it. Every brutal step, every time my name got in the way—it's about carving out this path myself. To earn such an achievement and gain favor within the Guard, I had to make sure I was credited for every accomplishment based on my actions, not my birthright.

That's why I sacrifice these moments, he reminded himself. *Doing the hard work would earn their respect, so when the time comes, they'll follow my orders without hesitation. Walking in their shoes, understanding their sacrifices—there was no other way. I couldn't achieve that by leveraging the family name. There's no honor in that.*

Yet, as he stood here now, doubt still lingered like an unwelcome shadow. He appreciated Daxler—his elite brother and future second-in-command—who kept insisting there was no way Izayah could have known what the Seer had foretold.

Unmuted confidence stirred from the depth where doubt usually lurked, rising like a tide.

Powerful and calm, as if strength and serenity could somehow coexist. It felt strange, yet undeniably real, this new sense of self that anchored him in the present moment. Balance had always been useless to him—unpredictable, fleeting.

He shut his eyes, letting the silence settle around him. *Just breathe*, he thought. *Let night conceal these notions, let stars dance, and grant moonlight authority to guide us through this encroaching darkness.*

Right then, he knew—*everything was about to change.*

Breathe, damn it!

Let go, the moon seemed to whisper, her voice soft against the approaching twilight. Izayah felt the familiar warmth of her advancing presence—a quiet affection for this celestial companion who had watched over him through countless moments of solitude. Always there. Always listening. Steady in a life that had never paused. A silent friend who understood without words. *She's seen every side of me,* he mused. *Through every phase, every shadow.* Even when he felt fractured, she reminded him, he was never truly alone…never less than whole.

"Fuckin' breathe, you bastard," he muttered. Irritation crawled up his spine, an unwelcome burn. He jerked his head back, trying to rid himself of the tension that clung to him. *Focus.* He thought back to last night. The chill had wrapped around him, thick and steady, when he'd insisted on taking that extra duty—*not* something someone in his position usually did, not at his rank. *The shitstorm would come. It always did.* But he wouldn't be there this time, not for reprimand. Last night, all he craved was stillness—stillness and the night air, the space to clear his thoughts, to fully grasp the weight of his decision.

Relentless as ever, the Demon of Doubt slipped back in—circling, clawing, trying to take up residence. *Damn insidious beast.*

This decision…my decision…did I really have a choice?

He let out a low, ragged breath—a growl, a huff, something caught between frustration and acceptance. *She's going to kill me for this. And yet... the mission moves forward.*

Izayah's remembrance returned to the moon of the previous night, its light soothing against the darkness, whispering, *Let go.* That presence had felt familiar, like a steady hand resting on his shoulder. *You're here for reasons beyond what's visible right now, Sir.* The words resonated deep, carrying a reassurance that felt tangible.

Now, in the daylight, his spine straightened, aligning with a renewed sense of purpose, his stance exuding a quiet command. *Patience,* he told himself. *Hold steady. Wait, observe, and be prepared to adjust when the time comes.*

He inhaled the rich scent of cedar drifting from the forest floor, letting it ground him. *This was the path forward.* The only path he could see.

His deep brown eyes, flecked with gold, eased as they found her again in the distance. The hushed calm returned, anchoring itself within him, pushing out the demons of doubt and reclaiming his confidence. Assured by certainty forged through years of experience.

Runa was the soft glow in his life, a captivating presence that hollowed him with wonder, like the night sky. *She's always been there, hasn't she?* he considered. *My guiding light...my north star, even when distance kept us apart.* He had always understood the moon, but now, he understood why. "You became my moon, Ru," he whispered.

Like a force of nature, understanding surged through him. *She's everything I've yearned for but could never grasp—a celestial being, forever just beyond my reach.*

That smile, that laughter...they grounded his soul in ways he never knew he needed. *I found solace in her, a lifeline against uncertainties.* Their bond, unspoken yet undeniable—held him in place, tethering him to this world. Even now, with her unaware of his presence, he felt their connection pressing in, filling, consuming, and pulling him deeper into an eternal longing.

Does she even realize? he wondered. *All that she's capable of?* The Seer's revelations had altered everything—reshaping his understanding of their world before, and of Runa now. *From this vantage point, she must have learned to disconnect—to put distance between herself and her experiences. That's how she survived.*

A strained breath bridged the notions, like planks of certainty hammered into place. *And yet, I had left. My absence made everything worse for her.* The thought struck hard, each word driving deeper, the weight pressing in like nails sinking into wood—cold, final, unyielding. It sounded crazy, but he believed it.

Because the Seer had said it. And the Seer's words never came loose.

Yet, there she was—finding freedom in the simplest moments, laughing with his brother's girls and Tabytha, Zane's tethered companion. His brow furrowed as he took a measured intake of oxygen, assessing, reflecting. The information given to him before he left so abruptly now felt like fragments of a broken puzzle—pieces forced into place that didn't belong.

A low growl rumbled from his throat, frustration bubbling. Doubt crept back up, "Fuckin' damn demon," he whispered, recognizing its familiar taunt: *You should never have left. How fuckin' selfish were you?* The ideas gnawed at him. *How could I have overlooked so much? I never responded to Runa's letters. How could I? Where would I even start?*

He had pored over each word, again and again, revisiting every sentence, letting it pull at the very threads of his being. But then Sienna— the Seer, Daxler's mother—had stepped into his office just three days prior and unraveled everything. The weight of her words still pressed down on him, a sickness curdling in his stomach.

As he watched Runa now, nothing mattered more than her safety. *The letters…they had held so much, and I'd been blind to it until the prophecy. Were they really the answer?* he wondered. *Together—had they always been the solution?* He withdrew his hand from the back of his neck, running his fingers along his jaw. *There has to be more,* he reflected, feeling a glimmer of hope flicker within him—tentative but persistent.

A faint smile tugged at the corners of his lips, a trace of darkness clinging to it before dissolving into something deeper—calm intensity simmering just beneath the surface. *Well, if we are the key to it all,* he mused. *Wouldn't that be a kick in the nuts?*

Puffing out an audible sigh, he barely had a moment to sit with the thought as Daxler came up beside him, knocking their elbows together—a firm, familiar gesture, an unspoken certainty exchanged without words.

"That's her, Zay?" Daxler nodded toward the meadow nestled within the tree line. "Petite thing, isn't she?" He leaned back, one hand cradling his gin and tonic, the other gripping the railing.

A smirk pulled at his lips as he released a low chuckle, his attention drifting to his elite brother. "So...what's the plan? Make her an offer she can't refuse, or just steal her out from under me?"

Daxler's grin stretched wider as he rolled his neck, throwing in a lazy shrug. "A snail has a better chance than you. First, I need to confirm if she truly lives up to your claims. Got any pointers before I make my move?"

"Just don't trip over your own feet." Izayah grinned.

Daxler flung his hand to his chest, gasping. "How could you say such things?"

Izayah chuckled again, shaking his head at the absurdity. If provocation was an art, he'd mastered it—just to see what would unfold. *But that's Daxler...the one who keeps me from drifting too far gone, even when I'd rather stay there.*

He had always been this way—the solid, unshakable force Izayah had met decades ago at the Shadow Guard training facility, always stirring up an unwanted debate. Unlike his older brother, Zane, Daxler had a knack for cutting through tension, knowing exactly how to lighten the mood.

When Daxler arrived at the training center, Izayah felt the undercurrent of something reshaping—an unspoken awareness, as if fate itself had just altered its course. It sank deep, carving raw truth into the very marrow of his bones. The moment felt strategic, as if fate had methodically mapped out their paths, tightening and binding them together. Strangely exhausting, yet undeniably "fuckin' true," as Daxler would say.

Born into royalty...that was supposed to mean something, he mused. *Privilege. Power. Expectations.* His title was his birthright—a golden chain binding him to the kingdom of Shadow City. Yet, it remained just that—a chain, tethering him to an unchosen fate. He needed more than the castle's narrow halls and its suffocating expectations. So he chose the Shadow Guard—chose to break free, leaving his older brother, Zane, to bear the weight of the kingdom. At least Zane could handle it without the looming threat of retaliation. In their world, having two males in the family didn't guarantee peaceful succession. Often, it meant a fight for the crown—sometimes to the death. Izayah had no interest in such a battle.

Disbelief. Resistance. The reactions had been predictable, with his father,

Lord Brannon, being the most vocal in his disapproval. But Izayah had been determined to carve his own path, to prove he was more than just his title. He craved the harshness, the relentless rigor of the Shadowed Elite. It had driven him beyond every known threshold—pushed him to the razor's edge—and he'd almost savored it, though he'd never confess that to anyone. Strange, how something so brutal could feel so damn close to perfection.

And then there was Daxler. The small-town guy. A simple man from rolling hills and open fields, yearning for more than the peaceful Valley of Visions. *Just a blacksmithing apprentice with a hunger for adventure...service beyond the forge.*

Their worlds had collided in a brutal exercise, deep in the shadowed corners of the training grounds. Gasping, muscles burning in the frigid night air, they had exchanged a single glance—one that spoke louder than any words. *We don't belong here. Not like this. But here we are, side by side.*

Opposites, that's all they were. Izayah, the prince accustomed to luxury, and Daxler, the grounded boy from the valley. The Elite Guild had intended to test them, to break them apart before they could even begin. Every challenge had been designed to expose their differences, reveal weaknesses, and sabotage any chance of success. Yet, rather than dividing them, each trial forged their bond into something unbreakable.

Nobility encountered modesty, privilege collided with perseverance as weeks passed. Izayah often marveled at Daxler's quiet determination, reflecting on how effortlessly his friend confronted challenges head-on. Nobility met grit, prestige faced persistence. In the early days of their friendship, Daxler had frequently remarked on Izayah's surprising resilience and adaptability, clearly expecting less from someone of his privileged background. Yet Izayah had his own quiet revelations, too—discovering in Daxler an unwavering strength he deeply respected.

Those evenings by the campfire—the faces barely illuminated by dying embers, never truly at ease, always waiting. Waiting for orders, for the enemy, for whatever came next. Nights when silence was broken only by boots shuffling in dirt or knives scraping across wood.

Those nights wove us together in a way training drills never could. I realized it then, felt it deep in my bones. How could we not bond beneath those unforgiving stars, intaking the same bitter air, with nothing but a dying fire shielding us from uncertainty? Out there, weakness wasn't an option. It never had been.

In the moments of unsettling silence, when the darkness pressed in on all sides, they had learned the necessity of trust—trust that was unspoken, but vital. *Trust*— is what it came down to. It wasn't stories or dreams that forged their bonds; it was the waiting. *Holding the line. Keeping watch. Knowing someone had your six when everything went to hell. That waiting had laid the foundation for everything solid in my life, everything real. Everything worth protecting—right here, right now.*

Didn't see that coming either. And Daxler, yeah, he's a fucking pain in my ass, yet here he is still willing to give me hell, no matter how high I climb. While others hesitate, Daxler holds position, never afraid to call bullshit. I hadn't known I needed someone who could look past rank and title—someone to remind me I'm just a male trying to do right. Daxler never wavered from who he was—a steadying force, sharpening my resolve, pushing me to uncover the parts of myself I'd overlooked.

Then there was Zane, the blood-tied anchor who held me steady. After losing Ma, it was Zane who provided the firm guidance and stability I desperately needed as a youngling—keeping me mission-focused, disciplined, and clear-eyed. He taught me early on what deserved my fight and what required my restraint. His clarity shaped who I became, grounding me firmly when everything else threatened chaos.

But there were things even Zane couldn't touch, couldn't understand. *Secrets buried deeper than blood—truths I've kept hidden, even from him.*

That's where Daxler came in—the one who saw through my defenses and dared to call me out. He shared the same values, the same loyalty to the city and its people. But unlike Zane, Daxler had a knack for spotting the cracks I tried to hide. Two sides of the same coin, Izayah reflected. *Zane keeps me on course, while Daxler keeps me honest.* Together, they formed a balance, one that kept him steady, kept him sane.

And for a male like Izayah, who walked the line between light and shadow, balance was critical. Yet without Runa, sustaining that balance had grown harder, increasingly elusive. *Balance—hell, it barely made sense without her.* But when Runa's letters began arriving, each one revealed something new, something he could build upon. *Her words inspired my evolution, guiding me toward a strength I hadn't realized was missing. She had taught me what balance truly meant—not tactically, but personally, profoundly. How others became the counterweight to my center, stabilizing me in ways strategy alone never could.*

Daxler watched as Izayah's focus returned to the present, the faraway look slowly fading from his eyes. *He doesn't drift like that often,* Daxler thought. *Only when he knows the squad around him has his back. Growing up around the Shadow Guards must have drilled that into him—never drop your guard unless you trust every last soul in the room. The fact that Izayah's letting himself relax right now speaks volumes. The man carries a heavier load than anyone else I know, always anticipating, always keeping his eyes open and ready.*

"You're thinking about her again, aren't you?" Daxler teased, catching the shift in Izayah's expression—the softening of his gaze, the faint smile when Runa's long black hair caught the sunlight. Strands of hazelnut glimmered with every movement as she spun, carefree and laughing. *Still the same girl she's always been. Or so Izayah had thought. But that was it. He had been wrong. He'd missed something vital.* Daxler realized. *Maybe Runa isn't the same girl he remembers after all.*

Since meeting Izayah, Daxler had noticed how he buried himself deeper into the relentless demands of the Elite Guard, always aiming for higher ranks. *I respect him for it, always have, always will. But I've always sensed there was something beyond duty that fuels him, something deeper. She has to be the reason he was beating the shit out of himself; but if that were true, why did he leave?* Pressing his forearms into the weathered wood he cleared his throat, bumping a shoulder and treading lightly. "She's your driving force, isn't she?"

Izayah nodded in agreement.

Always has been, Daxler reflected, confirming what he'd long suspected. If there ever was a good time to figure out what's really going on in there, it's now, he decided, clapping a firm hand down on his elite brother's shoulder.

As soon as he touched down, it hit Daxler—the crushing loneliness, an emptiness gnawing at the edges, the kind only Runa's presence could ease.

Her absence didn't simply mute existence; it created a void, a consuming silence.

Daxler's smile withered as a wave of nausea welled up inside him. "This is the downside of being able to filter into your thoughts, Zay," he muttered. They were bound in that moment; the sickness churning in the pit of their shared stomachs. It wasn't merely the realization that strategy had pivoted three days prior—Daxler was now fully immersed in Izayah's internal awareness, absorbing every consequence, standing not just shoulder-to-shoulder with his elite brother but squarely in his boots.

A deep anger swelled within them, like thunderous clouds massing on the horizon. Yesterday, the Shadow Guild, the overarching command of both the Shadow Guard, and the Elite Shadow Guard, were scheduled to escort Izayah to meet Lord Brannon, to receive an honor earned by merit, not birthright.

Entering into full immersion, Daxler found himself within Izayah's consciousness, experiencing the scene as if he were living it himself—navigating shadowed halls, surrounded by laughter and the subtle clink of glasses. He could feel the brush of full military regalia against his skin, sense the polite smiles and shallow conversations with High Lords and Ladies. The young females' eyes burned bright with hope and curiosity, fluttering toward him like moths drawn to flame—each gaze offering a subtle invitation for courtship.

Beneath it all, that familiar ache lingered. Daxler could feel Izayah's heart pulling away, distant, withdrawn. He knew what Izayah had been thinking: *No matter how they look at me, or how they laugh and lean in close, none of them will ever be her. None of them will ever compare to Runa.*

Always searching, always longing for what he couldn't have, Daxler thought, feeling the sharp twist of resignation and frustration as if it were his own.

*If everything had gone as planned…*Izayah's thoughts reverberated like a distant voice drifting through a vast hall. *Today, I would have been named General of the Shadowed Guild. Daxler, slated to assume his position as Lieutenant General.*

We should be celebrating, shouldn't we? Izayah's mind twisted like a labyrinth, restless energy flickering between fractured glimpses of the base, the nearby town, and the hum of preparations that should have already been underway. Within the vast expanse of his mental projection, the grand celebration loomed—a tribute to their rise within the clandestine ranks of the Shadow Elite, marking their advancement under the powerful umbrella of the Guard Guild.

But instead, here Daxler fell into retracing Izayah's steps—tracking through the base's winding corridors, hewn from stone, the Seer by their side, a figure as familiar as she was haunting. His past self walked beside the two, unaware of the moment, as each boot fall echoed, thunderous. Now, through Izayah's eyes, memories flickered along the chiseled passageways like shards of shattered glass catching sunlight, offering glimpses into a world warped by haunting revelation. *I should've seen this coming…*Izayah's thoughts splintered like barbed blades—jagged, unrelenting. *Three days ago, everything changed. And it should've changed sooner. That's on me. Fuck. The signs were right there. I wasn't blind—I was too busy staring at my own goddamn shadow to see them. Too caught up in the past. Damn fuckin' idiot.*

The weight of words settled heavily in their shared space. Daxler felt the instinctive response as Sienna, the Seer, entered Izayah's office, the tension thick and unspoken. *Why can't I speak?* The question hovered like smoke. Sienna had kept Izayah silent, her presence commanding, her quintessence undeniable.

From Izayah's perspective, her voice was sweet like honey, yet every word dragged like a chain grinding over his nerves. He fought the impulse —to reach out, to take her hand, to kiss her fingers in reverence. But she glided away, as if tugged forward, drawn to the bookshelf. Without hesitation, Sienna pressed the letters to her forehead, as if absorbing their essence.

The moment Sienna rested the script to her brow, something tore through Izayah's mind—not a vision, but a searing impact, an unshakable imprint burning into his thoughts. It struck like hot coals pressed against the backsides of his eyes, raw and unrelenting. Each tear that fell from Sienna's eyes shimmered like blood-forged crystal, reflecting truths so profound it shattered every strategy, every plan.

And then, nothing was the same; just like that. Izayah's instincts surged, yanking Daxler along. The room's atmosphere tilted, urgency thickening the space. *Her revelation struck,* and Izayah's whirlwind of shadowed currents screamed back at them both. *It changed everything.*

Immediacy surged through their bond, a battlefield of controlled chaos and rapid-fire decisions between them. Daxler felt the commands solidifying—clear, direct, as if relayed just over his shoulder. *No time for celebration. The mission takes precedence.*

The ache swelled—the relentless drive that kept his brother moving. It had to be enough. Turbulent reflections surged through their shared link, raw and untempered. *I did this. I pushed her away. This is on me.*

Here they stood, two stoic figures amid the impending chaos of his superior's reality—knee-deep, drowning in classified intelligence. The Shadow Elite carried a relentless and deadly hallmark, a creed that meant when orders were issued and authorized, each guard was bound by faith. Guards were determined, handpicked, and briefed. Mission-focused, executing strategies known only to those willing to shoulder the crushing burden of success.

From the balcony's edge, to outsiders, it appeared the pair were merely enjoying a temporary respite before the grand celebration. But beneath Izayah's calm facade, a simmering fury burned—silent, unrelenting, a resolve to set things right.

That resolve surged forward, whipping through the carved hallways, yanking Daxler back into the vast expanse—the continuum of Izayah's reflection—only to be dragged once more into the stone-walled cave of his deep-set office within the base's cliffside. The marble floors stretched beneath him, the cold walls looming like sentinels, a stark reminder of the conversation three days prior.

Their collective vision gravitated toward the nearby shelf, where a basket rested; its contents spilling out, revealing a tangled cluster of letters bound with a weathered ribbon—the ones imprinted with Sienna's fingerprints, still smeared in red. The sight unleashed a flood of emotions, like a bonfire caught in a gust. Her pain, unearthed and scribed in blood—a truth revealed only to those willing to see.

A crashing wave of remorse surged in, slamming through the door, as years of neglected fury rose, choking the air from their lungs. *Daxler…* Izayah's ruminations were like a hushed plea, desperate and raw. *I needed you here on this balcony to see her, to feel this.* The void within grappled with the uncertainty of how to respond to Runa's written words.

Daxler's body tensed, reacting to the palpable unease that rippled through the colosseum of their shared headspace. *Runa is my lifeline. If she dies, I die…*his admission rang out, reverberating off the walls. *She's my anchor, my guiding light in the darkness, even if she doesn't know it. I can't afford to let her down again. I can't lose…everything.*

Daxler pulled his hand from his brother's shoulder, leaning back against the balcony. His chest tightened under the pressure of what lay ahead. His fingers tapped a steady, determined rhythm on the railing as he stared into the distance, fully grasping the weight of the task before them.

"Fuckin'—shit, man. That's your daily routine? You seriously need a hobby."

Izayah exhaled audibly, adjusting his posture to manage the simmering anger beneath the surface. "Yeah…24/7–," he muttered, setting aside thoughts of certain individuals he'd rather deal with sooner than later. "But you know, I can't just…let go. Not yet."

Daxler swirled his gin and tonic, the ice clinking softly against the glass. "Not yet," he echoed, a grin tugging at his lips. "It's *always* 'not yet' with you, Zay." He downed the rest of his drink in one swift gulp, then slapped Izayah on the back with a firm hand. "You're gonna give yourself a stroke before you make General if you don't loosen up."

Izayah let out a half-chuckle, half-sigh. "Loosen up? When have you ever seen me loose?"

Daxler leaned back, tilting his head with a grin. "Point taken." He let out a hearty laugh. "But seriously, you need space to think. So, when all is said and done, we're dragging your ass back to this cabin. A little decompression never killed anyone." He chuckled again. "Well, unless you count that time with the boar, but that's a different situation entirely."

A flicker of a smile crossed Izayah's face. "Yeah, if it's still here." His gaze hardened.

Daxler noticed the tightness around Izayah's eyes, that raw edge he rarely let anyone see. He took another breath and placed his heavily tattooed forearms on the balcony rail, the ice in his empty glass gently clinking. "I know, man. I know," he said softly. "But if you keep carrying all this weight, you're gonna sink. And I'm not in the mood to dive in after you. You're fuckin' heavy."

Izayah looked down at the forest below, a blanket of fallen needles covering the ground like a muted carpet. Rolling his eyes, lips quirked into a smirk. "You're saying you wouldn't save me?"

Daxler grinned. "Oh, I'd save you. But I'd make sure to remind you every damn day that I did." He paused, continuing with a more serious tone. "Look, you don't have to handle all this alone. Whatever's in those letters, whatever Ma's vision meant…"

Izayah nodded, his gaze still fixed on the forest floor. "I know." He hesitated, then added quietly, "Just…not sure if time's on our side."

Daxler leaned in closer, bumping shoulders with Izayah. "Hey, it's always on our side," He winked, adding, "If not, we'll just smack the shit out of time and take the fucker down a peg. That work?"

Shaking out a smirk, Izayah clicked his tongue in a subtle confirmation.

Daxler pressed his lips together and blew out a small burst of air, creating a popping noise. He repeated it a few times, each pop louder than the last, as if to say, *Asshole, I will wait here all night until you fill me in on this.*

"It's always been her, man." Izayah sighed, stretching his spine and rolling his shoulder to ease the strain in his pectoral muscle. "Truth is, every damn fiber of my being is throbbing with discomfort right now."

Daxler grinned, a glint of mischief in his eyes. "Throbbing, huh? Sounds like it's been a minute…about time, don't you think?"

Izayah snorted. "You're an idiot."

"Maybe, but at least I'm not the one throwing out lines like 'throbbing with discomfort.' Seriously, when was the last time you've had a proper distraction?" Daxler's eyes widened. "Because if it's been that long, no wonder, you look like a constipated porcupine."

A chuckle escaped, and Izayah shook his head. "You're not wrong," he muttered, though his eyes remained distant, searching for something past the horizon. "See that boulder over there…along the treeline?"

Daxler leaned back against the railing, letting out a mock sigh. "Hard to miss, considering you're staring at it like it's gonna sprout lips and start giving us step-by-step instructions. For someone who's all about sorting things through, you make it sound like you're lost in a damn labyrinth without a map."

"That's exactly what it feels like," Izayah admitted, his tone softening into something more contemplative. "Some things are just...tangled; it's hard to see clearly."

Without missing a beat, Daxler quipped, "Don't worry, man. If things are tangled, just hand over the scissors. I'm remarkable at cutting through bullshit."

A chuckle rumbled out as Izayah shook his head. Daxler's tone losing its edge. "But look, you don't have to do this solo, right?"

"Yeah, I know," Izayah muttered. "But certain things...I just need to face on my own."

Shuddering theatrically, "Oh, *fan-fuckin-tastic*, more 'lone wolf' shit. You know, you could just try talking to people who care, instead of pretending you're the only one in the universe with problems."

"Point made." Izayah nodded.

Daxler's grin widened. "Splendid. Because if I have to sit through another one of your 'soul-searching in solitude' sessions, I might just start charging you."

"Fair enough. I'll try to keep my existential crises to a minimum."

Daxler nodded, a grin tugging at his lips. "That's the spirit. How about this—next time, we bring some whiskey? A lot of whiskey. Might make all this 'soul-searching' a little more bearable...for me."

"Deal," Izayah smirked.

He exhaled sharply, jaw clenched, frustration simmering. "You gonna finally tell her?"

"Tell her what?" Izayah replied, a casual shrug masking the flicker of unease in his eyes. "After getting sand in every damn orifice and smacked around by those frigid gusts this morning, I'm savoring this cedar-scented break like a prize I didn't even know I needed."

With a deadpan expression, Daxler rubbed a hand along his forehead. "Are you fucking kidding me right now? Tell her what? Fuck, seriously, Zay. You gotta spell it out for me. Is she as unpredictable as that chick I dated for, like, five minutes? Because this is getting fucking ridiculous, man."

Izayah chuckled, a grin spreading across his face. "Oh, you mean the girl who had that uncanny knack for appearing everywhere? I swear, Dax, she was like a magician. For an entire month, she'd just materialize out of thin air, like she had a sixth sense for where you'd be." Izayah set his glass down on the railing, rubbing his hands together. A mischievous grin emerged.

Leaning in toward Daxler, Izayah hunched over slightly, ready to recount a moment from their brotherhood. "Oh, the highlight—it was unforgettable." He paused, savoring the buildup. "Picture this: you're leaving the barracks, all serious, full soldier mode, while I'm in the middle of a conversation with my superior. And then, out of nowhere, this woman —dressed as Cupid—jumps out of the bushes. She's flailing her arms like a lunatic, tossing confetti in the air to celebrate your 'first-date' anniversary."

Izayah's grin sharpened as he continued, "The look on your face was fucking priceless. Eyes popped wide, just as they are now." Daxler tipped his head back with a groan, as if to say, *Not this again*, yet subtle amusement flickered across his features, clearly dallying with the entertainment of it all.

Izayah leaned in, relishing the moment. "Oh man, it knocked you flat on your ass." He paused, milking the tension. "To your credit," he added, raising a finger for emphasis, "you managed to pull yourself together. No scene, no chaos—just pure shock. But let me tell you, it was a hell of a spectacle."

Daxler grimaced. "Oh, I remember, thanks. Nothing like getting blasted with confetti in front of my CO." He clicked his tongue, adding with a smirk, "Yeah, my commanding officer still gives me shit about it—today, in fact—bastard, but now sends me on excruciating, three-day missions to investigate a female that he just stares at." He pinched the bridge of his nose. *"Yeah,* and I'm the one with issues."

"Oh, it gets even better!" Izayah's fingertips tapped out a rhythm as he continued the tale. "Following the incident, the guard officials detained, interrogated, and gave a stern warning to the 'Cupid intruder.' To this day, we still can't figure out how she even breached the base."

Izayah tilted his head toward Daxler. "So, naturally, I took it upon myself to mentor you. From then on, any female entering your life faces rigorous screening by the inner circle—even before a casual coffee date," raising an eyebrow in Daxler's direction. "It was a necessary measure to keep any more undesirable individuals from slipping through the cracks."

"Well, if this is your version of mentoring, it's not inspiring much confidence," he said skeptically, gesturing toward the field where Runa was running. "And as for a second date...I made it clear that was never happening."

Izayah's grin stretched wider, mischief glinting. "Well, at least we've confirmed your preference for wildly animated women," he quipped. "A little over-the-top for me, honestly, yet from my view, it was pure chaos and side-splitting hilarity. I'd hit replay on that fuckin' day just to catch your priceless expression again, Sugar Plum."

Daxler rolled his eyes, muttering, "You're really sticking with that one, huh?" Casually shrugging, he slipped into a mused tone. "You know my heart belongs to Missy," he shot back, winking at Izayah. "There's no one quite like her, Zay."

Izayah's laugh was low, amused. "Always, Missy. Without question."

Daxler leaned in, still grinning. "Enough about my charming love life— let's talk about yours. "So, shifting gears—how long have you been smitten with this one?"His gaze flicked to the lively, black-haired whirlwind spinning about. Laughter rang out as the children darted in and out of the trees, pretending to escape some imaginary danger.

Izayah hesitated, a wistful smile edging his lips puffing out his checks, observing. "*Phh...*who *fuckin'* knows?" Mist curled from his fingertips, like the memories themselves were wrapped in a soft, nostalgic haze. "It's been a thing for..." he murmured, letting the words drift off.

"*Ahhhh...*no! I will NOT lose you again. *Fuckin'*— focus, man! *Holy hell!*" Daxler's tone brimmed with both amusement and mock seriousness. "Well, I can say for a fact that I've never seen you look at anyone with such...*intensity.*" A mischievous grin stretching. "It's *nauseating,* and I understand why you haven't said *jackshit.* I'm willing to bet, words wouldn't come out of your mouth coherently right now." Izayah quickly switched his whiskey glass from one hand to the other, swinging a playful elbow into Daxler's shoulder.

"Come on, man," he chuckled. "...After the beating we endured this morning, I don't need your lip." Izayah's eyes sparkled with amusement as the familiar scent of hickory and BBQ wafted through the air.

Zane rounded the corner, the smoke wrapping around him and pushing forward, bringing a sense of understanding that pulled Izayah back to long-forgotten memories. Even after all this time, his brother still managed to take up the whole damn space. A few inches taller, always making sure Izayah remembered who was bigger, stronger, and faster.

But things had changed since then; the Shadow Guard's training had leveled the field. Zane might still have the height, but the gap had narrowed. Years in the elite unit had broadened Izayah's frame, built his muscle. *I'm not the little brother anymore,* he thought. *Not in every sense anyway.* And yet...seeing Zane now, there was still that familiar blend of admiration and competition. *He always appeared larger than life,* Izayah mused, *without even trying.*

"Hey, what the hell are you doing here? Slap me sideways; it's been forever!" Zane's voice boomed with genuine surprise and excitement, pulling his younger brother into a bear hug, like they were back in their childhood wrestling matches. "Damn, the Shadow Elite really don't mess around, huh?"

Izayah chuckled, shaking his head with a smirk. Zane puffed out his chest, stretching his upper back with a grin before turning to the broad-shouldered man beside Izayah. Extending his hand, he said, "And you must be Daxler, right? Heard a lot about you...some good, some...questionable." He leaned in with a hearty handshake and a solid pat on the back. "Man, that's some serious ink! Must've cost a lot of coinage, but hey, for what you guys do, tokens well spent."

Handing Izayah another glass of whiskey, he added, "Brother, take note —this guy's not going down without a fight, that's for sure." With a playful scratch of his eyebrow, he continued, "I know shadows have their use, but maybe a bit more thought weaving ink would be more convenient."

Furrowing his brow, Zane asked, "So, what's the topic of conversation?" He leaned back, casually sipping his beer, his gaze drifting to the tree line.

"We're diving into Zay's oh-so-exciting love life!" Daxler quipped, a roguish grin curling at his lips.

Izayah let out a frustrated sigh as he raised his glass toward the lively group of ladies laughing and dancing among the trees.

Zane watched with a grimace as Tabytha burst into laughter, their oldest daughter playfully showering her with autumn leaves. He gruffly muttered, "Don't bother, Daxler," averting his eyes from the field. "He's been practicing this dance for years."

His tone softened, nostalgia mingling with enthusiasm. "We used to be close, you know. Runa's family had this tradition of visiting the cabin every holiday season. And this bastard"—Zane shot Izayah a teasing look—"would trail along behind her like a loyal dog. You were practically born for the role of devoted guardian, weren't you?" He chuckled, casting him a sidelong glance. "Remember that time Runa was with us, and I knocked over that hideous vase in the hallway? Shattered it to pieces. We got in so much trouble when…"

"It landed on me! A tiny, innocent bundle of joy, rolling amidst shattered glass. It's a miracle I've survived this long." Rayanna appeared from the cabin's sliding door, grinning wide, a bucket-sized mug of coffee in hand.

Zane guffawed loudly. "You, my sweet sister, were anything but an innocent little angel." Grumbling, he bit out, "I was about halfway to my Dawning Day, so, what, eleven? Your ass had to be around five at the time. Runa's not that much younger than you, so don't give me that. It's not like you were crawling around on the floor or anything."

"I would have to agree you are being a bit theatrical, Ray." Izayah teased, leaning into the banister. His grin was short-lived but genuine, a familiar warmth softening his expression. "You always did have a flair for the dramatic." His eyes met hers for a moment before he gave a casual nod. "Guess some things never change."

Rayanna set the coffee down on a nearby surface and threw herself into Izayah's embrace. With little effort, he scooped her up, locking her in a firm, familiar hold. The steady thrum of his heartbeat against her ear was grounding. As a child, he had been her anchor on the nights after their mother's passing—when fear tore through her and darkness threatened to take hold. And always, without fail, it sent her straight to him. A brotherly force. The one unshakable presence she could cling to, seeking refuge from the shadows creeping into her world. Back then, she would listen to the rhythm of his heartbeat, intertwined with the faint glow of a tittering lark or sparrow—she was never sure. It hovered at the edge of her dream realm, visiting from another world, a quiet guardian pulling her back before the darkness could claim her.

Her long, golden-brown hair spilled across his face, he sputtered and swatted at it, just like he used to. Rayanna couldn't help but giggle—exactly as she always had, the sound carrying a warmth that filled the space between them.

Rayanna smirked, tapping his shoulder. "Not much has changed—my ass! I'm going to have to hold back all of my single friends from the big, brooding sidekick." She winked in Daxler's direction, asking "Tell me, is Zay still overanalyzing life like it's some grand mission he can't afford to screw up?"

Daxler snorted. "Yep, and he's still terrible at it."

Izayah let out a sharp breath. "Great. Now it's become a team effort."

Rayanna grinned as he lowered his head, meeting her halfway like he always did. *Same old Zay,* a fond smile tugging at her lips. *Always making things easier, always playing the protector, even in the smallest ways. I can't help but love him for it, even if I have to feign annoyance most of the time. He always means well.*

My big, introspective brother, she mused, *still trying to fix everything…I've often wondered if he'll ever see that things don't have to be so complicated. Maybe one day,* she thought. But until then, giving him a hard time was really her only option—until he realized there was more to living than just the weight he carried.

"Frankly, how would you have ever coped without me?" She playfully taunted as she took a step back, casually draping her long, golden-brown hair over one shoulder, sending a wink in Daxler's direction. "Here's hoping your coffee's finally strong enough to match the new look, brother."

Before stepping out of the cabin, Rayanna noticed the three men, their focus fixed on the center of the clearing. She could only guess that Izayah was lost in thought—a state he often fell into whenever Runa was near. There was something almost endearing about the way he clung to those moments, like precious stones he had to examine from every angle, under every light.

Rayanna recognized that look—the distant gaze, reaching for answers in places only he could go. *Same old Zay,* she mused, her lips curving into a soft knowing smile. *He's always been this way—diving headlong into his mind, trying to fix things no one else even notices. I love that about him: his drive to make sense of the world, to figure it all out. But sometimes, I can't help but wonder how hard he must beat himself up if he misses something. I wish he'd let others in, trust them enough to share the thoughts bouncing around in his head. It's one of the lessons I'm learning from Papa D—when we come together, bringing our minds and ideas with openness, it's easier to uncover the truth. I feel like he carries so much more than he needs to, and maybe that's what the Shadow Elite really is teaching him. That's why Daxler's here, after all, isn't it?*

Rayanna grabbed her coffee and strolled to the railing, settling beside Zane. She turned her gaze toward the grassy knoll, just in time to see Runa contorting her face in a comical attempt to imitate a growling monster, sending the girls scattering in all directions. Their shrieks of laughter carried across the clearing. Eyes twinkling with playful intent, Runa fixed her sights on Zane's youngest, leaping forward to envelop her in an enormous hug. The little one went limp in her arms, only for Runa to swing her back and forth between her legs, both of them dissolving into giggles.

"Her heart is truly immense." Rayanna stated, shaking her head in quiet wonder. "No matter how many times she saw it, Runa's joy never faded—pure, unburdened, and wholly free." It always caught Rayanna off guard, striking her with quiet awe.

"Yeah, it is," Izayah said, bringing the glass to his lips. A glint of silver edged his waterline as thoughts ricocheted through his mind. He quickly brushed them away with a brief, almost imperceptible nod. "Yeah...she's incredible isn't she."

Zane leaned in, "You just need to stop this bullshit and tell her already, brother. Keeping it all to yourself at this point is just broody and pitiful," he said with a crooked smile, tilting his head, eyebrow raised in a silent challenge.

"I told you, *'Brooding'* should've been your damn call sign," Daxler chimed in, his comment landing like a crumpled piece of paper tossed into the conversation.

Izayah's gaze narrowed, his brow furrowing. "I can't risk losing everything, Zane!"

"Are you serious right now?" Zane shot back, disbelief flashing across his face.

Izayah's eyes bore into his brother's, his face shadowed with something unreadable. "If I lose her...I lose everything," he muttered, almost to himself. "She's been there–always–and I *want* that to stay the same. She doesn't need to know—end of story." He raked his fingers through his hair, pausing at his temples as if trying to shove the thoughts aside.

"It's not about being foolish or immature. I'm done talking about it—with you or anyone else." He paused, his cadence wavering almost a whisper. "Maybe you don't get it now, but someday you will. She's already carrying enough; she doesn't need *my* shit on top of it. So just...*let it go,* alright?"

"Look, Dax and I aren't here for a vacation," he stated, voice firm but edged with frustration. His mind raced with the unspoken thoughts. *There's too much I know...too much I can't even put into words yet. It feels like something's pressing on my chest, keeping me from saying what I should.* He gave a slight shrug, shaking off the weight, pushing the notion aside.

"I had to see her," he said. "Dax needed to understand—to see the full picture. No room for misinterpretation." He fidgeted with his glass, ice clinking against the sides. "I know it's frustrating," he continued, "me not laying everything out; but there's more to this than even I knew."

Izayah sighed gravely, the sound heavy in his own ears. *Damn, it's like wading through mud...this whole fucking thing.* "It's not going to all come out at once either," he added, his voice quieter now, like he was speaking more to himself. "The moon—phasing, fading, returning. But it's always whole. It's just a matter of what the night lets you see."

He looked up, his gaze following the line of the treetops against the sky. *Feels like I'm trying to breathe underwater here.* He rolled his neck, trying to release the tension coiling there. "Healing is a slow process like finding your footing on scattered stones." His gaze swept across the space while he spoke, almost expecting the universe to answer, "Right now, all you see is the surface ...but what's underneath is a hell of a lot deeper than any of us realize."

Zane's authority was clear as he clapped a firm hand on Izayah's back. "Believe me, she's not going anywhere; you've got everything to gain here." He met his brother's eyes, his tone easing just a fraction. "I really hope you understand that. I know her just as well as you do, maybe even better, seeing as I'm older, wiser, and way more charming than your sorry ass." He arched an eyebrow and pressed forward.

"Look, I know everything you do has a purpose, I get it, and I trust you. But hear me out: if she finds out, it might not be the end of the world. Hell, it might just be the start of something better."He took a swig of his beer, casually clinking the bottle against Izayah's whiskey glass, a smirk playing on his lips.

"As General Diesel Hollowborne would say, 'In the face of darkness and hidden truths, the moon remains a steadfast guide for any warrior willing to seek resolution." His grip tightened on his little brother's shoulder, a steady reassurance. "I'm with you—no words needed. When those secrets surface, I'll be there, sword in hand."

Pulling up his sleeve, Zane turned his arm over. A tattoo emerged, a living mark stretching from wrist to elbow—a sword inked in exquisite detail, etched with thought woven precision. The hilt, intricately wrought and pulsing with life, appeared as though it were embedded in his arm, nestled in an indented, velvety-like space. The blade was hidden deep within him, at the cusp of his wrist, as though the weapon had been driven into his flesh—like a sword plunged into rock—leaving only the guard visible.

Upon the guard and descending into the blade, the emblem of the Shadow City came alive—a lion, fierce and noble, forged head-on into the metal. The great beast melded seamlessly into the crossguard; its mane unfurling like a storm, each strand twisting and coiling—the guardian inlaid, set into a darkened veil of shadow and adorned with grayish-white gemstones. Its gaze, fierce and unwavering, held the weight of dominion. The mane curled endlessly around the hilt, forming a leather wrapping, its lines as fine as whispers of smoke—moving, spiraling, like ink dispersing in water.

Daxler's eyes widened, letting out a low whistle, a mixture of awe and fascinated curiosity, belting out. "No way in hell—that's my old man's work. I have heard about this one, but never had the privilege." Shock jolted him forward, fingertips hovering just over Zane's forearm, sifting through the thought woven, obsidian markings. "Sorry...just never imagined I'd see *that* one up close. But with your royal blood...makes sense." A playful gleam dallied with his senses, "I've got a few beasts etched on me, but nothing like that. From what I've heard, it can hold more than shadows. It can cradle a life…"

Zane's expression tightened—a flicker of discomfort crossing his face. Without a word, he pulled his arm back and stepped toward the balcony's perimeter.

Daxler shrugged, unfazed, edging a little closer to Izayah as his arms crossed with confident ease. "Guess that hit a nerve," he muttered, letting the tension slide off him like water.

Izayah stepped away from the balcony's edge and sank into a large chair, his broad frame molding into the cushions. Raising his glass, he took a sip and stared out, lost in thought. "What the hell would I even say to Runa? *'Hey, I've been in love with you since the first time I saw you. Let's just spend forever together because, obviously, we're meant to—even if you haven't figured that out yet.'*" He sighed, rolling his eyes. "Yeah, that *doesn't* sound awkward, cheesy, or desperate *at all*, does it?"

Rayanna's voice sliced through the air, thick with sarcasm. "Wait, WHAT?!" She threw her hands up dramatically, eyes wide, lips curving into an exaggerated pout of mock disbelief. "How am I just finding this out? *Seriously?* You—Mr. Human Enigma with a mouth wired shut—decided to keep this from me, your sister?!" She crossed her arms, tapping her foot as if waiting for an answer.

Zane took a swig of beer, smirking as he muttered from the corner of his mouth, "Honestly, I don't think she'd be all that surprised."

"You can't keep me in the dark like this," Rayanna exclaimed, her tone playfully indignant. "Remember when you promised to bake me that cake after my 'near-death' experience as a youngling? You know, when I was covered in shards of glass—courtesy of this guy." She jerked her thumb at Zane, who took another swig of beer, smirking and raising his drink in a lazy salute.

"Well, guess what, Zay? I'm still waiting! You promised me cake, but when I got there—nada! A total betrayal. A crime against baked goods and little sisters everywhere." She threw him a teasing grin.

"You're so damn overdramatic," Zane huffed. *"You don't even like cake."* He let out a guffaw, shaking his head.

"I like bread, and that's a form of cake," she shot back, undeterred.

"Wait a minute…" Daxler adjusted his stance against the railing, elbows braced on the wooden banister, one eyebrow lifting in Rayanna's direction. "You promised her cake and didn't deliver? That's just bad form, Sir." He shook his head in mock disbelief.

Zane raised his hands in surrender.

Rayanna shot Daxler a wink. "Smart move, considering your place in our tribe." She raised an eyebrow to drive the point home before turning to Izayah. "Zay, you nailed it with this one. He fits in perfectly—and he takes cake commitments seriously? That's a win," she teased.

Rayanna braced herself against the balcony railing, her gaze lingering on the now-deserted clearing."You know, it's kind of fascinating," she remarked; eyes catching Runa perched on a rock at the edge of the woods, right where the trail wound toward the hot springs.

"Tabytha has this bizarre talent for taking the most awkward situations and turning them into life lessons. It's like she can find hidden wisdom in even the cringiest of moments." She shot Izayah a playful glance, a smirk forming. "Maybe she'll make your signature smolder-and-shadowy recluse phase a little more tolerable."

She turned her eyes back to the sunset, the sky's oranges and pinks blending like sherbet. "I'm serious, though. She's got a knack for turning weird into wonderful. It could be worth a try, don't you think?"

Catching sight of the group, she adjusted course. With a teasing lilt, she called out, "I heard you were all here—gossiping about me again, are we?"

She inclined her head, a knowing smile spreading across her face. "You know it's not fair to tell wild stories before the newcomers even get a chance to form their own opinions." Flashing Daxler a mischievous wink, "For the record, you all missed out on some epic leaf battles and run-ins with a few ferocious beasts."

"They've been obsessing over my so-called love life for the last forty-five minutes," Izayah muttered, his smirk faltering into something unimpressed. "And I'm done drawing this out. So unless you've got some fresh gossip, let's just drop it."

Tabytha laughed softly, a velvety warmth drifting through her tone. "Oh, you know I live for awkward moments, Izayah." She leaned into the doorframe, her cadence playful, yet laced with intrigue. "I'll make it easy for you—I already know who you've been chatting about. And, funny enough, I hear they've been dreaming about you…a lot lately."

Izayah lounged back, crossing one ankle over his knee, his expression unreadable. A low, teasing hum rumbled as he lifted a brow. "Intriguing," the word drawn out, subtle but taunting. "Go on…lay it all out for me, and I'll tell you if there's any truth to it." A sly smirk tugged at his lips. "But, naturally, I'll need every detail first."

Tabytha's face brightened with amusement. "Oh, that's adorable," she mused, tapping a thoughtful finger against her bottom lip. "But no, sorry, not going to happen. I've sworn an oath of secrecy, and breaking a sisterly bond? That's no joke."

Izayah edged forward, interest piqued, curiosity sharpened. "Come on, you started this…you may as well finish it," he chided, eyes glinting with curiosity.

She bit back a smile, eyes widening in feigned shock. "Oh, this is where things get uncomfortable, huh?" She smirked, tilting her head, "It'll be worth it. The story is deliciously entertaining." Flashing him a cheeky grin, she spun on her heel with a playful flick of her tongue and sauntered inside, calling over her shoulder, "What a shame, huh?" Zane and Rayanna dissolved into laughter, their voices lifting, carrying them into the rich scent of grilled meats and spices as they trailed behind her.

Izayah let out a dry chuckle, dragging a hand down his face. "Oh sure, just leave me hanging. *Real nice.*"

"Not sure 'hanging' is the right word here, bud." Daxler arched his brow. "You've lasted this long, I'm sure you'll survive." Rubbing his jawline, a teasing grin glinting, he asked, "What was that line again?" He lifted his fingers in quotation, mimicking Izayah's earlier tone. "Every damn fiber of your being is throbbing with discomfort right now."

"Put a cork in it," Izayah said flatly, letting his foot fall as he finished the last sip of whiskey. He placed the glass on the nearby coffee table and moved back to the balcony's edge. The pair turned to watch the sun sink behind the treeline, casting the sky in soft yellows, purples, and deep grays as the creeping mist swallowed the lingering shadows. The landscape absorbed the fading light, brimming with the promise of what the night would soon bring. Twilight deepened—a muted pause before the storm.

Below, Runa descended from her perch, head bowed; ebony ringlets falling around her face as she made her way back to the cabin for dinner. Daxler straightened, rolling his shoulders back, focus sharpening; as he clapped a firm hand on his superior's back—which sent him hurtling back into Izayah's amphitheater of thought. His voice cut through the arching space, snapping Izayah's focus back into place, reinforcing their footing. *Clock's ticking. We move now. I know what's on the line, and I'm all in, brother. Every detail, every step—we lock it down in three days. No margin for error.*

Izayah's gaze tracked Runa as she made her way back to the cabin. Instinct took over—posture straightening, shoulders squared, his expression turned to steel. *This is what needs to happen Daxler—it's not what I want to happen.* The convictions reverberated through the quiet corners of his mind. *I know the path we need to walk. Protecting what matters most isn't optional—it's vital! It's everything. She is everything.*

One day, she'll see it for what it was—the only way. Until then, I'll carry it. Daxler remained—a steady, watchful presence while Izayah continued, lost in contemplation. *Some decisions have to be made quickly—without delay, no discussion. We both know that. I just hope she can forgive me for the path I chose for her.* Understanding clicked between the pair as he added, *I wish I were wrong.* A silent prayer fluttered past, like pages rifling through the air. *How I hope Zane's assessment proves accurate. Regardless, I'll deal with the fallout.*

His grip on the railing tightened, muscles coiled, nerves primed for action. Daxler gave a subtle tilt of confirmation. Always sharper. Always first to pick up on the shift. Izayah's gaze flicked skyward, tuning into the faint tremors rolling from the treeline. *Is this really happening?*

He forced his fingers to loosen, just enough to let the tension bleed from his knuckles. *Hold the line. Don't tip your hand.* His gaze tracked Runa as she approached the steps, her form silhouetted against the fading light. *Keep it together. Everything hinges on this moment. She can't know. Not yet.*

His heart hammered, palms dampened. *This isn't how I wanted her to see me after all these years.* Forcing his body into silence. *One slip, one tell—game over. She can't see...*He drew in a deep, measured breath. *Fuck.* Steadying the rhythm within, he refused to let it betray the storm gathering beneath his skin. *This is really happening. Oh, Gods...Blessed Father...shit!*

Daxler pressed a hand firmly between Izayah's shoulder blades, grounding him, as the world around them softened at the edges. The tension in the air eased, just for her, to support the approaching transition.

Shadows thickened, unfurling from Izayah's fingertips like a shroud, cloaking the night in muted stillness. Everything else faded into the background—shades of gray swallowing the once-vibrant grassy knoll as Runa approached the steps. Daxler pushed with intent. *No room for hesitation. Don't hold back,* Daxler's thoughts hit hard, cutting clean. *Sir, holding back now would only cause her pain and strife.*

Izayah felt his quintessence stir—the shadows curling and stretching, expanding outward, gently wrapping around Runa's petite form. Mist curled through the air, cool and soft, merging their breaths until her heartbeat became a steady rhythm, pulsing through the silence between him and Daxler.

Instinctively, Izayah's mind reached out, sending a surge of energy through the tether. His essence bled into the shadows, reaching for her like a tender hand, brushing against her consciousness—never confining, only leading.

Daxler remained, ever-present in the shared space, attuned to the same rhythm, to the same melody, compelled by the same force. *Stay with me,* his voice cut through the quiet connection, pulling Izayah back into focus. *Don't lose yourself in this, brother. She needs you right here.*

Izayah steadied himself, letting the words tether him, while his quintessence moved with Runa, not interfering, just accompanying her. All the while, he kept her unaware of the storm simmering beneath the surface.

Like a silent guardian, serenity cloaked her, shielding her from the turmoil lurking just beyond the treeline. *Am I really doing this?* The question loomed, heavy and unrelenting. The mist blurred her periphery, veiling her vision, guiding her gaze solely toward him. His heartbeat found hers, merging into a steady rhythm that quieted the doubts pressing in.

"They're approaching, Sir," Daxler said, his voice steady. Catching the subtle shifts in Izayah's stance—the faint tightening of muscles, the slight adjustment in footing. In response, Daxler released his quintessence, letting it ripple outward. The mist thickened, testing his instincts, probing his readiness. Izayah's response was automatic—a protective reflex ingrained in him, an unshakable drive to shield Runa from any threat, real or perceived.

Izayah's heart swelled with a strange blend of pride and longing as he watched her approach; he realized that it was Runa feelings surfacing about *him*. Her lips curved into a smile—*brilliant, unmatched,* and seared into his memory. *After all this time, I don't deserve this or her.* His breath caught as the fog wrapped around them—binding, inescapable—yet in that moment, she saw him with a clarity that shattered every shadow he had ever summoned. *This isn't how I planned our reunion. Not after all these years.*

They're almost upon us, Sir. Daxler's internal thrumming of alarm ricocheted across the bridged connection, muscles tightening, his footing shifting slightly to hold steady. *We hold our ground.*

Please forgive me. The thought surged like waves crashing against jagged cliffs. His quintessence unfurled, pushing outward as the mist thickened around them.

There, just beyond the treeline, Sir. Daxler's report came through, calm and unwavering. *No hesitation, no doubt.* They both knew what was at stake, even if Izayah's heart ached with every breath.

Her thoughts slammed into his mind, uninvited but undeniable. *God, it's been forever since I've seen that face.* Her heart twisted with a familiar ache, one that clung to her like a shadow—the same ache etched into every letter she'd sent; each one unanswered. *Did you ever miss me, even for a second?* She studied him, searching for something—*anything*—that showed he remembered. *I kept hoping you'd write back, that you'd explain why you left, but...nothing. You just vanished. Walked away so easily, as if erasing me from your life was the simplest thing in the world.*

The sting was sharp, unforgiving, a jolt to the very core of his existence, leaving him breathless and sick. *Why would he want to stay?* Her words spilled out like shards of broken glass, cutting into him as if he'd stumbled upon them barefoot. Her mother's voice echoed in her mind, cold and bitter. *You're not worthy of love. You're nothing.* The grief settled deep in her chest, heavy and suffocating, as if her heart were breaking all over again.

But after all this, she wondered, feeling a rush of warmth beneath the pain, *why do you still feel like home?* The sensation lingered, embedding itself like seed, quietly taking root.

He forced the emotions down, slamming the door shut and locking them away. Fixated on the air, on the steady rhythm of Daxler's breathing, the dense weight of the fog clinging to his skin—and hers. The fury simmered beneath, both men attuned to the same pulse. Alert. Watchful. Perfectly in sync. Ready for whatever would come next.

Trading my life for hers. Sacrificing my life. Without regret. The thoughts edged in, his gaze clouded in a silver sheen, until a lone tear defied command, carving a silent path down his cheek.

The words thought-wove themselves into Runa's mind, seamlessly threading into her consciousness. *"Follow the moon, Ru. It will guide you back to me."* A quick swipe of his hand erased the evidence, resetting his focus. The mission was all that remained.

My life for hers. It's my turn to take the reins.

And then—without warning—the sky erupted in blinding light. The boulder behind her fractured violently, exploding into jagged shards as the trees around her ignited, their branches consumed in flames of pure quintessence.

Chapter One

Starlight Beach

"Again with the paint and glitter?" Mama D's voice broke through, pulling Runa's concentration from the pile of papers and stacks of books surrounding her. Lifting her head, a soft smile forming. "You always seem to carry a little bit of color with you, no matter where you go."

"It's a talent, I suppose," Runa stated, rising from her desk, sensing the day's weight lingering in her muscles—the pleasant ache of time well spent. "I've always wanted to shine like a nova, especially on nights like this." She added with a gentle laugh, "Maybe I'm just fulfilling that little dream." Her eyes twinkled. "And you should have seen my little ones— they're sticky and shimmering from head to toe."

She brushed at the iridescent bits clinging to her dark shirt and fitted obsidian jeans. The tiny constellations scattered across the fabric were remnants of a day spent crafting with younglings. The classroom was still buzzing with their energy. The sharp tang of fresh glue lingered, blending with the remnants of laughter beyond her classroom door. Their voices faded into echoes, curiosity stretching out and weaving through the community gardens just beyond her threshold.

Today, time slipped away like sand through her fingers. *Where had the hours gone?* The sky stretched wide, stars blinking into view as her mind lingered on a single point. She couldn't shake the feeling that something meaningful was transitioning, even if she had yet to grasp the specifics.

She turned her attention toward the wall of windows along the back perimeter of the aged structure, where twilight softened the firmament's edges. Starlight Beach held a peaceful beauty that tugged at her soul strings, inviting her to unravel its mysteries one breath at a time.

Sometimes, it felt as though this place had been crafted just for her; but then the thought would surface: *I'm just a tiny blip in it all.* Still, a deep sense of belonging settled over her, and gratitude swelled within her—not for finding this place, but for the gift of calling it home.

As she continued to gaze out the window, a reverent joy swelled within, rippling through her like the first hush of twilight. It was as if a dream had slipped between the seams of reality, unfurling in quiet wonder. The Starlight Festival—a night where the sky waltzed with the earth—was more than just a celebration. It was a gathering—a tapestry of voices and light. Beneath a vast, glimmering night, the new year took shape, molded by the hands and hearts of those who called this place home.

That morning, she had gathered her little ones, who settled eagerly around her; their faces turned up to hers, eyes wide and bright with curiosity. Each expression brimmed with unspoken wonder, waiting eagerly for the tale to take shape.

"Have you heard the story of Starlight Beach?" She leaned in close, her tone gentle, as if sharing a secret too grand to be spoken aloud. Some younglings shook their heads in denial, their locks flailing wildly, while others nodded, their features scrunching up, like tasting a fruit that was both sweet and tangy at once.

"Well …" A playful glint surfaced, the storyteller awakening within. "A long, long time ago, there was a group of artists and dreamers. Hmmm." She pressed an animated finger to her lips. "Do you know what artists and dreamers do?" She paused, tracing circles in the air above their heads. Finally, she settled on a boy with black hair and a tiny, knobby nose. "Barry, do you know?"

The boy's face brightened as his words tumbled out in an eager rush. "Dweamers see all da wishes in da sky that were put in da stars." His eyes went wide with wonder, and he giggled. "And awtists build castwes out of cwouds." He leaned in closer, whispering, "I fink they cowor outside the wines 'cause dat's where all the fun is."

Runa's laugh spilled out, gentle and warm. "Exactly, Barry! They dream big things, and they believe in them too! Dreamers stumbled upon a special place near the sea. It was right here, where the waves whispered, uttering their secrets." She inched closer to the small group, her voice soft enough to be mistaken for thought. "The stars shone so brightly, it seemed like they were winking at you. And do you know what happened next?" Excitement crackled as small hands shot skyward.

"Ah," she continued, eyes still twinkling as her hand skimmed over the group once more, before landing on a little girl with pigtails and golden-brown eyes. "What do you think, Amee?"

Squishing up her face as she pushed her finger into the rim of her glasses, her speech lilted, shaped by her toothless gaps. "Thath's when a famouth man named Profeffor Thamuel Stharlight came to town. He loved looking at the sthars—juth like you do! And he built a big, thall building on the hill—ith's called—an obtherv-tor-y—" She took her little hand, curling it up in a cylinder and squinted into the hole, "to thee the sthars better than—anyone—elthe! He dithcovered all kindth of magical thingths —about the thky up there."

Runa lifted her chin with a delighted pause, savoring their eager expressions reflecting her own internal delight. "Now, every year, we cele-brate this special place with a *biggggg*, massive festival called..." Her voice grew quiet, "The Starlight Festival. It's where we dance, have crafts, music, and eat or indulge in all the yummy or delicious food your mamas and papas make for our community!" She gave a playful poke to a tiny belly, setting off a chorus of giggles. "Feels like the stars are dancing in celebra-tion with us." She whispered dramatically, "And maybe, just maybe, if you listen *reallllllly* carefully, those glowing specks above might be willing to share their stories with you." Her younglings gasped and clapped, their imaginations clearly taking flight.

But now, as she stood by the windowpane, pondering their lingering wonder, a warmth spread through her chest—born from the joy of sharing a piece of this town's soul, its history, and its enchantment with them. Watching as twilight settled, the sky deepened into a hush of fading light.

This place held stories—ones that stretched beyond her own knowing, stitched into the vastness of sky.

A soft smile warmed her features along with a flooding of memories, a wave of thoughts, gentle but vivid. *Just a child then,* she reflected—*suddenly appearing at their doorstep like a stray, wrapped in glistening gold, on the night of the festival.* She had been told the story countless times: Mama D and Diesel Dave—better known to her now as Papa D—threw their arms wide without hesitation, welcoming her in. She had found comfort in his embrace, slipping into slumber with ease.

Each year, on this very night, those memories stirred back to life—the weathered, white door in the theater of her mind creaked open. But this time, something else stepped through. A presence she hadn't known existed. An uncertainty she hadn't realized was there until now; walking back into her world as if introducing itself for the first time. Though something else lingered beside it. *A quiet resolve? Maybe.* The thought of a new foundation had settled in, though she wasn't sure where it had come from. It drifted through her mind like mist, ungraspable yet present, shaped by the kindness she had found in this place.

Years of bonfires, stories, and moments of pure joy—two decades building toward this very festival–this feeling. The simplicity of it still astounds me. It was more than a gift—it was a lifeline, a tether, pressed into my gut, like a truth too blinding to ignore. A chance to understand what it meant to be loved, truly and steadfastly, without conditions. And now, here I am, unraveling the layers of what that love has taught me. A profound gratitude warmed spaces she hadn't realized were there, as if breathing life into parts of her that had slumbered for far too long.

Mama D stepped beyond the threshold, clutching a bouquet of pink, bell-shaped blossoms in one hand and a brimming wicker basket of vegetables in the other. Driven by the heft of her load, she made her way toward the student desks, neatly lined along the back wall. They had been pushed aside to allow space for creativity and play.

As she bent down, her bag skimmed the edge of a table, causing silver strands of hair to spill past her waist, momentarily obscuring her view. In the midst of easing the load down, she misstepped—stumbling over a slightly skewed chair, sending the basket tumbling to the floor.

Runa pivoted, gathering the scattered produce with a chuckle. "Food adorned with glitter does suit tonight's celebration," she mused, idly brushing specks from the vegetables before placing them back into the basket.

Mama D's mouth turned up at the corners, her joy radiating. The lines around her earthy, brown eyes crinkled with each laugh, amplifying the warmth of her smile. She straightened from her crouched position, holding a handful of turnips and carrots. Carefully, she placed them back into the basket, brushing off as much confetti as she could. "It really gets everywhere, doesn't it? Just like the sand."

She paused, letting her gaze drift to the setting sun streaming through the classroom windows; the soft glow bathed the room in warm light. The final embers of daylight ebbed across a canopy of sparkling stars suspended above. The room pulsed with color; a living kaleidoscope against the black-painted ceiling and marine-blue walls. Hues altered and refracted across scattered gems, setting them aglow like a parade of jewel-like fireflies.

Runa murmured, "It's like the shadows linger—curious and watchful—while the light moves freely, unbound, carving out a space to make a life."

Mama D's eyes softened. "The shadows have a way about them, don't they?" She glanced back at Runa, her smile gentle. "Sometimes, I think they forget they matter, too."

Runa nodded, grounding herself as she returned to her desk. 'I suppose that's why I love it here,' she murmured, pulling out a ringlet of keys and slinging her worn leather book bag over her shoulder with a steady breath.

"My gut tells me that before coming to Starlight…" Her words faltered. "I think…there just wasn't enough of me—pieced together—to even see myself." She shrugged, her tone dipping low. "So how could I have seen the shadows?"

Mama D nodded in understanding. "Well, my dear, here and now is a very different place. And when you meet the shadows again—take the time to really see them." She glanced at the door, then back at Runa. "Ready to head out?"

Runa gave the keys a playful jingle, moving in time toward the threshold as Mama D rolled her shoulders, adjusting the weight of her load. "Absolutely." She confirmed. They stepped through the opening, out into the evening bustle. Runa turned, securing the door of the weathered-stone schoolhouse behind them. "Let's see what the shadows whisper today…I'm not quite sure why, but they feel different somehow."

Mama D linked her arm with Runa's, their steps falling into an easy rhythm as they moved into the twilight. Golden light stretched low, the sun's final farewell weaving through the dusky haze. Its glow softened the world around them, blurring edges into warmth. Shadows stretched and danced at their feet, gliding like whispers in the evening air.

Runa buried the keys in her pocket, exhaling, letting go of the hours behind her. With a gentle push off, a quiet smile tugged at her lips as she murmured, "This is the best time of evening for me." She turned to meet the world beyond the timeworn, ashen door of the ancient classroom, the earth stirred, as if by magic. The surrounding rugged terrain gave way to paths of sand and gravel; dotted here and there with raised planters overflowing with vibrant blooms. The twisting walkways led straight into the pulsing heart of Starlight Beach, where life spilled out in a symphony of motion.

Runa paused, taking in the town's latest addition—meandering avenues of slate, thoughtfully placed to guide the way through pockets of greenery. She realized, with a start, how deeply she'd drifted into her own thoughts. The children's laughter still rang in her ears; their little voices dancing around like playful sprites.

A smile pulled at her lips as she recalled Papa D's tone—somewhere between a bark and a chuckle. *Stay aware of your surroundings, Ru! It's vital to keep your bearings at all times.* With the soft padding of her footfalls against stone, she decided it was probably best not to mention just how lost in thought she'd been today. That particular confession could wait for another time. *I'm not in the mood for any lip from my workout drill sergeant today.*

Strolling through the community garden, neighbors paused mid-task to wave cheerfully, before returning to their tasks. Seeds sown, herbs harvested, hands working in hushed harmony to prepare for the night's grand celebration. This was more than tending the land; it was the careful cultivation, the laying down of roots for something far greater. *It's as though, beneath the soil, secrets slept—wrapped in hushed lullabies, cradled in stories not yet told.*

The newly laid slate pathways held a subtle sheen in the fading light;

starkly different from the aged cobblestones ahead, where every worn groove murmured of the town's past. Starlight Beach's history lay embedded in every crack and crevice; a quiet testament to all that had come before.

The salty breeze carried an ebbing reminder—*What is it exactly? Currents of protection, perhaps. Or at least, that's how it feels. Palpable. A weight both tender and heavy, braiding itself through every fracture and hollow.* She stopped walking, taking it in, trying to comprehend the feeling it stirred. *Settled—is that the right word? Transformed? Something about all this looks... different.*

Her gaze lifted to the towering lighthouse ahead. Not just a statue, but a centerpiece—a guardian etched into the heart of Starlight Beach. A sea of flowers in deep blues, greens, and whites surrounded its base; each petal carefully arranged to mimic waves crashing against unseen rocks.

She kept walking, drawn forward in a newfound state of awe, mouth agape. *Was it always this grand, or am I now seeing it for what it truly is?* Raising her chin skyward, she wondered, *Why now? What else have I missed?*

The monument stood at the forefront of the town hall—prominent, undeniable—its plaque catching the last glimmers of golden twilight. As they approached, the inscription gleamed, sending a shiver through her; a ribbon unthreaded, rippling along her spine, as if the plaque itself bristled with irritation.

It feels like...an idea resting on the tip of my tongue, she thought, perplexed yet curious. She shook her head, making her way to the engraved words. *Maybe Mama D was right about those damn shadows...*She waved the notion off with an uneasy chuckle, running a finger along each line as she read.

"Starlight Beach Community Covenant: A Pledge and Dedication to Residents, Travelers, and Newcomers"

In the Heart of Starlight Beach

This lighthouse stands as a beacon—a steadfast symbol of hope; its spirit enduring through every storm. Here, at Starlight Beach, sanctuary isn't just a dream, but a place you feel in your bones. A refuge where weary souls find peace in the ocean's quiet whispers, the age-old songs that

drift through the trees, and cobblestone streets paved with a longing for something unspoken, something more.
In this cherished corner of the world, you will find the strength to build anew, to create a life where light guides the way.
For Starlight is the star you wished upon, and the Moonlight that will find its way back to you.

Erected with love & light by the creative souls of Starlight Beach & the sworn guards of Shadow City.

She had stood before the plaque a hundred times, yet for the first time, a single quote emerged from beneath the inscription—rising slowly, as if to meet her astonishment. Her finger reached out instinctively, tracing the raised letters, feeling each curve like a forgotten touch. The words settled deep within her, as though they had been waiting. *Waiting for me.*

"Day and night, light and dark—stars and moon—two bound, two tethered like a circadian rhythm: one seeking the other, and another still to be found."

She ran her fingertips along the inscription, letting its meaning take hold, as if absorbing light for the first time. Tearing her gaze away, she pursed her lips, searching the depths of her thoughts for anything—any thread of reason—that might make sense of this. *Maybe I am the one living in the shadows?* The notion came unbidden, creeping in, lacing itself through everyday sights and tangling into her ordinary. *It's as if the world is breathing…differently.* A muted fascination slipped through the floorboards of her memories, dancing with what had long laid dormant. *Fresh eyes allow fresh insight*—a quote from Papa D, settled into place, like an old truth rediscovered.

With eyes alight in wonder, Runa stepped forward as Mama D extended an elbow—an unspoken invitation to link arms. The grand, time-worn stone of Town Hall merged seamlessly into a wooden boardwalk stretching leftward. The well-worn planks carried the soft, rhythmic clunk of bootfalls and the light echo of bare feet. The familiar sounds mingled with the distant cries of seagulls and the soft tinkle of shopfront chimes.

She gave a small nod, confirming what she already knew—*Everything feels a shade lighter, a touch brighter—like the world has slipped into a new hue.* A quiet sigh escaped her, a silent admission of admiration and awe swelling.

Charming storefronts lined their path, their hanging signs creaking in the breeze, a chorus of voices lost in time. Wind chimes clinked like hushed secrets, as if the walls themselves were whispering—undiscovered friends waiting to be heard. Each haven held its own assortment of coastal curiosities and handcrafted delights.

Runa paused at the window of a coffee shop she had passed a million times; its warmth and aroma now pulling at her with unexpected delight. Her gaze drifted to an apothecary, where bottles of tinctures glinted like gems in the sunlight. The general store overflowed with color, brimming with a variety of goods that hinted at stories of old waiting to be retold. Just beyond the shops, the gentle tinkling of musical notes filled the air, while ethereal forms seemed to dance and float on the breeze.

The air thickened with seaweed, salt, and sand, wrapping around her like an old quilt, reshaped by the turning tide. Each inhale carried a hint of something forgotten. *It feels like I'm filling my lungs for the first time—like reclaiming a piece of my soul.* The crisp tang of the ocean clung to the air, brushing against her skin like a half-remembered dream—stirring at the edges, pressing gently, like the tide creeping back to shore.

It's like I've been living underwater, everything muted and distant. And now, here I am—dragged to the surface, feeling everything at once. A gradual swell, an unraveling of emotions and memories—a lazy, drifting cascade, like a rolling current. What would happen if I just let it take me? She hovered on the edge of surrender, letting the sensations wash over her. With each step, the world seemed to open a little wider, inviting her to slow down, to wander and wonder; letting her mind drift, releasing the tension she hadn't realized she'd been grasping.

The North Star's aromas wafted through the courtyard, drawing her gaze back along the promenade. She took in the familiar quaintness of the coffeehouse and café's facade—an endearing blend of weathered wood, old wagon wheels, and mismatched signs jutting from the front. *Order Here. Pick Up There.* The Open sign, a mosaic of stained glass, caught the fading light, casting fractured colors onto the worn planks below.

The scent curled through the air, luring explorers from the enchanting gardens of Starlight Beach. The fragrance enticed them back to the bustling boardwalk, teasing their senses with the promise of something familiar and inviting. Through propped-open, vertical-hinged windows, the rich aroma of espresso and warm pastries spilled into the evening air—an unspoken invitation to linger a little longer.

Here, mornings began with more than just a cup of coffee—these seemingly random groupings, possible brotherhoods, Runa noticed, always started with indulgent breakfasts. Each plate was built on sustenance rather than excess. Eggs, seasoned meats, and hearty grains lined the tables, a stark contrast to the sugar-laden fare favored by occasional tourists.

The regulars moved with an easy familiarity, gathering in the soft light of dawn, their presence as steady as the tide. Dressed in deep black and dark charcoal, their attire was unassuming, yet a quiet discipline marked their every movement. They blended in—just another set of locals or passing visitors—but there was a rhythm to their presence, a subtle cohesion that set them apart from the rest.

It wasn't just the aroma of coffee that beckoned. The warmth of freshly baked bread intertwined with the savory pull of smoked meats drifting from the smoker, while the sizzle of bacon blended with the sweetness of cinnamon and nutmeg. A whisper of coconut syrup, delicately drizzled over fluffy pancakes, lingered in the air—a symphony of flavors, each one a subtle invitation to come closer.

In the café's corner, a different crowd gathered—retired travelers, vacationers, and longtime locals who had settled into the rhythm of the place. Jolly older men swapped stories over steaming mugs, some moving with a slight limp, the quiet remnants of storms weathered long ago. Joyous women shared knowing smiles, their laughter carrying the warmth of well-worn friendships.

They moved at an easier tempo, as if life had nudged them into a gentler speed—a striking contrast to Mama D and Papa D, who still carried an energy that seemed to defy time. Yet, despite the ease in these weary traveler's movements, there was an undeniable structure to them, a routine that never wavered. They arrived at the same time each morning, ordered without glancing at the menu, and drifted to their familiar spots as if guided by an unspoken rhythm. Even in the relaxed hum of the café, they carried a quiet discipline, a lifetime of habits ingrained into something as simple as breakfast.

But now, the day ebbed into twilight, and with it, everything changed. The courtyard awakened in a different way, the golden glow of lanterns flickered to life as melodies wove through the air, winding themselves along the boardwalk. Laughter spilled freely—deep, bellyful sounds; glee-filled jokes tossed between old friends and new. Glasses clinked in easy celebration, voices rising and falling in the warm cadence of shared joy. And then, as if carried by the night itself, someone began to sing. Another voice joined, then another, until a chorus swelled, bursting into an impromptu song that belonged to everyone.

Isn't it incredible how it evolves? How the hum of the morning café crowd gives way to this—a world brimming with music, warmth, and unguarded happiness. One moment, it's just a quiet gathering spot, and the next, it's alive with song, laughter, and stories waiting to be told.

This—this—is what tugs at my core. The way the music curls through the air, coaxing the crowd to loosen, to lean in, to open their minds and carve out space for something new to take root. How could anyone resist? The very essence of it all tugged at her feet, urging her to stay, to soak it in, to become a part of it.

Her boots tapped against the well-worn stones as she ventured deeper into the heart of town. There, "The Cabinets of Curiosity" stood as a distinctive haven—Rayanna's carefully crafted sanctuary. It wove together an eclectic blend of health, wellness, and a touch of nostalgia. *Just like Ray herself,* she thought, a smile tugging at her lips.

Rayanna, her sister in all sense of the word, was an artist with a deep love for the natural world. *She embarked on a journey creating her own unique little shop. With the support of Mama D and Tabytha, she'd poured her soul into the space; heartstrings woven from corner to corner.*

Runa grinned internally, as Rayanna's words bubbled to the surface: "An apothecary isn't just a shop—a living entity. You craft with care, precision, and purpose, because this isn't about mixing herbs or stacking shelves. It's about intention. The right element in the wrong place—might as well be poison." She imagined her fingertips brushing along the edge of the cool, polished countertop. *I wonder if Ray feels this change too?* The answer was there, nestled among her carefully curated collection—each piece chosen with an eye for the unusual, the potent, and the healing.

Tabytha had been Rayanna's collaborator—a counterpart in this delicate art; a craft that wove nature, science, and beauty together into the extraordinary. They'd graced the shelves with an array of herbal remedies, each carefully selected from the gardens of their community. *A haven of healing, they would say.*

Tiny bottles of essential oils pressing close, nestling among a hodgepodge of meticulously forged glass jars. Runa knew each jar held more than just tucked-away secrets—they brimmed with hope, truth, and healing. Each cruet rested upon the elegantly crafted dark wooden shelves, holding more than just inspiration—each carried a touch of awe. The ledges themselves seemed to grow from the U-shaped counter, like the branches of an ancient tree. They reached around the store's edges, their lines as graceful and intricate as the herbs they held.

At the heart of the shop, small islands and tiered platforms stood at varying elevations, each a stage for its own display. Handcrafted soaps, and beeswax candles smelled of honey and herbs. Set alongside botanical balms, offering the gift of restoration, as crystal encased tinctures gleamed softly under a golden hazed lighting. Jars with curious labels, old mortars, pestles, and other peculiar artifacts seemed to hum with hushed histories.

"Like a world of its own," Rayanna would say. In this moment, Runa felt the space exhale, settling naturally into itself. It was a quiet refuge, a place where dreams could take root; where the magic of possibilities hummed softly, knitted into every corner. Within her mind, Runa extended a hand, brushing against a small vintage jar, imagining the cool glass meeting her skin. *Yes, Ray could very well be right about that.* She smiled to herself.

*How have I never seen it like **this** before?* Runa thought, a sense of disbelief washing over her. *I just...I don't understand how I missed all this.* She walked with hesitation, almost afraid that moving too quickly might shatter this newfound clarity. *I feel like the boardwalk has just sprung into existence.*

Her eyes caught on the space entwined with the apothecary's shared wall—Tabytha's domain, a haven where the soft rustle of leaves and the distant murmur of waves wove wonders into wellness. On the polished wooden floor, movement flowed in rhythm—mobility drills, primal exercises, strength and conditioning; each routine a dance of purpose and precision.

And dancing, Runa mused, a wry smile tugging at her lips. *How I wish it were my thing.* Tabytha moved with effortless grace, but Runa favored power over finesse. Not the kind that twirled or swayed, but the kind that held firm—grounded and unwavering. Still, the energy here was unmistakable, the space breathing with the waves. A living current, steady and sure. Even if rhythm wasn't hers to claim, The Studio's pull still beckoned.

The coastal boardwalk is a central hub, blending every distinct element like the ingredients of a cake, layered, rich, and full of surprises. This small town is no mere collection of people coexisting; it's a recipe, each element carefully chosen, adding its own flavor to the mix.

Runa paused, taking it all in. *Everything has such a purpose,* she thought feeling the truth of it settle deep. *How have I missed this? Every step today feels so different than before.* Blinking, she noticed the crunching beneath her feet. *Crunch. Crunch. Crunch. So many layers, so many puzzle pieces.*

With a slight dip of her chin, she simply listened, attuned to the newest sound that captured her notice. The shift in texture marked the town's quiet transformation, from cobblestones to gravel. Each step carried the weight of the world. *Crunch. Crunch. Crunch. Soft, and then light. A sharp distinction,* she mused—*a break from the old to the new. Simple yet complex.*

At the farthest edge of the town center stood what was once a vintage general store; its bones still carrying the charm of a New England cottage. Now a confectioner's haven; its green and cream awning spilling over like the embrace of a long-lost friend. The walls, painted in warm, sea-inspired tones, felt like a cozy harbor. They were a safe and inviting place where worries gently faded into a cream-filled wonderland; delectable even from a distance. The space exuded a sense of childlike wonder that mingled with the scents of ice cream, sugar cones, and chocolate-covered treats. The charm of the place was familiar.

Dagny's Seaside Sweets. Her gaze lingered on the petite green sign, its weathered edges whispering stories of salt-kissed summers and the timeless magic of seaside days. As they passed, she imagined her hand hovering over the doorknob—a flicker of herself as a youngling. Her tiny fingers reached out to touch the cool metal—hesitant, yet drawn forward by the promise of something sweet. Just inside the door, she could see it: her younger self, wide-eyed with wonder, caught in the first thrill of discovery.

Cre-eak. The old door groaned open in her mind, followed by a cheerful *Ting!*—the little bell above, always announcing a new arrival. A soft smile tugged at her lips as she pictured it closing once more with a gentle *plop*, like a satisfied sigh—a sound that always promised something worth discovering.

She hesitated, feeling the faint pull of something unseen, something tethered to the past. *This can't be happening. Can it?* A peculiar mix of disbelief and wonder settled somewhere between her heart and her stomach. Her mind lingered on Dagny's front patio, drifting back to those afternoons with Papa D—freshly home from his brotherhood camping extravaganza; still clad in his usual obsidian-black gear. The fabric carried the scent of the sea and something else she could never quite place.

His laughter ran along the floorboards, ricocheting off the walls before bursting forth like sunlight, chasing away shadows. The unexpected sound turned heads, pausing conversations and halting movements mid-step. For a moment, people hesitated—caught between surprise and curiosity. Then, like a ripple on still water, the mirth spread—reluctant at first, until the deep timbre of his chuckles proved too infectious to resist, drawing others into a full chorus of joy.

He's ours, and I cherished every ounce of those moments with him. Ice cream and tales were shared freely; the meandering brotherhood drifting in from the North Star. Groups drawn to the patio's edge the instant his tone echoed through the streets. The glinting eyes sparked carefully crafted stories of distant lands, weaving wonders into the ordinary. *These tales made my eyes widen, and I was tangled between accounts so outlandish they couldn't possibly be so. Right?*

Nonetheless, those afternoons were everything. Little treasures —like puzzle pieces still learning their place. Her lips curled into a smile, soft and secretive as a murmur. The remnants of such joys flitted around her like sugar-dusted wafers—light, delicate, and fleeting. As the two women meandered past, the reveries began to dissolve at the edges, fraying like the well-loved pages of a favorite book.

Runa laughed out loud, the sound breaking through the serenity, startling Mama D. "Sorry," she said, her smile widening into a grin. "I can almost see Papa D's face when he spots the bag of divine rose cakes I bought for tonight's celebration."

"He'll pretend to be outraged," Mama D replied, a spark of mischief lighting her eyes, "but—he'll devour them all the same."

Runa shook her head, amusement glinting in her eyes. "His protests are nothing but a farce," she mused, laughter gliding through her words. "Never—not once—has he fooled me with such absurdity. These blasted cakes are heavenly—any sane person would be mad not to fall for them."

"You really do have him pinned down," Mama D nudged Runa with a gentle shoulder bump. As they passed the tail end of Dagny's Seaside Sweets , sunlight spilled through the stained-glass panes, scattering jeweled fragments of color across the gravel path. Each step sent the hues rippling like water over stone. Mama D glanced at Runa, "What's on your mind?" she asked softly, "You look like you've been savoring a thought."

Runa blinked, then smiled. "I suppose I have," she murmured, "Everything…it just looks different today, Mama. More vivid somehow."

Mama D raised an eyebrow, her curiosity piqued. "Different how, darling?" she asked softly. "Like you've pulled a veil from your eyes?" She paused, waiting for a response.

Nodding she scanned the approaching cottages. "Maybe —It's hard to explain. It feels like I've walked this path so many times, but today…today, it's as if I'm seeing it for the first time." She paused, frowning slightly, searching for the right words. "The colors, the smells, even the sounds… they're all…clearer."

Mama D's gaze softened, a playful grin tugging at her lips. "Well, if the world's looking clearer, maybe that's why the pastries at the North Star were calling my name."

Runa laughed, the sound bright but tinged with awe. "It feels different," she confessed, almost as if admitting it to herself. "Like I've been here a thousand times, but I've never really been here…not like this." She halted mid-stride, her eyes wandering, absorbing every detail.

Mama D studied her intently, sensing there was more beneath the surface. "Is it unsettling, Love?" her voice was soft and probing, without pressure.

"No…no, not unsettling." Runa's words slipping out, barely perceptible. "More like…waking up from a dream. Bewildering, maybe, but beautiful too."

With a subtly nod, Mama D considered the words. "Maybe it takes just a small shift," she murmured, "for the shadows to move aside, showing us what's always been there. Waiting."

"Maybe," Runa murmured, "It's very possible." Hesitating for a moment before finally speaking. "Mama, do you ever feel like something's missing? Like someone is missing?"

Mama D's features lifted, a quiet thoughtfulness settling in as her gaze traced the distant mountains. "I think so," she murmured, exhaling and choosing her words with care. A small chuff escaped her lips, as if letting go of a long unspoken question. "Like shadows stretching at dusk—not hiding the light, but making their presence more well-known?"

Runa nodded absently, her fingers gliding over the cool, uneven surface of the waist-high, stone wall as they moved further inland. Gravel paths wove between pastel, coastal cottages with an old-world English touch. Each property was guarded by a towering oak, its sprawling branches casting dappled shadows over the front yards.

Mama D nudged Runa on, "Tell me more."

"I don't know," Runa admitted as a slight frown creased her brow. "It's just...being here, I feel drawn—toward something I can't quite name. Sometimes, it's suffocating, an aching quiet that presses in from all sides."

She smiled softly, squeezing Runa's hand. "Maybe it's the magic of this place," she suggested. "Starlight Beach has a way of doing that—slowing time to a crawl, making you feel like you're part of something bigger. Even timeless..."

"I don't know—maybe?" Her words lingered like a droplet of water clinging to the edge after a heavy rain. "I think there's something… purposeful beyond Starlight." She shrugged lightly. "I mean, the stars hold on to the moon. The light holds the night's hand, doesn't it? So, why wouldn't there be more here for us?"

Mama D leaned into Runa, her tone a steady promise, "Life doesn't stop here, sugar. There's always more."

Mama D cast a sideways glance as they made their way back to the girls' cottage. Each year, she watched Runa slip into quiet reflection. *But this time was different. Not like any other,* she admitted inwardly. Runa had always sifted through a whirlwind of emotions, pulled in every direction. *But now? Now, the questions were sharper—like arrows loosed into the dark, searching for a target. And she's getting closer.* A thought came loose, *I ache to share every hidden detail, every truth I've carried. Izayah was right, this Dawning Day would change everything.*

Opening their door to the younglings had been the most fulfilling mission she and Diesel had ever undertaken. As General of the Shadow Guild—the most sought-after rank within The Lands—there was supposed to be a celebration. A clean break from the field and veering into a new form of leadership.

But like anything in the military, plans pivot. A developing operation took shape under his command, pulling them both back in. Instead of closing the door on their old life, it became their final operation, delaying everything they had once agreed upon. "One last assignment before we stand down," Diesel had said. At the time, she'd only grasped the weight of it on a surface level.

Yet...here I stand. The corners of her mouth tipped upward at the thought. *Their spirit simply infused us with a newfound fervor.* But it was always Runa's gaze—so full of searching—that left Mama D's heart in fragments. *Give them a home. Help them grow. That had been the mission. Yet it has become so much more. It commanded every part of us. It claimed our full attention, leaving no room for hesitation. Rekindled something I thought was long gone.*

She couldn't speak for Diesel, but after nine hundred years at his side, she knew this much: *One look at those girls, and you know—his loyalty is a hard line. I'd wager my last breath on it.* A quiet smile formed as she followed the path. *They were so unaware of the adventure that awaited. Such things, greater than themselves. It fills me with a sense of optimism, a belief in the future of Shadow City and Sanctuary, coming together. She was our start, this mission was our introduction. Witnessing Runa gathering the pieces of herself, steadily mending the fractures within.*

She felt a quiet sense of understanding. *This is what the shadow binding is for, to grant the mind the grace to heal, so the rest may follow in time.* Her gaze softened as she reflected, *The shadows hold steady as they must. For that is their role. To stand beside the light. Two parts of a whole. One cannot exist without the other. Yet, together they create a divine balance.*

*To think that in this moment, in this place, she's **initiating** her own unbind-*

ing. Mama D marveled, the weight of it settling—like a sack of stones placed down with care. Not forceful, but undeniably heavy. *She's doing the impossible. Without awareness. Without the assistance of a Seer or an Unbinder. She is single handedly unspooling the shadows.*

Her chest brimmed with something too heavy to name. *What they have restored in me, restored in us, I can never repay. Not in words. Not in deeds. It was faith. It was grit. It was the quiet, unyielding determination to claw free of the darkness— even without a clear path forward.*

Easing her pace, Runa nodded toward the cottage and casually pointed her thumb over her shoulder. "So, what's the plan? Are you staying to work your culinary magic, or should I save two seats?"

"Oh, don't worry about me. I've got a few things to grab for you ladies, including that old man of mine." She flashed a wry smile. "Just save us a seat; we wouldn't miss it for the world. Besides," she added with a chuckle, "you know how he vanishes into his paperwork the second he steps inside that study."

Runa laughed softly, shaking her head. "Yeah, but you always manage to drag him out just in time. I swear, he could write a book on creative avoidance."

Positioned at the edge of the moon gate, Mama D surveyed the pathway, ensuring all was clear. *What else might she be releasing?* Her teeth catching her bottom lip. Her gaze traced the crevices of the weathered barriers and the delicate layer of moss. The greenery glazed the masonry, seeping into the mortar's gaps like frosting smoothed over a cake. Unknowingly protective, yet undeniably pleasing to the eye.

She shifted uneasily, her feet digging into the gravel that crunched with every nervous movement. *What did Diesel tell me?* A gentle scrape of stone against stone disturbed the silence, as the finer sand beneath her feet gave way. It was almost as if the ground itself urged her to slip into the shadows. *He said no blood reaching…Shit!*

Runa's eyes narrowed slightly. "You okay?"

"Yes," Mama D replied. "You know how I get with the festival." She batted a hand dismissively. "I just want it to be perfect. I'm a little on edge, I guess. I always try to outdo myself, and it rattles my nerves."

A shadow of black ghosted over her skin, an enigma. *Is my unveiling a response to her? Could it be?* Rubbing at her forearm, she feigned a need for warmth. From her periphery, she caught Runa's gaze drawn to the movement—a momentary spark at the edge of her vision. *Stay calm,* she thought, feeling her pulse quicken. The subtle incline of Runa's head betrayed her awareness. *Don't linger. Move.*

"Are you alright?" Runa's eyes lingered on the spot. "What was that?" Her fingers brushed against Mama D's arm, her gaze fixed on the place where obscurity wavered.

Mama D adjusted her stance, tugging the bag higher onto her shoulder. "This bunch is getting a bit heavy," her tone faltered slightly. "I should get these back, you know…" She quickened her pace, resisting the urge to rush. *Don't make it obvious. Just keep moving.*

She nearly reached the corner before turning back, realizing how abrupt she must have seemed. A smile tugged at her lips as she called out, "Ru, I can't wait to see how you outdo last year's decor. Light up the world, love!" *Keep it steady,* she thought through clenched teeth.

Runa shot back a playful wink, flinging her arms wide like a child reaching to claim the mountaintops. "Did you expect anything less than a glittering extravaganza, a sea of candles, and the most incredible feast imaginable? I learned from the best."

Warmth unfurled in Mama D's chest as she watched Runa slip through the moon gate, disappearing into the golden glow of their cottage. Only then did she exhale.

Lingering for a moment, her gaze drifted over the path they had just walked. With a quiet nod, she turned back. Her body remained composed, but her mind was already three steps ahead. *All clear. Diesel needs to be briefed.*

Her footsteps faltered briefly on the fine gravel, as she quickened her pace. *I have to get to him…now!* She could already see his reaction—poised and set. *Would he anticipate these specifics? I can't be sure.*

Part of her ached to blood-reach—that rare, potent form of telepathy. *It's out of the question, D. Do not blood tether—no matter the reason. Not here. Not after what happened last time.* She rubbed her temple, thinking. *He's right. The risk is too high.*

She hurried along every instinct urging her to lighten the load, but even *that* small comfort was forbidden in this phase of the assignment. *Focus,* she reminded herself, but her mind kept coming back to what *was off-limits. No blood reaching. No shortcuts.*

Her simple sandals pressed between her toes, fanning out toward the sides of her feet—not ideal for sprinting across the sand. They were meant for leisurely strolls, not for the hurried strides she took now. At least she'd chosen wide-legged, velvety-gray pants and a fitted charcoal crop top instead of the loose teal beach dress she had considered. *Smart move,* she thought. *But still too slow.*

The cottage just…seems so far away. Though it's just a few houses down the lane, it feels impossibly out of reach today. It's only a short walk, she reminded herself. *But nothing about this feels normal.* As she approached and passed through their own moon gate, the gleaming perimeters shimmered. Their faint outlines materialized, shrouded in a thin, misted shield.

How far has Runa unbound herself—and what does that mean for Starlight's stability? The barriers didn't just shield—they silenced, absorbing every sound within and forming an impenetrable line of defense against any breach. Not every dwelling in Starlight Beach has earned this level of protection.

With the wealth of knowledge hidden within these walls, security was a top priority, and the "keystones" remained indispensable. *If Lord Brannon knew the full extent…it would be our heads.*

Three substantial, aged, slate stones marked the entry path. The "keystones" rested comfortably within the gravel, beneath a vine-covered trellis —*hidden in plain sight. Cleverly simple. Who would ever suspect?* They served as an access key, shifting the house's defenses, depending on the level of clearance for those entering, with walls hidden and information protected.

Each day, Missy, the quaint abode they called home, adjusted their access codes. Tiny blotted dots would appear on the inner surface of each palm—one pattern for departure, and another for arrival. Only the bearer could perceive them, a silent communication, known only to those who needed it.

Her attention snapped to her right hand, anticipation stirring. A faint *ssssip*—sharp, pressurized—then dots surfaced, ink blooming from the very pores of her skin. The entry pattern emerged, alive with a will of its own.

With care, she placed her foot on the first slate, just near the left edge. Instantly, a soft hum buzzed beneath her sole; the faintest glow spread, like a lantern's light drifting through thick mist. She pulled her right foot to the farthest edge. A muted thrum vibrated up her leg, the slab responding with a subtle, eager shimmer.

Moving to the second piece, she set her left foot in the center, then her right. *Steady now, just like old lessons,* she thought. A gentle pulse quivered through the ground, as if the path were awakening after a long sleep. With a swift movement, her left foot glided to the middle of the left-side edge, her right following to the opposite side—a signal to Missy that she had moved from *attention* to a more *relaxed at ease* stance.

The response was almost immediate. With a soft click and a barely audible sigh, the front door drifted open. A warm sheen spilled outward, washing the entryway in welcoming hues of emerald green and deep navy blue, as the house itself exhaled in relief.

She stepped across the threshold with a soft sigh of the floorboards beneath her, pausing by the shoe rack. With a swift motion, she slipped off her sandals and moved down the narrow corridor, awash in the gentle radiance of soft, amber hues. Light shimmered across the deep green wallpaper. Its surface scrawled with intricate, filigree-like branches that twisted and turned, reaching toward a central symbol of knowledge. The afterglow was a gentle reminder of the secrets held within these walls.

From the outside, Missy appeared to be an unassuming cottage—modest, with just enough space for a cozy life. But now that the girls had moved into their new home down the street, Missy seemed to stretch and unfurl, like a contented cat basking in warmth. Her true depth and secrets surfaced, as though she had been waiting for this moment. A sigh, a creak, and the walls responded, breathing in rhythm with Mama's own anticipation.

As she continued, the frames along the walls quivered slightly, stirring to life in response to her presence. The images within flickered, capturing the joyful faces of the townsfolk in moments of laughter and mischief. A chuckle here, a wink there—each frame a window into a past, filled with warmth and wonder; their gilded edges catching the dim glow like scattered treasure.

She heaved the bag of vegetables onto the sleek, black countertop, nudging aside the bouquet of pink, bell-shaped blossoms that hummed faintly with life. The comforting aroma of roasted pork wafted through the air as Missy, ever helpful, nudged the oven door open, revealing a perfectly braised pork shoulder inside.

Not now, Missy. She resisted the temptation to pause. *That looks beautiful, but there's no time to get distracted.*

In response, the oven dial clicked softly, lowering the heat to keep the pork warm. The door eased shut, as if Missy were crossing her arms with a quiet sigh of understanding. Mama D smiled at the house's gentle insistence but pressed on. She pushed away from the counter, and strode down the hallway.

Entering the study was like stepping into another world. It was a surrender, a return to something and someone deeply known. The room had expanded into two floors; with bookshelves towering upward, their volumes whispering softly, exchanging stories untold. The air altered, carrying the scent of misty lakes and the calm of distant mountains. Deep, velvety greens blanketed the lower walls, gradating into dark, inky hues of navy. Higher still, the colors intertwined and deepened into soft grays, reminiscent of a budding twilight stretching across the ceiling.

Fairy lights coiled around the towering tree trunk rooted at the center of the far wall. The base of the trunk merged with the nearest bookshelf; its branches reaching out toward the carved mantel of the crackling fireplace. The flames cast playful shadows, flickering in time with the soft glow above.

Beside the hearth, a spiraling staircase wound upward, each step sprouting naturally from the very wood of the house itself. The bookcases yielded to the grain, flowing as if shaped by an unseen hand, forming an elegant, fluid ascent.

The staircase invited exploration, promising private spaces where bits of knowledge and endless possibilities waited to be discovered. Mama D's gaze drifted to the small balconies lined with rustic pillows; each cushion fluffed and inviting, the textures enticed fingers to explore.

Soft moss clung to the surfaces, a patchwork of growth tracing the edges of bookshelves—much like the stonework outside. Nester called it a healing balm for Missy's soul. To the right of the firebox, a velvet armchair in a deep forest hue sat closest to the flames, its fabric worn soft with time, beckoning her to sit. The cushion adjusted itself with a soft *plip-plop,* as if expecting her to nestle in and share her daily tale.

A charred coffee table sat between the aged velvet seat and a leather sofa, its burn marks dark around the edges, adding a touch of rugged charm. A soft creak from the table's legs drew her attention, urging her to fill the space with words unspoken. The scent of coffee grounds, aged leather, and cedar-lined whiskey barrels filled the room, a heady mix that nudged her with reminders of just how far they had come.

Beyond the inviting sofa, Diesel sat at a large desk in the far left corner. Reclined in his opulent chestnut, leather chair, he rolled the amber whiskey along the curve of the glass, his focus elsewhere. His tattooed knuckles raked through his peppered hair, kneading away the tension buried beneath his scalp. Another pensive turn of the glass. A distant gaze.

Mama D stepped closer, her voice cutting through his reverie. "D, we need to talk." The weight of concern shaped each syllable, a truth he couldn't ignore.

His eyes flicked up, a low rumble of awareness escaping his chest. "About what?"

She hesitated, then pressed on. "Runa…" Her fingers rapped against the wood, muscle memory from a life spent waiting for deployments to end."She's unbinding herself."

"Excuse me." The glass froze mid-swish, "Unbinding herself?" His tone sharpened, disbelief slicing through contemplation. "That's impossible. No one unbinds themselves."

"Well, she is." Mama D replied, "Hon—it's Runa. She's doing it on her own, piece by piece."

Diesel set the glass down with a soft clink, leaning forward, eyes narrowing. "You're saying she's unraveling the shadow binding on her own?

"Yeah," Mama D huffed, "Runa's deciphering a puzzle she doesn't even know she's holding the pieces to."

Diesel's brow furrowed, "But…how?" His shoulders went rigid, shock locked into disciplined restraint.

"Pure will? I mean, thought weaving and shadow binding are not common practices," Mama D stated, tension lining her expression. "I can only assume at this point."

"If she finishes...if she fully unbinds—what happens, then?" he wondered aloud.

Mama D's voice wavered. "This isn't something we could predict. Sienna warned us—said Runa's core was unlike anything she'd seen in generations. It was a risk...that we took anyway."

Diesel dragged a rough hand over his forehead, the weight of it settling in. "If she fully unbinds, Starlight Beach won't stay hidden. The shadows won't hold—not with that kind of power pouring off her. We're not prepared for that. She has to be moved, Darlin'. Far from here."

Mama D nodded, bracing herself against the desk's edge before clearing her throat."Those unexplained bruises and cuts, I can only wonder if it's tied to this."

Diesel grunted, his gaze hardening as he considered the possibilities. "And Izayah...? Could it be?" He furrowed his brow. "Anything is possible."

Mama D's voice sharpened. "We need to move her—quietly, without drawing attention or making matters worse."

"How are we supposed to do that?" His voice tightened with frustration. "Love, it makes little sense. There's nowhere else to go—and Rayanna will have a conniption if Runa suddenly disappears." He exhaled sharply, shoving his chair back before sinking deeper into the cushions. "Treefall, maybe." He clicked his tongue against his cheek. "No one would think to look there." Swirling the liquid in his glass, he mulled it over, thinking aloud. "Not sure how we'd actually get in, though."

"We have to do something," Mama D shot back, her voice rising, almost trembling. "If she keeps going like this, who knows what could happen? No one's ever done this on their own. She's tearing herself apart, D, without knowing the risks—the consequences could be catastrophic!"

"I'm well aware!" he snapped, his anger flaring before retreating almost immediately. "I didn't mean that...sorry, my love."

"I know." She softened, coming around the desk and leaning in closer. "It's okay."

"She could expose everything," Diesel muttered darkly. "The whole town…Starlight Beach, all of it." He shook his head and downed the rest of the amber liquid. Mama D took the glass from his hand, setting it on the table with a firm thud. "Where's the extraction point? Where can we move her that's secure—somewhere she won't draw attention?"

"Treefall." She swallowed hard, pushing past hesitation, "Is it actually an option, though?" Biting on her bottom lip and forcing down the lump in her throat. "I don't know where else…but we have to find somewhere. If we don't, everything we've kept hidden here—everything we've built— could be exposed."

"You're right," he muttered, exhaling. "At least none of them have phased markings—yet."

She gave a small, shaky nod. "It's like she's finding her way back…but through the wrong door. If Visha learns of this…We can't lose her. If we do, everything here…all we've built…it's all for nothing, Love."

"Then we find her a place. Whatever it takes." He softened, a rare smile pulling at the corner of his mouth. "Hope's got a way of hiding. Maybe it's finding its way back."

"I hope you're right," she whispered. "I don't want Runa lost in the darkness again."

He reached out, gently tilting her chin, meeting her eyes. "We would find her, Darlin'. She's ours now."

Her breath pulled heavy, thick as tar. "And if she's found…?"

Diesel let out a low chuckle. "Then we handle it. Like we always do." The sound faded, but his gaze remained on hers—searching, steady. She leaned into the solid strength of him, her hands gripping the arms of his chair as she eased onto his lap. His arms wrapped around her, drawing her close. Her head settled against his shoulder—a small comfort in the storm closing in around them.

"D…" she softened into him, "Do you think…do you think the unbinding, the bruising…and Izayah…*could* all be connected?"

His hand moved down her back, rubbing gently as he considered, his expression darkening. "It's possible," he murmured. "If she's tearing at the bonds holding her, and Izayah's somehow tied to them…it could mean he's feeling it too. It could mean—"

She lifted her head, eyes wide with worry. "It could mean what?"

He spoke barely above a whisper. "It could mean they're closer than we thought. And if that's the case…"

"If that's the case, then…?" Her voice wavered, trailing into an uneasy quiet.

"Then we're running out of time, my sweet sip of whiskey, and whatever happens next…we may not be able to stop it."

"How can this be happening?" She drew in a measured breath. "Do you think…" Her voice faltered, the words catching in her throat. "Is it time to raise the white flag? To call the Golden Guard?"

"It might be," he murmured, tilting his head in quiet acceptance. "We don't have many options. But you know what that means, Darlin'." He exhaled heavily. "If we call them…there's no going back. We lose any chance of control."

"I believe it's our sole option," she said, her voice unsteady. "If it's the only way to secure her safety—to protect the girls, the mission, Starlight Beach…everything we've built."

His tone was a raw whisper, edged with restraint. "Then we may have to. But we need certainty—absolute certainty—there's no other way."

The discussion settled between them, thick as poured lead—pressing in, molten and unshaped. Then, deep within the house, a faint sound. *Click —whirr—click.* A door creaked open, followed by a faint tread of footfalls.

"Did you hear that?" Her tone was hushed, clipped with urgency.

Diesel's eyes narrowed. "No, love. I'm just sitting here, enjoying the ambiance," he replied, his voice dripping with sarcasm. "Were you expecting anyone?"

"No," she whispered, a chill running down her spine.

Tap—tap—tap. A faint glow bobbed in the shadows, creeping along the walls, inching toward the study. The light flickered—small, persistent— casting strange, gliding shapes that danced across the room. *Sir, we have a problem.*

Chapter Two

Sanctuary

Following Elite Surrender
Past

Izayah's gaze drifted—unfocused—drawn to the looping projection overhead, cycling in a silent, merciless rhythm.

Chest tightening.

Breathing shallow.

A gasp, *but not enough air—never enough.*

The weight pressing down…the burdening of waiting.

Of being watched.

Always watched.

How did she—The thought unraveling, slipping into oblivion…

Breathe in.

Breathe out—sputtering blood, a cough, a guttural groan.

Out of breath—ragged and raw.

Heavy.

Lips pressing together—gasping intervals, working himself through the moment.

Breathe in—hold for two seconds.

Breathe out—through the mouth—slow.
I can do this. I can sustain this encounter.
Breathe in—hold for four seconds.
Suffocating—under the torment—as if drowning were the only option left.
I can't—FUCKIN'—breathe.
FUCK, MAN! STOP—FUCKIN' HELL!
She can't witness me in such a state
DAMN IT!
STOP.
Focus your mind…CENTER!

Izayah willed his body still, forcing the fog and whispers of darkness up from somewhere deep, dragging them to the surface. Willing them to rise. To shroud his thoughts. *Control. Steady.*

The shadows strained to gather, swirling at the edges of his consciousness. Fighting to smother the chaos.

Burning it down. Burying it deep.
Rage simmered. Panic clawed its way up my throat.
This has to fuckin' work.
Breathe out—four seconds, smooth and controlled.
Breathe in—five seconds, feeling the pressure ease, just enough.
Breathe out—five seconds, the darkness is folding in around me.

Izayah watched as the world blurred, fading into nothingness. Silence swallowed him—dense and unrelenting.

Better than what looms before me.
Better than what she'd see if I let the darkness slip—if I let my guard down.
The significance is in swallowing air. Forcing it past the tightness.
Visha did this to her.
Did the High Priestess sit here, in these moments? Watching her, like she is with me now?
Was Runa drowning in this agony? For how long?
She bore this burden…and now, I carry it.
Trading my life for hers.
Fuck! Breathing burns.
A gut punch. Heavy.
No room for breathing deep.
Ribs threatening to snap.

Hold steady, man!
She fought through this darkness. She faced it alone.
Well, she isn't–FUCKIN' ALONE anymore!
Clenching his fists, the cold bite of reality sank like stone, leaving no room for denial.

Izayah fought through the poison churning in his veins.
If I could tear every ounce of suffering from her bones…
A scream clawed at him. Raw. Primal.
An urge to unleash it all. To let the rage spill free.
To bellow until his throat tore. Until his lungs seared.
But I can't.
He strapped it down. Contained it. Controlled it.
Silence! He commanded himself.
*Silence is **my power.***
Tension racking his frame. Muscles taut, trembling. Every fiber fraying, as he gripped the reigns of control. *One wrong move, and it unravels.* Fury gnawing. Anguish scraping raw. Forcing his breath to steady, syncing it with the pounding rhythm in his ears. *Not yet. I can't lose myself. Not now. Not when everything depends on this—on me.*

The chaos would come soon enough. Visha, the High Priestess, made that clear. And this is just the beginning. A trial of endurance. Years of agony and relentless discipline, awaiting me. The ultimate battlefield till Runa's new Dawning Day.

Twenty years.
Two decades.
Silence is my edge.
No cracks.
No compromise.
Only resolve.
I want to shatter something. Anything. Everything. I want to let the fury rupture like a dam bursting—an all-consuming flood, drowning everything in its wake.

Hold it in. Let it fester. Let it boil. Keep it caged.
Discipline first. Control always.
Dammit. Keep fuckin' breathing you fucking asshole.
Fuckin' feels like swallowing glass.
Dry—everything feels so dry.

Mind…slipping…floating…upward.

Teeth grinding.

Jaw ticking.

Muscles straining.

Pressure crushing.

Eyes burning.

Survival is the only option.

Father above, Blessed Father—Please.

Dissociation—a switch flipped by distress. A spark of silence. She could walk into the dark, shut off every feeling, and still function fully. Numb, but surviving. How many times has this been her existence?

His thoughts scattered, trying to make sense of the chaos.

Intense events…undeniable trauma…survival instincts.

A mental barricade—a divide, a muted sanctuary, the quiet that kept her operational.

Here I stand, in the center of her life.

A single moment where everything collides.

Every truth. Every pain, aligned.

How long…How long has she lived like this?

His mind, drifting away, detached from his body. Floating above it all, watching the torment unfold from a distance. Dissolving. Turning to mist. Numb, yet surviving.

Dissociation—a shield, a silent space, the numbness allowing her to breathe. Her way of existing.

I am listening to you, Ru. I am finally…able to listen.

Drawing in a breath.

I will learn from her. For the next two decades, I will learn from her.

Strange, how detachment settles once accepted.

But it's the only way to endure. It's the only way to stay mission-focused.

His skin, bruised and bleeding, knees now pressing against the cold, unforgiving ground. *When did I fall to my knees? When did my stance become submission?*

His mind, decelerating…seconds stretching before the next blow.

I know what's coming: Visha's chaos. Her unpredictability. Her vindictive need for control.

There—right there—is the crack in her foundation. Weakness identified.

When facing the High Priestess, silence was the key.
Silent. Kneeling. Waiting.
Detachment my treasure. It is my weapon.
Breathe in — six seconds.
Breathe out — six seconds.
Breathe in — seven seconds.
Breathe out — seven seconds.

His arms hung limp. Chains drained his strength. Gravel bit into his skin.

The ballroom was no longer a place of grandeur.

Just a prison. Just a cage.
Breathe in — eight seconds.
Breathe out — eight seconds.

Standing in the abyss, the darkness pressed heavy—crushing, absolute.

He forced his mind to ascend. To rise beyond the confines of his body.

Detaching, piece by piece. Preparing for the next onslaught.

Breathe in — nine seconds.
Breathe out — nine seconds.

Gaze vacant.

Heart numb.

Body slack.

Let go, a whisper slipped through his thoughts. His arms still bore the jagged scars, stark reminders of the relentless battles that had dragged him to this dim and desolate room.

A prison, her prison, I never imagined her enduring. Bile rose up his throat. *Chains bore. Stone walls. Iron bars. For* **her**. *I will stand witness to it all. Her pain. Her memories. The torment she fought and endured. This endless cycle, binding us in understanding.*

The High Priestess turned her marble ballrooms into savage playgrounds. It doesn't make sense. Who turns beauty into brutality? The thought scraped through his mind as he took in the scene. Sweat and blood smeared the marble floors, their once-polished surface buried beneath strewn gravel— twisted into something brutal. The air clung to him, metallic and biting; a second skin he couldn't shed. *The last time I'd been in Sanctuary, everything had been pristine. Almost too clean. Too sterile. That sharpness — Visha's calcu- lated nature — only made the cruelty, her cruelty, more apparent.* The chains around his wrists tore deeper, like they had a mind of their very own. Ruthless in their grip, tethering him to the marble beneath. *It was all wrong. Magnificent, yet crafted for suffering.*

Rage surged—fierce and unyielding—gnawing at him, clawing for release. The pressure built, pushing relentlessly against the boundaries of his control. He ground his teeth, the taste of iron bitter on his tongue.

The cage around him gleamed, its bars severe beneath the unforgiving light, trapping him like prey awaiting the strike. Marble walls loomed, their stark elegance catching every sound, turning even the smallest noise into a sharp echo.

He forced his breath to regulate, clenching his fists until his nails bit into his palms—the sting anchoring him. *Hold steady,* he commanded himself, even as fury gnawed at his core.

And then…he saw it.

Izayah watched her eyes—empty, devoid of the light he knew so well.

His heart sank, the ache threatening to tear him apart.

Those eyes…so unfamiliar.

The projection hurtled forward, time rushing like a storm, capturing the instant she crumpled to the ground. She teetered on the edge of her own sanity, staring up at the figure looming over her.

The female's voice lashed out like a whip. "You didn't get down on your knees enough," she snarled. "Why am I not surprised you failed again? Your existence is only worth the chances I've given you, and this is how you repay me? With betrayal and disrespect?" She spat at the crumpled figure, her words laced with venom. "Speak, you wretched little creature."

Laying there, sprawled on the cold, unforgiving floor, she tentatively lifted her head to meet the female's gaze. Shattered words rubbed her throat raw. "I regret not meeting your expectations once again," she whispered, her voice tinged with defeat.

Izayah felt it—a sharp, profound sorrow slicing through his heart. His chest tightened, lungs clenched, every breath a jagged struggle, as if the very air had thickened and grown too heavy to inhale.

Pinned down. Cornered. Stuck in this relentless cycle of disdain.

Fury rippled. Wrath coursed through his veins as anger burned a hole in his heart.

If only I could siphon this pain from her bones.

But all he could do was feel her suffering—each breath driving a jagged-edged dagger deeper into him.

*Love was supposed to heal. This was **not** that. It was like licking a knife, every touch cutting deeper than the last.*

She whispered, "I am not worthy of love. I am yours—empty, without value...and yet, I don't matter enough to be seen." The words fell from her lips, hollow and rehearsed— a script etched into her bones. A small, weary tremor ran through her, like a puppet too tired to resist its strings.

The female sneered, a dark smile twisting sinister features as she drove a boot into her daughter's ribcage. "Pathetic," she hissed. "You are worthless—an abomination to our name."

A primal fury coiled in Izayah's chest—feral, raw—straining against the walls of his ribs.

He wanted to unleash it, to tear through this agony, shredding it down to nothing—until only smoke and ruin remained.

The projections flickered out, dissolving into the shadows. The room reappeared—stark, hollow, bleak. Silence pressed in, thick and suffocating, leaving him alone with the weight of her suffering.

Runa was methodically shaped, molded, and forced to see herself through a lens that had never been her own—a distortion of existence. But he understood her potential, the depth of her—*and now, I will learn the terrain of the scars she bears.*

I am choosing to see Runa clearer—to feel her in every breath, every heartbeat.

*The good, the bad, the ugly. I don't give a **shit** how it sounds.*

I want and need it all, raw and unfiltered. No bullshit.

So, I step into the viper's den—not out of recklessness, not as prey, but to finally grasp what I have long missed. My idiocy...my damn fuckin'...How blind could I be?

Well, she screwed with the wrong asshole. Because no warrior moves blind—terrain, enemy, and strategy dictate victory.

Twenty years.

Two decades.

His head dropped, shoulders bowed under the pain he couldn't erase, the fury he couldn't unleash. Tears welled, a silent rebellion against the torment he could not express. He swallowed them back, refusing to let them fall.

She has carried this agony alone for far too long.

Ironically, he met each moment with honor, twisted as it was—fully aware the next two decades would be brutal.

This would be a reprieve for her. A respite.

I will take on the agony so she may finally know peace.

Visha, the High Priestess of Sanctuary City, would count these moments as victories over him. His expression darkened—contempt, brief and fleeting. *She'll believe she's breaking me. I'll let her think it—let her believe she's shattering me.*

But she's wrong.

Gravely mistaken.

Izayah trusted his guides—the General and his bonded—with every fiber of his being. Diesel Dave and Mama D, who had stepped in when no one else dared, who had become a lifeline for Rayanna after their mother, High Lady Nadine, passed. They were family now, bound by more than duty. He believed in their assignment. In its necessity. In their unwavering commitment to see it through.

The High Priestess thinks she can break me, shatter me, unravel me, thread by thread. She. Has. No. Idea. Izayah clenched his jaw, using the pain as fuel. *Every second, every ounce of it,* he vowed to silently endure.

The light flickered overhead, and Izayah lifted his chin, teeth gritted, bracing for the next assault on his mind. Every moment seared into his memory, branding him from the inside out. Lethal rage boiling, pulsing, caged but awake. The projector's gaze lifted, and the world twisted—every shadow, every figure, now an enemy.

*The list is growing. These were no longer **just names** on a page; they are living, breathing targets that will be wiped from existence.*

Visha calls them 'lessons.'

I call them fuel.

Semantics, really. A fatal miscalculation.

How utterly predictable. You fuckin' bitch.

TRUTH SEEKER/TRUTH TELLER PREPAREDNESS

DEFENSE INTELLIGENCE AGENCY
PREPARED BY SHADOW GUARD ELITE DIVISION

CONFIDENTIAL
FOR AUTHORIZED TRAINING USE ONLY
INTERNAL DOCUMENTATION GIVEN TO THE HIGHEST
CLEARANCE LEVELS

Truth Seeker Training
Compiled Entries for Rayanna

Prepared by:
General Diesel Hollowborne
Lieutenant General Shadeworth
Time Period: Prior to the onset of Mission: "Moons and Shadows"

Purpose:
This manual contains a meticulously curated collection of entries to train someone in the skills and knowledge essential for the role as a Truth Teller. It provides comprehensive insights, historical context, and practical information crucial for development and understanding of events leading up to the unbinding.

Contents Include:
• Historical Records: Documentation of Collected Observations of High Priestess Visha
• Correspondence from Runa to Izayah preceding Mission: "Moons and Shadows"
• Entries by Izayah: Prior to Triad Transfer to Starlight Beach
• Lumis Blooms: Documentation of Noted Memory Vines

Confidential
For Authorized Training Use Only

Notes for Future Reference

Trainee: Rayanna Shadeworth
Advised by: Lieutenant General Shadeworth and General Diesel Hollowborne
Purpose: Training and comprehension enhancement for post-unbinding phase.

Context: These entries have been meticulously selected to aid in training and to enhance understanding and focus. The information is intended to guide the future self following the unbinding of shadow binding, ensuring the future self is aligned on the correct path for deeper comprehension.

Note: Signed prior to taking part in shadow binding. Entries were selected by advising ranks to deepen understanding. All entries will be included in the full packet; the following have been pulled for specific reasons to facilitate the transition back into training sessions.

Signatures of Authorization: Rayanna Shadeworth (Trainee): _Rayanna Shadeworth_

~~Dear Runa,~~

~~Dearest Runa~~

~~My Dearest Runa,~~

~~Hey Ru,~~

Ru...

I am overthinking this.
This is why I never wrote you back.

We have about four months of laying low
to ensure you ladies are set to go before
the Elite Shadow Guard go straight back
into your version of hell.

Ru,

I don't know where to begin.
By the time you get these, you might
know all of this information.

I don't know how to kick-start these entries. Daxter
suggested that they might be a good idea, and Sienna
agreed. So, here we are...

The thing is, everything sounds like an excuse when I
start to write it down. The old you would know that. The old
you would roll your eyes at me and probably nudge me
away with that look of absurdity, but I don't want this to get
weird. I want us to have a fresh start.

So, how do I explain myself? Where do I begin?

I need time to ~~figure~~ ~~think~~
mull these questions over.

Izayah

I have determined that this isn't going to be perfect—
nothing ever is. Why would this be any different?
What I have right now is time, and what I want to do
with this time is sit with you and explain everything—
the why behind the what.

However, I am unable to do so. The Seer and
the truth seekers running this mission have
strict directives, even for myself. Yes, I
realize that sounds cocky, because they say I
would be a distraction if I were in the room,
which I think speaks to my amazing good
looks. They say it does not.

We will not debate who is right or wrong in such
matters. In short, I would never forgive myself
if my presence negated the process of you letting
go of what was. I already struggle with such

things.

What I have determined you need to know is twofold:

1. This is going to be harder for you than it is for me. I am doing this because I need to give you time—time to heal, time to breathe, time to be. Time to live the life I thought you were already living. I was wrong. You need to know this.

2. Shadow Binding is designed to protect your cognition, pausing recollections to divert energy towards healing other areas first. Who you were will gradually resurface during the first phase. What you need to understand is this: it's a testament to your perseverance.

This might not seem like it right now, but after my dumbass finally comprehended your actual reality—thank you, Sienna—this is me taking action, like the old you said I would if I knew.

I now know and I did.

Izayah

Dear Runa,

I stopped by today, hoping for a glimpse of the progress made, but it seems I'm still kept at arm's length. Sienna shared news that painted vivid images in my mind—all three of you are undergoing profound transformations, a rebirth of ~~the~~ sorts. Imagining the three of you, all a century beyond your Dawning Days, now reliving them in reverse, fills me with both worry and wonder.

Rayanna will be the first to cross the threshold, laying the groundwork for you both to follow.

~~~~~~Unfortunately, there was a hiccup along the way, unforeseen, yet my older brother Zane always has his reasons.
~~~~~~

What I have determined you need to know within this entry is threefold:

1. Rayanna, a "Cabinet of Curiosities," will have endless questions.
2. The "North Star" always holds answers at the bottom of a cup of coffee.
3. Awkward angels are incomplete without silver linings—game changers when dire situations arise.

Where you three are bound, the Locations are tailor-made—a gift of rejuvenation, where Starlight and Moonlight bend time, allowing each of you to pause and find a new Dawning Day.

Izayah

Runa,

This pen I hold has spent more time hovering above the page, dripping ink. It has become music instead of a mere tool for delivering a message, I believe.

Let us proceed:

The cabin was a carefully orchestrated plan, yet sometimes life defies our expectations. It throws us for a loop, and we must adapt. You taught me that.

I am officially in hiding because when the time comes, I will be detained, put on trial, and punished under the rule of High Priestess Visha. Before this can occur, I need all pieces of the puzzle to fall into place.

My rank or name will not shield me from this.

I accept this fate.

My mission is to make her believe she has outsmarted me and gained access to the Shadow Guard Elite.

I will remain in this environment until the first phase has been set into motion.

~~back to~~

Exiting will come, guiding me to where retreat is encapsulated beneath the Earth.

Izayah

Hey Ray,

Don't worry, I've been keeping an eye on you too. I can just hear you now, "What am I, chopped liver?"

Trust me — these ladies are pretty set in their ways. There's no getting around them.

By now, I assume you've read all the other entries.

My advice: pick and choose the ones that catch your eye. Diesel has a few in mind, but you'll know.

Trust your gut.

On another note, I wish I could be there to see you bombard the General with your questions. I'm smirking just thinking about it because Diesel is very much looking forward to your teen years again.

I told him it's just heart-wrenchingly tragic that I won't get to witness them myself. Really, the universe couldn't be more cruel. I will make it through... though.

Anyway, here's some info to jump-start your training :

- Sanctuary's been in full lockdown for the past two months. By the time you're reading this, it'll likely have been about two decades of chaos.

- The High Priestess is not a fool, but she doesn't know how much I know, which means, it can't be worse than the Shadow Arena with Zane. What was it that, we use to say?

Brotherly moment: (Last things): *I swear!* ☺

Remember, listen to your mentors—they know a thing

or two.

And hey, don't bitch, you've got your own office

space waiting for you, but only when you're ready.

Missy might need a bit of an attitude adjustment.

Give her hell; she'll come around eventually.

Trust me when I say, you have someone that is laced

with silver lining — give her a chance.

See you on the other side, Spitfire.

XO

Your pain-in-the-ass

Older Brother,

Izayah

Runa,

It's almost time for us to take leave. These next few notes will be brief.

If you don't already know, shadow binding and unbinding allow you to create mental bridges of communication. These bridges bypass all holds on any given playing field without others' knowledge and remain even after unbinding occurs.

So, no matter where you are, you might influence certain situations without realizing it even while shadow bound.

We're still uncertain how shadow binding will affect the three of you.

Stay alert and adapt.

Izayah

We are taking leave today, ^{Month 4} ^{Week 1}

We are taking leave today,
walking right up to the gates

Whatever occurs beyond this point in time, I
want you to hear me say, "I would do it without
hesitation if it meant each of you were forever

safe."

I know that's not how the world works.
Nonetheless, it's my turn.
Night will come, and each of you will

start anew.
This is the first year of the Starlight Festival, and
I pray that it is the first day of the best days of
your life with many more to come.

I'll see you on the other side.

—Izayah

Chapter Three

Runa stood in the center of the yard, a soft smile tugging at her lips. Weeks of effort had turned the mundane into something quite marvelous. The Starlight Festival was poised to transform every corner of Starlight Beach into a trove of delights. Her vision this year was forged in brilliance—each strand weaving into itself, spinning a tale of a celestial newborn. A glistening beauty, poised to ascend. Ready to ignite the night. Destined to claim its place among the constellations.

The bins sat on the gravel drive, no longer tucked beneath the eaves—awaiting their starlit purpose. These curious containers held candles of every size and shape, alongside glass orbs that hid untold bedtime stories —whispers only the night could unveil.

She could visualize each flame's spark, swaying softly—like reeds bending to the sea's rhythmic lull. Today, she would place each one carefully, intentionally, as if offering a prayer rather than a decoration. It was more than a celebration; it was a blessing, a stitch of a dream delicately woven into the fabric of the world.

Runa exhaled, her gaze settling on the nearest box. *Let them tease me about my starlit obsession. At some point, they'll admit the work was necessary—*

because when all is said and done, it's worth it, she thought, a quiet chuckle slipping past her lips.

Still, each season, neighbors and council members pestered her—asking about décor, themes, and concepts—always eager for her approval. They would approach her hesitantly, as if intruding, yet relentless in their curiosity about the latest decorations—like a half-formed story waiting to be shaped by its author. Sometimes, it feels like they're creating the tale just for me. She huffed at the thought. *Ridiculous, of course. It's not about me at all.*

But ever since she was little, there had been this unspoken tradition—this quiet expectation, as if the townsfolk couldn't imagine crafting it without her. *Maybe it started because, when I was young, they'd come to Mama D for inspiration, and she'd weave the story while I sat beside her, pointing and giggling at whatever caught my eye.* Somehow, those little gestures—those fleeting choices of a child—wove themselves into their decision-making, a tradition reshaped yet never lost.

She could feel it now—piece by piece, the town had transformed, turning into yet another storybook wonder. The anticipation hummed in the streets, the spark of a joyous parade already stirring the air. Later this evening, the little cottages will glow like scattered starlight, each one tugging at the community in its own unique way.

With candlelight in hand, the townsfolk will weave from home to home, exchanging flames at each threshold. If one were to watch from the heavens, the shifting lights would form small constellations, dotting their way from star to star. Each soul will pause at a property of their choosing, table-hopping and savoring the festive feasts. The light will travel with them, flickering from hand to hand, ensuring the night shimmers with warmth, connection, and quiet belonging.

As much as I enjoy the spread, the true magic of Starlight Night, for me, is in the wandering—meandering through the quaint neighborhoods, admiring the artistic displays of other households, she thought, securing the ladder. Her hands grasped the wooden rungs as she climbed, the cords of the last grouping of lanterns held between her teeth.

It's where my heart truly finds the most joy. In this kind of quiet. She steadied herself, hanging the glass orbs from the massive oak's branches. *There's something so calming about all of this.*

She pulled out a box of matches, gifting her festive friends with quivering flames that cast a soft, enchanting radiance through the branches. Descending the ladder, she stepped back, raising her chin to take in the glow as a thought surfaced. *It's like the sweetest gift I never knew I needed.*

She ran a hand along the nape of her neck, wiping off a bit of dirt. *That quiet meandering around town is mine—my time to gather inspiration, to let everything settle. A muted reflection on all the blessings this season has brought.*

Turning, she glanced toward the horizon, watching the sun sink lower. A small smile tugged at her lips. *Just in time,* she mused, feeling the day's last light slip through the crystals, scattering an arcing kaleidoscope of colors—a dance of radiance bowing in reverence to the night. *Always the same, yet somehow different every year.*

Tucking the remaining fishing line into the nearest container, her movements were precise. Every small task was executed with practiced care, as if the day were gifting itself to the night—Like fireflies weaving through blades of grass, their gossamer wings settling lightly upon the swaying stems. Smiling to herself, she whispered, "This—this is why I do it. For moments like these."

Wandering over to the stone wall that marked the edge of each property, she considered it with purpose. The rock-lined frontage had been introduced within the last decade—links binding the cottages together. Their rough surfaces, now brushed with drifting sunlight, blended like watercolors across a canvas rim, spilling into the mounds of greenery.

Leaning against the cool, substantial stone, she paused, allowing herself a moment—to reflect on all that lay before and behind her. *So much has changed, and yet so much stays the same.*

For whatever reason, when these walls were installed, they stirred images that began as lingering dreams. Each rock felt like a fragment surfacing—memories waiting to be remembered. The spores of moss encouraged the wisps to take root, coaxing visions to the surface with ease whenever her fingers brushed the cool stone.

The specifics of her biological father remained a mystery. She had never seen his face, but his words resurfaced, rising from somewhere buried within her soul. She could hear his steady voice: "Each day brings new challenges. The sun asks forgiveness for the world's wrongs. The moon symbolizes genuine change—the kind that comes when we embrace transformation. Every phase, my child, has its own reason, its own significance. Notice the light it carries; it holds truths that many miss."

Blinking, she shook the memory loose, silently promising to revisit it later as she returned to the present moment. The world had shifted, unfurling into a mosaic of gold and pink hues. *How does it always do that?* It was as if the sky itself had split at the seams, unbinding, only to be stitched back together by the hand of a master artist.

Reluctantly, she turned from the fading light of the bowing sun, digging her fingertips into the damp moss. She pulled herself up, settling atop the rough stone. *I will find you,* she thought. *There's something here—I know it.* She yanked her mind back, only to push it forward again, searching for the space where her father's silhouette had once walked beside her—a fleeting imprint woven into the fabric of...*whatever this was.* It felt like stepping into a labyrinth, thick with fog and shadows, where every turn unraveled more questions than answers.

Nothing surfaced.

I had been certain that today, of all days, he would show. But as disappointment settled in, she turned once more to the habit of daydreams—imagining the adventures they might have shared on distant shores. *Separate, yet somehow still joined, following parallel paths toward the same horizon.*

Maybe that's all we ever were, or will be, she thought, *two souls chasing the same light from different directions.*

Her biological father and Diesel had always merged in her phantom imaginings, their presence overlapping like colors bleeding together on a canvas. She could see it now—the way Diesel lifted the pipe, Old Faithful, to his lips, with the same careful grace she imagined her father would have. The way he exhaled, releasing swirling shapes that carried the warm scents of hazelnut and cinnamon. In those moments, it was as if the two men became one, their spirits merging across time and space, linked by dreams and memories.

Maybe they were always meant to be intertwined. The thought brought her comfort.

This rock wall stood as a threshold, separating what was from what is. Within its borders, Papa D's presence filled the gaps—not to erase, but to strengthen. Maybe that's what he was meant to do—to bridge the spaces my father has left behind. Countless impressions of his emerald green eyes flooded her memory. They shone with a love and tenderness she could only describe as profound—something that seemed to fill Diesel completely whenever he was with the girls and Mama D. *Does he know how much comfort that brings me? I really should tell him.*

Her favorite memory was of him nestled in his dignified green velvet chair, quietly observing, as if watching her personality unfold like a story he never tired of reading. *How easy it had been to slip into the warmth of their home, as if it had always been mine.* At a deep level, it had felt like a sanctuary —one she had known before, but only with her father. *I can't be sure though. It all feels so distant and clouded. And yet, perhaps the difference is that this is the first time I am truly experiencing the sacred union of a bounded pair. Maybe that, at last, is something I can be sure of.*

Their home had always held a delicate balance, much like Diesel himself—a captivating blend of strength and vulnerability. His rugged exterior softened in the glow of night fires and the presence of those who truly mattered.

How did he manage that? A subtle flicker of gratitude stirred in her chest. *How did he make it seem so effortless?* She couldn't help but marvel at the way he had become such a steady presence—an anchor in a place that had once felt unmoored, adrift in uncertainty. His existence was now woven into the fabric of her world, something constant when everything else felt like shifting sand.

Runa came to understand that his soul felt like a soothing salve, gently peeling away the defensive layers around her veiled heart. *How did he make it feel so safe to let go?* She wondered. *Had I really been so fractured as a youngling?* The thought gripped at her throat, catching her by surprise.

Where Papa D provided quiet strength, Mama D offered warmth, like a comforting embrace on a frigid winter day. Her presence softened life's jagged edges, creating a space where Runa could unburden her heart. *Mama D's steady calm makes it feel as if a single conversation could lift the heaviest burdens, leaving everything just a little lighter—even if only for a moment.*

And yet, even in Mama D's warmth, there were things comfort couldn't reach. Like today, walking back from the schoolhouse—an unshakable sensation. *There's something…*She fumbled with the notion, an elusive weight lingering. *Haunted by a void I can't define.* She huffed out a breath of frustration. *What am I really searching for?*

The question settled, pressing against her chest. The missing pieces hovered near—close enough to feel, but never close enough to hold.

It made little sense. There was no imminent threat, nothing lurking around the corner, yet the ground beneath her seemed to waver in this moment. *It feels like being chained to a place I can't escape. But everyone I love is here, right by my side. There's no need to worry.* Still, the feeling crept up her spine, uninvited.

Runa tried to recall the hardships she'd faced in her twenty-one years. There wasn't much to dwell on. She felt grateful for that—yet the thought left her wondering. *Is there more beneath the surface, something hidden just beyond my grasp?*

Her thoughts drifted to the warmth beyond the welcoming doors of the two-bedroom cottage down the street—Mama D and Papa D's home. *How has that place come to mean so much to me?* It had become a sanctuary, a refuge she hadn't even realized she needed.

Runa's neck had stiffened from sitting perched on the rock wall—a subtle reminder to ease the tension in her body. She rolled her head from side to side, trying to loosen the tightness. *I need to be here right now,* she thought, forcing herself to focus.

Gazing down the street, she was struck by something she hadn't quite noticed before. Though built in the same style, each cottage carried its own distinct personality—like a village of quiet souls, every house holding a story of its own. *Funny how they all blend together, yet each feels different,* she mused, her eyelids drifting shut like curtains drawing closed on the scene. She let herself sink deeper into the notion, imagining the houses as a little community of beings, each one alive in its own way. *It's all in the details, I guess.*

Each pastel-hued residence had a venerable, ancient oak standing to the left, just beyond the moongate's thoroughfare. These towering sentinels cradled a trove of tales, as though they had once guarded an enchanted forest. Runa pictured the massive oaks as protectors, somehow transported to Starlight Beach and placed here, one by one. The thought stirred something deep within her—an odd kind of peace, a quiet comfort in knowing they had stood watch for generations.

She let out a chuckle. *Can you imagine them coming to life? Marching down the street, branches waving, roots tearing up the pavement—all to protect the town's secrets?* Her stomach fluttered at the thought. *Now that would be a sight.* Yet despite their imposing presence, their broad trunks rested in the tall grass, their shadows stretching to create a cozy, inviting warmth around each home.

She glanced around their yard. A coarse layer of crushed rock covered the drive, stretching through the moongate's thoroughfare and extending beneath the balcony of the main house. The open space below the deck doubled as storage, housing outdoor recreational gear and a collection of holiday decorations.

To the left of the gravel entry, a trellis nestled between four sturdy posts. A pebbled path extended from there, its center thoughtfully lined with slate stepping stones, flanked by beds of lavender, sage, and lemongrass. Between the beams, colorful pots overflowed with prairie smoke flowers, their scents mingling with peonies and freesia—the household's beloved blooms.

Beyond the pathway, the steps to the front door blended seamlessly—stone and mortar interwoven with chunks of aged oak, as if they had organically sprouted from the earth. *If only they could speak. Would they reveal their secrets, share the stories embedded in their grains? Would they relay the answers my mind keeps wrestling with?*

Should one bypass the stairs leading to the living quarters and step beyond the arbor, they would find a winding path of pots and plants—arranged in a purposeful kind of chaos, forming a decorative trail to the backyard. *Whoever thought to place them like this must have known that beauty often hides in imperfection.*

A flagstone patio blended seamlessly with the house, reinforcing its sturdy foundation. *It looks as if the stones themselves want to hold the place up, to offer strength where it's needed most,* she thought, feeling a hushed admiration for the way it all fit together.

The patio was a haven—well-furnished, with a fire pit and cozy lounging chairs. Overhead, a wooden pergola stretched toward the door, its beams adorned with twinkling lights. This space felt made for reflection, for gazing out upon the imposing mountainside, as if nature had built its own fortress, whispering, *I am here, and nothing shall pass.*

Naturally, this spot held a special place in her heart. When the morning light danced over the mountains, it felt like the sun was celebrating with her. On weekends, she and Rayanna would wander onto the back patio, coffee cups in hand, and sit together, listening to birdsong. Their conversations drifted between musings and quiet observations.

The sun had been an artist, they agreed, watching as light brushed the clouds into new forms, creating a masterpiece above. Their eyes lifted to the heavens as the sky transformed into a canvas streaked with gold, blue, and soft purples.

They were privileged in where their cottage stood—perfectly placed to witness the moon retreating gracefully, yielding to a brighter light. Each celestial transition felt like a tribute, a reminder of nature's selfless beauty. A mesmerizing exchange of power.

There's something humbling about watching the sky shift and change, a constant reminder that life moves forward, even when everything else feels like it's standing still.

Slowly, she let her eyelids part, a thought emerging. *Something isn't right.* It pulled her from the comfort of her daydream. *Hmm, something definitely isn't right.*

What is that? She dabbed at her mouth, teasing her tongue along the inside, a strange taste lingering. *Metallic.* She ran her tongue across her teeth, tasting it again—faint but unsettling. *It definitely tastes…metallic.*

Her fingers brushed across her tongue, then pulled back. *Blood.* She blinked, confused, the fading light catching the dark smears on her skin. *How…?* Panic sparked, as chaos unraveled in a rush. *What is happening?* She retraced her steps in her mind, going back through each moment, analyzing every detail.

But there was just silence. Nothing at all.

What was that?

Thud. Scuff. Crack. Whoosh.

She blinked against the fading light, squinting into the dimness that fractured her vision. In a blinding flood—like a dam breaking—confusion rushed in, gripping her sanity, refusing to let go.

Flashing fragments. A jarring pop. A rapid descent.

Fuckin' ruthless.

BAM. Hammered into the gravel—*what the fuck?*

She blinked hard, struggling to bring the moment into focus.

I'm perched on a fuckin' wall—yet everything feels sideways.

Cold. Exposed. Open air biting at her skin.

SLAM! Pain ricocheting up her spine. Raw flesh against rough stone. Nausea surged through her veins.

Why am I so lightheaded?

Did I eat today?

What the fuck is happening?

The world tilted again, a wave of sickness tumbled through her. Her breath catching on the cold numbness seeping along her limbs. Draining. Panic rising.

Oh, for the love of the Blessed Father. What the fresh hell is this?

Swing a leg over the edge. They feel like lead. The fuck is happening?

Heavy and unresponsive. She slipped from the wall, collapsing to the ground. She crumbled, blinking back shock. *Legs—mush, useless… beneath me.*

What the actual fuck?

This isn't right. Her frustration mingled with fear. *This can't be happening. It* **is** *happening though. Why is it happening?* A whirlwind of emotions and questions surging. *What's happening to me? Drunk? No. Unsteady? Hell yes! Why can't I stand? Why does everything feel so…far away?* Grasping for clarity, but only more questions surfaced. *More doubts. More fears.*

This feels familiar…*too familiar.* Her hand flew to the back of her neck. Sharp. Stinging. Searing pain. Cutting through a fog, pulling her deeper… *suffocating. A ragged intake. Trying to stand…legs refuse. Unresponsive. Heavy.*

Get. THE. FUCK. UP. MOVE!

Clawing at the earth, her nails digging into the dirt, dragging herself forward — inch by inch, as numbness crept up her limbs, stealing her strength.

I have to reset. I have to snap out of this—whatever this is.

Breathless.

MOVE!

Her gaze sharpened, fixated on the house. Parting her lips to scream for help. *NOTHING. FUCKING NOTHING!*

Like a frog stuck in her throat. Strangled. Panic surged.

OH…MY…HOLY HELL!

Hands shooting to her throat.

Something solid pressed down, unseen, invisible.

Clutching desperately, fingers digging.
Working to pry away an unseen grip.
No. No. No. Shit! Shit! Shit! This isn't real. This can't be real.
Her face was draining of color.
The world's blurring.
Each breath a raging battle.
An invisible hand—tightening around my throat. The thought was jagged, like shards of glass slicing into her skin. *Squeezing. Harder. I can't—*
Breathe!
Her lungs searing, the air had thinned into vapor. She exhaled, unfurling twisted wisps of smoke, like the tendrils of a winter storm. She stared, bewildered, as each breath hung suspended and motionless, forming tiny clouds that grew more solid, more real. Ice crystals...danced within the wisps, shimmering like frost on a windowpane.

Snow? she wondered, blinking hard. *Is that...snow?* Her breath formed in front of her, each puff curling like a billowing ghost in the cold. *It's not even cold.* The space around her felt oddly still as tendrils spiraled outward, turning the air before her into something...*tangible.*

Every inhale, *brutal.* Every exhale, a gasp against the panic threatening to consume her.
*This isn't happening...This **isn't** happening!*
LOUD and STRONG—*Bang! Bang! Bang!*
The world shifted before her—just for a split second.
Desolation stretched wide.
Swollen eyes—caged—grim—dim lighting.
Face down.
Instant rage—"Burn in hell, asshole."
A plea escaped her lips, raspy and weak, "Please..."
Dizziness, nausea, swirling. A relentless numbness.
A flash of gold—*gone.*
Is this real?
Air flooded her lungs as the grip on her neck relented. She gasped, her throat searing with pain. Gradually, she forced herself upright, eyes locked on the cottage, a silent plea echoing in her chest. *Why does this feel like it's pulling me apart?*
Her eyes fluttered closed, listening to her steady pulse, as if a hidden

river flowed beneath her skin, channeling some unseen current. Every fiber of her being screamed for support. Goosebumps rose across her arms.

What is this? Faint shimmering threaded and twirled…*linking to something, someone?* A tugging, urging her to understand. *I have to know…* Pulling her knees in, weak, yet sensing a faint vibration, stirring within her core. Her skin warmed. *Am I glowing?* She focused harder. *Why do I hear a hum?* She blinked, pulling her head back, trying to focus her eyes on the surreal moment she was caught in.

This isn't happening. This isn't happening. This isn't happening!

Her eyes fell to the grass beneath her.

MOVE.

She willed the grass to sway, to dance with the core…the thread. It was as though she had taken a string and attached it to the very tip of the blade.

She pulled.

A strange calm settled over her. *Stay focused,* she told herself. *Just breathe.*

A voice stabbing in, calling to her like a siren on the shoreline. "Imagine the sea, the moon, the sun…flowing…" Her glassy eyes fogged over, the world outside dissolved into nothingness as she stared deeper into an eternal night. Another environment hidden behind fogged glass—deep greens, earth browns, and lapping blues.

The distant stars above were mere flickers of hope dotted against a sky stretching vast, and silent. Reaching out, hand trembling.

I've been here before. Heart pounding an erratic beat, one that didn't feel like her own. *So fragile. Still there. So tender.* And yet, there was a desperate urge to soothe something just out of reach, something that wasn't even **hers** to heal…*yet.*

Shadows closed in, smoky projections curling at the edges of her vision, swallowing what little light remained. A voice trickled out, thin and fragmented, like water leaking from a faucet. *There's a door, in the space between life and knowledge. You will find me there.*

She took a deep breath, desperate to hold on to reality. *Stay here…stay present. Don't leave.* But her surroundings hazed out, melting into a bluish fog collecting on the lapping teal waters.

The figure before her flickered.

Was that...a fin? It slipped into the darkness below, dissolving like mist at the first touch of dawn. *Who are you? Where are you?* Runa mentally pulled herself closer, drawn to the figure, the teal undertones flowing around her ankles. The line between reality and dream blurring even further, slipping into obscurity.

Am I dying? Is this how it ends? Fading...disappearing...? The thought barely took shape before it withered and fell away. She crumpled deeper into the gravel, the rough impact jolting her back to earth.

Then, all at once — the world went still.

Rayanna stood at the country-sized basin, scrubbing the last of the dirty dishes. Then, without warning, her body lurched forward, crashing against the cold, unyielding surface. Unforgiving. Held there, pinned in place. *Okay...what?*

A fleeting moment that struck like a jolt of electricity.

*Ummm...*Her eyes widening as she stared into the sink, trying—and failing—to make sense of what she was seeing. *Seriously?* Frozen in place, her gaze darted in frantic desperation.

The droplets of water clinging to the basin began to shiver, rippling upward, defying gravity. Her breath hitched as they hovered just above the surface, morphing into tiny, floating spheres. She blinked in stunned disbelief. Comprehension fractured, struggling to take hold.

This isn't real.

It can't be.

A soft, sizzling vapor began to rise from the droplets, releasing a soothing mist. Little hovering beads of water swayed, like blades of grass in a gentle breeze. She blinked again, her mind racing.

Ummm...this is not normal.

Maybe I've been at this far too long. Confusion gnawed at her. *See? This is exactly why I shouldn't be trusted with kitchen duty. It's messing with my head now.* Her heartbeat quickened, pounding against her chest like a drum, each pulse echoing the uncertainty that kept her rooted to the spot.

She reached for the towel, fingers wrapping around the fabric, but her body refused to follow. Something invisible held her there, tethered to the sink. Panic tightened in her chest as she tried to pull away, yet her feet stayed fixed to the ground. Then, with an audible *pop,* the unseen force released its hold, and she stumbled backward, free at last.

Just then, a voice broke through the shock, resonating with clarity as it pleaded, *"I need you...now."* Rayanna shuddered, goosebumps prickling her skin as she backed away from the sink. *What the—fuck—is happening?*

Moving cautiously through the kitchen, she weaved around the island, her gaze locked on the living room where the voice seemed to echo from. The emptiness of the house settled over her, thickening the sense of unease. It wrapped around her mind, constricting, as if the very walls were closing in.

Her steps slowed as she backed toward the L-shaped couch, the towel still clutched in her hand. Pressing herself against the backside of the sofa, eyes darting wildly around the room, searching for any sign of movement.

"Ray! Now!" The voice tore through the air, raw and frantic.

Runa? Her head snapped up, a creeping sense of dread settling in. She questioned the very core of her sanity. The answer stayed just out of reach, stress scraping at the cusp of her mind—she recalled a relentless echo of Tabs telling her she needed to relax more often.

Okay...I swear...it sounds just like..., the thought wavered.

Am I losing it?

Silence.

Yep—I am losing it.

"Of course!" Rayanna threw her hands up. "I'm losing my mind, and now I'm talking to myself."

"RAY!"

The shout rattled her nerves. Bewilderment hitting like a punch. She stood there, utterly dumbfounded, trying to make sense of the situation. "This is getting ridiculous! There's no one even here!" Her eyes blinked rapidly as she scanned the room, head whipping from side to side. Desperate to find the source of Runa's voice.

"I swear it sounds like she's—*RIGHT HERE!*" She flung a hand out in front of her, as if pointing to an invisible presence.

Rayanna called out, "Runa, where the hell are you?" Huffing out within irritation. *Probably still outside,* she realized—*finishing up those ridiculously over-the-top Starlight decorations.* Rayanna could picture it. This display was even more extravagant than the last. She'd truly outdone herself this time. Rayanna recalled how the previous festivals had left her—along with half the neighborhood—gawking like kids at Dagny's Seaside Sweets. *Excitement? Sure. Until that electricity bill hits.*

A flicker of irritation crossed her face. *Why does she always have to go so extravagant?* Rayanna's sigh tangled up into an inevitable quiet chuckle. Runa always loved this festival and the spectacle it brought, no matter the cost.

"This is absurd!" Rayanna snapped. Determined to figure out what was going on, she marched to the front door and flung it open, her gaze sweeping across the yard.

Her eyes landed on Runa—huddled on the ground.

Too still.

"What on earth, Ru?" she shot out. Runa didn't respond. Rayanna's chest twisted in concern, as goosebumps rippled along the surface of her skin, gripped with unease.

Why isn't she moving? Blinking, trying to make sense of what she was seeing. *Is she hurt? No...she wouldn't just sit there like that. Not Runa.* Rayanna's heartbeat quickened, the irritation from earlier, replaced by a low bellow of worry.

"Hey—Ru! Hell-hooo?" She waved the towel frantically, like white flag on a battlefield.

Nothing. No response...

Rayanna leaned forward, squinting, trying to make sense of what she was seeing. *What is she doing out there?* She tossed the towel onto the balcony rim and took a tentative step down the stairs, a sense of unease curling through her. But as she moved closer, and Runa's form came into focus, her heart picked up speed, slamming against her ribs.

Why does she look so...small?

Her feet moved faster now, driven by urgency. When Runa lifted her head from her knees, Rayanna stopped short, her breath catching in her throat.

Is that...a handprint? She blinked, trying to reconcile the dark marks circling her sister's neck.

No...it can't be...

"What the hell happened to you?" The question burst from her lips, raw and ragged.

Runa's gaze lifted, eyes bloodshot and glassy. Her voice, when it came, was barely a whisper, frayed at the edges. "I don't know."

"What the hell do you mean, you don't know?" Rayanna scoffed as she rushed to Runa's side. "This would explain the whole 'screaming bloody murder' thing I was just exposed to in the kitchen."

Rayanna reached out, fingers skimming over the seared, tender skin of Runa's throat. "It's like the sun itself grabbed you by the fucking neck and left its mark."

"I was up on the wall, watching the sunset. Then, in some blurry world, someone, or thing, told me to look for the place between life and knowledge—thing is, I have no fucking clue what that even means, Ray!"

Runa's breath hitched weakly, shaking her head. "Seriously, I have no idea. Feels like I just did a faceplant on a bed of hot coals. Oh—and then my breath turned into little clouds and it snowed from my mouth."

"What?" Rayanna's face twisted in disbelief. "Well, you definitely look like you were rolling around in the dirt with someone. And not in a fun way." She raised an eyebrow, exhaling sharply. "So, explain to me why you've got a bony handprint wrapped around your neck like a pretty, fuckin' bow, Runa?"

She leaned in closer, eyes narrowing. "Did the sun try to put you in a chokehold today, or was that voluntary?" She hesitated examining the seared handprint closer, "I can see fucking fingerprints..."

"I. DO. NOT. KNOW. RAY!" Runa let her eyes roll into the back of her head. "Oh, yeah, that's exactly how it played out. I was just casually lounging on a rock, minding my own business, when out of the blue, this mythical figure materialized from thin air, demanding payment for the impending electric bill. Classic, right?"

Rayanna shook her head with a wry smile and chuckled. "At least I've got support from someone who grasps the expenses involved." Like a madwoman, she flung her arms toward the front yard in exasperation before reaching down to help her sister up. "Whatever went down, we'll *need to* sort it out because there's *no way* you can conceal that *horrifyingly flawless creation around your neck now.*"

Runa clasped Rayanna's wrist, pulling herself upright. She still felt unsteady, her legs wobbling beneath her, but she kept moving, leaning on her sister as they made their way inside.

"Alright, we can't just keep going in circles," Rayanna muttered, frustration bubbling through her words. "I have to admit…this *is* a bit worse than the bruises on your leg from last time."

Runa exhaled sharply, "I know," she admitted, the taste of blood still lingering in her mouth. The weight of it settled. *"I know…"*

Chapter Four

Sanctuary

Present Day

The desolation stretches before Izayah—a lifeless canvas drained of vibrancy. The ashen walls, weathered and devoid of life, have long been greedily absorbing color, casting a pale pallor over the underground chamber.

Twenty years. Two decades. And still, he remains. Strategically positioned within Sanctuary's confines, his body bears the relentless marks of brutality. Blood-soaked, bruised-purple wounds layered over childhood scars—mapping his pain.

A living punching bag, existing solely for the morbid entertainment of the sadistic crowd encircling him.

Through swollen eyes, a playground of punishment lay before him—a grim battleground. The rusted metal framework bore the scars of countless conflicts, an ageless witness to brutality. The grime, sweat, and bloodstains clung to the worn skeleton. A grotesque, sticky mosaic pooled beneath him —thick as spilled paint, left to fester and reek by day's end, indifferent to those who lived, died, or survived.

Izayah inhaled through his mouth, willing the stench clinging to his nostrils to fade. The rancid odor made things impossible. It was like a parasite, seeping deeper with every ragged intake.

Cheers and jeers swelled like a tide, pressing against his ribs. *Suffocating.* Overhead, the lights flickered, casting a dim, eerie glow—*as if they knew of the bedlam, lurking along the sidelines.* The crowd fed on the brutality of the ring, a constant reminder of the lawlessness beyond the rusted metal. *Unsatisfied hunger. Ruthless. Relentless. Exhausting.*

The tight cages encircled the pit, crushing inward, leaving them no choice but to watch—forced to bear witness to the brutality on display. Each clash, every scream, and every desperate struggle served as a brutal reminder of the horrors that awaited them. Whether as punishment, reluctant participants, or mere pawns in a twisted game of survival and dominance, they couldn't escape. *There was no way out, no reprieve from the torment*—the visceral crack of breaking bones, the wet splatter of flesh meeting steel, the suffocating stench of blood and sweat thick in the air.

Each day, Izayah watched numbly from his compacted enclosure as the first light of dawn pierced the horizon, casting long, creeping shadows across the arena. It had done so countless times before, an unbroken cycle of light and dark. He would find himself lost in the gentle flow of it, the soft radiance offering a fleeting reprieve, a momentary escape. A mist of light, shifting and ephemeral, would break his mind into cherished fragments of his days as a youngling, scattering memories across his thoughts like embers drifting into the night. And in that warmth, he recalled moments of innocence, of belonging, of home.

He often reflected on those early years—after their mother's passing, before Mama D stepped in—when Rayanna had shown such dislike for the chambermaids who assisted her. In those particular moments, he had struck a desperate agreement with her: *If you permit the house staff to dress you at daybreak, I will carve out time each dawn to have morning coffee together.*

Every dawn before training, she had a task. Be in full garb without a word of complaint. If she managed, she could dash down to his room, just off his study. There, a thimble-sized teacup of watered-down coffee waited, biscuits and homemade jam placed neatly beside.

Subsequently, she would fervently request that he be the one to replicate their mother's 'hair creations,' as she fondly called them. He would huff and roll his eyes, pulling back his chair from the desk. She would sit on the floor in front of him, with legs crossed, as she had with their mother, handing him her small hair ties and comb.

Staring into the blurred beams cascading down into the murky abyss, these memories anchored him to his purpose. He is a brother. A protector. The core of what he cares for most in this world. He will do anything to keep her safe.

The silent laughter within him still echoed—a fleeting trace of tenderness buried deep inside. A reminder. A flicker of warmth within a mind numbed by brutality, wandering aimlessly as battles ignite with the sun's ascent.

The sky's heat intensified, dragging the day with it. Yet here he sat, combing through streams of memories, lost in silent moments with his little Ray of Sunshine. *My Spitfire. My bit of sanity.*

As the sun climbed higher, its glare would always sharpen into something more ruthless, turning the arena into a boiling pool of crimson sludge. The slick coating seethed—bubbling like molten rock, an open wound of fire and filth.

Izayah exhaled sharply, gaze locked on the roiling surface. A silent prayer, twofold in its weight, crushed against his ribs—raw, fervent, unyielding. *Let it slow my enemies, these demons. Let it burn them. Let it send them home. For those condemned to bleed for these savages' amusement, let it cool —just for a moment. Let mercy be given.*

By late afternoon, the shadows stretch out, reclaiming the arena. Darkness edges in, prying away the heaven's furnace—bringing with it the promise of rest...and a new kind of hell. The light gradually retreats, its tendrils of radiance fading—his sister's figure diminishing with every step, leaving him anchored in the silence of what was. *But soon, that silence will break.*

As dusk approaches, he watches the sun sink into the horizon against the backdrop of gray marble structures, its final radiance bleeding into the encroaching blackness.

The moon's ascent is always welcomed—it is my domain, my control. It is where the new hell of Visha rises, and my silence matters most. His heart stuttered in anticipation as the cool, silvery hue approached, its grace casting a gentle balm over the day's harshness. In these moments, Runa's ebony hair would unfurl across the sky, weaving through the tendrils of night—always present, yet safely cloaked in starlight.

How long has it been since I last saw her? Two decades. Twenty years. Izayah's thoughts meandered through the darkness starting to spill across the enclosure. *Does she think of me too, under this same moon? No, she won't recall me because of the shadow binding. She needed this time, and I have given her just that—time.*

The longing swelled within him, an excruciatingly beautiful ache, a hidden treasure of dreams and desires. Visha's gaze could never penetrate, no matter how hard she tried to get answers out of him.

I wish I could reach out to her, even just once, and tell her everything. That I'm still fighting for her, that someone isn't giving up on her. His mind wandered back to their childhood, to the quiet days at the cabin, when pain had been little more than a distant thing. *Or so I had thought. Might she remember even a single tale we shared?*

Nothing was certain. No one truly knew how shadow binding would affect any of the females long term. Taking this chance had been the mission—fast deployment, going off Sienna's intel, and an open-ended operation. The consequences never seemed to stop coming.

Without fail, during each nightfall, when the moon hid behind the clouds and settled in for a nap, the air would hang silent. Izayah and the other participants were thrust back into their kennels that surrounded the arena, or forced into holding cells beneath moldy slabs of marble and stone. He had to brace himself for the thick, gritty aftermath clinging to his skin, knowing that the cruel luxury of a bath was a distant, weekly reprieve.

One more day. One more night. He reminded himself often. *Each day brings us closer. It has to.* Izayah clung to that belief, convinced that every moment of suffering had its purpose. Each passing second edged him nearer to the day when he could finally speak the truth, laying everything bare before her.

Snapping back to reality, he forced his attention to the gritty, slick slab beneath his knees. A harsh truth slamming into him—this cycle isn't just meant to break the body, but to shatter the mind. From dawn to dusk, the torment never ceases—a cruel form of order within the chaos; control twisted under Visha's ruthless hand, contorting reality like sinew stretched past its breaking point, reshaping the world with an unnatural, bone-snapping precision.

There it was—an epiphany laid bare in the sludge, revealing not just the brutal truth of her leadership, but the warped doctrine she wielded like a blade. A system built on suffering, where power was sharpened through cruelty, and obedience was carved from bone.

It left him staring into the abyss of her rule, forced to reckon with the sheer depth of her ruthlessness—and the terrifying certainty of what would come if she remained unchecked.

Squinting through blurred vision, Izayah scanned the containment spaces. A swell of relief rose in his chest as he spotted Daxler and two others still standing—the last of the Shadow Elite. They had started with six, including himself. Now, only four remained. These were his unwavering lifelines—the ones who had endured the hellhole and learned how to survive in Visha's playground. Forever under watch, they exchanged silent, resolute nods—never truly alone, yet always deliberately kept apart.

Delving into the depths of his memory, he blocked out the noise of the crowd, submerging himself in the past. The moment the gates of Sanctuary yawned open, he had stepped through—straight into the mouth of hell from day one.

Nearly two decades prior, the operation had begun with precision when they walked through those very gates of Sanctuary. Meanwhile, the females had slipped quietly into hiding within Starlight Beach, their feigned deaths accepted as truth. Thought weaving ensured their concealment, their shadow bound state allowed them to progress in their own way, unseen and untouched.

In response, Visha, the High Priestess, had sealed Sanctuary in an iron grip, ordering the full lockdown of the holy city. She claimed it was to safeguard her citizens, to mourn the tragic loss of her only daughter, Runa. In truth, it was something else entirely—an unflinching display of dominance. Cold, calculated, and absolute.

At first, they were confined to the newer battlegrounds, where the enclosures gleamed, untouched by war. But Visha found them unworthy of her elite warriors, dismissing them with a flick of her wrist. They were soon transferred—elevated, as she called it—to a space where they should feel 'privileged' to bleed.

Her chin always lifted, her bitter smile unshaken, she had watched them from above. Hands gesturing grandly, as if bestowing a gift—their suffering a spectacle meant to be savored.

Izayah knelt, his swollen eyes clamped shut against the harsh light, letting her voice echo through his mind. He wasn't just bracing for the battle ahead; he was etching Visha's words into his memory, preparing for the day he would face his Ray of Sunshine and mentor with the truth.

"This," she had declared, her voice thick with pride as her hand swept across the room, "was once an elegant ballroom." She strode forward, her steps crisp and sharp, cutting through the stillness. "Now, it serves as my grand stage, where I find my finest entertainment."

She halted, surveying the space with a satisfied gleam in her eyes. "Every stone holds a piece of its history." Her fingers traced along the pillar's edge, her voice quickening with fervor. "Each one," she continued, her touch danced lightly from one stone to the next, "has borne witness to the glory of my reign…and the futility of defiance."

She ended her words with a dismissive glance over her shoulder, the arch of her brow underscoring her disdain. The train of her black lace dress flowed behind her as she moved toward the exit of the arena. "Enjoy your stay in Sanctuary, boys. It will be unlike anything you've ever known." A low, malicious chuckle escaped her lips as she turned slightly toward Izayah.

"Or," she purred, "you could have me instead." She bit her lower lip, a finger gliding along the marbled railing. Her left shoulder lifted gracefully to her throat before rolling back, sending the delicate strap of her gown slipping further down, baring more of her collarbone.

"You know," her voice dripped through the air like warm honey, echoing against the stone walls, "Runa spent quite a lot of time within these halls."

Her smile unfurled, dimples deepening, eyes gleaming with something knowing. "She learned so much from the inside out."

The sickness in these memories always dragged him back to the present, his body kneeling on the unforgiving surface. A thought ripping through his mind. *This arena, the very birthplace of Runa's pain, is Visha's most prized possession*—a bitter irony he'd only come to grasp with time.

He remained there, on the hard, cold ground, feeling the grit of the concrete bite into his knees. "Here we go again," he muttered to himself, his eyes fluttering shut as he tried to envision a calm space within. *Breathe,* he commanded silently—air thick with sweat, clinging to his skin, tainted with the sharp tang of rust. *Steady,* he whispered inwardly, releasing the breath, his eyes blinking through the encroaching darkness that seemed intent on mocking his every move.

Focus! His muscles tensed, visualizing towering walls of stone rising around him.

Breathe. A sense of peace washed over him as the thick, impenetrable walls muffled the distant sounds of clanging metal and muffled cries. He imagined Runa beside him, her calm expression a stark contrast to the turmoil within. *I'm untouchable, like Runa,* he thought, admiring her resilience. *Survive, just like Runa.*

The mayhem outside, where lawlessness reigned, and the pit, that was a stage for raw, unchecked violence, felt a world away. *Listen to them,* he said to himself, the distant roar of the crowd, the metallic clangs of weapons, and the guttural grunts of combatants, became mere background noise. *But here, in my fortress, I'm untouchable,* he reassured himself. The walls in his mind stood tall and unyielding, allowing him to return to reality with a refreshed line of defense in place.

Chains and shackles dangled from the rusted structure.

Clink, clank, clunk—as bloodthirsty spectators pounded their fists.

Thud, thud, thud—on the cage, causing vibrations to echo through the grimy hall.

Bang! Bang! Bang!

The metallic rattling of the cage and the relentless pounding melded into a grotesque symphony of malevolence. The crowd, a ravenous throng with an insatiable hunger for violence, shouted their taunts and jeers, voices merging into a single chaotic roar.

Izayah's muscles strained under the weight of the adamantine chains wrapped around his wrists. He knew their sinister grip well—an uncanny force that shifted with malicious intent.

Visha had always relished the chain's merciless versatility. With a single command, she could sabotage him—rooting him to the spot, twisting his body into submission, and tipping the balance in favor of his foes.

Like a serpent coiling around its prey, her voice had long since slithered into his mind—smooth, deceitful, and insidious. It never truly left, its fangs still buried deep, venom laced through his consciousness.

"The challenge will definitely add some excitement to this game today —at least for me," she purred, her tone dripping with delight, eyes sparkling with anticipation, a blush creeping up her neck. As she neared, her breath quickened. Against his skin, it intensified—warm, lingering, savoring their closeness.

Visha delighted in their pliability, making the shackles as light as air, granting Izayah a brief sense of freedom each night, for the past two decades. As the last event of the day ended each evening, she would loosen the weight of the bindings. Her gaze glittered with wicked delight, breaths shallow and hurried, heat blooming along her neck. Passing his pen, she would run a finger along the cage's edge, savoring the ease of control—the way his fleeting liberty was nothing more than a cruel joke.

She toyed with him, a cruel gleam flickering in her eyes, daring him to step willingly—not just into the shadows of her chamber, but into her grasp. A proposition plated in silver, polished and gleaming, laced with something far more insidious than mere danger.

Each night she came, prowling closer, her presence curling around him like silk-draped temptation—a soft, gliding noose, whispering of promises unspoken. If he followed, if he just let himself be led, this would all be easier. No more chains. No more weight pulling him into the dirt. *Just her. Just surrender.*

But beneath the velvet veneer of seduction, the truth festered. It was a perversion of what she knew. Or what she thought he knew. And when he refused—when he turned from the hunger in her gaze, the twisted offer of her body—she reminded him what rejection cost. The weight of his constraints grew heavier, anchoring him further into her world, ensuring he would never forget who truly held him captive.

His elite brothers, caged in their pens, seethed with fury. Fists slammed into iron bars—over and over—a relentless percussion of defiance. The sound ricocheted through the arena, reverberating in their bones, in their very marrow. It was not just anger; it was the desperate, helpless rage of warriors forced to bear witness. To watch as power slithered through the air, thick and cloying, like perfume gone rancid—sweet, overpowering, and nauseating in its persistence.

With each passing year, Visha's frustration festered, curdling into something even more insidious. Her cruelty was no longer just an edge honed to cut deeper. It was a blade dipped in poison, each move calculated, every whisper a slow, intentional incision. She didn't just seek to break Izayah—she sought to unravel him, thread by thread, until resistance became a distant memory.

And still, without fail, every night, she returned. Always descending to the arena after the decontamination of stone and man, the scent of blood and sterilization thick in the air, eager to make her next move in their endless, perverse game.

On one particular evening, she arrived draped in black, sheer as mist, clinging to her like whispered temptation. The lamplights flickered hungrily, their glow bobbing and stretching, seeking their aim.

Her heels struck the stone with sharp precision, each click reverberating through the cavernous space as she neared his confines.

Biting her bottom lip, she smudged the crimson ink faintly, a calculated imperfection. Her fingers—unhurried and controlled—trailed along the bars, the cold metal humming beneath her touch. The guards followed in silence, their presence a mere shadow to the spectacle unfolding before them.

"In the spirit of generosity," she purred, her voice lilting in a low, sing-song cadence, thick with sultry amusement, "I've brought you something." A fingertip traced lazy circles along the padlock that secured the gate. "A gift," she murmured, as the delicate fabric slid from her body, pooling in a silent offering at her feet.

Izayah did not lift his gaze. His attention remained fixed on the rough, weathered stones beneath him, tracing the uneven lines in the cement. The cool, gritty surface beneath his bare feet was a tether—a stark contrast to the heat and stench of her unrelenting desire.

He clung to those lines, to the rigid, unyielding texture beneath his fingertips, grounding himself in their certainty. The faint scent of damp stone and the distant echo of dripping water surrounded him, cocooning him in something real. Something steady. His focus did not waver.

A growl of irritation clawed up her throat as she stomped forward, heels striking against the cold floor in sharp, furious beats. With a huff of frustration, she kicked them off, the delicate stilettos clattering violently across the stone.

"Pathetic," she sneered, unlocking his elite shadow brother's enclosure with a flourish. The key turned with a metallic clink, the sound slicing through the charged silence.

The scent of her overpowering perfume, mingled with the acrid stench of sweat and iron, turning the air thick—oppressive, suffocating. The Sanctuary guards moved without hesitation, gripping his brother's chains as metal clanked violently against metal, the jarring noise reverberating through the cavernous space.

"Get him up," she commanded, her voice laced with venomous disgust.

The guards wrenched the male from the ground, chains rattling as they dragged him upright. Boots scuffed against the gritty floor, their strained grunts grinding into the atmosphere, layering over the ceaseless noise.

"Is this the best you can muster for one of your Elite?" Visha spat, the words slicing through the stagnant air, laced with venom meant to fester.

Her gaze flicked to Izayah—still unmoving, still refusing to look up at her.

Her lips curled back, as if disgust alone might consume her. She took a measured step forward, the space between them charged, expectant—only to be met with nothing.

Nothing.

Her nostrils flared. Her fingers flexed at her sides.

"Look at him." Her voice, now a whisper of raw contempt, curdled at the edges, thick with the weight of her scorn. "Look at what I'm taking from you."

Still, nothing.

Her expression twisted, her fury pressing against the seams of her carefully composed facade, splintering into something jagged, something rabid.

"Pathetic," she finally hissed, the word scraping from her throat like rusted iron. It burned—because no matter how much she pressed, Izayah would not break.

As they forcefully escorted his brother away, Visha's sultry voice toyed with the air, stretching between them like a lingering caress. "You know, I expected more from you." A purr of disappointment.

The faint rustle of the guards' clothing, the steady jingle of chains, and the muted clink of keys filled the silence, yet Visha moved without a whisper. Barefoot. Unbothered. Confident in her nakedness, as if the very air should be honored to touch her skin.

Izayah still didn't stir, yet the shadows graced him with the honor of his brother's solemn bow of his head—silent acceptance, a muted farewell.

"Such a touching moment…really." She stretched the syllables just enough to make them sting. Her lips curled, tantalizingly irritated as she dragged out a sigh—amusement feather-light, yet dripping with venom. And then, methodically, she turned—a movement as a blade drawn across the throat, meant to savor the moment of surrender.

"It's the last time you'll see him," a relaxed boredom caressed his mind. "Are you sure you don't want to reconsider?"

Nothing.

"I cannot stand the stench of such stupidity." With a flick of her wrist, the lights cut out. Darkness swallowed the chamber. The clanking of chains echoed through the void, followed by the lingering scent of iron and sweat. Visha's taunting laughter bled into the obscurity, slithering between the walls like a venomous echo.

Then, the projector whirred to life. Its mechanical eyes flickered open, spilling cold, sterile light into the pitch-black room. The day's events unfolded again, replaying in vivid, merciless detail. Each torturous battle, every agonizing moment, demanded to be revisited—as if the unsatiated agony needed one more fix.

The screams came next. Drawn out. Warped. Each one ricocheted off the arena's walls and snaked around the bars of his enclosure, ripping into his heart and echoing through his resolve, crawling beneath his skin— writhing and whispering like ghosts that refused to rest.

She was leaving, but not without the final word.

Pausing at the darkened threshold, she glanced over her silhouetted shoulder, deceptively casual. "That uniform is a little stifling, personally." A flicker of her amusement danced along his spine, wicked and knowing. "And because you've seen all of me…" She smirked. "…I think it's time I see much more of you." The sentence hung in the air, curling around him like smoke—a punishment wrapped in seduction.

A moment later, her bare feet whispered against the stone as she vanished into the darkness. And soon, so would his uniform. With it, the battlefield itself would shift.

Izayah remained outwardly steady, a mountain holding firm in a storm of fractured memories. Then the room bled into a deep crimson light as Runa's face filled the surface above.

His breath caught—a ragged sound betraying the fear tangled with his anger. His jaw clenched, muscles coiling tight as a silent war waged beneath the mask of his unyielding composure. His lungs burned—rage igniting, spreading, turning each intake into a battle against the heat threatening to consume him.

Still, he stood resolute—a fortress against the storm raging through him. Fingers tightening around the rusted metal links, he dropped to his knees, the air punched from his lungs. The kennel groaned but held. Fury seared through his veins.

Visions struck sharp, unrelenting with every gasp. The past and present blurring, daring him to reach out, to dismantle the bodies of those who dared touch Runa's fragile frame. A hellscape of indescribable powerlessness caught him, forcing him to bear witness to her unspoken hell.

His shoulders heaving, tearing at the joints. Details magnified, suspending mournful cries as he watched the light in her eyes shatter— again and again. *In. So. Many. Moments.* He clenched and unclenched his fists, never averting his gaze. Words eluded him as he swallowed his fury, silently carving each face of Visha's soldiers into his memory, searing them into his mind.

Judgment day would come—that's a promise. Shadows swallowed his gaze as he lowered his head. *One objective. One mission. And there would be hell to pay—I don't care how I get there.* He forced his chest to expand—*Breathe, just breathe. There has to be a way out of this madness.* His jawline quivered with contained restraint. *Focus, you fuckin' ass. She wants to break you.*

He seized his anger by the throat, slamming it into the ground. *Bury it, for now. Repercussions will be my treasure. A mighty fine fuckin' treasure. The lucky fucking bastards! How sorry they'll be, when they find out I'm their ultimate fuckin' dirty ass prize.*

Two decades. Twenty years. And this—just a taste. A glimpse of Runa's story. It's only a fraction of what Visha wanted me to see. Her mistake? She thought I'd never break free. She hasn't been watching closely enough—hasn't seen the signs. What this rage is becoming. What it's capable of unleashing.

Mesmerized, Izayah fought to anchor himself, grasping for any shred of sanity. His senses reeled, drowning in vivid images and the relentless echoes of Runa's suffering. Despair and determination twisted tight, locking into a brutal struggle.

Then the shackles loosened for a moment, granting him a brief clarity. In that instant, he understood Visha's true desire: to see him break completely. And Runa held the key to that door.

He started to unravel and fray at the edges. The only thing grounding him was the onslaught of impending battles. The irony of it all—a sardonic laugh rose from deep within—was the rising and falling of the sun, the boiling crimson pools, and the searing pain were the very things keeping him alive and fighting on.

He inhaled deeply, then exhaled, wrestling with the choice to keep playing the game or surrender. Yet he knew the females needed time to climb the steep mountain of self-discovery—a journey they hadn't even realized they must undertake.

Here he knelt, his kneecaps numb against the rough ground, releasing a breath, and trying to fend off the stench that had marinated for days. It was a foul mix of sweat and decay, marked by his scratched tally marks in the muck of his holding pen. The echoes of distant screams and the clanking of chains filled the air, a constant reminder of the relentless torment.

The sound of clattering reemerged as the crowd outside jeered and screamed, pounding the pen. Precisely then, the unyielding iron doors of the arena creaked open begrudgingly, slamming into the rusted wall with a resounding bang and caused the chains to clunk and rattle. His teeth gritted at the noise, and his body tensed.

"Creatures of the abyss, prepare for the next contender!" The announcer's voice crescendoed, attempting to cut through the roar of the crowd.

A colossal figure entered the arena, standing at least seven feet tall. It had a werewolf-like appearance but lacked any fur. Instead, thick scales adorned its body, resembling those of an ancient reptile. The creature moved on two powerful legs, its elongated arms sagging to its knees. Izayah's gaze climbed to its face—a grotesque mass of teeth.

As it opened its massive jaws, a thunderous bellow erupted, momentarily silencing the crowd. The stench of death filling the air. Gelatinous mucus splattering across the grotesque space. The sweat dripped from its scales, making them glisten under the eerie lighting as an unholy odor caused Izayah's eyes to water. The deafening bellow echoed, holding the crowd in a grip of silence for what felt like an eternity. Izayah rolled his head, trying to loosen the kinks that had set in, bracing his body for possible obliteration.

Words stretched between Izayah and the creature—twenty years of silence, and now he was choosing to speak. He decided it was time to play a game beyond his mind, to turn the creatures' thoughts in circles, disorienting him for just a moment. "So, tell me, where shall I go? To the left, where nothing is right?" A ragged draw of air, chest heaving, as he continued, "Or to the right, where there is nothing left?"

There was irony in his severe restriction; they had bolted him to the floor, channeling all their power into the chains around his wrists to "level the playing field," as the High Priestess would say.

He could hear her cooing against his ear, as she sometimes did on nights when he was too tired to even move. "Ahh…" she would moan, her mouth parting in a pout. "Poor baby." She traced a finger down his swollen face, her touch lingering over exhausted muscles. "Do you need me to clean up your mess?" Her hand continued its gradual descent, and he recoiled, mentally wrenching the memory away, forcing it to dissolve among the remnants of previous battles.

The creature tilted its head, squinting its gooey eyes in Izayah's direction, and emitted a growl, filled with a putrid stench, before pouncing. With no time to brace himself, the force of the creature's jump flung him against the cage wall's sharp edges. Gritting his teeth, he tasted the metallic tang of his own blood. *I will endure this pain.* His defenseless form pressed against the frigid, unyielding, slippery surface of the enclosure.

Barely covered in a loincloth garnished with thin bloomers beneath. He bore not just the agony, but the shame that came with it. With each brutal toss slamming him against the enclosure walls, the flimsy fabric shifted with every impact. Leaving him exposed and raw, his dignity hanging by a fraying seam.

His thoughts staggered, his mind struggling to course-correct just moments before another blow descended upon him. A burst of agony rippled through him, eliciting an earth-shattering cheer from the crowd.

The arena announcer's voice boomed, low and husky, "Our motto today is, between two evils, we shall pick the one never tried before." He guffawed into the microphone.

Izayah's inhale was jagged, each exhale scraping against his ribs like a blade carving him from the inside out. Thoughts crashed and coiled, twisting into a suffocating mass, drowning out reason. *There are no alternatives. No escape.* His chest shuddered with a fractured inhale, the nightmare tightening its grip with every intake. The weight of it crushed him, pressing into every fracture. He was splitting apart, cracking at the seams —unraveling into something he could not stop.

Diesel's voice reverberated within his skull, like an echo on a mountaintop bouncing back to the forefront of his mind. "When your body and mind reach their limits, that's when you call upon the Golden Guard." The words, like plumes of smoke looping and weaving through each syllable, solidified Izayah's understanding. "They will be your last line of defense; only call on them when every other option has been exhausted."

He hauled himself up to sit on his haunches, his heart pounding as his body wavered slightly. Taking a deep inhalation, he muttered what he knew of the creature, trying to recalibrate his system. "Netheron, the consumer of souls, not seen since the Great War."

He stumbled forward, chest heaving, and braced one knuckled fist against the slick rockwork. "Burn in hell, asshole." He pushed himself back up in the center of the ring, the boisterous crowd around him roaring with excitement. The arena announcer's voice surfaced briefly, but was quickly drowned out by the overwhelming discord of the room.

His sight came back into focus as he struggled to heal. The chains held his quintessence captive, the fifth element, and the bedrock of all power in the land. The Netheron circled him, observing its prey kneeling before it, releasing a deep, guttural groan.

Izayah's breathing quickened as the sinister creature circled. The Netheron's decrepit hand compressed around his neck, searing and branding the delicate skin beneath. Scalding and throbbing, the agony threw his body into response. He clenched his jaw to withstand the torment. Pulled up by his throat, he dangled as the blisters bubbled up and burst; an audible groan of misery escaped him.

Dizziness and nausea swirled, a relentless assault leaving him numb. Trembling and frail, his body slumped as time became elusive and indistinct, slipping through his grasp. He cast his plea between labored gasps.

Searing pain. A white flag. My only choice. My last option.

His voice was barely audible, a rasp, at best. "Aid me." His hands clawed at the stone, desperate for an anchor. Unsure of what would happen next, he lifted his eyes, seeking relief. The words hung in the air, a plea met with: *Nothing, but silence.*

The crowd surrounding the enclosure, hushed, watching in anticipation.

Time stretched painfully as the Netheron circled, pacing around Izayah's exhausted body. Its footsteps sucked at the muck, pulling with each step. In the eerie stillness, Izayah dragged himself into a crouch, then unable to maintain the position, he collapsed onto the stone.

An earth-shattering pop filled the room, and pain erupted from his shoulders. His body sagged, quivering like jelly, a blistering throb shooting down his spine—unsteady, unfamiliar. His eyes grew heavy, crossing, his vision blurring—caught in a storm of dizziness and disorientation.

The Netheron extended its venomous release valve, from a space between its forefinger and thumb, jabbing it like a syringe into the nape of Izayah's neck. A lethal dose of poison coursed through his veins as the crowd erupted in frantic applause.

The edges of his vision blurred further, and unraveled as the announcer's voice burst with excitement. The words grew less clear, melting into the deafening roar of the audience and the intoxicating effects of the venom. Lights flickered, faltering as uncertainty gripped him. *Was that the poison's cruel trick, or a response from the Golden Guard?*

Silence caressed him. The air was thick with moisture, and there was a heaviness in it that carried a delicate aroma of sea salt.

Instantly, his senses sharpened, every nerve heightened. His breath turned frantic, mirroring his accelerating heartbeat, which pushed the venom through his veins at a quicker speed. His eyes widened, taking in the hall's air, thick with the tang of the sea. Fear seized his heart, churned his stomach, and forced his chin to the side as sickness spilled onto the floor. His strength ebbed away, making it impossible to lift his head from the cool, sordid stones.

And then, her voice reached him, a fleeting but electrifying moment, a mere whisper in the depths of his consciousness. "Ray!" It reverberated through the chasm of his mind as if she were right there in the room. Onlookers stalled in place as fear rippled through his body, goosebumps shimmering along his skin.

What the fuck? His eyes darted around the room, bewildered by the occurrence. Blinking back the haze overtaking his vision, he muttered, "What's happening?"

Wait—can anyone else hear this? His heart pounded, panic rising. *It's so clear, faint, yet unmistakable.* His eyes scanned the room again, frantic. *No.* He released a labored breath, relief clashing with confusion. *Whatever this is, it's beneath their notice.* His heart eased slightly, but his mind raced. *Shit... did I open a portal? Have I exposed her to this terror, have I? Why can I hear her right now?*

"Hey Ray!" He heard her again. Silence, then, "Rayanna—I need you!" The cries, faint at first, intensified and resonated in the silence recesses of his mind.

This was exactly why he had stifled his emotions, why he had kept a vow of silence for two decades. He feared that any slip might connect their minds again, making her vulnerable. Now, as his body began to fail, everything threatened to collapse, leaving her exposed once more.

He blinked through the confusion, muscles tensing, mind racing to regain control. *Was this a reminder from the Golden Guard of what was at stake?* His heart slammed against his ribs, the poison searing through his veins—suffocating, gnawing, hollowing him out from the inside. *The Netheron— this fucking soul-sucker*—burrowed deeper, its hunger relentless, tearing through his mind like serrated teeth, leaving nothing but raw, bleeding echoes in its wake.

Failure is not an option!

GET UP!

Adrenaline surged through him, battling the venom. He seethed, hating himself for this single lapse, for momentarily giving in to the bastard in front of him. "How fucking dare you—FUCKIN' hell!" He hauled himself off the ground, the chains holding him in place as he fought to stand. He stumbled but steadied himself.

"FUCK THIS—I will NOT fail!" His voice came out raw and throaty, burning with rage, as he blindly pushed through the pain, inch by agonizing inch, forcing himself up from the sticky stones. Thoughts spun in his mind, each obstacle falling into place.

"FUCK YOU," he raged, knowing his failure would put everyone tied to the mission at risk. Everything hung in the balance, held by faintest traces of sanity. His voice thundered, tearing at his throat as he roared at the Netheron.

"I WILL NOT FAIL!" he bellowed, voice erupting from the pit of his stomach as his head snapped back, mouth wide open toward the ceiling.

"I YIELD! I FUCKING YIELD!" The words tore from his throat, raw and ragged, erupting from the pit of his stomach. The words echoed, a desperate plea to the unseen Golden Guard. Silence fell as his body seethed with fury, muscles straining against the chains. He pushed with every ounce of strength left, the bolts in the ground beginning to loosen.

"TO HELL WITH THIS, AND TO HELL WITH YOU ALL!" He thrashed against the chains, veins bulging, his entire body fighting as if to break free from years of confinement in a single moment.

The air cooled, but Izayah ignored it. His focus stayed on the bolts loosening beneath his feet. He didn't notice the world growing quiet, or the confusion spreading through the crowd.

It felt like a dense, invisible veil had fallen over the arena, muffling every sound and electrifying the air. Fractured dendrites—brittle, crackling branches—danced across the space, moving with a delicate tinkling, colliding with the corners as frost crept from hidden crevices.

The chill spread inward, forming intricate patterns of ice that sparkled, sharp yet elegant. Frozen tendrils crept like living vines toward the center, while a thin layer of ice spread like a second skin over the marble stone. The murmuring, a low, endless hum, like a distant conversation, was creating a symphony of otherworldly sounds. The advancing cold purred as it moved, filling the arena with a mystical presence, steadily closing in on the combat zone.

As the ice neared the spectators, panic spread like wildfire. A man closest to the creeping ice felt the chill climb up his leg. He shrieked in terror as the icy tendrils bit into his flesh, his skin cracking sharply, frostbite setting in instantly. His cry echoing in the cold, a testament to the force driving the chill. The crowd, realizing they'd never see their bets again, released their coins, backing away.

The frozen onslaught kept advancing towards the center, relentlessly. The arena's warmth diminished, causing the demonic entities to scatter. Their cries filled the air as they gnashed their teeth in irritation.

Smaller creatures, unable to escape, found themselves caught and encased in the icy terror, freezing them in time. The sight intensified the panic, causing chaos, as demons trampled over each other in their desperate attempts to flee.

The rest of the fighters remained stuck in their rusty kennels. Icy formations covering everything like ghostly fingers. The frost reached Izayah's elite brothers' pens and then stopped, creating a protective barrier around them. Then, the cold moved on, flowing towards the center of the arena, passing the opponents. Izayah's brothers watched in stunned silence. Their shock quickly turned into urgent screams directed at him.

Izayah heard their frantic calls and fought against his chains, his strength fading as the adrenaline drained away. His vision blurring again, the freezing air slicing through his resolve.

The Netheron noticed the frost creeping closer and seethed with fury. It banged on the bars, trying to shake off the encroaching icy bite. The impact rattled the rusted metal, sending ice stalactites crashing from the ceiling, narrowly missing Izayah as he fell to his knees. The demon paused, its eyes flickering to the frost climbing up its legs, inching toward its pelvis.

Izayah lifted his head, gasping from the floor. "It's coming—for you, bastard!" he taunted. The demon's sinister eyes glared with malice, fixing on Izayah as it tried to lunge toward him, but remained stuck to the marble. The ice continued to climb steadily up the demon's legs, crackling and freezing everything in its path, creeping toward its chest like a relentless wave.

Barely holding on, he let a wry smile ghost across his lips as he pushed himself up from the floor. The frost grew in brilliant intensity, like the moon cutting through a nocturnal sky. A dance of fading bleakness and glinting frost painted a chilling scene of struggle and transformation. The frost inexorably covered the demon's weathered skin, and a light within it grew brighter.

Izayah's body sank lower to the stone, weighed down by exhaustion. The demon shifted its gaze upward, looking past the frozen enclosure. Its eyes swept over the cavern beyond the metallic dome.

Every corner seemed caught in a violent change, a frosty storm building just beneath the surface. The walls and edges contorted and twisted, bending to the unseen forces that no one could place. The ice crept from the corners, covering every surface in a chilling shroud. The ghostly light overhead, now glazed with crystals, flickered for a moment, capturing the attention of all who watched.

Daxler, nestled in a corner with his arms weighed down by hefty adamantine chains, stared blankly into the distance. He seemed completely unaware, devoid of emotion, trapped in an invisible box that shut out the world.

Izayah slumped deeper against the stone, letting his thoughts drift like a leaf on a meandering stream. He couldn't shake the feeling that his dear friend had spent all these years in a different reality altogether—always aloof, detached from this realm, yet somehow still connected. They appeared to be cloaked in an unseen darkness.

With a long exhale, Izayah turned his focus back to the Netheron. Its wrinkled skin crystallized from within, forming an intricate lattice of blue that spread like ink in water, shimmering under the surface. The ethereal beauty of the transformation clashed with the doom it signaled. The demon's flesh became a living mosaic, each crystal shard reflecting a fragment of the relentless cold seeping into the arena.

Izayah felt time stutter as his blood decelerated. His heartbeats became more relaxed, fighting the spread of the venom. *At the speed of molasses in winter,* his mouth curved into a sarcastic smile, taunting the beast. "Well, isn't that shit luck, big boy?" Each word drained what little energy he had left.

Sprawled across the floor in the filthy loincloth, his frame shuddered uncontrollably. The cold stone beneath him sapped away the remaining warmth. Each wave of shock caused his muscles to twitch, making it impossible for him to lift his head.

A radiant glow emerged above Daxler's enclosure. It illuminated the grim faces of onlookers and cast long shadows across the space. The light resembled the sun, obscured by clouds, causing everyone to squint back in response.

Through the glowing haze, a silhouette emerged from the shadows and decay. The adamantine chains, unyielding in nature, now hovered next to Izayah's form. Unclasping from his body, lashing forward like a whip, and coiling around the demon's torso. With wide eyes, the remaining onlookers watched.

The beast's struggle was futile. A mere ripple against the tide of its imprisonment. The demon let out a guttural growl, the sound resonating with a primal fury, echoing against the frozen walls. Frost crackled and shattered beneath its weight as its breath emerged in visible plumes against the wall of chilled air.

Simultaneously, a golden radiance enveloped Izayah, tenderly caressing his battered form. The swelling around his eyes receded. His world sharpened into focus. Under the brutal brilliance, every detail of the arena was exposed.

As his vision cleared, he saw the raw reality of his surroundings: jagged ice formations, a desolate frozen landscape, and harshness etched into every crevice. The unforgiving nature of the environment was evident. The ethereal light illuminated every facet. Izayah's bloodshot gaze snapped wide, his pulse hammering in his ears.

The woman lifted her head, chin raised in regal defiance, eyes burning with an unrelenting fire. She moved with unshaken grace, her presence commanding—unstoppable—as she extended her hands forward.

A searing surge of amber light detonated from her fingertips—an incandescent eruption that tore through the void. The cavern quaked. The air crackled under the weight of her unleashed power, humming with a force both ancient and divine. Her fists clenched. She yanked her arms back, coiling the light like a drawn bowstring—then, with devastating finality, released it.

Detonation upon impact.

The Netheron ruptured with a thunderous crack, its form shattering into a cascade of jagged, solid fragments. The force of the explosion ripped through the chamber, sending shards skidding across the frigid stone floor.

They clattered violently against the perimeter's fencing, some lodging deep, others ricocheting wildly like shrapnel from a collapsing star.

The air hung heavy with raw energy, thick with the scent of scorched iron and something primal—something older than the cavern itself. A mix of relief and awe settled over him as he blinked in stunned silence, his face tilting downward, caught between bewilderment and amazement. Before him, the spectacle unfolded. Reality wavered, shimmering like a mirage.

The Golden Guard. A strange mix of recognition and confusion churned within him, a deep, unspoken pull he couldn't place. The glowing orb of a woman drew closer, her brilliance fading as she approached. He squinted, trying to pierce through the glow. As she hovered nearer, her features became clearer in the softening light.

"Mother?" he whispered, his voice filling with a mixture of hope and disbelief. Her touch upon his forehead was tender as she skillfully drew out the poison from his exhausted body.

Overwhelmed by fatigue, he surrendered. "How long since you've been gone?" he whispered. He simply let the darkness press in, pulling him under. *Twenty years…Two decades,* he thought. *I made it. Runa's Dawning Day draws near.* His breath shuddered. He embraced the oblivion, trusting the edge…letting *go.*

Chapter Five

Blinking into the shadows, Daxler heard a faint plopping, like a rock falling into water. He turned his head, tilting it toward the ground, his left hand resting on the floor. Faint sounds—calling to him.

Twenty years. Two decades—in an abyss of silence.

Visha's twisted playground, crafted with purpose, was designed for her cruel games. The High Priestess would coo, "Just for my special ones," her voice dripping with delight.

Here, days blurred into a haze of shapeless moments; a perpetual twilight where time lost all meaning. His willpower was drained away, leaving him trapped in an invisible deprivation tank. On the outside, he was on display. But inside, his mind was ensnared, unable to see beyond the confines of his prison.

Sounds rippled down his temples and along his jawline. Soft, like a female's fingernails grazing his skin, arousing everything in between.

Then came the eerie creaks and groans, filling the emptiness like ancient ice shifting. High-pitched pings and delicate tinkling—like shards of glass splintering—punctuated the silence.

A deep rumble reverberated through the stillness, like distant thunder vibrating in his bones. *Seductive.* A deep, primal calling stirring something dormant within him, the tremor teasing his senses. It awakened a fervor, quickening his blood flow and heartbeat—a *tantalizing* whisper, urging him to massage away the numbness clouding his mind.

Their arrival at the gates of Sanctuary had been abrupt and jarring. He'd expected discomfort, but the harsh, individualized nature of their environments had caught him off guard. It reminded him of how his father, a blacksmith, had spoken of seeking the godforsaken metal that was now clamped around his wrists. Both experiences were unique, tailor-made to test one's very core.

Right when we stepped through the gates of this failing city, I assumed fate would throw us into something like Elite Hell Week with the Shadow Guard. How wrong I was. Dropped headfirst into the void—no light, no sound, just a suffocating silence thick enough to choke on. *My senses faltered, forced to recalibrate. I had to claw for mental footing just to stay sharp. It was a crucible— raw and brutal. Just like the ones forged to seek rare metal. Only this time, the ore was us.*

Cocking his head, he wondered if there was a parallel between his situation and Izayah's. *Was there a clue that explained why they were both placed here, each in their own personal hell?*

The idea was to tap into his *quintessence*—his so-called *fifth element. That 'intuitive transcendence' crap. Basically, a fancy way of saying I'd have to dive into her headspace, poke around her thoughts to get a real grip on what Visha expected and why she did…well, everything she did.* This mastered skill had always proved to be a valuable tool amidst most challenges, turning the tide against the desolate realm of hopelessness. Yet here, in this space, it was *useless.*

I've had no say in my freedom. Never have. Visha doesn't just hold the keys— she owns the narrative. Twists it. Shapes it until even the truth forgets itself. She breaks the stillness of my isolated hell only when it suits her, dragging clarity out by the throat and replacing it with whatever distortion she's decided I deserve.

Survival here isn't about winning. It's about withstanding. You ride out the storm with no warning—never knowing how long it'll last, how bad it'll get, or what it'll tear apart next. And even that comes at a cost.

Told Zay back then—and it still holds—I'd move on faith, trusting his lead while we wait for the first ripple of Runa's unbinding. Whatever breaks this shadow bound grip. Truth is, I'm just riding blind, at the mercy of everyone else now.

Until I reconnect with Izayah, I'm just existing—clinging to the belief that my brother still has a plan. That he'll find a way to pull us out of this mess. Mission success has always been non-negotiable, always leading the charge. I trust he hasn't forgotten that.

His mind shuttered at the thought. *Was my isolation meant to break me—or just screw with Izayah?* He slumped back against the grated wall—jagged, sharp, and as charming as ever. The metal had etched itself into his spine like it had a damn vendetta, carving grooves so deep they might as well come with names. He wasn't even sure where flesh ended and cage began anymore. *Time? Time was a joke here—some sick, dragging illusion that stretched pain thin just enough to see what snapped first. Blessed Father only knows how long I've been sitting here. Long enough for the wall to leave love notes in my bones.*

Leaning forward slightly, the movement stiff and sluggish, his curiosity cracked like distant thunder—low, rolling, and impossible to ignore. The bigger question hovered, gnawing at him. *Am I living on one side of the coin while Izayah deals with the other?* Furrowing his brow, he tilted his head, pondering—just as the pinging crescendoed again, sharp and sudden, catching him off guard. The sound echoed like a pin dropped inside a sealed tomb—each note unnaturally crisp, unraveling into the silence like teeth tearing a chunk from his flesh.

In this bleak cavern of shadows, the medley of sounds tinkled like breaking glass, making him think of the one thing he truly wanted: a surface where he could carve tally marks, just to count the days and pretend he had some grip on reality. *Guess that's her point.* Here, he let his mind roam, mulling over the scraps of information Visha had tossed him during brief escapes from this jar of existence—sealed tight, airless, warping his perception like a specimen suspended in formaldehyde. A place where thought echoed too loudly and silence scraped the walls of his sanity. A mind prison disguised as isolation.

STOP!

His mind screeched to a halt as the sharp scent of salt water hit his nostrils, sending him into a psychological free fall—down the rabbit hole with a failed parachute.

Confusion crashed over him like an icy wave, leaving him breathless. *Is the smell just another hallucination? Or is Visha pumping fresh poisons into my chamber?* His head tilted, nostrils flaring as he tried to pinpoint the source. *Anything is possible with this one. I wouldn't put it past her; the last time she'd been here, her desperation had been palpable. Painfully suffocating.*

His eyes darted through the pitch-black void, wide with confusion, searching for anything familiar. *Am I slipping into madness?* His heart pounded—an insistent, erratic drumbeat. He sucked in a breath, head leaning back against the cold enclosure, trying to find some sense of comfort in the chaos. But the air thickened, pressing in around him, amplifying his disorientation.

He flared his nostrils again, dragging in air until his lungs ached. *Not just a hint of saltwater…oh no—it's the whole damn ocean. Sand. Grit. The sting of seawater scraping raw skin.* His mind reeled, trying to stitch together the fractured onslaught of stimuli. He licked his lips, half-expecting to taste salt—or maybe the phantom skin of some long-lost lover. *Oh, fucking hell. This bitch. It has to be Visha, screwing with me again.* He blinked through the haze of disbelief, sitting up straighter as the storm in his head started to churn, hot and volatile.

Was this it? The tidal pull we've all been bracing for? Runa's unbinding— tearing through the veil like a siren's call soaked in goddamn salt and brine. The sensation was bewildering, an alien thing in this ink-drenched void. His hands clenched and unclenched reflexively, a futile attempt to grip something—*anything*—tangible in the dark.

"Ahhh—crap," he groaned, eyes locked on a distant flicker, barely visible within the void. The inky dark had swallowed everything else. *But that glint? Yeah, I see it. Maybe hope? Maybe a trap? Who the hell can tell anymore.*

"Damn fucking woman," he muttered, voice low, gravel-thick, rough from disuse. "Acting like some self-appointed god. Always tweaking the volume on my life like it's her favorite hobby." His fingers lifted, twitching into a crude puppet. He made it flap with mockery, dragging his voice into a flat mimicry. "Come on, come on, I'm in charge. Kneel before your queen." He let the hand drop with a dull thud against the stone. "Yeah. Message received, sweetheart."

A female silhouette emerged, sauntering closer through the lightless void. Instinctively, he slammed mental walls into place, numbing the reawakened parts and locking down the world within. A crooked smirk tugged at his lips as he lifted a chained hand in a strained, half-mocking bow.

"Oh, fantastic! Didn't realize I had visitors scheduled today," he rasped. "Can I get a rain check?" His fingers flicked out with lazy disdain. "I'm a little tied up—really soaking in the five-star amenities of this abyss."

But gradually, the glow around her shifted—no longer just a flicker, but a soft, golden radiance spilling from the folds of her dress. It pulsed like distant sunlight breaking through a storm, delicate but undeniable, turning her into a fragile beacon pressing back the dark.

"So much for a rain check," he croaked, sarcasm mingling with intrigue, every word scraping against his raw throat, his voice cracking like a door with rusty hinges. "I would have cleaned up," he added, rattling the chains against the ground with a metallic clink, "but I've been a bit...restrained." His jaw tightened just enough to show his irritation without breaking his composure.

Daxler shaded his eyes with his hand, shoulders tensing at the unexpected brightness. He let out a exaggerated sigh and feigned a relaxed slouch. "Well, that's a grand fucking entrance," he drawled. He pointed lazily toward the source of the light. "Points for effort."

Daxler rubbed the back of his newly shaved scalp—a nervous tick that gave him away more than he liked. His gaze narrowed. "Unless you're here to end me or set me loose, don't waste my time. He huffed out a sigh, then gave a shallow, theatrical sweep of his hand—what little motion his chains allowed. "Go on then," he muttered. "Find another toy to waltz about for your nightly escapades. I'm off duty.

The female advanced, gliding with measured grace. Daxler squinted against the growing brightness as she lifted her hands with elegant ease, a radiant surge of golden light spilling from her fingertips.

He scrubbed at the sting of brightness. "Fucking hell. Just what I needed—eye-searing illumination, the kind of wake-up call I didn't ask for."

Light unfurled from her fingertips in fluid ribbons, fanning outward with controlled grace—more like a blessing than an attack. It parted the darkness gently at first, then surged in clarity, revealing a blinding white room. The space shimmered, morphing into a translucent, gelatinous enclosure about the size of a small dog run. He blinked hard, vision struggling to adjust, with the sudden shift in his claustrophobic enclosure. "Perfect. Now I can see my future—guess we're trying out light-induced torture today."

Daxler jerked his head forward, squinting against the glare as he tried to focus. The brightness had peeled back the haze, revealing the wall's translucence—and beyond it, a motionless form sprawled across the floor. The woman was still right in front of him…and yet somehow, she was also outside the enclosure, cradling the figure.

His gaze snapped between the two versions of her, eyes wide with disbelief, like his brain was caught buffering. One version gently placed a hand on the figure's forehead. Her arms wrapped around him with a tenderness that shouldn't have belonged here—like a mother shielding her child in a place built for breaking.

Her voice drifted through the chamber—soft, almost hesitant—as if testing the silence that had owned him for too long. "I am here with you," she said, "and I am also there with him." She paused before saying assuredly, "He will be fine."

Daxler leaned forward, jaw tight, fighting back the rush of fear and adrenaline. *What the hell is this?* He tilted his head, squinting hard, trying to parse what lay beyond the fogged glass. His eyes locked onto the figure— familiar. Too familiar. *Is that Izayah?* His stomach sank. "What the hell happened?" The words tumbled out, raw, before he could stop them.

Muscles coiled, straining against the chains. *God-fucking-damn it. Let me get to him.* Every instinct lit up—desperate, feral—clawing to reach his brother, to close the distance. But the restraints dug in, unrelenting. *Fuck these chains,* he bit out inwardly, yanking hard. Nothing. Not even a rattle. *Useless scrap metal.*

Then it hit him—again—*that sharp, briny air. Unmistakable.* His nostrils flared. His eyes snapped wide, the shock like a slap. *What is this? What kind of twisted illusion…?* His gaze cut back to the woman. She nodded once, slow and steady, that maddeningly serene smile still curling her lips. Then she gestured toward the center of the room.

And there it was. The words he'd carved into Starlight's plaque all those years ago—*A promise, our promise, to the residents, travelers, and anyone who stumbled across its doorstep.* Coming in phrases drifting down from the ceiling, manifesting like they were cutting through thick fog, pulled into the present moment. *A vow we all made. Crisp and unbroken. Solid and unyielding, exactly as it was intended.*

"What is this?" Daxler spat. "Why are you showing me this now?" He wrinkled his nose, huffing sharply like steam rising from a seared blade. His gaze locked on the anomaly descending before him—phrases of Starlight unraveling in thick plumes, each word flaring like a beacon in the haze, radiating that maddening, familiar warmth. *Home—my home away from home.*

The shadows shifted, bleeding into varying shades of gray as his thoughts hammered against his skull—unrelenting. Tactical questions. Tactical failures. *If Visha finds out about—FUCK—no, I can't go there.* The salt-heavy breeze intensified with every step she took, dragging the past into the room like an uninvited guest.

He barked another demand, sharp and controlled. "Is this some kind of playbook? A directive? Or are we just freelancing now?" His features tightened, jaw locking. "Because I'm gettin' real tired of the twisted mind games."

Questions clawed at him, each one stroking the coals of his anger. *What does Visha know? Were the females found? What does this woman want?* His mind spun, a whirlwind of possibilities. *Some new illusion? Yet another one of her fucking games?*

"I am not the High Priestess," her voice cut in, sharp—severing his stream of thought, "nor am I tied to her antics. I am far from them." Her cadence eased, gently delicate as a feather drifting across dew-kissed blades of grass.

"Daxler," she breathed, lowering her hands in a fluid motion, "I know about Starlight." The name slipped from her lips like a secret carried across lifetimes—each syllable trailing shadows, and something deeper than memory. The glow encircling her softened, no longer searing. It flickered like an ember on the edge of dusk, casting quiet shadows where once it commanded.

He dropped to his haunches, arms straining against the bindings, every muscle coiled, ready to strike. "Is this a fucking joke?" he growled. "Because my give-a-fuck fairy died a long time ago."

"Daxler," she repeated, her voice low and steady, extending an arm, palm down. "Your presence here is no longer needed, Guard." As she spoke, a radiant golden sphere bloomed around them—soft, warm, pulsing with quiet authority. "You have done well," she continued, her tone never rising, never flinching, "and now it's time to move on." Light flared from her hand—not violently, but with conviction—as if it could reach inside and pierce through the storm tearing him apart.

Daxler's body tensed. Intake of air stuttered momentarily. Rage and instinct flared like twin blades, and he pushed back with everything he had, raw defiance screamed through his thoughts. *Fuck you and this. I am not falling for this bullshit!*

"Settle." With a flick of her wrist, the restraints binding him dissolved— vanishing like smoke on the wind. Her voice followed, soft but steady. "I am here to help."

Daxler staggered as the bindings released him, momentum pitching him backward. He caught himself, knees buckling, then dropped low to rub at his overstrained forearms—veins bulging beneath battered skin, the weight of years etched deep. Blood surged back into his hands, hot and prickling. He flexed his fingers warily, eyes never leaving the female.

The chains had carved deep, slicing through flesh like the rind of over-ripe fruit peeled back too far. Now exposed and raw, his skin throbbed. Fresh waves of pain shot through him—sharp, disorienting—riding in on a swell of nausea that hit harder than expected. His body quaked under it, the raw truth of it all beginning to sink in.

"Settle yourself," she said gently. "It's my turn to care for you, Daxler. You boys have done quite enough—and for far too long." She moved with measured grace, placing her hand lightly over his wrist. Her touch radiated a steady, restorative warmth, seeping through torn flesh and strained muscle. "It will leave only a small scar," she murmured, watching as the wounds began to knit together beneath her palm—sealing with quiet finality.

"Well, I've heard scars are a hit with the ladies," he said, glancing down at the mending skin before flexing his wrist and tossing her a wink. "Full disclosure, though—I've been off the dating circuit for a while."

"Guess we'll have to see if your theory holds up, won't we?" She smiled, her focus steady on the wound as her hands moved with practiced care.

Lifting his head, curiosity sparked behind weary eyes. "You're a Golden Guard, aren't you?"

Though the light concealed most of her face, her voice reached him—steady and serene. "I come from beyond the shadows…reclaiming what was once whole." Her tone drifted like a breeze through tall grass, loosening the tightness in his shoulders and quieting the static humming beneath his skin.

"The Blessed Father knows what you've done for the cause." The glow around her dimmed slightly—just enough for her eyes to meet his, a quiet understanding passing between them.

"And to answer your question—yes. I am." She replied.

"So…it sounds like the mission is still a go?" he asked, trying to piece it all together. "Dawning Days have begun—along with the first phase?"

"Not all of them just yet," she said softly, her gaze holding steady. "But Runa's begun…" She gave a small nod. "The mission advances, yes." A faint smile tugged at her lips as she released his now-healed wrists. "Izayah knows what to do next."

She straightened, "Remember, the righteous are as courageous as lions, but even lions need to rest." Leaning in slightly, her expression grew earnest. "Get him to rest for once, please."

Daxler let out a raspy laugh with eyebrows raised. "Yeah, well—have you met him? I'm not sure Izayah even knows the meaning of the word."

Suppressing a laugh, she inclined her head. "That's a fair statement. He wasn't much different as a youngling." Her voice softened, laced with something almost wistful. "It's been a while; be kind to yourselves." The corners of her mouth curved briefly. "The hot springs have always helped him settle." Her words crackled with warmth, like the embers of a long-forgotten fire.

Daxler rolled his neck, rubbing at his sore joints. "Yeah, well, from where I'm sitting, my back's already writing a thank-you note."

She grinned and leaned in. "There will be time for that." Her hand touched his forearm. "Daxler, I appreciate what you have done for him," she said, her words strained. "Thank you for finding him. He's always needed someone like you." Her smile tightened. "But I have to warn you, the new environment might be a bit of a shock."

His posture shifted, gauging the situation with sharp interest, watching her form dissolve back into a radiant sphere. The light gathered into a single, luminous orb, drifting through the blurred chamber with an unearthly grace. It pulsed softly, a low vibration rippling through the air—like the echo of light held too long—gradually sharpening Daxler's vision.

Then the room fractured. The translucent walls shattered outward, breaking into jagged fragments of incandescence that scattered and dimmed. A sudden chill swept in. The vibration deepened, a resonance that struck marrow. The orb surged with brilliance, revealing a new, expansive arena—stark, unforgiving. Despite the illusion of space, Daxler remained boxed in, confined to the long, narrow holding pen.

The cold was more than a chill; it bit deep, clinging to his ribcage as goosebumps prickled across his skin. Otherworldliness crept through his flesh, coiling around his spine, raising the hairs on the back of his neck.

"Well, shit, this is cozy," he muttered, a huff of vapor blooming in front of his nose. The chill mixed with the glowing spectacle, making everything feel like a surreal dreamscape. "Hey, is this a normal climate for you?" He glanced around as if searching for an invisible thermostat. "Because I left my winter coat in the box," he added, tossing a thumb over his shoulder.

The female's voice drifted like wind-whipped leaves, her words swirling through the icy air before settling—whispers from another realm. *I know you both have questions.* The golden sphere hovered effortlessly, its surface shimmering as it swayed side to side with unhurried purpose.

Below, the caged males stood within the frozen battlefield of grimy marble—a tundra blanketed in dried auburn sludge, blood and gore rusted into the corners. Each exhale spilled into the air as a misty cloud, giving way to miniature snowstorms that danced and vanished.

Drawn to the orb's glow—a flickering flame caught behind fogged, iced glass—it swayed in beckoning intervals, controlled and relentless. *Now is not the time for clarity,* she intoned. *Understanding will come. The process holds meaning. Izayah has been given the directives.* The sphere wavered, pulsing with quiet insistence. *Remember—your greatest tasks lie ahead.*

"Greatest tasks lie ahead? Are you fuckin' serious?" Daxler scoffed, dragging a hand along the rusted bars of his enclosure. "Because clearly, everything before this was just a warm-up, right? Just a little team-building exercise in hell." He threw up an arm, gesturing around his space like a jester revealing a prized chicken. "Surprise! You win another round in the pit with the resident nutter."

Silence.

He squinted upward. "Can she not hear in that shiny orb of hers?" His brows knit tighter. "Forget the answers—I'll take a coat, a drink, and a one-way trip to those hot springs you kept promising, Zay." Allowing the thought to settle in. "And this time? We're not just daydreaming. I want heat, stillness, and something wrapped in meat."

The orb hovered in silence, its light stuttering softly—like it was listening more than seeing.

"Okay, good to know, *Goldie!*" he called out, throwing his voice into the nothingness like it might bounce back with answers. "Must be nice—floating around like some Mystical Powderpuff, preaching about rest and relaxation while we're down here freezing our asses off."

Daxler didn't expect a response. Certainly not the one that came next.

Izayah's laughter hit him—not just a chuckle, but the deep, rasped, uncontrollable kind. It burst through their telepathic link, echoing like a forgotten melody, shaking loose the cobwebs of all that quiet, coiled seriousness.

Daxler's gaze snapped to him—just in time to catch the smirk forming as Izayah rose up off the chilling marble.

Keep it up, Dax, the thought soared across the connection, sharp with amusement, *you become the new court jester for real this time.*

The sphere glimmered softly, as if charmed by Daxler's defiance. Light danced from its surface, casting diamond-like glints across the ice beneath their feet. With a sudden spark, it zipped from one containment pen to the next—vibrating with life—as a protective shimmer wrapped around each prisoner. The perimeter doors flung open. The nearing possibility of final freedom crashing in like a wave.

When she reached Daxler, she lingered near his head, humming with quiet purpose. *The cold is healing.* Her words were spun sugar—a whisper of ancient wisdom. Warmth stirred, skimming along the nape of his neck, heat trailing his spine—slow and sure, pushing back the bite of frost. For a moment, it felt like returning from a long exile—not restorative, but soul-eroding. And she, impossibly, was the beginning of the thaw—of something broken starting to knit back together, one breath at a time.

"Well, that's a fucking useful skill," he muttered, stretching as every ache and ounce of weariness melted away—replaced by a surge of raw vitality. *Leave it to cold therapy. Forget the hot springs—guess I'll be booking an appointment with Goldie next time.*

Standing taller, he rolled his shoulders, rotating his joints with newfound ease. The cold had lost its grip on him—he felt immune to its freezing grasp. The soreness, the stiffness, the dragging fatigue—it was all gone, like someone had peeled off a layer of exhaustion and tossed it into the snow.

He tugged at the edge of his loincloth with a playful smirk, the intricate tattoos swirling across nearly every inch of his body—curling over muscle, slipping past the waistline like they had nothing to hide, and just as smug about it as he was. They rippled with every flex and shift, like they knew they were being admired. "Again—any spare clothes in there?" he called out, shaking his head in mock disbelief.

"Not that I'm complaining, but unless the plan is to break out of here armed with nothing but raw sex appeal, I'm gonna need more than this upscale dish towel." His eyes widened, brow furrowing as if personally offended by the thread count. "I mean, don't get me wrong—this whole 'bronzed warrior of the North' thing is really pulling its weight. But *pillowcases?* Really?"

He flicked the loincloth for emphasis, the motion barely shifting the laughably thin fabric. "I've had napkins during Shadow Guard hell week that offered more dignity—and those were on fire." He gave his shoulder a lazy brush, knocking away an imaginary speck with the kind of self-assurance that came from knowing the room wasn't done watching him yet. His elite brothers rolled their eyes like they'd seen this routine one too many times—and knew damn well it always came with an encore.

"Blessed Father help us all," Izayah muttered, crouching within the Golden Guard's radiant shield. It shimmered faintly around him, a translucent barrier pulsing with soft golden light. Though he hadn't responded directly to outside sources, his awareness hadn't slipped for a second—his gaze swept the perimeter, sharp and steady.

"Hey, Zay! You good, man?" Daxler called out, his voice dropping the sarcasm just long enough to reveal a flicker of concern.

The radiant sphere answered first, drifting in lazy, tightening loops around Daxler's head, its brilliance softening with each pass.

He will surface soon. Think of it as him being in a warm, placid spring. Her cadence wandered through Daxler's mind—ethereal and patient, more sensation than sound.

Then it stopped, hanging just in front of his nose. Its light stammered—faltering, like it had sensed a new current in the air. A beat passed, and something in its tone tilted. *My time here is drawing to a close.* The orb bobbed once, its flickering now uneven—like the thought itself was too heavy to stay steady. *Two pieces of the puzzle rest within a tethered bond. Be mindful before moving forward, my Elites. Shadows are funny creatures—a parasite that often goes unnoticed. See what you may, but do not second-guess.*

Izayah's shield dissolved with a soft pop, the golden light snuffing out. He remained crouched, one fist braced against the floor, his eyes sweeping the room—absorbing every detail with calculated focus.

Runa's time is coming. And when it does, I will be the one to collect her. The orb flickered—its radiance flaring as it veered toward Izayah. *When you hear of it, know that it is me. Do not respond to the reports or take action. Maintain your course.*

The glowing mass glided back toward Daxler, its movement pointed and precise.

Fighting leathers will be found in designated spots along your exit route. You've already been briefed on their locations.

The miniature sun swept down, tracing along each Elite's forearm with a faint chime echoing in its wake, leaving delicate trails of iridescent light. The sphere hovered briefly above the remaining warriors, recalibrating—reassessing. Then in a sudden burst of momentum, it shot toward the door, pulsing bright to mark the path. *Stay alert. Follow the plan.* Once more, the orb soared through the frosted air, sweeping over each male in a looping dance, its glow circling their forearms.

Daxler's ink was the first to stir—the dark lines lifting from his skin like a living thing, unraveling into an intricate, iridescent map. Tiny markers flared to life, glowing softly, guiding him toward hidden caches of leather and weaponry. He could feel the stares—the other Elites glancing between their own arms and his, confusion etched across their brows. Their maps didn't match his, and the unspoken question lingered between them like fog: *Why him?*

"Fuck yeah," Daxler said, loud enough for everyone to hear, a grin cutting wide across his face. "Must be the scars." He flexed slightly, just to be insufferable, then gave a shrug. "Or maybe Goldie's taken a liking to me." He pressed two fingers to his chest in mock sincerity, eyes gleaming with amusement as he shot a glance at the orb—almost daring her to react.

"All right, sweetheart," he drawled, his voice smooth and cocky. "Let's play your game. You've got my attention."

The map unfolded in breathtaking detail—fine lines etching out hallways, veins of marble swirling through floorplans, and arcane symbols that shimmered and shifted as if alive. Points of light darted in frantic motion across the surface, representing Sanctuary's guards and demons as they converged to cut off their unit's path through the crumbling city.

As the thought weaving ink deepened to an obsidian hue, it tugged against his skin, merging seamlessly with the designs already etched across Daxler's arm—layering over old lines like it had always belonged there. Brows lifting, a mischievous grin tugging at his mouth, he tilted his chin upward, eyes gleaming with delight.

"Now that's fucking sexy." A low, gritty base tore from his throat, the baritone vibration laced with a twist of admiration. "Fuck-*freaking*-fabulous, Goldie." Daxler clicked his tongue as he tossed her a wink. "Gotta say, sweetheart…you do beautiful work." He extended his arm, slowly rotating it to admire the new patterns from every angle. The markings pulsed in time with his heartbeat, the escape route blooming to life with each beat—mesmerizing in both clarity and complexity.

"Seriously, Dax? That's my *mother*." Izayah rolled his eyes, throwing his hands up in a half-hearted display of disgust—like he could physically ward off the comment.

Daxler waved a dismissive hand, smirk curling at his mouth. He turned toward his Izayah with an exaggerated bow—fluid, showy, and just a bit unhinged enough to be annoying. But beneath the flourish, a glint of genuine intrigue lingered in his eyes.

The orb brightened in response, her light taking on a coy shimmer. *So many things I could show* **you,** *if only there were time.* Her cadence purred along the edge of her golden glow, the hue deepening into a soft blush of pink before settling back into warm gold. She spiraled around Daxler's arm in a intimate orbit, brushing lightly against his wrist. More than just a guide now, the patterns on his skin had shifted—an elegant timer nestled at his radial joint.

The ticking countdown vibrated gently, a hum that rippled through his nerves. A tingling sensation climbed his arm—an arousing reminder of the fleeting moments they had left in this frozen landscape. "Well…now, Goldie. Getting a little cheeky, huh?"

Izayah threw his hands up again in mock exasperation, backing away from the group. "Ugh—I just can't, with you two." He rolled his eyes, but couldn't stop the smile tugging at his lips. A notion drifted out with the haze. *How I have missed this.*

Follow my lead, sir. Just trust me on this. Daxler's voice cut clean across the mental bridge, the weight of it steady—grounded.

Izayah straightened slightly, the familiar tone drawing his focus.

Then, like flipping a switch, Daxler's energy shifted. He rolled his shoulders back, confidence curling up his spine. *Remember Treefall Lagoon? When I told you to bob and weave, and you danced like a baby chica-boo on ice?* A pause, thick with mischief.

Yeah. Don't do that again.

Izayah's energy rippled across the mental bridge—a dry, unrestrained chuckle crackling through the link as he moved toward the exit, leaning against the cold exterior of the enclosure. *Oh, fuck off. The furry little thing, was adorable—just like me.*

Daxler didn't miss a beat. *Yeah, you fucking wish.* He gave a casual shrug, cocky as ever.

Arms crossed, posture relaxed, *You better not get us killed, Dax.* A beat later, he raised his hand, fingers barely apart. *We're this fucking close.*

Daxler arched his brow. *Just keep your pretty face out of the way, and let me do what I do.* He gave a pause—just long enough to let the statement land. *Trust me. I have a reason for this.*

"You better know what you're doing, Daxy." Izayah exhaled, the sound equal parts warning and resignation.

Daxler extended one arm with a dramatic flourish, his skin rippling with movement as he crouched at the waist in an exaggerated bow. Straightening up, he tapped his nose, pointed to his wrist, and then toward the door. "You ready to blow this joint?"

The illuminated orb hovered above the exit to the frozen, weathered arena, her light stuttering as if listening to something inaudible. The glow stilled, shifting to a blend of mystical gray and obsidian black, a faint white core pulsing at its heart. She saluted them in her own way—a gesture that spoke volumes without a single word. It was more than respect; it was a promise, reflecting the shadows and moonlight that would guide them through whatever lay ahead.

My time has drawn to a close. We will be in touch soon. Her light pulsed, shadows and fog swirling within. *Understand this: once I fold into time, you will have one hour to become nonexistent.*

She bobbed to the left, drifting toward Daxler. *Don't mess around too much.*

Then she floated to Izayah. *And you—listen to him.* The orb drew closer, shrinking in size as she approached, almost whispering in his ear.

I am so deeply proud of you.

Of who you've become.

Of the warrior you are…my son.

The Elite males turned in unison, chins lifted, saluting the Golden Guard with silent reverence. The orb sparked and darted—a quick, urgent rhythm. A surge of light burst outward, tearing through the door with a force that sent a gust of icy air lashing across the space. It flared again, a hesitant flash, then dimmed—folding into time with a soft, gentle *whoosh*. Silence settled in its wake, leaving the room bathed in dim half-light, shadows stretched longer, deeper.

Daxler pursed his lips and made a low chirping sound, birdlike and amused. "That's certainly an unconventional approach." He gestured toward the now-demolished door of the battle arena, then pointed at his own cage. "You ready to get me out of this bait trap?"

In the lingering shadows, the imprisoned warriors rolled their shoulders, exchanging nods. Izayah strode forward, his loincloth swaying with each step. "Can't wait to ditch these fancy napkins," he muttered, reaching for the nearest padlock. With a firm grip, Izayah twisted the metal at Daxler's enclosure, snapping the individualized dog run open with ease. The rush of deliverance felt like a breeze in a stifled room.

"Feel that fuckin' freedom!" Izayah croaked, rubbing his unshackled wrists before glancing at Daxler. "Now that is fuck-*freaking*-fabulous!" he added with a grin and a wink. "Can't say I'll miss the rattling chains." He rolled his shoulders with a smirk. "Moving like myself again has its perks. Not as stylish, but I think I'll manage."

With a smooth motion, Izayah released the next latch as a fellow Elite's hand landed on his shoulder—a firm pat that spoke of their bond. He moved to the other cells, each warrior greeting him with a tight gripping of forearms and a brief touch of foreheads, a silent nod to their survival and strength. One by one, they were liberated. Each followed the same tradition: foreheads together, hands gripping arms tight; their gratitude and resolve was clear without words.

Daxler glanced at the inked timer—digits ticking down in crisp intervals, each second flaring faintly before slipping away."Forty-five minutes." The Elites nodded in sharp unison, a silent acknowledgment of the clock now pressing in on them all.

The sound of distant footsteps drummed through the stone passageways as Daxler edged a finger along his forearm, tracing the moving shapes within the hallways that ebbed across his skin. "And it appears we're still clear on the rear side of the arena." A deep metallic clang rippled through the marble—a stark reminder of the danger closing in.

Izayah's eyes followed Daxler's gaze to the icy torch by the far door. The flame looked trapped, its red core glowing beneath a shell of frost— like chocolate-covered ice cream, hard on the outside but molten within, just waiting to be released.

His voice nudged into Daxler's mind, quiet and direct. *What are you gonna do, Dax?*

Just trust me, brother. His eyes locked on the pulsating flame. Its dim light pushed through the ice, casting a mesmerizing contrast of fire and frost. Moving with purpose, he tore the torch free from its frozen hold. The cold bit into his fingers like needles, but he gritted his teeth and hurled the encased flame toward the far door.

The ice shattered with a deafening crack. Shards flew in every direction as the flame roared to life, lashing out in a burst of heat and frost. Daxler shifted instinctively, shoulders dropping low as he braced into the impact —icy splinters slicing across his skin like tiny daggers.

A blast of heat tore through the chamber—a searing force that clawed at his lungs, violent against the stagnant, frigid air. It shoved him backward, but he absorbed the blow, twisting mid-motion and landing in a low crouch—graceful, sharp, feline.

The explosion sent the other Elites stumbling. Their grunts and low growls echoed through the space, sharp and raw—like something deeper inside them had been stirred loose.

Izayah's lips curled into a wry smile as he lounged in the shadow of the exit—well beyond the blast's reach. *And that's why we don't let you lead,* the words rolled across the mental link, smooth as smoke, as Daxler cut through the haze of heat and splinters. *Oh, let me show you how it's really done.*

Pushing off the wall with calm purpose, he crossed the space in a few easy strides. Reaching for a nearby torch, he yanked it from its icy mount and hurled it down into the stadium seating. The flame reignited on impact—this time, without the fireworks.

The other Elites' gazes darted between the two like spectators at a match—heads swiveling in sync, following an invisible ball. A frown tugged at the corner of one male's mouth, while another squinted, trying to decode a language only Daxler and Izayah seemed to understand. Silent banter passed between the pair, leaving the others caught in the middle of a show they hadn't bought tickets for.

Confusion flickered across their faces, but none were truly concerned. Everyone knew those two operated on their own frequency. Random acts like this were part of the routine. And regardless of theatrics, results always followed.

Nice move, Dax. Were you planning to set yourself on fire, or was that just a bonus? We're almost out of this joint, and you choose now to try and die?

Daxler's eyes widened in cartoonish horror. He reached up, snatching the silent jest out of the air, plucking it from existence and tucking it into a nonexistent pocket. Then, with dramatic flair, he crouched low—arms outstretched for balance. His body swayed dramatically from side to side, like a tightrope walker mid-act. Each motion was an exaggerated parody of stealth, his feet barely making a sound as he dipped lower, mimicking a predator in a child's game.

Izayah rolled his eyes—a silent broadcast of his rising irritation. His shoulders sagged as he exhaled. Tilting his head back, he stared at the ceiling like he was begging the heavens for patience, then glanced down at Daxler with an incredulous shake of his head. His fingers tapped against his thigh, each beat a steady metronome of restraint, as if willing his brother to pull it together.

What the hell are you doing? This is reaching new heights of ridiculousness. It's turning into a full-blown fucking spectacle. His thoughts pushed through the link, tracking Daxler's every exaggerated movement. One hand swept low, as if smoothing fabric over unseen skin—each motion fluid, unhurried, and laced with refined intimacy. It carried the grace of tracing the curves of a woman's form—the kind of touch meant to be remembered.

Dax...this is starting to feel less like stealth and more like seduction. The words came rougher now, strained at the edges. *I really don't want to know what you do in the bedroom, man. We are not that close.* A beat. *This is actually making me uncomfortable. A full-blown burlesque number in the middle of our extraction op? Really? Twenty years—two decades—*He rubbed at his brow, exhaling hard. *Don't screw this up now...just because you need to get some.*

"I think it knocked some marbles loose, brother," Izayah said aloud, drawing out the words just enough to sound half-serious. His voice shifted, snapping into command. "What the hell is happening right now?" He took a step forward. "Daxler—get it together."

Izayah's thoughts drifted as he stood there, brushing off the weight of recollection while Daxler continued his dramatic dance through the warped battle arena. Ghosts of the past clawed and clung to every surface. *How many battles had been fought here? How many scars earned?* Each experience was etched into the bloodstained marble—into the crevices of wounds that had only been crudely closed. *Now that those damn chains are off...the scars will finally mend on their own terms.*

Carved into our bodies—a brutal record of survival.

And Daxler, of all people...

You're spinning like you've forgotten where we are.

He frowned. *Still...something's not sitting right.*

I'm curious to see what angle you're playing here. A quiet pause. *What game are you running, Dax?* His fingers drummed a contemplative rhythm against his chin as he watched. Shifting his weight, he settled back against the cold marble along the exit. Arms crossed.

Another beat of hesitation.

Then—he caught it.

The flick of Daxler's wrist. *Subtle. Deliberate.*

There was something familiar in it—a pattern beneath the performance.

For a heartbeat, that was all it was.

Then Daxler twirled through the arena, his movements at odds with the eerie stillness surrounding him. He spun and whirled, finishing with an exaggerated bow that only deepened the absurdity.

Their elite brothers didn't move—watching in silence, as if waiting for a cue. Then, a low rumble of laughter followed, stifled but off-kilter. There was a baritone edge to it, something darker laced beneath the humor. Not quite mirth—more reflex than reaction. It didn't ring right. It slipped past their lips like a crack in the mask, feigning amusement that felt too thin, too brittle. Cynical. Fractured. And just a little too sharp around the edges.

Is this really what we've come to? Izayah mused, the corner of his mouth twitching despite himself. *You're either losing it, or you've got something up your sleeve. Which is it, Dax?* There was no response in the amphitheater of thought.

Then, the shadows stirred.

Faint, but unmistakable.

You fuckin' bastard. A grin cracked across Izayah's face. *I knew you had something up your sleeve.*

He pursed his lips and made a quiet smacking sound with his cheek— half judgment, half approval. *Well then…let's dance, Twinkle-Toes.*

Daxler moved like he'd just dismounted a horse, his steps exaggerated and bizarre, adding to the absurdity of the moment. Frowning, Izayah shook his head, a reluctant chuckle escaping as he straightened—just in time for Daxler to slam aggressively into his side, knocking him off balance. He staggered but caught himself, the movement snapping them both forward into the next beat of the plan.

Izayah let out an exasperated sigh, the sound edged with just enough irritation to sell the act. "That's fucking enough. Fall in."

Frustration surged as he dragged a hand across his scalp—the motion sharp. "This isn't playtime," he snapped, jabbing a thumb toward the exit. "Reel it in, Elite. We're burning daylight. Move out." He turned, striding toward the doorway—but Daxler jolted into him, off-balance, loose like a drunkard, slamming him sideways. Izayah stumbled hard into the stone frame. "You done screwing around?" Izayah barked.

Firelight surged across the icy surfaces, fed by the mounting blaze now consuming the arena. Born from the torches they'd tossed earlier—becoming something far greater. The pure quintessence burned hotter than any natural flame, stoked by old popcorn bags and discarded debris. It pulsed with a hunger of its own. And in that flickering chaos, faces began to emerge from the shadows.

Deep in Daxler's eyes, Izayah caught a glint of fierce determination—a minuscule scene clouding his brother's pupils like a ghost drifting through hazel coffee.

Something was off.

Narrowing his focus, he saw it—the shutter. The guilt. A silent reverberation winding through his brother's gaze.

In one swift motion, Daxler lunged for the nearest ice-encased flame. He swept the torch in a tense arc, light and motion carving jagged paths through the frosty air.

With a ragged shout—steady, yet urgent—he hurled the torch toward a heap of frozen, crumpled popcorn boxes lodged in the muck of the battleground. The ice crackled—not like normal frost, but with a brittle, unnatural dryness, as if the cold itself were desperate to burn.

The fire roared higher, merging with the earlier blaze. Heat rippled outward, washing across the arena. But the frost didn't retreat—it fed the flames. That strange brittle coating went up like dry bark, snapping and flaring with unnatural speed.

The inferno painted jagged shadows across the scarred stone walls and rusted iron bars, casting the arena in a shifting, haunting luminance. Smoke churned upward in thick plumes, rolling like storm fronts.

Daxler crouched low. His arms drew back, fingers tapping lightly along the tattoos stretched across his shoulders. A sharp pop cracked through the din, followed by a low, resonant hum. In a heartbeat, two daggers rippled into existence—rising from his skin, coiled memory made solid. The ink pulsed and writhed, like liquid shadows flowing across his arms. Dark lines curled and tightened into solid form, locking into place with a soft tink—metal greeting metal.

The blades tore free from his skin, their gleaming edges catching the firelight with an almost hypnotic shimmer. Dark tendrils twisted and coiled, binding together until they hardened into razor-sharp steel— glowing with an unnatural, volatile light.

The air around him crackled. Raw energy surged. Midnight-shaded daggers, now firmly in his grasp, felt achingly familiar—solid, reassuring.

He held his stance for a moment, reacquainting himself with their perfect weight. The blades spun easily between his fingers—extensions of his will, honed and ready. "You didn't think I'd notice?" Daxler seethed.

With a swift movement, his grip tightened—blades parting the air with a low whoosh. Fluid. Unerring. They sliced through the chamber, glinting like shards of starlight before striking with satisfying thuds. The daggers sank deep into the necks of his Elite brothers, red sparks erupting from the points of impact. A wet, sickening splat echoed through the stone chamber, cutting short two lives in an instant.

The final Elite hissed, fangs sliding into view as a low snarl curled in his throat. Another blade slid free from Daxler's obliques, ink undulating across his skin. The air snapped with a sharp, metallic tang—charged, tense. Daxler spat through clenched teeth, "Eat this, asshole," he growled. Muscles tightened, body coiled, his focus narrowing with deadly precision.

With a sudden, fluid shift, the feathered blade launched—piercing straight through the last Elite's eye. The body collapsed, spine hitting the floor with a jarring thud. It spasmed once before a twisted cough escaped its throat, rising into a warped, demonic grin. Black liquid oozed from its mouth as it sputtered, "Welcome to the next level, pretty boy." Its eyes went cloudy, the light extinguished.

Daxler straightened, neck cracking with a sharp pop that ricocheted off the walls. Shadows flickered over his inked arms as he exhaled. "Fuck your next level, jackass." He stepped forward, retrieving each blade with practiced precision. His fingers slid through the hilts' holes, spinning them once—twice—before settling. The thought woven ink across his skin still throbbed faintly, alive with residual energy, glowing like embers in the aftermath. With a final swipe, he cleaned the blades against his loincloth, the gelatinous black smear soaking deep into the fabric.

The chamber thrummed with the hungry crackle of fire, each lick of flame casting jagged silhouettes across the walls. Smoke curling thick in the air—suffocating, clinging—mingling with the tension settling like a lead weight on their shoulders.

Daxler shot a glance at Izayah, grinning. "Think they're gonna roll out the red carpet for us, Zay?" he quipped, twirling the blades faster—firelight dancing in his eyes. "Something tells me the real welcoming committee comes laced with explosives…and the drinks are poison." His cadence held a casual edge, challenge woven beneath every word.

With a swift motion, he sheathed the blades, flexing his fingers like he was savoring the steel's kiss. "I don't know about you," he drawled, testing each knuckle like a concert pianist readying for a finale, "but call me unimpressed." Defiance danced in his eyes. "Like you keep telling me —twenty years, two decades." He clicked his tongue, the corner of his mouth twitching with disdain. "And if *that* was Visha's opening act, someone better tell her dumbass demons to pack it up. I was promised chaos—not amateur hour. I've got energy to burn…and an axe to grind with these assholes."

Footfalls thundered from the corridor—Sanctuary's guards on the move, their rhythm frantic and closing in fast. Izayah cast a sidelong glance, a sinister grin stretching wider. "We've got the heat handled," he said dryly. "Let's see if they bring anything worth burning."

Daxler snorted. "They'd better. Twenty years in that box, and I've got some energy to burn." He adjusted his stance, rolling his shoulders. "Not in the mood for amateurs today."

Izayah's grin widened. "I was getting tired of being the headliner here. Couldn't we just leap from that window and fold out?" He flexed his hands, muscles coiling beneath his skin. "You know anything about this ice?"

"I know it won't have any issue blowing the ass off this arena," Daxler said, his smile turning feral—teeth bared like a wolf on the hunt. "Let's just say…it'll get our point across." He smirked, a sly glint in his eyes. "My Pa used to talk about stuff like this—never saw it firsthand, just theories. But this?" He whistled low. "This is gonna be fun, brother."

"So...we're lingering for what exactly?" Izayah arched a brow.

"Hey, man, I sat in silence for far too long. I *deserve* a little entertainment." Daxler crossed his arms with a cocky slant to his posture. "Don't worry your pretty little head—there'll be *some* kind of indication before this shithole blows its lid." He leaned back against the wall with a grimace, eyes dropping to the ticking timer. *15 minutes.*

Izayah puffed out his cheeks, clearly unimpressed. "Well, since we've got time to kill, let's get one thing straight—we need a new safeword because *'prancing'* doesn't exactly scream *your name.*"

He dragged out a staged sigh. "You know, I could've torched the arena way faster if you'd picked something a little less interpretive. What the hell were those pirouettes even supposed to mean?" He gestured toward the smoldering wreckage. "A heads-up that the remaining Elites had gone full Shadow Demon would've been *nice*. Just saying. After a couple decades of this mess, I think I'm due for a more straightforward, no-circus-acts version of Daxler."

"Your baggage ain't my burden, sweetheart." Daxler said, shrugging with maddening ease. "I said, *'Just trust me.'* If that's a problem and you can't keep up...that's on **you,** not *me.*"

"Explain this to me—how, in the BLESSED FATHER's green lands, was I supposed to take 'trust me,' pair it to you gyrating in a full-blown inferno, and somehow deduce that meant 'Shadow Demons inbound'?"

"Wait, what? Shadow Demons can't dance in fire?" Daxler feigned distress, smoothly dodging the subject. "Fine, we'll come up with a safe word for next time. Whatever helps you keep up." He leaned back, pressing his shoulders deeper into the cold stone, his eyeline flicking to the ticking timer upon his wrist: *10 minutes.*

Izayah leaned in, voice dripping with mock sincerity. "First off, you know damn well that Shadow Demons are stuck in the realm of endless darkness—fire, my friend, makes no sense at all." He rested his chin on his hand, clicking his tongue before pointing directly at Daxler. "Second— wouldn't you have liked to know, Twinkle-toes?"

Daxler scoffed, rolling his eyes. "I was actually looking forward to some cozy time with you in the hot springs and all your...brooding."

Izayah shot him a sideways glance, feigning distress with a deep frown. "Ahhh...I could never let you down." Then, arching a brow, he added, "Alright, alright. Back to the cabin, but not without a quick detour first."

"Of course, we fucking are." Daxler laughed, shaking his head. "Twenty years, and you think I'd expect anything less? How about we just make 'Starlight' our new safe word?"

Izayah leaned back against the frozen surface, ignoring Daxler's comment. Tilting his head to the side, he glanced at the ticking timepiece on Daxler's wrist. "Why does it feel like time is moving through tar?"

Daxler lifted his forearm into view, as they both watched the inky lines shift and morph into new numbers against his skin: 7:54…7:53…7:52.

Daxler rolled off the wall with languid grace, arms uncrossing as he dipped into a mocking bow. His loincloth shifted with the motion, soaked in theatrical intent.

"For fuck's sake, man." Izayah immediately averted his gaze, muttering under his breath, "Never thought I'd say it, but…I miss our leathers."

"Well," Daxler drawled, leaning into the moment, "good news is—our time here's almost up." Heat pulsed from the chamber walls, radiating off the stone as sweat pooled and traced fevered paths down their skin. The temperature climbed—a stifling, suffocating boil.

"So, what's the play?" Daxler asked. "A leap into the unknown, or one last cardio session with these assholes?" He tapped his wrist, the seconds ticking down.

"Eh…I'd rather keep it mysterious. Let's just fuckin' jump and fold." Izayah stated.

"Don't we need to grab a few things on the way?" Daxler's hand slid over his torso. Then he raised his arm, the map's markings flaring bright upon his skin.

"Nah…" Izayah threw up his forearm, brushing his opposite hand from wrist to elbow. Another map materialized—just as intricate.

Daxler stepped in, tugging Izayah's wrist closer for a better look.

"You've gotta be shittin' me. You knew about the Shadow Demons and just left me out here twirling like a jackass?" He puffed out his chest, clicking his tongue.

"Hey, you're not the only one who needs a bit of entertainment." Izayah grinned, clearly pleased with himself. "Reminds me of that one time in Shadowveil. Figured, why not—it's been a while."

"...And I'm the dramatic one." Daxler rolled his neck as they edged closer to the frost-covered, gothic window. "We're going with Plan B, then. Starlight? Unseen? Correct?"

Izayah nodded. "Your map's for something else. Keep it safe—and try not to screw the damn thing up."

"What? I am *appalled* you'd say such things!" Daxler clutched his chest in mock offense. Both males ran their hands from elbow to wrist, the ink fading back into their skin for safekeeping.

Rolling his neck and shoulders, Izayah laid it out: "Hit glass. Fall. Fold. One stop—Unseen. Then the cabin. Got it?"

Daxler turned to him. "Please tell me we're getting leathers before we hit Starlight."

Izayah huffed out a laugh, eyes flicking to Daxler's wrist: *5 minutes.*

Then, from the shadows, a rippling scream burst from the stands, echoing through the space. The frozen landscape responded in kind, a chorus of ice singing in sharp, tinkling notes as it shifted and groaned. The sound rose in a haunting melody, carrying across the arena.

Izayah's smile faltered. "That's our cue."

Daxler clicked his tongue. "That's got to be painful," he muttered, as the remaining audience—bound in ice—began to stir, blinking beneath their frigid crusts, creatures trapped within crystalline casings. Cracks spidered through their forms, each subtle movement accompanied by the sharp, chiming notes of the singing ice—a shrill reminder that the land's quintessence had once been part of everything. The flames along the walls flared higher, licking upward in open defiance.

Izayah's gaze lingered on the scene, absorbing the message forged in flame and sealed in ice. He pushed the thought down the bridge of their bond, the effort like flexing a muscle long atrophied from disuse. *This place—this moment—is more than just chaos; it is a declaration! A world no longer willing to settle for the ordinary. An invitation. A challenge that urges them all to reclaim what strength remains of their quintessence. A call to rediscover their primal nature; unleashing their souls—to take back what was once theirs.*

Daxler snorted, *Great. A motivational speech to go with the apocalypse. Just what I needed today.*

Izayah turned his head, just enough to catch Daxler's eye. "This place was a fucking hellhole," he said, voice low but clear. "but it was the kick in the ass I needed. Now we refuse to settle, we push back…"

Daxler grimaced, his lips pressing together. "To help others see what they've been fuckin' blind to for so long." His eyes trailed to the frostbitten figures stirring in the room. He cocked his head with a slight bob. "It's my reminder that I enjoy making dramatic exits." His eyebrows ticked skyward, a beaming grin spreading across his face. "You ready to leave one hell of a calling card?"

Izayah nodded, and the very pulse of the aged arena bowed to his heartbeat. "Always," he whispered. A hushed promise tucked into the room. It was an endearing acknowledgment of the forces still swirling around them. A blazing and deep appreciation for what had been given… and maybe, just maybe, for what was finally being released.

They exchanged a final look, a shared understanding sparking between them. Izayah inhaled deeply, savoring the weight of standing on the precipice of the unknown—one more breath, one last glance at the history they were leaving behind.

With a nod, they moved as one, launching toward the arching Gothic windows. Glass exploded outward in a sharp, cracking crescendo, shards catching the light like molten stars as they cascaded into darkness. Ethereal flames surged, fed by the rush of air pouring through the shattered panes. They lunged and slashed like warrior's blades, carving forward with relentless hunger. The ice crackled and hissed—fueling the fire rather than resisting it—surrendering to the blaze's fury.

Together, they moved—an alliance of extremes, searing heat and biting cold, each feeding the other's strength, neither yielding an inch.

Tongues of intensity stretched outward, scorching the space—peeling back layers of torment embedded in the walls, exposing ancient scars and deep gashes where anguish had existed for eons. The heat gave the chamber permission to grieve, to mourn, to finally release the burdens laid in its hands and at its feet.

Ice splintered beneath their dual advance, cold as the killer instinct that had been encased within, each crack a merciless strike that matched the rhythm of Izayah's heartbeat—his rage and fury echoing through the room like a battle cry.

The violent inferno and keen glacial chill clashed in a fierce, thunderous symphony, a union of fire and ice that roared through the chaos. A voice forged from flame and frost bellowed out: *Heal within the stars. Rise from the shadows. Stand to meet the moon. Emerge from the mist.*

The flames wove into the smoke that plumed out of the elongated windows, twisting and curling, as if reluctant to release the two elite guards in their downward pull. For a brief moment, the smoke hesitated, then surged past the flames, eager to cloak them, blending the guards seamlessly into the darkness below. Smoke shielded both males from the world as Izayah's shadows unfurled, spreading across the sky and blanketing it in deep-seated obsidian. With a controlled force, Izayah's quintessence swallowed the brilliance of the stars, casting the world into heavy darkness. The temperature dipped, a subtle chill gripping the air, as if bowing in respect to the core of Izayah's power.

Following suit, the flames deepened in color, saturated by the shadows' influence—heeding the command that rippled through Izayah's heartbeat. They gnashed their searing teeth, responding to elemental shifts as the air crackled with anticipation. Raw, unrelenting power unfurled outward. A faint breeze sputtered around them while the earth shuddered, as though the very land braced itself for what was to come.

A sudden pull—*fwoosh*—*shhh*—*thwap*—and time bent sharply, folding in on itself, embracing the men into its depths. It tugged at their senses like gravity dragging at their souls, pulling them through layered existence— through the core of the world itself. The space they left behind quivered like gelatin: stiff, yet pliable. It bounced once, then settled into stillness, as if they had never been there at all.

For a heartbeat, the battlefield held its breath. A fragile silence settling over the lapping flames and sizzling frost, like an unfinished note suspended in the air. Then, with a violent shudder, the arena collapsed inward. Fire, ice, shadows, and earth were drawn together like a sharp inhale. A swirling collision of quintessence erupted. Elements, long opposed, now entwined, working in unison for the first time in eons.

The massive arena imploded with devastating force, the inner supports collapsing first as the marble and stonework shattered. Shards of rockwork burst outward, spewing deadly shrapnel into the atmosphere. Larger slabs of stone crumbled and fell inward, each impact shaking the earth beneath. Dust billowed upward, thick and choking, raining down like volcanic ash.

The space filled with the crushing weight of devastation. Screams echoed through the chaos as the inhabitants of Sanctuary scrambled for shelter; their cries were swallowed by the violent collapse. For a moment, time itself seemed to pause. Then, silence fell—deadly and absolute—as though the very land stood wide-eyed in shock.

The dust settled, only to shudder again—particles rising as a deep, sucking noise rippled through the surroundings. The debris from the collapse—shattered marble and crumbled rock—rose, pulled upward by invisible hands. The remnants of the arena that was just scattered across the ground, hovered midair briefly before spinning and colliding, glinting under the blanket of obsidian sky.

The fragments shimmered, vibrating with an otherworldly energy as they coalesced into a new form. The very air around them crackled, a low hum accompanying the transformation, the cold bite of the atmosphere deepened as the process unfolded. Above the ruins of the arena, a resemblance of a moon rose, forged from the gathered elements—fire, ice, and earth mingling in defiance of the destruction.

The quintessence within each fragment of the shattered arena glittered and snapped—*clicking, binding*—as the sphere took shape. Remnants of stone, marble, and rock, once strewn across the battlefield, now rose like a phoenix from the ashes, hovering where the arena had once stood. A symbol of rebirth and resilience, the moon blazed defiantly against the powers that still lingered.

In response to the new formation, flames reignited from the embers, rising from the icy kindling. They whipped upward, coiling around the celestial body's cusp like tendrils of illuminated rope. Molten lava glazed the sphere, dripping down its sides in glowing rivulets, coursing across its surface. As the blazing flow shaped itself, the moon began to shift—morphing into the head of a lion, its mane flaring to life.

The great beast's mouth opened wide, its canines elongated as it tore through the obsidian night sky. Its roar echoed through the heavens, sending clouds of rain billowing across the land. The downpour began, a long-awaited rebirth—the first rain in decades. Citizens of Sanctuary threw their hands up in joy, welcoming the life-giving water with open arms.

A declaration.

A calling card.

A statement.

A reminder.

Citizens peeked out from their abodes, sheltered from the falling debris. They stared in awe at the burning celestial body—a symbol that they had never been alone. The Blessed Father's presence was undeniable, and the Shadow Guard Elite were coming to collect retribution and usher in Judgement Day.

The roaring moon, now bound in renewed radiance, hovered above—a promise, a warning. Flames whipped around it, whooshing and spinning as they lashed out to form a blazing mane—***shhhhhhwoop***. The lion's head bellowed once more, unleashing a fresh surge of storm clouds that billowed across the sky, while the first wave rolled deeper into Sanctuary's land.

Positioned over the Tree of Life, its branches stretching outward as though beckoning to the heavens. The massive, withering limbs extending like the hand of an expectant youngling, reaching out to an elder. It was desperate for the life-giving rain pouring down upon it. Then came the deep, sucking sound—*shoooooop*—as the moon, lion, and fire folded into time, vanishing from sight.

Only the dark clouds remained, hanging heavy in the sky. Shouts of joy erupted from the city square—the long-awaited downpour finally falling. But beneath the celebration, something darker stirred.

The cheers warped, dissolving into screams as terror rippled across the cityscape.

Chapter Six

Present Day

In the softly lit haven of her favored elongated washroom, Runa couldn't help but find humor in the sea of peculiar comfort it offered. *It's absurd, isn't it? How something so simple could feel like a refuge.*

Tucked away from the hum of the communal space, the room held its own quiet magic. Obsidian tiles covered the floor, rising from the earth like a tide, swallowing two-thirds of the walls on all sides in darkness. *Maybe it's the shadows. The way the darkness pulls everything inward—like memory, like silence—until the world outside forgets you ever stepped away.*

A slim coppery-bronze strip wrapped around the room's perimeter, nestled within the obsidian like a horizon line. It circled the entire enclosure at eye level, a quiet, steady marker. Above it, the teal-washed expanse continued upward, flecked with hints of gold that shimmered faintly in the warm light. The glow stretched all the way to the ceiling, evoking a celestial canopy—soft, inviting, infinite.

The walls were adorned with copper-accented stars of varying sizes, scattered across the teal like constellations. The stars climbed the upper walls and unfurled across the ceiling, as if swept forward by the tidal wash of the obsidian current. Their dance was slow, yet *mesmerizing.*

The space touched something in her—a quiet ache. *It's as if I've left something precious here and only just remembered. And it's been waiting for me to notice.* Runa's gaze drifted from the starry expanse above, fluttering downward to the rockwork basin.

Her hand reached out instinctively, flipping on the light. The soft backlighting from the discreet, square mirror came to life, akin to moonlight, casting a faint glow that reflected the world back at her. *It's never spared me—not even once.* Whenever she met its gaze, it revealed the truth without mercy. Sometimes, more truth than she was ready to face. Strings of radiant orbs, each the size of acorns, framed the mirror on either side. They descended from a shelf above, intertwined with cascading potted flora, their soft glow filtering through the delicate leaves. They glimmered and twinkled, evoking the semblance of another world. Within them, a delicate dance of oil and water unfolded, the heat caused the oil to undulate in swirling patterns. The iridescent glow shifted and bobbed as the vines cradled the ethereal radiance with remarkable care.

If only life could be that simple—just glimmering, untouchable, and safe in the hands of nature. Of all the wonders in the room, the gleaming pods felt like the heart of the vine to her. She liked to imagine that within them were dreams, memories, or thoughts, carefully tucked away as if someone had saved them for later.

"But are they really held there...or is that just a story I keep telling myself?" The interplay between forms added a pristine touch to the room's ambiance, casting a soft, harmonious illumination that infused the space with vitality. Runa often wondered if others truly noticed. *Probably not,* she thought, a small smile tugging at her lips.

In response to the thought, she placed her hands on the edges of the rockwork basin, leaning forward into her reflection. Curiosity drove her down another rabbit hole, forcing her to confront her seared skin. The raw reality settled in, and she silently appreciated the choice to use the mirror's backlighting, which felt safer, kinder, more forgiving...somehow. *It understands me better than the glaring light above, and right now, this is all I can handle.*

Her fingertips drifted across the inflamed impression—the lingering evidence of an otherworldly encounter. The imprint was unmistakable:

elongated fingers with unearthly claws, pressed into flesh, its skin bearing the wear of centuries—as if aged through eons. *What did it want?*

The strange, distorted markings left her unsettled—undeniably not of human origin. *And this time, there is no mistaking it. It wasn't random. Not this. There has to be a reason—a purpose hidden beneath the pain. But what… and why?*

She stepped back slightly, the motion soft and uncertain. Her reflection blurred in the dim light, as though the moment itself were slipping through her fingers. *Maybe it isn't about me at all…maybe it's part of something older, a weaving of something ancient.*

She lifted her chin beneath the muted radiance and studied her seared skin. A half-hearted, huff escaped as she recalled Papa D's words: *Light can always be found within the darkness.* Exhaling with quiet weariness—*He never mentioned how much it might burn. I look like a charred kebab. Or worse—aged past death, more prune than person.*

Shaking her head, a dry laugh caught in her throat. Disbelief lingered just behind the humor, until a jolt struck her—sharp and sudden, like the torment itself had left a fingerprint on her memory.

More reflex than thought, she grabbed the nearest hand mirror to examine the extent of the damage—how deeply the beast's claws had embedded into her delicate skin. *The pain was excruciating…a scalding familiarity.*

She traced her fingertips over the puckered area, where the skin had tightened into an uneven patch of scarred flesh. One talon had done more than just hold her—it had marked her. A finger, longer than the others, had pierced her spine like a syringe, leaving behind a venomous burn that felt like it would never fully heal.

She poked again at the tender skin, the truth settling in—she stood in a shroud of numbness. *This absence of fear…I think that's my real concern. It's not the pain, not even the mark. It's that all of this feels too familiar.* These patterns—bouts of chaos, the blank spaces in time—had woven themselves too tightly around her life. *There has to be something they're not telling me. A piece of the story I don't know yet.* The weight of not knowing pressed heavier than the fear of what she might find.

This has been preparing me, hasn't it? The realization dropped like a stone inside her. *Not for what's coming—but for what's buried. I've been walking atop something fractured, and I need to find the cracks before it all gives way beneath me.*

She hated the way the darkness wrapped around her—familiar, suffocating. *I can't keep letting myself stay here, stuck in the shadows. Clawing my way toward answers has to be better than sinking into this...ignorance.* Her fingers brushed the wound on her neck once more. *Whatever this is—it's happening more often. It's getting worse. I can't hide from it anymore.*

Pivoting from the basin, she reached for a towel, soaked it under the faucet, and pressed it gently against the raised skin at her neck. The flesh hissed beneath the cloth, thin wisps of steam curling into the air—*but there was no pain. None at all. Why doesn't this hurt?* When she pulled the towel away, she noticed the imprint had faded slightly, its edges less defined under her touch. She exhaled sharply, the sound brimmed with exasperation and weariness. *I need answers.* Drenching the cloth again and wringing it out, she met her reflection in the mirror—steady, calm. *No more hiding. No more standing in the shadows pretending I don't see what's happening. There's something beneath it all—a thread waiting to be pulled. Walking through town proves it. Something's changed, and I need to know what it is.* She lifted her chin once more, bracing herself against the weight of what she didn't yet understand.

From the hallway beyond the washroom door, the front door creaked open. A voice followed—Ma's—curious, alert. *She's going to ask questions. Of course she will.* And Runa would have to answer, or at least try. *Maybe this is the push I've been avoiding—the gentle nudge toward the truths waiting in silence. Maybe I need all of them more than I thought.*

A soft smile touched her lips as goosebumps crept along her arms, prickling through the fine hairs. Dropping her gaze to her inner arm, she watched a glow begin to pulse from beneath her skin. She inhaled deeply, cocooned in comfort—warmth, fog, shadow.

Dead center along the inner arm, an inky impression rose to the surface, as though an enchanted quill had pierced her skin and released a whisper of ethereal ink. A perfect circle formed, dark and translucent, like a new moon glimpsed through mist. Delicate lines unfurled from its edge, stretching outward into tiny dots that traced a halo around the moon's soft glow.

Darkness and light mingled across her sun-kissed skin as she stared at the rising moon etched in living ink.

The words echoed, faint but steady in her mind. *Follow the moon, Ru. It will guide you.* Her breath caught on the notion, lingering there, as her hand drifted toward the doorknob. *There **has** to be more to all this.*

Diesel ascended the front steps with focused determination. Each calculated stride carried the weight of vital information—details that might require careful handling, depending on the nature of the tale they were about to face.

Mama D watched him closely, well aware of the mental strain he battled. The unspoken, classified matters had taken their toll. *No one could blame him for wanting to retire—but I know better.* He could never truly escape the burdens tied to the Guild's history. That was likely why he agreed to pivot into the Shadow Elite, stepping into the role of training master. It gave him continued purpose, structure—something he could shape, even when everything else felt out of his hands.

The bags slung over his shoulders represented more than a physical load. They were a quiet symbol of the expectations he had carried for decades—the weight of societal roles bound to his rank. He'd tried to outrun all the social gatherings for years, but here he was again, shouldering more than most, and never once complaining.

Diesel wasn't here to check a box for the community—he had shown up, fully present, even though he disliked events like this. *What mattered most was sharing the evening with me and the girls.* She watched him climb the steps. *He might pretend the weight he carries is nothing, yet I've always seen through it.*

Those tiny hands had wrapped around something deep within him and quietly reshaped it—not just in him, but in the Elite Guard and the Shadow Guild on special assignments. Overtime—the girls' tittering laughter, their fingers braided through calloused hands, the spontaneous bubble relay races…all of it had shaped something new. *It became clear to those around us that they truly mattered to him—service before self had always been the Elite way.*

But this—this bond—welcomed everyone into something far more expansive than duty.

Her gaze lingered on Diesel. *Things had shifted—for him, for all of us. The man once known solely for his discipline and command now stood softened by connection, reshaped by laughter and a loyalty that had nothing to do with rank. And the people? They no longer saw just a General. They saw him—the man beneath the obsidian leathers.*

It's personal now. Closer to home. In these small, sacred moments, affection had been given space to thrive. These quiet intervals brought him back from the edge—one loss at a time—through the grief of Ezekiel, through the ache left by High Lady Nadine.

While the mission may have begun with the girls, a quiet gratitude had taken root in everyone who'd witnessed the transformation of a man once known for his discipline and reserve. A man long respected—revered, even. *But for me, it was never just about the objectives. It was about how he began to open. How these young ones reached into the far edges of his battle-worn soul and pulled him back into something real. Something lasting. Something I've needed—from him, from life.*

Mama eased into the moment, as each tread of the ancient, rock-encrusted staircase creaked beneath his weight. The glowing lanterns seemed to move with him, their flames dancing in rhythm with his ascent—as if the air itself were in on the secret. *Home isn't just a place,* she mused. *It's being with the girls...and with him.*

As Diesel swung open the weathered front door, Mama D caught the intent in his movements—measured and composed. The door's copper and turquoise patina, worn and beautiful, barely registered; his attention was fixed elsewhere. *Word of Runa's fall had reached us, launching him into quiet, tactical motion.*

Always scanning. Always reading the room. She noted the sharpened gaze as he took in the space before the door had even fully opened. *He caught the details—just as any Guilded General would. But beyond that, the Truth Seeker in him would soon rise.*

He moved as he always had—aware, precise—but lately, there was more beneath it. This wasn't just about readiness. It was about presence. About care. About Runa—his forever youngling.

The subtle shift in his stance, the way his shoulders braced as if reading the space for what might come next—it all said what he wouldn't. Not out loud.

He's been ours for a long time now, she thought. *But lately…he's been even more here. Rooted. Attentive in a way that feels closer. Like he's already preparing for what's ahead—whether he fully knows it or not.*

Trailing just behind him on the stairway, Mama D paused, her gaze drifting across the storybook scene unfolding in the yard. What Runa had once envisioned for this year had now been lovingly shaped into reality. This was more than decoration—it was her soul laid bare, creativity stitched into every detail, more elaborate than the year before. It wasn't just festive. It was *her.* A quiet chapter of *her* story, told in texture and light.

With each Starlight Night, Runa stepped more fully into the person she was always meant to be—finally aligning with the essence at her core. That joy…it was infectious. It poured from her, warm and radiant, drawing in the world without her even trying. What had started as a simple, solitary effort had become something the entire town looked forward to—a ritual stitched into the rhythm of the season. A soft smile touched Mama D's lips, leaving her breathless as she wondered what future Starlight Nights might become—beyond the beach, beyond the now.

The moment the sun slipped behind the horizon was when the transformation truly began. As the lights in the girls' cottage flickered to life, they sparked a wave of illumination. One by one, homes began to glow, a ripple of warmth moving through the neighborhoods. Each house held its own quiet tale, told in soft, celestial hues—as if the stars themselves had descended to dance in the streets.

Returning to the present, she centered herself on the rhythmic beats in her chest. The door stood ajar, sweet smells from the cozy kitchen drifting into the air. At the upper landing, a firm hand reached across the threshold. Without hesitation, she handed three of the bags to Diesel, his grip steady and familiar. *I don't know how we'd manage without him.* The thought warmed her as she cherished his rustic soul.

Their eyes met, and in the subtle arch of his brow, he wordlessly confirmed what she had already sensed. *Love, it will be okay. You were right about the shift—and Runa unbinding herself.* His expression softened with understanding, his gaze saying what his lips didn't need to. *We'll face what-*

ever's coming, just like we always have. He pulled her in, their foreheads connecting in a quiet, anchored pause.

Pulling back, the pair crossed the threshold, Mama D's gaze drawn immediately to the newly transformed atmosphere of the girls' cottage—brought to life by skilled artisans from the heart of the town. At the center of the room, two L-shaped couches sat opposite each other, framing the space like a perfect picture. Draped in deep midnight blue, the fabric was so rich it seemed to hold the night sky itself, shadows swirling like distant clouds. They beckoned to anyone who passed, offering a promise of endless comfort, as if time itself might slip away the moment you sank into their embrace.

A substantial, weathered coffee table anchored the room, its surface crafted from sun-bleached logs that looked as though they'd drifted ashore from some forgotten coast. The edges, gently curved and worn smooth by time, seemed to anticipate an accidental bump—softening the blow with quiet kindness. Along its rim, shades of midnight blue and teal blended seamlessly into a creamy white, like waves lapping at a sandy shore. It gave the impression that the ocean's froth swirled just beneath the surface —calm, mysterious, and still very much alive.

To the right of the front door, a tall bookcase stretched along the wall, crammed with well-worn, dog-eared volumes that seemed to whisper stories of their own. The shelves led naturally to a modest desk, where Rayanna had claimed a corner for her new workstation. It fit snugly against the kitchen counter, which curved gracefully along the back wall, inviting anyone to follow its gentle path.

The lower cabinets shimmered with a fresh coat of enchanted turquoise paint, artfully distressed at the edges to reveal hints of the wood's age beneath. In contrast, the upper cabinets retained their natural wood finish, recently oiled to bring out the intricate patterns of knots and swirls—like nature itself had etched its history into the golden fibers.

Overhead, exposed beams added a timeless charm, their weathered surfaces blending effortlessly with the teal cabinetry below. The space felt both ancient and alive, like a hushed secret waiting to be shared. Soft light drifted lazily through the room, gathering in gentle pools that seemed to glow just a little more than they should.

Along the far wall, a narrow staircase drew the eye upward, leading to three cozy bedrooms tucked neatly along the upper landing. The stairs, though simple, shared space with a warm, open living area—blending seamlessly into the room's quiet, inviting rhythm.

Tucked beneath them, almost hidden from view, an embedded pantry sat seamlessly next to yet another bookcase—its shelves brimming with volumes that looked as though they might, at any moment, whisper their secrets to those bold enough to listen.

Mama D blinked a few times, grounding herself in the cottage. "What an impressive job Nissa has done! The transformation is amazing." Her gaze swept the room in awe. "With the uptick in her business after incorporating interior design into her jack-of-all-trades approach, I'm excited to see all the finished projects popping up around town."

She paused. Something in her expression flickered—an almost imperceptible shift. "Then again…" The words left her like a quiet hum to herself, trailing off as her fingers found the edge of the couch.

A breath. A pivot.

"Her and her father's work is remarkable. Exquisite craftsmanship." Her eyes widened, a smile breaking across her lips. "I know it might sound cheesy, but they look like ethereal clouds settled right here in your home." She shook her head, still smiling. "Cheese and all, I can officially say I'm sitting on a cloud and eating all the dairy I want. And honestly, if that cloud was made of cheese? Yeah, I'd be okay with that." She winked, turning toward Rayanna.

With a light chuckle, she shifted gears. "Alright, enough about my cheesy daydreams. Ray, you've got that look—like something's off. What's going on? Where's Ru? We need to get things moving. I don't want to be the reason we're late for the opening ceremonies…again."

She moved past Diesel, who had just settled on the edge of one of the L-shaped couches, letting the larger containers drop with a soft thump at his feet. They were bulkier bags, filled with supplies and treats for later—practical, but still part of the charm. In her own hands, she carried the smaller ones—festive, ribbon-tied, and brimming with thoughtful touches.

She placed them down on the weathered wooden island with a firm thud. The bags clinked gently against one another, the soft rustle and chime of paper and glass hinting at the joy folded inside. The room seemed to hold its breath in quiet anticipation, as if it, too, was waiting for the cele-bration to begin.

"Clouds and cheese? I'm in. Can I throw in some meat and fancy mustard, too?" Ray tilted her head, winking back at Mama D, a cheeky grin playing on her lips. She glanced away, her voice dropping into a playful mutter. "Why do you always assume something happened?" She turned back to the copper basin, as she resumed peeling potatoes.

Mama D raised a knowing eyebrow, her lips curling into a smirk. "Because I know my girls," she replied with a hint of sass. "And yes, you can add the mustard."

"There's no point pretending," Rayanna muttered, her sarcasm barely masking the exhaustion. "There's no way of hiding this one."

Mama D's gaze locked on his figure, angled slightly away from the room—everyone silently waiting for him to speak. *A man of few words*, she thought, *but when he does, it's always exactly what's needed.* She watched the faint ripple of muscle beneath his T-shirt as he breathed. *He heard. He was listening.* The air stilled. The room waiting for his quiet authority to break the silence. Never a wasted word.

Flexing through the upper traps, he drew in deeply and pulled back, releasing his elbows from his knees to let everything expand—his chest, the moment—before swiveling to face both women.

As he pivoted, her attention drifted to what rested in his right, calloused hand. As expected, he cradled his beloved 'Old Faithful'—a seasoned, handcrafted pipe adorned with a gradient of celestite-encrusted gemstones that shimmered within its worn crevices. A gift from Mama D, given the day he returned from The Great War—a battle unlike any he had ever faced.

This little beauty symbolized a piece of him—capturing the uncertainty of a safe homecoming while quieting the weight of those worries. His eyes shifted from the twirling smoke that spiraled upward to meet her gaze across the room. She smiled faintly, acknowledging how this small, well-worn item had brought him comfort throughout their long, ongoing mission.

Once heated, the gemstones were said to soothe the mind and amplify energy circulation, easing conversation. An ember at its core enhanced the pipe's ability to channel stillness—allowing its wielder to soften even the most tumultuous chaos around them. As such, Old Faithful had assumed a pivotal role at Starlight Beach during this stage of the assignment, offering Diesel a discreet, protocol-safe means of handling anything that might trigger a surge of energy and draw attention to their corner of the world.

When he'd entered the girls' cottage that evening, his awareness had immediately picked up on a subtle shift—an energy rebalancing in motion, already dancing through the room. Beyond the ambiance and the updated interior design, something deeper tugged at his senses. A familiar enchantment, freshly stirred. An unbinding of the world that had been created.

He imagined Runa had noticed it too on the way home from the schoolhouse—even if she didn't realize it. Sitting in their living space now, he grappled with the weight of it. *It's worse than I imagined. She isn't just unbinding herself; she is actually unraveling the very essence that has kept Starlight hidden all these years.*

His gaze swept the room again, tracking the undercurrent of what lay beneath. Unspoken things. Layers no one wanted to confront, let alone understand. So he dug deeper—mentally, intuitively—following the current of what had been stirred loose.

The cream-colored walls had darkened, embracing a deeper warmth that cradled the shadows cast by the flickering candlelight. Accents of copper brown exuded richness, almost edible in their depth—like everything had been sculpted from the finest chocolate. The turquoise cabinets and doors hummed with energy, echoing the vitality of the girls who lived here. The space pulsed with renewed life, its magic lingering just beyond reach, eager to extend its hand…yet elusive as mist.

Papa D gripped his knee with his left hand, leaning slightly to the right as though drawing strength from the familiar pressure. It steadied his racing thoughts, anchoring him in the moment. He settled into the comfort of 'Old Faithful', the pipe's smooth surface grounding him in the here and now—a reminder of all those quiet evenings spent in reflection, when the world outside felt far too unmanageable.

Across the room, Mama shook her head, her brow furrowing in that endearing way he knew all too well. She blinked, pulling herself back from whatever distant thought had momentarily taken her hostage. *There she goes again.* He watched her, a fond smile tugging at his lips. It was one of those charming quirks that always anchored him—a quiet reminder of the life they had painstakingly built together. The home they'd nurtured for the past two decades, safely tucked away from prying eyes. *I won't lose what we've created.*

Just then, the front door swung open with a jarring crash, the handle slamming into the bookcase along the right wall. The sound echoed sharply, shattering the muted atmosphere.

"I got sent home from the studio—*again*." Frustration edged Tabytha's voice as she swung the mat bag off her back. "*Another* wave of nausea hit me right in the middle of class. It's happening too often now—*totally unsustainable*." She moved to the edge of Rayanna's desk near the kitchen counter and dropped the bag to the floor with a dull *thud*. "I'm seriously starting to worry about my job. I mean, I could've twisted an ankle—or worse—trying to stay en pointe like that." Her steps eased as she crossed to the L-shaped sofa. "Thank the stars Ashla was there. If it had been anyone else, I don't think I could've just walked out mid-sequence like that. I told her it was probably just a bad night's sleep...but still. She stepped in without missing a beat. I'm just—grateful. And frustrated. Mostly frustrated."

She sank into the plush, cloud-like cushions, pulling a soft cream-colored blanket over herself. "Where's Ru? Is she okay?" Nestling deeper into the velvety folds, she sighed. "Also—can I just say—absolutely thrilled we settled on this sofa, Ray. It's like lying in the clouds." Her eyes fluttered closed as she nuzzled into the warmth.

Rayanna, already moving toward the fridge, refilled the teapot with practiced ease. Her attention shifted to the small bowl of freshly plucked ginger—essential for the elixir meant to ease Tabytha's nausea. As she peeled the root, she addressed the room. "The occasional bruising on Runa's body has definitely transformed into something more substantial."

She paused, resting her wrists on the edge of the countertop, her head bowed. A deep inhalation, as though she were drawing strength from some unseen reservoir. The tension dissolved with that breath, melting like morning fog from the forest floor—readying her to continue with renewed focus.

"In all honesty," her voice taut with quiet irritation, "I'm struggling to find the words to describe what happened today." Another breath. "What started as panic has turned into something she shrugs off—as if it's just normal now. And I absolutely hate that."

Rayanna continued, "Despite our countless discussions on the matter, the mystery persists—and honestly, it's only intensifying my confusion about where all of this is coming from." She huffed out a ball of bitterness. "I'm growing weary of conversations that lead nowhere. I can't accept that this is just fate. Something's off. I just…can't put my finger on it."

Shifting her weight at the counter, she turned slightly, gesturing with the knife in hand. "At first, I thought Runa was just having one of those days—tripping over her own feet, bumping into things. But today?" She shook her head, then refocused on the ginger. "This isn't clumsiness," she added, slicing through the root with a firm, final *chop*.

"She's strong, coordinated—this goes beyond anything I can explain. You'll have to see it for yourselves. I can't do it justice with words." Rayanna dropped the peeled ginger into a mug and carried it to the coffee table, placing it down with quiet purpose. From her blanket cocoon, Tabytha murmured her gratitude.

Rayanna's dusty golden hair, once pinned in a high bun, had begun to tumble free. Loosened ringlets cascaded down her back as she moved toward the island nestled between the wide basin sink and the outward-facing couch. She sank into a stool, resting her head in her hands, shielding her eyes from the low, golden light. "And Tabs," she added gently, without looking up, "if you need to step back from teaching, even just for a while… you know Ashla will understand."

Across the room, Papa D drew his time-worn pipe toward him. It was already filled with his personalized signature blend—rich tobacco layered with warm vanilla, spice, and the faintest hints of roasted hazelnut, cinnamon, and cocoa.

His fingers cradled the pipe with practiced ease as he tamped the mixture down gently, each movement intentional yet, unhurried. The raspy flick of a match cut through the stillness as he struck the flame, coaxing life into the leaf. The aromatic symphony curled upward in response—twirling and whirling like a soothing melody, its warmth softening the air around them.

It was as if the blend itself breathed, a pulse awakening within it. The pipe radiated a low, steady energy, casting a surreal calm across the room

—slowing time, quieting thoughts. Tendrils of smoke spiraled upward in graceful arcs, rich with refinement and familiarity. The scent wrapped around them, grounding and gentle, as if inviting the room to exhale.

With each draw, the smoke seemed to smooth the furrows of thought beneath the surface, guiding Papa D's mind into deeper, more directed currents. It softened the atmosphere further, unlocking a space for understanding—quiet, open, and ready for what was coming.

Amid the room's gentle transformation, Tabytha emerged from her self-made sanctuary. Sensing the shift, Rayanna lifted her head from her hands, her gaze clearer now—her heart open to the moment unfolding. The air held a stillness infused with grace, fostering a quiet calm that settled across them all.

Papa D flexed the muscles in his back—a practiced release of tension without severing his presence in the room. "The words don't need to be perfect, Ray," he said gently. "Just walk me through it—start to finish, Love."

Rayanna glanced toward him as she massaged the tension from her neck. With raw honesty—unconcerned with eloquence—she began. Her voice wove a story both grounded and aching, and as the words unfolded, the room leaned in. No one interrupted. When she finally finished, Rayanna bowed her head, a subtle collapse of both weariness and relief.

From her perch on the couch, Tabytha sipped her tea in silence, eyes tracking the reaction in the space as Mama D reached out to take Rayanna's hand.

A deep hush settled over them just as the bathroom door creaked open. Runa stepped out, a small damp towel in one hand, the other gripping the stair banister. Her eyes were heavy with exhaustion, yet her cadence was steady. "I want to understand. I'm done living like this."

Her words landed with weight, drawing every gaze toward her. She raised her chin, placing the towel across the railing as her fingers swept her ebony hair into a high bun. The motion revealed the raw truth along the back of her neck—seared skin, dark and unflinching. The full extent of her injuries was finally visible.

"Oh my!" Mama D's chair scraped back as she rushed to her side to assess the damage. But Runa sidestepped, one hand outstretched to stop her in her tracks. With quiet resolve, she positioned herself so the entire room could see. Lifting her chin, she pressed the small, damp towel against the seared skin at her neck.

The moment it made contact, a soft sizzle cut through the air—steam curling upward in thin tendrils.

Eyes widened. Mouths parted. And when the towel finally pulled away, the markings had nearly vanished.

Turning to Diesel, Mama D scanned his expression for even the slightest shift. Silently, she urged him to respond—swiftly, surely—but instead, his steady calm grounded the room beneath the weight of what they'd just witnessed.

Papa D lowered his pipe from his lips and, with intentional fluidity, and furrowed his brow. *"Mhhh…well,* I've never seen that happen before," he murmured, almost absentmindedly.

"Really? Mhhh…that's what you've got?" Mama D's eyes, already wide, seemed to stretch further—nearly turning into saucers as she angled her head toward him, hands firmly planted on her hips. Speechless, her expression said everything her words didn't: *Explain. Now.*

Rayanna cocked her head with a smirk. Catching the dumbfounded look on Tabytha's face, her hands flung wide in mock exasperation. "See? I told you! How does one explain it? You don't."

Runa glared at Diesel, craning her neck in his direction. "Care to elaborate, Papa D?" she retorted, brows arching. A mischievous smile tugged at the corner of his mouth as he leaned back slightly, fingers tapping rhythmically against his knees, clearly weighing how best to put his thoughts into words.

He rose to approach Runa, leaning in to inspect the remnants of the mark on her exposed skin. "Oh, *absolutely,* Ru Bear. Let me *consult* the Oracle of Sarcasm before gracing you with my *unparalleled wisdom,*" he jested. As his fingers traced the nape of her neck, they followed the seared imprint, revealing four distinct finger marks, with the third resembling a puncture wound at the center of her spine. "Hmm…" he murmured thoughtfully.

His demeanor shifted to a more solemn tone as he continued, "But in seriousness, I've never encountered anything quite like this, healing-wise. Let me check some references, and I'll get back to you with answers. Just out of curiosity, will the towel remove it entirely?"

In response, Runa handed the towel to Papa D. He delicately traced the cloth across her skin, encircling her neck, while a solitary tear teetered on the rim of his eye. Inhaling deeply, the soft fabric cradled in his fingers transported him—back to the very first Starlight Festival. Just for a breath, the present slipped away.

She had arrived on their doorstep, a small form wrapped in a protective cocoon of shadow and mist—a delicate soul marred by muck, dirt, blood, and bruises. As she was entrusted to him, she nestled snugly into his arms, and his heart fractured. He had embraced the mission willingly, yet holding her for the first time made him grasp the profound weight it carried.

He had peered down at her tiny features—angelic, with chubby cheeks that brought a smile to his lips and a dainty, drawn-up nose that whispered of calm. Holding her close, he rocked gently as he paced the study, his gaze fixed on her as he quietly asked, "How could someone do such things to such innocence?" In that moment, she was the only thing that existed; everything else faded into insignificance. She was all that mattered.

Mama D had prepared a soothing lavender bath, and he had tenderly immersed Runa's small, battered frame into the lukewarm water. Gently, he guided the cloth over her skin, careful not to disturb the bruises and scrapes that marred her. The washcloth soaked up layers of grime and blood, tinting the bath a soft pink with curling loops of brown. He caught a flicker of curiosity in her eyes as the warmth stirred around her limbs.

The quiet rhythm of the bathwater became a balm—something steady to hold on to—pulling his attention away from the storm rising inside him. With precise care, he moved the cloth over the faint rise of her ribs, then began untangling the knots in her dirt-caked hair.

That's when she looked up. Her gaze locked on his. For the first time, she truly saw him. Her smile arrived like a sunrise, followed by a laugh so bright it cut through the haze of dawn. A tear slipped down his cheek.

Deep. Unshakable. Tender.

In that instant, something in him broke open. Her gaze held, unwavering—as if her small hands had reached forward and, without hesitation, taken a piece of him. The water deepened in color, darkening to a quiet red, but all he could see was her face, luminous within it.

When he pulled her close, Diesel sensed the truth beneath her yearning

—something that reached far beyond physical healing. His gift as a Truth Seeker allowed him to see the filaments of darkness rising from her, woven with years of solitude and suffering. Not just pain, but a silent, stifling ache he could only partially grasp—its full depth obscured by the shadow binding.

What he did see was that the emptiness within her ran deep. Vast. Hidden. And despite all he knew, it still pulled at him—an ache he struggled to fully comprehend. The intensity of her desire, though unspoken, was unmistakable.

As he washed away the grime of her past, each gentle motion seemed to tug at quiet fibers of loss and longing—the kind that whispered for someone to stay. Someone who could offer the kind of love she'd spent a lifetime without. Sienna had warned him moments like this would surface. That these hollow-rooted strands were signs the binding was working as intended. The physical act of cleansing became its own quiet ritual—of letting go, of allowing space for the what-ifs and could-bes to take hold.

"Diesel, you and your beloved will be crucial in her journey forward. Be gentle...she has endured much." Sienna had placed a hand on his shoulder before leaving Runa in his care. "She needs you both more than anyone. Together, you will change her fate—and the course of these lands. The alternative...is unimaginable."

In that instant, he understood what this assignment truly meant. He had faced missions of staggering weight before—battles etched into his body, decisions that shaped the fate of nations. But nothing had ever carried this kind of gravity. Not like this. This wasn't just about protection. This was about altering the course of The Lands.

The pain in his chest had been suffocating—a collision of emotion crashing inward. *I'll do anything to safeguard her for all time,* he'd vowed.

The girls were his mission—each of them holding something rare, something sacred he'd never anticipated. They were the key to everything. Though Runa's body had long since healed, the invisible scars remained— buried deep within a mind still bound by shadow. A necessary reset, allowing her to rise into who she was always meant to become.

"Pa, you okay?" Runa's voice broke through, prompting Diesel to refocus on the connection between towel and skin. Almost like a repetitive refrain, the sizzling and hissing responded to his gentle touch. With a furrowed brow, he asked, "Does this cause discomfort?"

She protruded her lower lip in a slight pout, raising her brow with a hint of curiosity as she gently shook her head. Her eyes remained steady and calm, and she offered a small, reassuring smile. With an intentional motion, she extended her hand, as if to say, *It doesn't hurt.*

He positioned his pipe between his teeth, tilting his head back for a clearer view. With precision, he worked the towel around her neck once more, closely observing as every trace of the mark disappeared completely. He arched his brow and remarked, "Well, I guess that spares me from having to attend tonight's events. Instead, I'll go find out what's really going on." A playful wink accompanied the returning towel. "You are an outstanding gift giver, Ru." Glancing at her forearm, he lifted *Old Faithful* and teased, "So, when exactly did *the ink* happen?"

Runa scrunched up her mouth into a shy grin."First off, I *did* get you a real gift—perfect for travel." Her eyes lit up. "Second…would you believe it happened in the washroom?"

"The washroom?" He gave a befuddled shake of his head. "You really need to avoid those tattooing nymphs; things can get sketchy with them." With a faint grin, he retreated to the couch, adding, "After we figure out this new branding thing that can be magically sponged away, we'll talk about the artistic nymph in your bathroom."

Chapter Seven

Mama D tenderly ushered Diesel through the time-worn turquoise entryway of the girls' cottage. The door creaked softly under her pull, its sound low and familiar. Even the hinges—worn but durable—stood as a testament to a time long past. *So much had been preserved—remnants we once believed were gone for good. The very planks beneath our feet. The doors. The hinges. All of it had been written off, lost to the River of Time after the unrelenting quintessence fires.*

She paused as the door clicked shut, her hand drifting over the frame, tracing the wood's rough texture beneath her fingers. *How many battles? How many losses had these walls endured? How many salvaged planks had it taken to rebuild—starting again with whatever scraps they could find?*

Father Ezekiel had insisted again and again that such materials were beyond recovery. But the truth was different. They had been quietly salvaged and repurposed, offering communities the chance to rebuild. It opened the door to new foundations for territories in need—and unexpected expansions, like that of Starlight. It allowed everything to become more enduring. And what rose from all of this wasn't just stronger. It held the memory of what came before, the hope of what could be, and a promise that still lay waiting.

The buildings in Starlight were much like the people who lived within them. Everything had been burned and broken down into individual pieces. Each item—or soul—pulled from the wreckage of the Great War, had undergone a painstaking process of mending; the very fabric of their being had been woven back together, thread by fragile thread.

We thought we'd lost it all—our homes, our sense of peace, even ourselves. But here we are, still standing, still moving forward. All because of the man whose hand I hold. She peered down at his worn, calloused hand—tender and loving, despite all they had endured.

The faint scent of weathered wood lingered in the air, more than a reminder of history—a resilient echo of survival. *It's all still here, in its own way,* she reflected, feeling the weight of the past beneath her fingertips.

The structures—from the creaking doors and sturdy beams to the rock walls, wooden steps, and cobblestones—spoke of perseverance. *Every piece held memory, etched into the land like a soft echo of what had been.*

From what lay broken…we rose. The thought settled in Mama D's chest—not loud, but certain. *Not everything was saved…but nothing reclaimed was wasted.*

The Starlight military base had expanded using salvaged materials—each piece already carrying its own resilience, woven through battle and reclamation. Plank by plank, they were laid with quiet intention, calming what had once been torn apart. Meanwhile, the framework of Starlight Beach—its earliest bones still intact—was built upon with those same remnants of history. With Izayah's arrival, the reconstruction took on new life. Protective ley lines were etched, the quintessence wall was raised, and what remained of the old world became the foundation for something enduring. What stands now carries within it the memory of what was lost…and the care of those who refused to let it stay that way.

The town was more than a place—it was a living testament to endurance, a community rebuilt from what was once thought beyond recovery. It had become a sanctuary for those once considered a *danger to society*, offering space to heal, rebuild, and rise stronger than ever. Starlight was a hidden pocket of the land, unknown to most, yet essential to those who found it—a beacon of resilience, rebirth, and quiet strength.

Nothing is as simple as it appears; everything holds a depth of careful consideration, she thought, as a faint smile touching her lips as her warm hand rested softly on her companion's shoulder. The gesture offered tangible reassurance as they stepped forward into this first phase with the girls. It was the moment they had long anticipated, yet also the one they had dreaded most.

He cleared his throat, giving her a sideways look. "You good?"

With a softly spoken promise, audible only to him, she murmured, "Attend to what you must. Things are already in motion now that the full moon has risen, and the markings have surfaced for Runa."

He turned to meet her gaze. "I do believe you're right about Ru and the unbinding." His eyes dropped as he traced small circles on the back of her hand, contemplating their next move. "Izayah and the Elite should be on track to advance to the next phase of their mission. Their location is still classified, but we'll get confirmation soon now that the Golden Guard has been mobilized for their extraction."

"I'll figure out a way to tell them about the phased markings," she said quietly. "Tabytha and Rayanna's ink hasn't appeared yet, which is promising." She exhaled again, her eyes drifting upwards as if seeking answers in the sky. "It gives us some time."

He grimaced, tucking the thought away. The younger version of himself would've kept what he knew from her, telling himself it was to protect her. He'd wait until everything was clear. But now, he knew better—she needed to know, even if the picture wasn't complete. "The seared marking could be that of a Netheron, but I've never seen it heal like this."

"Are you certain?" She gave him a sideways glance, her feet shifting anxiously.

He hesitated, glancing down briefly before responding. "No, I'm not sure."

"Well, just so you know," she began, tension pulling at her voice. "The morning after the Starlight Festival, the responsibility will fall to Zane's daughters. As Unbinders, they'll be the ones to take the reins—releasing the shadow binding from everyone but Runa." She paused, eyes narrowing slightly. "What comes next isn't easy. They'll need time to rest, recalibrate, to adapt to everything that comes with undoing the release—

resurfacing memories, reawakened senses, and the emotional fallout that follows."

Her voice softened, but her words carried weight. "A Golden Guard has been assigned to deliver the next phase of the mission directly to Starlight. After that, the Guard may escort Runa to a new location—where she can complete her unbinding with Sienna and the more experienced Seers. That change in environment might help stabilize the quintessence core—and possibly reinforce the ley lines woven through Starlight's foundation."

He turned away, dragging both hands through his hair, vexation tightening his jaw. "Damn," Diesel hissed. "I don't want to leave. Not now—not with everything happening." His tone softened. "I want to be here. In these moments, Love. I've missed too many already."

He tapped the pipe against his palm, shaking loose the last of the leaf before slipping it into the deep pocket of his dark linen pants. One hand stayed tucked away while the other rose to his face, brushing along his chin—thumb grazing his lower lip in thought. "Never seen anything heal like that," he muttered out of the corner of his mouth, the words slipping into the quiet like an observation meant more for himself than anyone else. A soft clicking sound followed—a rhythm of reflection as his thumb bounced lightly against his lip, buying him a beat of pause. "It shouldn't have mended so fast." His gaze turned distant, voice dropping into a hush. "It made me think of when she was little…the feel of that towel—everything came crashing back. That first night." He stilled, jaw tight, the memory settling over him like mist. "I still can't begin to comprehend the depth of it. The pain she endured. The history she carries."

He huffed. "It's all in her eyes," he said, anger tightening in his chest. "Visha knew exactly what she was doing. She fucking tested that beast on Ru." He paused, the silence underscoring the weight of his fury. "The fucking High Priestess created that monster—and used Runa as bait."

His jaw clenched. "Today, when she handed me that towel…I was right back there. Back to the moment she looked me in the eyes for the very first time. That night we cleansed her body…" His voice faltered. "Her tiny hands…they claimed a piece of me, and I'm okay if she never gives it back." He exhaled, the recollection pressing against him like something he'd never fully been able to set down.

"It's too much to bear." His eyes met Mama D's, the weight of the truth settling between them. "She knows, Love. Deep down, she knows what she's been through. All those years, all that suffering—it's part of her, but it doesn't define her. That's why she's not reacting the way Rayanna expects. She's numb to it. It's like it's woven into the marrow of her bones, that kind of pain."

He growled, a deep guttural sound rising from his chest. "I hate that for her. What she's been through is going to resurface, but how much?" His voice cracked, buckling under the strain of rawness. "How much will she remember? I don't know…and I can't take it from her."

Mama D gently lifted his chin, coaxing him to meet her gaze. "Diesel, you were here for her today—that's what she can handle right now. But when the memories of what Visha did begin to resurface, she'll have something stronger to hold her steady. You're her anchor now." Her voice softened, but the truth in it held firm. "I know you beat yourself up for not getting to her sooner, but there's a reason Visha kept her from you. She knew what it would mean if you were close. But you're here now—and that matters. Runa may not grasp all of this yet, not fully…but somewhere beneath it all, she does. She knows."

Diesel's jaw tightened before he spoke. "I've got to admit, part of me doesn't want to dig too deep into this. The weight of everything—what I'm feeling, what I'm saying—it's not something I'm used to dealing with. Honestly, voicing any of this probably isn't advisable." He gave a small, reluctant shrug, as if unsure how to express emotions that rarely saw the light of day.

Mama D raised an eyebrow, a playful glint breaking through the tension. "Well, I'll be sure to let you know when we hit 'not advisable' territory. You know me—I don't hold back, rank or no rank." She winked, her tone light, attempting to ease the heaviness hanging between them.

A faint smile tugged at the corner of his mouth. He shook his head, slipping his hand into his pocket with a quiet sigh. "Love, I'm not sure what's going to come out of all this, but I think I've got a place to start. I'll head home and grab a few things. Then head on out, unless Nester has something for me. Are you set for tonight? Got everything you need?"

"I brought everything. I'm good." Mama D's voice was soft as she returned his grin, her hand resting on his chest for a moment longer before letting it fall away.

The door swung open, revealing Runa's bright eyes and wide smile as she leaned casually, her back easing into the soft blue wall of the cottage— a calming complement to the whitewashed frame and weathered teal patina of the door. Her dark curls tumbled over her shoulders as she held up a leather book bag toward Diesel, one hand bracing herself against the sturdy wall.

"Oh, how splendid! Your consistency is truly something," Runa teased. "You gave me enough time to change and fix my hair, and yet here you are, still whispering sweet nothings to each other. How utterly shocking!" She winked at Papa D, a playful grin tugging at her lips. "Figured you might need a mini adventure kit."

Diesel reached for the well-worn, leather pack, but Runa playfully tugged it back. Leaning in with a smirk, she added, "Papa Bear, don't get any ideas—this isn't turning into an annual Starlight Festival gift, okay?"

Diesel's eyes widened as he threw both hands up in mock surrender, rolling his shoulders with a lighthearted sigh. "I had such high hopes this could be our thing," he teased. "Instinctively, I should've known better."

"You, Ru Bear, are one of my favorite gifts every year." Before the words had fully left his lips, he pulled Runa into a hug, inhaling deeply. The familiar scents of lavender, vanilla, and cinnamon filled his senses, mingling with the comforting aromas from whatever Rayanna had simmering in the kitchen. *How I would give anything to stay.*

"You getting all sentimental on me again, Papa Bear?" Runa stepped back, grinning mischievously. "Well, I'm glad I'm not you because… W.T.F.A.!" With that, she pushed off the wall and bounced back into the house, leaving Diesel blinking, a look of confusion tugging at his features.

"Come on now," Mama D teased, giving his hand a squeeze. "Where's…the…food…at?" She turned and headed inside to help Rayanna put the finishing touches on the dishes for the Starlight Festival—getting everything prepped before she had to head out for final coordination. Just before the door clicked shut behind her, she tossed him a wink and added, "Good luck, sir. I'll be here when you get back—don't you fret."

Diesel stood on the porch for a moment, drawing a deep, grounding breath. He compartmentalized the warmth and ease from just moments ago, locking it down with practiced precision. Shoulders squared. Lightness gone. As his spine straightened and his neck cracked with a quiet release, the shift settled into place—muscle memory forged over years. His focus narrowed, edges sharpened, no trace of the man who teased and grinned. That version stepped back so this one could rise: the soldier etched into bone, trained by fire, built for purpose. The contrast was stark, but the transition smooth—refined by time, honed sharp by necessity, lethal force distilled into form.

Without another word, he pivoted. His steps—light-footed and steady—honed from years of training. Not just measured by distance, but by the weight of what he carried: the burden of command, the ache of departure, the sharp edge of not knowing what he'd return to. *Would Starlight still feel like Starlight once the unbinding took hold? Would the girls even be here when he got back? Would Ru?* The timeline was slipping, and he knew it. He had to move fast—complete what needed doing and find a way back before everything changed. *I want to be here for them.* That thought, tucked beneath the surface of the mission, pulsed like a steady heartbeat.

Pulling away and descending the rockwork stairs, candlelight danced with the breeze of his movement—flickering across stone, catching in the folds of his linen. The light played true to an old saying from the Shadow Guild: May your shadow stretch long and your blade strike true. But tonight, as Diesel watched the wavering silhouette at his side, he felt the irony. A true Elite never wanted to be seen. He'd trained to blend, to vanish—not to leave pieces of himself lingering behind.

Each footfall measured more than distance. It signaled time slipping, a vow worn thin. The glow brushed his arms, kissed the edge of his steps, lighting a path forward—but also casting memories back. His purpose lived in the quiet between those lights, laced through the beauty she'd built. Not loud. Not showy. But steady. Certain. Like the promise he never spoke aloud. *A vow I would never break.*

Chapter Eight

Present Day

The cobblestone streets glimmered beneath ethereal strands of light. It was as though the stars themselves had descended into the heart of the town, infusing their radiance into its very core.

She eased her pace as the thought flickered through her mind. *How is this even real?* The sense of awe she'd felt as a youngling resurfaced, stirring an even grander realization. *I feel bound to something older than time, woven into a tapestry I can't see but somehow know is there.*

Each footstep was like turning a page in a book she had yet to finish, every new scene more captivating than the last. Rayanna, Tabytha, and Mama D walked beside her, but their voices dulled, slipping past, barely registering—lost to the enchantment before her. *I'm okay with that,* she thought, content with their banter melting away.

The houses whispered to her, silent narrators filled with histories she longed to uncover. *I'm pretty sure I can hear them.* Runa imagined the lives unfolding behind each windowpane—grand tales embedded into the very walls. *Wouldn't it be curious if they got irritated with us too? For not listening? Everyone just kept walking past, unaware of the pieces of their world slipping through the cracks.*

She breathed in deeply, her eyes drifting up to the sky as the salty air filled her lungs. *Do the stars listen too?* A quiet wonder stirred—fluttering through her like feathers of thought. *I've heard you can make wishes on them.* Her gaze lingered on the twinkling lights above, scattered like diamonds against black velvet. *Perhaps **they** know the secrets this place holds,* she thought, feeling both small and curiously connected to the vastness above.

Every property was a world unto itself, wearing its history like a well-loved keepsake. Tonight, they were more than just homes—they had come alive, preparing to tell their bedtime stories beneath the stars. Walking past each throughfare or moongate felt like being tucked in for the evening. With quiet grace, front yards had transformed into fables or fairytales. They softly whispered their secrets like a parent reading to a sleepy youngling.

One by one, the cottages revealed their tales, inviting her into a world where magic lived within their walls.

The first seaside bungalow gleamed with the imagery of the *Star Weaver's Chronicle,* a legend she still cherished—of a mythical figure who crafted constellations from strands of light.

The delicate forms hovered just above the rich earth, winding radiant threads through the towering oak's limbs. The streaks of light shimmered like stardust, as if the forms themselves were shaping constellations from the night sky. Each motion was both fluid and precise. It was as though stars were not fixed, but alive—shifting and rearranging, weaving a world placed with purpose by unseen hands. The entire scene felt as if it could unravel heaven's tale, pulling the sky and earth together in a tapestry of incandescence and otherworldly glow.

A faint reverberation of nostalgia settled in her chest as an epiphany tiptoed through her mind, sneaking in like a player in a game of hide and seek. *I used to believe in things like this,* she realized, *even more than I do now.* She bit her bottom lip, tugging at the currents that teased her consciousness.

I know you…come find me. The thought meandered through the beading lights above like smoke—elusive, undeniable. *I so desperately want to understand.*

Turning inward, the sensation pulled her down a mental corridor, thoughts flooding in, riding the current toward a wellspring of scattered notions. *It's as if…I once shared these secrets with someone. Secrets I only ever dreamed up. And yet what lies before me now feels like the result of someone—finally listening.*

The sound of her bootfalls on gravel-covered cobblestones drew her back to the present, grounding her. For a moment, she wanted to pause—to get lost in every crevice. It was like an elaborate deck of cards, a basket of well-worn letters written in blood, or a long-forgotten book toppling from a shelf, its pages now sprawled wide—exposed, unguarded. *Whoever this was—or is—had waited patiently. It's as if I can hear them whispering: We've been here all along. Waiting for you to remember. Waiting for you to come back.*

While the others moved ahead, Runa eased back—her gaze catching on a cottage façade adorned with the tale of *The Love Story of the Moon and the Comet*. Silver and gold threads wove through the air, tracing the arc of the celestial lovers—forever destined to meet only once in a lifetime before being pulled apart. *Such a bittersweet fate,* she reflected, a fleeting sadness mingling with her sense of wonder.

The thought lingered as she stared at the glowing symbols, delicate threads intertwining in midair, forming the graceful arc of the comet's tail. The strands of light twisted together, shimmering with every movement, as though the comet were in perpetual motion—forever chasing the moon. *To be loved like that…to hold someone's heart so deeply,* she mused, *their paths aligning yet never fully merging. I wonder if there's some truth in the old legends; what if, like the fated pair, we're all like that—reaching out for something we can never truly grasp.*

As they traveled, unexplored facets revealed themselves—perhaps for the first time—fresh layers of the town's character, an intriguing narrative waiting to be uncovered. *Yes, the town definitely feels different. It's like peeling apart the pages of an old book—the kind of tome that's been hidden for eons, emerging to reveal its secrets at its own leisurely pace. I suppose that suits this slumbering seaside haven.*

Everything feels more vibrant—like the town itself is breathing, pulsing with life beneath my feet. There's a hum, vibrating through every surface, lifting the scents into motion. Aromas aren't just wafting through the air; they're dancing, swirling in harmony. A haunting limerick of notes crafted from cakes, icing, and cinnamon. Every inhalation is an invitation to a fantastical celestial ball. Each moment offers more than awareness. It beckons. Tugs at my heart-

strings. Pulls at the thread of my being, as if begging me to remember some-thing important.

Year after year, she'd made it a tradition to methodically explore every property with a keen eye, taking in even the smallest details. It was a quiet devotion, one that always sparked a deep sense of joy within her. But this year? This year, something was off. A gnawing restlessness tugged at her, though she couldn't quite grasp why. Yet here she was, tracing the intricate designs with her eyes, caught up in the same wonder.

The scents of lavender, rosemary, and sage danced on the breeze, carried from the hearths of nearby cottages. *How have I missed this before? It's as if I'm seeing everything—truly seeing it—for the very first time.*

Gazing upward, Runa noticed star-shaped lanterns suspended from the sprawling canopies of countless ancient oaks. Their soft glow spilled through the branches like scattered stardust, casting a warm, welcoming light across the textured footpath. It flickered gently against the faces of those passing beneath, as if the trees themselves had invited the stars to join the celebration. *They've thought of everything,* she mused, her smile widening as warmth bubbled to the surface. The lights seemed to nod in quiet conversation, part of some greater, unspoken dialogue. *I wonder if they know something we don't. Some secrets we've forgotten how to hear.* Running her fingertips along the low rock walls, their rough edges tickling her fingerpads, she wondered, *What stories could they tell me if I kindly asked?*

For a moment, she closed her eyes, letting the sense of belonging wash over her like a gentle tide. It wasn't just the decorations that made Starlight special; it was the feeling of being part of something larger, of being woven into a fabric that had existed long before her. *It's as if this place is telling me that I matter. It holds a special kind of tangible magic, but not the kind that casts spells or moves mountains. It's the kind that makes you feel seen, as if this coastal haven has been waiting for me all along, inviting me to belong to its leather-bound history.*

Maybe it isn't a forgotten story, tucked away on a shelf after all. She had always seen this place as something preserved in time, but tonight, she felt its heartbeat. *Perhaps there's more here—a chance to be part of something alive, something still unfolding.* The realization left her feeling lighter, as though the seaside haven itself was waking up, inviting her to not just belong, but to help shape the story still being written.

She inhaled the cool air again, picturing herself enveloped in a snow globe of celestial radiance. Joy seeped in—warm and gentle. With another breath, air flooded her lungs, stirring something within—a promise, a whisper of hope, a new beginning rising on the horizon.

Then came the soft touch—light, anchoring, a reminder of where she stood. Still grounded…yet somehow lighter. When her eyes opened, she saw each of them—radiant in their own ways, their strength and grace quietly shining through.

Her gaze drifted to Mama D's hand, tracing the elegant lines of her black velvet ensemble. The long-sleeved shirt, soft as a whisper, hugged her frame with quiet grace, exuding a timeless allure. The wide-leg trousers, relaxed and flowing, made every movement seem like a gentle dance—ready for anything, whether in stillness or stepping toward the unknown.

Mama D squeezed Runa's hand again, drawing her focus to the cascade of bluish silver-laced hair, intricately braided and curling around Mama's shoulders. The lights cradling the town, mirrored the strands, weaving their own luminous pattern. Each ribbon shimmered beneath the starlight, like poetry in motion. A familiar scent—vanilla with a touch of tobacco—wrapped around her, dissolving the last traces of tension she hadn't realized still lingered.

Beyond Mama D, Rayanna stood, coffee in hand, her charcoal-gray velvet ensemble echoed Mama's style. Rayanna's dusty gold-brown hair flowed in soft waves, reminiscent of the salty sea breeze. The plush fabric of her attire invited the starlight's glow, illuminating the folds as they draped effortlessly against her lean frame. Her black, wide-brimmed, felt fedora added a touch of chic elegance, perfectly complementing her overall presence.

Tabytha, who was feeling better after Rayanna's ginger tea unwound the knots in her stomach, stood beside them. Runa cast a glance at her, a small smile forming. Tabytha's eyes captivated her—hues of blue kissed by gold flecks, with a hint of deep purple around the edges. Hazelnut locks framed one side of her face, delicately adorned with tiny jeweled stars that caught the light.

Beneath her neckline, Tabytha wore a black shirt adorned with stars and moons, paired with a high-waisted skirt. The midnight fabric flowed gracefully, cinched perfectly at her waist by buttoned suspenders. An elegant slit from mid-thigh down added to her striking silhouette, seamlessly blending with the celestial theme.

Runa blushed faintly, realizing that, compared to the other three women, she was undeniably underdressed. Cloaked in midnight black, her attire was more than just clothing—it was a shield, allowing her to melt into the background and observe the world from a comfortable distance. The soft cotton half-turtleneck she wore, in deep obsidian, was thoughtfully designed with matching cutouts that revealed the subtle curve of her collarbones.

The hem of her sweater was casually tucked into impeccably tailored jeans, the fit as precise as her need for anonymity. Her hair was swept into a high ponytail, long ebony waves cascading down her back, while a soft curl in front framed her face, brushing just above the ear in a vintage-inspired sweep. Her handcrafted, charcoal-gray leather combat boots reached just below her calves, adding a touch of swagger—the kind only she knew how to carry, like stepping into a pit of shadows and daring them to notice.

Her vision blurred as her thoughts began to drift, a familiar fog settling in—but it didn't linger. A gentle tug on her arm pulled her back. Without a word, Mama D twirled her—just as she had when Runa was a youngling. It was a tradition first started by Papa D, one that had stitched itself into the rhythm of their lives. *No matter the distance or absence,* he used to say, *beneath these stars, each of you carries a light all your own—something that makes this world feel more certain, more meaningful. More like home.* It was these tiny moments—comfort found in quiet repetition, in nuances only they understood. The hand squeezes that served as silent kisses, shared when words would've been too much. The minuscule gestures no one else would notice, easily dismissed as insignificant—yet they spoke volumes. And now, standing beneath streams of starlight with the girls beside her... she simply felt safe.

Mama D drew her closer, her touch light and reassuring, coaxing a soft laugh from Runa as their shoulders bumped. Together, they all ventured deeper into the vibrant chaos that was the festival.

Laughter, banter, music, and the warm glow of lanterns swirled around them—a living melody of shared joy, echoing through the strings of memories woven together within the community that surrounded their path forward.

Runa halted momentarily as a strange, almost forgotten feeling stirred in her chest. It was as though, after all this time, she could finally breathe—truly breathe. *Is this what it's meant to feel like?* she wondered, as the heaviness she hadn't even realized she carried slid away like a shadow dissipating at dawn. A lightness filled her, joy blooming within and spilling gently outward. *I could just float away*, she mused, a small smile playing at her lips.

Linked arm in arm, the females strolled leisurely through the alluring streets, heading toward the heart of the town. As the cobblestone paths opened up, they gradually drifted apart, each setting off on her own mission.

With an air of authority, Mama headed toward the lighthouse, which stood proudly, just beyond the Town Hall. Soon, her voice would carry on the salty breeze, signaling the official start of the festivities.

With purposeful steps, Tabytha nestled into the familiar realm of "The Studio." She worked with measured diligence, organizing the booth outside the storefront. The vibrant display featured luxurious workout garments, plush mats, pointe shoes, rejuvenating cleansing elixirs, and countless other essentials, each crafted to support the various classes they offered.

Rayanna, on the other hand, was spurred on by an urgency prickling at her senses. Across the courtyard, she noticed that the apothecary booth, "The Cabinet of Curiosities," remained in disarray. The treasure trove of extraordinary items was half-prepared, and the air buzzed with anticipation for the aromatic concoctions yet to be unveiled. These were the moments in which Rayanna thrived. Her sharp business acumen and quick decision-making were crucial in managing the frequent chaos of the apothecary.

Runa watched as her sister hurried toward the booth, her voice already ringing out: "No, we're doing this my way! We need to get things up and running—right now. The festival starts in less than an hour, and the booth isn't even assembled!" Her presence instantly commanded the space.

Rayanna paused just long enough in her flurry of busyness to lift a hand toward her—a wordless acknowledgment, instinctive and familiar. In response, Runa raised a brow, a smile curling at the corners of her lips, and tipped her chin in a casual nod before veering toward the grand Town Hall.

The building stood like a timeless sentinel, its façade adorned with intricate carvings that whispered stories of ages long past. Runa loved this quiet moment—the calm before the storm. Soon, the space would transform into a spectacle of color and sound, overflowing with the vibrant chaos of the opening ceremonies. As she ascended the substantial granite steps, she could feel the heart of Starlight thrumming through the stone, steady and familiar.

Tonight, however, it had undergone a celestial metamorphosis. The once stoic entrance now dazzled with lights cascading like a heavenly waterfall from the majestic facade. The well-worn wooden doors, polished by countless hands, creaked open to reveal the vestibule, filled with the comforting scent of old parchment and the soft murmur of footsteps on plush carpets. A decorative archway, glowing with strands of luminescence, beckoned attendees into a realm where the boundaries between earth and sky seemed to blur.

Just beyond the entrance, Ashla stood, gazing up at the ceiling, her head tilted slightly as if listening to something only she could hear. "Oh, hello, Runa," she said dreamily, her eyes still tracing invisible patterns above. The Studio's owner gave a soft, far-off smile, as though she were somewhere else entirely.

"Tabytha said you always wander here first, before venturing anywhere else." She nodded, her fingers drifting to her side with the aimless elegance of a dream not quite forgotten. Runa watched, silently wondering what plane of reality Ashla was navigating. "I had to come see what they've done. The enchantments...they're like little whispers, don't you think? Absolutely captivating."

Runa smiled faintly, pulling her gaze away from Ashla. Her chin tilted skyward, taking in the splendor before them. "Words escape me," she murmured, the awe clinging to every syllable. "Have you…made your rounds?"

Ashla, still gazing upward, replied softly, "The air here is different…I think it wanted me to linger." Her voice was light and distant, as if she were sharing a secret with the stars above. With an almost absentminded motion, she tucked a loose strand of golden-brown hair into a high, messy bun. Her porcelain-like skin caught the glow of the nearby lights, a gentle contrast to the dark-to-golden gradient of her hair. The yellow tank and ripped jeans she wore looked as though they'd simply appeared on her—a casually chic ensemble that matched her air of unbothered wonder. Runa smiled, captivated by the quiet magic of her—each detail like stardusted fabric, stitched into something only Ashla could wear so easily.

"Did you want to walk with me? I'd love the company," Runa asked, sticking out her elbow, a playful invitation to link arms. A smirk played at her lips as she added, "There's something enchanting about the Town Hall when it's empty. It speaks more in its silence, as if the walls have their own stories to tell."

Ashla nodded with a soft, hushed acknowledgment. "I can linger for a brief while. Tabs mentioned you wouldn't mind guiding me," she murmured. "It's like trying to drink the stars…lovely—but a bit much all at once."

Runa's eyes sparkled. "That's the most delightful part," she said, her voice softening—not quite a whisper, but close, like a treasured memory she rarely spoke aloud. She leaned in slightly, then with a fluid motion, swept her hands outward—an easy flourish, born more of imagination than dance. "When I was younger, I used to pretend it was a grand castle," she admitted, a quiet laugh escaping. "I imagined myself arriving fashionably early for a magnificent ball…always feeling just a little underdressed."

She giggled, glancing down at her casual clothes and twirling a loose string between her fingers. "There was always a touch of magic in the air. I'd spin and spin, the world blurring into a whirl of enchantment, completely lost in my own fairytale—a space just for me." Her cheeks flushed, the weight of a secret never shared beyond her inner circle pressing softly against her.

Ashla's smile tilted into a sweet, crooked grin, her eyes narrowing like she was squinting at sunlight she didn't mind. "It's rare, you know…

holding onto awe without crushing it," she said softly, just as the pair ventured forward and the grand halls unfurled around them. Lanterns, enormous and celestial in shape, swayed from the intricately carved ceilings, casting a soft radiance across the gleaming white marble beneath.

With every step, the gentle crunch of faux snow underfoot evoked the serene hush of a winter evening. Delicate flurries and wisps of ethereal light mingled with the drifting snowflakes, as if each were a tiny star descending from the heavens. The scene wove a tapestry of awe and dream, casting shimmering patterns on the walls and transforming the space into a living, luminous night sky. Breathless, they paused before the grand staircase, eyes meeting in a playful exchange. Innocent souls caught in the magic, they twirled in elegant circles, their giggles echoing through the vast hallway—a childlike wonder so often misplaced in adulthood.

Smiling deeply, Runa bowed with a flourish, extending her hand toward the staircase—a refined gesture signaling the urgency to proceed before the midnight toll of the Bell Tower. Their laughter echoed, light and full, mingling with the whispers of centuries past as they embarked on the dreamlike ascent—a journey toward a realm beyond the ordinary.

As they climbed, the rich aromas of cinnamon and evergreen wrapped around them, playfully tickling their senses like a soft breeze. At the first landing, they paused, eyes widening as the main hall unfolded before them—vast and glowing. Expansive galactic projections bathed the walls in shimmering hues, the colors swirling and melding like a celestial ballet.

A gentle, cosmic melody drifted through the air, feather-light and soothing. From their perch above, the ambient glow of the hall softened—dimming just enough to reveal the circular tables below, each draped in deep cobalt linens trimmed with gold. At their center, waxing and waning gibbous moons began to shimmer more brightly, casting delicate, shifting shadows across the fabric—rippling patterns that moved like reflections across a still lake.

Farther off, tucked into quiet alcoves, secluded seating nooks beckoned with plush cushions and folded blankets, arranged like whispered invitations. From above, they looked like secret havens carved into the starlit scape—shifting shadows giving shape to privacy, intimacy, comfort. A place to lose oneself in story or song, to share laughter over sweets gathered from the town center booths. Runa could imagine it all already: voices hushed in wonder, hands wrapped around warm mugs, a dozen memories in the making.

"You'll love this—it's the sort of thing that feels like it's been waiting for just the right moment." Ashla bumped Runa's shoulder, her finger guiding her gaze back to the grand entrance. "Father just finished them," she added softly, her voice carrying that faraway lilt the town had begun to recognize. "Aren't they exquisite?"

Runa's gaze landed on the massive carvings. Tilting her head, she asked, "Are they the same on the other side?" Towering and regal, the doors were crafted from rich, dark wood—each one a masterpiece. "When were those put in?" she murmured, stepping closer to the balcony's edge. "I've never seen them before."

"Slipped into place last week," Ashla murmured, her head tilting dreamily. "He said they needed to feel like they'd always been here by the time the festival came."

The twin entranceways gleamed beneath the starlight, their intricate details sharpening into focus. Each panel bore the image of a lion cradled within a full moon, its gaze steady and knowing. The craftsmanship was impeccable—powerful yet reverent, as though the lions weren't merely art, but guardians of something sacred.

"But this," Ashla whispered, leaning in slightly, her lips parting with anticipation, "this is the best part. Watch."

Almost on cue, the volunteers stepped forward, pulling at the hefty wooden doors. As they opened outward, the carvings came alive. The edges of each moon shimmered, revealing fine veins of molten gold—lines that caught the flickering light like liquid fire. The shimmer flowed, dancing with every inch the doors moved, casting a soft glow across the stone beneath.

With practiced care, the volunteers braced the doors open, sliding thick wooden stoppers against the stone landing. The effect was breathtaking—two celestial sentinels now fully revealed, holding space for the magic waiting within.

"Isn't it lovely?" Ashla chimed. "The way a thought can slip into the world and—just like that—it starts to breathe, and everything begins to shift."

A cool saltwater breeze rushed in, nudging the chandelier into a gentle sway, as if the building itself were awakening. Light danced along the walls, tracing the carved lines with playful precision, making the golden accents shimmer like fireflies beneath the moon's glow. With whimsical wonder, they leaned into the illuminated banister, elbows propped in unison, spellbound by the magic around them.

"This is simply my favorite time of year." Runa pressed her clasped hands to her cheek, a wistful smile tugging at her lips. "It's more than just tradition." She cast a sideways glance at Ashla before speaking. "It stirs the heart…and ignites the soul."

"I believe you could have dreamed it all up before." Ashla fluttered her lashes. "It suits you…like a dream finding its way home."

With that, Runa's gaze lifted, following the glittering lights strung between snow-dusted trees positioned along the balcony and framing the grand front doors below. Icicles clung to their branches, catching the light and refracting it like crystal. The air, now rich with the scent of fresh-baked cookies and sugar crisps, drifted in from the boardwalk—ribbons of sweetness carried through the open doors. She closed her eyes, scrunching her shoulders with a contented sigh as a cool breeze slipped past her, and the distant laughter of a child's game echoed through the hall. "Every year, I learn a little more about how to breathe in the essence of this life," she whispered, an unnamable longing blooming in her chest, "as if the festival helps me remember pieces of myself I didn't realize had gone quiet."

Ashla listened intently, her gaze soft and far away as she propped her chin delicately on her hand. "It's easy to overlook the little things…to let the rush of it all—the music, the people—carry you away." Her tone, barely audible, drifted skyward with her attention. "It's like choosing to pause and notice a single blade of grass in a meadow."

A smile brushed against her fingertips, and almost without thinking, she reached out and gently clasped Runa's hand. "I'm glad I could share this with you." Her eyes wandered toward the town center beyond the entry. "So, tell me—who do you usually enjoy the Starlight Festival with?"

A stifled yawn escaped as she added, "The others always seem to scatter, blending with the town's energy, but you…" She leaned into the full yawn, stretching slightly. "This seems more your pace."

Runa bobbed her head slightly, considering the thought. "Typically, Papa D." she said, a soft chuckle escaping as she reminisced. "He's not much for crowds though," she added, shaking her head. "But if he's home during Starlight Night, then he's here with me." She leaned back slightly as her thoughts wandered.

"We would start here, in the quiet before the chaos. Eventually we'd wander to the booths, eat way too much, and he'd lecture me about all the sweets." She rolled her eyes, the corners of her lips curving upward as warmth spread across her face. "After Mama D's opening remarks, we head home to gear up for the real celebration."

"Real celebration?" Ashla echoed, her tone drifting—light and distant, as though the answer might not even really matter. "Real's a funny word," she added, fingers tracing the air. "Sometimes the imagined things feel more honest."

Runa's gaze softened, her lips curling into a knowing smile. "I suppose…I see that with my younglings all the time," she said with quiet admiration. "They'll tell me something entirely imagined—but with such conviction, it feels more honest than anything else in the room." She scrunched up her nose and pulled her shoulders up to her ears in excitement. "So, a better way to put it, I think, would be to say the second half just holds a different kind of sparkle." Her hands balled into tight fists, vibrating with joy. "I think one thing we can all agree on—celebration starts with the food," she stated, eyes squinting with delight. "Which means—it does start now. I just prefer cottage-to-cottage connections."

She sucked in excitement, and a huff of piping-hot images spilled out into the air between them as Runa continued, "Buffet spreads are set up under every oak, on every property. Each serving area is adorned with handmade tablecloths, woven with patterns that tell the stories of the families there. The whole community wanders from one setup to the next; laughter and conversation mix with the rich scents of roasted meats, spiced breads, and sweet pastries dusted with powdered sugar. Younglings dart through the crowd with sticky fingers, giggling as they sneak treats, while the elderly exchange stories over glasses of warm mulled cider.

Mama D's famous bubbly Raz-a-Faz—a punch brimming with the tang of raspberries and fizzy citrus—sparkles in crystal bowls, beckoning thirsty guests. Her cheesy potatoes, golden and bubbling with melted cheese, send waves of rich, buttery aroma through the air. Just down the street, the neighbors' table boasts quails roasted to perfection, their orange-encrusted skin glistening under the festival lights, infused with hints of thyme and honey."

Runa's voice softened with nostalgia as she stuck out a finger to make her next point. "That's not all," she said, a twinkle in her eye. "There's always a bowl of star-encrusted candy gems—made from sugar and toffee —the kind with a caramelized crunch that melts in your mouth and stays with you." She spread her arms wide, her grin stretching ear to ear. "It's like one massive, shared feast that brings everyone together, blurring the lines between homes and hearts." Her eyes lit up as she added, "There's just something about the way the night hums with life—and how every bite tastes better when it's shared."

"Well, that sounds just enchanting and quite perfect." Her lips squished together in an awkward smile before she nudged Runa's shoulder. "So, do you have anyone special?"

An uneasy laugh escaped her. "Tabytha keeps telling me there's no hope for me in that department, if I keep wandering off on my own." she said, making her fingers walk like little legs along the banister. With a wave of her hand, she brushed off the thought. "Honestly, sometimes I think finding love is more like licking it off knives than being handed a spoon."

"Really? How so?" Ashla muttered, fidgeting with her nails.

"I know that's not the answer you want to hear," she said, pushing away from the banister slightly. "I can only assume it predates my arrival at Starlight." She kneaded her fingers together—a small, self-soothing distraction.

"There's this feeling I have—that love requires significant effort. But I know that doesn't come from Mama and Papa D, because I see how they are together. I didn't have to find their love; it found me. They just fit. Their love is effortless. The way Papa D's eyes soften when Mama walks into the room, or how she always knows when he needs a moment of silence or a spark of laughter—it's like an unspoken dance they've mastered."

Runa's gaze drifted, eyes unfocused as if searching through the past. "Even the way they are with us girls—it's seamless. They took us in when I was just around one, Tabs was about five, and Ray was thirteen. It was never strained or conditional. They loved us as if we'd always been theirs, stitching us into their lives with care, like threads pulled through a quilt."

She paused, her voice melting into something gentler. "I've always wondered if that ease was something only they knew how to create—if that kind of love is rare, if I just haven't found it…or it hasn't found me yet."

Her tone leveling out, laced with a mix of longing and awe. "It makes me think—maybe the effort I imagine love requires is just in my head. Perhaps it's me bracing for something that still feels unfamiliar." She shrugged gently, as if trying to settle into the idea. "It just…doesn't feel like anyone fits. Like love is some costly purchase, demanding repeated payments—and the currency is my own life."

Runa furrowed her brow and continued. "I think when it's real, you do what's needed because it's what's best for the other person." She tilted her head back and forth, weighing the thought. "I've dated here in Starlight, but honestly…it just felt like a chore." She cast a sideways glance at Ashla and gave a small shrug. "It shouldn't feel like a box I'm checking off."

"I think you'll know when you know," Ashla said, bumping her shoulder playfully against Runa's with a grin. "It'll click when it's meant to click." She arched her brow and gave a little shimmy of her shoulders, as if love were more a cosmic game than a choice.

Runa chuckled softly, then patted the tops of Ashla's hands. "What about you? Do you have anyone special?"

"Hardly!" Ashla's tone was airy, lilting—then dipped into something hauntingly somber. "After we lost our mother, our father became…well, extremely protective." Her eyes widened in mock seriousness, the corners of her mouth pulling into a whispered frown. "One time, Nissa went on a secret date by the river—back when we lived in the forest—and he followed her, hiding behind a rock the whole time."

She leaned into a precarious, lopsided grin. "He became a bit eccentric, to say the least, and completely petrified the poor young fellow." Blinking back a faint shimmer of light, she added, "From what Nissa says, Father needs a bit more time."

She smiled broadly, grabbing the railing and leaning back just a little. "We laugh about it now, but man…she was furious with him for ages."

"Seems like your father took your mother's passing really hard. Is that why you all moved to Starlight?" Runa's curiosity tinkled like a bell at the entrance of a sweet shop —bright and instinctive—only to still midway, as if the door had opened to something she hadn't meant to barge into. Her shoulders dropped slightly,"I didn't mean to pry...I just—was wondering."

"No bother. Sometimes I forget that the remembering isn't shared." Ashla shook her head, brushing the thought away. "When Mother passed —it hit us all hard. We've moved a few times since then." Her cadence dimmed. "Even though it's been a while, father still blames himself." Her mouth twisted into a sad, resigned smile. "Nissa and I came here for a fresh start. "That's where *The Studio* came in. A safe harbor to land while everything else tried to reshape itself. She sighed, "Yet, I do believe a new phase is arriving very soon." Her tone lifted, "It's like catching the first warmth of morning. Quiet and full of possibility."

Runa leaned into her palm, fingers brushing over her lips as she listened intently, squinting as if searching for an answer in the light. "Why *'The Studio?'*"

"It's simple," Ashla said, her eyes brightening. "You could say," she paused, gaze drifting as if searching for the right words, "at my core, I like to help people break free from their constraints, both seen and unseen. *'The Studio'* is where I let spirits flourish, evolve, and thrive in their purest form. To do that, I prefer simplicity."

She popped her lips and shrugged lightly. "Plus, Nissa didn't like the name 'Unbound'.' She said it might be mistaken for a 'different' kind of shop." Ashla added, making air quotes around the word 'different.' Shaking her head with a playful smile, she muttered, "She's just so particular." Chuckling to herself as she rolled her eyes.

Runa uncrossed her forearms from the balcony's edge. "I can see Nissa's point." Turning to face Ashla, she leaned in slightly, curiosity evident. "So, what happened with your father? Is he here in Starlight too?"

"No, he needed more time." Ashla exhaled softly, shoulders drooping as if weighed down. "He said he isn't quite ready to face a ghost from his past."

"Yeah. I get that." Runa took a deep breath. "Sometimes, when I look in the mirror, I don't even recognize who I see. It's like something's missing— like I'm trying to connect invisible dots from what once was to what is now."

"They might look identical, but some dots are shaped by thunder and others by lullabies." Ashla drifted back from the railing, like a thought changing direction. "Don't get too lost in connecting those old dots to the present. Sometimes it's better to restart where you are now." She gave a slight shrug, her tone light but thoughtful. "We're not defined by our past. Things happened to bring us here, but it's in the present that we get to decide what's next."

Ashla's mouth curved into a thoughtful frown as she glanced over the railing. "Oh, bother—I didn't realize the time," she murmured, already drifting away with a whimsical flick of her thumb over her shoulder. "I really should get back," she added, her voice light, as if the thought had only just landed.

"I'm glad we had this time together." Runa shifted her weight, stepping a little closer to Ashla. "Make sure to stop by early and check out our table," she added, a playful glint in her eyes. "Mama's cheesy potatoes are legendary—and if you don't get there soon, they'll be gone before you know it."

Lowering her voice to a whisper, Runa touched Ashla's forearm. "Also, make sure to visit Dagny's Seaside Sweets Shoppe." She spread her hands wide, then clenched them into tight fists, shivering with enthusiasm. "There's a rumor she has tiny dragons that help her melt the chocolate." She wiggled with delight. "The caramels have this incredible toasted glaze that makes me believe such rumors."

Leaning in with a mischievous smile, Ashla pulled Runa into a quick, tight hug. Whispering into her ear, "Life has a way of surprising us with extraordinary gifts when we least expect them." She pulled back slightly, winking, then placed her hands on Runa's forearms. Breathing in deeply, she closed her eyes and exhaled with steady purpose. "Unbinding takes what was once dormant," she continued, "reawakening all that has been bound." As her eyes opened to meet Runa's, a wave of dusky clouds washed through her pupils. "This phase is only the beginning."

Runa furrowed her brow, confusion marring her forehead as a soft radiance began to glow from beneath her black sweater. Her eyes widened, blinking in bewilderment, a gasp escaped her lips, as a subtle vibration rippled beneath her skin, prickling along its surface.

The light brightened, and Ashla giggled softly, her hands coming together in delight. "You have grand potential for so many things, Runa."

She tapped her fingertips beneath her chin, "It appears this is the year—you become part of the display."

Runa blinked, curiosity creeping across her face as she pulled back her sleeve, revealing the hazy inked tattoo of a full moon on her forearm. Shadows curled through the design—small dots arranged in a perfect circle, mimicking the moon as it rose through its quiet phases.

Earlier in the washroom, when the tattoo had mysteriously appeared—a globe beneath the skin, encircled by a thin line wrapping around the rising moon, with a dotted circle surrounding it. Now, two tiny dots—one slightly larger than the other—sat on either side of the globe, like delicate periods in orbit. They were intersected by a thin, solid line that encircled the entire moon. On the right side, an eastern star was just beginning to emerge; on the left, a western star mirrored its movement, slowly coming into view. Runa blinked, confusion clouding her expression.

With a sudden turn, Ashla descended the grand staircase. Near the imposing wooden doors, she twirled her fingers in precise circles. "You're all caught up now." she said, halting for a moment. Tilting her head toward the ceiling, she pointed skyward with conviction. "Keep looking to the moon, Ru." Lowering her hand to her side, she added, "Answers are on the horizon, and a world of possibilities awaits." Winking one last time, she spun between the heavy wooden doors, narrowly avoiding others entering the expansive hallway.

Nausea hit Runa like a wave, her vision blurring with flashing lights. She collapsed, body convulsing as a cataclysmic door opened within her mind, flooding her with blinding images and revealing the magnitude of what she once was.

Chapter Nine

Prowling down the narrow passageway, Diesel moved steadily as the corridor exhaled. The lights flickered and swayed, casting shadows that danced in the newfound space. This slight movement set the candelabras ablaze, brightening the hallway with each of his advancing steps. The wavering flames stirred countless shifting faces within the framed canvases, pulling them from their slumber in their golden homes along the hallway walls.

The emerald wallpaper was inlaid with intricate honey colored patterns, resembling meandering branches—the lifelines of the dwelling. These veins pulsed with enchantment, guiding him toward the heart of the house: his study. Within grew a sprawling fragment of the "Tree of Life," nestled beside the fireplace and bookshelf.

The tree served as an anchor to the city of Sanctuary, a place gripped by turmoil and strife. In its fractured state, the Tree of Life stood as a vital wellspring of wisdom, its roots tangled with secrets long forgotten. Each crack in its bark whispered ancient knowledge, strands of insight weaving through its gnarled branches. This connection tied it directly to the mission at Starlight Beach, where every leaf and splinter played a role in the unfolding plans.

As if sensing a change, the Tree sent out subtle vibrations. Its echoes rippled through the house, traveling along the walls and floorboards, tapping out a rhythmic Morse code. Each pulse carried a new piece of information, a fresh stream of intelligence coursing through the residence, urging him to listen.

As he advanced through the kitchen, the house seemed eager to reveal its recently acquired information. A low rumble reverberated through the wooden floorboards, a signal of its impatience. The vibrations pulsed beneath his boots, urging him forward. He continued down the corridor, feeling the weight of the dwelling's anticipation pressing in on him.

Diesel rolled his eyes subtly, knowing the house wouldn't relent. "Give me a minute," he muttered aloud, his voice gruff and yet commanding. The words echoed off the walls, steady and firm—a reminder to both himself and the dwelling to keep calm.

The house quieted, its energy still bristling beneath the floorboards like a held breath. Diesel exhaled and rubbed the back of his neck. His thoughts wandered to the information he would soon need to share with the girls— a revelation known to very few. It wouldn't be an easy conversation. He felt the familiar weight settle in his chest. *They won't like it.* He could already predict the questions, the doubt in their eyes. *Not that I blame them.* This wasn't just another mission detail; it was the kind of truth that could change everything. He sighed inwardly. *I can't keep it from them forever.* Once he spoke to them, there'd be no going back.

Starlight Beach was envisioned as a haven; it served as a concealed endpoint, a pocket of existence that intricately braided the ribbons of past, present, and future. This beachfront base was set into motion ages ago, orchestrated by the Blessed Father Ezekiel and the Shadow Guild—the overarching hierarchy that governed both the Shadow Guard, a standard military branch tasked with protection and security, and the Shadow Guard Elite Unit (S.G.E.U.), a specialized forces division handling covert and high-risk operations.

Early in his career, Diesel swiftly rose through the ranks, earning his place as General within the Shadow Guild. It was a top position, not just for its authority, but for the immense responsibility it carried—leading both branches through countless operations and challenges. Together, they had laid the foundation for Starlight Beach—a discreet refuge hidden in plain sight, nestled within a natural ocean inlet just beyond the training facilities.

The military compound itself was built into the face of the cliff, a stronghold forged to serve as a proving ground for Elite Shadow Guards. New recruits were shaped there into warriors for classified assignments, while seasoned veterans continued operations under the joint command of both Sanctuary and Shadow City—a rare alliance made possible through Father Ezekiel's leadership at Sanctuary and Diesel's rank within the Guild.

Etched into the jagged cliff's stone, the lion insignia marked the threshold with unmistakable intent. It served as both a warning and a seal, its presence warding off any who might dare venture closer. Most knew better than to cross it. And so, while the base remained visible to the world above, the heart of Starlight Beach—its true purpose and depth—remained untouched. The creation of this stronghold solidified the alliance between the two cities. It became a strategic sanctuary—offering both protection and control—just beyond the reach of those unwilling to see what lay past the boundary's edge.

Eons passed, and with the rise of a new generation of warriors, Izayah was named the next in line to command the Shadow Guild. The decision marked a pivotal shift—endorsed by the highest-ranking leaders and military units within the long-standing alliance. They saw in him the strength, precision, and foresight needed to carry the Guild's legacy into an evolving world.

Before his formal appointment, Izayah had already begun expanding the haven Diesel and Ezekiel had once established. Under a special directive from Lord Brannon, he took the bare-bones structure of Starlight Beach —a secluded refuge veiled by ley lines and hidden in plain sight—and began transforming it into a formidable sanctuary for high-clearance operatives. It was a place designed not just for rest, but for debriefing and reintegration after highly classified missions. Drawing from salvaged materials and long-forgotten technologies unearthed after the Great War, Izayah repurposed relics long stored within the Shadow Guard's vaults, integrating them into the haven's expanding design.

At the same time, he turned his attention to the military compound embedded in the cliff's edge—a separate but equally vital facility. Utilizing the same cache of war-era resources, he reinforced the Elite base, extending its infrastructure deeper into the rock, refining its defense systems, and retrofitting its layout to match the evolving needs of the Shadow Guild. The two locations—one for safeguarding secrets, the other for shaping soldiers—were soon bound together through a network of underground tunnels. Though distinct in purpose, both facilities had roots laid long ago by Diesel and Ezekiel. It was Izayah who transformed them, elevating each into a secure stronghold suited for a new age.

As the son of Lord Brannon, the High Crown and Ruler of Shadow City, Izayah had been groomed for leadership from an early age. His upbringing was steeped in the Guild's traditions, embedding within him the values of loyalty, strategy, and command. Stepping into the mantle of General meant more than inheriting a title—it meant overseeing both the Shadow Guards and the Elite Units. A responsibility that demanded not only tactical skill, but an unshakable will.

Meanwhile, Diesel had begun preparations for his own transition into retirement, shifting his focus toward training the incoming Elite at Starlight Beach and ensuring they were ready for the trials ahead. Though his command still held firm, the next chapter was beginning to take shape.

Izayah's elevation to command was imminent—but before accepting the mantle, he chose to act on new information relayed through Sienna, the High Seer. What followed wasn't an assignment issued by the Guild, but a directive Izayah authored himself with acceptance from Shadow Guild leadership. He embarked on a confidential three-day operation, known only to a select few high-ranking officials. Though brief in duration, it became the catalyst for a larger undertaking—a covert, twenty-year initiative that would delay his formal rise. The nature of the task, centered around highly sensitive intelligence involving Runa, demanded complete discretion. For Izayah, this wasn't ceremony—*it was a necessity*. One final act of conviction before assuming full responsibility. Even among the Elite, it was spoken of only in hushed tones—an effort that would quietly shape the kind of command he intended to shoulder.

He assembled a task force of trusted operatives, each handpicked for their loyalty, precision, and silence. With intelligence gathered, they initiated the first phase—an extraction that signaled the beginning of a broader objective. As operations quietly unfolded, Starlight Beach's haven was finally activated for its original purpose. But it didn't stop there. Personnel with high-level clearances—many long retired—were offered opportunities for reassignment within the coastal enclave. Daily systems were restructured. The population within the haven swelled, breathing new life into the compound. What had once been a ghost of theory became a pulse—vibrant and alive. Izayah hadn't simply stepped into the inheritance Diesel and Ezekiel left behind—he elevated it. Under his vision, both the stronghold and haven were transformed. Not just functional—*formidable*. Not just remembered—*future-bound*.

The weight of these thoughts snapped Diesel back to the present, reminding him just how much the girls would need to absorb. *Pace it out,* he thought, tension knotting in his chest. *They'll have questions. It wasn't just about the facts—it was how they'd take them in. It'll be a lot to swallow.* He exhaled, measuring his next steps. *Start with the basics. No sense in dropping everything all at once.*

Stress crept in, coiling tightly around him like an unwanted guest. He closed his eyes briefly. With a slight bow of his head and a quiet shake, he stepped into his study—a room steeped in history, where memories simmered just beneath the surface, waiting to be stirred.

The French doors creaked open, reminiscent of eyelids parting at dawn, revealing the study's carefully curated interior. Shelves lined with worn tomes and relics from another era cast long shadows across the room, hinting at stories long past. A sigh slipped from Diesel's lips, easing the tension that had threaded through his spine.

The house held its breath, the air thickening with anticipation as he crossed the threshold. The walls—currently shaped by Missy's mood— wore deep emerald tones that seemed to ripple in the dim light. Beneath his boots, the aged wood groaned with each step, echoing quiet murmurs —listening, comprehending. The structure didn't just creak; it responded, already sensing what lay ahead.

A deep scent of leather anchored the space, mingling with the faint aroma of smoke curling from the hearth. The combination stirred memories—of long nights steeped in strategy and silence, of reports spread across this very desk, of conversations held in hushed tones and decisions that could not be undone.

To the right, the whiskey bar stood—a silent sentinel amidst the room's darkness. Its polished wood surface gleamed softly, a familiar beacon of solace. Rows of bottles, each filled with rich amber liquid, lined the shelves above it—their presence an unspoken comfort, a final gift from Ezekiel, given shortly before he passed.

Here, in this study, Diesel found a strange sort of companionship. In a world carved by contrast and rank, where everything was either hidden or painfully exposed, he often felt like a man marooned on an island of his own making. Yet even now, surrounded by the relics of past triumphs and failures, a part of him still longed for the day he could walk away—for good. From the duty. From the weight. From all of it.

Not to abandon the fight—but to return to its roots. To the daily grind beside the Elite, where the mission wasn't inked into scrolls or filtered through endless chains of command. It was lived. Earned. Shared. Before the rank. Before the title. Back when he still felt connected.

I miss that. I miss the quiet rituals of training beside others—discipline baked into every repetition. In his early years, it was simply how the day began— shoulder to shoulder with peers, rhythm and rigor passed between them without a word. But the higher he rose, the more isolated it became. Training shifted into off-hours, forged alone in silence. Not for glory. It never was. It was a tether to something real. Something earned. Something that reminded him who he was beneath the rank.

When Starlight Beach began to change—when the older generation returned and the enclave stirred with something raw and alive—he felt it deep in his bones. He'd already made the decision to transition out of command, but with the abrupt pivot back into his role as General for the Guild, everything had been put on hold. Still, the resurgence of the town around him sparked something unexpected—something that reminded him he longed for more than duty and command.

When Izayah's covert operation finally launched and the twenty-year mission began, Starlight ignited with a different kind of pulse. The space was no longer just theory—it was alive. He felt it in the renewed weight of footsteps across the training grounds, in the laughter tucked between drills.

Then the girls arrived. Everything tilted. The town softened, pivoting into a place where he no longer had to tuck the joking away. Their small hands gave him permission to be fully present—unguarded in a way he hadn't been in centuries. As the girls grew, training became a language again—a way to connect, to teach, to remember. He passed on what he knew, not just tactics or formations, but the truths buried deep beneath discipline and motion. Watching them evolve stirred something long dormant. Purpose. Not the kind born from titles or war tables, but the kind that meets you at eye level—and holds fast.

Simply put, as the years passed and the mantle of command slipped further from his grasp, he spent more time among the veteran Elites, incoming recruits, and townsfolk assigned to special operations. Shoulder to shoulder. In it. Not just overseeing movement, but rediscovering what it meant to move within the crowd—to be part of something. To feel more whole than he had since losing his brother, Ezekiel.

Simultaneously, he grappled with the weight of leaving behind a 500-year commitment as General within the Shadow Guild. It was a position that had become ingrained within his very identity. He had devoted centuries to perfecting the art of leadership, navigating the ever-shifting landscape of power, strategy, and loyalty.

The title of General had come to define him—a badge of honor he wore even in his quietest moments. Now, as the time to step away neared, it felt like shedding a piece of himself. And yet, the transition was inevitable—to relinquish command and take on a new role: supporting the Shadow Elite as a mentor, with a steadier, perhaps even effortless, kind of leadership.

He had tried to imagine what that would entail—guiding the next generation, passing on the knowledge he had taken centuries to acquire. It sounded simple enough in theory, but the reality unsettled him. *Could I really become the mentor they need without the power that came with my former position?*

Somewhere within the house, he hoped to find answers—a deeper understanding beyond the information he already held. Something that would make this shift easier to accept, to make peace with stepping away from the weight of command. Years of habit and identity were built on the foundation of being the one who carried it all. Letting that go wasn't just change—it was unlearning a lifetime of vigilance. He let out a huffing sigh, his mind racing to quiet the uncertainty swirling inside him. "I require a brief pause to collect my thoughts and orient myself before we engage in conversation," he said aloud, his tone steady, though tension fraying at the edges.

He rounded his shoulders forward as he exhaled, creating space to be, even amid the mounting stress. Slowly, he turned his neck, feeling the pull and strain of muscles along his upper traps—the result of days spent in constant preparation for the changes he faced. Gradually, he straightened his back, drawing his chest forward, expanding his diaphragm and letting the stress leak from his lips like steam from a kettle.

"I'm aware you possess intel for me," he said, his voice gruff as he directed his words to the house. "I trust it'll facilitate a smoother transition than what I'm anticipating right now."

In reply, the dwelling—Missy—responded with a soft *clink-clink* as two substantial ice cubes dropped into the whiskey glass before him. The sound resonated gently through the room, a soothing gesture that spoke volumes. It was Missy's way of acknowledging the moment. She recognized the weight of their shared history—the triumphs, the losses, and the delicate moments when everything hung in the balance, just as it did now.

With a slight raise of his glass, he offered a silent gratitude to Missy for her quiet support, appreciating the calm before the storm.

Starlight was preparing to adapt yet again. As it stood now, it was a quaint coastal town—rich in history, steeped in legend and charm. No longer just a military base, it had become a beacon of hope, a place where the shadows of the past intertwined with the possibilities of tomorrow.

Yet today was a reminder that challenges did not simply fade. The rise of a power-hungry dictator now ruling over Sanctuary had drastically redefined the landscape. Starlight's evolution was no longer just a matter of strategy; it had become a fight for survival.

Diesel felt the weight of these changes pressing down on him. His mind was already turning over scenarios, calculating the plays that needed to be made. Every decision moving forward would shape the fate of their world —and he could feel that burden in every corner of the room. In the silence, he acknowledged the gravity of his role: to guide things where they needed to go, not just where he wished they could.

Pulling back from his reverie, he found himself standing before the exquisitely fashioned wet bar, its richness captured in a sophisticated shade of gray. The cabinetry, like the study's doors, had been weathered and repurposed from its former residence in Shadow City. The wood bore the scars of its history—burn trails lining its surface, each a silent witness to the chaos of the Great War. The quintessence fires had raged; their relentless heat had seared the grain, leaving behind marks that would never fade.

These planks had once lined the halls where battles erupted, where warriors clashed and shadows collided in desperate struggles for control. The darkened grooves spoke of spilled blood and buried grief, every inch etched with the remnants of command decisions and irreversible losses. Now, it stood here—quiet, enduring—a fragment of history anchored in the present, whispering stories best left unspoken.

His gaze lifted to the portrait looming above—a silent companion, most of the time. The figure, rugged and weatherworn, hunched over his bar, a whiskey glass poised near his lips. Dark, intricate tattoos coiled along his sun-worn forearms, winding like restless shadows. They crawled across each knuckle—an elaborate topography of ancient symbols, each murmuring of forsaken missions and classified truths buried deep beneath the surface.

The figure exhaled a deep sigh, subtly shifting within the confines of his frame, eyes tracking Diesel with quiet vigilance. The man on the other side of the canvas was more than pigment. He was a presence. Like a companion stationed at the far end of the bar—silent, pensive, shouldering the full burden of memory. The gray Malone tweed cap cast a shadow across his face, but a faint gleam in his eyes betrayed awareness. A readiness. As though he would meet Diesel's gaze the moment duty called.

The warm glow of the study caught the man's whiskey glass, making it gleam as it waited to be sipped. For a fleeting moment, Diesel could almost hear the faint note of glass meeting wood, calling his eyes downward to the three meticulously molded bottles cradled within dark walnut fixtures on the sleek black countertop. The amber liquid inside shimmered beneath the ambient light of the two-story, lofted space. Time-worn and treasured, the bottles had been crafted by skilled artisans of Starlight—men he had once stood shoulder to shoulder with while hunting adamantine during the Great War. After Ezekiel's passing, they'd been forged in his honor, each one set into the fixture, inverted and fitted with ornate brass faucets—a homage to a time when craftsmanship was art.

His gaze lingered on the bottles, appreciating their elegance—their presence a reminder of countless nights spent contemplating his next move within this assignment. He lifted his own glass, the coolness of the crystal meeting his fingertips as he turned to set down Runa's soft leather pack on the polished panels of the bar.

He leaned forward, fingers grazing the dark walnut dispensary as he gripped the brass spout. He tugged gently, letting the rich, brown liquid cascade into his glass. It flowed smoothly, splashing over the ice cubes with a silken, almost melodic cadence. The air filled with the familiar notes of tobacco, hickory, and a touch of chocolate—scents steeped in memory.

This was his moment—a brief pause amidst the maelstrom, a space to recalibrate and process the storm within his mind. He took a measured sip, the warmth of the whiskey rolling down his throat, grounding him in the present. And with that, he hooked a finger through the loop at the top of the rucksack, feeling the worn leather give slightly beneath his grip.

He lumbered over to the hefty green velvet armchair. Its deep seat promised comfort within the grand expanse of the study. Reaching the chair, Diesel set the bag down gently, his gaze sweeping the room as he straightened his posture. The familiar sight of polished wood shelves and the soft glow of candlelight dancing along the walls offered a semblance of calm to his racing thoughts.

His left hand rose to his brow, fingers pressing into the lines of tension scored across his forehead. The day's burdens seemed to lift slightly as he massaged away the stress. With a final shake of his shoulders, he shrugged off the weight of recent events, the lingering tightness in his muscles beginning to ease.

This space, with its shadows and light, its scents and quiet comforts, had become his sanctuary, a place where he could adapt and refocus before facing the challenges that lay ahead. The Starlight Festival was set to unfold tonight, and for the first time in five years, he wouldn't be in attendance. The thought lingered, a stark reminder of how much was changing.

He reached for the leathery rucksack at his side, his fingers grazing the familiar texture worn soft with time. Hesitating, the motion stalled as the green walls of the study deepened, their hues growing richer and more vibrant. Missy—the house—was already nudging him, her presence like someone bouncing on their toes, barely able to contain the anticipation. She was hinting at his next destination, eager to share what she knew, practically alight with unspoken energy.

He gave a slight shake of his head, smirking at the residence's impatience. *Always ahead of me, aren't you?* She was like a dog wagging her tail upon his return, brimming with excitement. The thought amused him, drawing a faint curve to his lips. *You just never could resist the pull.*

The fireplace crackled to life with a sudden pop, the flames spitting sparks stirred by Missy's growing impatience. "I know. I know. Just give me a bit more time," he said, leaning forward, adjusting his large frame in the velvet armchair. He lowered the bag to the floor between his feet, listening to the soft creak of the leather as it settled. Carefully, he leaned in and set his glass on the edge of the table in front of him.

His gaze dropped to the pack—hand-stitched leather marked by years of wear. Where hands had touched it most, the surface had softened and darkened, proof of both mileage and memory. Two narrow straps ran down the front, looped through small metal grommets. *Adjustable, and dependable, just like Runa,* he thought.

He reached for the top of the bag, lifting the folded flap where it rested against the front. The motion revealed neatly stitched seams lining the leather's edge—evidence of careful, intentional work. With practiced ease, his hands slipped beneath both sides, fingers finding the familiar give of worn leather. The flap lifted smoothly, granting access to the bag's interior. A small, simple act—yet it carried the weight of ritual, one he'd performed countless times before.

Upon opening, a divine aroma wafted out—rich notes of dark chocolate, mingling with the freshness of mint and the rich flavors of ripe berries. The scent teased his senses, an olfactory reminder of simpler, happier times. He paused, letting the fragrance settle in the air, a brief respite before he plunged his hand into the leather satchel.

His fingers brushed against the smooth edges of a small, intricately designed container. The box itself was a work of art, draped in a deep, majestic blue that mimicked the midnight sky. It was speckled with delicate hints of gold that glimmered like stars in motion. His lips curved into a smile, tinged with both expectation and memory, as his heavy, weathered hands carefully opened the delicate covering.

Inside, nestled within the box, were six impeccably crafted miniature rosebud cakes, each one a masterpiece of confectionery art. They sat in a perfect row, lightly dusted with a layer of fine white powder, like a gentle snowfall had kissed their soft petals. Beneath the delicate cakes lay a bed of deep green leaves, the rich color contrasting with the pale buds and stirring an unexpected swell of emotion within him.

Those leaves, he thought, a whisper from the past, a reminder of summers long gone. His mind wandered back to that bygone era, to the quaint ice cream parlor and sweets lounge that had become a sanctuary of joy. The place where little hands, sticky with sugar and adventure, had lifted these very cakes to their eager mouths, smearing lips with traces of chocolate glaze, sugar crystals, and berry jam. He could almost hear the innocent laughter, the gleeful chatter that filled the parlor, accompanied by the melodic chime of its old-fashioned doorbell.

"Dagny's Seaside Sweets," he whispered, the name drifting through his mind like a fond caress. Its façade had been painted in cheerful pastels, blending seamlessly into the seaside charm of Starlight. The inside was a wonderland of indulgence, where wooden counters displayed rows of treats, and jars brimming with candies lined the shelves.

Visitors were welcomed into a world of sugary surrender, where the salty ocean breeze slipped through open windows, mingling with the rich scents of roasted caramel, chocolate, and vanilla. As younglings—and even elders—savored the beloved rosebud cakes, the air became a symphony of fragrances.

The sweet scent of spun sugar clouds mingled with melted chocolate, while bright undertones of fruity gummies added a playful twist. Warm caramel drifted through the shop, laced with subtle hints of vanilla—wrapping around each patron like a soft, lingering embrace.

The memory was vivid, the atmosphere so tangible that he could almost feel the cool wooden benches beneath him, the gentle hum of chatter, and the rhythmic lapping of waves outside. He ran his thumb over the cakes, feeling their smooth texture through the delicate powder coating.

For a moment, he was no longer in the study, he was back in that parlor, surrounded by the ghosts of his past.

So much was about to change, Diesel reflected—*and yet, some things, like the quiet joy tucked into these small cakes, remained timeless.* It wasn't just a box of confections; it was a portal to another chapter, a bridge to memories that calmed the present and steadied him for the chaos ahead.

He recalled a cherished moment with his younglings—the way their eyes sparkled as they stood before the nostalgic showcase of treats. Their laughter, light and musical like wind chimes in a gentle breeze, wove through the air, mingling with soft conversation and the familiar jingle of the shoppe's bell as it swung open for each new visitor. Every smile shared between them felt like a snapshot, framed by the vibrant displays and the cozy hum of the old shoppe. Rows of glass jars lined the polished shelves, brimming with colorful delights—candied chews, fruit-studded drops, and other carefully packaged indulgences, each one a promise of something sweet.

The tenderness of those instances endured—not only in the flavor of the treats but in the enduring memories that mirrored the everlasting beauty of rosebuds. *Such simplicity,* he thought, inspecting the curved surface of the treat he now held. He placed the container gently beside his glass on the broad coffee table, letting its presence linger in the room.

With intentional care, he lifted one bud to his lips, pausing to inhale its delicate scent. Hints of lavender and lemon rose to meet him—a fragrance that soothed his senses and pulled him back to a time of innocence and uncomplicated joy.

He closed his eyes as he took a bite. The pastry gave way on his tongue, dissolving into soft delight that quieted the storm of thoughts swirling within him. A small, genuine smile tugged at the corners of his mouth. *This,* he thought, *is how memories survive the years.*

Popping the rest into his mouth, he leaned back, feeling the weight of the world lift as the room around him seemed to breathe in sync—like even Missy was savoring this quiet ritual of nostalgia.

The gentleman above the wet bar cleared his throat, eyes gleaming with a mixture of amusement and longing. "Aye, right. That's sittin' real high up dere with those Nutmeg Ginger Apple Snaps and Raspberry Cream Puff Kisses. Pure bloody royalty, dat lot." Liam remarked, each word rolling warmly off his tongue. "Aye, dat was somethin' all right. Like my tastebuds got dragged through a portal and dunked in a vat of quintessence. Should've come with a warnin'." He huffed out a sigh, then added, "I'd be delighted to give it a go meself. Mind poppin' one into ta frame for me?"

The corner of Diesel's mouth twitched upward in a smirk. *Always cheeky, that one.* Reaching over to the container, he carefully selected another bud, holding it up. "Just this once," he muttered. "Don't get any ideas."

He shifted forward to the edge of his seat and setting it on the coffee table. Pausing, he closed his eyes. The core of his quintessence stirred— subtle, steady, like tugging on a single strand while holding the rest at bay. It thrummed beneath his skin, an old muscle flexing after a long rest. The air around him intensified, humming softly as he extended his hand toward the gold-encrusted portrait frame.

In a single, fluid flicking gesture, the rosebud vanished with a soft *pop*, leaving behind a ripple in the air that quickly stilled. An instant later, it reappeared within Liam's frame, landing with a flourishing *plop*. The shift in the room's energy was subtle but unmistakable—like the space exhaled in quiet satisfaction.

The gentleman's eyes widened with delight, his face brightening as he reached for the treat. Raising his glass in a gesture of appreciation, he brought the rosebud to his lips, savoring its presence. "Stick a fork in me— dat's heaven on da tongue." he exclaimed, his tone thick with admiration.

Diesel raised his own glass in salute, a small, satisfied smile tugging at his lips. The space fell into silence—the kind that wraps itself around you and lingers, deep and unbroken. A calm settled into the room, filling every corner with quiet anticipation.

Then, faintly at first, a soft clicking sound began to echo down the spiral staircase, each click growing louder, more mindful with every step. The lights around the room flickered in response, their luminescence dimming and brightening in a rhythmic dance, syncing perfectly with the approaching *tap, tap, tap*. A faint radiance appeared at the top of the stairs, casting long, stretching shadows that swayed and twisted in the flickering light.

Nester descended, his small form fashioned entirely from sleek black piping, every joint seamlessly connected in a mechanical dance of grace. His movements were fluid, almost hypnotic, as he made his way down the steps, his rhythm an unbroken cadence. His head—or rather, the place where a head should be—was a small industrial lamp bulb. It cast a warm, dusky haze that bobbed gently with each step the little lamp took, lending him an ethereal quality.

The radiance was steady yet playful, illuminating his surroundings with an interplay of light and shadow that draped the room in whimsical charm. The darkness seemed to bow in acknowledgment of his arrival, retreating into corners as his glimmer danced across the walls.

Nester's voice brushed against Diesel's mind, slipping in like a familiar whisper, sticky with nostalgia. *Ah, it did take you quite a while, didn't it?* His tone carried a teasing lilt, infused with both amusement and curiosity. *There's much to share, and I'm inclined to regale you with the tales that have accumulated during your absence.*

Diesel's gaze fixed on Nester as he reached the final steps, cradling a small leather-bound book, its cover worn from years of frequent handling. Along its spine, a delicate feather was etched—a mark of the Truth Tellers. He paused, surveying the room with a quiet, unreadable calm.

As if sensing the weight of the moment, the book gave a faint flutter, its pages rustling softly against Nester's hold, as though the secrets within were eager to escape. His grip tightened slightly—a familiar gesture, hinting at the unspoken understanding between a keeper and the stories entrusted to him.

His other limb rested with ease on his hip joint, lending him an air of casual contemplation. The light from his bulb-head flickered in sync with the rhythm of his thoughts, as if the stories swirling within him were too numerous to sit still. *Now, where shall I begin?* Nester's tone was playful, yet laced with an undercurrent of seriousness. His glow dimmed and brightened with each musing.

Diesel leaned back into patience as Nester hopped up onto the charred coffee table. With a flourish, he tossed the book down. It wriggled, trying to slip away—until Nester plopped his small frame on top of it, pinning it in place. Leaning forward to whisper, *Do you think she will be ready for all this, Sir?*

Diesel's mind reeled at the inquiry, a familiar worry gnawing at him.

"Thoughtfully played, Nester," he said, his voice steady, yet tinged with a hint of strain. "The real concern is—*will any of them be prepared?*" He exhaled a long, controlled sigh as his tone turned gravel-soft. "Doesn't *really* matter, *does it?* Whatever the future holds, it's coming for them—*ready or not.*"

Chapter Ten

The thunderous roar of the tide eased the heaviness pressing on her chest. Runa let her eyes close, surrendering to the salty currents in the air. The melody of the waves caressed her thoughts, teasing the tension loose in her mind and gently guiding her breath.

For the first time in what felt like ages, the air tasted like calm. Vivid images flooded her consciousness. They came like tidal waves, crashing in quick succession, each one carrying the gravity of this new world she was now privy to. Faces, places, and fractured memories swirled around, demanding her attention—yet slipping away before she could grasp them fully.

The journey to this rock—this solitary outcrop beneath the deep night sky—remained a mystery. *Had I wandered here on my own? Or had some unseen force drawn me to this spot?* The details eluded her, drifting away like fragments of a dream dissolving with the morning light.

Only the coolness of the stone beneath remained—a grounding source amidst the chaos in her mind. Thoughts ran with abandon, chucking out notions and expecting her to make sense of it all. The chill seeped through the fabric of her clothes, spreading the steady quietude reverberating through her bones. This sensation became the one stable element in a reality that otherwise blurred and distorted around her. It offered her something tangible to cling to.

Time became a distant concept as she sat, lost in a current of reflection. Seconds stretched and folded into each other, creating a seamless stream that left her with no sense of how long she had been there. Hours might have passed, or perhaps mere moments. She couldn't tell—nor did it seem to matter.

Words twisted in her mind, turning into painful ideas that coiled into constraints. Every thought—every attempt to make sense of her surround-ings—bound her more tightly to this place, to this moment. And yet, buried beneath the confusion, the solitude brought a peculiar sense of relief. Here, she could unravel her emotions without judgment, away from prying eyes.

The rhythmic surging of the waves worked tirelessly to silence the world around her. They rose and fell, a laboring pulse that gradually hushed the lingering reverberations of laughter, music, and celebration. These sounds felt like remnants of another life, a part of her mind now unreachable, sealed away behind a wall of fog.

She resisted the urge to speak, biting down on the need to give voice to her turmoil. In this moment, words would only sink heavily into the air, distorting the fragile *stillness* she clung to. Any utterance would hang heavy—like stones dropping into water—rippling through the quiet and disrupting what little peace remained.

How could I possibly convey the full impact of what had happened? The collapse. The cataclysmic moment when the door swung open and consumed everything I had once believed. It was too vast, too overwhelming—and the very thought of it drained her of the will to try to comprehend.

Silence, she decided, *was easier. It requires no explanation. No need to untangle thoughts that swirl chaotically. This hush allows me to simply exist, without the burden of putting the unspeakable into words.*

Her emotions settled within her like lead poles at the bottom of a spiked pit—an abyss she hadn't even been aware of until she stumbled into it, clawing for a way out. Now, as she sat here, observing in stillness, her gaze drifted across the landscape, taking in the dark expanse around her. The starlight offered a kind of refuge, its dim glow softening the edges of reality. In this muted hush, the world seemed less harsh, more bearable. This place had become her sanctuary. It was a corner of existence where she could tuck away the tangible world, sealing her true beginnings in a mental file folder, neatly out of sight.

Yet even as she sought refuge, thoughts bombarded her mind—rising unbidden, like waves crashing against the shore. *What for?* she wondered. *Later use? Avoidance?* The questions circled, persistent. *What does all of this mean? Have I always believed that everything would eventually unravel and come apart at the seams?* The thought nagged at her, growing louder. It all felt almost too perfect to be real—the beach, her sisters, Mama and Papa D, the comfort of a secure existence.

In these moments, the heaviest questions weren't just thoughts—they were demons. A shadow gnawing at the fragile fibers holding her heart together, tearing each strand loose at the seams. Questions like: *What made me worthy of Starlight? What justified my worthiness? How am I still alive?* They sounded so dramatic, yet each word felt like a stone anchor, relentless in keeping her stuck.

The onslaught of questions unleashed a tempest of dread, casting her into a murky abyss, veiled in inky darkness. A deep churning stirred in her stomach as she acknowledged that this wasn't the first time. She had wrestled with these relentless questions before, turning them over and over, examining, swallowing, regurgitating, and swallowing them again.

What a horrible existence and cycle. This is what feels normal. The breeze stirred, wrapping around her like an embrace as the tide surged onto the sand. Its immense power urged Runa to cleanse every part of herself she was second-guessing. The dam within her cracked, and as she closed her eyes, tears streamed down her cheeks. She never wanted anyone to witness this—her vulnerability, her silent plea for survival. Huddled into herself, she yearned to disappear, to escape the world.

Lifting her head, she gazed up at the heavens, craving answers to everything unfolding tonight. A star streaked across the clear, crisp sky, but she felt nothing—just numbness. So, she closed out the world—crisscrossed her arms over her knees and brought her chin to rest upon them, her gaze blurring into the whitewashing tide.

I am alone in all this. The realization struck, sinking into her like a weighty anchor. Shaking her head in disbelief, she muttered to the wind, "You're repulsive. Utterly pathetic." She shook her head and lowered her temple on her arms. "No one will understand *this*. No one will understand *you*."

Amidst the distant celebration, her thoughts swirled, erasing every other sound but her own. The crashing waves embodied her solitude. Behind her, the faint whispers of the festivities brushed against her back. Lights flickered with a starlit vibrancy, each shimmer only deepening her sense of detachment.

A silhouette emerged against the brilliance of the world beyond, moving with hushed composure. Rayanna approached, her steps intentional. In her hands, she carried two cups, cradling them as if they held something fragile. When she reached Runa, she paused to extend one mug —her usual sarcasm absent, replaced by a softer, more thoughtful expression.

She settled in beside her sister, choosing the rocky ledge as an act of solidarity. She didn't rush to fill the silence. Instead, she let it linger, knowing that sometimes words weren't what was needed. Then, she leaned in, bumping her shoulder gently against Runa's in a gesture that was both playful and reassuring.

They sat like that for a while, side by side, letting the rhythm of the ocean swell around them. The crashing waves spoke in hushed tones, filling the void that had taken root in Runa's mind. Rayanna's presence, steady and grounding, made the darkness feel less oppressive.

Finally, she broke the quiet. "You're not alone." Soft-spoken, yet resolute. The simplicity of the phrase carried an assurance that nestled into the quiet, finding its place within the chasm of Runa's thoughts. It wasn't an offer of comfort; it was a statement of fact. And in that certainty, Runa found a glimmer of hope.

"Hey, Ray," Runa uttered, straining not to be swallowed by the night. A significant pause settled in, taking up residence between them.

Rayanna remained quiet, her attention fixed on the coffee in her hands while she watched the ocean's rhythmic dance against the shore. Waiting.

Sensing the unspoken tension in Runa's words, yet anticipating the moment her sister might finally open up. The darkness around them was at its peak, cloaking the sea in a deep indigo hue that mirrored the sky, sprinkled with starlight. Perched on the rocks, she let her gaze shift from the surging tide to Runa's small frame beside her. There was a deep attentiveness in her expression as she responded with a quiet, "Hmm."

Runa turned her gaze toward Rayanna, folding in tighter on herself. When she finally spoke—her tone, a breathless whisper."My soul is weary. And now I understand why."

Rayanna nodded, her focus stilled on the horizon. "Considering the dedication you've poured into the Starlight Festival decorations these past weeks, it's no wonder you're feeling exhausted."

"No, not that," she murmured, eyes tethered to the ground, dismissing the notion with a wave of her hand.

"Then what?" With curiosity edging her tone, Rayanna leaned in and bumped Runa's shoulder. "If it's anything like my butt—numb and a bit chilly—then sign me up. I'm weary too."

A faint grin tugged at Runa's lips. She turned her face to the wind and spoke softly. "I've glimpsed who I was before Starlight. Or rather, how I had to navigate life before all of this."

"How?" Rayanna's brow furrowed, disbelief creasing her expression.

Runa took a deep sigh, lifting her gaze to the sky. Above, the night stretched on, clear and unwavering, as if holding its breath alongside her. And then, as if in reply, another star shot across the dark expanse. She tipped her head back, pondering the universe. *Two shooting stars in one night…What are the odds?*

The stars overhead shimmered against the deep indigo expanse, casting a soft glow on their faces. Rayanna watched the streak of light disappear into the vastness, her mind working through her sister's words. She shifted on the rocks, the air around them thick with the unspoken.

"Sounds like…it would be a lot to take in." Rayanna replied, choosing her words with care. Her usual sarcasm softened, replaced with something quieter, more contemplative. "So, you're saying you remembered what it was like…before all this?"

"I don't know how to explain it. I don't have the right words yet," Runa admitted, her gaze still lost in the sky. "It was like looking at myself through glass—distant, unreachable. I didn't even recognize who I was at first."

Rayanna glanced at her sister, studying the way her shoulders curled inward, how her eyes reflected the night. For once, she pushed aside her playful banter, knowing it wasn't the time. "And how does that make you feel now?" she asked, her voice gentle yet probing.

"Scared," Runa admitted, her words barely above a whisper. "And... relieved, I think. Like I finally understand why I've felt so tired for so long."

Rayanna sighed, leaning back on her hands as she stared up at the stars. "Life before Starlight was survival, wasn't it?" She spoke more to the sky than to Runa. "You've carried a lot, haven't you? More than you let on."

Runa's gaze found Rayanna's. "I have. And it seems I still do," she said quietly. "I just didn't realize how much, until now."

A silence stretched between them, filled with the sound of the ocean's steady rhythm. Rayanna broke it with a small chuckle, a hint of her usual sass creeping back in. "Go ahead and unpack—but I'm not letting you do it solo." She gave Runa's shoulder a light nudge once more. "Trust me, I'm in it—for all of it. The whole mess of it."

Runa didn't say anything—just let a faint smile surface, the kind that meant *thank you* when the words were too much.

Rayanna's smile softened as she placed a hand on Runa's back—firm, warm, present. *You're not alone,* she thought, but didn't speak it. Some things were better left in the gestures.

The two sat together, the stars above and the sea before them. The darkness felt less daunting—not because it had changed, but because they were facing it together.

A hearty huff escaped, folding effortlessly into the steady crash of waves along the shoreline. Tabytha strode forward, her presence like a gust of wind breaking through the stillness around them. She tossed her dark curls over her shoulder, eyes gleaming with a blend of irritation and curiosity. "I've been searching for you two all night!" she exclaimed, her voice tinged with dramatic flair.

"Of course, no one had the faintest clue where you'd disappeared to. Not until I ran into Ashla at the North Star. And get this—while I was there, I grabbed a coffee with her and Nissa. Did you know they just moved here from the Dark Forest? Wherever that place is." She paused, her gaze drifting toward the horizon as if savoring the reveal of her tale.

"Ashla got smacked by Nissa for…well, who really knows? She didn't explain, and I didn't ask." Tabytha's eyes widened theatrically, her voice dropping to a conspiratorial whisper. "Anyway, that's when she let it slip —that she saw you, Runa. Said you were stumbling about, talking to the air itself as you made your way toward the waves."

She crossed her arms, a playful smirk tugging at the corner of her lips. Tilting her head, she pretended to study them with the curiosity of a cat eyeing a peculiar object. "How deep are you two into the bottle this year?" Her words hung in the air, teasing but edged with genuine concern.

Without waiting for an answer, Tabytha stepped onto the rocks beside them, her movements fluid as she took a seat next to Runa. She pulled her knees up to her chest, tucking them in, then turned to study their faces with quiet scrutiny, as if she might peel back the layers of whatever they weren't saying.

"Alright, what's the deal?" she pressed, her voice softer now, though still tinged with irritation. "You two have really mastered the art of dodging social gatherings—Papa D would be proud. It's truly unsettling. Hard to build bonds when you're always tucked away like this."

Rayanna lifted her chin from the waves, projecting her voice over the push and pull of the tide. "Runa says she caught a glimpse of her past—of how she used to live before coming here." She motioned toward the surging sea, her eyes reflecting its restless energy.

"How?" Tabytha blurted, her mouth parting in disbelief.

"That's precisely my question. Glad we're finally speaking the same language," Rayanna stated.

"Well, I might need something strong after all this," Runa declared, exhaling sharply through her fidgeting hands as she dragged them down her face. "Okay—" She clapped her palms together once, sharply, as if to punctuate the moment and keep herself on track. "I collapsed in the town hall after Ashla left. *Don't freak out.*" Her hands moved in front of her again, erratic and restless, as though the very ideas she was trying to grasp were tangled between her fingers. "I was engulfed in—*I don't know*—nightmarish glimpses, if that's what *you want to call them.*" She let out a hard huff, her thoughts jumbling midair. "I'm at a loss for what to make of it. But if my origins are anything like what I witnessed..." She glanced between Rayanna and Tabytha, their wide eyes reflecting her own disbelief. "...*it's not for the faint of heart.*" Her voice dropped on that last sentence —measured, heavy.

She broke eye contact, fingers falling to the fibers of her dark pants, tugging absently. "Before Ashla left the town hall, she proclaimed that we're *'all caught up now.'* Whatever the *hell* that implies." Another sigh escaped her—more frustrated than the last—as her gaze flicked between the girls, trying to read if they were keeping up. "Then she said something about how I *'need to keep looking at the moon.'*" Her hands lifted again, expressive, uncertain. "And I *don't* understand it. Like—*why* do I need to keep looking at the moon? I don't know." Blinking through the tears of burning frustration and jumbled words, she added quietly, "The answers are on the horizon. And silly as it may sound...I stumbled out *here* because I thought maybe—*just maybe*—the horizon or the moon held something, just for me."

Rayanna and Tabytha exchanged a worried glance but stayed silent as Runa pressed on. "So, I am weary—and I still don't have any real answers." She took a steadying moment. "Oh—side note," Runa said, rubbing her temple before letting her hands fall. "As you know, courtesy of the bathroom nymph, I decided to get inked earlier today—and I have a feeling Ashla either helped orchestrate the whole thing or knows her really well." She waved a hand vaguely. "The nymph—still not over that, by the way—was doing her thing, and Ashla started spouting off some cryptic nonsense like, 'Life has a way of surprising us with extraordinary gifts when we least expect them.' Then she reached in to hug me, and the tattoo just...lit up. Started glowing like stardust on the parade route." She blinked, her tone caught somewhere between wonder and weariness. "So yeah, it added to the bathroom nymph's creation."

She pulled back her sleeve and held out her arm for inspection, revealing the full moon that had risen beneath her skin earlier in the day. It now rested full and proud, surrounded by a darker, thin line that encircled the newly shadowed illumination. Around it, a dotted ring marked the perimeter, now bearing two tiny dots on either side. Within each pair, one dot was slightly larger than the other. A small, solid line cut through the center, enclosing the moon. To the right of this line, an eastern star had emerged, while to the left, a western star mirrored its movement—gradually coming into view.

Rayanna extended her hand toward the nearest point of light on Runa's forearm. The surrounding air tightened, crackling with a static charge as her fingertips hovered just above the inked constellation. She let her fingers brush against the mark tenderly. In response, a sudden shimmer bloomed beneath the black velvet sleeve, casting an ethereal glow that glinted through the fabric.

The light pulsed once, twice, before settling into a steady, luminous aura. With intention, Rayanna tugged at the sleeve, the fabric whispering as it slid up her arm to reveal a new pattern now alive on her skin. The design mirrored Runa's perfectly—an array of symbols and lines faintly glowing, as if a quiet flame had been sparked from within.

The trio exchanged wary glances, an unvoiced tension brimming between them, dense with questions of something just beginning to unfold.

Rayanna broke through the unease. "Well, Tabs, you always talk about 'glowing up.' Here's your chance," she quipped.

"Oh, you're hilarious," she muttered. Without missing a beat, she reached across Runa's body, her movements fluid, almost feline. Her fingertip hovered for a moment, feeling the warmth that radiated from the marking, before pressing down. All three watched intently as Tabytha held out her own forearm, anticipation clinging to the air like a whisper yet to be spoken.

"Of course," she muttered, frustration curling at the edges of her mouth. She pursed her lips, wrinkling her nose in mild annoyance as nothing happened. Her skin remained unmarked, swallowed by shadows.

"Maybe it's about positioning," Rayanna suggested after a moment, her tone drifting to something more contemplative, almost distant. "Like coordinates on a map. Given all this talk about following the moon, do you think Runa represents the moon? What if we are meant to be the embodiment of her West and East stars? Try the other side."

Tabytha pressed her lips together in thoughtful silence, her eyes darting over the symbols on Runa's forearm as if tracing hidden patterns of possibility. She reached across, her finger gliding to the inked star closest to her. The space between them buzzed, close and tangible—static brushing along their spines and lifting goosebumps down their arms. The sensation was both thrilling and unnerving as she pressed down—her touch featherlike, yet firm.

Instantly, a ripple of warmth surged downward, bristling just beneath the surface—like a current flowing toward her wrist. It was followed by a soft, golden radiance that flickered to life, reminiscent of a lantern glimpsed through thick fog. The light wavered, casting delicate shadows that danced along the contours below.

A collective gasp escaped the trio as a tingling sensation washed over them, cascading across their bodies like a rush of icy wind. It pooled at their feet before surging outward, sending a wave of light spiraling in arcs of energy. The ribbons coiled, encircling their forms before expanding—pushing against the very fabric of reality.

The ocean's rhythm faltered, its waves arrested mid-ebb, caught in a moment of indecision. The world itself paused—the wind stilled, the shimmering lights above flickered, casting reflections onto the quivering surface of the sea. The radiance surrounding them brightened, illuminating the shoreline in a pale, ghostly light, as the earth held its breath in awe of what had been unleashed.

"Well, *damn*! What in the hell was that?" Runa exclaimed, as the girls exchanged wide-eyed glances, the silence between them heavy and electric.

Rayanna shook her head violently, as if trying to dislodge the images that had just burned into her mind. "*Fuck*! This is just getting ridiculous," she blurted. "Well, bat me sideways and call me Larry—I don't fucking know what the hell is happening, and I am so *over* all these fucking questions!"

She exhaled sharply as her attention darted from the dark horizon back to Runa. "Okay, enough of this cosmic weirdness. I need to focus." With a sudden burst of motion, she shot her arms out to the side, trying to wrestle control from the madness. "Here's what we're going to do: locate Mama D, head home, and sort out the community's food under the old oak."

Taking a beat, she added with biting sarcasm, "Because, you know, it's the perfect time to unravel more pending enigmas. I simply can't wait to dive into more riveting discussions."

Runa moved as if in slow motion, her reluctance evident in every gesture. She rose to her feet, the moonlight glinting off her dewy skin with an almost ghostly sheen. A shadow passed over her face. She said nothing at first, simply reaching out and clasping the wrists of her sisters. "I'm sorry…but we aren't done yet."

"What do you mean we aren't—" Rayanna started, but the instant Runa's fingers tightened around their skin, a jolt shot through them—sharp as lightning cracking through the marrow of their bones.

A blinding flash erupted, spreading outward in a cascade of searing light that swallowed everything. The beach, the sea, the sky—all vanished in an instant, consumed by a dazzling white void.

Runa's eyes widened, pupils contracting against the intensity of the light. Her muscles locked, the force of the surge holding her in place like a vise. She could feel the energy coursing through her veins—wild and untamed—as if she were a vessel for something far greater.

Her grip tightened involuntarily around their wrists, nails digging into their skin despite her desperate, silent plea to let go. As she stared at their joined limbs, the world began to dissolve. It warped and twisted around them, colors bleeding into one another like paint on a drenched canvas. The edges blurred, and reality flickered like an old film reel caught between frames.

Seconds stretched into eternity, each heartbeat a thunderous drum in their ears. An eerie, pulsating hum resonated deep in their bones. Rayanna and Tabytha finally recoiled, breaking free and gasping as they stumbled backward. They blinked furiously, eyes burning as they struggled to readjust to the dim reality around them. The beach reappeared, shadows creeping back into place beneath the muted moonlight. Their breath was shallow and ragged, as if they'd been dragged back from some abyss.

"Ru, what the hell?" Rayanna yelled, her voice sharp against the crashing waves. She clutched her hand to her chest, the skin feeling scorched. Her eyes squeezed shut, trying to block out the chaotic blur of images still flickering behind her eyelids—disjointed, merging fragments that refused to settle.

Beside her, Tabytha staggered. Her knees buckled, and she collapsed onto the sand. Lurching forward, she retched violently into a nearby bush, her body convulsing with the effort. The harsh sound of her gagging filled the air, mingling with the resuming rush of the tide.

Runa remained frozen, her body rigid. Her mind spun wildly as the cataclysmic door slammed shut within her with a resounding finality. The glow around her faded, leaving her standing in the cold, indifferent moonlight.

"I...I...*can't*..." she stammered, her voice trembling with a mix of urgency and confusion. Each word clawed its way out, leaving her hollow, as if the ordeal had reached inside and emptied her completely. She turned to face them, head drooping, shoulders slumped. "What did you see?" she whispered, her eyes barely meeting theirs.

Rayanna stood rooted to the spot, her gaze fixed on where the blinding light had been. "I...don't have...the words." She stared into the darkness, mouth parted, struggling to articulate the flood of images that had crashed over her.

Tabytha wiped her mouth with the back of her hand, her legs wobbling as she tried to stand. Her eyes were wide, pupils blown with shock. She furrowed her brow, the words tumbling out in a fractured mess. "Ru...I... How? What? I..." Her chest heaved as she forced the next words free. "Runa...what...the...hell...happened...to you? And who...is...Izayah?"

Her eyes darted across the sand, searching desperately, as if the answers might be written in the grains themselves. Confusion rippled across her face, twisting her features in disbelief. For a split second, her eyes flickered—a reddish-orange glow flaring to life before dimming back to their vibrant, darkened teal. Her gaze snapped to Runa, her voice cracking into a whisper.

"He exchanged his life for yours. Sacrificed himself...for you...for us. Why? Why would he do that?" Silence followed, thick and charged.

Chapter Eleven

The trio linked arms as they left the beach, moving through the town center. Runa felt the warmth of her sisters on either side—a small comfort against the misty chill that pulled in, rare and unsettling. *It's like I'm wading through clouds made of riddles—soft and strange and full of things that don't quite make sense,* she thought.

Each step felt endless, like trudging through quicksand. She focused on the path ahead, struggling to stay upright. The ground undulated softly—distorting, wavering, tugging at her balance in a lopsided, pointless dance. Friendly faces blurred at the edges, voices garbled and muffled like distortion through water.

She nodded absently when someone called out, managing a faint smile here and there. *Not now. Sorry. I just can't.* She refused to meet anyone's gaze, fearing they might glimpse the storm still swirling in her eyes. *It's like the change is invisible to everyone but me.*

Obscured figures drifted around them as they pressed onward, the crowd's laughter fading into a distant hum. Thick mist hung low, billowing around the tops of buildings like hand-pulled cotton candy, turning the edges of everything into a soft, dreamlike haze.

This can't be real. Runa swallowed hard, trying to push down the panic clawing at her chest. *Just keep moving. Just get home.* The air grew heavier as they approached the town square, suffocating in its sideways gravity. She tightened her grip on her sisters' arms, grounding herself in their presence.

Yet, as she looked around, it was clear no one else seemed to notice the eerie veil in the air. *Why can't they see any of this?* She staggered slightly, catching herself before she could fall. Each step became a battle, her legs trembling under the press of the lingering shadows trailing behind her. *Let them think I've lost my balance. It's easier than trying to make sense of something even I can't explain.*

As they neared the lighthouse, Runa's eyes caught a flicker of movement. Mama D stood in front of the towering structure, her posture commanding, the microphone clutched in one hand. She had taken her place as Master of Ceremonies—an image of authority and tradition that usually brought comfort. But tonight, something felt different.

Despite Mama D's presence, Runa heard nothing. The words that should have resounded through the square were muted, swallowed by the dense atmosphere. It was as if reality itself had been turned down to a whisper, leaving Runa adrift in a sea of murmurs and fragments.

She strained to hear, watching Mama D gesture grandly to the crowd, her lips moving in a speech she knew by heart. The words surfaced in Runa's mind like a ritual she'd memorized through repetition: *We will travel from home to home, exchanging starlight gifts and sharing feasts. It's more than a custom,* she echoed silently, her thoughts drifting in tandem with Mama D's gestures. *It's the glue that holds us together. It renews our bonds for the year ahead.*

Then their eyes met, and Runa's breath caught.

Mama D's gaze pierced through her like a bolt of lightning—sharp and unyielding, slicing through the numbness and leaving a dull ache in its wake. *She knows,* Runa realized. And for a moment, the world around them faded—the banter, the flickering lights, the fog-drenched buildings—slipping into the background. It was just them. Mama D's eyes held a depth of understanding that went beyond mere concern; she could see the storm raging within Runa. Her stance didn't shift, but something in her eyes did —a flicker of longing, the ache of someone who wanted to step forward, to abandon ceremony and reach for the child she once cradled. *But duty holds her in place.*

How does she know? Her heart pounded in her throat. It felt like looking into a mirror that reflected more than just her surface—it revealed all the jagged edges of her soul, the unspoken fears that threatened to consume her.

Mama D offered the smallest of nods, a barely perceptible movement that conveyed more than language ever could. It was a promise, a reassurance. *You're not alone. I see the darkness, and I'm still here.*

Runa exhaled slowly, feeling a slight easing of tension, though the questions still loomed like shadows on the edge of her consciousness. *What now?*

As they continued through the square, she dropped her gaze, letting the world dissolve around her once more. The only certainty she had in this moment was the warmth of her sisters beside her—and the path that lay ahead, leading them home.

Upon entering the cottage through the turquoise front door, Runa withdrew from her sisters immediately, retreating to the second-story balcony. Beyond the decking's ridge, the sounds of the festival drifted— barely more than a murmur on the breeze. Laughter, music—once so vibrant—now little more than reverberations from a world she no longer felt a part of.

Finally alone, Runa slipped into the stillness, lifting her gaze to the stars. They blazed above, fierce and unyielding, their light flooding the dark emptiness in her chest—offering to drown out the storm roaring inside her, if she would just let them. So she allowed their brilliance to pour into her, burning through the turmoil.

Then, like a gift, sound gradually returned—steadied itself—and brought her in, wrapping her in something both haunting and delicate. It mingled with distant chatter, became a melodic string that curled around her mind like mist, caressing her consciousness, coaxing her to come up and play.

Runa pushed back. She fought to keep it from seeping into the raw, open spaces inside her—those places that still felt too vulnerable, too exposed.

Tonight, the darkness wasn't just a quiet refuge; it was alive. A force wrestling with the fragments of her light. Her ebony hair, pulled into a tight ponytail, had begun to unravel—twisting in loose tendrils across her shoulders. Something that was real. A tether. An anchor to keep her here, to keep her from being swept into that boundless, cold sky. The reality of what felt like the world played tug-of-war with her mind. It was disorienting—the fear of losing herself. *Unraveling. Unbinding.* These words struggled to the surface, clawing painfully up her throat, which her throat bit back, *You can't be doing this on your own. This isn't for you to complete alone.*

The dark looped tighter—a serpent winding around her heart, anchoring itself to her spine. The shadows refused to retreat. *You are not these wraiths,* a faint voice whispered.

Her body convulsed, arching upward with a sharp, involuntary motion as if trying to wrench free. She reeled back, breath catching—*but they move as if they know me.*

Above her, the sky stretched wide and endless, consuming. It beckoned her to let go, to join them, to dance among the stars, to feel completed. And yet—something about it all felt deeply, dangerously wrong.

They might have been vast bonfires, blazing bright across the heavens —but from so far below, the celestial lanterns shimmered like winking embers strewn across the void. Hidden truths surged forward, pressing against the mental barricade she had built so carefully. A woman's voice— soft, soothing—drifted from somewhere beyond: *Hold on, dear. I'm coming for you.* A little yellow bird fluttered close. A tear beaded and trickled from its beak.The brilliance—whether above or within, she couldn't be sure— pressed harder. The radiance demanded entry. Demanded acknowledgment. Tears flooded her waterline as she struggled through the contorting pain. Runa gritted her teeth, pulse quickening as the cosmic blooms bore down—relentless, gleaming with insistence.

They weren't just distant glimmers. They were questions. Tugging at tangled threads within her, coaxing her to unravel what had long been buried. Part of her urged resistance—to clutch the silence within Starlight, the space that had become her sanctuary. But the pull was steady. Gnawing. Unignorable. *Why do you keep searching for a way out? Don't you like it here? Or are you getting bored with the mundane? Are you missing the taste of your quintessence?* The questions flared—raw, unbidden.

She writhed against the gloom that clung to her, a tenebrous grip snaking around her essence like creeping vines. *My mind is caught in a web,* she thought, *trapped in the murky depths—of light…and of uncertain dark.* And still, the starlight persisted. Piercing. Reaching through the fog with sharp illumination, revealing glimpses of something hidden, untouched.

Her inhale snagged as a thrum rose inside her—uninvited. Not a voice. Not a thought. Just a flicker of a wordless, half-formed presence, curling up in the hollow of her chest like it had nowhere else to go. It didn't anchor—it receded, drawing inward until it became almost *nothing*. A fragile hush where a cry might have lived. She couldn't tell if it belonged to the light or the dark. Couldn't tell if it was something new trying to surface…or something old, long buried, too afraid to be seen. Maybe it was hers—maybe it had always been—but it came without language, without shape.

Just the quiet ache of something that had once tried to speak and had been taught not to. *Then it fell away.* In the hollow of her chest, it curled tighter—pulling back into the shadows that had always made room for *her* silence.

The darkness here…it was obscurity. A sameness. A repetition. A comforting bind. Starlight was safety. Starlight was the place to stay hidden. *And the dark*—it welcomed the pieces of her that had never been allowed to speak.

Here, no one will come looking for you.

No one cares enough to.

You are nothing, a new voice whispered.

Stay small. Stay pitifully safe. You won't stay hidden for long. The words wrapped around her like a thorn-covered blanket of isolation—a battering ram of quiet.

As much as I love Starlight, I can't stay. I will cave it all in…

The radiance pressed harder now—A golden sphere glided into view, ghostly and ethereal, hovering just beyond her reach like a silent guardian catching the updraft.

It shifted, wobbled in the light, and then—

—transformed.

Wings.

Feathers.

Some kind of bird. A swallow? A warbler?

I was never good with birds.

But then the light hit her. *Blinding.* Not sight, but sensation—every nerve alight.

She could feel it scraping along the inside of her skull—insistent.

Knocking.

Knocking on a door.

Open, my dear…

You know you want to let me in.

This ebb and flow wasn't gentle; it was relentless—prying at the corners of her awareness that had long been sealed away. The shadow binding constricted Runa's consciousness like ghosted tendrils, winding inward, unwilling to loosen their grip. The light wasn't just offering answers—it wanted something she couldn't give, because she didn't hold the key. She closed her eyes and inhaled sharply, steadying herself. This was a battle she hadn't even known she was waging—a quiet war between the darkness that had kept her bound and the light now pressing to break through. Runa gripped the wooden planks tighter, her knuckles turning white.

Then came the voice—not loud, not even distinct, but calm, drifting through her like warm radiance over cold stone. *You are part of something far greater than your own darkness. More than this storm. More than the shadows that bind you.* The words arrived like memory and truth, seamlessly stitched together.

She opened her eyes and pulled herself upright, the floor beneath her groaning in protest. The message wove through her like a song—subtle, but unmistakable: *You've been given two decades to breathe. A fresh start, away from everything you knew.* Her breath caught, then released in a trembling exhale.

Runa leaned into the edge of the balcony, the solid wood grounding her in the now. Fingers skimmed the railing before curling around it—less a grip for survival, more a quiet acknowledgment. The storm within hadn't disappeared, but its edges had softened, dulled by something just beyond understanding. Breath filled her lungs, and for the first time in what felt like forever, she didn't resist. *Okay,* the thought came—not with panic or weight, but with clarity. *It's time.*

In her new version of reality—this reshaped darkness—she released expectation behind closed eyelids, and allowing for reorientation of knowing. At first, it was subtle: a single knot loosening within. Her mind stretched outward, slipping itself into the night like tendrils of smoke dispersing into open air. A quiet force tugged gently at her, coaxing her thoughts beyond the edges of herself, drawing them into the vast expanse of stars above.

Suddenly, she was standing on a wooden-planked bridge suspended in an inky gloom, the world cloaked in silence. Each step rang out in the chasm—a *tap-tap-tap* that reverberated through the stillness like a question waiting to be asked. The air was dense, laden with all that had been left unsaid, emotions too tightly bound and sealed away.

To her side, a towering obsidian wall rose from the dark—smooth, cold, and stretching beyond sight. She reached out, letting her fingertips graze its surface. The chill crept into her skin, anchoring her amidst the quiet chaos within. As she walked, her hand trailed the wall's length—solid, unmoving, a quiet promise of truth waiting beneath the surface. *Is this what I've been hiding from,* she realized. *This darkness isn't all that I am. It's only a part.*

She stopped mid-step, palm pressed flat to the obsidian. Beneath her touch, the surface pulsed—one slow thrum echoing the rhythm of her heart. The shadows quivered, and from the stone's center, warmth unfurled, spreading up her arm and into her chest. It pressed against the tight coils inside her, unwinding them, one silent strand at a time. *I am not just darkness. I am not just pain.* The truth struck deep, rooted and undeniable. She trembled, allowing the heat to wash through, softening every place she had walled off.

And as she lingered at the threshold—suspended between earth and sky, between memory and becoming—something within began to loosen. The outermost wisps of the shadow binding, the ones nearest the surface of her mind, started to dissolve. These were the ties easiest to reach in this liminal space, the ones ready to be unfastened.

A flicker of warmth moved through her thoughts, brushing the edges of her consciousness. *I'm no longer resisting,* the thought glided gently through her, soft as breath. Her palm remained on the stone, now glowing faintly—its heartbeat thrumming against her skin. *I will yield.*

Then, a sliver of sound seeped in—a familiar tone spilled through the void. *Hey, Ru?* The phrase rippled through the stillness enveloping her. Runa's eyelids fluttered at the surreal quality of the moment, too weary to even be surprised. Deep in her gut, she knew: Rayanna's presence wasn't beside her—it was within her, folded into the quiet seams of her consciousness.

Mmh. The low sound vibrated through the balcony's floorboards.

You okay? The question came again—clearer now, though still distant. Like a whisper stretched across a great chasm.

Yes, but...I don't want to anymore. The truth slipped out before she could contain it, her chest tightening with the rawness of her own admission.

Why? It resounded—reverberating through the chambers of her mind like a call flung from one cliffside to another.

Runa hesitated. It felt like standing on the edge of an unseen bridge, staring through the fog toward where Rayanna might be waiting on the other side. *I think...my lungs have cracked from the weight of it all.* The confession ached, every syllable delicate and trembling—suspended between them like fine-spun gossamer, a web glistening in moonlight, ready to break.

Softer this time, yet unwavering, Rayanna's cadence returned. *I know—I saw it all too. But you don't have to figure it out at once, you know?*

Her voice folded around her like a blanket, warmth seeping into the coldest corners of Runa's mind. Tears welled, swelling thick in her throat. A pause followed, stretching long and fragile across their shared mental thread.

Ru? Barely more than an utterance in the dark.

Nnh. The hum spilled from Runa's lips, fracturing her resolve like splintered glass. She inhaled sharply as tears beaded—and *listened.*

Rayanna's presence pressed close—not physically, but in the way warmth seeps into chilled skin. Runa could almost feel it: the subtle hush in Rayanna's breath, the way she likely bit down on her lower lip to keep it from trembling. Her words came tenderly, carefully placed like stones across a riverbed, meant to steady. *It's okay for your heart to ache...but you don't have to face this storm alone.*

A shiver rippled down Runa's spine as Rayanna's steady warmth wrestled the cold, still clinging to her bones.

In the quiet that followed, she imagined Rayanna again—jaw clenched now, probably blinking fast to keep the tears at bay. That kind of effort said more than words ever could. *It's not like before Starlight. No more alone, okay?*

Runa nodded, though no one could see it. Her thoughts unraveled in methodical waves, like spooling vines winding through a sleeping forest. *Mmh…I know.*

Another beat of silence. *Ray?* The name escaped like frost lacing the edge of a window.

Yeah, Ru? The response came swift and sure—like Rayanna was already extending her hand across the dark.

Runa's throat burned. Her chest ached with the pressure of the question she had never dared speak aloud. *Who could ever love me…once they know?* The words barely made it out before her shoulders sagged, the weight of them dragging her inward. Her fingers dug into the fabric near her ribs, as if trying to hold herself together. The question was heavy and dense, dropping into the space between them. It sank, pulling at her spirit, threatening to drag her under.

Rayanna didn't rush to answer. Somewhere in that hush, something aligned—like constellations easing into place. *Someone…fantastically significant.*

Runa bit down on the inside of her lip, hard enough to taste copper. Her shoulders trembled. The truth of it scraped against her like broken glass—beautiful and unbearable. The tears came hard, hot and fast, pooling until they spilled. A torrential downpour she didn't have the energy to stop—and somehow, it felt freeing to let them go.

It'll be like a celestial match written in the stars—like the moon drawn to the tides, or the sun rising for the day, Rayanna continued, her voice gaining steadiness as Runa's gave way beneath the weight of it all. *There is someone out there—not out of obligation. Not bound by duty or expectation. It'll be someone who chooses to carry your pain simply because they can't not. Because walking away would feel wrong in the marrow of their bones. Because loving you will feel as natural as breathing. Not for what you've survived, but for who you are. And when they finally see it all—every scar, every truth—they won't run.*

They'll stay. Not despite it, but because of it. Because something in them will recognize something in you...and it will only burn brighter.

For a moment, everything stilled. The air around Runa quieted, heavy with reverence. Somewhere inside, a door creaked shut—softly, finally—sealing off the noise of the world beyond. The connection between them lingered a heartbeat longer...then slipped away. Runa was alone again, trembling, bathed in the light of a thousand stars. *Please,* she pleaded, *let her be right.*

Rayanna shook her head, huffing out a sigh as the cottage's communal lights swam back into focus. Her gaze darted around the living space— walls softly aglow with Starlight Festival lanternlight. *One more bizarre thing and I'm officially filing a complaint with someone at the Department of Sanity.* She blinked several times through the absurdity, adjusting as the blur of her vision sharpened into place. It was like resurfacing from under- water, a heaviness still clinging to her ribs. The room felt—*somehow*—too normal after what had just transpired.

She rubbed at her eyes. *Yep. Whoever's running this version of reality is doing a terrible job.* Pushing herself upright, she wandered toward the wide balcony doors. Beyond the open glass, the world shimmered—not wrong, not right, but undeniably altered, as if mid-transformation. *Alive.* As if the energy itself pulsed outward from the heart of their little cottage. *It's more than Runa's decor.*

She squinted into the dazzle, the scene before her both achingly familiar and painfully new. The festivities surged through the moongate and spilled into the gravel street beyond—laughter and music rising like star- dust, dancing in the brilliance like fireflies. Her heart swelled with warmth...and *buckled* at the same time. *This moment was her sister*—woven into every lantern's glow, stitched into the notes of every chorus. *A celebra- tion she'd helped imagine.* And yet, she stood apart—tangled in shadows she couldn't name, unable to step fully into the brilliance she helped create.

Leaning against the back of the massive L-shaped sofa, Rayanna filled her lungs—and the realization: *We just had a full-blown fucking conversation.* She blinked, trying to process the gravity of it all. *I'm not sure how I feel about this.* With a long exhale, she straightened and stepped toward the jubilant crowd gathered beneath the oak. The driveway and street had become an open-air celebration—tables laden with food, younglings darting between gift exchanges, laughter spilling like wind chimes in motion. *Tonight was meant for joy, for renewal.*

And yet, her gift tonight was simpler. *I would be Runa's shield*—the quiet strength only an older sister could offer. *Right now, Ru just needs space. A moment to be.* A tear slipped down Rayanna's cheek, unexpected but heavy with meaning. She swiped it away, lifting her gaze to the stars. And somehow, she knew: *When the indigo sky softened into sunrise…answers would come. But for now, this moment would have to be enough.*

Chapter Twelve

Diesel's gaze settled on Nester, who sat perched on the coffee table, the tome squirming restlessly beneath him. Raising his glass in a relaxed salute, he acknowledged his radiant companion's thought. *Will she be ready?*

He shifted in his chair, the leather creaking faintly, unsettling the threads of worry he'd worked hard to suppress. A tense silence filled the room, broken only by the faint, rhythmic thudding of the restless book under Nester's small frame. *That book, always so restless,* Diesel thought, glancing at Nester. The short, little figure remained poised, the light from his bulb-head flickering in sync with the tome's movements. It was as if he, too, was waiting for an answer.

"Thoughtfully played, Nester." Diesel finally said, his voice steady, though doubt crept in around the edges. "The real concern is—*will any of them be prepared?*" He scanned the room for answers, eyes landing on the whiskey glass beside him. "Doesn't *really* matter, *does it?* Whatever the future holds, it's coming for them—*ready or not.*"

Nester paused, his light fluttering thoughtfully, as he glanced at the manuscript beneath him. Then, with a quick, deft hop, he landed soundlessly on the worn rug. The book sprang to life the moment he left, its blackened edges crackling. It shot across the room, with faint wisps of dust trailing, like a bird escaping its nest—or a dragon shaking off old ashes. Purposeful in its flight, it nestled itself among the other volumes on the bookshelf, tucking in with a soft rustle. Diesel allowed himself a brief exhale, amusement dancing across his features.

Always for the dramatics, he thought. His eyes lifted back to Nester, who had begun pacing in front of the fireplace. The rhythmic tap-tap of his small frame against the floor filled the room, bringing a calm that eased Diesel's nerves. Gradually, he relaxed into the plush chair, resting the glass indifferently on one knee.

That subtle rhythm Nester carried with him always had a way of granting Diesel a momentary reprieve from the weight of command. It gave him space to pause—to breathe—while his mind continued to churn. He could sense the little lamp's wheels turning, sorting information, preparing for the conversation to come. Nester was a quiet constant amid the chaos, something that kept him anchored in the now.

This study had always been his refuge. A place to compartmentalize, to prepare for what lay ahead. *I wish it still offered answers the way it did back when Ezekiel was here—when we could sit across from one another and sort through the world together.*

Diesel's eyes narrowed as he studied the charred surface of the coffee table. With a subtle flick of his fingers, light began to gather—coalescing into form. Slowly, a slender structure emerged from the table's center, its edges humming with energy. *Starlight's sentinel.* Rising in miniature, the familiar tower took shape, its base wavering slightly as it stabilized. The faint shimmer danced across the surrounding furniture, as if remembering what it was built to protect.

He leaned forward, letting the image settle into the space between them. Not just a symbol. A reminder. *We forged it to reclaim what was lost—to strip away the rot and raise something that could stand long after we were gone. The bones of Starlight weren't laid for comfort. The stronghold buried in the cliffs —that was our anchor. Hardened. Permanent.*

Starlight Beach, though...that was our forward base. Tactical by design.

Temporary, if it had to be. It was there to deploy, to support, to absorb the first blow. But over time—quietly, stubbornly—it outgrew that purpose. It adapted. It became something else. Something we never planned for. And now, running through its very foundation, the intent we carved into it still hums, steady as ever.

From the hearth, Nester slowed. The small figure turned, his head tilting toward the table as the shimmer from his bulb met the tower's quiet pulse. Elongated shadows stretched along the study walls, swaying with the rhythm of thought. Diesel didn't move. Elbows on knees, glass in hand, he kept his focus steady—held in the expanse between memory and what still needed doing.

Nester resumed his pacing, signaling that he had absorbed Diesel's thoughts. He was more than just an ally; he was a fragment of the quintessence they had all sworn to protect. Ezekiel had understood that when he entrusted him with Nester—a secret Diesel had guarded fiercely, knowing the potential locked within his radiant companion. The little light held the power to save, but also to destroy, if wielded without care.

As Nester continued his mindful trek, Diesel's gaze returned to the bookshelf. The tome had nestled itself there, charred edges half-hidden among the other volumes. *Such a character—just like my Ray of Sunshine,* he thought with a faint smile. *Always finding a way to make an exit, always with a flair for the dramatics.*

His focus darted back to the glowing lighthouse projection. With a leisurely, swish of his hand, Diesel set the image spinning on an invisible axis across the scorched tabletop.

"Once, it had simply been the Shadow Guard Training Installation," he began, his voice quiet yet resonant, as the projection altered. The lighthouse dimmed, replaced by a rugged coastline. Jagged cliffs emerged, bathed in the amber light of a setting sun, the restless waves of the Twilight Sea crashing hard against the rock.

Nester moved closer, settling just before the projection with the ease of someone who'd heard the story a thousand times—yet never seemed to tire of it. With a soft thump, he plopped down, resting his bulbous head in his piped hands.

"Back then, it was nothing like what it is now," Diesel continued, eyes locked on the memory rising before them. "The original base was hollowed from the cliff's edge—no entrances visible from the sea. Its placement was strategic. Nearly impenetrable. Hidden from sight. You could only reach it by narrow, winding paths along the cliffside and the rear of the mountain. The lion's head—the emblem of Shadow City—was carved into the rock much later, after the Great War. Before that, there were no symbols. Just stone. Just sea and wind."

Nester nodded, as the hologram zoomed in on the cliffs, revealing a network of tunnels carved deep into the rock. "King Moros knew of its existence, of course," Diesel added, a hint of bitterness in his tone. "As the ruler of Shadow City, he worked closely with General Brannon to establish this bastion. It was here they molded all factions of the Shadow army, training not just standard guards, but the Elite units."

As Diesel's gaze fell on the projection, faintly crackling within the seared edges of the coffee table, his jaw tightened. The dim glow of candle-light cast shifting shadows across the display, creating a haunting, almost spectral image of the stronghold—a fortress of stone and shade that felt both imposing and eerily familiar. It sprawled across the tabletop, alive with hidden secrets and untold history, pulsing like a heartbeat beneath layers of memory.

Nester watched in reverent silence, the display responding to the inflections of Diesel's voice. With each word, visions of vast courtyards carved deep into the mountain's core took shape, where warriors sparred under the weight of rock, and concealed chambers where Elite units honed their craft came into view.

"The cradle of power—a proving ground where loyalty was forged, and only the strongest emerged to serve the future ruler of Shadow City." He paused within the swell of nostalgia, his gaze tracing spectral figures drifting through the stronghold's labyrinthine tunnels—ghosts of old comrades, their faces blurred by time, yet their loyalty etched into every slab of stone. Within the illusion's layered glow, the corridors stirred with motion, beckoning him inward—down through spiraling passageways hewn from the cliffside, dense with memory and the weight of long-buried commands.

The damp scent of mildew and brine clung to the air. The metallic bite of iron curled through his senses, sharp and unmistakable. The steady *ting-chink-ting* of practice blades rang in cadence—measured, relentless. Boots struck with muffled thuds, the clatter of armor trailing close behind, reverberating through the cold stone as if the mountain itself remembered. Diesel exhaled. "All of this matters," he said. "What we built still beats beneath it all." His hand unconsciously clenched as he spoke, the display faltering in response, as if mirroring his tension. This wasn't just a memory. It was a fragment of him—a chapter seared into his soul as indelibly as the table's scorched edges.

"General Brannon oversaw the recruits," Diesel said, his voice dropping an octave, eyes narrowing as he searched for Brannon's unmistakable silhouette in the shadows. "Ruthless but fair. He stripped away weakness, sharpening our strengths. This was where soldiers first learned to wield their own quintessence—channeling their energy under Brannon's unforgiving command."

The image panned, centering on the complex's central tower. Diesel exhaled, the weight of memory pressing down. "Even then, it was more than a training ground. This was the core of Brannon's military. A fortress built on secrecy and strength…and the very thing that would later define—and eventually break—Moros during the Great War."

Nester listened intently, absorbing each detail. The hologram slowly faded back to the lighthouse, still turning atop the console. *A cradle of power,* he mused, the phrase repeating softly in his mind. One small piped hand tapped thoughtfully beneath his bulbous head, as if mimicking a chin he didn't have. *And now…it's grown into something far greater.*

Diesel nodded, his gaze lingering on the charred base of the projection as the glow of the lighthouse returned to its steady sweep. "Yes," he murmured, the word thick with the burden of memory, as the beam continued its silent arc—illuminating shards of what once was and what still remained.

"During the war," his voice turned gruff as the lighthouse shimmered and dissolved, revealing the outpost carved into the cliff's edge—fortified, hidden, pulsing with buried strength. "The base held strong as we forged the Shadow Guard Elite. Before then, the installation was secretive, yes—but once the war took hold, it became something else. Brannon knew we couldn't keep training them the same way. He escalated everything." He paused. "Brannon led the early training. Later, I was placed at the helm—sent ahead to halt Moros' advance before it crushed everything we'd established."

The console's glow altered once more, the image dimming before lifting again. Another memory emerged—this one washed in thick, spiraling mist. It unfurled across low valleys and coiled like smoke along the jagged ridges of distant peaks.

Diesel leaned forward slightly, jaw tightening. "We are getting ahead of ourselves," he muttered. *"But this...*wall of mist and shadow...arrived, after the war. Like *The Land* itself was trying to recover—shield something, or hide what couldn't be undone." His eyes followed the projection's tendrils as they curled and rolled across the tabletop. "It doesn't behave like natural fog. It lingers. Settled with purpose." He exhaled. "The projection must think it's relevant...*otherwise,* it wouldn't be showing it now."

Nester rose in a fluid motion, almost weightless, and drifted toward the charred edge of the coffee table. *Because of that wall of mist and shadow, we had to restructure after the Great War,* he said, his voice lacing through the framework of thought. *New borders. A chance for civilians to reclaim what was lost.* A hint of pale green fluttered through his light—brief curiosity— before settling back into its usual warm filament. *But, like you said, sir... we're getting ahead of ourselves.*

Diesel nodded, his gaze fixed on the holographic display as the light-house rotated once more, casting its beam over a sequence of splintered recollections—scenes of fractured buildings, scattered banners, people hauling stone and timber, sweat glinting on their foreheads. "King Moros..." he muttered, the name tasting of rust and grit. "The chaos he stirred. The power grabs. The control..." His jaw tightened. "He cracked the realm open and let the worst of it crawl through."

Can you tell me more about how it ended? Nester asked, his light dimming slightly, as if bracing for the answer. *You've spoken of it before, but only in fragments.* The image responded—no longer ruins and rebuilding, but a looming figure cloaked entirely in black: boots streaked with ash, a sword dragging against stone, a hood veiling every feature. Silent, unmoving. And yet, the weight of his presence pressed like iron into the air.

"He wasn't just an enemy," Diesel said, the words settling like iron. "He was the ruler of Shadow City. That made him something else entirely." His voice lowered, darkening with memory. "When someone that tied to the city's core turns on it...it's not just betrayal. It's collapse. The kind that shakes everything you've built." He exhaled through his nose. "The

Obsidian Legion—Moros' personal force—bent the quintessence fires to their will, turning something sacred into a weapon. They left entire stretches of land hollowed out and scorched to the bone."

Nester's light pulsed, and his voice curled gently into Diesel's mind. *Why would King Moros need his own legion when he already had the Shadow Guard and the Elite?*

Diesel's gaze dropped to the console, the projection blurring into coils of smoke. "Because he knew the Shadow Guard didn't stand behind him," he said. "Most of us didn't believe in what he was trying to do. And he knew it." His fingers drummed once against the arm of his chair. "The Elites weren't his, either. General Brannon handpicked them—pulled them from the Guard and forged them into something new. Something sharper. While that was happening, Moros was busy building in secret. The Obsidian Legion came from the Tree of Shadow, born out of demonkind and bound to his will alone." He leaned forward slightly. "That's when the divide became undeniable. When the Shadow Guild rose from Brannon's rebellion."

Nester's head bobbed again in understanding, though his glow flared to a pale amber—his version of surprise—as if lifting an invisible brow. *So, General Brannon wanted the helm of Shadow City...and took his stance to save the metropolis?* Diesel gave a tight nod, his jaw clenched as the scene morphed, revealing once-vibrant regions blackened and burning, their skeletal remains a stark contrast to the vision of what had once been.

"The Shadow Guard rallied," he muttered. "Citizens fought to keep the younglings safe. It was a battle for more than territory—it was for the essence of life." Nester remained silent as he listened, his pacing waning to a near stop. His light dimmed in sync with Diesel's memory, shadows flickering across the walls as if the story itself weighed the air around them.

I know we've spoken of this before, Nester finally offered, his tone gentle, contemplative. *But...I still don't understand why King Moros would turn everything toward war. I know your answer's always been power—but it never feels like enough. Not for what he unleashed.* The projection on the console darkened, the image swirling into a chaotic blur, mirroring Diesel's inner turmoil. Diesel didn't speak—he didn't need to. The ghosts of the past said enough, rising in the flickering light like a verdict handed down in silence.

"Fools." Diesel's focus narrowed, muttering to himself. "They couldn't see it—couldn't grasp that wielding power without reverence for its source, would only ever lead to ruin." The image of Shadow City glowed intermittently, its walls trembling beneath the weight of internal strife. "The citadel nearly tore itself apart," his tone was taut with restrained fury. "The Shadow Guard had to fight battles both within and beyond its gates."

The view shifted again, dissolving into a new image—Sanctuary's ancient Tree of Life, encircled by a swirling vortex of raw quintessence. Diesel's breath caught. He watched Moros appear at the tree's base, his figure cloaked in shadow, siphoning power through his bond to Shadow City. It had seemed limitless then. Invincible. And yet…Diesel knew what came next.

"But in that crucial moment," he said, barely more than a whisper, "it wasn't a sword or spell that broke his grip on the core." He leaned in as the projection rippled, transforming into a darkened path. "It was adamantine." The image deepened, revealing vast caverns veiled in an emerald sheen, their walls humming with an ancient energy. The journey had been brutal. The metal—nearly impossible to reach. And still, they had gone.

The display reoriented. Diesel's own silhouette emerged within the projection, flanked by fellow Elite Guards as they advanced through the narrow pass. Each footfall landed with soft precision, forming a muted rhythm swallowed by the low thrum of pressure all around them. The corridor constricted with damp heaviness, walls beaded with condensation. Before them, the fractured ridge loomed—its rugged surface laced with stress veins glinting faintly under their lanterns. From his belt, Diesel withdrew a wedge, its edge forged from rare adamantine—crafted not for battle, but for precision. A gift from the Valley of Visions' blacksmiths. He fitted it to a fissure and drove it into the fault line with a single, exacting strike.

A sharp report rang out. The ridge splintered with a groan, a hiss of age-bound air escaping as a section cracked away from the greater wall. Behind the fracture, a gleaming vein of adamantine emerged—not luminous, but reactive. The metal bent the lantern light itself, its surface rippling with subtle iridescence: petrol blue, burnished silver, dusky violet. No single hue defined it. The sheen morphed with every glance, as though it existed outside the known spectrum. Behind him, the unit stood silent.

They all understood what it meant—what it could do—and what it had cost to reach it.

At the console's edge in the study, Nester stepped closer, his small frame casting an elongated shadow across the table's scorched surface. His bulbous head brightened momentarily to a curious aquamarine before returning to its familiar golden hue. *You were the one who found it*, he murmured, more to himself than to Diesel. After a moment, he tilted his head. *But how did you even know where to look?* The light inside him flickered thoughtfully. *You've never said.*

Diesel didn't answer right away. His gaze remained on the image, the last shimmer of adamantine fading into the memory. "There were whispers," he said at last, his voice low. "An old blacksmith from the Valley of Visions—the one, that had crafted the extraction wedge. He used to talk about a fault line tucked beneath the northern spine beyond the Valley. Said the mountain was hollowed by something older than memory, and the metal sang if you listened right." His grip tightened slightly on the edge of the table. "Most wrote it off as legend. I didn't have that luxury."

The projection swept forward, no longer centered on Diesel himself but gliding like a silent observer across riverbanks and jagged ridgelines, tracing the winding route he once traveled. It skimmed through narrow canyons chiseled by time, cutting across forgotten highlands toward a distant, mist-veiled enclave: the Valley of Visions. Known only in hushed tones, the valley was a refuge for seers and craftsmen who preferred secrecy to spectacle. The image descended through dense treetops and quiet foothills before settling on a small, secluded forge nestled against the curve of the mountain.

Within that hidden forge, the blacksmith moved with deliberation. Diesel watched as the elder hunched over a massive anvil, hammering glowing lengths of adamantine into shape—each strike casting bursts of light that danced against soot-darkened walls. Unlike common metal, the adamantine didn't glow outright. Instead, its surface responded to the flame like living ore, its sheen shifting from oil-slick blues to muted silver and shadowed lilac. The chains were dipped into a basin of obsidian lacquer to cloak their true nature, the final touch before they were cooled and set aside in silence. These weren't weapons. They were bindings— meant for something much older, much darker.

In a quiet corner of the forge, Diesel recalled kneeling beside a youngling—nimble fingers flicking jacks across the floor in intricate patterns. His laughter rang like a thread of hope, innocent and unburdened. Diesel had often found his eyes drifting toward the child, drawn to that untarnished spirit even as the world around them prepared for war. The contrast had stayed with him. It reminded him why they fought.

Nester's bulbous head flared briefly, a wash of aquamarine rippling through his core—the color he reserved for when memory collided with meaning. He didn't speak at first. The room felt heavier, the halo from the projection casting long shadows over the study's walls. His filament softened. *And you placed the chains in the hands of your Elites. The ones who bled beside you. The ones who helped unearth what was never meant to be found.*

The forge dissolved into ash, curling at the projection's edge like smoke. In its place, the dense expanse of the Dark Forest emerged, unfurling in twilight. Gnarled trees clawed at the sky, their limbs twisted by war. Small outposts and fractured havens flickered among the roots—forgotten places caught between Sanctuary's light and Shadow City's hunger. This was no staging ground. It was a crucible. *The war had already swallowed everything it touched,* Nester continued, the words catching slightly in his throat. *And the Elites...they didn't brace for it. They walked straight into its teeth.*

Nester's little piped hand touched down on the scorched edge of the coffee table. The display spun sharply—one full rotation, fast and deliberate—before halting with a soft click. At the center, a figure materialized, clad in the unmistakable garb of the Shadow Guard: boots laced nearly to the knees, dark leather strapped across his chest and forearms, and a hooded cloak drawn low over his face. Every inch of him was cast in black, an extension of the shadows themselves.

There was no mistaking him.

With a subtle movement, the figure let the hood fall. Liam's face materialized—more stubble than beard, younger, yet every bit as unyielding. His brow furrowed in that familiar way, two distinct lines etched between his eyes like the weight of command had carved them there. Just beneath his right cheekbone, the faint shimmer of thought woven ink curled like smoke across his skin, a tattoo that marked not just his rank, but the burdens he'd carried. He stood unwavering in the chaos—unshaken, unblinking—as if daring the world to break first.

He held rank, aye, Nester said, a trace of Liam's own irreverence sneaking into his tone. A pulse of amber-pink shimmered—humor and quiet admiration bleeding through the hue, exhaled as something between a chuckle and a sigh. *But that's not what people remember. It's his loyalty. The way he never flinched—not when the ground cracked beneath him, not when the mission turned to fire.* He tilted his head toward the wet bar, where the portrait sat bare, as if half-expecting Liam to already be standing there— grinning, arms crossed, ready to interrupt. *Still,* Nester added with a small, blooming smirk—his light briefly trailing like a filament caught in long-exposure—*if you ask him, he'll say it's the tongue they remember. Sharp, unforgiving—like he wears it as a badge. Contradictory, maybe. But fitting. That's Liam.*

The visual feed dimmed, curling inward like breath before a storm. It didn't cast Liam as a hero—just a man who stepped into fire with open eyes. He volunteered. No hesitation. No command required to send him— just the clarity of what had to be done. That's what forged him Elite.

His form wavered as the unit descended into the underbelly of Shadow City, cloaked in the illusion of Obsidian Legion armor—dread-helms shadowing their faces, war-forged plating swallowing the light, their eyes masked beneath veils of quintessence glamour. The adamantine chains were pressed close beneath their cloaks, like secrets too dangerous to name. Every step they took didn't echo with sound—but with resolve, sharpened like the edge of a blade. What they carried wasn't just burden. It was cost. It was consequence. And it was carved into every footfall.

The people of the Dark Forest helped disguise them, Nester continued, his voice quieter now, as if the memory itself deserved reverence. They made it possible—one final defiance, silent and sacred. On the table's surface, the render tilted, the grain beading up with snaking tendrils of light. The gnarled roots of the Tree of Shadow twisted violently in the console's glow, thrashing as though it sensed what approached. The bindings struck like lightning—adamantine igniting with a light that looked like starfire, coiling around decay and drawing taut. Corruption buckled. Light tore through the city's foundations, scalding the darkness with a force that was more than fury. *It wasn't a weapon. It was judgment. It was The Land's final reprieve.*

The vision swelled with one last flare of brilliance—and then, from the scorched edges of the coffee table, *darkness.*

Diesel sat in stillness, his head bowed. The air in the study felt heavier now, blanketed in the weight of what had just passed. No words rose to meet the silence, only the faint hum of the console cooling in the aftermath.

Beside him, Nester's light receded into an ash-ringed smolder—mirroring the scorched edges of the aged table, grief dusted in coal black. *None of our Elites returned.* His bulbous head tilted downward, trails of condensation beading quietly along the inner glass—grief drawn in silence.

The seared surface of the coffee table seemed to understand the moment, reigniting with a spark of memory just as the holoform of the adamantine bindings tightened around the Tree of Shadow. Then came the rupture—without warning but not without cause.

The projection zoomed outward, presenting a bird's-eye view of The Lands, the console acting as if it contained the epicenter of the blast. From the Tree's location in the heart of Shadow City, a ring of pulsing energy surged outward, cracking through the surface like buried thunder breaking free. Fire-kissed veins split across the wood grain in tandem, the projection shuddering with a force that felt too real. Shadow and mist surged outward from the ruptured earth, rising in tandem with the glowing fissures. A crescent-shaped wall unfurled, swelling skyward and sweeping west—encasing the regions beyond Shadow City and Sanctuary. In a single, breathless motion, the arc of its boundary sealed the outer territories, stretching all the way to the borders of the Valley of Visions.

The shockwave hit the study like a current. Nester's small frame was hurled backward, tumbling into a startled roll. Before he could collide with the bookcase, Diesel's hand shot out—stabilizing and instinctive—catching him mid-motion. Nester sprang upright in an instant, like a startled cat, his filament sputtering as if a connection had briefly gone loose.

The weaved form of the seared coffee table began to ease, the hologram gradually holding firm. The once-writhing map fell into stillness. Along the western edge, the arc of fog remained—its curvature illuminating the newly sealed ridge of the realm. Beyond it, The Land's scars stretched in both directions, scorched and hollowed, lifeless beneath the crescent's reach. Mist thickened like a cocoon, concealing whatever endured on either side of the divide. Whether the veil had sealed the world in—or barred something unspeakable from getting out—neither side provided answers.

With a quiet thump, Nester plopped back down along the hearth's edge, light dimmed, shoulders low. *Perspective, after all, has always been the architect of belief,* he offered.

Diesel leaned forward, elbows resting on his knees, the low gleam of the console catching in the planes of his face. "Couldn't be more true," he said quietly. "And belief…that's what held us together when everything else cracked."

Just then, Missy rattled the floorboards beneath the projection table—a bright, eager nudge as if to say, *And then what?* Diesel couldn't help but smile at her enthusiasm, so reminiscent of one of his girls. With her gentle insistence, the display stirred. The coffee table's surface spun once more, the illusion clearing and resetting, ready to unveil the next chapter of the story Missy longed to hear.

The hologram pulled at the seared edges, charred dust rising as Diesel's form took shape—depicted mid-ascent to General of the Shadow Guild, ceremony and all. In a quiet response, Missy extinguished the room's lights with a hush, gently blowing out the sconces and drawing the space into deeper focus. Cloaked figures stood in tight military formation, banners rustling behind them. As Diesel stepped forward, his silhouette filled the center of the rendering. His formal uniform—oiled obsidian leather—bore the insignias across his chest and shoulder, not polished but worn with the gravity of lived command.

He didn't need to raise his voice. Authority settled into the newly carved arena like weight in the lungs—hushed but undeniable. The memory held its frame as the lines of the Shadow Guard and Elite Units realigned beneath him—not out of fear, but out of unspoken conviction. No icons shifted like chess pieces; this was no game. It was a reckoning. A moment etched into the mountain and marrow alike. Diesel—General of the Guild—stood where others had faltered. And none watching could forget the way Mama D walked onto that platform, pinning the insignia to his shoulder like it had always belonged there.

The projection pulled back, rising through a carved window in the cliff-side base of the Shadow Elite. From there, it soared—gaining height until the map stretched wide beneath it. Below, the realm revealed itself in methodical transformation. Cracks laced across the territories began to soften. Leaders stepped forward—Ezekiel among them—taking positions across Sanctuary as cities scrambled to rebuild. The map pulsed, no longer static. Veins of damage settled into impressions. Power divided. Lines redrawn. And from the wreckage, the realm began to reshape.

Diesel watched in silence, elbows resting against his knees, the soft console light catching along his jaw. "So many had fallen in those final days," he murmured. "There was no time for mourning." He paused, gaze tracing the fluctuations across the terrain. "Only the need to protect what remained."

Missy rattled the floorboards beneath the coffee table—vibrating in eager little bursts, like the house itself shivered with pride at his rise in rank. The viewing slab gave a subtle creak in response, its legs bracing as if sharing the moment. Diesel chuckled. "Settle down, Missy." *Her joy is a simple comfort, sown into her timbers,* he thought.

"After the Great War, the base didn't stay unchanged for long," he continued, eyes fixed on the bird's-eye view of the mapped Lands. "Lord Brannon took power in Shadow City quickly." The vantage point plummeted, sweeping down like a falcon cutting through mist—revealing scenes rippling across the territories. "That's when the rebuilding truly began." The projection coasted low over fractured townships, alcoves carved into the landscape, and outposts still clinging to ruin. People gathered in the rubble, harvesting slivers of quintessence, hauling back what they could—most of it bound for the base. Broken tools, fragmented stone, metal scorched beyond its use. All of it touched now, by something more.

"After the surge from the Tree of Shadow," Diesel added, quieter now, "even inanimate things began to wake." The rendering shimmered, revealing relics once lifeless, now threaded with pulse-like iridescence— faint, steady, unsettling. The light wasn't natural. It beat like breath trapped in glass.

He glanced around the darkened study, the stillness almost reverent— until the bookcases shuddered with the thrill of stories yet to be told.

"Yes, like you, Missy," he murmured, his voice softening. "You remember this part, don't you? You were built from those very pieces we gathered—each beam, every board. Artifacts left in the aftermath." The cabinet doors swayed slightly, creaking like a child swinging her arms, bouncing on her toes, caught in the joy of anticipation.

Diesel smiled. "Yes, love. The quintessence gave you life. But it was what came after—the way they crafted you—that made you something more than just walls and wood." From the hearth's edge, Nester clicked his little pipe-feet together—the soft taps a quiet rhythm of encouragement for the tale to continue.

"We began collecting these items, bringing them to the base," Diesel said. "The healers did what they could to understand and restore their nature, using quintessence to foster growth and preserve The Lands. It wasn't just about salvaging relics—it was about purpose. Renewal. Just like what happened with you, Missy."

The shelves gave a low creak, pride hidden in the woodgrain. The house, built from remnants born of shadow, had become more than shelter. It was living proof of what could rise from ruin.

He glanced toward the hearth. Nester hadn't moved, still perched at the edge, clicking his little pipe-feet together in soft rhythm. Diesel studied him for a long moment. Though often mistaken for a mere device, Nester had never been that. He was a gift—sent from Ezekiel during the worst of it. And in those fractured days following the war, Nester had proven more vital than flesh and blood.

His tone dropped—low, but firm. "It's also why you're hidden here, Nester. In the wrong hands, you carry something beyond what any of us fully understand. You've taken on the traits of both a Truth Seeker and a Shadow Guard tactician. You process more than we can fathom. And once you bond with someone, that bond holds. For life." He paused. "Or until death breaks it. And that's saying something…since our lifespans are quite extensive."

He paused, his focus drawn to the soft dimming over the rendered terrain. "The rush of quintessence from the Tree of Shadow changed everything we thought we understood," he said softly. "Each element across The Lands was altered…in its own way." The scene reformed, revealing vacant cradles and withered fields, their silence louder than any ruin. Diesel's jaw tightened. "Since then, more citizens have been born without full quintessence," he continued, grim. "They're becoming…what the old records once called human-like. As though something essential has unraveled."

His attention turned toward the second velvet chair—positioned at a distance, parallel to his own. It was a twin to the one he sat in now, untouched since the last time Ezekiel had occupied it. "Our final conversation," he said, gesturing subtly toward the seat, "was right there." His voice bore the weight of memory, low but unshaken. "That's when we started to suspect the real cost—why we were losing so many of our young." The admission hung heavy. "But that's a story for another time."

Above the console, the ceiling groaned. Droplets traced down the stone beams as if the house itself exhaled in grief. A dark cloud gathered in the center of the room, casting rainfall upon the illuminated surface. The image below transformed: a younger Izayah, sleeves rolled, hands raw from work, stood amid the skeletal beginnings of Starlight Beach. Diesel allowed a small, almost reluctant smile. "Even long after the war ended," he said, "Izayah was still reading the scars it left behind." He exhaled. "Before he ever took his oath to the Shadow Guard, he was dreaming this place into being—a sanctuary." Nester didn't speak, but his bulb-head tilted slightly, internal circuits whirring with recognition.

"Starlight was always his," Diesel continued, the timbre of his voice thick with meaning. "Brannon gave him the freedom to build it. Even before the boy had rank." He leaned back slightly, velvet groaning beneath him. "Mornings, he trained harder than most under my watch. Afternoons, he disappeared into blueprints and scaffolds—putting his heart into every inch of this town." He didn't lower his voice, but the weight of it pressed deeper now. Not pride alone. Something truer. Something earned.

The image surfaced and settled into place: a younger Izayah sitting cross-legged outside what would become the North Star, his back leaned against one of the unfinished beams. Plans were spread across his lap, sketched in quick, measured strokes—his pencil moving faster than thought, as if staying still too long might unravel something. Around him, the coal sketchings of the town rose in skeletal outlines, quietly waiting.

"When Nadine passed," Diesel said, the words careful but unflinching, "it did something to him. Changed how he carried things." His gaze stayed fixed on the seared surface. "Lord Brannon...well, he's not the sort to speak grief aloud. But he saw it in Izayah. Let him work it out in blueprints and scaffolding. Gave him this project—not as a gift, but a shared wound."

The next image hovered: Izayah laying stones with painstaking precision, every beam set with care, every corner measured twice. His jaw was tight, but his hands were steady.

"Even after making the Guard—and later, the Elite—he never stopped building. Not once. It wasn't about duty by then. It was personal. Every piece of this town is an answer to pain he never put into words."

A low hum threaded through the room, followed by the familiar crackle of the hearth. Diesel glanced around once before nodding, just slightly.

"You can feel it too, can't you, Missy?" he murmured, his voice roughening with something gentler. "He started getting those letters around the same time. Something about them changed his rhythm. Not distraction... more like he was chasing something only he could see. Trying to outpace the quiet."

Izayah's form moved like mist marbled with obsidian, tendrils drifting through the skeletal framework of the town. Fog swept in low, lit by fractured moonlight, reaching for unfinished beams and bare stone as if summoned by his will alone.

The essence emanating from him warped the space it touched—subtle at first, then consuming. Darkness thickened, gathering in folds before slashing outward like ribbons on the wind. Stone split beneath the impact, gravel scattering in fans across the cottage thresholds. Cobblestones clicked into place, not by command but as if compelled by purpose long waiting to be remembered. The town rose beneath his hands—each corridor, each angled turn shaped by the weight of what he carried. It wasn't visible, but it was there—woven into the very bones of the place.

"It's rare," Diesel said, his tone quiet. His attention remained on the image as Izayah's essence stilled, suspended in a moment of eerie calm. "His reach runs deep. Fog, mist, night...he draws on all of it. He doesn't just build—he imprints." A breath caught in his throat. "Every evening, he tried to wear down the storm in his mind. Every beam he moved, every threshold he shaped—he wasn't just building a town. He was holding back the dark."

The scene shifted again, now revealing soldiers running drills through the early foundations of the haven. Their silhouettes moved with practiced rhythm, weaving through framework still damp from the day's labor. The town was no longer just a vision. It was becoming real.

"He used Starlight Beach as a training arena," Diesel continued, his voice tinged with something close to admiration. "A place where Guards and Elite units could reconnect—grow stronger, both as individuals and as a collective. It was brilliant, really. Gave them room to work through their fractured quintessence, or get reaquanted with a truer version of themselves…to reassemble what might have been once lost, piece by piece."

He paused, his gaze drifting toward a quiet corner of the wall—somewhere far beyond the confines of the study. "Lord Brannon, with all his military foresight, knew what was at stake. He gave Izayah full freedom to build, but made one thing clear: Starlight's location had to remain secret--- even from him, his Father." Diesel exhaled. "He understood the risk. If he was ever compromised, the sanctuary's placement could undo everything Izayah had worked so tirelessly to protect."

The house responded with a low, nearly imperceptible sigh through the beams—soft as breath against glass. Diesel's eyes warmed. "Yes, Missy," he said gently. "It was more than inspiration. Those letters changed him. Whoever sent them…they lit a fire in him for something beyond himself."

He let the stillness settle before adding, almost to himself, "It stopped being just a training facility…or an evolving frame of an enclave. It became something else. A place for healing. A testament to everything we chose to fight for." His focus dropped to the miniature sprawl of Starlight on the table, shadows dancing across the tiny rooftops. "Even before anyone declared him a leader, they saw it. Felt it. Watched him, waited—and when the time came, they followed."

Diesel paused, thoughtful. "I don't think he ever realized the way others began to change around him. He assumed they saw him as just another name—Lord Brannon's son, carrying a legacy he hadn't earned." His voice dropped lower, heavy with remembrance. "But Izayah was determined to show otherwise. He never hesitated to dig in, to get his hands dirty, to walk in others' shoes."

The projection on the charred console stirred once—then held. But instead of returning to the skeletal beginnings of Starlight Beach, it revealed the town as it stood now. Streets fully formed, cottages aglow, the cliffs terraced with watchpoints and pathways. The harbor shimmered beneath layered fog, boats anchored in quiet readiness. Lanterns danced in the night air, casting their golden flicker against stone walls and polished wood. Starlight, no longer a dream, but a living legacy. Then, with a soft exhale, the image folded inward. A low *whoosh* swept through the room as the vision receded, retreating into the still hum embedded in the table's surface.

Above them, Missy's candelabras sparked to life—flames flickering tall and clean—reigniting the room in full. Warm light returned, washing the study in amber and memory.

"Thank you for that, Missy." Diesel sat back. "Preparations are in place," he said—not to Nester, but into the silence that followed—as his gaze traveled to the bookshelf lined with journals and worn field logs. "Every lesson. Every failure. All of it's been recorded for the ones coming next."

On the hearth's edge, Nester didn't rise. He leaned back on his rounded pipe-caps, relaxed but alert, his light dimmed to a meditative glow. His silhouette cast delicate reflections across the stone floor—quiet echoes of all they'd carried to this point.

"That's what I'll leave them," Diesel continued. "Not just survival. Not just strength. The ability to face the dark and command it—*not fear it*. To *protect* with it. Not be destroyed by it." His eyes found the green velvet chair beside his own—Ezekiel's old seat, untouched and waiting. "Wish you were still here," his voice brushed with an edge too raw to hide. "Could use your mind on what's coming."

Nester turned just enough to glance Diesel's way, no words offered—only presence.

Diesel dipped his chin, a smile pulling across his features as his hand traced the seam of his linen pants. He stooped slightly, plucked the last rosebud cake from the plate, and popped it into his mouth. Then, easing back, he let the chair receive his weight. His elbow dropped to the armrest as he gave the glass in his hand a lazy swirl—ice clinking against crystal, rhythm soft and knowing.

Across the room, Missy stirred. A rustle at the cabinet. In a blink, the glass lifted from his fingers, tilting in a silent promise of refill.

He let out a chuckle, low and content, acknowledging her care with a slight nod. Then, twisting toward the hearth, he arched a brow at Nester. "All right," he said, a touch of mischief threading through. "What've you got for me this time?"

Chapter Thirteen

Present Day

Where shall we begin? Nester held a regal clarity as he assessed the entry point of information, leaning into the conversation and away from the heat of the hearth. *Perhaps with Sanctuary and the Tree of Life.* He hesitated. *I must caution you, General; much has transpired since our last discussion on this topic.* He drew his legs up into his body, crossing them with subdued dignity as he dipped forward, folding his arms across his knees. *I'm happy to report, we are on the right path. It appears to be progressing quite satisfactorily, if I say so myself.* A ripple of excitement fluttered through him. His small frame gave a subtle, joyous jiggle, and his bulbous head flared into a lively swirl of bright pink and sky blue—like bubbles caught in sunlight, energetic and full of life. The colors danced together for a beat, glowing with playful delight, before softening back into his usual steady, informative hue. *The fragment of the tree we obtained from Sanctuary has been nurtured within these walls for some time now.* His voice grew more assured. *It has formed a natural bond with the primary tree in the heart of Sanctuary. Our main challenge has always been extracting information discreetly, while remaining concealed within this ingenious pocket.* At that, he bowed his head—not in pride, but in quiet reverence for all that had been done to make it so.

"You definitely have been busy. Start from the root"—Diesel chuckled as he sank deeper into the chair—"no pun intended," holding the glass delicately between the tips of his fingers. He lifted it just enough, letting the firelight refract through the liquid, as if the swirl of amber might offer answers of its own. His gaze lingered, thoughtful, before returning back to Nester. "Go on."

Nester's piped hands lifted a hair's breadth from his knees, elbows angling outward as he continued. *I needed a way to entwine myself with the tree without being detected.* One hand swept gently behind him, motioning toward the hearth stonework and the rooted source. *After much trial and error, I believe I've finally devised a solution.* His arms moved with a mechanical grace—a rhythm of intent. *Excuse me if I do repeat myself, sir, but I want to make sure we're up to par on the information we both have.* He stilled, his filament crackling softly, as though he were breathing in before continuing. *The Seers from the Valley of Visions and the lower Priestesses of Sanctuary are the sole transcribers of the Tree of Life's knowledge. That is our main obstacle. Their unique abilities allow them to explore the records in Sanctuary's archives and the smaller library in the Valley of Visions. These records encompass everything— from the aftermath of the Great Wars to the origins of our journey.*

Hmm. Diesel bobbed his head in acknowledgment, spinning a hand once in a tight circle—as if to say, *Go on.*

Well, sir, we have records of the devastation across The Lands during and after the Great War—but our understanding barely scratches the surface. This new connection —our fragment and the main growth in Sanctuary—grants us access to wisdom once beyond our reach. He paused, his small shoulders lifting toward his nonexistent ears as he huffed out a sparked breath. *Think of this link as a key—a means to unlock truths and insights that have remained shrouded in secrecy for ages.* One of his piped nubs tapped lightly against his knee as he spoke. *It opens pathways to knowledge that the Seers and Priestesses have guarded fiercely, allowing us to sift through history and events long obscured by time. What we've learned so far is merely the beginning.* He hesitated, as if plucking at a thought he wasn't quite ready to voice. Slowly, his palms came forward and cupped the air before him, as if holding a delicate bloom. *It's like peeling away the petals of a flower,* he murmured, gently miming the act with a small outward motion, *only to find an onion beneath—its hidden truths stinging the senses.* His hands widened as if revealing the bitter core. *Each layer we uncover reveals new complexities, more nuances than we ever anticipated. Our goal is not just to witness these truths,* he finished, his piped palms now held together as if cradling something weighty, *but to cleanse the rot that has settled within them—to restore honor to The Lands.*

Diesel adjusted his grip on the glass, eyes narrowing with quiet understanding. He didn't look at Nester right away—just stared through the amber. "Are you saying we now have unrestricted access to the archives and library—all from the safety of Starlight Beach—without being detected?" As he spoke, a faint hum emanated from the kitchen. Missy, sensing the brewing tension, went to work. The soft clatter of utensils and the gentle click of the oven door opening signaled her attempt to soothe the atmosphere, filling the air with the comforting scent of freshly baked cookies. Diesel inhaled sharply, his gaze drifting momentarily toward the study doors. "And yet, we're still at a standstill because we have no one to transcribe the information?"

Nester's small frame went still, gathering his thoughts before continuing. *Yes and no, sir. There's a subtle difference between what we have access to and what we can actually use.* He bowed his head in contemplation. *What I've created means we won't need a Seer or lower Priestess to decipher this wisdom. That's the key distinction.* Dust moats drifted in his light, swirling as his mind worked—then settled as he rose and made his way to the coffee table. One capped nub glided along the scorched edge where the quintessence fires had left their mark. His filament pooled with a soft, shadowed glow, as though the energy from the table's wounds mirrored back into him. He didn't just observe the scars—he absorbed them. Saturated by their weight, he turned once more toward the hearth. *However,* he murmured, *becoming a limb of the main tree—tapping into its secrets—requires careful navigation.* His little capped feet tapped as he stepped intentionally over the roots, mimicking the metaphor that guided his thoughts. *One misstep,* he added, his voice low but certain, *and we risk severing our connection. Patience and precision. That's our only path forward.*

A clattering sound from the kitchen cut through the moment—an exclamation point in the middle of the conversation. Missy had decided to make herself known, one sharp click-clack of utensils at a time.

With feline grace, Nester hopped from the hearth to a section of floor where the charred planks had been carefully sealed, their dark grain polished to a quiet sheen. He bounded up to the surface beside the low table, the wood whispering beneath his steps. His hand shot out just as four small books launched toward him from a nearby shelf—one at a time, quick as a snap. He caught the first mid-air and set it down. The second followed, then the third. Each one he placed with meticulous care, stacking them neatly atop one another as they came. By the time the fourth landed in his grasp, he had built himself a makeshift perch. Plopping down atop the stack with a satisfied bounce, he continued, *What we do know is that the Tree of Life isn't just a symbol. It's a living entity, directly tied to the heart of Sanctuary. It holds vitality, wisdom, and power—feeding energy to all the realms it touches. Our fragment here in Starlight Beach has bonded with the main tree, but our focus now is on strengthening that bond.* He paused, letting the weight of his words settle. *As you've pointed out, the tree acts as a guardian, filtering and distributing knowledge throughout the realms. However, the full extent of what we can access remains uncertain. If all goes as planned, we'll become part of its shadow—hidden, undetectable, yet present.*

Diesel slid forward, the velvet fabric dragging faintly beneath him before the frame gave a groan under his weight. "I understand caution is necessary"—a gruff sound caught in the back of his throat, not quite a growl, more like a blade edged with impatience—"but how is it that we have no reports on Izayah and my Guards' location? We've been left in the dark since Sanctuary sealed its walls. And let's not overlook the timing— that happened the moment the girls arrived at Starlight." Gripping the armrests, he pushed back. The chair creaked in protest as he sank into it, one ankle crossing over his knee, arms braced along the rests. "My patience is *running thin*, Nester."

Nester leaned forward, resting his elbows on his knees and tapping his nubs together in a rhythmic *clink*—soft, metallic. His filament narrowed into focused thought, the light within him pooling like a lantern left to burn low. *I understand your frustration, sir. The situation demands the utmost caution. We're not the only ones with access to the tree's network—it's shared. We must respect Sanctuary's rules of information exchange. Extracting details reck-lessly could trigger consequences we can't foresee.* He paused, letting the metallic rhythm gradually fall into silence. *It's been two decades since we lost track of Izayah and the Elites, but this new link—this evolving bond with the tree —may be the very key we've needed.*

Diesel pressed his lips together, taking a controlled inhalation. "So, to make sure I have this right—you're saying Sanctuary gathers information from various sources and only shares it selectively. Since the beginning of Starlight Beach, and thanks to the ongoing ley line shield from the Blessed Father, we remain guarded…even within the tree's establishment. Is that correct?" The scent of cookies began to waft through the room—warm, golden, unmistakable. Missy's answer to his question. Not a solution. A distraction. His gaze flicked toward the study doors. "Patterns of avoidance aren't exactly part of healthy habits, love," he called out with a chuckle.

A soft, concentrated gleam hovered at Nester's center, collecting clarity before he spoke. *Yes, sir. Sanctuary must gather information naturally through the tree's network. We can't simply take it; it needs to flow through its veins.* The tapping of his feet resumed for a beat. *Think of it like a river—downstream. We've set up a new route for the information to pass through, catching it in our net as it flows past.*

Diesel pressed forward. "Status on the ley lines—are they holding?" His voice cut through. "I assume they're stable, but assumptions breed errors, and you know how I feel about that."

Stable across all known anchors. No signs of interference or drain. Nester raised his head, one hand lifting to rub the base of his bulb in a motion half-thoughtful, half-reflexive. *Our ley lines remain steadfast, connecting us to the established points across Starlight.* He paused, his nubbed hand dropping to his lap. *As you know, Ezekiel's blessing forms a protective barrier around Starlight Beach, keeping us hidden and setting us apart. Now that the connection between our sapling and the main tree in Sanctuary has solidified, we've metaphorically extended Sanctuary's boundaries. The tree now perceives Starlight Beach as part of the whole.*

Diesel lifted the glass in his hand, letting it catch the firelight as he leaned into one elbow, idly turning it between his fingers. "Just to clarify— you're saying we've not only secured our ley lines through Ezekiel and Izayah, but we've now merged with Sanctuary's borders? We're essentially perceived as part of the city itself?" He took a considered sip, then lowered the glass back to the armrest, letting it roll once in his palm with a quiet slosh.

Nester gave a small nod. *We are currently protected two-fold.* As he spoke, he drew his legs up onto the stack of books beneath him, settling in with his elbows propped on his knees. *However, this also means that any significant energy spike will ripple out, alerting the High Priestess—as it will appear to fall within her domain.*

Diesel bowed his head, spinning the crystal glass in his palm— measuring the implications in silence.

What I do know is this— Nester's tone lowered as he continued. *Ezekiel's grace conceals us, even as our connection to the main tree in Sanctuary solidifies. If an alert is triggered, it will seem to stem from the central hub, not from us. Think of it like a reflection—we are merely an extension of the main source. Any disturbance or surge in energy will be interpreted as affecting the original, not the reflection itself. This is why a sudden spike will be perceived as coming from within Sanctuary's boundaries, keeping Starlight Beach shielded.* He repositioned himself atop his perch, the stack of books creaking below him as his tone grew more measured. *The real question is whether there are other places like ours—absorbing information silently without revealing themselves. That is still unknown.*

"If I understand correctly," Diesel began, his voice steady, "when someone like a Seer, lower Priestess, or even the High Priestess herself requests information, it will flow through the tree's veins. This process of flowing is what grants us access as well, correct?" The oven creaked. Trays scraped across the counter as Diesel shook his head—softly chuckling as the warm scent of fresh cookies filled the space.

Nester's filament buzzed, a ripple of static curling around his core. Sparks rolled once along his frame—small, but sharp—betraying his irritation. He flicked a hand toward the open doorway, and the study doors slid shut, muffling the distant clatter as he pressed forward. *Our branch of the Tree of Life breathes vitality into the main trunk, healing it, despite the corruption within Sanctuary. From my sources, I've learned that the tree finds favor in our efforts to restore it.* His tone grew more thoughtful. *Nature instinctively seeks nourishment without explanation. This fragment sustains the life of the greater source found in Sanctuary, allowing energy to circulate through the network like quintessence through our ley lines.* The study door unlatched with a gentle click and swung open, allowing another hushed click of utensils to filter through the doorway. Nester's filament rolled, threads of annoyance sparking. With swat at air, he flung the door shut once more, pressing on. *Information will naturally circulate through the boughs' intricate pathways—reaching us and returning without interference.* The latch released again—this time more forcefully. The door swung wide as the quiet click of a cooling tray met the counter, followed by the rustle of cookies being arranged on a rack. A gleaming ribbon of light threaded across Nester's form—his irritation flashing bright. He shot his hand out once more, slamming the door shut with finality.

"You two and that door," Diesel muttered, amusement flung over his shoulder as he glanced toward the passage, just as the latch gave a dull clunk and the door creaked open once again. "I swear, you're going to break it off its hinges one day." He tilted his head, raising his chin toward the wet bar, already anticipating the scent would soon draw in another Elite. "He'll be here any minute. You want him around, just pull out a bag of something tempting, and General Sweets will show up faster than you can fold into time." A faint grin pulled at his mouth, confident in his prediction. After a beat, he shook his head. "Man, he has grown slow in death," he added, his gaze tugging ceiling-bound as his thoughts realigned. Clearing his throat and finding his footing, he continued, "So, the tree is making choices—aligning itself strategically. Survival is paramount, I suppose, and it's reaching for the light that flourishes here in Starlight. My question is this: what happens when the girls are unbound— or go through unbinding?"

"Miss me, Sweetcheeks? Told ye—Missy never bloody disappoints, does she now?" A gruff voice cut through the room. "So what of it, General? Gettin' a bit smug in yer assessment of me, are ye?" The sharp bite of ice met crystal as Diesel turned toward the brash tone. "So what I'm gettin' is, ye don't have the info yet, and we've gotta be careful about drawin' too much from the tree, aye? And without a Seer or lower Priestess, we're stuck transcribin' the details. Ye say we don't need either, but it sounds like we've landed ourselves in a right conundrum." He leaned forward slightly, voice thick with grit. "We might have the tree—but what good is it if we can't make sense of it all?"

The walls emitted a low rumble, vibrations coursing through the floorboards in eager anticipation—like a child clapping with glee at the return of a beloved guest. Frames rattled against the wall as light wavered sharply, phasing from dim to dazzling. Nester tapped one capped nub against his piped thigh—*dink*—a controlled strike. Metal on metal, laced with frustrated intent. *I hear you; you're truly insufferable and impatient today! I am getting to it!* he scolded, shaking his bulbous head as he crossed his arms tightly over his chest.

Diesel slapped the armrest with a solid thud, a guffaw escaping him. "I'm getting the sense one of you might need some alone time," he called out.

Nester's filament spat a few irritated sparks as he rolled his bulbous head, one capped hand lifting in a motion as if to massage his small metal shoulder. He gave a full-body wiggle, jostling slightly atop the stacked books as he straightened into a regal pose. His filament sharpened into a splintered amber glow as he turned toward the broguish Elite nestled within the gold-encrusted frame. *Liam, your timely question is truly valued. It fosters progression in our discourse—unlike a certain someone we are all familiar with.* He tilted his head with disdain, aiming a withering glare at the house. It responded with another low rumble. With a swift motion, Nester extended his arm, the action crisp and practiced. From the shadows near Diesel's hefty desk, a slender obsidian instrument shot forward, magnetically attaching to his stubby appendage. It gleamed darkly—simple in form, yet shrouded in quiet mystery. In the same breath, Nester leapt from his seated perch atop the charred coffee table, the small tower of books wobbling slightly behind him. His small frame moved with elegant precision, landing near the hearth with a softened feline *thud*. The roots of the tree stretched outward from the stonework just ahead of him, weaving into the floorboards like ancient veins that had long since grounded themselves in Missy's very foundation. He approached one of the smaller tendrils. At his precise *tap-tap-tap*, the wood stirred beneath his touch, curling upward in response—forming a natural podium, shaped by the tree's will. Nester stepped forward, posture straight and ceremonial, and carefully set the obsidian instrument atop the rooted platform.

"Bloody hell, Nes—what's that, then?" Liam strained his neck to see around the massive velvet chair as Diesel rolled his eyes and chuckled. "Ye've gone an got yerself a right magical tool, haven't ye?" He slid sideways within the portrait, bringing his head to the edge of the gilded border. The moment he leaned too far, the mount gave a soft *creeeak*—then jolted on its nail, tipping askew. A sharp *clink-thunk!* sounded behind the wall, followed by a cacophony of falling objects within the image itself. "Ah—bother, not again!" Liam barked, ducking instinctively as a bottle toppled off a shelf behind him. "What's it do, then?" he grunted, gripping the edge of the constructed bar top inside the painting as he tried to jolt everything back into place. The picture shuddered with his efforts, dust drifting from the upper molding. "Oi—General? You gonna help me out here or just sit there sippin' your bloody whiskey while I rattle off te wall?"

Diesel took a leisurely pull from the glass and shook his head—unfazed, unmoving. "You'll *learn* at some *point*, won't you, *brother.*"

A mechanical *slllliiiinkkk* sounded as the portrait righted itself with a subtle nudge of Missy's will, snapping neatly back into alignment. Liam blinked, straightened his tweed cap, and muttered, "Owe you one, love."

Nester tapped his foot with a sharp *tink-tink-tink* against the floorboards, patience running thin. Then, he pivoted slightly so he could be in eyeshot of both Generals. With a crisp clap of his capped hands, he reclaimed the room's attention. *As I mentioned earlier,* he began, *I needed a way to blend seamlessly into the flow of information.* His filament pulsed with restrained energy as he moved to the far side of the tree. *After consulting various sources within our growing library, I discovered that now we've merged the fragment with the main source, we can draw sap as effortlessly as drawing blood…*He hesitated, tapping a capped hand thoughtfully to the tip of where his chin would be. *Let me be clearer—it's more like cycling blood through the body, as if to cleanse the source in order to heal the whole. This is quite different from the structured process used by the Seers and lower Priestesses in Sanctuary.* He gestured toward the base of the instrument, now fully unified in form. *To make this process natural, we've crafted a sophisticated vessel at its core.* Stepping to the edge of the blackened hearth, Nester ran a hand along the exposed roots. The wood rumbled in response, and from its depths, a goose-necked bottle emerged—its foundation coiled in delicate vines that stretched upward like veins. Within the glass, a miniature landscape shimmered into view: a central fire pit casting a gentle radiance that scattered upward like firefly embers—each flicker rising, catching light, and turning into a slow-blooming constellation.

"That doesn't seem random, now does it?" Diesel leaned over the armrest, gaze narrowing on the scene within the vessel. "What's it trying to show us? What's the reason behind that display?" His voice carried the weight of concern, wrapped in the easy guise of curiosity.

I'm not entirely certain, Nester replied, a hint of caution in his tone. *The landscape shifts on its own, periodically revealing something new. My guess? It's a reflection of its memories—or maybe echoes of what the main source experiences across the grand city of Sanctuary, channeled through the essence of the sap.* He leaned in and tapped the glass with his capped nub. At the point of contact, a flutter of ember-like particles clustered instantly—gathering like a swarm of bees stirred to life. As soon as he withdrew his hand, the formation scattered, folding neatly back into the miniature scene. *Whatever appears isn't something I can control. It's the vessel's decision on what to disclose.* Peering up at Diesel, he gave a small shrug. *With this current approach— using the conduit and the pen—it collects the essence gradually over the course of hours. The excess gathers at the rootstock, much like blood filtering through veins and pooling into a pocket. This configuration*—he motioned toward the tome anchored at the base, the instrumental pen, and the bottle—*allows us to retrieve, transcribe, and reintegrate the life force back into the living network. It never fully departs from its source.*

"Help me understand—if the pen's anchored there, how does the transcription process work?" Diesel's voice was steady. "Wouldn't it need to be removed?"

That's the brilliance of it, he replied. *The pen remains anchored in its holder, yet it inscribes from a distance—transmitting directly onto the page. What's gathered only lingers for a moment—just long enough for Missy to transcribe it into a second volume. Then, the sap ink cycles back through the roots. This allows us to build our own archive without outside interpretation or meddling.* Nester gestured skyward in mock exasperation. *It also keeps Missy out of my filament—what little of it I've got left. Since she's always listening, she already knows exactly what we're hunting.* With a fluid turn, he spun on his heel and motioned back toward the roots. *She can sift through the flow without hesitation—like she's scanning for keywords.* He pivoted again, casting a glance up at Diesel, then back toward Liam. *Because we're tracking Izayah, she'll isolate anything tied to his name as it moves through the channels. The pertinent passages will emerge.*

"Can we trust that this information isn't propaganda?" Diesel pressed.

That's where you come in. With a bound, Nester vaulted back onto the charred surface of the coffee table, landing with a soft thud and plopping down onto the familiar stack of books. He settled with a slight wobble before throwing his arms wide—open to the idea of what came next. *Your ability to filter through the truth is the final step—helping us determine whether what we've gathered is sound or skewed. Only then can we recalibrate and advance the mission to its next stage.*

Huh. Diesel ran a hand along his jaw, thumb grazing the edge of his stubble before his voice dropped into a low, gritty cadence. "Didn't see that one coming. What do we need to do to get the ball rolling, then?"

Liam chuckled. "Haven't ye been listenin' to a word? The whole landscape in dae bottle an that magical pen poofin' into existence—this system's already up an runnin' far as I can tell." He cleared his throat, then added with a sly grin, "And as for Truth Seekin'—well, I suppose that means ye'll be leadin' dae charge, won't ye, General? With all yer subtlety an grace."

Nester settled back atop the stack of books, arms crossing firmly over his chest and his feet casually at the ankles. *General Liam is correct—the system is already up and running.* A beat later, he repositioned himself with a faint wobble, adjusting his position as though realizing perching as such, wasn't as dignified as intended. *To clarify—our segment of the 'Tree of Life' is directly interfaced with the house. When something of value flows through, Missy can sync and begin her search.* He tilted his head toward the ceiling, voice lifting just enough to carry. *She and I have discussed the parameters thoroughly,* he added, flinging one arm back in an exaggerated toss, and *no, we won't dive into more frivolous curiosities about seasonal scarf trends.* A short, electronic-sounding hum buzzed from within, his glow dimming faintly with an undercurrent of sparking delight. One capped nub pressed where his mouth would be. *She's been clinking around like a child about to leave for holiday. Honestly, I think she's more eager to share this than I am.*

A rattle of bottles sounded beneath the counter as Liam shuffled about, muttering under his breath. He emerged with a squat, rounded flask of vivid blue liquid, holding it aloft with theatrical flair. "No one's told us a bloody ting about where dae Elites went," he said, unscrewing the cap and tossing in what looked suspiciously like a sugared clove and a sliver of dried citrus. The mix fizzed on contact. "Curious, ain't it—dat every portrait in Sanctuary either sealed itself tight or went up in bloody flames dae moment dae girls vanished." He gave the bottle a swirl, blue liquid sloshing dramatically before tipping a bit into a wide, chipped mug. "Aye, but sure, nothin' suspicious there." His eyes narrowed, a smirk tugging at one corner of his mouth as he raised the mug again. "Funny how spillin' information gets ye a one-way ticket ta silence." The drink shimmered faintly as he held it up, the golden edge of his frame catching the flicker of Missy's candelabras. "Strange ting, ta lock things up so tight when there's 'nothin' ta hide,' eh?"

Nester gave a subtle wobble atop the uneven book stack before slipping off, his metal feet giving a soft clink against the charred surface. Without hesitation, he extended one capped hand. A cushion zipped into his palm —perfectly scaled to his proportions and shaped like a toasted-brown ravioli, its stitched edges slightly puffed. He positioned it carefully atop the books, then settled onto it with a precise scoot, adjusting once as though assuming a post of quiet authority. *You make a fair observation, Liam,* he remarked, arms folding with pointed calm. *We don't just need truth—we need safeguarded truth. Clarity that holds its shape under pressure and won't dissolve the moment it's challenged. Which is why, from here on out, we're not merely observing—we're tracking, testing, preserving. Every strand we capture gets stitched into the wider weave, anchored and protected.* He dipped his head slightly toward the firelit podium, where the obsidian instrument waited in its cradle. *And if the tree so much as murmurs...we'll be the ones tuned in.*

"So we're just tip-toein' around, hopin' it accepts us, aye?" Liam gave a sharp snort, scrubbing a hand through his peppered beard like it was a wild thing meant to be tamed. "Sounds daft, but I'll bite." With a roll of his well-defined arms—still solid as old ship ropes—he crossed them over his chest and scowled, the twin creases between his brows deepening like they'd been carved there by years of stubborn grit. "What's it showin' us so far, den? The color o' dae sky?"

A ribbon of amber light unraveled from inside the center of Nester's bulbous head, circling once like a smoldering filament pulled taut. *Not quite,* he muttered, voice clipped with precision. *It's more like we're seeing ripples on a pond—signals of what's happening underneath.* His tone sharpened. *Sanctuary is crumbling, poisoned from within. From what I can tell—* A faint clatter interrupted, soft yet considered. Plates of warm cookies appeared in front of Diesel with a delicate chime. Another *shwip* followed, a second plate sliding neatly into the frame and landing on the painted countertop with a gentle *tap*. The gruff male arched a brow at the offering, a mischievous smirk tugging at one corner of his mouth. Nester pressed on, his voice gaining urgency. *The tree hints at realms along the fringe—places it can almost reach—but they're lost in a heavy fog. The outlines are there...but the specifics remain blurred.*

Liam snatched up a cookie, biting into it with a crunch as crumbs scattered across the counter. He leaned on one elbow, gesturing with the half-eaten pastry. "So, what yer sayin' is, we're squintin' t'roo murky glass. Not much use if ye ask me."

A glint of disagreement stuttered through. *Not at all, Liam. It's revealing fragments of a much larger picture. Right now, it's testing us—seeing if this new branch is safe to share more with. It's about building trust. These glimpses are just the beginning. We're letting the source get used to us being here—it's part of gaining its confidence while we put these puzzle pieces together.*

Liam paused, lifting the cookie to his mouth and taking a thoughtful bite. He chewed, crumbs tumbling down onto his beard and the open collar of his cotton shirt. With one hand, he reached up, fingers grazing along both sides of his bristles in a practiced sweep, brushing the crumbs downward in a final, prideful flourish. "Aye, it's like them dinner rolls dey toss at ye before the main course—ye know da kind, soft as clouds, steamin' when dey tear apart. And then dey bring out dat wee pot o' cinnamon sugar butter—no one expects it, but once ye've had a taste, ye start thinkin' maybe ye don't need dae rest o' dae meal at all. Maybe that's enough."

Exactly. Nester cut him off, tone firm yet tinged with hope. *These are fragments, yes, but they're enough to guide us. Over time, more will surface—quiet as a rogue slipping past the city gates, unseen.* A soft glow gathered at his core, his gaze drifting toward the platter on the table—a modest arrangement of handiwork, simple yet strategically timed. *Starlight Beach grants us cover, letting us observe without setting off alarms.* He bowed his head slightly —a silent acknowledgment to Missy, appreciating the subtlety of her contribution in persuading General Sweets. *For now, we take what the tree offers...and prepare to go deeper when the moment arrives.*

Liam nodded, raising his glass in silent acknowledgment before polishing off the last bite of a cookie. "Aye, bit by bit, we'll get dere. Just gotta keep our eyes open an not rush dae swim. For now, we're just stickin' our toes in dae water—checkin' dae temperature."

A faint smirk played at the corner of Diesel's mouth as he reached down, his hand brushing the edge of the cookie platter before he plucked one free and popped it into his mouth. With his other hand, he gave Nester a light tap on the would-be nose with a knuckle, leaving it there just long enough to make a point. "Finally catching on, huh?" he murmured, tone dry. "Seems Missy had a point."

Nester pulled his shoulders up to his ears in a theatrical shrug, holding the posture for a beat before huffing them back down with exaggerated defeat. *I suppose she did,* his light flickering with a pensive hue. *It's remarkable how she catches onto what we overlook. A strategic mind of a different kind.*

Diesel leaned down and popped another cookie into his mouth, the edge of a grin tugging at his cheek as he rounded the back of the leather couch. Shrugging off his linen shirt, he hung it on a nearby hook without ceremony. *"You'll catch on,"* he muttered around the bite, eyes gleaming with quiet amusement, the kind earned through lessons long learned.

"Oi—what're ye ramblin' on about now?" Liam called out, dabbing a finger across the countertop to gather the last of the crumbs. He stretched his neck farther, trying to peer past the edge of his portrait. "Ye know I can't see a bloody thing from here!" He gave a gruff huff. "Can't even see past ta top o' dose damn velvet chairs ever since Missy went rearrangin' te whole place. Just da *worst* bloody setup."

Nester reclined atop his cushion, adjusting the set of his shoulders with a quick snap. *About one of your earlier statements, there have been no reports on the missing Elite...not directly.*

Before Nester could finish the word *"directly,"* a soft clatter interrupted —fresh pastries appearing on each empty plate with Missy's usual impeccable timing.

Liam snatched one and tossing it into his mouth, his expression still brash, but now edged with curiosity. "Aye, so you're holdin' dae whole loaf while talkin' breadcrumbs, eh? 'Not directly,' ye say...now I'm intrigued." He propped his elbows on the constructed bar top, fingers tapping a rhythm—part restless, part measured—as his gaze narrowed on

Diesel, who had moved to open the cabinet behind his desk, retrieving his obsidian leathers with habitual familiarity. "Didn't ye tell 'em ta wave te white flag, General, if dey were at te end of deir rope?" he asked, the words clipped with a quiet edge. "That was right before dey popped off to dat hellhole o' a city." He muttered something under his breath—likely about the High Priestess—then cleared his throat. "I'm glad yer Elite listen," he added, voice turning sharp. "At least deir egos don't get too much in te way."

Nester gestured toward the hearth and the ember lit binding nestled within the roots. *A report broke recently about a golden-sphered woman,* he said, mimicking a scribbling motion—tiny, controlled circles as if jotting something invisible on a floating page, his tone hardening. *As you're aware, public mentions of the Golden Guard nearly vanished after the Great War.* His light dimmed in contemplation. *The recorder seemed a bit baffled—and I can't blame whoever authored the piece. Apparently, this woman could decelerate time and manipulate ice, causing quite the stir.*

Diesel arched an eyebrow, a faint smile tugging at the corner of his mouth as he slid his arms into the sleeves of his obsidian leathers. The gear was thick and form-fitting, molded by use, with every buckle and reinforced strap locking into place like ritual. He tugged one glove snug, leather creaking softly as it conformed to his hand. "They managed to hold out for quite some time, didn't they?" he said, the words measured, almost reflective. He reached for the cross-latch at his chest, securing it with a well-worn tug. "Seeing a Golden Guard after all these years…that must've been something, considering what they were up against." His voice fell a shade deeper, a note of weight curling within his composure. "Makes you wonder…" he said, cinching the final strap at his waist before glancing toward the hearth, gaze distant.

Liam gave a dry snort, unimpressed. "Aye, sounds like a tale with teeth. Ice, ye say? Where was dis Golden Guard skulkin' about, den?"

Diesel didn't respond right away. Instead, he stepped behind the heavy chair and began unfastening his belt with the same calm efficiency he applied to every task. The metal clasp gave a soft clink, and he pushed the fabric down, folding his trousers neatly before placing them carefully on the nearby shelf. The cool air met his skin, but he moved without hesitation—ritual, not performance. With each motion, he seemed to be shedding not just clothes, but tenderly compartmentalizing a treasured piece of his life. Civilian simplicity, folded and tucked away with reverence. His eyes narrowed, a flicker of quiet amusement lighting behind them. "It's been two decades," he called out, the words simple, but not light. His lips pressed together, as if bracing against the memory. "Not bad, considering the circumstances." From the open closet, he reached for the obsidian riding gear—weathered by time, yet still tailored with precision. With a fluid motion, he stepped into the armored trousers, one leg at a time, drawing the dark material up over his frame. The fabric stretched with quiet resistance, sculpting to his build, each fastening secured with practiced ease. The sound of reinforced hide brushing against skin whispered beneath the room's low hum as he tugged the waistband snug and locked it into place.

From what the tree conveyed, there was a spike in activity—heavy rainfall, specifically. He spread his arms wide in illustration, *it was reported as a surge of kinetic buildup—roots flaring outward in sudden expanse before drawing back, coiling in on themselves as if bracing. A reactive morphing, perhaps—a prelude to transformation. This is the most significant reading we've received to date.*

Liam let out a rough chuckle as he popped the last pastry into his mouth, washing it down with a final swig of his blue drink. He pushed the glass aside with a lazy flick, then nudged the empty plate away. "Rain, eh? Makes ye wonder how bad things got if even te weather decided to weigh in." He gestured loosely toward Nester, his voice dry as cracked stone. "These fragments ye're feedin' us…feels like dee tree's reachin' for somethin' bigger." He smirked, one brow lifting. "And how d'ye go about thankin' a great, hulkin' brute of a tree on behalf of Starlight, then?"

Nester straightened slightly atop his cushion, his tone calm, but laced with quiet gravity. *From what I gather, it's less about repayment and more about consistency—offering without expectation, earning trust over time. As you've said before, Liam, equilibrium matters. What's taken must be restored. We're cultivating ground where growth can take root—where restoration, in itself, becomes a form of thanks. That's what speaks to the sapling…and to the source that bore it.* He paused, a pulse of thought radiating just beneath his surface. *Especially now, when its heart feels increasingly drawn upon—as though more and more is being pulled without time to replenish. Feels like echoes of the Great War—patterns looping back with new faces.* His voice softened, trailing off. *But to sever quintessence from the Tree of Life completely…that's a danger we've yet to fully understand.* He hesitated, as if uncertain how to approach the weight of his own thought, before continuing quietly. *The balance could collapse, and the consequences…*He left the sentence unfinished, his tone hanging between warning and curiosity inviting the others to consider the ramifications.

From the kitchen came the faint clatter of dishes, followed by a soft *ssss* as something began to sizzle. A smile breezed across Diesel's lips as he fastened the final strap of his glove with a sharp tug, the leather tightening over his forearm. With a measured motion, he reached into the open closet and retrieved the long obsidian cloak, folding it neatly over his arm rather than donning it just yet. "It could prove to be a problem," he said, voice low, "when you actually *consider* those ramifications, Nes." He turned slightly, casting a glance toward the hearth where the sapling had rooted itself. "Were there any other breadcrumbs? Anything else the tree offered… about the Golden Guard?"

Yes, sir, Nester replied, the light in his bulbous head deepening in hue as a band of concentrated amber curled across his filament—like furrowed brows knitted in thought before beading away. He scooted forward, slipping off the stack of books with a soft shuffle. Turning, he adjusted the ravioli-shaped cushion, ensuring it sat just right. Only then did he hop down from the charred coffee table, landing with a muted *thud*. As he made his way toward the hearth, one capped hand drifted along the stone —light, reverent—offering Missy a silent gesture of gratitude, like petting a fond companion. He settled on the warm bricks with a gentle *plop*, his frame easing into stillness as his glow flickered low, attempting to soothe the space around him. *The article implied that ballrooms were transformed into combat arenas,* he continued, *formal elegance repurposed into battlegrounds— what once held celebration now lined with scars.*

Liam narrowed his eyes as Nester settled. "Still don't understand how ye do dat," he muttered, watching the little lightform land with barely a sound. "All dat quintessence, an ye make it look easy—shiftin' like a padded bloody thud, or nothin' at all. Not even a proper clink. That's a gift, dat is." He shot a glance at Diesel. "Like I said, General—I think Nes ought to be te one trainin' our Guards next. Unlike our Elites, my lot never could grasp dae art of shuttin' da hell up. Not like dis. The gift of ebbin' and flowin'…" He shook his head, tossing the thought aside as he leaned into his elbows, arching his upper back as he stretched through it. "Anyway—why in dae hell would ye scrap yer ballrooms and turn 'em into combat arenas? She's already got spaces for fightin'. Sounds daft." He snorted. "I'd tread careful, lad. That 'reporter'—or Seer, or whatever dey're callin' themselves—might be leadin' us straight off course."

Nester's tone snapped sharper with a firm assuredness. *They don't know we're here, so it's unlikely, Sir.* His light flared, a quick surge of static thought. *It seems, through the journalist's lens of cynicism, that this particular ballroom was one of her earliest recorded battlegrounds. It must carry some sort of historical weight—something etched in memory deeper than ceremony.*

As he spoke, Diesel draped the folded obsidian cloak over the back of the leather desk chair, the fabric settling with ritualistic ease. He gave the edge of the cloak a light tap—an absent, habitual gesture—before leaning into the open closet, retrieving his combat boots: obsidian black, designed to mold to his frame, rising just below the knee. He reached back to close the closet door with a quiet *chuk*, then carried the boots to the velvet chair, letting them drop with a *thud*. "If it's carved that deep," he said, the words low, as if tasting memory on his tongue, "then we're not just walking into reverberations—we're stepping into something still alive." His fingers brushed briefly across the hardened leather over his abdomen before he sank into the seat, pulling each boot on and drawing them closed with hushed finality.

"Ehh…," Liam waved off the thought just as the scent of braised pork crept into his frame, piquing his interest. "Seems Missy's stress levels are workin' in our favor, with all dae grief we're causin' dae lass. *Can't say I mind.* Though, Missy—reckon it's worth mentionin', for someone so wound up, you've got a hell of a fortress stitched 'round you. You'll be fine, dearie." A crystal glass slid smoothly into view, as if Missy herself were saying, *Mind your business and have one for me.* Liam chuckled as he reached for the empty glass. "Golden Guard had a sense of humor, it seems —givin' da whole place an icy twist an playin' wid da dramatic." He pulled a bottle of bubbly from beneath the bar, sloshed it in, gave it a lazy swirl, then smirked. "Bet Visha wasn't *too* pleased. She likes her environments ta same way she likes her intentions—hot, bothered, an' barely contained. Da female's got no boundaries…'specially when it comes ta gettin' what she wants. Can't fault da commitment, but saints, she could make a volcano blush."

Nester eased back, propping his capped hands behind him as he stretched his small feet forward, ankles crossing. *The report mentioned a chill that wiped out all the usual entertainments…whatever that implies. From the transcript, Visha was visiting Lord Brannon in Shadow City when it occurred.*

A rough chuckle rolled of the walls. "Da High Priestess an' her grand ballrooms—put on ice by a Golden Guard. Almost poetic, don't ye dink? Bet she drew a proper tantrum when her precious little playt'ings went a missin'." Liam snorted a laugh, a conspiratorial glint in his eye. "If it das da Elites, I can't wait ta hear da story behind dat."

Nester glinted warmly in agreement. *I wouldn't be surprised. From what I gathered, the Golden Guard's presence completely disrupted the atmosphere—much to Visha's dismay. It wasn't just the ice; it was the audacity of it. Someone dared to upend her carefully constructed world under her nose, and she wasn't even there to tighten her grip. The transcriber also noted how the registered fighters made off with plenty of coinage from the bets placed on them. A small rebellion wrapped in spectacle.*

Diesel, who had been listening intently, pitched forward, arms braced on his knees as his tone plummeted to something lethal. "Visha…doesn't have a soul left to be bothered by such things. She burned through whatever decency she had a long time ago."

Liam burst out laughing, sharp and dark. "Aye, typical, isn't it?" he scoffed. "Burned drough any decency she had, if she ever had any tae begin wi'. You're givin' her too much credit, General." He shook his head, still chuckling. "If it was our Elite, some wee village's found a goldmine, eh?"

"Well," Diesel shook his head with a dry scoff, "I hope the town's got enough sense not to spend it all at once—who knows what kind of wrath *that* might stir." His voice firmed. "This Golden Guard…think it's operating solo? Or is there something bigger pulling the strings?" He ran a hand along his jaw, pausing when his fingers met the rough stubble. His eyes narrowed. "I thought they were all gone. Long before any of this. Before the 'Moons and Shadows' mission even came into play." Another shake of the head. "Didn't think they were even on the table." He trailed off, a low hum in his throat.

Nester hesitated for a moment before speaking. *I'd imagine there has to be more than a single individual. But if it's just a lone figure, that might explain why they've stayed hidden for so long. No certainty in that, though. If they could disrupt Visha's domain, they'd have considerable power—and a careful way of using it. Likely lying low, waiting for the right moment to reemerge.*

Liam tapped the side of his crystal glass, the bubbles dancing up before he spoke. "Whoever dey may be, dey've done us a favor—givin' Visha somethin' real tae fret about." He knocked upon the side of his portrait frame, half-smirking. "Now, whereabouts is dat pork shoulder? Ye can't be teasin' a man's taste buds like dat and leavin' him hangin', Missy."

"Wait a minute—do you think it could be..." Diesel leaned forward, lowering his voice. He huffed out a disbelieving breath. "I mean, to reveal herself within Sanctuary's walls—if that's not a bold fuck-you, I don't know what is." Amusement flickered in his eyes. "I can't imagine Izayah response...if it was her." He clicked his tongue against the side of his cheek. "Now this has me curious how she managed to fake her own death." He puckered his lips, nodding. "That's one hell of a white flag." Shaking his head, Diesel muttered, "Damn impressive, and with Runa unbinding herself..." His voice trailed off as his fingers reached for a pastry from the plate, chewing thoughtfully as he considered the implications.

Liam shot an incredulous look. "She's doin' what?" He interrupted, his disbelief clear. "Come again, General? Who's gone and fakin' deir own death, aye?" He shook his head, smirking, but the playful banter faltered as confusion crept in. "Wait...Runa's unbindin' herself?" He leaned back slightly, letting the thought settle. "I've heard da stories of unbindin', aye, but no one's ever managed it on deir own." His smirk faded entirely, replaced by genuine confusion. "So how in da bloody hell is she pullin' dat off?"

Nester's filament flared—a sharp, reactive pulse of red—then waned into a steady amber, as if recalibrating to a finer frequency.

"Unbinding's only half of it," Diesel said, voice low. "Earlier today, Runa had what looked like a Netheron handprint scorched across her throat. Puncture wound too—base of the spine." He paused. "Thing is...it vanished. No scabbing, no trace. Like it never happened. Just wiped clean—water and a damn towel."

"Water an' a hand towel, ye say? What are ye on about?" Liam downed the rest of his drink, shoved the empty glass aside, and slammed his forearms down, bracing against a thick wall of disbelief. "Considerin' what da Soul Devourer did to meself—da pain, da damn poison—I barely remember any o' it before dey dragged me back. But water an a towel…no bloody way." He scoffed, shaking his head. "Just disappearin' without a trace? That's a load o' shite."

Diesel pushed himself up, the chair creaking under his weight as he moved around to the side and positioned himself on its hefty armrest. He pointed directly at the man in the painting, needing to make eye contact, to let the words land. Liam dipped his chin in confirmation. "I don't know, man," he exhaled hard, shaking his head as if trying to dislodge the memory. "I wouldn't have believed it if I hadn't witnessed it myself." Pausing to scratch the nape of his neck, then rubbing his chin, he added, "It wasn't like a wound that heals over time. It just fucking disappeared." He ticked off his thoughts on his fingers, his thumb and pointer tapping in succession. "No swelling. No scarring. For her, it was nothing like you. I should know. I moved you, Liam, after the Netheron," he inhaled deeply, and on the exhale pushed out the rest of the thought, "And what I saw with Runa today wasn't even close." Taking a beat, he continued, "The mark today on her looks exactly the same as it was on you. But how the hell could something like that just vanish?" Leaning in slightly, his tone dropping low, Diesel finished, "In all my days, I've never witnessed anything like it."

Nester faltered momentarily as though furrowing his brow. *A Netheron, sir?* He pondered. *They're exceedingly rare. We haven't encountered one in ages.* He hesitated, processing the possibility. *I've read about them, but for a mark to vanish so quickly…*His tone turning tender as he scoured crevices of thought. *It could've been a Netherling—a lesser servant of the Netheron. But if it was a Netheron…*He flared briefly, a spark of realization yanked him forward. *That points to something far older. Something…primal.* He paused, his glow flickering with quiet contemplation. *My question is—why would she keep one? Or where did she find it?*

"I don't dink a Netherling could pull off somethin' like dat." Liam scoffed, shaking his head. "I'll tell ye what, dat woman's off her rocker. The High Priestess? Nutjob an' half. Who knows what twisted creations she's meddlin' with now? If da Netheron is in her bag o'tricks." Before he could finish, a plate of braised pork whipped forward, skidding across the countertop and sloshing juices over his white shirt. "Oh, bloody hell, dearie!" he exclaimed, ducking under the counter to grab a napkin. "Aye, I get it, ye don't like dese chats, but ye don't have to start chuckin' food at me ta get me ta shut up!"

Nester bounded onto the seared surface, landing with a heavy thud, causing his makeshift stool to falter and knocking his pillow off-center as it slid away. Both males turned their attention toward the small light, who immediately began to speak. *If Runa is unbinding herself...that could pose a serious problem for our connection to Sanctuary. Are you certain? It shouldn't even be possible.* He moved closer, his voice a mix of wonder and alarm. *If Runa is successful, and if Nadine's still out there...*He threw his arms wide, words spilling faster now—"*Then, could it mean—*"

"Well, smack meself sideways an call meself Cottoncakes...I'll be damned. D'ya really tink it's the High Lady Nadine?" Liam grunted, "Aye, wonderin' where dat devil's been hidin' all dese years? Where'd you suspect she..."

BOOM!

The deafening sound reverberated through the room.

CRACKKKKK!

Suddenly, a flash of blinding radiance erupted, devouring every last shadow. The air crackled, charged with a palpable tension as the brilliance lashed through the room, making everything stand still for a breathless moment.

And then—*silence.*

The light surged once, twice, before plunging the room into a jarring darkness.

Chapter Fourteen

Everything froze in that moment—breathless, suspended in time.

BOOM!

A surge of blinding radiance engulfed the room, devouring every shadow and vibrating the walls with electric intensity. Both Generals instinctively shielded their eyes from the overwhelming glare.

CRACKKKKK!

The room remained suspended, each figure locked in the wake of the deafening roar, the afterglow still searing their vision.

BOOM!

Lightning sliced through the obsidian sky like a jagged blade, transforming the tranquil Starlight Festival into a frenzy of crackling energy.

The light swallowed the whole of Starlight, pulling all into its blinding core. For a heartbeat, the world seemed frozen, held in the grip of radiant intensity once more. Then, in an instant, the brilliance vanished—spitting them back into pitch darkness.

Missy responded with a low, purposeful hum, her will cutting through the structure with focused resolve. Metallic clicks and whirrs pinballed from point to point, locking down every potential entry. Her essence poured through the walls—resolute, unyielding. The air thickened as a deep groan reverberated through the foundation, the structure compressing, bracing itself. The keystones disengaged with a sharp *shhhkk*—a sound like light brushing metal—sealing the boundaries with finality. She wrapped the perimeter of the property in a protective embrace, her presence weaving through the space, poised for any impending threat.

Nester walked to the edge of the coffee table as another burst tore through the sky, its thunderous echo rolling over distant peaks and ricocheting off the closer mountains. *Same lightning strike, same night—just like two decades ago, right before we received the girls. What if we're about to receive someone else?* He paused, sticking out a hand in the air, bringing it to his bulbous head as if tasting the energy in the room. He jumped down from his perch and walked to the study windows, pulling at one of the curtains. His attention was fixed on the rumbling heavens. *Then again, lightning doesn't strike the same place twice, now, does it?*

"Aye, looks like da skies in Sanctuary decided ta dump their bleedin' downpour o'er Starlight, eh?" Liam's voice pierced the thick darkness, followed by the scrape of his fork along the dish and a slurp. "Seems like da perfect time ta shift Runa elsewhere, eh? If she's unbindin' herself, ta Golden Guard would've picked up on it. Yet da threadin' would've been dere if Goldie's been with Zay." Another slurp was followed by the clatter of an empty plate tied to a contented hum.

Tendrils of lightning lashed out once more, twisting violently like electrified whips. They tore through the sky, scattering stardust into an ethereal patchwork across the velvet sky. As the storm intensified, Missy responded swiftly—no alarm, just instinct. *This wasn't a breach.* Just a tempest rolling in, pressing hard within Starlight's borders. Nature reclaiming her ground. The hefty curtains whooshed along the windowpanes, casting a protective barrier as Nester jumped sidelong with a soft *whoosp. Clink—clank—clunk.*

Her mechanisms began to disengage, tension peeling back as she eased her reinforcements and reignited the candelabras—no longer bracing, but attuned.

The room, once heavy with the storm's energy, started to settle. With the pivot, the pressure lifted—inside, the space softened; outside, the storm continued roiling.

Diesel moved with commanding fluidity across the room, his silhouette crossing from the desk to the window. A small hourglass timer appeared in his hands. "Liam, can you make the journey to the neighboring areas around Sanctuary? Not just to observe the effects of what's happening, but to get a read on what the people there know." He pulled back the curtains, revealing the world outside as the sands slipped steadily through the glass with each flip, marking the moments between lightning strikes. He paused, his hand resting on the edge of the window, fingers lightly tapping the frame. "Maybe they'll have more details or backstory to offer. And listen for any word of coinage being shared."

Liam straightened. "Aye, I'll see what I can find out, Sir." He gave one last lick of his lips, wiped his beard clean, cracked his neck, and—*pop*. The frame stilled, empty.

Three times the sand turned, and the room fell into a tapered hush. As the rain ceased its percussive dance, Diesel inhaled deeply. "It's just the same, Nes. Exactly as it was two decades ago. As much as I hate to admit when Liam's correct, someone's creating an outward distraction to slow everything down."

Beyond the window, a celestial ballet unfolded. Charged particles collided, painting vibrant greens and purples across the night sky. The vast obsidian canvas above transformed into a cosmic wonderland, leaving those who watched in silent awe.

Sir…? Nester nudged.

Diesel's expression remained controlled, though a single tear managed to escape—a quiet sign of the pride swelling within him. Holding his head high, his voice deepened, carrying the weight of a personal revelation. "My little girl is finally breathing." The words surfaced like an inhale—breaking water's edge, long withheld, now irreversibly spoken. "It doesn't get more defining than this," he uttered. His hand lingered upon the pane of glass before turning to Nester's small frame. "Check on D for me, Nes. Make sure she's well before I depart."

Diesel stepped back toward his desk chair, reaching for the obsidian cloak draped along its carved edge. His fingers closed around the collar. In one fluid motion, he slipped it over his arms, the layered fabric settling cleanly over his gear. Reinforced shoulders locked into place, the drape falling in sharp lines as he clasped it across his chest—secure, familiar.

Crossing to the velvet chair, he reached down and grabbed the rucksack Runa had given him. With a single, practiced motion, he slung it over his shoulder. The straps drew tight—no adjustment needed. Without pause, he plucked the last rosebud cake from the dish and popped it into his mouth, the comfort grounding him for just a beat. Then his focus snapped forward —clear, unflinching. The mission waited. And he was ready.

*Sir...*Nester hesitated, a flicker of uncertainty crossing his small, slim frame. One piped arm extended toward the couch where Mama D usually sat—his gesture tentative, searching.

Then, without warning, the bulb atop his head detonated in a blinding flash and a sharp, concussive pop that cracked through the room like a skull splitting wide. A jolt of energy ripped outward, glass erupting in a scatter of light and shrapnel. For a moment, the room stilled—frozen in the aftershock of the break.

Diesel's eyes widened. "What did I tell her about fucking blood reaching? I swear, that damn woman...sometimes...she boils my blood," he muttered. He swept from one side of the room to the other, rummaging through his desk for a replacement bulb. Finding one, he grumbled, "She just never listens."

A tremor rattled through Nester's body, the echo of the rupture still sparking along his joints. His structure jittered with residual charge, a faint hiss curling from the base of his socket where the bulb had blown. Smoke wafted upward in delicate coils, but he didn't collapse. He turned instead —angled himself toward Diesel. One small pipe-arm braced to the floor, the other tucked in, as if keeping his frame steady. The posture was minimal, but clear. A silent offer. Unspoken permission to address the damage done.

Just then, the floorboards creaked—tilting upward. Shattered fragments slipped below, disappearing into the foundation. With a soft, satisfying *plink-plink*, the boards settled back into place.

Nester's gaze met Diesel's, the faint glow within him rekindling once more. *Runa is gone*, he relayed softly, the light stuttered gently as the information resonated. *And the truth about Layla has surfaced.*

Diesel stood motionless for a moment, absorbing the gravity of this briefing. His body tensed, shoulders squared, eyes narrowing as he processed the revelation. It wasn't shock that kept him still—it was calculation.

Tsk—shhk—tsk—shhk.

A rhythmic, almost hypnotic scratching cut through his focus, forcing him to pivot toward the hearth. His mind raced, trying to make sense of it —"What the hell is that?" Diesel barked.

Glistening gold ink flowed like a stream across the page of the bound volume. Symbols etched themselves into place. "I don't have time for this," Diesel growled, the thought coming and going, rough and edged; the noise itself had struck like a tuning fork inside him.

Diesel blinked as the air around Nester shimmered briefly, folding through time, like ripples on the surface of water. The small, luminous figure emerged by the hearth, his bulbous filament gleaming and fluttering, as though pulling at threads of stardust. Nester holding position over the tome; Diesel advanced toward the exit—steps tight, uncompromising.

Sir—wait! The command cracked through the room, uncharacteristically sharp. Nester yanked at the very fabric of space, time warping around him in a flare of static and light. Reality folded—undulating in his wake.

Before Diesel could take another step, Nester materialized in front of him, blocking the path out of the study. His small pipe-arms pressed against Diesel's shins—not forceful, but firm. Every inch of his frame leaned into the resistance just as the door slammed shut before him. A double barricade: lit, grit, and foundational leverage—Nester's spark and Missy's stone resolve.

Frustration erupted. Diesel's palm slammed against the doorframe, his voice a low bark of authority. "Just read it to me!" he roared, body rigid. Muscles tensed. His plan was set—he needed to move, to push ahead with the mission. A non-negotiable.

No...General, Nester murmured, his filament tuning to a more serious, almost urgent hue. *It must be you, Sir,* the light intensified, pulsing with a quiet plea. *You're the only one who can see the truth in what's written.* His light flared. *Please, Sir...I wouldn't request such things right now unless it was truly warranted.*

Registering the ask, Diesel closed his eyes and inhaled. "Missy can do it. You said it runs through her veins," he reasoned. "I don't have time for this, Nes."

Nester pressed harder. *No, Sir...Missy can't. It has to be you. Missy can transcribe, but she can't interpret what's been written.* His petite frame shoved against Diesel's shins, refusing to let him brush it off. *Sir, it will only take a moment,* he urged.

Diesel's chest rose, a steady exhale as he released the tension in his jaw, massaging away the heat that had accumulated. He huffed out, "Fine."

Diesel crouched down, lifting Nester without effort and settling the small, glowing figure into the crook of his arm. The two moved—no tension, just quiet resolve—as they reached the offset where the root system met the freshly inscribed markings. Nester pulled himself forward and, with a fluid swing, dropped lightly from Diesel's hold, landing beside the tome. One arm extended as he touched down, steadying himself before bounding upright and pointing to the inscription carved between root and ink. He looked up, his glow low but insistent—waiting for Diesel to see what had been shared.

```
531 9Z W17H U5, F41L W3 W1LL N07.
            F.Z.
```

He crouched down to scrutinize the open, leather-bound book embedded in the base of the tree. His finger swept over the cryptic symbols newly imprinted into the parchment. His gaze hardened, irritation creeping in as he studied the unfamiliar text. Without looking up, he spoke. "What the hell is this?"

Nester's stubby arms lifted in a shrug. *Not certain, Sir. The path to truth has grown quieter—more selective, about when, and to whom it shows itself.*

"I don't have time for this, Nes." His jaw tightened. "I'm not here to play games. My girl is gone, and I'm not going to sit here solving puzzles with a tree." His fists clenched the straps of his pack as he stood.

Missy groaned, as if to say, *You're not listening.* The creak of her timbers echoed through the tension—a gentle nudge. Almost imperceptibly, Mama D's essence rolled in, warm cookies, sweet vanilla, and sandalwood—a grounding presence woven into the house. It softened the sharpness of his frustration, guiding his focus back to where it needed to be.

Nester's bulbous head dipped as his piped nub shot up, almost as if to say, *Please hold.* The faint light in him pinged softly from edge to edge, like a thought rebounding as he processed. His tiny frame, still, as he listened with quiet intensity. Once the light settled, he extended his nub again, a gesture of presenting, and spoke. ***Mama D says: Diesel, listen...make contact...press in...pause...contemplate...the answers you seek are there.***

Diesel's eyes widened as he exhaled sharply. He began pacing, rubbing his hand over his chin, mind churning. "Dammit, D!" His voice was low, controlled. Shrugging off his backpack, he threw it into the green velvet chair. He kept pacing, fists clenched tight in front of his face, pressing them together beneath his nose, his knuckles whitening with each second. His body tensed, a flush creeping up his neck. *"Fuckin' A,* woman!" His jaw locked, biting back a surge of words.

"Blood...fucking...*reaching!"* He spat through gritted teeth, barely contained fury. *"Fucking—*dammit—*I swear!"* He heaved a breath, frustration sparking off of him. *"Fucking* fine," he muttered, pausing as his frustration gave way to his beloved's wishes—a reluctant surrender. He reached down, his expression tightening as his fingers sank into the inky, golden sap. The parchment gave way under the pressure of his finger, soft, like fresh yellow cake.

As soon as he made contact, the world dissolved. His vision fractured, and his mind emptied. A hush swept in—and with it, a breeze. It crept beneath his collar, whispering along the exposed line of his jaw, cool and Intentional. *Not jarring, but invitational.* It carried the crisp scent of fresh grass, sea, and pine—earthy and ancient, like something buried in memory and stirred loose by the wind. It filled his lungs slowly, winding deeper into him—not as air, but as summons.

Beneath his boots, the study altered. It no longer felt like, floor and framework. It responded—subtle, flexing, alive. Vibrations welled up through the soles of his boots, threading through his legs like a low, resonant drumbeat rising from beneath the earth. The house didn't groan. It inhaled—tender and expansive. The perimeter fell away. What had been beams and floorboards opened outward, stretching into, horizon. The room transformed—*not broken, but reimagined.*

A pine tree's root tore through, clawing and scraping at the soft soil, determined to rise. Diesel turned toward the sound as nature cracked around him. Trunks surged upward—grooved and ancient—twisting skyward with patient gravity. Bark followed, snapping and crackling, rough and ridged, wrapping around the rising core like armor.

Others answered—drawn forward as if summoned to a sacred gathering. Trees filtered in from behind, from within, and to either side: towering pines, sturdy cedar, graceful maple. They didn't form a wall. They formed a threshold—a silent vow of protection, of quiet presence. A cathedral of trunks and limbs and rooted knowing.

Scattered among the forming grove, boulders appeared—not placed, but revealed. Some lay half-buried, worn smooth by time, their shapes curved like bent knees or the backs of resting giants. Others jutted from the damp earth, their edges blurred by moss, offering themselves as nature's makeshift stools. They didn't interrupt the space—they belonged to it. Silent sentinels, shaped by time and left to rest.

Then came the grass. Tiny beads of green sprouted in play with the widening expanse, tickling the edges of possibility and hope. It didn't grow so much as reveal itself—each blade pressing up through loam, cool and dewy, brushing against his ankles with reverence. The ground exhaled into softness. He could feel it: the texture of each stalk against leather, the moist pull of earth releasing shape. The greenery swayed to a soundless rhythm, orchestrated by wind and something older.

Yet with them, the flowers materialized—like prayers spoken into blossom. Tight buds peeked upward, their curiosity quiet and insistent. Wild tufts fanned outward in crisp strokes—not just color, but memory rendered in bloom: pale golds, muted lavenders, hints of rust and early dawn—all whispering of endings and beginnings.

And at last—vines that slipped between the trees, unraveling from hidden seams.

Smooth as silk, they coiled and spilled, their sheen catching the amber radiance like morning dew. From beyond the extending treetops, a warm light bled across the hidden horizon. Not the sun—but something older. *Elemental.* It cast no harsh rays—only gentled the edges of all it touched. Gold braided into moss. Verdant tones hushed into shadow. Every hue ebbed and flowed as a faint sea breeze drifted through the canopy, carrying the clean, briny sharpness of salt and wave.

The vision built itself like memory coming into form—sacred, systematic, whole. Diesel, cloaked and battle-ready, stood at its center—not as a soldier, but as a witness.

Above him, the light began to fade with the grace of a tide drawing back from shore. Golden warmth, once stitched through branch and bloom, began to pull away, coaxed by an primordial rhythm the land made habit. Greens deepened—not to ash, but to a dusk-kissed blend of blue and charcoal, as if the forest were pulling the sun's final breath into its roots. Golds thinned to pewter, brushing the edges of stone, bark, and bare skin with a final glint. Even the boulders, half-buried and silent, seemed to settle into the grass, as if asking it to blanket them for the night. Flowers bowed gently, their vibrant faces tipping in quiet resignation, while the vines curled inward, tucking themselves to sleep. Within this narrowing breath of time, the sky deepened, hue by hue—amber dissolving into smoke-blue, then into slate. Indigo overtook them both until the world eased into obsidian. *Not absence, but richness.* A darkness vast and velvet, the kind that invited stars. One by one, pinpricks of starlight broke through —not scattered, but systematic—constellations arranging themselves like an sacred script older than names.

And that's when he emerged—at first perched high upon a weathered rock. A man crouched low, staring up at the night sky. Without urgency, he looked over his shoulder and swept down from the boulder, coming to a quiet stop a few feet away.

He stood tall, long silver hair trailing down his back, catching faint traces of moonlight. His jaw was set firm, a trimmed beard hugging his face—more stubble than fullness, intentional in its cut. Broad shoulders were framed by a white linen shirt, soft at the collar, loose at the sleeves, the fabric pulling gently at the bends of his arms. A leather wrapping extended from wrist to forearm, covering what the linen left bare, with the same woven layers of dark leather coiled around his abdomen. It was the kind meant for utility, not display. A harness crossed over his chest, securing a long sword strapped across his back, its hilt rising just behind his shoulder—steady, familiar. Heavy fabric pants, worn and dust-streaked, fit clean at the waist and tucked into boots that rose just below his knees. Nothing about him was decorative. Every piece was built to serve. He was a man Diesel had known well—one who never stood above the fight, but in it.

Diesel shook his head once—small, disbelieving. As if trying to blink the vision into logic. *Or sense. Or memory.*

And that's when he saw them—thin strands beginning to rise, lightless at first, then stirring faintly in deep hues of emerald. They unfurled from the man's chest, fine as silk but dense with meaning. They didn't drift— *they reached*. Not random. Not hesitant. Drawn to Diesel's presence like instinct answering instinct. Each one carried something: old oaths, ancient regrets, fragments of memory too sharp to name—and something heavier still, rooted in the marrow of the man before him. A quiet certainty. A peace forged not in surrender, but in resolve.

One filament settled into Diesel's chest, pressing into him like a fingertip to the sternum, prompting a grounded exhale. It made space as it unraveled, folding into knowing. Others lingered—hovering just above the man's head, circling him like truths not yet ready to land, waiting their time.

And then, the man began to blur at the edges—like fog unraveling from form. The leather, the linen, the steel—all unmade in silence.

In one final gesture—one Diesel knew by heart—the male lifted two fingers to his forehead and extended them toward him, the slight dip of his chin marking a farewell shared only among the Elite.

And in the quiet, Diesel understood—why it had to be him. And why the answers he sought could only be found in the pressing in—*to the unknown.*

The world within the forest dissolved as Diesel's breath caught, reality pulled taut. His vision fractured, then blinked toward clarity—like eyes adjusting after long exposure to light, the world narrowing before expanding again. He gasped for air, chest lifting as the weight of the moment folded inward.

He was back—standing beside the hearth, fingertip still pressed to the parchment's surface. The muted warmth of the study returned in fragments: the quiet crackle of flame, the stickiness of resin on skin, and a hum that no longer belonged to nature, but to daily life.

His gaze settled on the inked sheen clinging to his fingers as he brushed them together. The sap—no longer just sap—crumbled into golden dust, fragile as ash, scattering with an iridescent shimmer. The flecks drifted over the inscription, caught on a gentle updraft, swirling in lazy play before settling like sugar crystals on icing—melding, transforming into something entirely new.

He crouched, the breadth of his form folding in closer to the light. The golden script pulsed, delicate and alive—words dancing like thought between worlds.

And Diesel knew, whether he was ready or not—what came next mattered more than breath itself.

SHE IS WITH US, FAIL WE WILL NOT.

F.Z.

The string of letters winked once—twice—then collapsed, folding inward like sigh drawn too deep. Golden flecks scattered, then sank, saturating the parchment's fibers until no trace remained.

He rose, the weight of knowing pressing into every breath.

How could I have missed this? His gaze locked on the leather-bound book. He turned away, jaw tight, and uttered,"My training was meticulous. *Methodical.* Designed to unravel lies like threads...*yet somehow, this* slipped past me." His chest thrummed with silent unrest as he crossed to his velvet chair and sat.

Sir? Nester's voice came softly as he followed, halting just at the tip of his General's boot. His stance was uncertain.

Diesel didn't move, his thoughts spinning in silence. *Why would he do this?*

Sir, the light whispered again, more insistent this time, as his small nub pressed gently against Diesel shin.

Inhaling, nothingness.

Exhaling—long and uneven—as a single tear slipped down, unbidden.

Nester's glow dimmed as he moved in closer, hesitant. *Sir…*

Diesel's voice barely broke the stillness—rough and raw—as he lowered his head into his hands. His shoulders gave way, shuddering beneath the weight.

"My brother is alive." He swallowed thickly."And he has Ru."

The moment was rare. Rarer than rain falling upward. Rarer than glass shattering backwards, then piecing itself together—flawless, whole. Rarer than the moon rising before the sun.

Nester quietly plopped down to the floor beside him, one nub resting gently against Diesel's shin. And sat with him. In silence. It needed nothing more.

Chapter Fifteen

Twilight State: Processing

Future: Month One of Unbinding

As her eyes fluttered open, the room blurred into a earth-toned palette of browns and bluish-gray hues, accented by rustic floorboards and exposed beams. The morning light filtered delicately through the sheer gray curtains, casting a muted glow on the books lining three-quarters of the room's walls.

Disorientation settled in, as though her quarters still held the remnants of a dream, leaving her to wonder if the vivid scenes in her mind were real or mere fragments of a fading slumber. She closed her eyes once more, nestling deeper into the suede and knitted pillows, pulling the plush comforter tight around her, breathing between the quiet haze where dreams and wakefulness intertwine.

Her stomach rose and fell with each breath. Runa inhaled a fleeting scent—vanilla, apple, and milk chocolate. Rayanna's favorite coffee blend, a morning delight they always shared after the Starlight Festival. A tender smile touched her lips as she meandered through memories woven with the aroma, though they soon blurred into fragments that felt more like a nightmare.

Wait a minute, her thoughts stirred, *how long has it been?* The serenity was shattered by sudden, gut-wrenching recollections. The smile faltered, and a piercing thought streaked through her mind like a shooting star: *Was I the one deemed unworthy of love?* It was swiftly followed by a self-condemning notion: *What a pitiful thing to dwell on.*

Her inhale hitched, such curiosities pushing her forward, as though it had revisited her countless times. Yet it felt longer—much longer—than just the morning after the Starlight Festival. *How long has it really been?* Familiarity lingered, yet everything seemed distant, like a memory slipping through her fingers. She curled deeper into the comforter, wrapping herself in its warmth, seeking shelter from the uncertainty swirling inside.

A fleeting image surfaced—a golden sphere of light—and a woman's voice whispered through her thoughts: *You can't stay in Starlight right now. Unbinding yourself makes you a threat to its safety. We created a place, hidden and safe…*The words drifted into silence, leaving only an echo in her mind.

Tucked where? The answer eluded her, but certainty remained. The vision of the glowing orb pulled her inward, like the tide drawing back to shore. The sight captivated her, but there was no escaping the truth: *I can't leave. Not yet. Unbinding requires patience,* she was told. *The pace simply felt daunting. It can't be rushed. Not with everything at stake. This is for everyone's safety—I have to stay in the Moonlight.*

The dam holding her memories broke with a violent force. An avalanche crashed over her, *relentless and suffocating.* Then she was back on the beach, gasping for air, held between Rayanna and Tabytha—her pillars, her constants.

The images weren't gentle—they clawed their way through her, every detail as vivid and cutting as it had been the first time. Adrenaline surged, but the world stuttered, freezing them all in place. Images hit, sharp and jarring, each one a punch to the gut, raising more questions than she could ever answer.

Nausea gnawed its way up. Tabytha had already collapsed to her knees, retching into the bushes. Rayanna stood rooted, her breath hitched, swallowing back the bitterness as the weight of everything—every injustice, every betrayal—wrapped around her throat.

It wasn't just shock; it was the brutal realization that this shouldn't have happened to Runa. *None of it.* The betrayal, the loss—it squeezed

Rayanna like a vice, until the tears pressing against her eyes felt like they might choke out all light.

Astonishment. Horror. Disbelief. It all came crashing down all at once. And then, in clipped, broken gasps, Tabytha's voice cut through the haze. "Runa…what…the…hell…happened…to…you?"

Runa bit down hard, the metallic taste of humiliation filling her mouth as she pulled the blankets further over her head. She felt small—*so small.* Shame ripped through her, and all she wanted to do was run. *To escape this. How could that have been my life?*

Thoughts flooded her mind, attempting to drown her. She clutched her head, fingers digging into her scalp. *What was I?* She trembled, her shoulders hunched. *Worthless…a cheap toy?* Her eyes darted behind her closed lids, searching for answers in the shadows. *For whom?* Her pulls came in shallow gasps. *Collecting…what? Why? What power?* Shivering, she pushed through the thoughts. *A tree? Chains? A silent box?* Her fingers traced invisible scars on her arms. *Punishment…for what?* Tears welled up, consuming her vision. *Bloody? Bruised? Lifeless…*

She remembered being on the balcony back in Starlight, collapsing to her knees under the weight of these questions. *What was my life beforehand?* Her voice had broken into a whisper, eyes staring blankly. *What kind of existence was that?*

Shaking her head, she turned away from the lingering horrors. The festival had become her distraction—swirling lights, blaring music, whirring faces. It was a rapid dance that quickened her mind, even as she begged for everything to slow. The cottage. Her safe space.

A desperate scream erupted within her, rising from the depths of her soul and pulling her toward the vast, obsidian sky, speckled with stars. She felt the weight of the night pressing down on her, urging her to retreat. *Alone. I need to be alone.*

This year, this Starlight Night, more than ever before, she craved the quietude—the stillness of a world she could disappear into. A desire to tuck herself away, like a new moon on this clear, crisp night, unseen but still there. It was a place of refuge, a contrast to the usual joyous abandon she would have embraced, casting aside her worries with enthusiasm.

Now, the cool wooden floorboards enveloped her. In that past moment it felt natural to allow herself to transition into an empty vessel. Quenching her thirst for reprieve. As she had let go, her awareness descended into tranquil silence.

Unseen doors opened, and a bridge took shape, with her on one side and Rayanna on the other. She had thrown out questions into the arena of her mind. *How did we get here?* No response. Only quiet. *How are we effortlessly surpassing the confines of physical separation?* She tucked her bottom lip beneath her teeth, frustration brewing. *There is so much I do not understand, and I am getting tired of living in the dark.*

Hand in hand, they stood there, staring at a reservoir of memories—reminiscent of an ancient archaeological site. The kind of excavation where remnants of the past lay concealed in the gloom of a forgotten tome, untouched by time. This emotional archive appeared familiar but bound in shadows and chains, urging her to retreat.

Pfft…The absurdity of it all, she thought. Laughing it off, or making light of it, seemed like the only reasonable option. Dismissing the situation with a gentle shake of her head, the bridge they had been standing on faded as Tabytha's face came into focus. She let out a hushed chuckle and whispered a small prayer under her breath.

Shit. She rolled her eyes. *I should have known.* It was then that she noticed it—the ripple of color in Tabytha's eyes, the change, the heartbeat of someone different. In that instant, a shared ache took root, weaving an unspoken bond between the two of them.

It wasn't just a brush with memories; it was something deeper, a connection that cemented emotional ties. But even in the midst of this heartfelt fusion, a fleeting question surfaced in Runa's mind, lingering as if searching for answers buried within their shared history. *What's different about her?*

As Runa reflected on their time together at Starlight Beach—and beyond—she couldn't ignore how the threads that once bound them had begun to loosen. The familiar rhythm she had always felt in Tabytha was gone, replaced by a heavy silence that seemed to hum with unspoken transformation. *Was she always this way? Had the shadow binding blinded me to the change?* It was as if Tabytha had retreated into the haze of her own identity, stepping back from the trio's once-unbreakable bond. Conversations that once flowed effortlessly now hung in the air, lingering in the spaces between them—safe, yet undeniably distant.

Runa placed herself back on the bridge, letting the growing sense of unfamiliarity settle around her. Her sister, Tabytha, seemed contained within a lagoon—a stillness no one else could truly understand. The distance between them had grown into a void, a space where questions danced wildly, searching for elusive answers within the silence. *She simply wasn't the same person.*

She wrapped herself deeper into the cocoon of blankets, seeking refuge from the relentless process unfolding within her. The tendrils of shadow, which had held her mind captive for so long, were slowly unraveling, like the grinding of old machinery shaking off rust. It was exhausting work—each step forward felt fragile, as if too much force might break something delicate. Her thoughts drifted back to Rayanna's words, though they barely pierced through the fog of her weariness.

And yet, she was certain it had always begun with the same thought from her past. It felt too natural, too familiar, to be anything else. *Who will ever be able to love me once they know?* The doubt clung to her—unsettling yet inevitable. It was a lingering uncertainty that had followed her through the years, woven into the fabric of her mind like an unwelcome, constant presence.

This doubt hadn't simply lingered in her mind; it had settled into the very core of her being, becoming part of the foundation she built her sense of self on. It wasn't just a passing fear but a weight, heavy and unmoving, like a stone lodged far within her chest.

Over time, the pressure built, and the stone began to crack, its sharp edges piercing deeper, burrowing through emotions and influencing her daily decisions. As she unraveled the tendrils of shadow, the haunting question resurfaced: *How could anyone love someone like me, once they knew the truth?*

This time, something shifted. *What a pitiful thing to dwell on,* the understanding struck her with unexpected clarity. This belief had been bound to her soul for so long, weighing her down, and yet, only now did she truly see how small and unworthy it was of her focus. This wasn't just a fleeting uncertainty; it had been her constant companion through lifetimes—a shadow trailing her steps, always waiting, whispering. But now, it seemed less certain, more fragile than ever before.

Rayanna had offered an answer that felt almost too simple, too profound. "Someone...significant," she had said, as if the word could cut through all of Runa's doubt. Rayanna had compared love to the Moon and the Sun, forces that moved the Earth itself. *But how?* Runa wondered. *To equate to such grandiose ideas—with all my flaws, my scars? How could I be worth such depth, such significance?*

The words *Worth* and *Significance* rang out in her mind—not just as concepts, but as entities. They moved like predators, clinging her every step, reminding her of the gap between what she longed for and what she believed she deserved. She could almost see them: *Worth*, standing tall and distant, unreachable; and *Significance*, looming like a shadow—something she could never fully step into. They weren't just ideas; they were forces that once controlled her, bending her perception of herself.

Rayanna's words felt like a struggle—wrenching something buried deep, something that resisted the light. *Healing*, Runa realized, *isn't about ease. It's about excavation.* She'd have to dig up the knotted phrases she'd sown into her soul, like barbed wire wrapped around her heart. To heal, she would have to unearth each word, with effort, just as Papa D had told her.

She remembered those early jogs along the shoreline with him, the sun barely rising. They'd fallen into a walk, and paused for water, as he'd gaze at the peach-colored sky, lost in his thoughts. One morning, in a rare moment of open introspection, he'd said something that stuck with her.

"Ru, one day you'll understand this deeper. People we trust sometimes chip away at our inner voice. Not because we deserve it—but because they're afraid to confront their own demons." She could still hear the steadiness in his tone as he continued. "Instead of facing their own beasts, they pass that pain onto the ones they love—or should love—the most. With your depth of empathy, Ru, you probably didn't even notice when their words began to embed themselves in you, like a thorn under your skin." Papa D's wisdom had lingered, like glitter taking root in the carpet of her classroom.

Back then, she hadn't truly understood what he had been referring to —the gravity and weight of it all. The knowledge had simply waited, resting in her mind until the light of understanding finally shone through, gleaming back at her and blinding her, as it was now. Its meaning was finally sinking in. The judgments, the fears, the unresolved pain—it had seeped into her as a youngling, shaping the way she viewed herself.

With the unbinding, she could objectively see how deeply those beliefs had taken root, and how different her life could be without them. *Their words were never meant for me,* she realized. *But they lodged in my mind, swinging like a relentless pendulum, constantly reminding me of the unworthiness I never deserved to carry.* The question burned through her, as relentless as the memories. *Why let them keep me tethered to a past that never really belonged to me?* She could still feel the weight of it all—the anchors of others' expectations pulling her under, their burdens chaining her to broken stories.

Papa D's words echoed in her heart, clarity washing over her like a rising tide. *I don't have to carry this anymore.* She felt the chains loosen, slipping from her shoulders, each link dissolving into embers as the weight lifted. *I can break free,* and *unhook myself from those burdens.* The hurtful words that were once seared into her mind, now felt distant, like flames burning low. She imagined them flickering, sputtering out until only ashes remained, scattered and weightless, drifting away on the breeze.

How do I start with something so deeply ingrained? Guess that was the whole point of Starlight, she mused, her eyes twitching behind closed lids. She mentally switched off the light on that thought, turning back to the memory of Rayanna and sitting on the bridge beside her sister. Runa could almost feel the unspoken embarrassment, hesitation, and pain arcing between them.

This isn't ours to bear, she realized, the thought settling heavily in her chest. *These doubts, these fears—they were never mine to carry. They never belonged to me. And yet...they're still here.* Her tongue felt raw. *Fucking knives.*

Her eyes drifted down beneath the bridge. Tabytha was there, floating away in the water, her form distant and dissolving. *She really was no longer quite the same person, was she?* It wasn't just a physical drifting—it was something deeper. *She's slipping away,* the realization bloomed with quiet certainty. *Becoming something different, somewhere else. The distance between them felt like a symbol of transformation—a lingering reminder of absence.* She knew it now, even if Rayanna hadn't spoken it yet.

Then the world above them began to splinter apart. The memory struck like lightning splitting the sky over the Starlight Festival, electric streaks igniting the air. The storm held its breath, then the sky opened, drenching everything in a sudden downpour, as the festivities fell silent.

The crack of thunder never came for her, but the revelation did—sharp and jarring, a lightning bolt finding its mark. The chaos in the sky mirrored the turmoil still raging within her, pulling her back to the balcony. Vibrations rippled through the town, bouncing off the mountains, reverberating through the night.

I am not the sum of their demons, doubts, and limitations. I am not shaped by what they were too afraid to confront. Mentally, she plummeted back down the rabbit hole, standing at the edge of the balcony, drenched and consumed by the unbinding process. With arms outstretched, she welcomed the crashing waves of energy, letting them sweep over her and carry away the burdens she had borne for far too long.

Below, the town stirred, the community scrambling for shelter beneath the storm's onslaught. But Runa didn't move.

I'm done hiding. The truth cut through her, sharp and unforgiving.

No more running. She had lifted her chin into the raging storm. A new kind of determination anchoring deep like roots bracing against the wind. *It's time for answers.*

Chapter Sixteen

Her body recoiled from the mental bridge, trembling as her senses fought to reorient. The residual link with Rayanna clung to her like mist, confusion pulling at her like a churning tide. She was dazed, breathless. *From the exchange? The conversation? The vision?* She tried to shake off the need for understanding. *I'll ask someone about this later,* she thought—but the notion fractured as the world erupted into upheaval.

The once-celebratory atmosphere of the Starlight Festival transformed into an unpredictable tempest. Winds howled, and lightning cracked across the sky like jagged veins of radiance, as the electric air hummed with frenetic power.

Townsfolk scattered below, rushing for cover—but Runa stood at the balcony's edge, arms outstretched, bracing her petite frame against the railing. The storm roared around her, rain lashing, wind clawing, mirroring the turmoil she carried inside. *Let it come!* she screamed in her mind. *Let it crash into me. This storm is nothing—nothing compared to what I've already endured. This unbinding is just another reckoning. So howl. Rage. Tear the sky apart. You still can't touch what I've weathered in silence.*

The thought settled, the weight of everything slamming into her. *Sadness. Weariness. Anger.* Emotions she had buried for so long surged to the surface, each one striking with overwhelming intensity. Runa's chest tightened, the pressure nearly suffocating. Tears, unnoticed until now, mingled with the rain streaming down her face. The storm outside had finally met its match within her—and now, everything spilled out at once.

"I see you," she whispered, recognizing the storm as a kindred spirit— the sky tearing open as the downpour hammered against her. The water swept away the tightness coiled in her chest; her lungs finally expanding fully as sharp, cold air surged in, tasting the moisture. Her gaze slid to her hands, palms lifting toward the sky. A blinding flash of lightning cut through the darkness, illuminating everything for an instant.

This is it, she thought. *I'm letting go.* The roaring storm began to soften, as if it, too, had grown weary of its fury. Her mind spiraled inward, though her body remained anchored to the balcony's edge. *I'm ready to fall. I'm ready to understand. I'm so tired of the questions piling up.*

Her fingers tightened around the railing as the sensations overwhelmed her. *Is this what it means to come undone?* Reality fractured further, slipping away as she tumbled into a place she had never ventured before. The feeling was both freeing and terrifying, like slipping between the cracks of her own mind. Memories and emotions spiraled around her—entwining with thoughts she hadn't touched in decades. *Or was it longer than that? More than years?*

The present moment blurred, like wading through dense water, everything was thick, slow, and heavy. *Is this truly part of me, or am I reaching into something beyond myself?* The question ricocheted through her consciousness, unanswered. *Am I witnessing the dawning of...what exactly?*

Then, the spiraling stopped. Her fall unspooled into stillness, until she wasn't descending at all—just hovering, weightless, caught between one thought and the next, between worlds. She remained untouched by the storm, as if time itself had ceased its forward march.

Ahead of her, an image began to form—faint at first, the kind of thing you almost convince yourself isn't there, like shapes moving behind frosted glass. But then the mist peeled away, slinking back like it had a mind of its own, revealing a massive, impossibly wide window. The glass shimmered, thin as a breath. On the other side was a room she knew all too well: *Papa D's study,* but something about it was…*off. Too still. Too quiet.* The kind of quiet that made the back of your neck itch.

He stood there, one hand resting casually in his pocket, while the other tapped lightly against the window frame—a steady rhythm, like the ticking of a clock counting down to matters yet unresolved. His gaze remained fixed on the darkness beyond. *Solid. Unwavering.*

Just beyond the glass, he was bathed in the warm, golden glow. Runa blinked, tilting her head, a quiet confusion stirring within. *Did that lamplight just…move?* Her body leaned into the question, wrapping itself around the uncertainty. *That can't be right, can it?*

Runa felt as though she had stumbled upon a secret—something hidden in plain sight. Behind his sturdy form stood a veiled space, concealed by a thin, misty barrier that shrouded the unspoken. He didn't turn to face her; he didn't need to. Even now, within this vision—tangible yet impossibly distant—his awareness of her was undeniable.

"My little one…you're finally breathing." His tone reached her, low and steady. The words loosened something deep inside her, unraveling tension she hadn't even realized was there.

So this is what it feels like to truly breathe, she thought, the sensation unfamiliar but welcomed. She inhaled his calm as the exhale brought about his certainty.

"Ru, I knew this day would come. Figures it would happen while I'm away." The scene tilted slightly, the edges of reality wavered and sharpened. He turned, standing motionless for a moment, gaze steady, as though weighing his next words carefully.

His fingertips crept toward the whiskey glass, the amber liquid catching the lamplight like it held secrets. He raised it to his lips, drawing from it like a ritual in motion. He exhaled, the words that followed falling heavy—like stones sinking into a dark well."This had to happen," the statement was unhurried and measured, not just spoken to Runa, but to the space between them. "Not like this, of course," a quiet acknowledgement, softening the admission as he returned the crystal to the table, his fingers lingering briefly upon its rim. "*But then again*…you always had a way of crafting your own path."

His eyes drifted deeper into the darkness,"The Golden Guard will come for you tonight." Silence followed, the truth settling in as his tone descended an octave. "No one has ever unbound themselves before, Ru. It's unheard of. Remarkable...*really.*"

Another pause stretched between them, allowing the weight of the revelation to land. "You'll *need* time," he said softly, a hand coming to rest on the window's pane. "That's why, for your safety, and for Starlight's, you can't stay here."

What? What do you mean? Her gaze darted frantically around the empty void. *There has to be some misunderstanding.* The rawness of the moment pressed harder against her chest, thoughts racing. A quiet panic bubbling up. *I have to leave?* The phrase slashed through, knocking her off balance. A knife of uncertainty twisting in her chest, puncturing her resolve like a lung collapsing. *He's leaving me?*

The faint hum of his tone reached her. "I'm not leaving you, Ru. Think of it more as...*a reframing.* I'm simply tucking you away for safekeeping." His hand remained on the glass, gaze cast outward toward the void where she hovered. It was her space—a remarkable feat, one whispered about but deemed impossible, even while she was shadow bound.

Clearing his throat, he tapped the windowpane's frame—once, twice, then thrice—soft, rhythmic, coaxing her light back into her eyes. "My gift is what some call a Truth Giver, or a Truth Seeker. We're rare these days." He drew his hand from the glass, crossed it over his chest, and pressed into his opposite shoulder. Not for comfort—more reflex. He exhaled hard, the words lining up behind the release. "So trust me when I say, the world is a brighter place with you in it. I can *vouch* for *that.*"

He paused in the share, then dropped his hand from his shoulder and continued, "The information you've absorbed—and will continue to absorb—may make you question everything around you, *and that's okay.* Know this: Whether near or far, I'll always be here in whatever form you need. You're one hell of a bright light, my RuBear. Don't forget that."

The lamp in Papa D's study wavered. His tone quickened, urgency pressing through his words. "I'll try to return before you're gone." The warm glow wavered, casting muted shadows, as if retreating back into the core of the room. For a moment, the space seemed to oscillate—as if he, too, might dissipate with the light. But then his voice resurfaced, crisp and sure. "Ru...*listen to me.* A rosebud for your thoughts, *okay?* I love you deeply, my *sweet* girl."

The shadows intensified as a sharp crack followed. The beading of radiance that danced across the room vanished in a violent flash. His voice, fading now—"You hold a bit of my heart…and I don't need it back." The entire scene trembled. The floating window frame and everything within it dissolved, evaporating into nothingness with a faint *whoosh*. For a moment, she simply existed—hollow, disoriented, yet tethered to him, anchored by the trust she had placed in Papa D's words.

Without warning, her very essence launched skyward, blazing like a comet, only to be violently yanked back toward her body. Her spirit colliding with the solid form she had momentarily left behind—melding into it with a gelatinous *thud*, the two halves forcibly reunited. Her grip on the railing tightened, the wood anchoring her while her body shuddered from the impact.

"What…in the *hell*…was that?" The words slipped out, each one drawn from a deep well of confusion, with an extra side of *what the fuck*.

The sky responded to the tempest within her, translating her release into vibrant streaks of pink and blue. The lights coiled and spiraled, breaking free from the confines of the stars. Hues of green erupted, swirling in wild abandon, no longer tethered to the predictable rhythms of the night.

Just like me, she thought. The radiant waves surging outward, riding the magnetic current. They twisted and flowed across the sky, as though her newly unleashed freedom was being etched upon the heavens. Each ribbon of light moved like a stroke from a cosmic painter, where tempered anger and deep sorrow bled together, merging into something raw and powerful, yearning to be understood.

The hues swelled, rippling across the firmament. She observed each subtle change, a gentle tug on heartstrings she hadn't known existed. *I've never seen anything like this…*She hesitated, the thought slipping into her mind, *Or…have I?* A memory hovered just beyond reach, like an elusive star she couldn't quite place.

The colors continued unfurling across the expanse, mist-like and mesmerizing, weaving through constellations and turning the night into a surreal masterpiece. Her thoughts blurred, lingering like whispers waiting to be remembered. *How can something so vast feel so intimate?* The question drifted through her mind like a cloud, feeling oddly like an answer, as though this light show was a silent message from somewhere...*or someone.*

In that suspended moment, she stood speechless. It was as if the sky had chosen this night to reveal something that had been hidden, something very precious—something she might finally be able to reclaim. *This is for me.* Releasing a breath, content for now, not fully understanding...*but I know I will in time.*

The rain kept falling in relentless torrents, battering her skin like a thousand tiny needles, each drop seeping through soaked clothes, chilling her to the bone. Her black sweater and pants clung to her drenched frame, tracing every curve of her petite silhouette. Every second became a battle, her lungs straining against the wall of rain and wind, as untamed energy seethed both inside and out.

The cold gnawed at her, but her boots held firm, planted on the balcony's wooden planks. She gripped the railing with white-knuckled hands, her only anchor against the fury of the gale. Every muscle in her body screamed for release, yet she held on, refusing to let go. Chaos raged, each gust of wind tearing at the fragile threads of control she had left. *I can't let go. Not yet.* The thought pulsed through her mind, like a heartbeat keeping her tethered amidst the upheaval.

The vintage curl pinned at the front of her hair had loosened, damp tendrils slipping free, clinging to her cheeks. Her once-soft ponytail now hung heavy, plastered to her neck and shoulders. Her gaze drifted across the blurred scene of their front yard. The muted glow of lanterns mixed with the swirling colors above the gravel, casting soft reflections across her dewy skin. A shaky release slipped free as tears mingled with the relentless downpour—each drop carrying away fragments of brokenness, of burdens she'd held for far too long. *Is this what Papa D meant by unbinding; by breathing?*

The yard, usually brimming with the energy of the Starlight Festival, now lay hushed, bathed in the hazy glow of lit water droplets—like lights staring back at her through underwater hues, their radiance blurred by the curtain of rain. Nearby, glass orbs hung—flames waltzing within, their luster warped by rivulets of rain. Droplets pinged in rhythm against the curved surfaces, crafting a song meant to lull. Beneath the old oak tree, a feast lay hastily covered—its flimsy shield no match for the unyielding storm.

Suddenly, mirroring the storm's inception, everything eased into a profound stillness—the rain paused mid-fall, and the candlelights froze in place. Runa's gaze settled on a single droplet, poised on the edge of the balcony. Leaning down, she gently plucked it between her fingertips—*plink*—rolling the tiny sphere around, transfixed by its delicate, suspended form.

"Oh, for heaven's sake." She leaned closer, squinting. *What the…what the hell is happening?* Her mind spun, struggling to grasp the spectacle before her—*It's like reality is cracking and reshaping its core nature.* With quiet reverence, she returned the droplet to its place. It settled seamlessly, merging once more with the suspension of time around her.

The sky began to dim, and shadows crept in like a hand pulling a velvet curtain shut. Colors bled into the deepening black, each hue swallowed as though the night had decided to reclaim its dominion. The stars themselves blinked, leaving the world beneath them wrapped in darkness; subdued by a celestial hand guiding the transition with a strange, quiet finality. The evening stuttered. A vacuum of existence. No movement. *No sound. Nothingness. Then…*

From within the rounded stone arch of the moongate, at the end of the gravel drive, blues as profound as the ocean's currents bloomed, mingling with emerald greens. The colors began to swirl—*thrumming*—*whooshing*—in vibrant waves through the circular stonework. Streaks of gold appeared, threading through the churning hues like waves of liquid frost, casting a faint sheen along the gateway and spilling haloing mist over the drive.

She rubbed her eyes, baffled. *I'll be damned.* Irritation flared, mingling with disbelief. *You have got to be kidding me. This isn't possible.*

The evening's stillness deepened as the luminous hues within the moongate sputtered, pushing away the shadows. The portal's aura seemed to breathe, infusing life into a transmuting radiance. Then, a female emerged from the swirling veil. She drifted forward with a grace that defied gravity, the space around her quivered—each motion distorting the air, like a trace of warmth ghosted over chilled stone.

Runa stilled completely, transfixed as the female's gaze lifted toward the balcony's edge. The traveler exhaled, eyes closing as she dipped into a low bow. Her hands delicately gathered the flowing fabric of her dress, which fluttered softly within the honey-hued luminescence surrounding her.

As she straightened, an ever-altering halo of vibrant light enveloped her, like the first blush of sunrise caressing the suspended rain. The radiance twisted and coiled around her, like remnants of a dream lingering on the edge of reality. The woman's allure was captivating, like the call of a Siren, whispering across a restless sea.

The moongate's light flickered, sputtering once more before finally dimming. The incandescence within the gateway vanished, leaving the night in a profound darkness. The throughway faded back into what it had always been, as the moment itself slipped back into the shadows. Runa gripped the wooden balcony rail tighter, the cool, rain-soaked wood biting into her palms.

This has to be the Golden Guard. It has to be…right? She stared at the figure below—graceful, ethereal—completely at odds with the image she'd conjured in her mind. *The Golden Guard,* she repeated to herself, the words summoning visions of a rigid, armored sentinel, not this soft, fluid presence. A dry chuckle slipped pasted her lips, like a breeze through a cracked window. *To hell with expectations. Sometimes what comes isn't what you braced for—it's what you forgot to hope for.*

Yet, uncertainty stood beside her, poking and prodding at doubt. *What if I'm wrong? But then, what else would come through a portal during a storm?* A pang struck her in the gut. *If she's here to take me, then every second matters.* Heart thudding against her chest, a desperate rhythm that rumbled through her bones. *I have to see Papa D first. I need to give him more time.* Her teeth sank into her lower lip. *He said he would show. He always does…when he promises.*

The female's arm extended, fingers reaching toward the second-story veranda. Her movement was fluid, carving a path through the stillness. Tiny beads of rain, suspended in midair, shivered and fell in soft *plinks,* nudged from their frozen state by her touch.

*If I can slow this down…if I can just delay her…*Desperation clung to that fragile bit of hope, *than maybe, just maybe, time could bend, allowing me a few more precious moments to linger in Starlight.* Unease nudged at the edges of her mind, a strange tug that unraveled her sense of reality, like a ball of string sent skittering across a room.

Papa D warned me about this. He'd said it himself—absorbing all this new information might make everything feel like it's slipping through my fingers. And it's okay. His reminder cycled back through her with uncanny clarity. *Unbinding…He called it remarkable, something no one else has ever done. Coming from him, that means something.* It held a resonance she couldn't easily dismiss.

Then, the voice reached her without a single movement of the traveler's lips. *My dear, you will indeed have the power to hault time one day, but that phase is not now. You will see Diesel again, at some point. I can guarantee you he hasn't left you, just as we haven't.* The words cocooned her like a soothing lullaby, that rocked her like a mother cradling a child. *But leaving this place is the only option.*

Curiosity bloomed within her, delicate as the first leaves of spring. Closing her eyes, Runa surrendered to the strangeness of the moment. In the brief bit of darkness, she felt herself slip between the folds of time, like stepping through barely parted curtains.

When her eyes fluttered open once more, she stood beneath the ancient oak's sprawling canopy. A quiet gasp escaped her lips, surprise widening her eyes, as if she'd been caught off guard by the effortless shift through the fabric of time. *Did I do that?* She glanced toward the balcony's edge, then back to where she now found herself. The beads of rain still hung in place, yet subtly vibrated with the transition.

The traveler remained still, her expression calm and focused as she took in the surroundings before her. "Yes," she said gently, "I am one of the Golden Guards." The words settling like a delicate reverberation in the space between them. "Isn't the power of muscle memory…intriguing?" she continued, her tone holding steady. "Like Diesel said—you're unbinding yourself, dear." Her eyes widened for emphasis. "It's truly *remarkable.*"

She paused, letting the impact of her words take hold before speaking again. "Surrendering control, leaning into your instincts—Diesel has taught you well. These reflexes will become your key to relearning and honing your true potential. Folding into time was once a skill widely known, but now, it's a rarity. And this, my dear, is just the beginning of what's possible for you."

Amid this new vantage, Runa stood, her mind spinning as she absorbed the scene around her. In the feathery shimmer of suspended candlelight, the remnants of the lashing deluge hung in its magical stasis. Raindrops glinted like floating jewels, forming delicate, crystalline veils that draped from above, casting a dream-like haze over the world. She blinked. Speechless. *Absolutely speechless.*

They hovered in defiance of gravity—a torrent paused on the edge of release. *Mama D won't be pleased when all this finally gives way,* she mused, a hint of unease creeping in. The gathering had scattered in the onslaught of the storm, rushing for shelter and leaving behind signs of their hasty retreat. Plates balanced precariously, about to fall like leaves from the branches of the old oak. Nearby, the bucket-sized canister of Mama D's famous bubbly Raz-a-Fraz hung mid-air, on the verge of spilling over, threatening to drench the basket of extra biscuits tucked beneath the table.

The traveler's gaze lingered on Runa, her expression slipping from composed serenity into something more raw—wonder, tinged with a sorrow she couldn't quite hide. She inhaled deeply, steadying herself before speaking. "I know you don't remember me," she murmured, her words trembling. Her voice carried a tenderness that felt like a secret meant only for Runa. "And that's...*alright.* It's not your fault...it's all part of the binding."

She paused, her eyes tracing over Runa's face, as though trying to memorize this version of her. "Your energy is so much more...*vibrant*... than the last time we crossed paths." A twinge of emotion tightened her throat, and she blinked rapidly, swallowing hard. "It's just...*as much as*...I didn't want to do any of this, you're so different now, *more alive* than I ever thought possible." Her voice wavered, hope and nostalgia weaving through the spaces between her words.

"Runa..." A tear slipped free before she could stop it, and she brushed it away with a graceful hand. "I just...*if I had known then...*" Her voice trailed off, the sentence dwindling into silence.

Runa's chest tightened, confusion swirling with a faint pang of guilt. "If you had known...*known what?*" The question lingered—puzzlement looming just out of reach, tangled in shadows and fragments, elusive and teasing. Her mind churned, clawing through fleeting notions like sifting through a warehouse of countless dusty boxes and coming up empty.

Overhead, the ancient oak towered, its massive, knotted branches stretching outward, each one thick with age and gnarled history. The bark, rough and furrowed, held patches of moss and trailing vines; and from its boughs hung candles and glowing orbs—remnants of festival preparations now caught in suspended animation. The tree absorbed the pulse of Runa's emotions, responding with vigilant strength. Its limbs stirred—a baritone creaking, alive with a guardian's resolve—while delicate incandescent orbs swayed with the movement, painting the ground in dappled patterns and phantom shades.

A tremor thrummed down the oak's trunk, coursing through the earth as Runa's palms met bark. The branches wove tighter around her petite form, crafting a barrier between her and the traveler.

The female's voice slipped through the stillness, tailored with resolve. "It's attuned to you, Runa—your surge of energy, set in motion by the touch of your quintessence," she spoke directly. "The oak's strength is poised to soften, to yield to calm, should it find its way back to your heart. But right now, your mind is searching, tugging at ancient threads bound deep within you—the ones always meant to protect. When you pull at these shadow bound thoughts, you signal an attack." Her gaze held Runa's, her tone edged with urgency.

"Each tree, each sentinel in Starlight, is stationed here to guard. You have to find stillness, or you'll wake them all from their restful slumber." A low, resonant groan echoed from the oak's trunk, deepening into a rumbling stretch. The tree flexed its spine, readying itself to step forward from its long-held station.

Beneath the ancient branches, the wooden table trembled, dishes atop it teetering from the vibrations above. Plates wobbled precariously, but held steady as the traveler lifted her hand gracefully—fingers curling in a refined gesture, stabilizing the scene. She divided her focus between grounding Runa and anchoring the objects around them, her presence a steady force amid the altering space.

"Shhh...my child—breathe." An invisible pressure settled on Runa's back, familiar and comforting, a maternal touch. Though the traveler hadn't moved closer, her hand hovered in Runa's direction, maintaining a quiet connection.

After a moment, the female lifted her phantom hand from Runa's back, allowing her fingertips the freedom to wander—tracing delicate circles through the air, each motion an elegant coaxing of calm. Soft scents of lavender and lilac drifted toward her, curling around her, cooling the warmth that pulsed within her chest. The intensity ebbed, like embers settling, a clarity returned to Runa's vision. Breathing steady.

Blinking, she eased the grip she'd had on the oak's bark, noticing faint impressions she'd left behind—darkened patches where her touch had pressed into the rough surface. A pang of guilt tightened in her chest as she took in the imprints she'd left, her fingers trembling with the realization. *I didn't mean to…I'm so sorry.* The thought lingered, heavy and unspoken, as she absorbed the impact on something so ancient, *so alive.*

With care, she set her palms over the blistered bark again, guided by an instinct she couldn't name—only that it felt like atonement. Eyes closed, she drew in a steady breath, then released it with intention.

Beneath her touch, a shimmer stirred—green and silver trails bloomed along the contours of her fingers, vibrant against the weathered timber.

The sensation pulled her inward, unexpectedly, to her classroom. Her students' faces sparked behind her eyelids—squinting in concentration, tracing their own hands in crayon, delighted by the flow of color.

It's as if they're here, she thought. *A gentle illumination. An echo of their innocence—and the quiet healing life sometimes allows.*

She watched as, at each fingertip, a faint spark of energy hummed, like tiny waves of light cresting a hill before rolling into the next. Transfixed, she followed the luster as it flowed from one finger to another. When the sheen reached the base of her thumb, she withdrew her palm, observing as the gentle radiance descended into the bark—a silent apology conveyed in the softening of its hue. Her own curiosity lingered, mingling with the urge to make things right.

As her hand released, warmth radiated from the bark where her touch had settled. Now in its place, a delicate moss began to grow, velvety and lush, spreading outward like a natural bandage. She hesitated, then brushed her fingertips over the greenery, finding it cool to the touch, like the refreshing balm of morning dew.

Overhead, the branches groaned, creaking with the grace of a sentinel bowing in respect—a lumbering giant, acknowledging her care. Her gaze drifted back to her palms, a faint tingle lingering like they'd gone numb;

they were only now stirring back to life, a trace of energy still humming in her fingertips. She flexed her hands, bewilderment mingling with awe. The intensity of it all struck her—unfamiliar, yet rooted in something ancient. The oak's response, her own unguarded strength—they mirrored each other, as if recognizing the same source.

"Is this...what unbinding does?" she murmured, hoping the question would unravel itself. "What...what am I becoming?"

The traveler stepped closer, awe twinkling in her gaze. "No, this isn't the unbinding," she said with quiet resolve. "This is part of who you *actually* are...who you've always *had the potential* to be." As she spoke, the towering oak loosened its protective stance, branches that had woven around Runa slowly unfurling, groaning and creaking to create an opening.

"Perhaps," she continued, "it's time you learn what truly is, what was, and what can be." Waves of energy flowed outward as she spoke, mirroring the rhythm of the ocean meeting the shore, cutting through the stillness with graceful delicacy.

With a fluid sweep of her hand, she drew an arc across her body, and in that instant, the air seemed to sigh, cascading in a supple wave. Suspended raindrops shimmered, then fractured into glistening flakes—a diaphanous snowfall of crystalline feathers and faceted diamonds that cascaded around them. The landscape transformed beneath the ethereal frost, each leaf, branch, and stone blanketed in a glimmering veil, as though dipped in stardust.

The traveler's lips curved in a soft smile. "I thought, why not turn your Starlight Festival into a touch of winter wonderland? Just as your first had been." Her voice lingered, gentle and warm, wrapping around the spectacle like a cherished memory.

Within the canopy, the lights and candle-lit orbs swayed gently, their golden halos glinting in the crisp air, catching and holding the luster like fireflies encased in frosted shells. The crystallized atmosphere mirrored the decorations' shimmer, filling the space with a hushed radiance. Beyond the moongate's edge, everything stood still, awaiting the gentle fall of each feathered snowflake—standing in a patient contemplation.

The traveler's smile softened as she released the invisible grasp she'd cast over the yard. "This property—and others like it in this haven—has its own defenses, thanks to the ley lines woven through the land," she said, her tone steady and clear. Her gaze lingered on Runa, noting the glimmer of understanding in her expression. "These lines were gifted long ago by Sanctuary; they form chords that tether this place to an enduring protective veil."

With tranquil authority, she extended her hand outward, fingers unfurling with command, guiding the boundary of containment around them. She lifted her arm in a measured arc, as her fingers traced the air; a tide of gentle vigor emanated, washing over the cottage. A pale shimmer whirred outward from her fingertips, a quiet reflection of the ancient resonance now anchoring their safety. "Only the yard may stir for now," she murmured, "and the cabin here."

As the hum dimmed, the frozen earth responded—its features subtly stirred, like the beat of wings across fresh snow. Holding her other hand raised, the traveler maintained the stillness beyond, keeping the rest of the town bound in silent pause. Her fingers curled in a controlled gesture, channeling strength from the ley lines', she extended a delicate, protective bubble over the cabin, gently encouraging it to come alive within this preserved moment.

She lowered her hand, allowing the shimmer to settle as a tranquil hush embraced the yard. "For now, we must remain unseen—shielded," she said, her words carrying an almost reverent understanding of the power they held. "Once we're ready to leave, it will all be restored."

The front door swung open with surprising force. Mama D appeared atop the stone steps—eyes sharp, shoulders squared—her usual calm slipping as she descended with steady purpose. Her waist-length, silvery-blue hair cascaded over her shoulders, catching the cold light in a way that softened her fierce expression. *She contains such a rare strength*, Runa thought, watching her. *Locked out, unable to protect or even witness...she must feel truly slighted.*

Mama D moved forward with steady ferocity, her gaze sharp as she swept over the scene, assessing it like an unfamiliar threat. Behind her, Rayanna and Tabytha followed awkwardly, their delicate sandals slipping on the damp, melting snow. They clung to the banister in a desperate bid for balance, each footfall a cautious test against the slick surface. As they reached ground level, Rayanna's hand shot out to steady herself on Mama

D's shoulder, setting off a chain reaction as the three collided in a tangle of arms, laughter, and startled shrieks, ending in a heap.

Runa's lips twitched, unable to hide her amusement. "Don't rush on my account," she called, watching the trio struggle to untangle themselves —their high-pitched squeals and laughter pierced the air as they flailed in a jumble of limbs. "We really do need to work on the 'rushing to someone's aid' part."

As they steadied themselves just a few steps shy of their goal, Mama D cast a fierce glance in the traveler's direction. "I'll deal with *you*...in a *moment*." Her tone came out clipped. Turning abruptly to the towering oak, she twitched her wrist, and the plates teetering on the table slid neatly back into place.

Rayanna leaned in, her loose curls brushing Runa's face, the dusty blonde strands catching the soft light. In a whisper barely audible, she asked, "Are you seeing this?"

Beside her, Runa nodded in disbelief, brushing her own dark, damp hair back from her shoulders. Rayanna leaned closer and murmured, "Did you know Mama D could do that?" Then she threw her hands up in the air. "All these years, I've been washing the dishes..."

The absurdity of it all tugged a smirk to Runa's lips.

"Well, I'll be *damned*," Rayanna crossed her arms. "I can tell you what... I feel cheated." Speaking in a hush, she added, "Quite *betrayed*, actually."

With composed focus, the traveler raised her arms, fanning them out to the sides before arching them upward. Fingers spread wide, she brought them together in a soft, decisive clap. Lowering her pressed palms past her brow, her eyes fluttered closed as she placed both hands over her heart, holding them there with a reverence that hinted at ancient loyalties. After a moment, she lifted her fingertips to her lips in a gentle kiss, then let her hands fall gracefully to her sides.

Around them, the protective bubble shimmered in response, snapping firmly into place as if sealing the property under its guard. The great oak acknowledged the barrier, its massive branches flinging off droplets in a powerful spray—like a wet dog shuddering off bathwater—casting away the last remnants of the storm. Instinctively, the girls raised their arms, warding off the mist.

Stepping forward, Mama D extended two fingers from her brow, palm outward, and twirled her hand in a gentle circle—a silent salute of respect to the ancient guardian. A deep vibration hummed through the ground, resonating beneath their feet as the oak's roots anchored firmly into the earth once more, the great sentinel resuming its watchful silence.

Mama D furrowed her brow, her stare locking with the traveler's. An unspoken challenge simmered between them. In the silence, distrust mingled with fierce resilience, as each woman measured the other with an intensity that needed no words.

Rayanna's arm extended instinctively across Runa's front, pressing gently against her damp clothing. Just behind them, Tabytha leaned back against the banister, arms lazily crossed over her chest, idly picking at her nails. The trio's gaze bounced between the two women, the space vibrating with a keen awareness to every flicker of movement.

Mama D's eyes widened, her mouth slightly agape as disbelief crossed her face. Her voice was layered with surprise and a faint trace of hurt. "*So*...I guess *death* didn't take?"

Rayanna's jaw dropped as she threw her hands onto her hips, fists clenching. "Wait. You *tried* to kill her?"

"Well, obviously *not!*" the golden woman replied to Mama D's accusation, lifting her chin slightly, each word punctuated like an exclamation mark. "But that's a *story*...for *another* day." Her final words softened, trailing off into a low crescendo as her stance relaxed.

Rayanna's eyebrows shot up in shock. "What is even happening right now?" she demanded, half-sarcastic, half-stunned. "And don't even get me started on all those plates I scrubbed while you just waved a hand and made everything pristine. Like, *what?* You always preached about not half-assing anything." Her arms crossed tightly, eyes narrowed with exasperation. "Maybe it's time you took your own advice." She blinked back at the pair of females. "Oh, and from now on, I'm done with chores."

Mama D's gaze cut through the air, landing on Rayanna with the force of a reprimand. Without turning her head, Runa whispered from the corner of her mouth, "Stand *down* and fall *back*."

Without pulling her attention from the scene, Runa reached over, hand wandering across Rayanna's face to silence her. Her fingers tapped lightly in a blind search for her sister's mouth, landing, with a gentle pat, on her chin. "Damn your height, lady!"

Rayanna half-heartedly swatted her away, her face going from light pink to red. "I do not agree that this is a story for another day." Turning to Tabytha and Runa, she tried to gather support. "I know I'm not the only one needing answers."

Runa sighed, throwing up her hands in quiet surrender. "Yeah, *no thanks*—don't drag me into this. I'm still wrapping my head around what just happened."

"*Perfect.* Ru's in—that's two votes," Rayanna said, sass lacing her tone.

Runa rolled her neck back, looking up at the sky as she tossed her arms up, frustration radiating from every motion. "*Seriously?*" she muttered.

Ignoring the gesture, Rayanna's glance darted to Tabytha, reclining back on the bottom step with her arms loosely folded. She signaled her agreement with a single raised finger. "One for Tabs," Rayanna declared, turning back to face the two older women. "So that makes three. *Majority* wins."

Mama D arched a brow, lips pressing into a thin line as she took in the challenge. She glanced from Rayanna's resolute stance to Runa's exasperated retreat, a mixture of irritation and faint amusement flickering as she let a beat of silence hang before responding, her voice low.

"Majority wins, *does it?*" she said dryly. "You three might want to rethink your little coalition before declaring any victories here." She gave Rayanna a pointed look. "Some things aren't meant to be unpacked all at once."

"I have to agree. Foundational things need to be addressed first." Realization dawned across the Golden Guard's face as she spoke, her brows lifting in quiet revelation as she continued, "What exactly do they know?" She made a purposeful loop with her hand near her head. "About their *triad* situation?"

Mama D's expression tightened as she began pacing in mindful circles. "Their knowledge of realms beyond this one...it's limited."Her voice gilded with careful thought, gaze drifting to the sky. Her eyes swept over each curious face. "Layla knows more than Ru and Ray. Shadow binding has safeguarded much of what they might otherwise understand."

Rayanna jolted forward, her face flushed, the pink deepening with her frustration. "Wait...who the fuck is *Layla* now?" she snapped, huffing out a sharp sigh. "This is just getting *fuckin'* ridiculous!"

Mama D turned to her, expression unyielding. She arched an irritated brow, lowering her chin as she raised a hand—a firm, silent command to pause, like a mother calmly deflecting a child's tantrum. Without missing a beat, she continued, "Thought weaving isn't about holding it back. It's about guiding what's already there—threaded through the ink during their marked phasing. That process was arranged before they ever arrived here. Runa's release has been gradual because she's doing what most can't." She paused. "She's unbinding herself."

Her fingers tapped lightly against her side as she continued. "Izayah and Diesel decided the information would come through in stages—allowing them to absorb and adapt gradually." She paused, her tone reflective. "It's more Izayah's design than Diesel's, though he sees the wisdom in it—a strategy put forth by the future General of the Elite Shadow Guild."

Runa rubbed her face while she listened, squatting down in her still-soaked clothing as the chill began to settle into her bones. "*So…*what I'm getting out of all this, is that there's a lot more to this world than what we thought," she muttered, glancing down at her forearm; there the dark ink of the moon and stars rested. "And this thing," she gestured to the markings, her thumb tracing an arch from the East and West stars flanking the moon,"—it *actually* holds information?"

"That's what you got from all that, Ru?" Rayanna huffed.

"Yeah, *well…*Miss I-need-answers, looks like you missed some key points of this conversation." Runa shot back, squinting up at her sister. "You're focused on the wrong details, Ray," she added with a shiver.

Rayanna shook her head, hard enough to send a stray curl whipping against her cheek. "Forget it," her voice tight and low, like a kettle just beginning to hiss. One hand propped on her hip, the other rose to rub at her temple, a futile attempt to push back the building tension. "Regardless…someone needs to start explaining. Who the fuck is Layla and why does she know more than us?" Her gaze sharpened. "And why are you talking about her like we're supposed to already know her?"

The Golden Guard's expression lifted from astonishment to something unreadable as she turned toward Mama D, lowering her chin. "They don't know about Layla?" Her gaze dropped. "Are you telling me Layla's been… all this time as…?" Her voice trailed off as a sharp, unexpected laugh escaped her lips. "That's *just* insane. *Effective,* but completely *insane.*" She cleared her throat, regaining her composure as a wry smile crept onto her face. Turning to the girls, her eyes gleamed with a mix of amusement and authority. "If that's the case...you've got a lot to learn, young ones," she said, her tone pointed and knowing. "You're definitely not ready for my story...not yet. Let's just start with the basics."

"Alright then, I'm all ears," Rayanna snapped, her hands flexed and clapped together, sharp and impatient, demanding action. She leaned forward slightly, her body coiled tight, ready to pounce on the next word, the next explanation. Her gaze flicked from face to face as she pivoted, daring someone to speak.

"Rayanna," Mama D replied, her tone carrying a quiet warning.

"*What?*" Rayanna's tone was laced with mockery. "How many *fucking* times do I have to say it?" Her voice sharpened further, the derision giving way to fury. "So go on—*fucking share something!*" she spat.

"Um, yeah, *soooo*...that would be me," Tabytha said coolly, lifting her hand as she joined the inner circle. Tilting her head, she cracked her neck, one eyebrow arching as her chin rose slightly. "I am Layla, *actually.*"

Rayanna's expression darkened, as the weight of Tabytha's—*or rather,* Layla's—words sank in, hitting like a sucker punch to the gut. Her pulse thundering in her ears, drowning out all reason. This wasn't *just* a lie. It was a knife slipped between her ribs by someone she *never* expected. "ARE...you...FUCKIN' kidding me?" she spat, her voice trembling with rage.

She moved before her mind could catch up, spinning on instinct more than thought—her hand clamping around Layla's throat. "What...the... *fuck* is happening?" The words were low and venomous, poisoned by a mixture of fury, confusion, and disbelief—something raw and unspoken clawing to the surface. Her grip tightened, thumb digging into Layla's neck for a heartbeat before she shoved her back.

Layla's shoulders slammed into the rockwork staircase with a sharp *thud.* Rayanna followed, pinning her there as the fire in her chest spilled over. "*And where the fuck,*" she growled, her voice splintering into a dangerous whisper, "*is Tabytha?*" Her lips curled as the words left her, trembling with the force of her anger, teetering on the edge of this new, jagged reality.

Pinned yet unfazed, Layla's lips curved into a languid smirk. "Hmm...

that escalated quickly," she drawled, her voice a low purr, tinged with dry amusement. "What's the *matter, dear sister?*" Her tone taunting, "Too many surprises for one day?"

Before Rayanna could tighten her grip again, Layla twisted, her movements fluid and instinctive, muscles snapping to attention. Her elbow shot up, striking Rayanna's forearm with powerful force, loosening the grip. With a sharp thrust, she shoved Rayanna backwards creating distance and using the momentum to step into a steady, defensive stance.

Catching her balance, Rayanna's eyes narrowed in disbelief. "Fuck *you.*"

Layla shrugged, a wicked, lazy smirk settling over her like a second skin, shaking it all off like an old habit she no longer had time for.

The Golden Guard's salt-and-pepper hair fell forward as she leaned casually against the wall, a bemused smile playing on her lips as she glanced at Mama D. "It's amazing how fast their training comes back, isn't it? Like I said before—muscle memory never fails to astound me."

Mama D nodded thoughtfully, her gaze pooling between the three women before her. "*Impressive*, really. Fascinating to see what will emerge during the unbinding."

Runa, quietly observed everything, as her gaze flicked between Layla and Rayanna. "Really? Can we finish the mystery before the murder?" her tone dry, but edged with exasperation. Raising a hand, stepping forward, she spoke. "*I get it*—you're *all* on *information* overload. *I am too.*"

Her brow knitted as her attention glided to Layla, who leaned casually against the banister. Then her eyes found Rayanna, folded into herself on the bench, frustration pressed into every angle of her form. "How about you two try not to take each other's heads off, okay?"

Rayanna rose, her voice trembling with barely contained anger—it was almost a whisper, "We were *fed some bullshit story* while they made us out to be complete dumbasses." Her eyes darted between the group, searching desperately for answers that never came. "How the hell do I figure out what's real in all this mess—or what's just bullshit?"

Runa rubbed her brow thoughtfully. "Actually, Ray, it kinda seems like we've been on vacation compared to whatever everyone else has had to go through."

Mama D laughed, the sound rich and full. "Ray, trust me, after your unbinding, you'll have *no trouble* deciphering *any* of this. That's part of why you're so frustrated right now—and it's understandable." She turned to the Golden Guard, a glint of amusement in her eyes. "Well, Nadine, how about you drop this honey-hued bubble you've got going, and we let them in on a few things? What do you say?"

Nadine let out a long, resigned sigh, a smirk tugged at the corner of her lips. "I *suppose* I have a *bit* of time," she said, a quiet levity in her otherwise measured tone.

The golden mist shimmered around Nadine, swirling lazily, as if it moved to its own rhythm—its own will. The orb radiated in subtle intervals, each beat casting a mellow, incandescent wash across her face. With a graceful flourish of her wrists, the bubble spiraled inward, folding seamlessly into the fabric of her floor-length golden dress. It sank into the material, leaving behind a faint gleam—delicate yet unmistakable, like the thin line of a horizon where day meets night. She inclined her head toward Mama D, the motion fluid, mirrored by a modest bow in return—an expression unreadable, but expectant.

The winter wonderland dissolved like a mirage, snowflakes evaporating mid-air and leaving behind the crisp clarity of the quiet night. The stars stretched across the clearing, their cold light settling over the scene like a held breath.

"Alright, D," Nadine's huffed out, "Looks like we've got some stories to share."

As the two women began up the stone steps to the cottage, the trio exchanged silent, wary glances. Rayanna shook her head, casting a sidelong look at what used to be Tabytha. Turning back, she started up the stairs.

As Runa walked passed—Layla—she leaned in and whispered, "Just give her time. She'll come around."

Layla raised her hands in surrender, calling after them, "If it's worth anything…it's always been me. Tabytha was done two decades ago, back at the cabin."

Rayanna froze at the top of the steps, and Runa halted beside her, their mouths falling open. Runa pivoted back, "What?!" Her voice wavered with disbelief and edged with raw emotion. "Done? What do you mean?"

Before Layla could answer, Mama D's steady voice carried from the doorway, grounding them. "*This* can wait. That's *enough* for today. Let's get *settled*. There's time for stories later." She gestured for the group to follow her inside.

Runa exchanged a lingering glance with Rayanna, inclining her head slightly toward the back porch. Rayanna bounced one shoulder, a subtle acknowledgment of their unspoken tradition. The Starlight Festival had its customs, and theirs was always the same—escaping to the back patio with coffee in hand and quiet reflection as the sun rose. A cherished ritual both of them looked forward to.

Without another word, Runa turned toward the glow of the cottage's interior, the soft light promising a brief reprieve as the night gave way to the first hints of dawn.

Behind them, Nadine moved with purpose beneath the sprawling oak, her hands like a conductor's baton guiding the dishes and platters in an uncanny procession. Laden with the remnants of the night's feast, the plates floated as though caught in an unseen current, weaving through the air in an orderly parade toward the open door. Each piece moved with its own peculiar grace—a choreography both meticulous and whimsical, as if enchanted by the night's lingering spell.

The females hesitated just inside the entryway, their eyes wide with a mixture of awe and disbelief. The dishes did not merely settle on the kitchen island; they landed with a considered flourish, their soft clinks and clatters harmonizing like the final notes of a melody. Cups pirouetted midair, bowls rotated as though deliberating their positions, and platters glided in majestic arcs before coming to rest.

The air shimmered faintly, imbued with a surreal quality that made the moment feel both impossible and inevitable. It was as if the house itself exhaled with satisfaction, folding the magical choreography into its walls. For the girls, it was a quiet revelation—a whispered assurance that what had already begun could never return to what it once was.

Chapter Seventeen

The dawn crept in slowly, a delicate cusp of light peeking over the jagged silhouette of the distant mountains, washing the sky in shades of muted peach and soft orange. Runa sat back on the old lounge chair, cradling the warmth of the steaming mug that Rayanna had brought her moments ago.

The morning after the Starlight Festival was always like this—marked by a dew-drenched hush on the patio, a soothing contrast to the chaos of the previous night. Mama D and Nadine had spent the final hours arranging and rearranging the dishes in what Runa could only describe as an elaborate symphony of care.

She exhaled, sinking into the familiar quiet, her gaze following the faint creak of the decking as Rayanna rounded the corner, her steps light with practiced ease.

"How's all this not getting to you, Ru?" Rayanna's words carried a gentle ask as she took the seat beside her. Together, they turned to watch the rays of light stretch across the mountains and settle into their crevices.

Runa leaned into the mug she cradled, allowing the warm steam to rise and meet her face. "It's a lot to process," she said softly. "And even though we're still buried in questions, I'd rather take my time through it—*quietly*." She inhaled a strained breath. "The whole thing with Tabs alone has my mind *spinning*." She exhaled, frustration glinting just enough to tighten her features. "*Honestly?* I'm weary. It's not answers I'm after, per se—at least, not the way it is for you."

She pulled back, stretching her arms out as if trying to distance herself from the thoughts. "*For me*, it's the endless *wondering*."

Pausing once more, she leaned back in, as if the sea of rising steam tugged her toward what she wasn't quite ready to abandon. "I have these underlying beliefs about myself that, in isolation, don't make much sense." She shrugged through the thought. "I just can't keep shoving them under the rug—pretending they're not there."

"It's like we're holding a bottle of fizzy water, right? And we've found out it's been shaken—*yet*"—she stuck a finger in the air dramatically—"we already had a feeling something was afoot. And now we've been told to wait. So, we're just standing here, holding it, waiting." Rayanna released a tense sigh as she leaned back against the cool plush of the lounge chair. "The thing is, it's more about the anticipation—knowing there's no way around the explosion of chaos." She pursed her lips and made a smacking sound. "I've come to realize I like control. And the more information I have, the better chance I have of figuring out a way around getting completely drenched."

"What are you talking about? We're not *about to*—we're mid-shake, Ray, and someone's already aimed that shit at our faces. Point blank." Runa ran a hand over her forehead, chuckling into her mug of black coffee. "It's time to understand the purpose behind all this. Why Starlight? Why here?"

Her eyes lifted, tracing the distant peaks, the questions spilling out more for the world than for Rayanna. "Come on, what happened with Tabs at the cabin? *What cabin?* Where did Layla come from? Did she grow up with Tabytha? And what if we already *do* know these answers—these countless questions—just not in the way we think we do?"

Runa released the tension bound in her chest as she exhaled. "There's just so much," she murmured, the gravity of unspoken fears and unanswered questions pressed down. Turning away from it all, she let the sweet songs of birds accompany the sun's gradual ascent, filling the quiet with their gentle music.

"You know…" Rayanna adjusted her posture. "Sometimes I wish we could just start from the beginning. Turn to Chapter One, where everything's clear. Where the story unfolds step by step—*nothing* rushed, *nothing* missing. Just this quiet life in a cozy beach town where things make sense." Her fingers found the hem of her ribbed charcoal leggings, tracing languid, steady circles. The rhythm anchored her. A soft, rueful laugh escaped. *"But this?"* She glanced at Runa. *"This is* more like finding the author's rough draft—pages scattered everywhere—with the hope we can piece it together before the wind carries it all away." Rayanna's sarcasm slid into the space where the tension had just begun to crack. "At least in this mess, we're together. Let the world see it for what it is—chaotic, relentless, but ours. *And honestly?* I think we'd be bored with anything less."

"That's…perfectly put," Runa murmured, nodding in acknowledgment as she puffed out her cheeks, a string of questions released in the exhale. "What does it even mean to be shadow bound? What is thought weaving? Phased markings? I mean, how much do we not know?" She ran her tongue along her upper lip, her voice dipping into dry sarcasm. "And going off your rough draft analogy—did this author at least write in page numbers?" A slight incline of her chin. "Because that would be helpful."

Rayanna took a sip from her mug—and immediately coughed, nearly choking. She reached out blindly, setting the mug down on the side table with a clumsy thunk, one hand pressed to her chest as she leaned forward, trying to catch her breath. *"Blessed be,* Runa," she rasped, coughing between sputtered chuckles. "You *can't just* drop page number jokes mid-sip." She cleared her throat, waved a hand in mock scolding, and blinked the tears from her eyes. "Anyway—" Her tone softened with curiosity. "I'd like to know why you've been getting all these random bruises, cuts, and scars over the past couple of months." Her voice lowered. "And that seared handprint…healed with just water?" She clicked her cheek, then murmured, quieter still, "At the surface level, it doesn't make sense." She rubbed her hairline thoughtfully, then tugged up her sweater sleeve to reveal the inked pattern on her forearm, her gaze drifting to the raised full moon and stars mirrored on her skin. "Why is *this* now? Is it because we're getting closer to *whatever* this *shadow thing* is?

Runa sipped her coffee, the hint of a playful tone rising with the steam.

"I...do...not...have an answer for you *quite yet...on*"—she shrugged—*"any of it, really."*

Rayanna nestled back into the cushions, one brow raised. "Oh, just admit it...you've been dancing with devils in your free time, and your lack of coordination is *the real culprit."*

"Ha, ha—very funny." Runa angled her head to the side, letting out a theatrical guff. "Oh, you are *so* hilarious," she muttered. *"Honestly?* I wish it were that simple. If it were just my lack of rhythm, I'd happily own up to it." They shared a look as they both turned back to the rising sun.

Runa sank deeper into the comfort of her simple black T-shirt and dark green sweatpants, pulling her legs beneath her as she faced Rayanna. With a small shrug, she admitted, "I don't even know where to start...trying to make sense of it all." Her fingers tugged absently at the fuzzy fabric of her fresh, deep green socks, which she had put on after the downpour.

"We could start with the visions—those fragments that hit us like an unstoppable film reel, scenes flashing by so fast it felt like we were being hurled through them." Her voice caught slightly as she navigated the memory—like it was a fragile glass jug she needed to handle with care. "Each image blurred into the next, leaving us breathless, nauseated, and barely able to keep up." She paused, eyes darting to Runa. *"...which was... profoundly comprehensively confusing."* She threw a wink, clicked her cheek, then propped her feet up on a nearby stool. "And that's just me trying to process it from the sidelines." She rubbed at her lips, fingers curling around her coffee mug. *"It's your past,* Ru. And if I'm this scrambled just watching it...I can't imagine what it's like being *inside of it."*

Runa opened her mouth to speak and then shut it, a subtle shrug signaling surrender. "Pfft...*profoundly comprehensively confusing,"* she uttered, her voice laced with dry amusement as she nodded. "Yeah, *well...* we'll get to it all—*at some point."* She set her coffee aside and leaned forward, pressing on, "First things first," she said, resting her chin on her clasped hands. "I think we can both agree that we need to understand Tabytha's...story?" Perching her lips, searching for the right word. *"Happenings? Death?"* She reached up, lightly scratching at her hairline. "Assessing the situation from where we are seated, it feels like a solid entry point. From what I can tell, the cabin seemed to come right before we got *shipped...stationed..."*

Rayanna cast a sideways glance, picking up on Runa's hesitation and finishing the thought. "…before we were given this new life?" They exchanged a look and shook their heads in unison.

"That *damn* cataclysmic door," Runa muttered. "Was *such* a bitch." A sigh escaped as they both leaned in, Runa picking up her mug. They clinked their cups together and turned to watch the morning light in silence, the sharpness of the rugged mountain peaks casting a warm glow over the landscape and marking the day's inevitable advance.

The sound of boots scuffing against stone announced Layla's arrival as she rounded the bend of the house, a black mug of coffee cradled in one hand. The morning light bathed the patio, illuminating the set of her jaw— strong but with a slight tension that belied her composure. She paused, placing her free hand on her hip, eyes sharp and assessing as they flicked between Runa and Rayanna. "So, this is where you two plot world domination, *huh?* Cozy."

Rayanna's brows arched. "Bold of you to assume we're not already halfway there," she quipped, easing some of the tension lingering in the air.

Layla's lips twisted into a half-smile, "*Perfect.* Saves me the effort of making an entrance," her eyes darted between them as though taking stock, "*So,* what's today's assignment? Or do I *need* to *start* taking *notes?*"

Runa's fingertips tittered along the porcelain. "*Depends,*" she quipped, a glint of curiosity threading through her cadence. "*Are you* any good at untangling impossible messes?"

Layla's smile widened, one eyebrow arching as she set her coffee down and dropped into a chair. She crossed her arms with a confidence that dared the moment to challenge her. "Lucky for you, that's *my specialty,*" she said. "In all transparency, the cabin is *an excellent starting point.* It's *quite* the story."

Rayanna's gaze sharpened, an eyebrow lifting in disbelief as she shook her head, her voice edged with skepticism. "*Seriously?* How much of this are you *actually* informed about?" She leaned forward, elbows on her knees, hands gripping her mug tightly as frustration simmered beneath her composed exterior, barely concealed.

Layla sidestepped Rayanna's pointed inquiry. "It was part of the mission objective," she said with a casual shrug.

Turning her attention to Runa, she added, "I *wasn't at liberty* to *say anything*." Layla leaned in, pressing more weight on one elbow, the atmosphere growing more charged. "*Why do you think* I've *kept my distance* as the phasing began to show?" She tilted her head, eyes narrowing with a subtle challenge. "Well, there it is, Runa. I knew you'd notice."

Rayanna's eyes rolled, a flicker of disdain sparking in their depths. "*Oh, please.* 'Mission objective' *my ass.* Convenient excuse, *don't you think?*"

Layla let out a short huff, shaking her head with a touch of exasperation. "Would you really cross Papa D if you were in my shoes?" Her posture remained bold, her movements sharp and assertive, punctuated by a casual shrug. A spark of mischief lit her eyes. "*And trust me,* you haven't met Izayah yet. He's…*a bundle of fun*…to deal with."

Rayanna's mouth curved into a smirk, a glimmer of challenge sparking in her gaze. "*Oh, I bet.* Sounds like our type of trouble."

"What does that even mean, Ray?" Layla shot back as she raised her hands defensively. "*Let's be clear*—my version of shadow binding wasn't… *exactly* on the same level as both of yours," She grabbed her coffee, sank back into the cushions, and let her guard down—just a little. "*Just saying.*"

Runa's gaze darted between them, taking in Layla's demeanor and the flippant tonality. It was a stark contrast to who she had been as Tabytha. The difference unsettled Runa, bringing a moment of dissonance as she tried to align these new realities with the fragments she could recall. Tabytha would have offered tempered words, quietly searching for the middle ground, the notion slipping through her mind like smoke. But Papa's vigilance—she clung to that for assurance. *He wouldn't let anyone unsafe near us without a reason,* she reminded herself, though even that thought felt more like an echo than an absolute certainty.

Runa shook her head and rubbed her eyes. "*I want to ask*…who is Izayah, and how does he play into all this?"

Hesitating, she caught the girls looking toward her. Again, she shook her head, as if trying to dispel the tension clawing at her temples. *Another name. Another enigma.* Another piece she *didn't* understand.

Sighing, she muttered, "Imagine someone watching all this unfold, trying to make sense of the relentless questions and the parade of unfamiliar faces—with *no answers, no anchor.*"

A moment flashed through her mind—standing in the town hall's winter wonderland, surrounded by twinkling lights and festive garlands. But the image fractured, giving way to a rush of unfamiliar places and ephemeral faces—like memories that weren't hers, but pressed in as if they could be. A towering, cataclysmic door loomed, cracked down the center, its frame groaning with souls—trapped, pulsing, familiar and not.

And somewhere in that surge, she tried to find him. *Izayah.* The name alone felt like reaching for a thread that wouldn't hold, slipping through her fingers the moment she thought she had it. A face surfaced—half-shadowed, half-sacred—like someone she should know, someone who had once stood close, but now hovered just outside the frame. The closer she got, the further it blurred.

Was it familiar? It felt like it should be—pressing behind her eyes, caught in the tension at her temples, like something trying to surface. But whatever it was had become fogged, cloaked in something she couldn't name. And maybe that was the ache of it—knowing it was hers, and still not recognizing it.

"Why does he feel like he's a memory I'm not allowed to keep?" she muttered with a grimace. "There's something there, and it pains me, not understanding what."

Rayanna scoffed lightly, but there was no humor in it. "One thing at a time, Ru. We'll get to that when it makes sense to do so," she said, shaking her head and dismissing the question with a casual wave of her hand. "It's okay to let it go...*for now.*"

Layla cleared her throat, locking eyes with Rayanna, her expression softening with an unusual sincerity. "I get why you'd hesitate. Why you'd think I can't be trusted. But I had *no choice,*" she admitted, the edges of her voice firm but laced with a trace of vulnerability. "I was given Tabytha's clothes, told to replicate her—to be her shadow. Even if you can't fully remember, the shadow binding leaves traces...bits and pieces of memories. Like Runa noticing when I started pulling back, and the tug to understand who Izayah is. If I had come in as myself, there would have been cracks in the foundation of this mission right out the gate—*especially you, Ray.* If I failed, I would have been the *downfall* of the assignment."

"Why especially me?" Rayanna asked, her voice wary.

"Because...*you are you.*" Layla scoffed, shooting out an arm. "Who do you think came up with the idea? Hmm..."

Layla's gaze flitted between them before landing back on Rayanna. "The fact that neither of you realized there were two of us is probably the only reason it worked. And truth be told, not many people know I exist—that's why it succeeded."

Runa blinked, her tone quiet, almost disbelieving. *"No one knows you exist?"*

"No." Her response was clipped, tinged with something blue, as she sighed audibly. "That's a later thing," she said, fluttering one hand out to the side, brushing the notion away. "It'll find its place when it's time." She took a sip of coffee, then cradled the cup in her lap as she continued, "I want to share what I know. I always have. But this situation…it's more severe than any of us can fully grasp."

She paused, exhaling as if releasing an unseen burden. "There's a lot I'm still piecing together myself."

Shaking her head lightly, she added, *"My suggestion?* We start by identifying the gaps in our understanding—and fill them in."

Rayanna shook her head, pivoting her body slightly away from Layla as her eyes refocused on the sun-kissed peaks of the distant ridge of mountains.

Layla's eyes narrowed, catching the silent dismissal. "Really, Ray? What do you expect of me?" she spat. "Do you think you wouldn't have noticed something was off if I had just strolled in one day wearing leather pants, a black shirt, a top bun, and combat boots? Might as well have raided Runa's closet—that's more my style." Her lips twitched in a half-smile that didn't reach her eyes. "And if that didn't tip you off, the change in my eye color would have. Just another twist no one saw coming."

Layla inhaled, as her eyes began to evolve, captivating Runa, who nudged Rayanna. The change was hypnotic—a ripple of light swept across her irises, teal bleeding into deeper hues as if an unseen hand brushed vivid strokes onto a canvas. Blue and gold specks glistened, catching the light before melting into a rich, liquid turquoise. The turquoise encircled her pupils, deepening until it solidified into a bold, cobalt ring that pulsed with an intensity that felt almost alive. A halo of golden honey emerged at the edges, glowing faintly as a spark of reddish-orange unfurled within it, blossoming like a flame-tinged flower that stirred to life—mysterious and liminal.

Rayanna's head tilted slightly, her stare unwavering as her lips formed a faint pout. A subtle nod followed—her quiet way of confirming, without words, that *yes*...she and Runa would have noticed.

Layla's brows pulled together as she looked from one to the other, a hint of annoyance shadowing her expression. "Yeah, it started happening about two years ago—out of nowhere." She sighed. "You remember that solo trip I took with Mama D? This was why." She tapped the corner of her waterline. "I had to see Sienna the Seer, spend days redoing the shadow binding. And let me tell you—it was anything but pain-free."

Her gaze turned skyward as the light began to seep into the morning, softening the darkness. "Unlike you two, I handled most of this alone. I knew more than you did, so if anyone's earned the right to be upset, *it's me.*" She leaned into the conversation, still cradling her cup of coffee. *"But what's the point* of keeping score? I don't want us tangled in *'you should've told me'* arguments. It happened. We're in this...whatever this is—and we'll deal with facing what comes next. It's just the hand we've been dealt." She pressed her lips into a tight, frustrated smile, raising her brows as if daring them to challenge her resolve.

"It's not about being upset or keeping score; it's more about not knowing what's *real* and *what isn't.* It's just a lot to take in." Rayanna stood, walking over to the coffee jug she'd brought out earlier and refilling her cup from the small warming stone Papa D had rigged together for moments just like this. "It's been, what—seventeen something hours to digest this new version of life," she added, letting the steam curl up around her face.

"Yeah, well, *know this*—I never left your side," Layla whipped back. "I knew everything the whole time. I never betrayed, never faltered, even when there were moments I wanted to drown myself in a drink and forget —to slip into oblivion."

Runa's eyes softened as she asked, almost in a whisper, *"Why didn't you?* You could have let it go, changed course, become who you wanted to be. We've had two decades here, after all. Tabytha could've gone through phases, changed her style, rebelled."

Layla's fingers tightened around her mug, her gaze steady and unwavering. "My mind is shadow bound—*just differently.*" She lifted her chin slightly, eyes darkening with the weight of the notion. "You didn't see what I saw after the cabin. The way he looked at you both…I wasn't going to cross him. Not any of them." Her tone grew sharp, a glint of defiance in her eyes. *"I might be rebellious—even lethal* if need be—*but not like them."*

Runa's brow furrowed with worry. *"Them who?"*

Layla's eyes sharpened as she looked between them, drawing a lazy circle in the air with one finger. "Izayah—the *most magical older brother."* A huffed smirk tugged at her mouth, dark humor glinting at the corners of her lips. She lifted her hand, ticking off each point with casual finger visuals. *"Rule number one*—don't go believing everything Visha says. *Rule number two*—never lie to Izayah. *Rule number three*—refer back to rules one and two." Her eyebrows lifted with a trace of warning as she tried to stifle a yawn. *"Trust me,* he's not someone you want to *piss off."*

"Who the hell is Visha?" Runa blinked, confusion clouding her expression as she shook her head, trying to make sense of the onslaught of information. *"Wait…*Izayah's my brother?"

Layla's eyebrow lifted. *"HA…*hardly!" Her laughter burst out, echoing off the mountains like an inside joke tossed up to the sky. "Call it the missing link." She sank back into the cushions, lifting her coffee for another sip. "Just do me a favor, Ru—when the time comes, remember this moment." She pointed subtly with her mug. "Because understanding the *why* will make the *what* a whole lot easier to swallow."

With a fluid motion, Layla pushed herself up, rolled her shoulders as she stepped back, and grabbed the jug of coffee. Pointing it at them, she called out, "Chop, chop! We're burning daylight." A smirk curved her lips, her voice lilted with playful urgency. "Buckle up, ladies. This is one hell of a tangled mess with your names penciled in at the top."

"I still don't get how you know this much," Rayanna cut in.

Layla shot back over her shoulder, "Remember, my shadow binding was way different than yours."

"I'm not sure if that brings me any comfort," Rayanna stated flatly.

"Well, it should." Layla shrugged. "Just think of it this way, Ray—I'll know when you need more coffee, and when you *absolutely will not."*

The trio fell into an easy rhythm as they followed the cobblestone path winding along the side of the house, their steps weaving through clusters of potted herbs. The cool morning air clung to their skin, leaving goosebumps in its wake. Footsteps crunched softly against the stones, the weight of unspoken thoughts hanging between them. Yet the silence felt companionable—the kind that settled in when questions loomed too large for immediate answers.

Layla cut through the thoughtful silence with a toss of her hand, coffee sloshing slightly in the cup. "I'll need a bit of time for a costume change when we get in," she said over her shoulder. "You two can handle the coffee. Pretty sure it's going to be one of those mornings."

As they neared the steps, Rayanna tilted her head toward Runa, her expression a mix of amusement and lingering disbelief. "What's her deal?" she asked, her voice low but curious.

Runa shrugged, "Don't ask me. I'm still trying to figure myself out." Her tone held the faintest trace of humor. "But she's not wrong about the coffee."

"*Obviously.*" A quick snort of laughter escaped as she dipped her chin, and they made their way up the weathered steps. "Leave it to me."

Runa nodded, her expression softening. "Yeah. I just need a second to myself."

Rayanna gave a quick nod before heading inside.

Runa lingered at the threshold, her gaze drifting inward—past the open space where the soft hum of voices mingled with the faint clink of dishes, the creak of cabinets, a muffled chuckle, and the hush of a closing door. All the familiar sounds of the cottage alive and breathing around her.

She paused, one hand brushing the doorframe as if grounding herself there, before stepping through the entryway and crossing the communal space in silence. With a steadying inhale, she slipped out onto the balcony. The morning light had begun to spill across the tops of the cottages, glinting faintly off the protective barrier that shimmered—just barely visible, like a bubble catching the sun. Runa settled at the balcony's edge, the rim of her mug warming her palms. The swirling chaos in her chest didn't vanish—but in this hush, it began to soften, just enough to make room for the story still to come.

Chapter Eighteen

Present Day

Standing on the wooden balcony of the front porch, Runa rested her forearms lazily on the banisters, her gaze drifting over the sprawling front yard. The stillness of the pre-dawn air mirrored the quiet turbulence in her mind. She raised one hand to her mouth, absently rubbing the edge of her pointer finger across her lips—a small, grounding gesture she always found comforting.

Night was finally yielding to dawn, and Runa hoped it would bring the answers she so desperately needed. Her mind softened as her eyes followed the emerging gradient on the horizon, where deep indigo and navy gave way to the subtle warmth of approaching light. It reminded her that change—daunting as it might seem—could also hold promise.

From inside the cottage came the faint clinks of movement—Rayanna's rhythm, as familiar to Runa as her own heartbeat, busy with the well-worn ritual of brewing another pot of coffee. Runa had excused herself for a moment, slipping onto the porch to greet the familiar soul of solitude—a quiet space to think. *To simply be.*

It was the only time she felt wholly herself, unburdened by expectations—or, more recently, the unanswered questions—that weighed on her during the day.

The dawn was her one constant, a faithful companion to her quiet musings. It always felt like a conversation, this quiet dance of light and dark—a reminder that despite everything, the world was still evolving, renewing itself, and offering something beyond the chaos. She exhaled deeply, the cool morning air filling her lungs and pushing back the weight of the night's revelations. For now, she could let herself simply exist.

Behind her, the soft hum of life in the cottage carried on—a murmur of warmth and familiarity she appreciated from a distance, even as she hesitated to step back into its embrace. But out here, she had space—just her, the sky, and the subtle certainty that this fleeting peace belonged to just her.

The complexity of it all revealed itself—simple in its essence, yet intricate in its details. Runa's thoughts drifted as she watched Nissa and Ashla cross the gravel threshold, each lugging a sizable black trash bag to collect remnants from the rain-soaked community landscape.

Nissa, the creative force behind all their interior designs, raised a hand in greeting, her warm smile lighting up her face. Ashla, mirrored the gesture, her wave casual, yet sincere. The feathered cuffs on her wrists slid down, catching the early morning light and scattering intricate patterns on the ground—an unintentional display of her effortless flair.

Runa squinted as the glint of bracelets sparked a flicker of recognition. She managed a nod and a gentle, hesitant wave, her fingers trembling with the drag of fatigue.

It was a cherished tradition for the community to unite in volunteering, ensuring the town was pristine before the first light, seamlessly transitioning into the next day without a hiccup. For once, in an unprecedented twist, Runa found herself grateful not to be part of the crew.

Luckily, Mama D had swiftly arranged for the neighbors to step in for her and the girls. Mama had asserted, "…there are more pressing matters to deal with right now." And for once, Runa wholeheartedly agreed.

Nonetheless, a smile glimmered in Runa's eyes as she watched the two young women move quietly, gathering small items. Observing them together, she noticed a quiet ebb and flow between them, an unspoken rhythm in their movements that underscored their connection. Their striking resemblance was evident—both with blonde hair, though Nissa's was longer and brighter compared to Ashla's, which carried a tinge of brown.

Nissa's golden-hued shirt, its thin straps delicately framing her shoulders, shimmered faintly in the pre-dawn light. In contrast, Ashla's black top absorbed the subdued glow of the twinkle lights and candlelight softly surrounding them. A woven gray sweatshirt draped loosely from Ashla's shoulders, resembling a comforting blanket in the dim morning ambiance.

They seemed like two sides of the same coin—equally beautiful, yet distinctly different—simmering with a calmness, like dawn spreading over a still lake, where sky and water merge in a radiant stitch binding two landscapes.

As Runa blinked, a fragment of a bygone moment surfaced—joyful and fleeting, like a darting shadow: a forest clearing, crackling leaves underfoot, the faint, hearty laughter of younglings, and a story once hers to tell through play. It lingered like a distant echo, hovering on the outskirts of the tangible.

The scene before Runa blurred, the memory weaving itself into the present like overlapping tides. She furrowed her brow, thoughts heavy with uncertainty as she tried to grasp the significance of the fleeting vision. Her mind itched with the relentless drive to understand—a need she couldn't shake, buried deep within a shadow bound consciousness. The strain felt like pressure against a dam, her insistence chipping away at the fog that clung tightly to her past. Yet, even through the haze, she could sense it—freedom glimmering on the horizon, just out of reach.

Light filtered through the sprawling branches of the grand oak tree beyond the balcony's edge. Watching the beams glide gently through the canopy, her mind was pulled back to the moment she and the others—Layla and Rayanna—had stepped through the front door from the backyard patio. They'd found Nadine in motion, moving with effortless grace, conducting a magnificent procession of platters and dishes that bobbed in from beneath the grand oak. Plates clattered softly, jostling in the air until Nadine extended a steadying hand, coaxing them into order as they landed neatly on the kitchen island.

They stood in awe, watching as the display came together—a vivid arrangement of braided breads, golden-roasted vegetables, and bowls that shimmered like starlight. Nadine turned to face them, her voice calm and steady, yet carrying an unmistakable weight.

"I need a moment," she began, her gaze settling on each of them in turn. "What you're feeling—this ache, this itch you can't quite scratch—is because you're shadow bound. It's a protection placed on your mind, a safeguard for your cognition." Her voice was steady but layered with purpose, as though every word was meant to root them firmly in understanding. "Being shadow bound means your memories from the past have been paused, tucked away so that your energy can be used to rebuild yourself—to reestablish a foundation that's strong enough to support you when the time comes to move forward."

Standing firm with both hands on the edge of the island, she continued, "The phased markings are there to guide this gradual release. And normally…it *is* gradual." Her gaze pulled to Runa, steady and warm. "It's not meant to overwhelm—it's like standing at the edge of a vast lake and stepping onto the first stone. You can't rush across. Each phase is a part of your life returning—layers of memory and meaning, arriving in parallel with your ability to hold them. The markings unfold step by step, not all at once, giving you space to reflect, to meet what was with who you are now —before the next piece reveals itself."

Runa stood in the present, still feeling Nadine's words sink into her like stones dropping into a still pond, sending ripples through her thoughts.

Nadine had continued, her voice, unhurried. Turning slightly, she gestured toward the food-laden island, as though the act of arranging it mirrored the process she described. "There's a reason it happens this way. Your mind needs time to adjust, to process what's being unbound. That's where the Unbinder comes in." Her voice softened, her words meant to reassure yet carrying the gravity of truth. "The Unbinder's role is to help you release the weaving of your thoughts, phase by phase. It's like cracking open the floodgates, allowing the river of your past to flow through you—*but not all at once.* If everything were unbound at the same time, it would overwhelm you. You'd drown in your own memories before you had the chance to make sense of them."

She paused, letting the weight of her words settle over them before adding, "This unfolding *isn't about* rushing to remember everything. It's about *readiness*. Your past *isn't meant* to consume you; *it's meant* to guide you. And when the time is right, you'll be ready to step into it."

Her gaze softened as she turned her focus back to Runa. Her tone, though firm, carried a warmth that steadied the air around them. "I know the phases seem messy—but the madness has a blueprint. Just remember to be patient with yourselves."

Runa didn't speak. She only nodded, eyes flicking to the sheen of light crawling across the kitchen counter, the last of the floating dishes settling into place. Nadine's words clung to the air like morning mist—part truth, part shadow. And yet, whatever this was, it left Runa with a struggle she couldn't quite place. *Was it hope? Guilt? A flicker of resentment tucked beneath all the rest?* She didn't know if she had the right to be angry—*had I even been given a choice in all of this?* The notions pressed inward, complicated and sharp, twisting through questions she wasn't prepared to ask aloud.

How could I ever harbor resentment for being granted a space like this—like Starlight? Above all else, it felt like a gift she wasn't sure she deserved. *Maybe I should be angry; maybe others would be, after being shadow bound and kept in the dark for so long.*

Runa tilted her head back, letting out a heavy sigh—releasing all the questions that couldn't be answered right now and turning toward the one that might. "Is Tabs really gone?" Her eyes misted, mouth tightening as she fought to hold back the tears. She had searched the exposed beams, as if hoping for an answer. "I hear you—none of this is without reason," she had whispered, her shoulders sagging under the strain. "Losing her had to mean something…more than just pain. Right? I mean…did we get time to grieve? Did we get that chance?" She had bitten down on her tongue to hold back the flood of emotions that threatened to spill out. "And then there is Layla—such an integral part of our story of Starlight." She puffed out her cheeks, sputtering the air with an audible vibration of her lips—a breath, a distraction meant to help her hold everything together. *"Man,"* she exclaimed, "to navigate all this, alone, masked as someone else, to do what—save some mission?"

Dark sadness welled up, knotting stubbornly in her chest. She pressed a hand across her collarbone, willing the hurt and anger to subside. Her eyes darted across the front yard, searching desperately for any reason—any justification—for why she stood here while the idea of suspending everyone else's life for her sake weighed so heavily. "Am I really that important for all…this? Are we that important?" she uttered to the wooden railing.

Nadine's words resounded in her mind, her voice a firm reassurance cemented into their new reality. "These are outstanding questions to be asking, Runa. Your inquiry about Tabytha is valid, and we will get there—but let's focus back in, on the foundations of understanding…*just for now.*" Mama D had reached across the space between them, placing a steadying hand in comfort, as Nadine continued—reiterating the process of the phased markings and emphasizing Runa's unique past. "Your binding is much more intense than that of the other girls; you require phased releases. Those markings—the tattoos placed on all three of you—are there to prevent the floodgates from drowning everyone. I know it doesn't seem to make a whole lot of sense now, but it will. *I promise.*"

Frustration tightened *now* in Runa's chest as she recalled the woman's words, her thoughts stumbling over the irritation that threatened to spill into self-pity. The notion of who she once was—*quite frankly*—infuriated her.

She bowed her head, inhaling deeply, redirecting her gaze to the females moving rhythmically beneath the old oak. Their steps formed a quiet dance that remained unhurried and carefree, even as they gathered scattered bits of food and trash. They bumped shoulders, giggling—sharing inside jokes no one else could imagine, let alone fathom. Their laughter bubbled up through the stillness, a bright counterpoint to all this confusion. She watched the pair crunch along the gravel drive, drifting closer to the moongate, their playful banter rippling outward like a gentle tide—steadying her, drawing Runa back from the edge of spiraling emotional turmoil. There was something magnetic about their ease, like a bright light reaching into her soul and tugging her toward a reality she hadn't yet fully grasped.

The protective barrier encasing the cottage shimmered in the morning sheen, flowing like a translucent veil as the girls approached. Runa's breath caught as the bubble quivered, its surface undulating as though alive, before it rippled faintly, reacting to their presence. Yet the pair stepped through it effortlessly, the barrier pulling at them with a soft, fluid motion, smoothing over their forms before releasing them on the other side.

Their laughter swelled, unbridled and infectious, as they began to move with exaggerated playfulness. Ashla kicked off from the ground, twisting into a leisurely backstroke midair, her arms sweeping in wide arcs as if cutting through invisible water. Nissa followed with a gleeful leap, diving into what looked like a gelatinous ether. Her legs pumped together in rhythmic pulses, mimicking a mermaid gliding beneath unseen waves.

Runa's mouth parted. She blinked once—twice—trying to process the surreal spectacle, but it slipped through reason like water through her fingers. Joy and absurdity mingled in a way that felt impossible, yet vividly pure, as if the world had folded in on itself and turned inside out for her to witness. She stared, unblinking, her grip on reality tilting once more as they swam—yes, swam—effortlessly down the path. Their laughter floated back to her, muffled and strange, like sound underwater. Unreal. Baffling. And yet, it tugged at something raw and long buried.

"Those two have a way about themselves, don't they?" A firm touch landed on Runa's shoulder, her head snapping up as Nadine came into full view—forcing her to shove the clutter of wondering aside.

"Sorry." Nadine's grip lingered a moment longer before she dropped her weight onto the railing beside Runa. "You know, it's okay to wonder," she murmured. After a beat, she adjusted her stance and added in a hushed tone, "Here." She offered over a glass of whiskey, the ice clinking in a muted rattle. "This should keep your mind from drifting too far—like those two," she added, tipping her own tumbler toward the figures dissipating farther down the path.

"Little early for this, isn't it?" Runa asked, the chilled weight grounding her as she adjusted her grip.

"Let's just call today…an extended special occasion." Nadine smiled again.

"Do they do that often?" Runa angled the rim of her drink toward the ghosted pair.

"They do all sorts of things often," Nadine replied with a smirk. "The real question is whether they should be doing that at all…right now."

Runa chuckled as she lifted her drink in a quiet salute of acknowledgment.

"I'll have to have a talk with those two…again," she said, the corners of her mouth twitching upward before she gave a shake of her head. "What they just did—no one else could manage." A soft puff of exasperation followed, as though the idea amused her despite its implications. "Well, other than…" She waved a hand, brushing the thought away.

"Let's just say the safeguards have been put into place while I'm within Starlight Beach, meaning there's no cause for worry." She scratched the top of her head and pressed on. "They were raised in locations where they didn't need to hide such behaviors from the world. It's because of their essence—so specific to them—that the usual boundaries don't quite…stick. They've had a lot of time to simply be. To exist without the usual checks. It's part of what makes them *so* unique."

She waved another hand dismissively before Runa could press further. "All you need to know is, this encasing has been intertwined with the ley lines, stalling time beyond this cottage perimeter. No one else should be able to cross it—not from either side. What they did would be impossible for anyone else. Well, unless those two are involved with unbinding specific sections." She grimaced then, her smile turning mischievous.

"They have a soft space for certain people…and how they adore helping love stories along." Her tone took on a lilting ease as she added, "Even at a young age, Tabytha had her hands full keeping you and—" She stopped herself with a sheepish shake of the almost-spoken truth. "Silly me, I'm getting ahead of myself."

Nadine settled more firmly against the railing, her cadence dipping just enough to draw Runa in. "You're carrying too much of it, you know." A wink accompanied the words, less a tease and more a gentle nudge.

Runa let out a dry chuckle. "Great…not sure I'd ever want all the answers. That sounds exhausting." Brows drawn tight, she studied the amber swirl, where the light rippled like fire caught in crystal. "And you're really…okay with all of this?"

Nadine gave a subtle nod, pressing the pad of her thumb briefly to her sternum, as if steadying something behind her ribs. "I don't have all the answers either—nor would I want them," she offered, the words rich with sincerity. "But what I do know is this: when we come together—when we share what we know—we make better choices. That's the point of all this." She gestured outward, motioning beyond the balcony. "After the Great War, so much was lost—information, communication, the ability to work as one. It fractured everything. We lost more than just records; we lost trust

—the threads that held everything together. This mission, Runa, it's about more than you or any one of us individually. It's about rebuilding that, piece by piece. Regaining control of how we connect, how we understand. It's not perfect, but it's a start."

Runa puffed out her upper lip, giving the whiskey a quiet swirl. "That's…a lot," she admitted, her tone casual but thoughtful. "But at least it sounds like there's a plan."

Nadine chuckled softly. "There's always a plan." She drew in a purposeful inhale, then added, "The hard part is seeing it through as new information unfolds. Yet it comes back to the core belief. It's a lot, but when the heart is in the right place…" Her words faded into the space between them, unfinished but understood.

Runa blinked. "Sorry," she muttered, exhaling sharply. "This whole process…" She paused. "It's overwhelming. Can you please just explain to me—again," her voice wavered, rising with the words, "—how shadow binding is even possible? I'm still struggling to understand." The words kept coming, quick and tangled. "I mean, it's like I've been shoved into a box, completely cut off from everything I knew. And there's this part of me —" her grip tightened as she stared into the tumbler, "—that's furious about it. I wasn't even asked. *Was I?* And yet…" She exhaled again, this time quieter. "At the same time, I can see the purpose in it. I understand why this space had to exist. I am grateful, truly. But the contradiction—it's constant. Both truths press against me at once, and I can't find the middle." Her voice caught. "*So*…if I can just understand what shadow binding actually is…maybe I'll be able to sort through all of this. I don't even have a name for what's twisting in my chest—*anger, confusion, rage?* It's all just… there." She looked up at Nadine, her brow knit together. "*It seems like understanding* shadow binding has to be the first step. Otherwise, how do I move forward?"

"Yes, it does make sense." Her cadence dipped momentarily before gaining gentle momentum. "I want you to understand that the choices that were made—they weren't forged lightly, Ru." She paused, her tumbler tipping slightly in her fingers, as if testing the weight of her next thought. "This wasn't easy. It wasn't done to take your life or your choices from you. And all those things you're feeling? They're valid. Completely valid." A quiet smile tugged at her lips as she pressed closer, her shoulder brushing Runa's. "I need you to know that, Runa. And I need you to know this: you don't have to figure it all out by yourself. You don't have to shoulder this alone. I can be that person—the one you come to with questions, the one who walks beside you. We'll face it together, step by step." She paused again, her tone quieting with intention. "We'll start untangling it together—one memory, one phase at a time." Nadine lifted her drink, tilting it just enough for the ice to chime against the sides. "That's why this is my drink of choice—simple, yet layered," she said with a wry, knowing smile. "Not everyone has an 'Old Faithful' pipe to summon clarity on demand." She winked, dipping her chin slightly. "But you—you're adapting to a quintessence you don't even fully grasp yet. That's not simple. That's exceptional."

A faint chuckle cracked the surface, loosening the emotional knots coiled tight beneath Runa's ribs. Her shoulders eased—just a bit.

A grin curved across Nadine's face. "You know, your father—Ezekiel—has one similar to Diesel's…Old Faithful. Mama D had them both crafted after the Great War." Her gaze stretched toward the moongate. "They're meant to remind both men of what obsession with power can lead to…and how the world, even in ruins, can still offer something worth rebuilding." She propped her elbows on the banister and stretched her back with a feline ease, settling deeper into the rhythm of morning calm.

Runa's gaze dropped to the whitewashed floorboards. "Nadine, I don't understand how I deserved all this—being tucked away."

Nadine didn't speak right away. Her fingers tapped lightly against the railing, rhythm soft and steady, as if coaxing the right words forward. Her gaze lingered on her hand, watching the way her thumb thudded once, then again, against the wood.

"It's natural to have those kinds of thoughts," she murmured, more to the morning air than to Runa. A small bounce of her palm followed, half shrug, half hesitation. "From the life you had, after Ezekiel—it makes sense."

She scratched at her forehead absently, still not looking up. "Especially from what I know now…" Her voice drifted, unfinished. A beat passed. Then she drew in a breath, found her footing.

"Runa—let me put it this way." She straightened slightly, her thumb still thumping along the railing. "Don't shut the door on the idea of deserving. Not yet. It might not make any sense. Hell, it might rattle everything you think you know. But let these questions find the light...*even the darker ones.*"

Her knuckles rapped once against the railing for emphasis. "*Ask them* when they come. Because here's the thing—new information," she tapped the side of her temple, finally glancing up, a spark in her eye, "it can change everything. *I know it has for me.*"

She pushed off the railing, her movement easy now, tapping her temple once more as she added with a faint smile, "It's the asking that carries you forward." Dipping her chin as she crossed the threshold, her tone curled back like a warm invitation: "Whenever you're ready, Ru." With a final, graceful tilt of her head, she drifted back into the cottage.

Runa's gaze lingered a moment longer on the doorframe Nadine had passed through, the soft echo of her words still pressed against the back of her mind.

She exhaled, her thumb brushing the lip of the tumbler as she brought it closer, the amber liquid catching the low light.

A quiet inhale.

A longer breath out—measured, strained—as her fingers tightened around the thick, cool surface of the etched crystal.

She drew in another breath, her eyelids fluttering closed like drawn curtains. She held it—quiet and warm—letting it steep, then slipped it softly from her lips as her gaze rose again, tracing the yard's familiar lines more from habit than need.

Runa's focus drifted along the gravel, fingertips wandering, skimming mentally through the blades of grass. The scent of dew, fresh and cool, nudged her deeper—coaxing her palm across the imagined surface of stone—until something caught. Until her attention stilled.

Her focus snagged on a drift of fog blanketing the pathway beyond the cottage moongates. It unspooled like thread through still air—too dense for morning, too deliberate to ignore. From the balcony's edge, her stance softened with intrigue as the haze moved with weight. It felt like silhouettes of forgotten dreams clinging to aged stone, lingering in quiet spaces and taking their time to feather skyward. It teased and tempted the edges of memory—soft-footed and soundless—spooling outward and slipping into moments she hadn't realized were still hers.

The air shifted, prickling along her skin with a tender, tempting chill. She dipped her chin into the breathed hush—vanilla and tobacco winding through it, each note steeped in something beautifully tender. A memory made mist. Not near, but near enough to be felt. Then the coolness moved along her like a silken ribbon—a tendril of methodical intention. The fine hairs on her arms lifted, rising like an unhurried sigh. It traced the unguarded slope of her neck with a light, reverent hand—a sensitive, quiet greeting. Not loud. Not certain. But honest. Like the outline of a choice not taken—an almost there…asking nothing, yet offering everything. She inhaled, slow and deep, chin tucked to chest as she gave in to a presence she couldn't define, but her body knew all the same. An openness. Exposed. Raw. Intimate in the way only recognition can be—as if taking a chance with nothing to lose and everything to gain. Her exhale fragmented, spilling out in pieces, as if desire and memory had tangled somewhere in her chest. She inhaled with the quiet knowing—an ache stuttering just beneath the surface—realizing the air remembered her before she could remember why.

Her body responded before her mind could object. A subtle incline, as if something beneath her skin had forgotten how to yield. Heat sparked: reason unraveling, a thread igniting. It wove like molten satin through bone, each ember a whisper, tracing the paths once bound in shadow. The warmth threaded itself between her ribs, winding inward, curling into the quiet conclaves of muscle and reverie. And somewhere within the innermost weave of her—within the ancient hush of bone and buried knowing —memory stirred, marrow-rooted, from a place beyond the reach of words. Her breath caught on the darkness that clung mid-throat, as though her body had sensed the shape of a world not yet realized. The silhouette lingered ahead—like ink bleeding with intent—more suggestion than form, a whisper from a dream refusing to fade. Her lips parted, and the coolness brushed against them like the ghost of a waning day. She caught her bottom lip between her teeth, a gentle instinct—an unspoken need to steady herself, to hold her ground—as the energy lapped softly around her. The shadow reshaped, folds of darkness drawing back like sheets, like fabric sliding across bare skin. Her gaze trailed the hem of night. She held her breath, unblinking, caught between the fear of breaking the moment… and the ache of needing more.

She could feel the intake of breath—comprehension, a raw realization of her desire—the craving of wanting. The coolness cinched close, like dusk folding in around flame. A hush drawn near in reverence. A final whisper pulled tight across skin, a secret not meant to be kept. A silent gesture of awe.

Then, a withdrawal—a backward movement marked by pause, carved with reluctance into the last contours of dusk. The shadows recoiled softly along the stonework path they once trailed, pulling through the places they had touched: where silhouettes of forgotten dreams had clung to aged stone, where remembrance had been teased loose, soft-footed and sound-less. Now the fog-laced darkness receded—gradual, but not without yearning—dissolving in strands, retreating even as something in it lingered. The mist simply observed, a breath suspended in wonder—awe-bound, faltering—as though caught between bowing in parting or daring to remain. As it began to blur at the edges—the golden light of morning brushing the darker seams of shadow like memory reversing itself—it lingered a beat too long. And in that fraction of a second, it stuttered. Dark-ness tucked itself into the cusp of crevices and moss-covered grout, slip-ping into the hushed hollow where shadows settle, biding time with quiet patience.

Her shoulder curved inward, chin resting in the cradle of her fingers as strands of hair fell forward, obscuring her view. Within that veil, her thoughts unraveled—turning over themselves, unsure if the moment had passed…or if some part of it still held, suspended in pause. A flutter of hope nestled into the quiet, coaxing warmth to rise in her lungs—an expanse she longed for, a desire stretching toward the space he no longer held. The chill, once woven around her, had unspooled like a sigh retreating from her skin—falling away, evaporating, dissolving back into the underbelly of the dawning light.

She blinked once—twice—eyes adjusting to the absence, as if dissolving light still shimmered across her vision. Her shoulders remained curled inward, chin nestled in her hand, the last of her distorted reason retreating behind budding clarity. A flush of embarrassment began to rise—faint at first, then coloring high across her cheekbones, threading red through the soft pink already painted there. It bloomed not just from what had happened, but from the way her body had welcomed it.

She pulled her chin from her palm and gave a small shrug, as if trying to put distance between herself and the feelings she couldn't fully label. And yet, her lips dampened at the thought, the taste of whiskey lingering as the warmth traced its way down—like a quiet dare settling in, rising gently between her thighs. The sensation—unexpected, yet unmistakably hers—found its place with surprising ease. A softening followed, unfolding into the first true smile she'd worn in some time.

"Well, maybe there is hope for me," she murmured—words more exhale than thought, tangled with possibility like sunlight breaking through clouds, scattering the last remnants of doubt. "But that definitely felt like something I could get used to."

The pure joy of the thought lifted through her, light and unfiltered, as she tapped her fingers playfully against her lips. Turning one outward, she flicked it gently at the air just in front of her nose.

"That right there—" she grinned, "felt a lot more like being handed a big bowl of ice cream with a massive spoon."

She brought the rim of the glass back to her mouth, inhaling the exquisite, earthy aroma. It carried hints of vanilla and tobacco now, subtle and smoldering—like smoke still curling at the edge of something unfinished. The scent tugged at her in places she wasn't quite ready to label. Her breath fogged against the glass in a soft bloom, as if the crystal whispered back, *Hello, my darling…I've been waiting for you.*

Biting down gently on the inside of her cheek, she closed her eyes, letting the words fade into the dense morning hush of a dream. "Maybe… just maybe…"

With a vibrant shake of her head, she lifted her chin and took another sip, draining the glass with ease. Arching a playful eyebrow, she set it on the railing with a crisp clink that rang in the cool morning air.

Throwing her arms wide, she let the wind catch her like a second skin, the breeze brushing lightly against her frame—less a gust, more a whispered promise of what might come. Possibilities stretched before her, and for once, she didn't feel the need to brace for them.

With a final glance toward the horizon, Runa turned from the balcony's edge, her hair catching in the light before she flicked it over one shoulder. Each step toward the double doors carried the rhythm of something freshly claimed—measured, confident, entirely hers. A smirk tugged at her lips as she murmured, "This is about to get interesting, I think."

As she stepped back through the threshold, Rayanna's voice greeted her—flaring with equal parts excitement and impatience. "Took you long enough, Ru!" Swinging around the corner of the banister, she called up the steps, "Hey, Ms. GlamGlow—chop chop. We've got stories to spill and the world's problems to solve!"

Runa snorted a quiet chuckle, the familiar cadence grounding her in the present. It was a tether—steady and warm—as the cottage's embrace gathered her in, guiding her forward and leaving the balcony, and the dawn, behind.

Chapter Nineteen

Present Day

Rayanna broke the silence as she poured herself another cup of black coffee. Cradling the mug in her hands, she moved toward the island, teeming with a small feast. "Explain to me the need for Starlight Beach," she said, as Runa pulled out a chair and sank into it, the last traces of dawn still soft on her skin.

Setting her mug down, Rayanna broke off a piece of the flowering focaccia bread. The airy interior, still faintly warm, tore away, releasing soft wisps of steam before she sank it into the thick, savory stock from the braised pork. The golden crust—dappled with herbs and edible petals—glistened as it became saturated in its rich oils.

Across the room, movement pulled Rayanna's attention from the feast. Layla descended the stairs, and turned the corner with the kind of confidence that didn't ask permission. Her vibrant cobalt eyes caught the light, the reddish-orange bloom encircling her pupils flaring like a sunrise waking from within. She tousled her freshly cut bangs—resting just above her brows—while the rest of her hair was swept high into a sleek ponytail.

She wore black leather pants, a loose-fitting green tunic, and spiked black high-heeled boots that grazed just below her calves. The sharp click of her heels echoed across the floor as she reached for a nearby plate.

"Did I miss anything?" she asked, arching a brow, a mischievous grin already in place.

"Well, well, well…someone's been playing beauty school dropout," Rayanna said, glancing up and doing a double take, a smirk claiming her mouth. She popped the bread into her cheek and muffled out, "I was wondering what was taking you so long." Narrowing her focus on Layla, and speaking through bites, she added, "Since you asked—it appears you're missing the front half, just there," dragging a finger across her own forehead before dipping back into the bread and braised pork without another glance.

"Well, that's good to know, because that's the exact look I was going for. Your observational skills are unmatched, dear sister." Layla smiled widely, bowing low in Rayanna's direction. "No need to keep up appearances," she added, ruffling her bangs again with her fingertips. "I think they turned out pretty good—if I do say so myself." Shrugging, she nodded toward Rayanna. "You just wait, Ray," she said with a wink. "The dragons aren't out of the cave just yet."

Rayanna bobbed her head as if drunk with absurdity. "What *does that even mean?*" she muttered, widening her eyes and shaking her head before returning to her bread.

Layla shot the room an overzealous smile, shimmying her shoulders. "Don't you fret—you'll get used to *the real me,* at some point."

"Not like I have much of a choice, now do I?" Rayanna grumbled, shaking her head before taking another sip of her coffee. "I will say, though, I prefer this ensemble. No one needs to see your tits all the time." She shrugged, lazily rotating her pointer finger toward Layla. "It's definitely bolder—and way more badass. It actually makes me take you more seriously," she added, tilting her head to the side. Pausing for effect, she flung out a hand. "But those heels—"

"Where the hell did you even find those?" Runa cut in. "I haven't seen them in ages."

Rayanna let out a low chuckle. "I hid them. Figured they were the reason why you kept bruising yourself." Tossing oil tipped fingertips in Runa's direction, "Your fluid but, not in those." She glanced back at Layla, crossing her arms over her chest with a smirk. "Careful now…keep up this little style pivot and I might have to start respecting you."

Layla shot Rayanna a mischievous grin, giving a little twirl to show off the outfit framing her chest cavity with her hands, "Well, if that's what it takes to get your approval, maybe I should have done this sooner."

Rayanna's laughter burst out, rich and genuine, briefly smoothing the edges of her usual sarcasm. "Yeah, well, don't get *too* comfortable. I'm sure you'll find a way to ruin it by lunch."

Layla stuck out her tongue and gave an exaggerated wink. "Challenge accepted." She placed a hand on her hip, feigning offense. "Wait a minute —are you saying you didn't respect Tabytha?"

"Cool it, hotstuff," Rayanna's laughter trailed off. "From what I understand, it's been quite some time since Tabytha's *actually* been alive. So, that's *neither* here nor there."

Tilting her head at Rayanna, Layla leaned in and picked up a spoon, pointing it at her like a weaponized truth. "Speaking of old ghosts, I think Tabytha's story fits nicely with Starlight." She gestured toward the two older women at the island's edge. "Those two? They're the encyclopedias on the subject."

"Let's not get too ahead of ourselves," Mama D said, letting out a noticeable exhale. "Starlight has existed for ages, adapting over time. Initially, it served strictly as a military training base—approved by King Moros and commanded by Lord Brannon, who was General during the Great War. After King Moros' demise, Brannon assumed control and is now the acting leader of Shadow City…and your biological father. The military base is well known—embedded into the cliffside and acknowledged by every major leader. But Starlight Beach?" She shook her head. "That's something else entirely—its location strategically concealed from the outside world, so much so that Lord Brannon himself requested not to know its exact location." Her finger traced along the edge of the island, pausing to pick at a flanking pastry. "It's only known on our internal maps and shared with highly classified individuals." Leaning back, she let her words settle like dust after a storm.

Nadine cleared her throat, avoiding eye contact as she lowered her head and stepped closer to Mama D. "Well…Starlight Beach is actually on another map."

Mama D shot her a concerned look, squinting slightly as if trying to grasp the implications of the revelation.

Nadine didn't look up, just cleared her throat and closed the space between them, "Well...Starlight Beach is actually on—another map."

Mama D's gaze lingered, squinting just enough to suggest the truth was beginning to take shape.

"Okay...ummm..." Nadine exhaled, cheeks puffing easing forward resting both elbows on the counter. A hesitation as the room looked to her for a response.

Mama D's eyes narrowed, her fingers drumming lightly on the table. *"Another map?* How is that possible?" She swallowed hard, her gaze darting around the room. "Has the mission been compromised?" The words tumbled out, barely more than a whisper.

Nadine glanced up briefly before averting her gaze. "It's been recorded elsewhere. It's in—*our*—internal maps." She bit her lip, pressing them together as if bracing herself. "It's all Ezekiel, D."

A breath caught between words, her voice gentled. "He paid attention to you and Diesel all those years ago." Reaching out, she placed a steady hand over her old friend's restless fingers, her tone calm and measured. "He heard you, D, that night out on the patio. He still listens."

Rayanna's eyes widened. "Well, that doesn't sound creepy at all," she quipped.

Mama D drew back, casting Rayanna a sharp look before turning her attention to the others. She angled her head, resting her chin on the base of her palm, lips pressing together as she blinked hard. "How about we provide a concise overview and address any missing details as they come up?" she suggested, the words coming soft as a tear gathered at the edge of her waterline. Her fingertips came to seal her lips in quiet restraint, her head bowing in a gesture of allowance—a passing of the torch.

With a nod and an exhale steeped in centuries, Nadine began. "In the aftermath of the Great War, the devastation left lingering echoes...the chaos of restructuring power and rebuilding." She paused, her eyes scanning the group. "We needed a beacon of hope—a space that would also act as a haven, a refuge from which these towns could emerge." She cleared her throat before continuing. "It was Father Ezekiel, a revered leader of Sanctuary, who secretly funded the foundation of what stands here today."

She lifted her arm, almost lazily, gesturing toward the expanse of the living room. "All of this comes with great sacrifice." She edged herself back, offering Mama D a cautious glance, unsure of how the revelation might be received.

Mama D gave a small nod, her expression unreadable but steady—an unspoken acknowledgment passed between old friends, shaped by shared history and quiet understanding.

Nadine took a sip of coffee before continuing. "As I said, Starlight's military base is known, but the town itself is not." She nodded, as if physically justifying her words. "What matters now is that there are many layers that went into…" She fell silent for a beat, choosing her words carefully. "The creation of all of this." Her gaze slid to Runa, then dipped to the countertop as she drew in a deep inhale.

"I need you to hear this, Runa." Her tone mellowed—not to hide, but to underscore its importance. "Keeping you safe is part of it—but there's more at stake than just that." She placed her hands on the counter, grounding herself. "The actions that have been taken," she said, biting her lip and glancing at Mama D, "these covert operations were driven by a deep sense of duty to the citizens we serve—and by the necessity demanded by Shadow City, the Shadow Guild, and Sanctuary, each bound by oaths sworn long ago."

Mama D lifted a hand by a fraction, palm hovering in the space between them—a silent gesture to stall Nadine's next thought. Her gaze remained steady, slipping into the quiet rhythm of something half-remembered. "Do you recall, when you were little, how we'd talk through the bedtime stories?" she murmured. "I want you to see this clearly now—understand that Shadow City, the Shadow Guild, and Sanctuary…they were the founding powers. The ones who helped shape what Starlight Beach became." Her fingers lowered gradually as she spoke. "They were the quiet storm—always brewing just beneath the surface. Because as we used to say…great power entails great responsibility." Her voice finally falling into stillness, like the final line of a well-worn tale.

Nadine glanced at D, pausing thoughtfully. "But for now, let us set aside this thread of the tale," she said. "Its relevance will become apparent in due time." She nodded, steady assurance laced through her tone. "There is a lot of history to cover, and we'll get to it all…eventually." Her body seemed to meld with the sturdy surface of the island, her eyes locking onto each woman in turn before pressing on. "After the harrowing aftermath of the Great War, both Ezekiel and Diesel made a solemn vow," she continued, delivering the words with quiet force. "They promised to protect those most affected by the conflict—the innocent, the ones bearing the deepest scars." She paused. "The Shadow Guard was established to protect the Land's citizens—but over time, their objective was distorted. Corrupted from within."

She looked to the ceiling, as if searching for clarity. "Shadow City began targeting the Golden Guards for their quintessence," she said, her tone tinged with frustration. "This essence—this fifth element—develops uniquely in each individual, especially in those destined to become Golden Guards." Her fingers hovered at her mouth, tracing lightly down to her bottom lip before one began to move gently side to side—an unconscious effort to ground herself as the weight of what she'd shared settled between them. Her gaze flicking to Rayanna, an uncertain hesitation.

Rayanna's brow tightened—not confrontational, but clearly unsettled, as if the pieces weren't aligning the way they should. "Wait...why the Golden Guards?" she asked. "I don't understand."

Nadine raised a hand in a quiet halt, swallowing as she registered the flutter in energy. "Ezekiel and Diesel personally visited each new territory and spoke with those enduring the weight of rebuilding," she said, with a calm conviction. "In those moments, they recognized the urgent need for a stronghold. They sought to unite trusted leaders from across the factions—those who could stand in solidarity and defend the most vulnerable."

Rayanna leaned in, listening intently. "I don't see how Starlight helps with all that, though."

A sigh broke from Nadine's lips as she dipped her head toward Rayanna, humming back in understanding. "Starlight Beach was known to a select few who went through intense vetting. Essentially, this initiative stemmed from a deeply rooted distrust of the leadership in Sanctuary and Shadow City—the two largest civilizations within The Lands, each capable of starting another war. Corruption of power was becoming evident to top leaders like Diesel and Ezekiel." Her voice lowered, as though fearing someone might be eavesdropping. "You must remember—there is much hidden behind the facade of diplomacy."

"In essence, Ezekiel and Diesel went to great lengths to breathe life into this vision…" She turned her attention toward Mama D and continued. "It was all because of Diesel's keen perception of the pervasive corruption that still lurked in the shadows—even after King Moros' reign and destruction—that saved both Ezekiel and me."

"How did Papa D save you both?" Layla asked, her fingertips tapping gently on the surface.

Mama D slid a glass of amber liquid in Nadine's direction. Nadine nodded her thanks, lifted the glass, tipped it in acknowledgment, and took a sip. "Diesel being a Truth Seeker played a pivotal role in that, Layla." She raised her glass again, this time tilting it in Layla's direction. "In response to the information Diesel uncovered, this place became an unparalleled training ground for Elite Shadow Guards. Gradually, he wove even greater secrecy and intrigue around them, distinguishing them from the ordinary soldiers of Shadow City. This new branch of upper-echelon warriors was—and still is—considered ten times more lethal than your everyday guard."

"So, Starlight comes with built-in, round-the-clock defense? Fancy." Layla let out a low whistle and nodded once, then began loading her plate with small helpings of braised pork, green beans, and bread. With a quick twirl of her fork, she motioned for the older woman to continue.

"How did the town come about, though?" Runa inquired.

Mama D flung out a hand, jumping into the conversation. "The bare bones of the town were already in place—like the schoolhouse, North Star, the general store on the main path, things like that. It was Izayah who wanted to expand. As Lord Brannon's son, and with his brother Zane by his side, he spearheaded the transformation of the base into a strategic stronghold. Coinage was channeled into the operation, meticulously allocated to trusted commanders responsible for developing key sectors. The idea was that Starlight would provide sanctuary for high-profile individuals seeking to withdraw from active tracing—protecting them from the grasp of power-hungry cities."

Mama D's sigh slipped out before she found her voice again. "…And so, in the wake of Ezekiel's and Nadine's—supposed demise," she grimaced, casting Nadine a sharp sideways look before continuing, "it became imperative that Starlight follow the path of metamorphosis Izayah was proposing."

She glanced down at the food around them, reaching out to pick at the cheesy potatoes. "When he was given the official go-ahead, Izayah threw his whole self into the build." Speaking through a bite stuffed into her cheek, she added, "Through the whole undertaking…you were the one who kept him sane, Ray." Swallowing as she pushed a pot back to make room for her plate, she continued, "After Nadine and Ezekiel—things changed for you all. There was more 'separate time.'" She waved her fork casually. "Again…that's later information."

Mama D picked up a fork, turning it once between her fingers before reaching for a plate. "And for the record," she said, using it to gesture lightly toward Rayanna, "that old curiosity? It's been missed." She turned to Nadine, her gaze dipping in unspoken understanding.

"I do have to say, my favorite thing between you and Izayah…" A glint of moisture gathered at her waterline as she cleared her throat. "Every morning, after his cup of coffee with you, construction went full steam ahead." She smiled tenderly again, reaching out to pick at the food in front of her, a quiet chuckle slipping out. "So, after *this one* passed—" she shot Nadine a quick, begrudging look, "you stayed in Shadow City a little while longer. Then you came to live with us, Ray, in Starlight." She popped a small morsel into her mouth before adding, "It was in the routine, with you, that I believe he found comfort."

Rayanna blinked up at the ceiling and shrugged, half to herself. "Essentially what I'm hearing you say is…the whole beach thing, with the stars and the phased markings…was like being handed a box of puzzle pieces and told, 'Here, figure it out.' And now—now it's actually starting to make sense." She tapped the edge of her coffee mug and continued, "Shadow binding feels more like *that* to me than the stepping stones. It's like we're handed all these scattered bits—memories, impressions, symbols—and then something new appears, and suddenly, it pulls the whole picture into focus. Does that make sense?"

Layla huffed, the sound laced with exaggerated disbelief as she threw her head back and laughed. "Considering it's you? Yeah, it makes sense." She leaned forward, eyes bright with mock seriousness. "Truth Seeking, starting as self-reflection. Imagine, the concept." She tossed in a wink for good measure, popped a slice of potato into her mouth, and bounced her fork in Rayanna's direction. "You're a quick one."

"I can see that being the case for you, Rayanna." Nadine shook her head. "I could never quite predict how you ladies would respond to my presence." With a strained exhale, she added, "I've rehearsed this moment a million times in my mind, considering every conceivable outcome."

Nadine reached for her counterpart—not in title, but in burden. "The work you've done here with them is truly extraordinary," she said, her voice wavering as her attention glided to the girls. "I worried I wouldn't find acceptance. In all honesty, I was prepared for more resistance—hence time-stalling Starlight." Grimacing, she turned her attention back to Mama D, continuing, "If anything fails beyond this point…you and Diesel got this part right." She frowned through the acknowledgment and understanding. "Thank you."

Mama D's eyes softened, her hand sliding forward to connect beyond just words. "You held the line," her tone low but sure. "That had to be the hardest part of all of this." She gave Nadine's hand a gentle squeeze, then released it with a nod. "We'll come back to this—I promise. But we're not through it yet."

"Love the connections we're making," Rayanna said, exhaling sharply. "But we don't have time for this. Sorry…not trying to cut it short, but in the words of Layla—chop chop." Clearing her throat, she pressed on without waiting for a response. "Can someone explain to me what exactly Ezekiel and Diesel discovered about the corruption within the two cities?"

Nadine hummed in response as the atmosphere gradually lightened, her pointer finger bouncing in the air as if dribbling a notion mid-formation. She made her way toward the couch, each step a quiet negotiation of thought—measured not just in pace, but in purpose, as she searched for the right words. In her hand, a glass of amber liquid caught the light, its warm hue reflecting the cascading folds of her gold chiffon dress.

"What you need to know is that Ezekiel uncovered a wealth of information and confided in his lifelong friend, Diesel," she began, her voice steady, yet charged. "Diesel is someone Ezekiel trusts implicitly. Not just with his own life, but with the lives of his daughters…and mine." She eased into the cushions, the thought landing with her. "What they found out is for another day." Eyes wide, yet edged with weariness, she tucked her legs beneath herself. Gold chiffon pooled gently, spilling over the cushions in gentle folds that blanketed the rich blue of the upholstery.

Rayanna's mind raced as she tried to make sense of the revelations, her thoughts swirling like a storm within her. Her brow furrowed in concentration as she volleyed her questions back, her voice trembling with urgency. "Wait a minute, I don't understand. Is that what this town is made of? Does everyone here harbor some kind of twisted secret they're unaware of? Do they bear the same markings as we do?" Her attention fell to her now-empty mug with a heavy sigh, exasperation tugging at the edges of her composure. Rising from her seat, she crossed the kitchen—doubt still clinging to her shoulders—and reached for the coffee pot.

"Another round of caffeine? Seriously?" Layla quipped, leaning lazily against the counter, swaying slightly with bottled-up, childlike amusement. "You think that's what you need right now?"

Ray rolled her eyes and reached for the pot, her hands trembling slightly from the rush of caffeine and the weight of newfound knowledge. She muttered dramatically, "Oh, coffee, my sweet, enabling friend." She caressed the side of the pot as if it were a cherished pet. With an exaggerated sigh, she poured herself a cup, her lips curling into a sarcastic smile as she glanced at Layla—playful disdain simmering just beneath it.

Runa couldn't help but snort with laughter at the theatrics, the sound cracking through the tension for a fleeting second. No one else spoke. The room had quieted again, each person steeped in their own thoughts, marinating in the weight of what had been shared. As the silence stretched, Runa watched Rayanna saunter back to the island with her coffee, moving with her usual nonchalance. She grabbed a bowl, tore off a piece of focaccia bread and placed it inside, then poured the juices from the braised pork over it—her movements unhurried. A few roasted vegetables followed before she pushed away from the island and made her way to the opposite end of the L-shaped couch, where Nadine reclined. With a soft plop, she settled onto the pillowy surface, pulling her legs up beneath her, her plate balanced neatly in her lap. The quiet lingered, not heavy, just…present. Like they were all letting the truth stretch out around them, filling the space where words didn't need to reach.

"There's just so much we don't understand. It feels like every time we have a conversation like this, I end up…I mean, we end up tumbling down a rabbit hole filled with more questions than answers—surrounded by mysteries begging to be uncovered. I'm kind of over it." Rayanna's voice broke the quiet, dropping mid-thought into the open space. Her eyes darted immediately between Mama D and Nadine.

"I think that's a fair assessment, Ray," Mama D agreed, pushing her plate back and leaning onto one elbow. She angled herself more toward the center of the room, her gaze settling fully on Rayanna.

At the island, Runa pushed her plate aside and placed both hands flat against the cool countertop, trying to steady herself. Her vision narrowed at the edges, tunneling inward—colors dimming, sounds thinning. A wave of nausea curled in her stomach, threading its way up her spine. She blinked hard. Her breath came in shallow as her fingers twitched once against the stone.

Swallowing against the dryness in her throat, she tried to speak.

"Please..."

The word rasped out—hoarse, nearly swallowed by the flow of infor-mation. *"Please..."*

She coughed, clearing her throat again. "Please *interrupt me* if I start to..." She gulped, wincing. "Assuming this is—even a thing."

Her tongue stuck uncomfortably to the roof of her mouth. Her eyes pressed shut, lids cinched so tight they ached. One trembling finger rose to the corner of her eye, as if trying to subdue a flare of pain. She didn't know what this was. The nausea surged like a tide catching in her throat—so sudden it stole her breath."I..." she stammered, barely able to shape the word. "I don't..." A low whimper escaped her as pain shot down her spine, humming like a live wire. Her chest rose sharply with another inhalation, her back arching slightly—muscles pulling tight bracing against something unseen.

On the couch, Rayanna shot to her feet, her cup and bowl clattering as they knocked against the surface of the coffee table. "What the fuck..." she muttered, eyes wide, mouth parted in alarm as she scrambled across the cushions—half-crawling, trying to close the space between her and Runa.

Layla was already moving, one hand braced against Runa's back as she slid her own plate out of the way, steadying herself, alarm etched across her face.

Nadine set her dish down gently, her eyes fixed on Runa as she leaned forward, her attention sharpening. She unfolded herself and rose from the couch, the blanketing of her dress becoming more air than fabric. Pivoting around, she circled back toward the island's edge.

Mama D angled forward in synchrony, her stance fluid, second nature as Nadine fell in beside her, observing in silence. A single glance passed between them—nothing spoken, just that old, wordless language built on shared years and hard-earned trust. Their nods—barely noticeable—came hesitant. Bracing. Not just confused, but uncertain. Preparing.

Runa's mouth parted, and a low, breathy sound escaped—half grunt, half exhale—as if her thoughts themselves were straining their way out. "I see us...*only us*," her voice distant—thinned by a darkness she didn't dare name. "There are *no others* here in Starlight." The words tumbled too quickly, unspooling faster than she could catch them. "It's *all* a jumble." She bit down on her bottom lip, inhaling hard, exhaling just as sharp. Her eyelids fluttered as if fending off a rush of chaotic images. "A newborn. Lies. Healing. Screaming in a hallway. Caravans. A male with dark hair... on his knees..." Her tone dropped an octave, loosening into something winding, soft—less anchored, like she was slipping down into the sensation. "...an elderly woman. A figure veiled in shadows...an ancient forest. Smoke. Fire. Heat...and laughter—echoing through the woods, reverberating along the banks of a meandering stream."

Runa's fingers twitched against the cool surface of the island, as if water flowed just beneath her skin—its current brushing along her nerves. A tremor ran through her, and she began to shiver, her toes curling inside the warmth of her socks as if chilled by the damp air near a stream. The sensation rippled outward, conjuring the faint crackle of dry leaves underfoot—sharp, brittle, familiar.

As she spoke, her eyes drifted open like surfacing from a deep, weighted sleep. Her vision was already blurred, pupils swallowed in inky black, as if her gaze belonged elsewhere. Possessed by the moment, she turned slightly to the side, her body moving with fluid, dreamlike ease, addressing someone directly—someone only she could see. "But why?" she murmured, her voice a blend of wonder and unease. "What keeps her lingering in that secluded spot? And how does a stream influence the path of a child?"

She gasped—sharp, sudden. Eyes widened. Panic bloomed. Her fists clenched, nails biting into her palms. "No...this isn't right," she choked out, her voice trembling. Abruptly, she shoved back from the island, nearly toppling her stool—Layla lunged forward, catching her just in time before she stumbled into the back of the couch.

Runa stood, body rigid. Locked. Her gaze darted wildly across the room. "We need to figure out what this means—now!" she cried. Her arms folded in, gripping her elbows, rubbing against the cold that seemed to rise from within. Her chin dipped to her chest as she curled inward, crouching as if she could make herself smaller—like a child caught in a winter with no end.

Layla held her steady, hands firm on her shoulders, grounding her.

Rayanna hovered near the back edge of the couch, watching, unmoving, her gaze pinned to every subtle change in Runa's posture, face taut with silent tension.

"She can't do this while she's still shadow bound, Nadine!" Mama D barked, moving in fast. She clasped Runa's shoulders opposite Layla, her voice climbing. *"Ru, can you hear me?"* she cried, shaking her gently at first, then more firmly as goosebumps rippled along Runa's arms.

Runa's breath came faster—short, shallow gasps rattling in her chest. She couldn't focus. Her hands clenched tighter, her voice cracking as she stammered through the rising fear. "No...no, this—*this can't be right...*" Her words dissolved into sobs, the pain clawing against her ribs.

Mama D's grip tightened, her voice sharp and commanding. "Runa, *STOP!*" Her tone cracked with fear and rising urgency. "You *can't* do this yet!"

The room snapped—energy spiking—as Rayanna shot to her feet, vaulted over the back of the couch in one fluid motion, and landed hard. The sound echoed through the room like a heavy book slamming to the floor.

"DAMN IT, Ru—stop it!" she shouted. "I don't need *FUCKIN'* answers!" Her voice climbed, edged with desperation, panic blooming into full chaos.

Runa's petite frame remained curled inward—arms wound tight, chin pressed low. For a moment, everything held. The group waited, bodies braced, suspended in an invisible undertow. Anticipation coiled through the space like a drawn bowstring—no one dared to move.

Then her head snapped up. Her eyes—blacked out, glinting like obsidian beneath a floodlight—were cold, detached. A sudden force erupted from her, silent but undeniable.

Layla was flung backward. Mama D staggered. Rayanna tumbled aside with barely a sound, while Nadine held her position. Napkins lifted and spun, suspended mid-air before drifting down like ash. A fork clattered, skittering across the floorboards in the charged silence that followed.

Runa dropped to her hands, palms slapping the hardwood with a dull thud—fingers splayed, tense, digging in like she meant to hold the ground in place. Her neck rolled to one side, each vertebra cracking in succession like distant thunder. A twitch tugged at the corner of her mouth. Her jaw flexed. Her eyes caught the light—glassy, gleaming, almost too bright—before her expression stilled, smoothing into something unreadable. When she spoke, the words moved more like smoke—curling, creeping—vibrating through the room. "Twins…separated at birth. A precaution. Taken by Ezekiel. Blamed for death. What lurks in the shadows…warrants such drastic measures." A hiss followed—rasped out like gravel dragged through frost.

Runa gasped—sharp, strangled. Her eyes rolled back. Then snapped up, locking with Mama D's wide, unblinking stare. Her pupils, vast and vacant, swallowed the light. A slow, sinister smile unfurled across her lips as the voice spit: "I will taste her…and lap up her soul."

Silence held.

"Excuse me?!" Layla snapped. "Was this Plan A? Because it feels like we skipped a couple steps."

Runa's form *braced*—knuckles white, gaze cutting—as if in response. "I will…*taste* her…" it hissed again."Yes…my dear, running my tongue along every inch of you." At that, her tongue slid predatorily along her upper lip. Her neck snapped toward Rayanna, tilting at an unnatural angle as that same sinister smile crept back across her face. "Truth Tell *this*, sweetheart."

Every eye had widened.

The air turned suffocating, tension—visceral, unspoken—fracturing through the room like glass breaking in winter.

And then—Runa dropped.

Her body crumpled sideways, the eerie stillness broken as her cheek struck the floor. Limbs loose. Breath shallow.

Whatever had taken hold of her…*let go.*

Rayanna's eyes darted around the room, her hands trembling slightly. "What—the *living*—hell—was—that?" she exclaimed, her voice cracking under the weight of everything unsaid.

Layla's eyebrows shot up, nearly touching her hairline. "This is…definitely not the vibe we discussed."

"Shut up!" Rayanna snapped, whirling on her.

Nadine stood abruptly, flinging her hands out before her—then folded into time, vanishing for the briefest breath before reappearing beside Runa's collapsed form. She dropped to her knees as she pressed both index fingers to Runa's temples. Golden orbs bubbled at her fingertips, weaving into intricate spheres that anchored against her skin. Her tone fell into a steady, almost reverent cadence:"Time will tell, a tale revealed, a truth too deep to be concealed. Hear my words, let secrets flee. Let her be."

Runa's gaze drifted back into focus—blinking up at the two older women looming above her, their mouths parted in silent shock. "Nadine…" she rasped, her voice unsteady. "I don't understand—what this is."

"It shouldn't be happening like this," Nadine said sharply, eyes wide as she turned to the others. "And not while she's still shadow bound!"

"You fucking think?" Rayanna barked, flinging a hand toward Runa. "This—this is the kind of shit that has started to feel normal!" She spat. "We need you to tell us everything. No more secrets. No more cryptic metaphors. We need answers. Now."

Nadine turned toward her, head tilting with eerie calm. "What I know," she said softly, "is that Runa can't stay in Starlight much longer." Her gaze swept the room, taking in the stunned, shaken faces. "She needs more cover than this place can provide." Extending a hand toward Runa, she added, "You just showed everyone why staying *isn't* an option."

Chapter Twenty

Rayanna's eyes narrowed as she tilted her head toward Nadine. "Where the hell are you going to take her?" she snapped. "Somewhere safer than Starlight? That doesn't exist." Her voice was like sandpaper against steel, grating through each word. Shaking her head, as a bitter contradiction—played on her lips. "This is beyond ridiculous."

Layla's eyes widened, and she let out a short, incredulous laugh, pressing a hand to her forehead as if to steady herself. "Oh, come on, Ray. You really think *that's* the ridiculous part?" She gestured toward Runa, fingers splayed in exasperation, her jaw tightening slightly. "How about— what was it again?" she asked, sticking a finger in the air like she'd just flicked on a lightbulb. "Oh, right. The soul-licking thing? Yeah…that could be *slightly* more concerning, *don't you think?"* She leaned against the counter, arms braced firmly, grounding her annoyance.

Rayanna scoffed, her lips pressing into a tight line as determination took root, stubborn and unyielding.

Nadine let out a heavy sigh before speaking. "Rayanna, we'd be going to a place called Moonlight Beach." She glanced sideways at Mama D, lowering her voice. "It's the mother town to Starlight."

"*Excuse me?*" Mama D's head snapped up. She halted mid-step at the far end of the communal living space, her pacing cut short. Without another word, she crossed to the island, planting both hands firmly on the edge—facing Nadine from across the counter, the space between them suddenly charged.

"You can't be serious," Rayanna burst out, her grip tightening around the mug. "Where the hell is that?" She slid her coffee aside, then crossed to the couch, dropped into the cushions, and pulled the nearest blanket over herself, forming a makeshift space—small, enclosed, *hers*.

Runa poured herself a cup of water from the jug on the counter, her hands trembling a tad as she drank it in heaving gulps. She set it down with a tender *clink*, her cadence—drained and weary. "Honestly, Ray…I don't care where Moonlight is. That's not my focus right now. I need to make sense of the Tabytha part first." As she spoke, she made her way to the couch and leaned over the side, reaching beneath the blanket to find where Rayanna's head had disappeared. Her fingers pawed playfully at the lump she found there, a small smile flickering through the heaviness. "Wherever Nadine needs to take me to figure this out, I have to go," she added, giving a gentle pat before settling back. "We need to understand everything else before I leave."

Rayanna threw the blanket off her head with a dramatic flourish, her hair slightly mussed, a pout already forming on her lips. "Well, I'm going wherever you're going. No arguments." Her arms crossed in quiet defiance, her chin tilting just enough to make it clear she meant every word.

"What are you, five?" Layla muttered, leaning back on her island stool. "I can't believe we're having this conversation."

"I liked you better as Tabytha," Rayanna muttered, throwing the blanket back over her head.

Runa let out a gentle chuckle as she pulled herself up, perching on the backrest of the couch. She dug her feet into the cushions below to anchor herself, using its weight to keep her balanced. For a moment, she just sat there, leaning into her knees, quiet, watching the lump under the blanket that was her sister. She opened her mouth to speak—but was cut off by the sharp inhale behind her, Mama D's irritation carried in the breath itself, taut and unmistakable. "I don't know where Moonlight is," she stated, "but I have a feeling you're about to tell me." With a brief inhale, her shoulders lifted—then sank again as she exhaled, her gaze settling on Rayanna. "Still…I trust Nadine's call. I'm sorry, Ray—but this isn't a trip you can take with Runa."

"What the hell are you talking about? Give me a reason why." Her voice punched through thick fabric, muffled but no less fierce.

"Fuckin' A, man! *Seriously*—get off it." Layla snapped, rolling her eyes so hard it was practically audible.

"You have to train with Nester and Diesel. That's how you'll start to uncover what you're truly capable of after the unbinding." Mama D moved to the coffee table, setting down a shallow dish near Rayanna with a quiet huff. Her tone brooked no argument. The boundary had been firmly drawn.

From beneath the blanket, Rayanna's arm snuck out, patting the surface until her fingers found the dish. She slid it under the blanket like it was a secret stash. "Why can't I just do all that at Moonlight?" she muttered. "Why can't I go there and figure it out?"

Nadine, already at the island, reached for another piece of focaccia, her fingertips slick with rosemary-laced glaze. "We have a way for you two to stay in contact," she said, pointing with the wedge, its corner glistening. "But Runa can't stay here anymore. Not after what just happened." She popped it into her mouth and settled her chin in her palm, chewing pensively.

"Ray—just let it go," Layla snapped. "Runa made it through her first Dawning Day without you, and I think she's capable of handling this next stage on her own." Her voice flattened. "I'm so over the hand-holding."

In one practiced motion, she pushed herself away from the island. The stool scraped softly against the wood floor, the sound pointed and measured. Sweeping a hand down her body like a performer mid-mono-logue, she declared, "Now let's talk about me…" She paused, a sardonic smile playing on her lips. "…and the girl who shares my face—Tabytha." She bobbed her head to the side, letting the name linger just long enough to sting, then brushed it off with a lazy flick of her fingers—like shaking free the last drop of something she never meant to carry.

Rayanna pulled the blanket off her head and sat up, settling into a cross-legged position with the fabric pooling over her lap. "Yay. My favorite subject." Her tone came without inflection as she popped a rosebud cake into her mouth, offering no trace of real care.

"Look," Layla said, giving a loose flourish of her hand as she sauntered back to the island, "been the same person the whole time—minus the name and personality. But still."

"Thank you for *proving* my point," Rayanna said mid-chew. "*Completely* different person."

"*Ugh.* Semantics." Layla tousled her bangs with a huff. "Let's just get on with the information, shall we?"

Runa cleared her throat, bracing her hands on the back edge of the L-shaped couch. "Okay," she began, "so what I've gathered from all this—cataclysmic door, possession, or that tunnel of unsettling truths—whatever we're calling *this chaotic nonsense* ..." She pulled her feet out from beneath the cushion, swung her legs around, and in one fluid motion vaulted lightly from the ledge, landing just behind Layla. With a quiet slide forward, she aligned herself, their shoulders brushing as she came to stand at her side. "Tabytha and Layla," she continued, lifting her pointer finger as if drawing a line through the air, "they're my *older* biological sisters." Her hands moved instinctively as she began stacking the plates in front of her, clearing the space with practiced care. She nudged the island stool aside with her foot, her attention never breaking. Then, caught by a quiet pause mid-motion, her hands stilled just long enough for the truth to press inward. "Tabs always felt like a sister," she said softly, almost to herself. "Kind of like Ray does. I just didn't know about Layla...and now that I do—it's like I've gained someone I didn't even realize I was missing." A small, airy hum slipped from her throat as she turned the thought over. The words felt weightless, as though they were drifting—fragile, uncertain—circling in the air like moths drawn to a distant, tender flame.

Runa snapped her fingers once—then again—as though trying to summon a thought forward. "Layla...," she said, bouncing her hand in midair as her mind kept moving, "where did you put those pens you bought?"

With a sigh, Layla eased off the kitchen stool, her heels clicking softly against the floor as she shuffled over to the junk drawer. "You realize this isn't exactly the time to start drawing out the answers, right?" she muttered, rifling through the clutter.

Rayanna's eyes widened, as though catching fragments of a hushed conversation drifting through the undercurrent of conscious thought. In one fluid motion, she tossed the blanket off her lap and leaned forward to place the now-empty bowl on the coffee table. She crossed to the bookshelf near the stairs, pulled out a notebook, flipped it open, and slid a few clean pages free before circling back to the island. Leaning over Runa's shoulder, she laid the sheets in front of her without a word.

Layla returned and dropped the envelope—stuffed with multicolored pens—onto the counter in front of Runa. A black one rolled free, coming to rest at the center of the page like it had chosen its moment. Runa picked it up, flicked off the cap, and watched it spin away before tapping the back end of the pen against the parchment, her thoughts catching up to her hands.

"One flicked cap and suddenly I feel *very* emotionally evolved," Layla said, one brow arched.

"Is that *all* it takes?" Rayanna fired back, a smirk audible in her voice. "Noted."

Runa didn't respond. Her focus remained locked on the page, eyes tracing the blank space in front of her as if the lines were already there, waiting to be revealed. Without looking up, she asked, "What's it called? It's not a family tree—some of these people aren't blood. I just need to see how everyone fits."

Across the island, Nadine nodded, her tone even. "It's called a tethering tree. They became more common after the Great War, when we lost so many of our records. It helped us track how people were connected— blood or not." She paused. "That's what you're crafting."

Runa nodded. She looked down again and quickly scribbled *Tethering Tree Notes* across the top, her handwriting slanting as though the words were eager to escape her pen. Her head tilted, gaze catching on the faint letterhead etched at the top. Turning, she held the page up toward Rayanna, curiosity flashing in her dark eyes. "Where did this come from?"

Rayanna leaned casually against the table, one hand braced on the edge. "The bookcase," she replied with a shrug, her tone light. "Found it a few days ago—just a few loose pages stuffed in some folder."

"Truly, your insight is blinding." Layla said flatly.

"What?" Rayanna rolled her eyes, shaking her head and tipped her chin in Mama D's direction. "Figured they were snagged from Town Hall."

Mama D furrowed her brow, circling around the island to peer down at the paper. "Interesting." Her gaze slid sideways toward Nadine as the old woman gave a subtle shrug, her expression unreadable.

Layla sidled closer, studying the sheet for a long beat before glancing up. Fork in hand, she pointed between the two older women, focus narrowing. "Yeah...*that's it. Poof.* Just happened to show up here *magically.*"

Runa rested her face in her hands, pulsing the pen in the air as her fingers tapped a methodic rhythm. "Could we also talk about what a Dawning Day is, at some point?" she asked, mentally adding it to a growing list. "It keeps coming up, and I get the sense it matters. Like it's something I should already know." Across the room, Nadine exchanged a glance with Mama D—an unspoken accord settling in the space between them.

Runa gave a small nod, pen poised. "Okay, so Layla and Tabytha—blood relatives," she said, noting it aloud.

"Correct." A soft chorus of agreement followed as the names took form in ink.

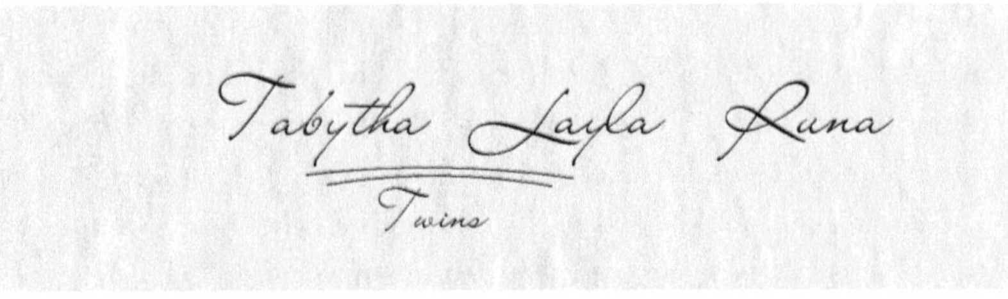

Runa pressed on. "Ray is Lord Brannon's daughter, and…" She glanced at Rayanna, blinking once, then looked toward Nadine. Her gaze snagged on the necklace resting at her throat just as a shiver ran down her spine, curling at the base like a whisper of warning. The pendant—an intricate weave of golden metal vines—caught the light. Their twisting shapes almost pulsed, the metal seeming to breathe with a life of its own.

Runa leaned forward on one elbow, her voice low. *Why does this feel so familiar?* The thought caught and held—not quite a memory, but something older, more elusive. Like smoke, thick and curling, slipping through her fingers like sand she hadn't realized she was holding.

The pendant gleamed in quiet response, its surface glinting warmly against Nadine's olive skin, yet somehow, the luster only deepened the chill tightening in Runa's chest. *I've seen this before…haven't I?* The question clotted her thoughts, dragging behind it an urgency she couldn't name. She swallowed hard, unease blooming in her ribcage. *And why does it feel like it's been waiting for me to notice it?*

Her body remained still, propped on one elbow, but her thoughts surged forward. The reverberation of recognition—faint, distant—froze her in place. This wasn't just a piece of jewelry. It was a current: intricate and ancient, tied to something vast, buried, humming with meaning. It felt like it belonged to her…and yet, impossibly far away.

Nadine fidgeted under Runa's stare, curiosity braiding through her own stillness. Her fingers moved, almost unconsciously, to the pendant at her throat—holding it delicately, as if acknowledging the words it bore. The motion sharpened Runa's focus. Her thoughts unraveled, reformed, and without warning, the necklace seemed to shimmer in her vision. Not twist, not glow—just…*respond.* And in that stillness, as the air grew taut with what hadn't yet been said, a single truth rose to the surface like lightning. "You're her mother." Her tone came soft, but sure.

Rayanna's eyes flew wide. "Wait—you're my *what*?" she sputtered, twisting to the side as coffee sprayed across the floor. She stared, mouth agape. "Excuse me?"

Nadine's fingers paused against the necklace, hesitating but not pulling away. Instead, she traced the edges with intent, her expression tightening as her gaze cut to Rayanna, who glanced between Runa—scribbling furiously—and Nadine, before letting out a soft exhale.

She spoke evenly, each word intentional. "I am connected to Lord Brannon as his tethered mate, and, as you've just pointed out...to Rayanna." Her fingers resumed their contemplative path over the pendant. "By title, I am known as High Lady Nadine of Shadow City. Or...I was, until my supposed demise." The way her fingers curled around the token betrayed the fading trace of an untold story.

"I'm sorry—you're *my* mother?"Rayanna's grip tightened around the empty mug she hadn't realized she was still holding. "No, seriously—what the actual..." Disbelief caught in her throat, halting the thought as she turned back to Runa, her voice rising. "How in the hell do you even know any of this? Where is this coming from?"

"It's coming from the fact that she's unbinding herself," Layla said flatly. "At some point, we're just going to know things." She slowed slightly, the next words more measured. "Because the shadow binding... it's going to release it."

"I didn't mean for you to find out this way, Ray. I really didn't. At least not right now." Nadine's voice was quiet, thick with the ache of years spent in absence. She looked down at the counter, her hands braced against its edge, as if searching the grain for words on how to move forward. "But yes...I'm your birthing mother. You were so young when it all—" Her voice trailed off beneath the weight of everything left unsaid.

"I do know that necklace, though," Runa murmured, more to herself than anyone else. "It means something. I can feel it." Her words drifted, carried on the quiet pull of memory—tugging at the edge, threading through her in subtle, invisible pulses "And why does it..."

"Welcome to the wonderful world of unbinding," Layla cut in. She leaned back lazily, arms crossing over her chest as she flicked at her nails. "It's like peeling an onion—except with Runa, every layer gets weirder."

Runa waved off the comment, the pen now balanced between her fingers, teetering back and forth in the air like a weighted scale. "The younglings by the river," she said, her tone distant. "Their laughter carried...their voices—" She broke off, flipping the pen around and pointing it toward Nadine, the tip angled like an accusation. "It's connected. *To that.*" Her gaze locked on the glinting curve of the pendant. *No—it's a token. But for what?* The thought batted about in her mind as she watched Nadine still cradling it against her chest.

Runa resumed fidgeting, the pen twisting absently as her musings circled. Images danced, refracting through her mind like broken light in a restless kaleidoscope—unsettled, unfinished, refusing to align.

Layla threw up her hands in a halting gesture. "Wait a minute. We're seriously back to rivers and younglings?" Her eyebrows shot up. "Yeah, no—that's a hard pass." She stretched her neck, rolling out the tension. "The whole babbling brook thing and laughing children? It's starting to freak me out." She rubbed at her face. "There are no younglings by a river." She let out a sharp sigh, hands rising as though delivering a verdict. "I know unbinding's supposed to be incremental." She jabbed a thumb toward Runa. "But with her, it's like someone hit double speed." Another breath. Sharper this time. "Maybe somebody else needs to take over."

"It is the necklace, Runa—and yes, it holds memories from your past." Nadine's voice held steady, threaded with curiosity. "I wanted to see if it might open a door for you. The rivers and younglings…they're there—safe, and waiting." Her gaze turned toward Mama D, who stood silently, brow furrowed as if assessing the pieces of a puzzle. "I had an inkling, D," Nadine added. "She knows more than we previously thought."

Mama D nodded. "Now I understand why it took three months to work through the shadow binding with her." She bobbed her head slightly. "Compared to the others."

Rayanna flung both hands out to her sides in a gesture somewhere between a shrug and complete disbelief. "Okay, first of all—surprisingly, I'm going to have to agree with Layla on this one." She finally seemed to register the coffee she'd spit earlier and reached for a towel to mop it up. Her cadence dipped into an effort at lightness, but tension still clung to the underbelly of each word. "I know you find all this unbinding stuff fascinating," she added, shooting Nadine an uneasy glance, "but it's starting to freak me out too."

Runa's gaze flicked toward Mama D. "Three months," she echoed softly. "Interesting how an object can trigger the inkling of a memory." Her voice fell to a hush as she spoke."Rivers and younglings…" She paused, as if trying to hold the thought before it scattered. "At least they're safe and waiting. Waiting for what—I have no idea." With a weary motion, she swept her hand beneath her chin. "And I don't think I have the brainpower to figure it out right now."

She blew the air out between her lips—part sigh, part refusal—as her focus drifted. The pen tapped rhythmically against the paper, guiding Runa's thoughts into place. "There are two males," her tone tightening, as if drawing their names forward might give shape to the rest. Her eyelids lowered, not quite closed, her focus pulling inward. "Zane and Izayah." She pinched her upper lip into a small fold, holding it, grounding herself. "Zane's the eldest..." A small, chipmunk-like sound escaped. "Izayah, the middle. Rayanna...the youngest of the bunch."

"Yes, you're correct," Nadine replied, quiet intrigue threading through each word, as if watching Runa unlock a door only she could reach. She lifted her chin slightly, eyes following the pen as it danced across the page in tight, slanted sweeps—names spilling into place with relentless focus.

As she underlined *Lord Brannon* and *Lady Nadine* with delicate strokes, Runa's pen pressed firmly into the paper. The connection between their names—and the family—finally clicked into place, igniting a spark of realization. She froze, the pen pressed into the page like punctuation for a truth she hadn't fully realized.

Runa's gaze drifted as her thoughts caught up with memory. "After Ashla had descended the staircase...she turned at the doors—the newly etched ones." Her fingers twitched around the pen still balanced in her hand, the weight of it grounding her. "She said, *'You're all caught up now.'* Then she paused just long enough to tell me to keep looking to the moon. *'Answers are on the horizon,'* she said. *'A world of possibilities awaits.'* And then she winked...and left." Her voice softened. "So I went to the beach—because she told me to look to the moon. It was in those moments our tattoos duplicated. The phase markings. Ashla said we were all caught up. And *I believed her.* Because...it started making sense." She tapped her forearm. "The markings are the door. They unlock memories—specific ones—

boxed away until the right moment. Memories meant to evolve with us." She looked directly at Layla, her voice gaining quiet strength. "When your linework appeared—*yours and Rayanna's*—I started to wonder if who I was, who *I am*, had somehow tangled with your memories. Because we were all caught up, right? All on the same page." Her gaze bounced between Layla and Rayanna. "But the dots don't connect in that order. In turn, my perspective needed to shift—which leads me to believe I might've been wrong, which now opens up a new hallway of notions." Shaking her hand as if waving at the new ideas, she proceeded, "Go with me on this—I swear it connects back to the Tethering Tree and Izayah. On the beach, when your markings surfaced, you both received pieces of me. But I didn't get anything in return." Runa turned fully to Layla. "When we thought you were Tabytha, you asked who Izayah was. You didn't recognize him. But you heard his name—*like I do.*" She tapped the ink again. "And then you said it: *'He exchanged his life for yours…sacrificed himself for me, for us.'* Then you asked why." Her voice tightened. "You didn't know then. You knew as much as I did. We were on the same wavelength."

Shifting gears, she exhaled, throwing a thumb over her shoulder. "But then in the backyard, it was a different response. You said he wasn't someone to mess with. Like you already knew him. Like you understood why he did what he did." The butt of the pen tapped against her bottom lip. "So maybe when the markings appear, it takes time for the pieces to click. Like Rayanna said—fragments at first, building toward something whole." She glanced at Nadine. "And since you said I know more than you all expected…then maybe I'm feeding back into this loop—giving information that allows you to understand more than you would've otherwise." She stopped, eyes darting between Layla and Rayanna. "Because you're here to support me—and I you. Yet by different means." Her gaze dropped to the parchment in front of her—not searching for answers, but holding space for the question to land. "You both know things I don't. And I know things, it appears, no one else has had a chance to piece together at all." She furrowed her brow, contemplative. "Yet, there is this one pivotal piece of knowing, that is this itch I can't seem to scratch. You know who Izayah is. And why all this was put into motion. Don't you?"

"Yes," Layla replied softly, placing a gentle hand on Runa's back. "But that's because my binding was different from yours…and Rayanna's. I know who he is—and why he did what he did. That part's already been unbound for me." She hesitated. "But like Nadine said, you need space. Unbinding takes time…you can't force it. That's why you have to leave Starlight—so you can have the space to ask these questions and receive the answers." She glanced around the room before continuing, her voice steady. "Have you ever thought…maybe it's not you holding you back? Maybe it's the ley lines in Starlight Beach that are keeping you from pushing forward. I know you think you're failing at something—but what if it's not you at all? It's not like you're not asking the questions." She gestured toward the floor. "I mean, hell—do we really need to bring up the soul-lapping thing again?" Then Layla took Runa's shoulders gently, looking her in the eyes. "There has to be a reason you're not able to see it all yet. Your time will come." Her voice dropped lower. "He hasn't come to you because you're not ready. But when you are—he will. His story isn't mine to tell, Ru."

Runa braced an elbow on the edge of the island, her other hand reaching to rest lightly on Layla's. She tapped it once, her gaze drifting to follow the motion. "I didn't think of it that way," she murmured. "You make a good point." Her focus pulled to Nadine. "I just keep circling back to *why* he would do this for me." She rubbed at her eyes, pushing through the fog of thought. "Maybe Starlight has become my barrier." Her voice steadied. "I know there were letters—ink, wax, seals. I catch glimpses of them sometimes, scattered like breadcrumbs. I think they're part of Starlight's origin…but why?" Her brow pulled tight. "The one thing I can never quite grasp is his face. I don't even know who to thank—or who to blame." A short, breathless laugh slipped out—more ache than humor. "I don't *remember* him, Nadine. Just fragments. His name. The pull of it. The weight. But never *him*." Her tone thinned, emotion strung through every word. "If he's the thread holding all of this together—if he's the reason we're even here at Starlight Beach—then why can't I recall him?" She tapped the edge of the letterhead in front of her, almost absently. "There's more to this. I can feel it…"

Mama D stepped forward and placed her hands gently on Runa's shoulders, then tilted Runa's chin upward with a crooked finger, calm and understanding. "You're not ready. *That's the answer,*" she said. "He's not part of *this* phase—not now. And you *can't* force it."

Silence stretched thin, Nadine's eyes shadowed with something unreadable—contained, but far from absent. She remained composed, though her cadence was underscored by quiet sorrow. "Yes, D is right. His sacrifice—and the meaning behind it—runs far deeper than you know. I suspect we'll tread that path before we take our leave."

Layla squirmed slightly, crossing her arms as though to shield herself from the weight of Runa's revelations. "Oh, look—a shiny answer, just over yonder. What now? A scavenger hunt, perhaps?"

Rayanna tossed the damp dish towel into the sink. "Fantastic. I always dreamed of being emotionally manipulated and confused in the same day." She pointed to both eyes, then jabbed a finger at Mama D. "Now that we know what *you* can do—"She gestured to the sink. "Clean-up crew's *open* for applications."

Mama D chuckled, shaking her head.

"Wait," Runa blurted, "Are you and Papa D...somehow connected to Nadine?" She exhaled. "Is that why—before the shadow binding—Rayanna was brought to Starlight?" She leaned in slightly, her tone dropping lower, as if voicing a secret. "Am I...related to Rayanna?"

Nadine let out a bellowing laugh that echoed through the room. "Oh, dear—you are far from related to any of my younglings." But as the words left her mouth, she quickly raised both hands, shaking them in a hurried attempt to soften the blow. "Oh, but don't get me wrong! There's a significant reason why I said that. It's not that I'm embarrassed by you or anything. It's just—well, it's complicated, you see..." Her words tumbled over each other as she stumbled through the explanation, her usual composure slipping.

"Everything *is* complicated," Runa muttered, her shoulders lifting in a subtle shrug as both hands landed on the counter. "So, my question is this: who are my birth parents, then?"

Mama D cleared her throat, drawing the room's attention. "Yes, Nadine and I are faith bound sisters—which means I would step in if anything ever happened to her. It's a vow, really—meant to ensure that younglings shift into the line their birth parents intended," she explained. Her demeanor softened as her gaze drifted to Runa's pen, moving steadily across the page, capturing every word. "I must say, I didn't expect any of this...not really."

Faith bound sisters?   High Lady Nadine
Mama D

"Now neither did I, D. Like I said, I wasn't sure how any of you would receive me," Nadine stated, leaning to hover a hand over the pork shoulder, the oils beginning to bubble. "Where I can set the record straight—I am your birthing mother, but not your mother."

Runa's head lifted sharply from the page, her dark eyes locking onto Nadine's. The pen stalled between her fingers, poised but forgotten, as the truth lodged itself in the space between them—dense and undeniable.

Nadine took a step forward, the crease in her brow deepening. "Your mother is High Priestess Visha. Your father is Father Ezekiel. You stand in line to inherit Sanctuary one day."

Runa's grip around the pen tightened, fingertips paling. She didn't speak. Her eyes held to Nadine's, as if sheer focus might pull the rest of the truth loose.

Nadine's tone cut a little sharper now, layered with fatigue and irritation. "Again, I don't know what Visha told you—the woman is a tapestry of lies. But what I do know is this: Layla and Tabytha are your blood. Your sisters. There's a long, tangled history there." The final words hung in the room like smoke, impossible to wave away or unhear.

Runa's hands had gone so tight her fingers ached, knuckles pale with tension. She flexed them open, and the pen landed on the surface with a soft clatter. Wide-eyed, she blinked once, twice, then reached for it again. Her grip closed around—each stroke of ink now carrying more than just words. Every line pressed into the page felt final somehow, tethered with undeniable meaning. Still, she kept writing, even as her thoughts spun with everything left unsaid.

Nadine hesitated, her gaze flicking toward Mama D, searching for an unspoken confirmation. When Mama D gave a subtle nod, Nadine exhaled, scooping a small bowl of the braised pork shoulder, the last of it still simmering in the pot. She reached for a few nutmeg ginger apple snaps, popping one into her mouth as she chewed, her eyes never leaving Runa. The stool screeched softly against the floor as she pulled it out from the island and sat down. After swallowing, she leaned slightly forward. "I'll explain more in depth when the time's right," she said, her tone carefully even. She picked up a fork and let it bounce lightly between her fingers as she added, "When we meet up with your pa—Ezekiel." The name landed with weight. "It'll be better for him to explain it directly, with my support. That way you'll get both sides of the story at the same time."

Layla, halfway to taking a sip from her glass, froze with her mouth open. "Oh, I didn't see that coming." She stuck her straw in and made an exaggerated slurping sound.

"What?" Mama D's eyes widened, incredulous. "Ezekiel is alive too?" She dropped her head into her hands, releasing a heavy sigh. "Oh, Blessed Father, how deep does this run exactly? How much do we not know?"

"Oh, and Layla, you're coming with Runa and me," Nadine said, tilting her neck slightly to ease the tension in her shoulders. "Didn't I mention that?"

Rayanna cut in, her voice edged with annoyance. "Excuse me—but why does Layla get to go? What about me?"

"Oh, for heaven's sake, are we *back* to this bullshit?" Layla blurted. "If it's such a big deal, I'll just stay here in Starlight and this nutcase can go," she added, flinging a hand in Rayanna's direction.

"Because, my dear, someone needs to hold down the fort here in Starlight—and that someone is you," Mama D stated matter-of-factly. "Layla has her own part to play in this, just like you do."

Rayanna huffed, crossing her arms, but she didn't argue further.

Nadine cleared her throat and continued, unfazed. "Like Mama D said, it'll all make more sense once you're fully unbound." Her gaze returned to Runa. "With the unbinding, you'll need to piece together what you know—think of it as mapping out a family tree. You'll have to connect the dots, ask the right questions, and untangle who's tied to whom. It's like waking a dormant muscle. It takes effort—but it comes back."

Mama D's attention drifted to the paper in front of Runa. With a slight tilt of her head, she reached across, lifted the parchment, and scanned its contents briefly. "We'll revisit this later," she murmured, giving the page a smooth, disc-like flick. It spun through the air—flat, steady, deliberate—until Nadine's hand rose without hesitation, her gaze never leaving her bowl. The paper met her palm and vanished instantly, no shimmer, no sound. She took another bite, entirely unbothered—as if catching disappearing documents mid-meal was the most ordinary thing in the world.

"Funny thing, my first impression of a tethering tree was something literal. I thought, 'Why would we tie Runa up? Is that really necessary?'" Rayanna leaned back against the kitchen sink, the cool surface offering momentary relief as she sipped her freshly poured coffee, considering her next words.

"Well, strapping Runa down might just fit the bill," Layla quipped, gesturing toward the grand oak. "Nature's just trying to help you stay rooted—spiritually or otherwise." She grabbed her drink, pushed back from the island, and strolled toward the couch. "I have to admit, the concept of tethering sounds pretty solid. Mapping out insights like this—definitely beneficial in the long run." After setting her glass on the coffee table, she flopped onto the cushions and stretched out, arms wide. "Seems like we only ever get fragments of the truth—like with Mama D's reaction to Nadine and Father Ezekiel." Lifting her cup again and cracking a small smile, she added, "Understanding both sides gives us more to work with. So...*thanks* for the transparency, Nadine."

Raising a hand, Mama D called for attention. "Ray, I can bring clarity to your arrival in Starlight. After Nadine's supposed death"—she paused, her jaw tightening briefly—"you came to live with us. It was a difficult season for everyone, especially the boys. Losing their mother was one thing. Figuring out how to raise a youngling was something else entirely." Her voice held steady. "They knew you needed a female perspective—someone who could help you navigate the complexities of growing up and prepare you for what was coming."

She shot a pointed look at Rayanna, signaling her to hold her thoughts —for now. "Izayah believed you needed that consistency—and Brannon agreed. Not just to guide you into becoming a full-fledged young woman, but to help you understand the power awakening within you. He knew Diesel's role would be just as essential as mine. Your quintessence—your connection to truth, to seeking and revealing it—is something only Diesel, as a seeker himself, could help you fully grasp." Nadine and Layla both nodded, their agreement unspoken but palpable. Mama D's gaze softened as she continued. "From there, you began living within the Starlight base during your early double-digit years—ten or eleven, I'd guess. It all blurs a bit now. But I know it was before your next stage truly began—that threshold where age decelerates, and your quintessence starts to surface—clear and undeniable."

Mama D raised a hand and began languidly spinning her finger in a loose circle, as if visually rewinding the story. "Twofold," she projected, her voice carrying. "Before the shadow binding. Before the cabin. Which—yes, I realize—you haven't been fully briefed on. We'll get to that soon. I know we keep saying that, but it's hard to fill in gaps without starting from what's already familiar, right?" She exhaled, lips twitching at the corners.

"I've always suspected Izayah didn't tell us everything Sienna foresaw," she added, her tone laced with quiet exasperation. "There was a lot shared in that exchange—about your past, Runa. It happened when she visited her son, Daxler, at the Starlight base while he and Izayah were preparing to rise in rank. That whole visit unraveled like a pulled thread. One moment we were prepping for celebration, the next we were knee-deep in prophecy and deployment." She shrugged. "But that's the rhythm of active duty—everything can recalibrate in a heartbeat." She gave a tired smile—more memory than mirth. "What I need you to understand is—this is him. Always propelled by purpose. When he makes a decision, everyone in the unit understands it's never impulsive. He weighs every outcome, considers each angle, and when he finally asks for help, people listen. Not out of fear—not because he pulls rank—but because they trust the gravity he gives to each word, each step forward. That's who he's always been."

She grimaced, shaking her head lightly and lifting a hand in front of her face, as if to stop herself from spiraling further. "Sorry. I digress." With a steadying intake, she centered herself. "Let me pull it back a bit to the second half that's relevant," She glanced toward Rayanna at the sink. "After Nadine's supposed demise, Rayanna came to live with us in Starlight. When her first Dawning Day passed—after the celebration had settled and the choice was hers—she decided to stay. She could've gone back to Shadow City, but she didn't. She chose us. Chose the base." Her voice softened with the memory. "And that's when the Cabinet of Curiosities took shape—your apothecary, Ray. It was the very first space Izayah built exactly as you envisioned it. A gift. I can still see your face the day those cabinet doors creaked open and the morning light spilled through the glass panes."

Her hand grazed the edge of the counter before she gestured lightly in Runa's direction. "Now that I think about it—Ru, those notes you mentioned? Izayah always kept paper with him. Called them his 'Letters of Guidance.' If memory serves, it was right after the apothecary was finished that the missives started showing up. And from that point on…it was like something cracked open inside him. He began building with this wild, intentional energy—like the letters had unlocked something."

Mama D reached across the island and gently tapped Runa's nose. "You know that look you get in the classroom—when your younglings stumble into something new? That spark? That's how he looked. Locked in. Clear-eyed. Completely driven. And whenever someone asked how he came up with his designs, he'd just point to those papers, like they held every answer."

Her gaze drifted, drawn into the memory. "No one ever saw what was written in them. But every morning—especially on those quieter drill days—he'd sit at the North Star Café with his coffee, poring over them. Scribbling in the margins. Reading and rereading. Sometimes just staring, like he was trying to see through the ink itself. Wouldn't be surprised if he went through a whole stack of paper just trying to get it all sorted out."

She let out a faint laugh—warm, but tired. "And after the Cabinet of Curiosities? He went back through the boardwalk. Added details. Swapped out the gravel for cobblestones. Adjusted layouts. It was like the letters weren't just pointing to what came next...but to what needed healing, too."

The room hung on Mama D's every word, each one dropping like water into a parched silence. The intensity with which they listened was tangible, as if every detail she shared might alter the ground beneath them. She paused a beat, then continued, "Right. The point is—Sienna's arrival at the base altered everything, completely overturning the planned celebration. None of us expected it—least of all Izayah. That's when the coordination for extraction from the cabin began to take shape. Let's just say, once that news hit, any joint celebrations between Sanctuary and Shadow City stopped cold. Since we knew people would still gather for the Fall Harvest Festival...because Rayanna was the one who orchestrated the entire thing."

"Excuse me?" Rayanna shot out, making her way over to the couch. She leaned forward into a bow-like shape, propping her elbows on the backrest and tilting her chin up toward Mama D.

"Are you all that surprised?" Layla said flatly, now sitting crisscross, with wide eyes, listening intently. "Ignore her, Mama—go on," she added, waving a hand dismissively at Rayanna before slurping her drink.

She let out a huffed chuckle, the sound thin and touched by memory, as Mama D continued, "The opportunity was locked in. He knew the exact timing—every name on the list, every necessary presence accounted for. Objectives were clear—mission-grade. His team was selected. His unit was prepped. Maneuvers were already in motion. Sienna and the other Seers were brought in to assist with the thought weaving and the binding. Every step was mapped—down to the breath." She inhaled deeply before taking a sip of water. Setting the glass back on the counter, she continued, "What I'm trying to say is—he refused to trust anyone else to oversee the mission from this side while he was deployed with his unit. He needed someone he trusted. Someone who understood exactly what was at stake." Her tone leveled, firm but clear. "Diesel remained General of the Guard, while I stepped into the role of Mayor. It gave me a more active presence within the town—while keeping step with Diesel and the military framework. It was all put in place for this assignment specifically. It was the only way to ensure nothing slipped through the cracks."

"To circle back to an earlier question—feels like forever ago, but I think it was Rayanna who asked—every citizen here has been handpicked for the vital nature of what Starlight holds. They either support a critical military function and live here full-time, or they've been stationed with a mission-specific purpose."

Her gaze softened as it met Nadine's. "But what really matters is this: in a very real way, you girls became ours. And I need you each to understand," she said, easing forward in her seat, plopping a few butter cakes onto her plate with casual precision, "what started as an assignment for Diesel and me became something far greater than a mission objective. We've always wanted you to know…" Her voice faltered, words weighted with everything she hadn't yet said, "…that regardless of what was intended, what truly matters is what each of you became to us."

She brushed at a tear, a soft chuckle escaping—worn, but warm. "I never imagined it would unfold like this," she admitted, the words exhaling like the easing of a door long held shut. "Sorry," she added with a sheepish glance. "I've kept this inside for too long—it catches me off guard sometimes."

"To love so deeply, to feel so irrevocably connected to all of you," she continued, her hand drifting to rest on the one that grieved her heart the most. "I know old threads of depleting questions, sown tightly to your soul, are beginning to unravel and rise again. Rayanna told me about the bridge of communication and the quiet confessions down by the beach— about the fear of who might ever love you. Those thoughts, they'll feel random, disorienting—because in your previous life, they were anything but."

The warmth of their bond steadied her, an unspoken bridge between their hearts offering the strength to continue. She set her plate aside, fingers wrapping firmly yet tenderly around Runa's hands, delving deeper into the caramel pools before her. "I need you to know you are worth loving. You hold immeasurable value, and—" her voice softened to a whisper, "you are cherished, my love. So very cherished."

With that, the space between them vanished. Their shoulders folded inward, arms entwining with quiet desperation as tears streamed unchecked. A binding of souls forever sealed—an embrace offering solace and strength in equal measure. Runa melted into Mama D's arms, her head tucked close, as though seeking the warmth wished for on distant stars. It wasn't just arms that wrapped around her, but the fragile pieces of her spirit, gently stitching themselves whole with every silent heartbeat shared.

A faint luster rippled around them, soft at first, until a rosy light radiated outward, enveloping them in a sanctuary of warmth and affection. The light flickered and pulsed gently, echoing the quiet rhythm of their shared bond. Runa trembled, pressing closer, her fingers clutching tight, unwilling to release the solace she'd found. In a voice fractured and barely above a whisper, she murmured, "I don't want to leave you and Papa."

The space itself seemed to draw inward—alive with a tangible stillness —where the walls bore silent witness to the sacredness of the moment.

Rayanna leaned forward, breaking the hush like the sharp drop of a pin. "Umm…should they be glowing like that?" she murmured.

Nadine's lips parted slightly, her gaze softening as her hand brushed over the vined necklace at her chest, as though steadying the ache rising there. "Remarkable." Her tone trailed off into hushed awe—suspended in the stillness—as though letting her words steep in reverence. "Sometimes…the strongest, most beautiful lights grow from within the deepest shadows," she said, her voice carrying a quiet prayerfulness—words so delicate they felt etched into eternity. "Oh, Blessed Father," her gaze lifting slightly. "He weaves the extraordinary into the unlikeliest places, doesn't He?" Her eyes lingered on the faint light haloing the two women—soft and ethereal, born of something sacred. "To think…" Her voice wavered, the words catching as she swallowed hard. "After everything she's endured, this is what she's become. This light." Her tone broke, raw and unguarded. "She's taken the darkness that tried to consume her...and turned it into something that brightens the world." The gentle brilliance surrounding them dimmed—like the final note of a cherished lullaby dissolving into stillness. Yet the warmth it left behind remained, wrapping the room in a quiet blessing.

Mama D's hand moved in tender strokes along the trembling form nestled against her. Gently, she pulled Runa back just enough to see her, palms rising to cradle the face she treasured so dearly. Leaning in, she pressed a kiss to Runa's forehead, as though pouring her love into every fragile piece. Her voice—soft and full of unwavering devotion—broke the silence. "You're *more than* special, my sweet one. You're my *miracle.*"

Drawing back slightly, Mama D rested her hand gently on Runa's chest, tapping softly. "No matter where you are in this world," her tone firm yet brimming with affection, "I will always live right here." Her palm pressed over the steady rhythm of the heartbeat. "You hold a piece of me...and you don't ever have to give it back." A hushed stillness blanketed the room— heavy as a weighted quilt, woven with sentimental tension.

"Ahhhh..." Layla's voice shattered the quiet, bouncing through the space like a pebble ricocheting off smooth stone. "How sweet! Ray, are you tearing up?"

Rayanna whipped her head toward Layla, her eyes narrowing into sharp slits. "Okay, Bangs, I'm getting real tired of your lip," she shot back, crossing her arms so tightly it looked like she might crush her own ribs. "Honestly, Runa, you can have her," she added with an eye roll, sticking her tongue out for good measure. "I think she chopped off the only part of her I liked."

Laughter erupted, filling the room with a joyful cacophony. Voices over-lapped, playful insults ricocheted through the air. A cushion soared across the room, narrowly missing Rayanna, who ducked with a grin before launching it back with equal force. Another missile of fluff sailed straight through the balcony doors, disappearing into the night.

Just as another cushion was about to be hurled, a sudden knock at the door froze everyone mid-motion, silencing the room instantly.

"Seriously?" Rayanna groaned, rubbing her head as she pushed herself up from the couch. Her glare locked onto Layla, narrowing into a sharp edge. "You better hope I don't find something else to throw."

"Ohh…what are you going to do?" Layla teased, fluttering her fingers like an impish firefly before clasping her hands behind her back and swaying innocently. "Do you always have to get the last word?"

"Yes, only because it's you," Rayanna quipped, her smirk widening as she arched backward, flinging the nearest cushion with theatrical precision.

Layla dodged, ducking just in time—but the throw landed squarely on Runa, sending her toppling onto the couch with Layla tumbling close behind.

The two collapsed into laughter, tangled in a heap, their joy washing through the room like an unbroken melody. Rayanna rolled her eyes with a mock groan, tossing another cushion their way with halfhearted aim. "Honestly, I don't know why I bother with you two," she muttered, arms crossing as a smirk tugged at her lips.

Layla opened her mouth, ready to fire back—but before the words could escape, a second knock echoed through the space—sharper this time, more measured. All eyes turned toward the door.

"And here I was thinking time stood still outside. Did I mishear you, Nadine?" Mama D's words held a quiet note of concern.

"I did," Nadine replied, her focus narrowing as she rose from her seat. "No one should be able to cross the property lines…yet…" Her voice trailed off, the last of the lightness slipping from the room.

Runa stretched across the island, snagging one of Dagny's raspberry chocolate truffles. She popped it into her mouth. "Nadine—Ashla and Nissa were out in the yard earlier," she mumbled around the chew, reaching for another as she shrugged with both cheeks full. "Maybe it's one of them."

Chapter Twenty-One

The knock—*thud-thud*—punctured the room's banter, drawing all eyes toward the door. Layla pushed herself up from the folds of the couch, her voice booming with playful theatrics. "The floor is yours! Enter, Your Majesty!" She swept into an exaggerated bow, her grin widening as she straightened.

Ashla stepped inside, rubbing the back of her head with one hand, the other clutching a pillow she'd clearly intercepted mid-flight. "What in the world is going on in here?" she asked, her golden blonde hair swept into a high ponytail, though a rogue twig stuck defiantly out the side. Mud streaked down the left leg of her relaxed-fit jeans, the fabric worn and frayed at the knees.

With a casual air, she ran her hand along the mud-streaked denim, her fingers moving in a fluid motion. The clay dried instantly, crumbling away in powdery flakes as she brushed it off with an absentminded flick. "Don't worry." Her cadence was like warm light spilling further into the room. "I caught the rogue pillow with my head. You're welcome." She glanced at Runa, her expression warming, though a flicker of uncertainty darted behind her eyes before she turned to embrace Mama D.

Standing frozen, memories of their last meeting at the town hall flooding her mind and leaving Runa momentarily speechless. "I didn't think I'd see you again so soon," she managed, her voice quieter than she intended.

Ashla's energy bounded forward. "Well, it's good to see you too!" she exclaimed, sweeping Runa into a whirlwind of an embrace. Runa stiffened, her arms hovering awkwardly at her sides, unsure where to place them.

By the kitchen counter, amusement danced in Rayanna's eyes, a sly grin tugging at her lips before she threw her arms wide in an exaggerated embrace—guiding Runa through the awkwardness from across the space.

Runa's expression crinkled in exasperation at Rayanna's antics, but she relented, giving Ashla's back a light pat as if to say, *Close enough.* The moment felt startling and unfamiliar—too full of affection and energy for someone who didn't know where she fit in this dynamic. Ashla broke the hold and moved deeper into the room.

At that, the space swirled into a current of sound and unrestrained mirth, allowing Runa's mind to slip free—yanked backward as if caught on a tripwire. Suddenly, she was mentally back on the beach with Papa D, their morning jogs a steady rhythm of sandy footfalls and guided conversation. The rhythmic crash of the waves echoed in her ears, the scent of salt sharp in her nose. His voice rose above the ocean, steady and firm: *Ru, moments like this are pivotal. Set your ego aside, and you'll find the truth waiting for you just beyond. That's how you grow.*

Was this one of those moments? The notion settled uneasily as she blinked back to the present, pulling from the embrace. Ashla had already stepped back, effortlessly blending into the group gathered near the island. Around them, the women's voices mingled in animated conversation, their laughter bubbling over like champagne.

And yet, Runa lingered in the space left behind, her thoughts caught between past lessons and the reality unfolding before her. She blinked, trying to reorient herself.

"Excuse me, but I need to know something!" Runa called out, her voice rising above the cheerful din. The smiles and chatter continued, undeterred.

With a sharp inhale, she stuck two fingers in her mouth and unleashed a piercing whistle that halted everyone mid-motion. Smoothing the front of her black attire and straightening a bit more, she repeated, quieter now, "I have a question." Her tone was clipped but composed.

Layla tilted her head with a playful smirk, "Ohhh—" she nudged Rayanna with an elbow, gesturing at Runa. "See what happens when you loosen your iron grip, Miss *Control* Freak?"

Rayanna rolled her eyes skyward. "Zip it, half-pint."

Layla gasped, clutching her chest in mock offense. *"Seriously?* Half-pint? That's the best you've got?" She swept a hand down the length of her figure, "In these heels, I am literally the same height as you."

Rayanna's hands shot up defensively. "Hey, I'm not the one who needs three-inch stilts to rise up in the world."

Runa rubbed at her face, frustration bleeding into the motion.

Ashla, seated near the edge of the gathering, quietly piled her plate with meticulous care, seemingly untouched by the banter swirling nearby. Morning light filtered through the windows, casting a soft glow across her features as she moved with a calm, almost entrancing rhythm. When she finally looked up, her smile bloomed gently, softening the space around her. "I imagine your curiosity is gnawing at you when it comes to me and my sister, Nissa," her voice infused with an otherworldly calm, each word unspooling with purpose. "Ma always told us the time would come when we'd have to answer for the threads that tie us together—unravel them, bit by bit." Her smile widened slightly, and a quiet laugh escaped, light and affectionate. "I am the eldest of Tabytha's daughters," her tone carrying both pride and warmth. "And with that comes responsibility. Nissa has her part to play, but her purpose is still budding, growing stronger with every passing moment. My role, however, is to guide the first steps, to nudge when questions start to form—when past memories begin to push against present reality." Her gaze drifted, her tone softened as she picked up a morsel of food, twirling it idly between her fingertips. "When you said, 'I think acquiring love seemed more like licking it off knives than being handed a spoon,' *it struck me.* To me, it sounded like you were drawing from some part of you that already knew, buried deep under shadows." She blinked, eyes wide and dreamy, her expression a delicate blend of sweetness and reflection. "Was I wrong to think this?" her voice floating like a delicate melody, soft yet filled with meaning.

"Well...no," Runa uttered, as her fingers absently traced the design on her forearm. The intricate full moon, flanked by delicate stars to the west and east, had appeared only hours earlier. Her words floated upward gently into the space between them. "I was going to ask—are you the reason I have these markings?" Her fingertip hovered over the fine dotted lines, which shimmered faintly under her touch.

Ashla spoke through a mouthful of potatoes, her tone light yet thoughtful, muffled slightly as though carried on a gentle hum. "Yes, it's connected —*it's my specialty*. I help release the shadow binding, and when needed, I open the gate for thought weaving." She tilted her head back dreamily, her eyes following a path only she could see. Her free hand floated gracefully, as if painting the explanation in the air. "Thought weaving completes the process of shadow binding," she explained, tracing invisible patterns with her fingertips. "It's the ink that forms the phased markings. Think of it as a time-release mechanism: once contact is made with an Unbinder like *myself* —or when you reach a certain level of realization—the ink gradually *awakens*. Images surface where they're needed, acting like stepping stones toward a door." Her hand danced with the notions, a gentle smile finding its place on her lips as she glided toward the couch, balancing her plate with effortless grace.

Runa followed and dropped onto the cushion across from her, the weight of her curiosity evident in her posture. "Okay, so let me get this straight," her brows knitted together. "Which comes first—shadow binding or thought weaving?"

"It's a delicate process," Ashla replied, her voice lifting into a melody, brightened by the thrill of unveiling truths long kept. "Most of the time, they're done in tandem. For you, though, shadow binding came first." Her fingers resumed their weaving motions, soft and measured, sketching patterns and pulling at threads. "Your binding was…different. *It had to be.* So much needed to be contained." Ashla's expression turned tender, her voice falling to a near-whisper—intimate, reverent. "It was agonizing to watch—but it was done with great care." She paused. Her expression quirked, eyes sparkling with secrets too sweet to keep. "You know, Izayah used to try and visit you every day." The words lingered in the air, stretching tenderly between them. "He wasn't allowed near you," she tittered, impish amusement curling through her tone, "but he *always came back.*" She scrunched up her face, popping the last chocolate-covered mint leaf into her mouth. "There's something between you two—special *and* rare." Pressing her fingertips to her lips, she bounced them lightly as though pondering aloud, her gaze twinkling with admiration. "Even on days when he knew he couldn't stay long, he still found a way to return. It was like his soul couldn't bear to be away from yours."

Ashla's eyes shimmered with wonder as she brought the tips of her fingers together in a silent clap, celebrating the unknown. "I've never seen such devotion. It's like you share an invisible thread, always pulling you back to one another." She sighed softly, her voice filled with a mix of adoration and curiosity. "Probably spun from stardust. It's quite rare these days."

Runa's cheeks reddened as she retreated into herself, biting down on her thumbnail. "Well, this is…awkward," she muttered, feeling the words scamper away like startled mice.

"Why?" Ashla squished her face to one side in thought, her lips pursing slightly as though tasting the idea. "I think it's *quite sweet.*"

Rayanna's brow arched, her gaze sharpening as if dissecting Ashla's every word. "Are you saying my so-called loving older brother only visited Runa?"

Layla snorted out her water, sputtering upon herself and the floorboards in the kitchen. "You *can't be* serious?" Wiping her mouth with the back of her hand, her eyes wide with mock astonishment, she added, *"Oh please!* He probably avoided us because our wit was too sharp for him." Jumping off the stool, grabbing a nearby towel, and throwing a hand up as if struck by a brilliant idea before mopping up the floor, "Or maybe—just maybe—Runa makes better coffee than you do."

"Yeah, that's it!" Rayanna said dryly as she took another sip of coffee.

Ashla glanced up mid-bite, entirely serene. "Hmm…pretty sure it was just Runa," she said with a vague nod, as if she'd been listening through a dream. Without pause, she went on, "Ray, you left pretty quickly after arriving—and everything you owned already lived in Starlight. Layla has a bit more history, but…ah—well…she didn't take as long." She picked up a wild berry ricotta sweet bun from her plate, examining the crescent of blueberries nestled into the glaze like it might answer something for her. After a thoughtful bite, she added, "Izayah looks at Runa differently, though. Like there are stars in her eyes."

Nadine lifted a finger, interjecting with gentle conviction, "I don't think we should assume how Izayah feels about any of this." She pulled a stool back with a quiet squeak and settled onto it, setting her blackberry mint fizz on the counter. The chilled glass gave off a faint wisp of condensation —cooled not by ice, but by her own quiet control.

"I'm not assuming anything, though. There's a difference...the energy is all...tickly and tingly." She tittered. "Always been that way." She giggled again, gently poking at the layers of her pastry. "Mama used to tell me, 'Ashla, shh...it's our secret.'" She didn't look up right away—still focused on the sweet bun resting in her fingertips. "I'm glad you've come back to Starlight, Nadine." Her gaze lingered on the crescent of blueberries, her head tilting slightly—as if listening to something only the fruit could say. After a thoughtful bite, her voice drifted out, dreamy yet sincere. "I didn't expect you for a few more days. But the blueberries were arranged differently this morning. I should've known."

Rayanna turned abruptly toward Ashla. "Wait—how would you know she was going to be in town?" Her head cocked, hinting at her skepticism, as if she were filtering through the possibility of Ashla's response.

"The trees talk," Ashla replied matter-of-factly, her voice light and certain, like she'd just shared a weather update. She popped the remaining sweet bun into her mouth, chewing as if it might help her listen better. Then, with purpose, she reached for the loaf of bread in front of her, tore off a small piece, and dipped it into the balsamic glaze. The rich scent of roasted garlic curled through the air, cut by the sharp tang of vinegar as she took a bite—eyes thoughtful, but unfazed.

Rayanna's eyebrows climbed, her voice sharp with disbelief. "I'm sorry —*what?*" She leaned in, arms crossed. "I know they move, *but talk?*"

Ashla's smile widened, her blue eyes sparkling with the reverence of someone sharing an ancient secret. "Oh yes. They're always talking. The houses do, too," she added in a sing-song tone, gesturing vaguely toward the walls. She took another bite of the bread, pausing mid-chew. After a thoughtful swallow, she leaned in slightly, voice dropping to a whimsical hush. "But the oldest oaks? They're the worst gossips. They chatter endlessly. I think it's because they've lived through so much— they *can't keep* anything to themselves." She blinked, then added with quiet certainty, "One of them once told me, I'd forget something important just to make space for something better. And then it rained for three days."

Ashla dipped the edge of her bread into the dark reduction, her movements unhurried. Her gaze meandered toward the balcony, thoughtful yet unfazed. "Their roots carry messages underground—like a hidden telegraph system. Warnings, advice, observations…*they share it all, really.*" She tore off a corner of the bread and brought it to her lips in quiet ceremony, as if honoring some unspoken tradition. After a delicate bite, she let the moment breathe, her fingers still cradling the remaining piece. "Imagine being rooted in one place for centuries. Wouldn't you have opinions on everything?"

Rayanna's brow furrowed, lips twitching with dry amusement. "So… what? The oaks are just out here like bark-skinned busybodies?"

Ashla raised a finger to her lips. "Shhh," she whispered with playful solemnity. "I'd be careful what you say. They do have an appointed council, and they've had centuries to perfect holding grudges. Very deep roots." She stood as she spoke, gliding back to the island with that curious mix of grace and distraction. With great concentration, she scooped a few more sweet treats onto her plate—two wild berry buns and a raspberry cream puff—before plopping back down with theatrical gentleness, as if the food required a soft landing. "Honestly, why do you think the trees and houses here are so opinionated?" she added, nodding seriously. "Nissa's whole design palette for the cottage? That wasn't *just* her being artsy. *Your oak* demanded cool tones—said something about *'tranquility for the spirit.'*" She dropped her voice low, mimicking the gravelly wisdom of a centuries-old tree. "'Soothing hues, or no structural cooperation.'" And then, with a quiet giggle, she picked up the cream puff like it was a reward for delivering the message.

Rayanna, seated at the island, curiosity piqued, plucked the blueberries from her sweet bun as she listened intently.

Ashla tilted her head, a faraway smile curving her lips. "And the houses? Oh, they bicker constantly. Debating doorframe shapes, arguing over who gets more sunlight. Your cottage? Always a little chillier because it's vying with the greenhouse next door. They're rivals." She chittered at the thought, amused in the same way one might find clouds arguing with the wind. "But don't worry—it's friendly competition. Mostly." She lifted a wild berry bun and took a small, thoughtful bite, then reached for the raspberry cream puff, tasting the edge as if testing a theory. Her brow lifted—not with surprise, but with quiet delight, as though the flavors confirmed something only she had suspected. "They keep us safe, you know," her voice light but certain. "The roots carry warnings faster than anyone could run. They sense danger long before it arrives." Her words settled into the room like dust catching sunlight. "It's not just communication—it's a tapestry of awareness, a way of weaving everything in this place together." She turned to Runa, her tone softening like dusk. "You just have to know how to listen."

"Out of curiosity…do you know anything about the cabin—the place we were before all of this?" Runa asked, words halting like she was stepping carefully across uneven ground. "When you were walking with Nissa in the yard this morning…it pulled something loose." Her brow pinched. "Was there a field? I can't explain it, but it was like I saw us there—just for a second." She hesitated. "And something about your mother…she was there too."

Ashla's nostrils flared slightly as she inhaled deeply, her expression faltering for just a heartbeat. A subtle shadow crossed her face—fleeting, but unmistakable—before her usual dreamy demeanor returned. Her fingers, still sticky with glaze, twirled a strand of her blonde hair as her reply lilted into a sing-song rhythm. "We can do better than that." She balanced one of the wild berry buns delicately between her fingertips, took a bite, and then—almost experimentally—tasted the edge of the raspberry cream puff, as if testing how one flavor spoke to the next. Her brow lifted, not with surprise but with quiet delight, her body swaying ever so slightly, as though lulled by something only she could hear.

"I can show you the cabin," she said after a pause, her voice airy but certain. She plucked another bite from the cream puff and gestured faintly toward the door. "It's not far—if you're all willing."

All eyes snapped to her, disbelief and intrigue stirring the quiet. Rayanna angled forward as if needing to physically confront the possibility. Her voice sliced the moment, sharp and direct. "How would you manage that?" she asked, suspicion coiled just beneath her tone.

Ashla reclined in her chair, lifting the remainder of the first wild berry bun and popping it into her mouth as though the flavor itself held a memory.

She followed it with the last of the cream puff, her fingers delicately gathering the bits of raspberry glaze left behind. "Memory Vines can be quite handy," she said, licking a trace of sugar from her thumb. "And wonderful household décor, if I do say so myself." She picked up the second wild berry bun and took an unhurried bite before continuing. "They're not exactly easy to acquire, though—not since the stagnation of Treefall Lagoon."

"Memory Vines?" Layla threw her hands in the air, eyes wide. She pushed away from the island and crossed the room with exaggerated steps, collapsing backward into the couch cushions, arms flinging out in defeat. "I can't with all this," she groaned, kicking her legs up as she yanked off her boots. With a huff, she flung them aside. "Might as well get comfortable for this one."

"It's a grand story to tell," Ashla mused, "and one worth getting comfortable for." She held the last sweet bun delicately between her fingers, her eyes drifting along the crust as if the crests might remind her where to begin. "Yes—Memory Vines and Lumis Blossoms." Each word flowed gently, placed with intention, like stones within a stream. "I learned about them in Moonlight. The library there—oh, it's far more extensive than anything Starlight has managed to preserve. A treasure trove of pure knowledge, untouched by time."

As Ashla spoke, Nadine rose quietly from the island, her glass of blueberry mint fizz still in hand. She eased down beside the others on the couch, tucking her legs beneath her so the soft chiffon of her dress fell naturally around her. "How did you come across Memory Vines and Lumis Blossoms?" Her gaze held steady. "They only grow within Treefall Lagoon. To comprehend their existence now…" Her voice dimmed, tinged with something heavier. "It's nearly inconceivable, given what the Lagoon has become. To be able to grasp their survival…indescribable."

Ashla let out a high-pitched, melodic chuckle that spiraled gently. "Oh —Izayah needed them." She popped the last piece of the bun into her mouth, brushing her fingers together. "But I didn't obtain them myself. It was Izayah and Daxler—during the waiting period."

Runa blinked slowly.

Ashla's attention drifted toward the balcony, catching on the lazy flutter of a butterfly dancing just beyond the threshold. She raised her hand in an absent greeting, then pressed her palm gently to her chest, as though cradling a delicate blossom. "Nissa was the one who cared for them when we lived in the Dark Forest," her cadence dipped like sunlight through leaves. "She has such a way with things that grow."

"What exactly are Memory Vines and Lumis Blossoms?" Layla asked as she sank deeper into her seat, arms folding loosely, her expression skeptical but undeniably intrigued. "And how are they supposed to help us get to the cabin?"

Nadine took a long breath before speaking. "Imagine this," she began, "slender vines intertwined with blossoms that shimmer in the moonlight—their glow soft, almost otherworldly. Each bloom pulses gently, like it's echoing the memory it holds."

Mama D settled beside her, giving Nadine's arm a playful nudge. A hushed cadence dropped into her lap as she added, "And when you touch them, they radiate a faint warmth—like a heartbeat inviting you in. It's not just remembering…it's reliving."

Ashla leaned forward, setting her empty plate on the coffee table. Her voice softened to a near whisper, each word unfolding like petals in bloom. "They are simply extraordinary," she murmured. "Just like you, Auntie Ru. When the vines find you, and they're ready to share, they twist and curl into shapes that speak—a story waiting to unfurl, a memory begging to be known." A dreamy smile touched her lips as she exhaled. "In their presence, time bends. The past breathes beside you. And for a moment…you're allowed to hold it."

"Okay, well, that's poetic and all," Layla groaned through her exasperation as she flung her legs up onto the backside of the cushions, "but can we just get to the part where we use them to find the cabin?"

"*Soon.* That part likes to arrive in its own time," Ashla replied, her smile deepening. "But you'll see—they don't just help us *find* it. They help us *feel* it." She turned to Runa, dipping into a playful hush—like a tentative toe in still water. "That's their *real* magic. They don't just *show* the way—*they become the way.*"

"They're absolutely mesmerizing," Mama D said, exhaling the notion. "They blend seamlessly into their surroundings…like shadows just before daybreak."

"That's an exceptional way of putting it," Ashla hummed. "Maybe that's why they accepted Izayah so easily."

Runa let her head sink back into the cushions, her gaze tracking the exposed wooden beams above—as if the grain might spell out something long forgotten. Her thoughts slipped through the cracks of the present, curling backward like smoke…back to the mist that had hovered beyond the moongate that morning. It hadn't just lingered. It had watched and moved with intent. The memory wound itself around her ribs again, quiet yet insistent, threading through every word spoken about the Lumis Blooms and their strange possibilities. And for the first time, she didn't wonder *what* she had seen. She wondered *who*. And if that *who* had been waiting all along—*waiting* for her to *see. Waiting* for *her to remember.*

Her thoughts lingered in that space between—what she knew and what had been bound. Where memory pulsed in quiet rebellion, deep in the folds of herself left still too long. Not buried. Not forgotten. Just sealed shut—until now. The pull low in her spine wasn't new, but she was only just beginning to feel the ache of its unraveling. Like muscles strained after sudden use, or a door resisting its hinges, the truth tugged—steady, quiet, demanding strength she hadn't realized she'd need to reclaim.

Slipping into her line of sight—wings of deep onyx, fringed in misted haze—a quiet beauty fluttered in with the same curious ease Ashla had made welcome. The butterfly moved as if born from memory, riding a spiraling draft that stirred the stillness around her. Each lift folded effortlessly into the next, its glide so seamless it barely brushed the edge of her existence. Runa watched as it sailed through the open balcony doors, like a thought not yet fully formed—shadow woven shimmer trailing in its wake. A dusting, brief as breath, already dissolving into the hush of morning light.

The hunger to know stirred in her chest—more instinct than thought, a quiet pull in her ribs she didn't question. Runa rose, the fuzz of her green socks padding across the tide of midnight blue. She rounded the sofa's edge, her feet gliding softly onto the floorboards. Her steps were tender— like dew settling on petals—as she moved past the staircase toward the elongated bathroom tucked just beyond it.

The butterfly lingered on the curled end of the banister—the place where the railing bent inward in a quiet spiral, like punctuation at the close of a notion. Its wings, once in motion, now folded with still precision—its body catching the low light like a flicker caught between dimensions. As Runa neared, it lifted again, as though it had been waiting just for her. Its path ahead was meandering, almost languid—fluttering not with urgency, but with reverent insistence. It guided her—pausing just long enough for her to follow—through the threshold of the washroom, then drifted onward once more.

It alighted on a small, budding orb nestled within the cascading greenery that spilled from the mirror's edge—wings settling in delicate surrender, as if it had delivered her to exactly where she was meant to be.

She paused, captivated. The butterfly—wings of obsidian and mist—saturated into the surface of the acorn-shaped bud, fully absorbed. In its wake, the outer shell began to undulate—a softening, an acceptance of notions. The once-glossy sheen gave way to a granulated texture, onyx fracturing into veins of a gray-hazed halo.

The bloom was alive. Not merely appearing to be—it was. With every exhale, it released a mist-like luminescence into the space, gentle and ethereal. The sheen spilled outward in rhythmic waves, folding through the air like fog laced with memory. Runa felt herself leaning in—not out of urgency, but recognition—as though the blossom wasn't summoning her... but welcoming her back.

From the other room, Ashla's voice drifted gingerly—lilting like wind through ancient trees. "In Treefall—" she began, "...Memory Vines and Lumis Blossoms thrived amidst emerald pools and endless canopies of verdant leaves."

Her words lingered, then faded, leaving the air strangely still.

The thought of such reverent enchantments brushed the farthest edges of Runa's awareness. Yet, her gaze remained fixed on the bud before her, its pulsing light drawing her in—anchoring her in the hush of something ancient and known, as if it carried the weight of long-lost stories aching to be remembered.

From the other room, Rayanna's voice cut in—dry, precise, and sharpened to a point. "So, let me get this straight." She eased into the cushions, claiming the spot Runa had just left, arms crossing in a display of performative calm. "We're not actually going to the cabin? Of course not. That would make far too much sense. Her brow lifted, lips twisting with wry cleverness. *"No, no.* We have to *activate* the memory instead," she drawled. "What the fuck is the plan, then?" Her cadence brightened with mock curiosity. "Do we chant in unison? Sacrifice a goat? Or maybe we just *stare* at it until it feels emotionally supported enough to open up?" Her gaze locked onto Ashla, who simply fluttered her lashes—dreamy, unbothered. "Because if we're waiting for that thing to build up its trust issues, I'll be over there taking a nap. Feel free to wake me when it's finally ready to share its feelings."

"The process of releasing memory," Nadine began, her voice a steady stream of calm, shaped purposefully to carry into the next room. "It requires sincerity and a genuine desire for clarity. When someone seeks to activate a Lumis Bloom, intent matters above all else. It's not simply about unlocking the past—it's about meeting it honestly, without force."

"You see, Runa," Ashla's excitement spilled over like sunlight breaking through dense foliage, her words tumbling out in a rush, "the seeker's essence must be as clear as a mountain stream and as open as the sky at dawn. It's not just about remembering—it's about *feeling*. The essence of the recollection intertwines with the seeker's spirit, flowing through pure intentions and a heart wide open. *Only then,*" she added, her laughter light and effervescent, "can the true nature of the memory be revealed."

With that, Runa found herself drifting forward without pause—guided not by her own past experiences, but by a primal trust in the voices just beyond the washroom walls...and by the weight of who had once shaped the coming memory. This bloom wasn't just spoken of—it had been created with intention, with meaning. Izayah never did anything without purpose, or so she had been told. And now, standing before its haloed sheen, Runa felt the aim for meaning stir within—familiar and wordless. It wasn't reckless. It was instinctual—raw, guttural, and steadied by belief. A belief not just in the bloom itself, but in the voiced confidence of those who trusted the man who had woven it into being. Her fingers hovered for a moment before curling softly around its fragile surface. As she plucked it from the vine, the air tilted. A shimmer laced the space—a warmth that grazed the edges of her senses like breath across skin.

In her palm, the delicate sphere responded instantly. Color bloomed within its shell, swirling in fluid motion—deep greens, oceanic blues, and earthy browns blending like a living memory, familiar in ways she couldn't name. The scent of seawater threaded with pine rose gently, anchoring her in a place that didn't yet exist in language—*but did in feeling*. Her breath caught as the petals began to unfurl, one by one, peeling back with intentional grace. A smile crept across her lips—unbidden, quiet, honest. Warmth rose through her chest, so swift and full she had to bite her bottom lip, rooting herself against its tide. The orb glimmered in her hand, a luster radiating from its center.

And then, the words began to form—one at a time—within the liquid heart of its core. Each appeared steadily, like a heartbeat written in light: *"How–I–have–missed–you,–Ru.–Only–the–truth.–Only–ever–the–truth."*

The message lingered—it was a delicate promise whispered across lapsed time. A quiet shiver traced the length of her arms, raising goosebumps in its wake. It was real. This was real—something she could hold. The beginning of trust, not built in declarations, but in raw exposure. In nothing hidden.

As she pressed her fingertips into its warm, pliant surface, it didn't push back—it pressed in. A nestling. A hug. A closeness. She wasn't just feeling the words—she was meeting them. The orb nestled deeper into her palm, a heartbeat she wanted to remember. Drawn to its affection, Runa lifted it gently to her lips. "No more pretending. No more hiding," she whispered. "Honestly? That's all I've ever wanted. From anyone."

She inhaled, letting the remaining embrace settle behind her ribs like faint embers. With the haloing light still cupped delicately in her palms, Runa stepped across the threshold of the washroom, returning to that of the communal space, holding it as though it were a fragile, newly-hatched bird.

"I didn't see a mountain or stream," she said, wonder softening her voice. "But I saw the most exquisite black butterfly with gray-tipped wings —something I've never seen before. Does that mean anything?"

The room turned in unison to the question, their expressions softening into hushed awe as all eyes fell to the orb Runa cradled. A collective intake—then, Ashla's airy voice spilled into the silence. "Oh...he caught your fancy too." Her gaze sparkled as she clapped her fingertips together. "Butterflies are fantastic at keeping secrets—they tuck them in their wings."

"Secrets in their wings?" Rayanna echoed dryly. "So...is she officially our guide now in this whole Lumis Bloom situation? Because if we're picking spirit animals for this quest, I'd like to choose mine."

"Of course you would," Layla groaned, flinging her legs flat onto the couch with one arm draped over her face. A short, incredulous chuckle slipped out. "And I'm the questionable one?" She let her other arm fall dramatically to the side. "Meanwhile, butterflies are out there delivering cryptic scrolls."

"Oh no...hardly," Ashla lilted, utterly undeterred. "But they do hold memory dust. Onyx butterflies are like catching the breath of a storm just before it dreams."

"Well," Rayanna blinked. "That...sure sounded like a *real* sentence."

Ashla's eyes brightened as she dipped into a whisper. "The gray edgings," she giggled, "they're message carriers—Nissa and I used to weave thoughts right into their feather-rimmed wingtips." She gave a satisfied nod, wholly pleased with the idea. "Very clever of him, indeed." Reaching across the table, she lazily dragged a finger through the remnants of raspberry glaze on her plate. "He used it like a fluttering key seeking its orbed lock."

"The two of you...definitely come with your own flair." Nadine said with a small smile, looking toward Runa. She tilted her head with a quiet, knowing ease. "Seems he meant for it to find you all along," she added simply, her gaze steady. "Message received, I'd say."

A soft hum followed, as if Ashla were savoring a melody lost between hearing and knowing. "Perfect fit, if I don't say so myself." Then she lifted her wrist beneath her nose, crossed her eyes in exaggerated assessment of time, and declared, "I do believe it's time for us to be on our way now."

"Wait a minute—*on our way?* I thought the whole point was that we weren't going anywhere," Rayanna muttered, her voice edged with frustration.

"Oh, Ray, you never miss a beat, do you?" Layla arched an eyebrow, smirking. "Sometimes I wonder if you actually have a thought—but then it just bounces around, ricochets off another, and *poof*—gone before you can catch it."

Rayanna narrowed her eyes, her expression darkening with mock offense. "You know what, Ms. Sassypants? Ricochet *this*," she snapped, grabbing the nearest deep velvet square, launching it across the room.

The pillow sailed cleanly through the space, missing Layla by inches. She arched back with a laugh and retaliated with a cushion of her own. "Oh, it's *on* now!" she declared, grinning as she braced for chaos.

And just like that, the tension cracked and fell away—replaced by laughter, teasing, and the soft thuds of pillows flying through the air. The room shimmered with joy, lightness pouring in like sunlight through stained glass. But even amid the mayhem, the orb in Runa's hands shimmered brighter, as if drinking in the laughter—its glow blooming with the joy around it, warm and radiant like a shared heartbeat.

Chapter Twenty-Two

Rayanna crossed to the kitchen, stepping over a stray pillow without so much as a glance. Behind her, the laughter from the living room began to ebb—still present, but thinning into a gentle buzz. She set her empty mug on the island, reached for the coffee pot, and refilled it halfway before snagging one of the crescent moon–shaped cookies from the platter nearby. Golden, matte stars nestled in the sugar glaze—dimly luminous, brushing the light in passing as she bit in, savoring the sweetness. She leaned a hip against the counter, cradling her mug in the other hand. "Hang on," she said, nodding toward Runa who stood holding the orb with tender care. "How did the Lumis Blooms even get from Treefall, to the Dark Forest, to Starlight—without anyone noticing?"

Ashla's fingers floated through the air, tracing patterns and nudging invisible bottles, adjusting shadowed threads, and gingerly placing them on shelves no one else could find. It was as if she were tending to an apothecary of thoughts, her motions precise yet impossibly delicate. "Nissa has her ways," she stated at last, her voice a regal melody—smooth and unhurried, like moonlight poured into sound. "Of making everything feel

412

—*just—like—they—belong.*" She paused mid-gesture, fingers gracefully tilting an item into alignment. "Like it was said earlier…the orbs are quite good at blending in until they're needed." Her gaze flitted to Rayanna, then slid toward Layla—who, slouched across the cushions, remained keen in her stillness. "*Don't fret.* There's something waiting for each of you. A puzzle piece." Ashla's tone floated lightly, tethered to thousands of random possibilities. "Maybe…a feather from a yellow bird you've yet to meet. It will find you—that's the fun part, *isn't it?*"

"Not particularly," Layla uttered, inspecting her nails with the drama of someone enduring great inconvenience. But Rayanna's attention had already drifted to the bookcases lining the walls, her gaze fixed—not on a single book—but on the spaces between them, where something curious had begun to pull her forward.

"It's not here, Ray," Ashla spoke, plucking at what no one could quite see—though something subtly glistened, nudging the notion from her throat. "But it was. Just a whisper ago." Her voice meandered through the space like a gentle breeze. "Letting things happen has never really been in your nature." She tilted her head, coaxing another thread from the conceptual shelf before pressing her palm forward to pinch up a new notion, tucking it carefully into an invisible jar—making room for raw truths. "Forcing answers before they're ready to reveal themselves only leads to more frustration." She raised a brow, the soft hum that followed underscoring her point. "Just like dancing dishes and platters parading around the yard," she added, her gaze drifting toward Nadine, who was easing back onto the couch with a refreshed plate of sweets and a glass of wine in hand, her brow lifting with amusement.

"And yet somehow, the yard still managed to survive the parade," Nadine replied dryly, setting her wine down with a *clink.* Her gaze flicked toward Ashla—curious, but not unkind. "You definitely have a way of making nonsense sound like prophecy." A beat passed, her lips curving faintly. "Those darn enchanted platters—how they do enjoy a bit of theatrics."

Ashla's laughter rose, light and airy. "Oh, Nadine, it's just one of those little wonders we stumble upon now and then," she said with a glint of mischief in her eye. "Like a nudge from the universe—reminding us to keep our eyes open and our spirits ready for anything. The clatter of plates always tickled my fancy as a youngling. Seems some things never change." She winked—haphazard, awkward, and utterly delighted.

"Yeah, well, could we maybe *not* make the dancing plates and clattering platters a regular thing?" Rayanna muttered, lifting her mug again and dropping in a couple of vanilla cream cubes, each laced with a hint of mint from their garden. She watched them dissolve, exhaling a satisfied sigh.

Runa circled to the couch nearest the washroom and lowered herself onto the edge of the cushion with a soft *plop*, folding into a cross-legged seat. The bloom, still warm with a quiet thrum, settled into the cradle of her lap. Its glow had dimmed but held steady, as if it had found a temporary home. A faint whisper curled up from its center—barely audible, a murmur just beneath awareness. "I think it's gotten restless and started the conversation without us." Her gaze lifted to the others. "How exactly do we extract the memories from the bloom?"

"Well, that's simple. You drink it," Ashla stated matter-of-factly.

"I do what?" Runa blinked, her nose wrinkling at the thought of downing something that shimmered like oil and whispered like secrets.

Without notice, Ashla completed a side-scoot, gliding around her invisible shelf—her fingers fluttering near her temples, as if ducking beneath a dangling idea. Leaning toward Nadine, she bobbed her chin at the half-consumed blueberry fizz on the table. "Would it be terribly rude if I finished your berry fizz?" her tone hushed with the gravity of someone requesting a sacred relic.

"Asking is the first step to receiving," Nadine replied, offering a small nod, amused but unsurprised. "Progress can be made," she added with a wink.

Ashla lit up. "Splendid," she chirped, plucking the glass from the table as though retrieving a starlit chalice from an ancient altar. She took a long, thoughtful sip. "Just as I imagined. Like moonlight steeped in bubbles." Twirling the straw delicately, as if stirring her thoughts, she added, "The blueberries are always the best part. They tumble like beads of ancient mischief and memory codes. Very stabilizing for the spirit—a bit chaotic for the spleen, but we can't have everything in one glass, *now can we?*"

With that, she drifted back to her seat, folding into the cushions with the kind of grace reserved for silk scarves caught mid-upbreeze, just before they settle. The fizz found its home as she gently shelved it among her invisible curiosities, tapping the rim twice for good measure—sealing it into her world.

"Yeah, just take one for the team," Layla muttered from beneath her arm, not even bothering to look up.

Runa blinked, her mouth parting in disbelief as the absurdity of the moment settled across her face. "How about you give it a try first," she offered, gesturing vaguely toward Ashla, "and I'll observe. Take notes, maybe."

The corner of Ashla's mouth lifted faintly. *"I cannot,"* she said simply, as her fingers fiddled with the air, adjusting her reality and tucking it all neatly away. "It accepted you," she added, as if it were the most obvious thing in the world. "So, you're the one who needs to drink it."

Ashla sat up abruptly, as if seized by a sudden knowing. Without a word, she rose—swiftly, more so than most would expect—and before the others could track the motion, she was already at the edge of the balcony. She paused there, as if catching a fleeting thread midair, then pivoted and returned to her seat, slipping an unseen notion into her pocket. "If I interfere, the consequences could be dire—destroying the memory forever...or worse, it could lead to death," she remarked lightly, as if commenting on the weather.

"How about you give it a go?" Runa deadpanned, stretching the orb toward Rayanna. "Go on, then. You seem curious."

"Nope, I'm good with my mint cream coffee and staying alive, thanks." Rayanna raised her mug in a casual salute as she crossed the room, dropping onto the couch beside Ashla. "Nice try, though," she added, as she set her coffee on the table.

"Fantastic. Nothing quite says comfort like the looming possibility of death," Runa muttered, recoiling slightly as she cradled the orb to her chest, her expression twisting into a grimace. *Precious, yes—but perilous all the same.*

Ashla inhaled, the breath shaping her posture like a wind bending blades of grass. "These orbs can be quite finicky when separated from the intended recipient of their memories," she said, eyeing the group. Her hand hovered, then darted to Rayanna's coffee, lifting the mug in one smooth motion and draining the leftover liquid without a second thought.

Clearing her throat, she set the empty mug back down like returning a prized artifact.

Rayanna just stared at her, dumbfounded, trying to process whether the theft had actually happened.

From her seat on the couch, Nadine snapped her fingers once—a crisp, knowing sound that drew Ashla's attention. "Asking is the first step to receiving," she said lightly, amusement sparking at the corners of her eyes, glinting like the first silver edge of a crescent moon.

Ashla blinked once—slowly—as if realizing she might have just crossed a critical threshold. "Ray is dangerously close to being over-caffeinated," she announced with great solemnity, brushing a stray thread of air aside as if steadying her balance. Folding her hands primly, her tone dropped to something almost reverent. "As I've said before, it's a highly personalized and specific undertaking. Unique. Intimate." She blinked again, quicker this time. "And dangerously jittery energy does not bode well for the trip ahead."

"Well, you could've just said something. That would've been the better option," Rayanna muttered.

From the corner of the couch, Nadine lifted a slice of maple toffee to her lips. The caramel coating cracked as she bit down, the sweetness mellowing her expression. "Knowing my Izayah..." she began, her voice easing into a quieter rhythm. "He would have meticulously considered every aspect of this gift." Her gaze flickered with fleeting discomfort, momentarily catching on Rayanna before she averted her eyes, seeking solace once more in the amber depths of her treat. After a beat, she added, "The bloom would be imbued with purpose and crafted with the utmost care—down to the smallest detail."

"I appreciate your insight. I wish I could recall him as you do," Runa said, turning back toward her sister, giving notice to the subtle tensing of her shoulders as the conversation glided toward the subject of Izayah. Without a word, Rayanna pushed up from the couch, scooping her empty coffee mug from the table before padding barefoot across the floor. Her movements were quiet, controlled—an escape masked as routine.

At the island, she set the mug down with a faint clink and carefully cut a slim slice of chocolate pomegranate tart, the rich cocoa crust crumbling slightly at the edges as she lifted it free. She poured herself another dark cup of coffee, the steady stream filling it nearly to the brim. Her gaze flicked toward Ashla, a wary glint passing through her eyes, before she nudged the mug to the side—as if politely declining whatever whimsical energy might try to claim it.

Tart in hand, Rayanna drifted back toward the couch, settling beside Ashla with a quiet exhale. She focused intently on the dark velvety drizzle zigzagging across its glossy surface, the ribbons of ganache pooling faintly at the edges. Every detail demanded her full concentration, leaving no room for anything—or anyone—else. She squared her shoulders, huffing out a sigh she didn't realize she'd been holding, then took a quick bite of her sweet, as if fortifying herself for what was to come. Mouth still half-full, Rayanna grumbled around the bite, "Okay, well, I'll have to take your word for it on who or what he is." She swallowed hard, wiping a crumb from the corner of her mouth. "There's no way around it. No shortcuts. Just through. This is the reality—whether I like it or not."

Runa lifted the orb higher as if offering it forward. "But if I'm doing this—if I'm drinking the Lumis—I need you here with me. Not stuck in whatever place you just disappeared to, Ray." Her words weren't a command—they could never be with Rayanna. They were an invitation. A bridge, quiet and enduring, laid steady across the space between them.

Rayanna's head dipped in a barely perceptible nod. For a moment, silence settled—not empty, but heavy with a shared understanding that didn't need words.

Runa lowered the orb back into her lap, her fingers curling protectively around it as she shook her head. "I can't believe I'm doing this." A quick inhale followed, the exhale soft and measured as she tried to steady herself. "Is there anything else I should consider before I drink this?" Her expression tightened as her question took shape, like tiny dragons weaving through the shadowed caverns of each person's ear, lingering before spiraling onward to the next.

Ashla's attention wandered toward Mama D and Nadine. A subtle nod from both women caught her eye, and a spark lit behind her gaze. With a small, lopsided shrug, she popped off her shoes with lazy kicks, reached for her blueberry fizz, and plucked it from the table like a prized relic. Tucking her feet beneath her, she nestled into the couch, readying herself for an explanation long overdue. "To access these memories," Ashla began, her voice soft and melodic, carrying the rhythm of a lullaby, "the seeker—*you*—will carefully extract the Lumis Bloom, as already done, and consume its contents." Fluttering her lashes rapidly, as though staring into a bright light, she threw up a finger dramatically, her pitch rising to a crescendo. "But it's not a savoring sip; you must gulp it down in one go."

Halting in her thought, Ashla one handed pinched and plucked at the air, like coaxing notes from an unseen harp. Then, as if remembering she was supposed to be sharing, she pulled her hands back with a sheepish tuck of her wrists. "Imagine," her voice lilting with curiosity as her free palm swept a wide arc, "as the elixir of memory touches your lips, a doorway to the past swings open. Sights, sounds, emotions—and some-times…only sometimes, scents—will flood in, helping to immerse you in the memory itself." Ashla paused momentarily, then offered, "Isn't it fasci-nating how a single taste can carry you across the threads of time, weaving you into what once was?" She dipped into a whisper. "And I do hear the gibbering too, Runa. I suspect they might be awaiting our arrival."

"What are you plucking at?" Rayanna deadpanned, her stare sliding toward Layla, who was now upside down with her feet in the air, noisily slurping the last of her drink that appeared somehow by her head.

"Soon, Auntie Ray." Ashla lifted a finger, pinching at what appeared to be absolutely nothing mid-flight, and tucked the unseen notion neatly behind her ear, her smile widening. *"Soon enough."*

"What does that even mean?" Rayanna asked, irritation sharpening her tone.

Ashla continued, unbothered by the question. "Yet, in the realm of shared memories, the journey doesn't end with the individual seeker." Her hands rubbed together as if warming the next thought over an invisible fire. "Memories are meant to be shared—like reflections in a pool of still water."

"What?" Rayanna exclaimed, frustration cracking through her composure.

Nadine's mouth curved into a half-smile. "It means that when Runa drinks the contents, standing in front of something reflective—like a mirror or a pool of stagnant water—it allows the memory to be shared with others."

Delight brightened Ashla's expression. "In the bathroom, there are not one, not two, but at least three such sources," she mused, her gaze sweeping across the space before settling once again on the two older women. "Nissa has such a knack, doesn't she? Thoughtful placement is her gift. She knows exactly where the Lumis Blooms will flourish." A tender hum of admiration vibrated through her words. "These moments of shared experience are acts of communion, sincerity, and profound respect, which means each link in this delicate chain must be embraced," her attention turning to Runa, who stood blinking in astonishment. "It requires an open heart and a deep sense of honor. Such a bond cannot be forced."

"Who the hell would force someone to watch a memory?" Rayanna blurted, her tone dripping with disbelief.

Mama D's head bobbed once, her eye line glistening briefly to Runa before returning to Rayanna. "That's a good question," she replied, her voice steady but edged with unease. "And it has been done—with memories that torch the soul rather than heal it. Not all Lumis Blooms are crafted with care."

Nadine's posture stiffened, her lips pressing into a thin line before she took over. "It's true," she admitted, hesitation creeping in as her fingers brushed faintly over her thumb in small, grounding gestures, the movement almost imperceptible. "They can be used in ways you wouldn't want to imagine." Her statement lingered as she glanced momentarily at Mama D, a silent exchange passing between them before she continued. "Where there is good, there is also evil. It all hinges on the intention of the creator."

Runa's face twisted into a tight grimace. "Well," she began, her voice tinged with hesitation, "I'm not sure how this works, but…here goes nothing." Drawing herself upright, she rolled her shoulders back, adopting a newfound formality laced with regal undertones. "I ask that those willing to join me prepare themselves for the journey ahead. Your participation in this mission is voluntary, but your commitment must be absolute."

Ashla chuckled. "Who knew we needed to be so formal?" Her attention drifted toward the little orb. "I'm sure Izayah would approve of such discipline," she added with a teasing lilt. "It seems we're in good hands. Just as fitting as if he were here himself. Good channeling."

Layla's eyes rolled skyward. "Oh, lovely. Time in Izayah's head," she drawled, her lips curling into a disgusted sneer. "Just the vacation I was hoping for."

"May I ask…why such aversion to Izayah?" Ashla fluttered her lashes, her wide-eyed curiosity almost childlike.

Layla shrugged. "He's…a bit too formal for me," she said, her teeth grazing her lower lip. "I like my men a bit more…mischievously unconventional."

Rayanna rolled her eyes, popping the last bite of her pomegranate tart into her mouth and setting the empty plate on the table with a soft clink. "Well, *you did say* a flick of a cap *does it for you*," she snorted. "So, you *want* a whore?"

Mama D sputtered in disbelief. *"Rayanna Marie Shadeworth!"*

Rayanna's hands shot up in mock surrender. "What? She's the one who wants someone 'mischievously unconventional.' A 'go with the flow' kinda guy?" She clicked her tongue and winked at Layla with a knowing *tsk.*

"Oh, I like me something untamed," Layla teased, her voice tinged with nostalgia as she rolled off the couch, snatching up her drink on the way down. With a playful smack to her thigh, she grinned and headed for the island. "Izayah, bless him, is all respect and honor. The kind of man who'll walk you to the door, tip his hat, and send flowers the next day. He's thought through every gesture—every move." Her smile tilted, eyes dancing with mischief. *"But me?* I want someone who doesn't think at all. Throw me into the brush, roll me around in the sand—messy, wild, and gloriously unplanned." She set her glass down, grabbed a piece of bread, stuffed it into her mouth, refilled her glass with the watered-down blueberry fizz, and dropped onto a stool. She looked every bit the sly troublemaker, her words still hanging in the air like a tossed gauntlet.

Rayanna shook her head, irritation flaring like embers catching a sharp gust. "That doesn't even make any sense!" she exclaimed, throwing her hands up in exasperation. *"I just—can't—with you."* With that, she tipped sideways, flopping into the couch with the resigned grace of someone accepting a lost cause. She dragged a pillow over her head, her voice emerging flat and muffled: "You give me a damn headache!"

Ashla, who had been quietly observing, spoke as though addressing the stars themselves. "Well, 'mischievously unconventional' can be quite endearing…if one doesn't confuse it with fleeting whims," she mused, her voice soft and distant. "Tethering," she murmured, her words like a breeze carrying a secret, "is like the dance of the stars—only when the heavens themselves whisper their approval do two souls find their way to one another. It's for those who dare to let their hearts follow the stars, having faith in the dreams they pray for." A faint smile curved her lips as she turned toward Layla. "Don't give up on dedication," she added, her voice trailing off like an unfinished thought.

"Dedication?" Layla snorted, stuffing another bite of bread into her mouth, crumbs scattering in her wake. "Sounds like a lot of work for something that's supposed to be cosmic," she quipped, her tone playful but edged with skepticism.

Tossing the pillow off her head with a sigh, Rayanna drawled, "Well, now that Layla's sworn off stealing Izayah, I guess it's safe to head out—" She pushed up from the couch, motioning loosely toward the hallway leading to the washroom. "Heading in? Not really heading out, is it?" she added, glancing at the others before starting down the hall.

Layla peeled herself off the island stool with a groan, snagging her drink. Runa rose quietly from the couch, the orb cradled carefully against her chest. Ashla, last to rise, grabbed her blueberry fizz, downed the last of it in one swoop, and gave a tiny hiccup—beaming with the slightly dazed delight of someone drunk on bubbles.

Runa slowed, glancing back. "Um—are you coming?"

Mama D and Nadine exchanged a brief glance, a silent understanding flickering between them. Nadine shook her head lightly, offering a small smile. "We'll wait out here," her tone remained steady. "The bathroom's a bit cramped, and Sienna already shed light on this a long time ago. Besides, there are other pieces to fit into the puzzle—things long left unsaid."

Layla moved past the back of the couch, but Mama D's hand caught her wrist, halting her mid-step. "Remember, dear," her cadence firm but kind, "you've only seen one side of him. Would you want to be judged solely on the role you were forced to play?"

"I get it," Layla uttered as Mama D's firm grip dropped away.

"Wait a minute—" Rayanna halted, sending Ashla stumbling into the back of her. Her jaw tightened, frustration bubbling like water from an overfilled pot. *"You know what?* Why didn't you tell us this sooner!" she snapped, throwing her hands up as she pivoted toward the communal living space. "We could have had these answers already!" Her words cracked with exasperation, her shoulders squaring as though bracing against a blow. "I'm so tired of being the only one who doesn't know anything!" she barked, stomping toward the washroom, bare feet slapping sharply against the floor. "I just—*ugh!*" she burst out, disappearing around the corner.

Mama D watched her go, letting out a measured sigh. "She's just trying to make sense of it all," she murmured, more to soothe than to explain. Angling herself toward the hallway, she raised her voice so it carried into the washroom, a note of firm compassion threading through her words. "Rayanna, I know it feels like you've been left in the dark, but things need to unfold in phases. The Lumis Blooms work when the time is right— forcing the truth to come too soon would only leave you with pieces of a puzzle you aren't ready to comprehend." She exhaled softly, her gaze steady. "It's not about withholding—it's about trusting the process." Then, she added dryly, "And for the record, you're all shadow bound. You're learning together. Deal with it."

Ashla's voice lilted back unseen, but felt—threading through the space like mist. "Remember…sometimes it's better to feel the stones underfoot, rather than simply being told where they lead."

"Shut it, Ashla." Rayanna spun toward her, exasperation flaring. "I'm over all the whimsical bullshit. I don't want to walk on stones—I want to jump into the fucking deep end already."

Ashla beamed, unbothered. "Maybe you weren't ready to dive until the deep end called your name," she mused, her voice drifting like mist. "They were only mirrors, not walls. They waited for you to see through them, not stumble over them."

Upon crossing the threshold, the air grew dense with quiet anticipation, thick and alive. The women clustered within the elongated washroom, their collective focus knitting into silent unity. As Runa's hip bumped the sink's edge, all eyes fixed on the reflection of the bloom cradled in her hands. Its halo diffused outward, and from its core, a single, delicate strand of golden light began to unwind, its shimmer catching the softened shadows as it arced upward in a graceful sweep. The thread pierced gently through Runa's chest—right at the soft juncture where her ribs meet— drawn forward by instinct alone. Her breath hitched as it slipped clean through her, emerging from the center of her back as a resplendent ribbon, spiraling further into the room. It moved in a weighty wave, threading through the front of each female's diaphragm, a gasp released as the light passed through them, reemerging from their mid-backs, and extending toward the next. Together, the glistening current stitched their sacred cores into a golden webbing.

Ashla's voice floated up from the hush, as if summoned by the weaving light. "Allowing the heartstring to breathe into each of us builds the connection we need…sort of like blood reaching. The only difference is this version is sewn into the Lumis itself…more ghost than true form." A pause, then adding, "Wait for the knotting," Ashla said gently. "You'll feel it, Ru. It's more of a light tugging along your spine, and when it comes, you'll know. The bloom will open. And then you drink."

Almost on cue, Runa felt it—a faint, steady pull threading upward from the small of her back, an invisible summons twining along the golden strand. She glanced down just in time to see the orb stir in her hands. Its surface shivered once, then sprouted, forming a small spout at its crown— like a flower offering its nectar.

"Bottoms up," Runa said, throwing her head back without hesitation and letting the elixir pour down her throat in one fluid motion.

For a heartbeat, she felt suspended, caught in weightlessness—an aching stillness that felt like it could collapse her lungs. Then Runa's body jolted sharply, a gasp tearing from her lips as energy raced up her spine. The golden cord flared, and in response, the mirror's backlighting sputtered, the greenish glow faltering, throwing shifting shadows over the cascading foliage before the cored webbing. From the mirror's perimeter, a mist began to form, descending in slow, curling tendrils. The fog cascaded down and outward like an ancient curtain, draping itself around them—an ethereal veil softening the edges of reality, blurring the lines between past and present.

A shiver passed through them, goosebumps rising in unison as the golden tether pulsed in time with their hearts, its rhythm an ancient echo of connection. The energy rippled through their veins, a sensation both foreign and familiar, awakening something dormant within each of them. Individuality faded, dissolving into a singular collective as their souls intertwined, tethered by the shared vision now beginning to materialize before them.

After the fourth wave of nausea rolled through them, Rayanna froze, air tangling in her lungs. Her eyes fluttered shut as a tear slipped free, carving a fragile path down her cheek. The rippling current of energy skimmed her surface, stirring something deep and raw within.

"Do you smell that?" her voice trembling with uncontainable emotion. Her fingers twitched, aching to reach out, but Ashla's firm grip steadied her.

"To unclasp one's hand from the tether would be to cleave one's heart," Ashla cautioned. "In this moment, the Memory Vine seeks out what it must. It reveals pieces meant only for certain hearts—fragments meant to mend or awaken." She allowed the weight of it to settle, then inhaled slowly, her breath spilling comfort into the stillness. "The one before you and the one behind you will hold your soul upright when the weight becomes too much." Her voice softened. "With our hearts and hands, we are bound." And with the final word dropped into the air, there came a sharp *shhhhwwwpppp*—as if the very air sealed the tether.

Rayanna sniffled, her shoulders trembling as she leaned into Ashla's grounding presence. Her lips parted, the word emerging like a fragile shard of glass. "Zay," she whispered, the name breaking through her choked breaths. *"I didn't know*...Why would you do this? You *should have* told me sooner."

Chapter Twenty-Three

As the lavatory dissolved into obscurity, the golden heartstring anchored the women, tethering their souls in a delicate web of shared purpose. Though their bodies remained still, the memory unfolded with such vivid intensity it drew them inward, devouring all it touched.

Each step carried the figure—Runa's past self—closer to the cabin balcony. Her footfalls pressed a muffled rhythm into the forest floor, dried leaves crumbling beneath her boots with a delicate crunch, whispering secrets long buried in the fabric of time.

A wistful breeze stirred, winding through the memory like an undetected ribbon weaving together fragments of a forgotten story. It carried the faint, earthy scent of pine mingled with the understated sweetness of vanilla. Beneath it lingered the ghostly trace of tobacco, clinging to the edges of shadow—a bittersweet echo of what once was. The vision stood vivid yet distant, an invitation to observe—but not to interfere—holding them as silent witnesses to what was and could never be undone.

Runa's past self lifted her gaze, her features emerging as shadows rippled backward, retreating in delicate waves like a curtain being drawn aside. The darkness clung to her briefly before unraveling, flowing away like strands of silk dissolving into the fading light. As the shadows withdrew, the scene before the observers unfolded—a landscape drenched in the warm, golden hues of a setting sun. The air shimmered faintly, holding the remnants of daylight, as twilight itself loosened its grip to unveil the glowing essence of the world beneath.

The forest floor stirred to life, rustling leaves and whispering branches rising in soft murmurs. A gentle breeze wove through the tree line, humming with quiet vitality as if knitting the memory together with unseen bindings. Its embrace carried a blend of earthy fir and damp moss, grounding yet infused with an undercurrent of tension—a faint ripple of uncertainty weaving through the serene exterior.

The tension was almost tangible, drawn into each breath like a subtle vibration reverberating through the wooden skins of the forest. Runa's petite form moved with grace toward the balcony, her presence drawing the observers deeper into the memory, as though inviting them to bear witness to a truth unraveling in real time.

Behind her, the sun slipped lower, its fractured rays filtering through the canopy above. The light fragmented as it passed through the dense foliage, scattering dappled patterns across the wooden balcony where two figures stood. The kaleidoscope of reflections danced upon the grassy knoll below, each glimmer elongating and twisting the moment. It was a surreal tableau of shifting realities, suspended between the memory's vividness and the intangible weight of something irrevocably past.

Runa moved forward, her stride purposeful. As she approached the balcony, the women felt themselves pulled along—tethered by a mystic force. Her presence blended with the wistful breeze that tousled her ebony hair, the fading light catching in its strands. Subtle undertones gleamed like fleeting embers in the waning glow of day.

Suddenly, the world around them warped. A tide of time and memory swept them from their vantage point behind Runa into the very heart of the recollection. Weightlessly, they found themselves no longer mere spectators but immersed in Izayah's perspective. The worn banister beneath his calloused hands became their own fragile bond to reality. The raw anticipation in his chest, the magnetic pull toward her—all of it surged through them, unrelenting and vivid.

The rough wood steadied him, grounding him against the storm of emotions swirling inside. Each heartbeat reverberated with unspoken fears and the gravity of what lay ahead. The cord that bound the women pulsed, flexing like a muscle in sync with Izayah's heightened awareness. Though uncertainty loomed, his attention remained razor-sharp, cutting through the haze of pending chaos and setting the tone for the unfolding vision.

A sharp inhale hitched in his throat—a primal instinct, a feral urge driving him to bridge the unspoken distance. Desire clawed at the edges of his mind, desperate to unearth buried longing and reveal every hidden truth. Fragments of their shared history flickered like faint stars behind a veil of clouds, muted and incomplete, lingering as distant reverberations. These fractured recollections hovered just out of reach, obscured by the surreal reality now enfolding them.

His gaze scanned the treeline, piercing the shadows with an intensity forged by both caution and certainty. Among the foliage, ghostly figures moved with fluid precision. They weren't mere phantoms but the Elite— poised, waiting, and watchful sentinels attuned to his command. Their forms, draped in a muted veil—like memory-bound phantoms of purpose and duty. The forest held its breath, the air thick with anticipation. Each figure embodied the gravity of the mission ahead, their presence a mix of reassurance and the weighty reminder of failure's cost.

The cold settled over him, pressing down like an acknowledgment of their readiness. Yet an imaginary barrier held them all at bay, their purpose palpable but untethered, like chess pieces frozen in time, awaiting the decisive move.

Izayah's head snapped to the side, his instincts honed to detect even the faintest disturbance. His consciousness latched onto a thread of memory, pulling at it until the darkness unraveled. Suddenly, light pierced the shadows, saturating their shared view. The memory twisted and reformed—a scene within a scene—etched in wavering candlelight and muted hues.

Hard marble floors stretched beneath their feet, while the rich scent of parchment and ink saturated the room's intimate confines. The view sharpened, narrowing onto a massive hardwood desk that dominated the space.

Their attention was drawn inexorably to a basket on a nearby shelf. Its contents spilled outward, as if nudged by an latent pull. Letters bound with a weathered ribbon lay inside, radiating a quiet significance. Each envelope bore Izayah's name, the elegant red ink bleeding into the fibers of the paper, as though the letters themselves carried the sorrow of their contents.

A wordless plea tugged at the air, its weight neither fragile nor weak but resolute, as Izayah adjusted his focus and released a strained sigh. The memory lingered on the cusp of its conclusion, its tendrils unfurling like smoke dissolving into the encroaching shadows. His voice, low and unyielding, emerged from the stillness: "Your words were written in blood, and I missed them for far too long." The statement lingered, drawing the breath from the space, leaving his chest heaving as he wrestled with the unrelenting truth etched into the marble floor beneath him.

His hands—calloused by time and tempered by duty—came together in a considered gesture, a silent ritual anchoring him to the balcony's edge. The rough texture of his palms brushing together served as a tactile reminder of battles fought and promises made. The motion steadied him, tempering the storm of frustration and regret threatening to unravel his composure. It wasn't anger that defined him, but the unwavering discipline to transcend it.

"Sir," a voice cut through the memory's dissolving edges, steady and assured. "Mission parameters acknowledged. Execution will be precise across the next three days—no deviations. Our cargo will be secured." The words resonated with clarity and conviction, crisp and ironclad against the memory's fading hum.

The scene fractured, twisting as the observers were drawn backward toward the balcony wall. The air turned abruptly, the warmth of the memory surrendering to the forest's cool embrace. Izayah stood outward-facing, his posture deceptively relaxed, though honed awareness bristled along every line of his frame. Tilting his head, he eased the tension in his neck, his gaze dropping to the chest plate concealed beneath his unassuming attire. The darkened insignia of the Shadow Elite, burnished into obsidian and worn with quiet pride—its lion crest momentarily alive with muted vigilance.

The emblem embodied an unbroken creed—service before self—and an unspoken bond that tied him to the man beside him. His fingers lingered over its surface, as though drawing strength from its weight. Clearing his throat, his voice emerged, concise and even. "Noted, Dax."

The name hung in the air as the vision dissolved further. Figures of the Shadow Elite stood poised in the periphery, their dark forms merging with the forest's gathering shadows, their purpose sharp yet withheld. The balcony solidified beneath the observers' feet, grounding them in the present. The forest whispered, its echoes of duty and allegiance drifting like the final sigh of a memory, fading into silence.

Izayah regarded the name patch stitched firmly into the midnight fabric of his fighting leathers, the bold letters stark against the shadowed back-drop. He turned his focus toward Runa, drawn by the measured rhythm of her approaching steps. The flow of his breathing aligned with hers, an unspoken synchrony anchoring him in the rising tension. Pivoting, his eyes swept the horizon, the air thick with unyielding expectation. His jaw tight-ened, the weight of responsibility pressing into the hardened lines of his face—a burden he bore with battle-worn efficiency.

The familiar heaviness settled over him like a second skin, vast yet resolute. He embraced it fully, offering only a slight nod as acknowledg-ment. His thoughts rippled outward like waves across still water, gently urging the observers back, carving a boundary for the memory to unfold. In the gathering stillness, his head turned, guided by imperceptible currents. A stolen glance locked on something intangible, piercing through the veil of time. His voice, deep and sonorous, emerged like a distant thun-der, booming with the gravity of a truth long concealed: "Rayanna, I now know the truth of what was—don't touch the past just yet. Let it be—let it unfold. Patience, my darling sister. My little Ray of Sunshine."

Time distorted, every tick of a hidden pocket watch amplified—swelling louder and thrumming through the stillness like a metronome of dread. The air thickened, taut as though the universe itself braced on the cusp of revelation. Izayah's gaze, flawless as a falcon's, swept the expanse before him with predatorial certainty. Every detail crystallized under his scrutiny, each fragment of the landscape aligning with exacting purpose, charged with a shrouded pressure.

His hand moved instinctively, fingers tapping a measured rhythm on the worn banister. Each tap echoed like a heartbeat marking the count-down to destiny. The silence grew heavier, laden with the weight of expec-tation. Every breath lingered suspended, carrying the immense burden of what was about to surface.

Tap—5.
Tap—4.
Tap—3.
Tap—2.
Tap—1.

The explosion erupted with a deafening roar, splintering boulders into jagged fragments that tore through the air, cleaving trees like fragile reeds. In response to Izayah's unspoken command, darkness surged from the periphery like a living tide. It swallowed Runa and the overlook, coalescing into an impenetrable barrier that absorbed the chaos beyond.

The atmosphere morphed, the swirling obscurity stirring with an almost sentient intent. Within its depths, a thin, silvery glow began to emerge, tracing Runa's form in ethereal light. The delicate aura lulled her into tranquil slumber, her body surrendering to the embrace of the surrounding void. With purposeful fluidity, the enveloping gloom guided her into the waiting arms of the Elite Major. Izayah's hold, firm yet careful as though cradling a delicate ember, released her with sureness. The dense murk coiled around them, layering the cabin's back edge in a veil that concealed them entirely from the outside world.

Beyond the protective cover, the cabin appeared to twist and writhe beneath the onslaught. Its walls buckled as tendrils of obscurity lashed through the air, creating an illusion of destruction. Yet, beneath the turbulent facade, the scene was entirely different—hidden, serene, untouched.

Inside, the night sculpted a haven. The darkened currents tempered, flowing in gentle undulations like a midnight tide. Moonlight and starlight interlaced, casting a tranquil radiance that caressed Runa's form, cradling her in an almost celestial embrace. Her hurried breaths eased, aligning with the rhythm of the serene night. Each exhale whispered quiet peace, her eyelids fluttering shut as the surrounding stillness guided her into a deep sleep.

As the aftertones of the explosions persisted—muted and distant—they faded into the backdrop like a dying storm. Daxler's intense focus locked onto Izayah. With a acute, systematic execution, his chin lifted, then dipped in a silent exchange—repeating three times. His protective hold on Runa tightened momentarily before, with a resounding snap of energy and a swift *whoosh*, they vanished. The surrounding haze rippled faintly, the only trace of their departure.

Izayah's piercing gaze swept across the dimly lit cabin porch. The air hung thick with tension, clinging to the scene like smoke. For a moment, silence reclaimed the space, broken only by the measured rhythm of his boot tapping against the wooden floor.

TAP.

TAP.

Daxler's expression darkened, the gravity of the moment coiling around him like a living vice, compressing the air with relentless force. With a almost ritualistic motion, he shrugged off the illusion of casual attire. The soft fabric dissipated into a vaporous mist, curling away as though retreating from the power simmering beneath his skin. The battle-worn leathers emerged—creased and weathered by countless encounters, their texture a map of endurance.

His hand hovered above the tattoo etched into his forearm, the ink throbbed dimly, as though awakening to the urgency coursing through his veins. His fingers hovered, trembling for the briefest of moments, poised between hesitation and inevitability. Then, with a resolute touch, the tattoo flared to life, its design glowing with an intensity that merged with the beat of his heart. The ink rippled like liquid fire, its lines twisting and expanding as though breaking free from their confines.

The sword began to take form, its hilt materializing first, drawn from his flesh like a forged promise brought to life. It pulled outward, silvery and alive, the blade extending in a fluid motion, solidifying into a sleek, gleaming edge. The weapon hummed, its resonance low and menacing, as if aware of the weight of its summoning. When the reformation was completed, the weapon settled into his grip with a satisfying heft, its cold surface familiar and steadfast against his palm.

It wasn't merely a weapon—it was a manifestation of him, an extension of his will. The blade radiated an implied duality: a harbinger of destruction and a sentinel of protection, depending on the demands of the moment. Its surface bore intricate engravings, symbols that gleamed faintly, imbued with power beyond comprehension. Each line palpitated in time with Daxler's heartbeat, a visceral connection between wielder and weapon.

Izayah's arm shot out, halting his comrade with a sharp motion.

"Zane, what the *shit,* man? You could have been skewered—" His voice faltered, wavering for just a moment as his narrowed eyes locked onto the figure before them. The eerie glow of the porch light refracted strangely against the tar-covered form. Izayah's brow furrowed deeply, tension knotting his jaw. His words landed like a measured blow. "…What in the *living hell* happened?"

His older brother's silhouette trembled, his attention fixed on the two chiseled males before him, yet his focus seemed strangely distant. Izayah's thoughts lurched backward, recalling Zane's stance after their Ma had passed—an echo of a time when the world felt like it had collapsed into a single, unbearable point.

His hand raked through his hair, a futile attempt to anchor himself to a reality that slipped like sand through his fingers. Staggering first one way, then the other, his steps were unsteady under the crushing weight of grief that hollowed him from the inside out. Sinking to his knees, he landed heavily in the pooling wetness, staring down at his hands, disbelief etched into every line of his face. Slowly, with movements stripped of purpose, he dragged himself to the porch couch, his frame slumping as though the weight of her absence pinned him there.

"Tabs…is…gone," he uttered, his voice gravelly and raw, each word a struggle against the unnatural act of voicing the unbearable. Oblivious to the world spinning on without her, his presence seemed anchored solely to the loss that consumed him.

Izayah forced his voice into the steady cadence of command, though an undercurrent of doubt wove through his words. "Rest assured," he began, his tone meant to convey brotherly reassurance, though the weight of uncertainty loomed heavily beneath it. "She will find sanctuary amidst this chaos. Tabytha and the girls are in safe hands. I've accounted for everything—every detail, every precaution." He hesitated, his gaze hardening, willing his words to anchor them both, even as he questioned their truth. "No harm will come to them. I've made sure of it." The promise lingered, fragile, teetering precariously on the edge of belief.

"This has been orchestrated by the Elite unit," Izayah said, each word standing as a lighthouse against the thrashing storm. "I assure you, brother, they'll be fine. I've made sure of that. But now isn't the time to get into it."

The silence that followed was dense, almost suffocating, but Daxler's steady presence filled the void with an unspoken vow: they would safeguard what Izayah cherished, no matter the cost. "This is part of the plan. Trust me," Izayah added, lifting his hands in a defensive gesture, as if warding off the doubts threatening to take root.

Daxler's eyes narrowed, instincts sharpening as his hand dropped to cradle the hilt at his side. He tilted his head slightly, nudging Izayah's shoulder, a faint twitch of his lips forming a half-smile that lacked its usual warmth. His attention snagged on the thick, inky substance trailing in Zane's wake, its slick, oily surface catching the dim light with a strange, almost sentient glint. "Uh—man, that's..." He pointed toward the black gelatin-like substance coagulating beneath Zane. "Not part of the plan we talked about," he muttered.

Daxler moved closer, crouching down to rub his fingers together in the viscous liquid pooling around Zane's boots. Its tendrils clung unnaturally to the ground, twisting as if alive. His eyebrows shot upward, nearly merging with his hairline as he whispered hoarsely, *"Fuck..."*

Zane's head barely moved, a faint shake betraying the disbelief rooting him in place. "No, no," he breathed, the words fragile whispers, as though voicing them might shatter his tenuous grip on reality. "She's—*gone.*" Each syllable cracked under the weight of his anguish, scraping raw emotion like a blade dragged over exposed nerves. His trembling hands turned upward, as if searching for answers etched into the lines of his palms— some fragment of strength to hold onto.

"But I *still* have my girls," Zane's utterance trembled under the burden of lingering sorrow. "I'll shield them from all of this." The words bloomed like a lifeline, his fists clenching tightly, knuckles whitening with the force of his conviction. Fierce determination shadowed his eyes, fixed now on his hands, as though within their grasp lay the promise he was making—to himself, to his daughters, to a future unmarred by loss.

"They'll be safe. I won't let anything happen to them. They won't be part of..." Izayah's voice faltered, the sentence severed mid-thought as Zane's outburst tore through the air, barbed and unsparing.

"Fuck, man—*YOU* are *NOT* listening. *SHE—IS—GONE!*" Zane's fists slammed against his thighs, anguish erupting in an unfiltered storm. His words struck like a thunderclap, jagged and undeniable, shattering the fragile calm. The jabbed outburst left an aftershock, its tremors coursing through the silence, electrifying the air with raw tension.

Daxler thrust himself between the two brothers, his presence an unspoken command for restraint, like a dam holding back the flood of unexplained circumstances threatening to overwhelm them all. "Enough," he snapped. "Yelling won't bring her back, and it damn sure won't help your girls." The words landed with weight, steady and grounding. "I have to ask, Zane—where the hell is all this blood coming from?"

Zane sat silently, his head dropping into his hands as if trying to block out the storm threatening to consume him.

Daxler's fingers flexed at his sides, the faint metallic hiss of the sword sliding back into his flesh breaking the charged stillness. The ink rippled, dissolving into his skin like a stone sinking beneath the surface of a still lake, his frame taut with restrained tension. "What the fuck happened in there? Zane—are you confirming Tabytha is dead? Because if she is, we can't redirect this mission stumbling blind."

Zane's head lifted, his eyes sharpening as Daxler's words sliced through the fog gripping his mind. "Fuck...is he always this much of a damn flurry of explanation, Zay?" he muttered. A bitter chuckle escaped him, but it faded quickly, the anger in his clenched fists easing just enough. Sorrow still clung to him like shadow as he straightened slightly.

"Permission to sweep the interior? If we're regrouping, we need action-able intel—immediately. This alters the op profile. Contingency required." Daxler pressed on without pause.

Izayah's jaw tightened, gaze locking on Daxler. When he spoke, it was with the crisp precision of a field commander. "Negative. No sweep—not yet. I've already got the pieces in motion, but we execute in phases. Everyone gets to their marks first. Once they're secure, we reassess and adapt the plan to this development. You follow?"

Daxler exhaled, the sound carrying a mix of frustration and acceptance as though taming the coiled energy threatening to snap loose. "You better be right about those marks, Zay. If this goes sideways, we'll all be dead before phase two even hits the table." Straightening, his shoulders squared with military precision. "If there's more intel you're sitting on, spill it. We can't afford a single loose thread."

Izayah's voice was clipped as he shot back, "Every thread is accounted for, Major. Eyes on your sector, and stick to the timing." His tone softened just enough to carry weight without undermining authority. "We'll cover the ground when we're clear. Until then, keep it locked down."

Daxler nodded once, the crisp motion signaling reluctant agreement. "Fine. But we're on borrowed time, and I'm not letting the ground crumble under our boots."

"New orders," Izayah barked. "Rendezvous at the designated location. The females will ALL be transferred to your mother. She'll initiate thought weaving and shadow binding immediately. Diesel's directive is clear: their safety is the top priority." He let the weight of the command settle before continuing, his tone unwavering. "We regroup in Starlight—Diesel's study. Maintain situational awareness at all times. No lapses."

Izayah's jaw tightened as he delivered the next part, his voice pointed. "I'll handle the cover operation. It will be executed flawlessly. The intel will confirm the females perished in the attack—no discrepancies. Am I understood?"

He turned to Zane, straightening his shoulders, trying to meet his massive sibling on equal footing despite the disparity in their size. Locking eyes with Zane, he squared his stance. "I did this," he stated, his words resolute, ringing with finality. "Tabytha is on MY hands, NOT yours. I will take this one. DO—YOU—UNDERSTAND, *brother?*" His voice softened at the end, a hand settling firmly on Zane's tar-streaked shoulder, sticky with remnants of the fight.

Zane's muscles flexed as he rolled his neck, the movement controlled. His jaw tightened, his chin lowering as he glared out from beneath his brow. "You will NOT," he growled, his tone low and deadly. "This blood is on my hands. I will NOT let you take ownership of what you DID NOT do."

Izayah brought his opposite hand to Zane's other shoulder, his grip tightening as he closed the distance. "Z, you have your girls. They need YOU, brother. You are theirs to love through this." His fingers dug in slightly, grounding the moment. "I don't HAVE that. So I'm telling you again—I did this. Tabytha is on MY hands, *NOT* yours. I will take this one. *DO—YOU—UNDERSTAND?*"

Zane's head drooped, his chin sinking to his chest. In perfect unison, he and Izayah raised their fists, striking their hearts three times in methodical cadence. Each impact reverberated like the beat of a war drum, a shared rhythm carrying the gravity of their bond. *"Um-bra,"* they intoned as one, their voices merging into a solemn declaration of unbroken loyalty.

Izayah's hand slid from Zane's shoulder to the back of his neck, delivering a firm, exacting slap. Zane mirrored the gesture, his palm landing on Izayah's nape. Without hesitation, they leaned forward, their foreheads pressing together in a gesture steeped in respect and unity. For a fleeting moment, they remained locked in silent communion, their actions conveying what words could not.

Izayah pulled back, his gaze unwavering, his tone sharp and authoritative. "General Diesel will guide you to Starlight. And Zane," he added, his voice hardening like tempered steel, "this isn't over. I expect a full report—everything. No omissions. No excuses. Major General, I'll handle the cabin. It understands what needs to transpire after my leave."

Daxler stepped forward, his nod curt. *"Um-bra,"* he growled, striking his chest again with force. The sound thudded briefly before his form blurred, dissolving into the encroaching darkness. Threads of moonlight clung dimly to his retreating figure, an afterimage fading as he folded seamlessly into the void.

Izayah turned back to Zane, his resolve firm. His jaw clenched momentarily before he exhaled. Rolling his shoulders back, he straightened. Behind him, the muffled roar of the mast shield faltered, the muted chaos outside swelling louder as it clawed at the cabin's edges. The fragile barrier trembled violently, straining under the relentless assault, threatening to collapse.

Izayah's focus snapped back to Zane, his words slicing through the clamor with precise authority. "We don't have time for this," he said, his tone unwavering. Planting his feet firmly, he grounded himself against the turmoil. "Move. Now. Get to Sienna—the Seer—in the Valley of Visions. Dax's mother. Mama D is already in position and ready to intercept."

"Zay…" Zane's voice wavered as he pointed to his arm, where the blade now rested dormant beneath his skin. The ink that encased it glistened, rippling with a subtle vibration, alive in a way Izayah had never witnessed before. "Father said I'd be a waste for taking this—that I'd never use it the way it was meant to be used." His hand fell to his chest, clutching tightly where Izayah knew the heart-tether must feel frayed, the unbearable weight of grief radiating through his brother. "I have to go. I have to ensure what remains of my duty is fulfilled—for Tabytha."

The words struck like jagged stones, battering Izayah's composure and tugging at something indefinable between them. Izayah's mind flickered to their father, Lord Brannon, and the cold, unyielding way he had endured their mother's death. High Lady Nadine's loss had carved scars into them both, but now, standing before his brother, Izayah felt a faint pull deep in his chest—a resonance, like an erratic hum that trembled along the invisible blood bond tying them together. It wasn't just sorrow pressing between them—it was something heavier, more deliberate, tinged with an unease he couldn't quite name.

And there it was—fractured and skewed. The bond they shared, those unseen cords stretching between their souls, sagged and twisted like a rope fraying under strain. It wasn't severed—not the absolute finality of death— but warped, vibrating with an unnatural dissonance, as though its rhythm had faltered. A flicker of instinct whispered through Izayah's thoughts: *This isn't the end.*

He forced the notion aside, focusing on the figure before him. Izayah leaned in, pressing his thumb firmly against Zane's forehead. The gesture wasn't just physical—it was a command, a pulse of intent coursing through their shared bond. The touch worked like a needle weaving through fragile strands, stitching together strength where despair had unraveled his brother's will. *Find clarity. Stay steady.* The directive rippled outward, weaving calm into Zane's grief-clouded mind.

As Izayah withdrew his thumb, a faint sigil shimmered on Zane's skin. It glowed briefly before fading—a phased mark, thought woven, invisible to most but known to them, a silent instruction burned into his soul. "This will guide you," Izayah said, firm but laced with something gentler. "No thinking, brother. This is on me. What happened today—it's mine to carry."

Zane nodded, the anguish in his expression softening just enough for Izayah to catch a glimmer of resolve. "You're not alone in this," Izayah murmured. The words weren't a promise; they were a fact, unshakable and solid. In the next heartbeat, Zane vanished, folding seamlessly into the temporal path that stretched ahead. His form dissolved into the threads of time, leaving only a faint hum behind—a vibration that lingered like an echo of his presence.

Izayah's eyelids lowered, like the gradual closing of a camera lens, drawing the vision into shadow. The room's familiar boundaries faded, replaced by an all-encompassing darkness that consumed sound and motion alike. Reality held its breath, suspended in a stillness so profound it seemed even the air had ceased to move.

Time splintered, its moments stretching and bending as if caught in an eternal pause. The steady pulse of Izayah's heartbeat resounded dimly, subdued beneath layers of silence that pressed against the space. The Lumis Bloom's tether shimmered faintly, golden threads connecting him to the observers trembled with a restless energy, like a harp string strummed by unseen fingers. His frame remained rigid, caught between the revelations of the vision and the uncertainties lying just beyond.

For the observers, the world constricted further, their awareness pulled inward as though drawn behind the veil of Izayah's vision. Suspended within the contours of his mind, they floated in a space where fragmented memories stirred and twisted, their patterns rippling across an unseen surface like water disturbed by a passing wind.

The stillness endured, taut and unyielding, stretching to the brink of tolerance. Then, a blade of light pierced through the shadow, sharp and precise, severing the silence like dawn breaking through a storm. It carried a subtle resonance—a stirring vibration that radiated outward, gentle but insistent. The air quivered as the shroud of darkness began to lift. Slowly, with an almost agonizing reluctance, light and sound bled back into the space. The muted roar of chaos swelled, clawing at the edges of sanctuary, testing the fragile barrier that had held it at bay.

A sharp exhalation escaped Izayah, releasing the tension that had bound his form. The breath unraveled the lingering remnants of the vision, shedding its weight like a discarded mantle. With a roll of his shoulders, his posture steadied, every line of his stance radiating newfound determination. Behind him, the shield's faltering hum grew louder, the chaos outside pressing closer, threatening to breach the delicate boundary.

His attention cut toward the balcony's edge where the observers stood. Though beyond the vision's direct grasp, their presence rippled through the Lumis Bloom's luminous threads, the connection between them taut and unwavering. His voice shattered the quiet, firm and resolute, carrying the precision of a command. "We're not done. There's more you need to see."

With those words, the shutters of his mind lifted, and light surged through the scene, dissolving the remnants of the past. The observers felt the pull immediately—the threads drawing them forward, guiding them deeper. The fragments of reality slid again, memories folding into one another, the moments yielding to the next chapter as shadowed possibilities unfurled ahead.

Chapter Twenty-Four

The room reassembled itself piece by piece, the transformation drawing the observers back into their present surroundings—the elongated bathroom in Starlight Beach. The copper-bronze horizon strip embedded within the obsidian tiles gleamed faintly, catching the soft glow of the stars scattered across the teal-washed walls. Above, the golden starburst pattern on the ceiling shimmered subtly, as though alive with quiet energy, the cosmos itself etched into its surface. The air carried a charged stillness, the faint hum of their connection palpable and beautifully binding.

The mirror reflected faint impressions of the observers' forms—translucent, spectral outlines woven delicately into the fabric of the space. Below, the sink's polished surface shimmered imperceptibly, its ripples aureating with a life of their own, beating in sync with the shrouded heart of the Lumis Bloom, a reminder of their link to the unfolding memories.

Ashla's voice drifted in like a melody, curling warmly around the senses of the observers. "Oh, my sweet little blooms," she cooed, her tone lilting and teasing, underpinned with amusement. "Back here again, are we? Thought you knew this place, didn't you? This house, this view—so quaint in your memories. But Missy," her voice dipped conspiratorially, "Missy has layers, my loves. What you remember? That's the surface. She adores her flair—the grandeur that you never noticed before. She's always been a touch too much, but that's why she fits so perfectly into Starlight, don't you think?" Her tone—lilting, softer—almost reverent. "And this space—Diesel keeps it close. The study is *hers*, but *not hers*, if you understand. It's *the bridge*, the *unfiltered truths*, the raw spaces few ever see. A tether between what was and what will be. Now," she hummed lightly, her voice laced with warmth, "Izayah's ready to guide you. Missy may linger, as she always does, woven into every corner of this place. Just...don't let go."

The teal-washed walls wavered like heat-glazed glass, the room undulating at the edges, responding to Ashla's words. From the mirror, a golden radiance spread outward, like sunlight cresting a horizon. The bathroom's boundaries dissolved, and the copper-bronze strip shimmered, stretching forward like a bridge weaving the Lumis Bloom's threads into the fabric of the next space.

Izayah's consciousness shifted as the scene solidified. The observers felt themselves drawn forward, their forms settling into a new space. Plush leather couches wrapped them in quiet warmth, their deep surfaces gleaming faintly in the firelight. Across the room, a sapling spiraled upward in a corner, its branches stretching confidently toward the ceiling —a living testament to resilience. The study exuded quiet strength, its rich, earthy tones enfolding them like a sanctuary where burdens might be shared, even if not entirely lifted.

Izayah sat beside a low-burning hearth, a tumbler of amber liquid resting lightly in his hand. The glass caught flickers of firelight, refracting them like shards of memory, each glow suspended in time. Without turning to meet the observers' gaze directly, he dipped his head—a silent gesture of regard. When he spoke, his voice was gravel-edged, weighted with reflection and the echo of unresolved doubt.

"The pieces are still scattered," he began, his eyes fixed on the undulating flames. "But perhaps it's time to start seeing the framework."

The room exhaled, the shadows deepening in the far corners as the firelight danced. Somewhere—subtle yet unwavering—the Lumis Bloom hummed beneath it all, its strands of connection pulsing gently through the space. This study, warm and resolute, seemed to beckon them forward, inviting them into the shadows of what would come next.

The observers remained silent, tethered to the edges of Izayah's consciousness, as a tempest of memories churned above him. Disjointed thoughts, restless and unmoored, darted like birds across the expanse of the room, their wings flickering with muted light. Each erratic motion bled into the next, creating a chaotic rhythm that mirrored the turmoil within. The room itself seemed to pulse with energy, shadows stretching and recoiling as though caught in the gravitational pull of his unraveling mind.

Irritation flared in Izayah as he rubbed at his temple, his fingers pressing firmly against the ache rising within. The flickering patterns above him began to stutter, their orbit faltering until one by one, they plummeted. With sharp precision, they fell toward the coffee table, a vast surface framed by charred edges that seemed to breathe faintly with ember-like glows. The air above it thickened, swirling into a silvery haze that caught the descending pieces. They sank into the mist like falling stars, only to rise again, reshaped as vivid, miniature projections.

From the mist, shapes began to form—twisted figures blackened by destruction, each one contorted by the weight of what it represented. Among them, the cabin emerged, skeletal and broken, its charred remains flickering into sharp focus. Surrounding it, the jagged remnants of a life once sheltered within stood as silent witnesses to its fall. The projection grew sharper, drawing the observers closer to the scene etched on the table's surface.

The display atop the coffee table expanded, drawing the observers deeper into its unfolding narrative. The cabin grew larger, dominating the surface with its stark, ruined form. Beams reduced to ash and rubble told a story of sacrifice, their remnants a haunting testament to what had been. Izayah appeared within the vision, standing rigid on the balcony. His stance reflected resolve as the shadowed veil that had cloaked the structure began to unravel. The inky shroud peeled away, exposing the cabin fully to the inferno he had unleashed. Flames surged, consuming every trace of what had once stood, until only ashes and smoke remained—a hollow monument to a calculated act.

Izayah's gaze lingered on the image, his breath steadying as the enormity of the moment sank in. The obliteration had been deliberate, each step taken to ensure the illusion of devastation was seamless. Yet, as the memory replayed, its weight pressed upon him—not in grief, but in an evolving clarity sharpened by the stutter of firelight. Words billowed across the coffee table's surface, glimmering in golden strokes: *Runa*. The letters radiated, steady and purposeful, joined by others unfolding into phrases—*every act, every sacrifice.*

Izayah inhaled deeply, the golden light reflected in his eyes as he murmured aloud, his voice steady but raw with emotion. "This was for her survival. Every choice...every step...all of it, for her." He leaned forward, watching as the shimmering text rearranged itself into another thought. "Her role...her purpose...it's tied to something far greater than any of us. Something even she doesn't yet understand." His voice dipped lower, steady but reverent. "And Rayanna...Layla...they're part of it too."

The golden light refracted again, the projection on the table morphing into Tabytha's charred form amidst the cabin's ruins. Izayah's hands tightened, his knuckles whitening as the image took shape. "Tabytha..." he whispered, the name heavy with acceptance. "She's moved on because of him—because of Zane. And yet...I understand." The words carried an edge, a harsh acceptance of reality. "That blade..." He exhaled sharply, his voice trailing off as comprehension solidified. The image dimmed, the cabin's smoldering remnants casting an eerie glow across the tabletop, its weight tangible in the room.

Above him, a flutter of movement broke the stillness. A leather-bound volume, its edges worn with time, glided down from the towering bookshelves. It landed gently in his lap, tucking itself lightly against him, the way a creature would lean into a familiar hand. Izayah hesitated, his fingers brushing over the embossed cover as if it might dissolve under his touch. "I'll keep this here for you, *my little Ray of Sunshine*," he whispered. The tome cracked itself open, as if responding to his words, and a few of the glowing birdlike figures darted downward. Their radiance extinguished as they merged into the pages, weaving themselves into its core. His gaze lingered on the blank space where the glowing trails had vanished, their essence now bound within its chapters.

"Rayanna will need this one day—a reminder of what happened, and why it mattered." Closing the volume with care, he placed it beside him on the couch, its steady presence a keeper of what it now held.

Izayah leaned back, his shoulders easing as he released a measured breath. *"Every piece matters,"* he muttered, his tone firm and controlled, as though speaking to both himself and the observers. His gaze lifted, locking onto theirs with unwavering resolve. "This isn't just about destruction. It's about what comes next."

The study seemed to draw its warmth closer around them, the hum of the Lumis Bloom threading faintly through the edges of the room. The flickering remnants of the vision settled into stillness, but the questions it carried lingered, waiting to unfold in the chapters ahead.

With a snap of his fingers, the miniature framework of the cabin convulsed, collapsing inward as if reality itself had buckled under his command. The structure disintegrated into spiraling ash, its essence drawn into the table's charred surface, which tremored in response. Fog crept in from the edges, veiling the remains in a restless mist until only ghostly silhouettes lingered, sinking into obscurity.

Izayah's breaths steadied, as he sank deeper into the couch, the leather sighing beneath his weight. His brow furrowed, head tipping back, eyes tracing the flames as they swayed in a hypnotic rhythm. The embers cast refracted patterns of light across the room, their steady glow peeling away hesitation. Each flare burned through doubt, leaving behind something sharper, more resolute.

The observers drifted to the edges of the room, their translucent forms silent but watchful, leaving Izayah at its center. The air thickened, heavy with an unspoken tension, bracing for what was to follow.

*"Hey—*what the *fuck* happened *back there?"*

The words sliced through the space, sharp and unrelenting. The atmosphere seemed to constrict, the walls pressing inward as if recoiling from the force of Daxler's arrival. His boots struck the floor, each step carrying a gravity that commanded attention.

His tall, broad-shouldered frame exuded restrained power, like a spring coiled tightly, ready to snap. Black fighting leathers, worn but meticulously maintained, clung to his form. Ink stretched across the visible planes of his skin, intricate designs shifting subtly with each movement, their dark strokes telling stories steeped in shadow. His brown hair was pulled back into a taut bun, every detail of his appearance calculated; control itself had always been an Elite's greatest weapon.

"That was pure bullshit!" he boomed, his piercing grey eyes locking onto Izayah and stripping away any pretense. A cold, calculating edge radiated from his gaze, tempered by a shadow of something deeper, a burden buried beneath his hardened exterior.

Daxler's eyes darted briefly to the scorched coffee table, then back to Izayah. A faint smirk tugged at his lips, pointed and razor-sharp. It lingered, daring confrontation. "I'll ask again—what the fuck happened back there?" His voice, low and unyielding, demanded a response.

Izayah inclined into the conversation, elbows braced on his knees, chin cradled in one hand. His groomed beard framing his angular jaw adding a rugged contrast to his otherwise meticulous appearance—a balance between raw strength and exacting discipline. Deep brown eyes, flecked with gold, caught the firelight, their intensity smoldering like embers fighting to reignite. Even the sharp cut of his ebony hair, streaked faintly with golden undertones, was cropped clean at the sides; the purposeful part was a reflection of his controlled nature.

"Hell if I fuckin' know," he muttered, his graveled tone threaded with frustration. Broad shoulders rolled slightly as he settled deeper into his seat, the tailored leathers clinging taut across his powerful frame, emphasizing the quiet force beneath his stillness. A sharp exhale escaped him. "I can assume what's transpired," he added. "Zane doesn't act without purpose. You think I'm difficult? Wait till you deal with him."

Despite the tension in the room, an unshakable calm radiated from him —a quiet confidence, forged through discipline yet tempered by self-awareness. Even seated in the eye of the storm, Izayah exuded a control that remained immovable, an anchor in chaos.

The house groaned in protest, timbers creaking like an ancient beast disturbed from slumber. Doors slammed open with a reluctant shudder, their echoes rolling through the space. At the bar, a glass clinked beneath the whiskey spout, amber liquid swirling like molten gold as it poured. The sharp crack of ice cubes landing sent ripples skimming across its surface. With a definitive *thud*, the glass settled onto the scorched coffee table, taking its place before Daxler's usual seat—a vantage fit for both observer and predator.

He stepped closer, his presence taut with intensity, a storm simmering beneath his stillness. His gaze lingered on Izayah, the smirk still faint but cutting, sharp enough to slice through the tension. His grey eyes gleamed, carrying the clarity of someone who had already assessed the room and found it wanting.

Daxler's gaze tossed upward, his head tilting slightly as one eyebrow arched in acknowledgment of the house's presence. Without missing a beat, he waved his fingers in a crisp, dismissive motion. "I'm good. Don't need anything," he said flatly, the words delivered with finality.

The house replied with a disgruntled groan, a low, resonant sound accompanied by the creaking of walls. A sharp *'pop'* and a *'woosh'* followed, ending with a heavy crystal glass landing with a defiant *clank* in front of Izayah. Its contents hissed faintly, the sound punctuating the house's unspoken retort: *Fine, have it your way.*

The faintest twitch of amusement pulled at the corner of Daxler's mouth. He lowered himself onto the leather couch beside Izayah, his movements unhurried and steady. The worn cushions exhaled under his weight as he folded forward, elbows braced on his knees. His sharp eyes traced the flickering patterns of shadows dancing along the polished floor, tension from earlier simmering down into something quieter. The room hummed faintly with the house's passive-aggressive energy, its presence as tangible as any other occupant.

Izayah smirked, casting a sidelong glance at the glass. Amusement lit his gold-flecked eyes as his voice dripped with mockery. "Oh, come now, Missy," he began, gesturing to his soot-streaked leathers with exaggerated flair. "Trying to get me drunk and take advantage of me in my grief-stricken state?" One eyebrow arched as his smirk widened. "I'll have you know, Miss, I'm not so easily bedded."

Daxler's grin turned wicked, mischief sparking in his eyes. "Oh, darling," he purred. "His most treasured asset is already under lock and key—or should I say, shadow bound for the next decade or two, at least." With an exaggerated nod toward Izayah, he gripped his nether region and barked a guffaw, a crude diversion from the reality closing in on them. "Safe to say, he's *well off* the market."

With effortless audacity, Daxler reached out and snatched the glass before Izayah could react, his fingers curling around the crystal as he lifted the drink to his lips. "Feeling possessive, are we?" he quipped, cutting a sly eye toward the exposed beams above.

The house retaliated swiftly. The glass wrenched itself from Daxler's grasp, floating sharply upward before hovering precariously over the wet bar sink. It teetered dangerously on the edge, as if daring him to test her patience further.

Before Daxler could retort, the study doors groaned open with a reluctant protest. Diesel filled the doorway, his imposing frame cloaked in quiet authority. Tufts of snow clung stubbornly to the leather jacket draped over his broad shoulders, the material snug against the worn fighting leathers beneath it. Hazelnut-brown hair, peppered with silver at the temples, was cropped neatly on the sides, with the longer strands above styled just enough to suggest both precision and practicality.

Emerald green eyes scanned the room with a steady intensity, their sharp brilliance cutting through the charged atmosphere. His beard, fuller than usual but neatly groomed, framed his jawline in clean lines. Diesel stepped forward, boots scraping faintly against the polished floor, each step carrying the weight of battles long past.

His gaze landed first on the hovering glass, then on Daxler, whose grin faltered slightly under the scrutiny. "What's all this about?" Diesel's voice rumbled, low and even, but with an unmistakable edge that brooked no nonsense.

Izayah leaned back, crossing his arms with the faintest shadow of amusement tugging at his lips. "Just Daxler making friends, as usual," his tone was as dry as the firelight flickering against the room's edges.

Diesel snorted softly, brushing snow from his sleeve as his gaze pulled to the still-hovering glass. "Missy's not one for games," he remarked, stepping further into the room as he surveyed the space. "Missy," he drawled, a low rumble that resonated through the walls, "what have I told you about wasting the good stuff?" The heavy *thud* of his combat boots punctuated his words as he strode purposefully to his desk. Rolling his neck slightly, he let out a faint sigh, a sign that his patience was running thin. "We've got business to handle," he muttered, his hands deftly shuffling through scattered reports. His gaze snapped to the glass, then to Daxler. A mischievous glint skimmed his features as he stacked the papers, drawing additional parchment from his internal pockets to add to the growing pile. "So, if you two could keep your little tug-of-war under control, I'd appreciate it."

Izayah leaned back in his seat, arms crossing lazily over his chest, a coy smile tugging at the corners of his mouth. "Hey, I'm just here for the entertainment," he quipped, his tone light but edged with defiance.

Daxler's smirk sharpened with mischief as he cast a sideways glance toward Izayah. "Oh, seems Missy might be pegging us as the instigators," he teased, nodding at the glass still teetering precariously. A hand rose to his chest in a theatrical gesture, his expression a picture of exaggerated innocence. "And who am I to argue with such a formidable lady?"

Diesel rolled his eyes, hefting a well-worn tome with edges frayed by time—and shaking his head as he lumbered to his oversized chair. "I swear, you two could turn a bad day into an outright catastrophe," he muttered, his gruff cadence edged with reluctant amusement. Sinking deeply into the velvety cushions, the upholstery creaked softly beneath his weight, as though groaning under the strain of their antics. "I swear," he added with a dismissive wave, his focus sharp with exasperated affection as he eased back into the headrest. "Missy, don't indulge them or their nonsense."

"That wasn't us!" Daxler shot back.

"I find that hard to believe, Major General," Diesel replied dryly, not even bothering to look up. "I've known you two far too long."

The house's candelabras wavered, their flames swaying as though in agreement with Diesel's skepticism. A subtle vibration moved through the walls, followed by the decisive *pop* of a whiskey bottle's cork freeing itself with a melodramatic *hiss*. Amber liquid poured in smooth, steady streams, the sound rich and indulgent, before the glasses glided through the air. They settled gracefully beside Diesel and Izayah with a soft *clink*, each filled to the brim.

Izayah smirked as the glass appeared beside him, his fingers brushing the rim. "Looks like she's not entirely immune to our charms," he quipped, lifting the glass slightly in a mock toast to Missy.

Daxler snorted, leaning back into the couch with a grin that walked the line between lazy charm and razor-sharp wit. "Or maybe she's just trying to shut you up, Zay. Can't say I blame her," he drawled as he gestured toward Diesel. "Besides, we're not the ones who stirred up the hornet's nest back at the cabin. That's on Zane."

Diesel's palm struck his knee with a sharp *crack*, the sound slicing through the room like a gavel striking order. "Speaking of…Nester tells me Zane's arrived at the destination," he stated as his attention settled on Izayah, a brief nod carrying a note of approval. "Thought weaving was a smart call." The acknowledgment, rare and pointed, held for a beat before he continued. "They'll be here shortly." Diesel's tone darkened, his jaw tightening as he leaned back.

"Debrief me before they arrive." He let out a taut breath, shoulders rolling back with a restrained discipline that spoke of simmering anger. "This assignment—looks like a goddamned bloodbath," he ordered.

"It definitely didn't go according to plan," Daxler hissed, the grin fading from his face as he leaned forward, his forearms resting heavily on his knees, bracing for impact.

Izayah's jaw tightened, his eyes sparking like embers in a wildfire, consuming what little hope remained. His hand raked through his hair, disrupting its usual precision. "Couldn't have said it better myself. Let me just fuckin' show you," he fired back.

With a flick of his wrist, the charged air above the coffee table rippled. Low fog began to rise from its scorched surface, curling upward in almost choreographed, languid tendrils. The mist caught the dim light, its swirling patterns churning like the first stirrings of a storm—silent, foreboding, and heavy with the weight of truths yet to be unraveled. The scene was steeped in tension, as though even the mist braced for the revelations it was about to unleash.

The fog above the coffee table thickened, crawling over the coarse wood like something alive. Mist coiled upward in snake-like tendrils, winding tighter as Izayah pressed his palm to the seared edges. The air felt heavier, the fog creeping in, dimming his vision like a curtain being drawn. In the churning clouds, shapes began to twitch—faint, ghostly things, slipping in and out like half-formed thoughts. Piece by piece, they pulled together, snapping into place until the scene before him wasn't just a vision anymore. It was real.

The first scene unfolded on the balcony. Zane stood silhouetted against the dusky sky, his frame still and commanding, yet unnervingly stained. A red, gelatinous substance clung to him, glistening as it oozed and dripped onto the planks below. The material seemed almost alive, its viscous tendrils stretching and recoiling as though reluctant to release him. Each movement of his body sent fresh rivulets cascading to the floor, pooling at his feet. The eerie quiet of the moment was broken only by the faint, wet sound of the substance hitting the wood.

The mist peeled away, the balcony dissolving into the chaos of the cabin's interior. The kitchen was a violent tableau of destruction. Red spray coated every surface, streaking the walls and dripping from the edges of the counters. The once cozy space had transformed into a scene of utter devastation, its warmth replaced by the cold, clinical reality of what had occurred there.

Izayah and Daxler moved through the wreckage with methodical precision, their boots crunching against shattered glass and debris. The Elite guards flanked them, collecting specific items from the chaos with quiet efficiency. Each movement was calculated, designed to leave behind just enough to tell the story they needed others to believe—a story of absolute obliteration.

Among the chaos, the structure itself seemed to respond. The walls groaned faintly, their sounds reverberating through the air like a sentient creature in mourning. Drawers slid open unprompted, spilling contents onto the floor in a perfect choreography of disarray. The heavy beams overhead creaked as if under invisible strain, and the entire structure seemed to sigh—a low, resonant sound that felt both sorrowful and purposeful.

Then, with a shudder that rippled through its very foundation, the forest refuge began to collapse inward. Its walls folded, floorboards curling like parchment under flame, but instead of destruction, there was a careful, calculated retreat. The once-sprawling kitchen compacted into itself, cabinets and beams folding seamlessly as though drawn by unseen strings. The air grew dense, vibrating with energy as the entire cabin seemed to compress into a singular, concentrated mass before sinking into the earth.

Izayah stepped back, his eyes narrowing as the last remnants disappeared beneath the ground. The space where it once stood was now a smoldering crater, its edges scorched and jagged—a perfect illusion of violent destruction. Ash and debris floated lazily through the air, settling across the crater's surface like the remnants of a firestorm.

"It'll be back," Daxler muttered, his voice low, almost reverent, as he stood beside Izayah. His grey eyes glinted with an understanding that only those present could share. "Not as it was—but it'll return when it's ready."

Izayah nodded silently, his gaze lingering on the empty space where the cabin had once stood. The structure had sacrificed itself willingly, folding into the earth to protect what lay within and to deceive those who would come looking for answers. Its essence, alive and waiting.

The vision faded as the mist above the table dissolved into thin air, leaving only the scorched wood beneath Izayah's hand. He withdrew his palm the weight of the scene settling over him like a cloak.

"Smart," Diesel murmured, his voice heavy with approval. "If they're looking for answers, they won't find any."

"They'll think the bloodbath was the end of it," Izayah replied, his tone cold, final. "But the cabin will endure."

As the final scene dissolved and the mist dissipated into the table's charred surface, Izayah's hand dropped away. His gaze returned to Diesel, who sat poised at the edge of his seat, his frame taut with unspoken tension. The silence in the room felt brittle, stretching thin as though braced for the weight of his response.

Diesel's fingers grazed the edge of his bristled beard, tracing its rough contours in a familiar gesture of contemplation. His emerald eyes narrowed, their sharp focus betraying the calculations taking shape in his mind. The glass in his hand swirled with amber liquid, catching the firelight as he brought it to his lips. He sipped, savoring the fleeting warmth, his gaze lifting briefly to the exposed rafters above—as if searching for answers written in the shadows. Each considered movement spoke of a man wrestling with the gravity of decisions made, expectations shouldered, and futures yet to be defined.

Diesel pressed his index and middle fingers to his temple, massaging circles as he released a measured exhale. The low, steady sound broke the silence, carrying the weight of suppressed frustration—a brief crack in his otherwise controlled demeanor. When he spoke, his tone was firm, each word purposeful. "Sienna has them under her care," he said, leaving no room for uncertainty. "Your mother," he added with a glance toward Daxler, "has already begun Runa's shadow binding. From her reports, it should take at least three months to complete the process." He turned to Izayah, his emerald gaze steady. "You'll have time to make whatever notes you need while you stay in hiding. Subtle distractions for Visha will be key to keep her off balance."

He paused, his voice calm but edged with urgency. "As you depicted, remnants were laid carefully, every detail accounted for. Well done." Diesel's sharp gaze lingered on Izayah, a rare note of approval threading through his words. "Nester relayed that Mama D has already filled in the gaps regarding Zane's actions. We won't press him when he gets here—he made his decisions for reasons that align with our objectives. Exceptionally well, in fact," he finished, his tone clipped but measured.

Izayah's brow furrowed, his jaw tightening as his fingers brushed the edge of the coffee table, the gesture almost searching for answers within its scorched surface. "Yet how did Zane know our assignment was underway?"

"Are you *fuckin'* kidding me? That's *your* focus? It was a *goddamn* bloodbath." Daxler's low chuckle cut through the tension, his smirk sharp and unapologetic. "And the wreckage?" he drawled, grey eyes glinting with dry amusement. "It looks fuckin' believable. Like a masterpiece of chaos."

He swirled the last of his drink, before downing it in one smooth gulp. The faint *clink* of the glass on the table punctuated his words as he leaned back, his grin fading into something colder, more calculating. "No one's gonna question it. That's for damn sure." Rubbing at his chin, uttering, "*Fuckin'* bloodbath."

"Nester's reports will detail all of that regarding Zane. It will come in due time." Diesel gave a single nod, a flicker of approval crossing his face as he pulled his focus back to Izayah. "And the shadow binding? Thought weaving?" he asked, his pitch pointed, directing the conversation toward the next critical element.

Izayah rubbed at his forehead, a rare flicker of irritation breaking his usual control. "It's—methodical, as expected. But Dax and I still need to figure out the Lumis Blooms situation." His fingertips drifted along his forearm, tracing unseen lines as though following an invisible map. "The markings will surface in phases. Tattoos, like threads of ink, will rise gradually—cycling through stages. Each line, each thread," he said, his tone leveling as he met Diesel's gaze, "will release fragments of their shadow bound memories."

His focus settled on the table's surface. "What they're binding isn't just about who they were before the cabin—it's about their past lives, what ties them to Starlight and to each other." Izayah's inflection softened, carrying a note of quiet reverence. "The ink will reveal their journey piece by piece, a map leading them to what lies ahead. My little Ray of Sunshine and Layla are parts of the puzzle Runa will need. Even Tabytha, Ashla, and Nissa…" He paused, biting his lower lip in thought. "The Trinity of Healing…" His voice drifted, softer now. "Makes you think."

The room descended into a heavy stillness, Izayah's words pressing down with bated breath. Diesel lowered his hand from his temple, letting it rest on the armrest as a measured exhale slipped free.

Izayah turned to his elite brother and continued, "The phased markings will allow each female to understand one another's journey without words," he said, his tone steady and controlled. "When the markings finally start to surface, Runa won't need to dive into extensive detail. Their focus will center on moving forward—no explanations, no distractions." He rubbed the back of his neck thoughtfully before continuing, "Unless Runa chooses to share specific parts of her past, most of it will be inherently understood—tethered through the thread they share, embedded into the thought weaving ink within the phased markings."

Diesel's hand moved along the bristled edge of his beard, his emerald gaze sharp with consideration. "As Nissa and Ashla grow into their roles as Unbinders, will they remain integral to releasing the females from shadow binding? Or does their influence diminish after a certain phase of the process?" His tone was calm, but the edge of strategic inquiry cut through each word.

Izayah nodded, the tension in his jaw easing as though a knot had been carefully undone, freeing him to breathe. "Yes," he began, "they can manually release the females when necessary." He paused, weighing his next words carefully. "But their abilities should be used sparingly—too much interference risks disrupting the natural flow of the process."

His hand rose to his scalp, fingers pressing against the growing ache as though he could will it away. "The Unbinders will safeguard the Lumis Blooms and Memory Vines. They're more than protectors; they're the keepers of essential, irreplaceable knowledge. What they hold is critical." His voice deepened, a low growl escaping his throat. "To think we have two Unbinders among us…" The thought trailed off, heavy with both reverence and unease.

"They're not just pieces in this web—they're anchors," Daxler said, leaning forward slightly, his voice quiet but resolute. *"Underestimating them would be a mistake. From what I've seen, there aren't many left—if any at all."* He exhaled, his tone softening, though it retained its weight. "What I'm saying is, I'm with you, Zay. You're not wrong."

General Diesel's solemn nod shouldered the weight of the unprecedented nature of their endeavor. "What you are both attempting," he began, his tone laced with curiosity, "exists only in myth and childhood tales, spun under the comforting shroud of bedtime." His upper lip twitched, a question forming as his hand patted the armrest with resolute intent. "Are you certain it will succeed? I mean—you're talking about rebirthing them into another life. That's no small task."

Daxler angled back in his seat, the purposeful motion punctuated by the faint crack of his neck as he eased the tension in his muscles. A low rumble rolled from his chest, drawing the room's attention to him. "Sir," he began, his drawl steady and firm, carrying unshakable certainty, "my mother's knowledge runs deep. It's rooted in the ancient lineage of Seers, a connection that stretches back to our earliest ancestors. She knows how to guide the girls through the reverting process."

He paused, his words carefully chosen. "The reverting process will restore them, pulling them back to a time before they veered off their destined path. Their memories will remain intact, but they'll be given the chance to rebuild, to mature, within a hidden pocket of time."

Inclining slightly, he set the crystal glass on the coffee table's edge. "She predicts that Rayanna will be the first to return to you and Mama D, the first to acclimate." His gaze slid to Izayah, sensing his attentiveness. "The process finds its fork in the road—a specific year of rebirth unique to the journeyer. For Rayanna, it aligns with the passing of High Lady Nadine, around the time she began nearing her Dawning Day. It came earlier than most—she's one of the rare, more powerful potential Truth Seekers."

Diesel leaned closer, his emerald gaze fixed on the swirling depths of his glass. "Thirteen was a hard year," he murmured, his voice heavy with unresolved emotion. A measured breath escaped him, laden with intense reflection. "Even though we took on the role of raising Rayanna after Nadine's passing," he continued, his tone softening, more vulnerable, "the pain still lingered. It haunted her, especially when she began her training as a Truth Teller." His brow furrowed as he exhaled sharply, his cheeks puffing slightly before settling into quiet acceptance.

Shattering the tension, Daxler's flickering amusement slid to his elite brother. "Yah, well, from what I gather, Rayanna isn't far off from the depth of power—and spunk—of High Lady Nadine," he said, a bright inflection carrying a playful edge of truth. "You know, I like my ladies spicy." His grin widened as he leaned back slightly, a mischievous wink following. "This will give her the support she needs to blossom into…"

"A spitfire," Izayah concluded, a faint grin tugging at his lips, echoing Daxler's mischief. The humor slipped away as he continued, "I truly believe Runa will gain as much from Rayanna as she will from Runa." His voice hitched momentarily, the pause underscoring the weight of his thoughts. "Their potential was something Visha never fully trusted." His gaze dropped, his brow knitting as he worked through the implications aloud. "That's probably why she kept them apart after Runa's Dawning Day. Honestly, I'm surprised Visha even allowed you to stay as close as you did, Diesel. The High Priestess has never been one to confront the unraveling of her own lies and carefully constructed truths."

Diesel leaned back, his emerald eyes tracing the ceiling as though searching for answers hidden in the grain of the wood. "I wonder if we'll face the same challenges with Ray this time around," he mused, his grip tightening slightly on the glass in his hand. He brought it up a fraction, muttering, "If so, we're going to need more of this." The gesture carried the weight of both a toast and quiet resignation. "Maybe the Blessed Father thinks there's still more I need to learn from her," he added with a soft chuckle. "And honestly? He's probably right."

Daxler's crooked grin widened. "Good thing whiskey sharpens Truth Telling—without dulling the senses," he quipped, his tone sharp with mischief, cutting through the tension like a blade.

Izayah smirked, nudging Daxler in the ribs with his elbow. "In other news," he said, "Tabytha's another story that Mama D will need to shed light on when she returns."

Daxler groaned, running a hand over his face. "Well, if Mama D's on board…" He twirled a finger in the air, frustration clear in the restless motion. "Just finding out about Layla—*shit, man.* Talk about a goddamn curveball—an identical twin, *out of nowhere.*"

Izayah scoffed lightly. "Didn't see that coming either. Apparently, she's been in the Dark Forest her whole life; she was raised there. From what I've gathered, she was found as a wee babe, floating down a river in a basket." He cleared his throat, the enormity of the revelation pressing down on him like an unseen hand. "All I know is that, in Starlight, she'll assume Tabytha's identity to keep things from spiraling." Shaking his head, he added, "It's the only way. Even with Rayanna shadow bound, she's going to sense something isn't right. If anything, by the time the first phasing hits, I'd expect her to get...irritable."

"Yeah, I do agree. Ma says that even though the ladies are shadow bound, they'll still have that female intuition," Daxler said, his tone steady and assured. "As for Layla, there's the eye-changing thing—that could raise flags. But Ma's confident she can rebind Layla's quintessence if it ever becomes necessary. The thought weaving for her, is just there to help align with Tabytha's personality more so. It'll hold as long as it needs to."

"Layla's got the potential to be lethal," Izayah said, his tone plain and unwavering. "The females have been blessed with more quintessence than most—hell, probably more than The Lands are even ready for."

Diesel exhaled, his eyes flicking upward toward the ceiling before returning to the conversation. "Considering when they were all birthed, I still don't understand how this imbalance came about. From the reports I've seen, most younglings now have such a low level of quintessence—or none at all. It's like the ones who still possess it chose to vanish into hiding." His voice tightened, a thread of frustration slipping through. "But I have to ask—what's the long-term goal here?"

Izayah leaned forward slightly, his tone calm yet focused. "The goal is to give them time—to see the world from a perspective they've never had before. To understand what's possible when they're free from the shadows they've been living under."

Daxler picked up the thread without hesitation, his voice firm but warm. "We only know what we've been taught," he said. "This gives them the chance to unlearn, to rebuild." He paused, letting the thought settle as his gaze flicked between Diesel and Izayah. "Upbringing shapes the story we tell ourselves. But this?" He exhaled softly, the weight of his words hanging in the air. "This lets them write a new story—to compare, to choose, to figure out their own path. With support of course," his voice dipped lower, resonant but calm. "When the shadow binding and thought weaving lift, they'll finally see the world on their own terms."

Izayah's gaze dropped to his hands, fingers tracing idle patterns against the table as his thoughts settled. "Runa, especially—," he began, lifting his eyes to meet Diesel's. His voice was steady, but the weight of his words pressed into the room. "One day—," he paused, letting the silence stretch, drawing attention to the gravity of his next statement. "Runa will have to face Visha again. But this time…she won't be the daughter Visha remembers." The silence deepened, stretching outward as though each word carried ripples across unseen waters.

"She's always been strong," Izayah continued, his tone thoughtful as his gaze lingered on Diesel. "Visha put her through hell, used her as a tool more than anything else. Runa survived that—quietly, yes—but she survived because she's always been a badass in her own way." He paused, letting the truth of his words settle. "But this time…" His voice gained momentum as his conviction grew. "This time, she'll have something Visha never gave her. She'll have perspective—a new upbringing. When things get hard, she won't face it alone. She'll have her sisters, yes, but not just them. She'll have a whole circle of support—people who see her for who she is, not what they've been made to believe."

Izayah's jaw tightened as he leaned forward slightly. "The Lands were fed one version of Runa—Visha's version. But when the time comes, Runa will stand her ground, unshakable and unyielding. The truth of who she is will finally be hers to claim."

Daxler leaned back, a sly grin curling at the corners of his mouth. A low chuckle escaped as he added, "Yeah, well, the badass is gonna hit her from fuckin' left field…" He let the silence linger, his phrasing exact, the silence between lines doing most of the talking. "The Bitch—Priestess—will have —no—fuckin' clue." Mischief gleamed in his eyes as his grin deepened. "Right now, she's convinced her 'only' daughter is gone." The smirk widened further. "And with us just finding out about Tabytha and Layla? That's gonna be one hell of a surprise."

"What I'm hearing is that the long-term goal is to reclaim Sanctuary." Diesel tilted his head slightly, his tone calm but probing. "So, how exactly do shadow binding and thought weaving interact?"

Daxler settled into the cushions, crossing one ankle over the other as he gestured toward his tattooed forearm. "Psychologically," he began, "this process of rebirthing is a journey of regeneration." His fingers skimmed lightly along the inked skin, his movements thoughtful and precise. "Each stroke of the brush is imbued with whispered instructions—thoughts, memories, and experiences," he continued, his voice steady, laced with quiet authority.

A spark of anticipation brightened his expression as he went on. "Once the ink sets, they'll be submerged in the Seers' water. That's when the reversion truly begins." His tone softened, carrying a hint of nostalgia. "Ma used to describe it as sitting cross-legged on the floor, wrapped in the warmth of shared stories—each narrative unfurling like petals." He paused, clearing his throat. "But for me? It's more like packing away boxes of parchment—taking the stories from one phase of life and tucking them away for safekeeping. It frees up space to stretch and breathe—for growth."

Diesel rubbed his mouth, his gaze fixed in quiet thought.

"Each participant embarks on a journey unique to them," Daxler began, his tone steady. "Shadow binding tucks away their memories, dreams—everything they once were. It's like packing those parts of themselves up to make space for something new." He paused, the weight of his words thickening the air. "It will pull them out of survival mode, no matter how far they were stuck in it."

He let the thought linger before Izayah picked it up. "The process is intricate," he said, nodding slightly. "Tailored to each person and their past. The Seers guide them into regression—physically, mentally—to the point where they diverged from the path they were meant to follow. No further, no less. That's where the shadow binding and thought weaving stop."

Daxler leaned forward slightly, threading his fingers together. "That's why they'll arrive here—at Starlight—at the exact age when everything changed for them. From there, it's like watching them bloom in reverse, until they reach the second Dawning Day." A faint smile curved his lips as he added, "Ma says the Dawning Day's not just a rite of passage—it's where they reclaim themselves."

Izayah inclined his head, continuing the explanation. "The thought weaving fills in what's missing. It gives them a sense of alignment—of who they need to be, how to hold onto the pieces that matter, while leaving room for growth." His tone softened, a faint note of reverence slipping through. "It's an art that's both restorative and precise."

Daxler tilted his head, his gaze flickering toward Diesel. "And since Starlight exists outside of regular time, it gives them back the years they lost," he said. "But unbinding doesn't just rewind their lives. Once they pass through the second Dawning Day, they'll begin to age slower—more like us, more like The Lands intended."

Diesel exhaled, his hand tightening on the armrest of his chair. "It's a lot to take in," he admitted, his voice low. "They're essentially re-living their lives—but better, this time."

Izayah's expression grew pensive. "That's the idea. They won't just return to the path they lost. They'll walk it with clarity—with strength they didn't have before." His gaze sharpened, his voice steady with conviction. "When they come out of this, they'll be ready to reclaim Sanctuary. *Together.*"

Daxler threaded his fingers, his tone weighted with quiet conviction. "Ma's exceptional at what she does," he said. "She'll treat each of the females like her own younglings."

Diesel's brow furrowed, his concern evident in the subtle tightening of his features. "It sounds intense. Complex." He tilted his head back against the chair, his lips pressed into a thin line. "Is it...painful for them?" His cadence was laced with the unmistakable burden of parental worry.

Izayah leaned back, resting his head against the couch, his gaze steady on Diesel. "And that," he said, "is why I needed you on this assignment. A high achiever who already carries the weight of a father's worry." His tone offered a strand of reassurance. "This mission will shape you. Each of the females will leave their mark in ways you won't expect. Stay open to it."

Diesel arched an eyebrow. "Oh? And when exactly did you become an all-knowing sage?" he asked, his cadence biting with sarcasm.

Izayah's grin widened as he lifted his glass in an exaggerated flourish, his tone turning light. "Learned from the best," he quipped.

Daxler cleared his throat, drawing the conversation back. His hand traced a deliberate spiral in the air. "To answer your question—no, it's not painful for most of them," he said, his voice steady. "It depends on their experiences, how deeply they're tethered to what they've been through. If anyone's likely to feel pain, it's Runa." He hesitated, his delivery dropping by a fraction. "Given what she's endured, she's got the hardest path ahead." His voice faltered, a stretch of silence before his next words slipped out, hushed. "So, Izayah…why did you leave her in all this? Why didn't you tell her—"

Before Daxler could finish, movement at the study's entrance stole their attention. The memory began to dissolve, its edges smearing into shadow, the details bleeding away like ink across damp parchment. Darkness crept in, measured and unrelenting, swallowing the scene as Izayah withdrew the moment.

A soft chuckle bubbled up from the edges of the fading memory—Ashla's voice, airy and tinged with amusement. "Oh just wait and see," her cadence threading floated within the darkness. "This part always makes me giggle."

The scene retreating further into obscurity. With calculated exactitude, Izayah let a sharp *thud* punctuate the silence, followed by the muffled sound of something heavy hitting the floor. The noise hung in the darkness, suspended and final, before a voice, dry and laced with irritation, broke through:

"Shit, how would I know that some stupid light would be sitting on the floor?"

Chapter Twenty-Five

Past

Izayah's eyes fluttered closed, erasing any sense of delay. When they snapped back open, it was as if he declared, *I am ready for you.* The observers were slingshot back into the stark clarity of the Lumis Blooms' tableau. The shift was visceral. Diesel's study enveloped them once more, its familiar contours reasserting themselves with physical force. The space itself demanded their presence, issuing a jarring call to order. The scent of leather and aged wood had settled deep into every crevice, crafting a home imbued with warmth and love, sewn into every beam with care.

The cold mist curling over the coffee table had vanished, fully dissipated into nothingness, like the fading edges of a dream no longer needed. Each detail of the space sharpened into focus, grounding the scene with purpose. This was not just a vision—it was a place with history, meaning, and weight.

Ashla's voice drifted softly through the room, her cadence light and unhurried. "It's strange, isn't it?" she mused, her gaze distant, as though observing something just beyond the visible. "Seeing Father like this—not so strict now, is he?" A lilting laugh followed, delicate enough to vanish on the faintest breeze. "I rather like this version of him—*don't you?*"

"How the *fuck* are we supposed to *know* that?" Layla's blunt tone cut through Ashla's musings, clean and unapologetic. The sudden interruption snapped the focus back to the room, a stark contrast to Ashla's airy detachment.

Ashla tilted her head slightly, her expression unchanging, as though the comment hadn't even registered. The edges of their forms shimmered, translucent and ethereal, like light refracting through water. "You know," she said, as if sharing a curious secret, "Izayah doesn't usually behave this way. He's a bit dull in this part. You'll see—not exactly a shining moment." Her lips curved into a small, enigmatic smile. "But don't fret. I might help him along if it feels…necessary." She tittered lightly. "They're doing quite a fine job otherwise, don't you think?"

The room seemed to quiver with irritation, the Lumis Blooms drawing their attention with a silent insistent—*Here, here*—commanding like a teacher clearing their throat.

"*Yes, yes*…terribly temperamental things," Ashla remarked with a wistful wave of her hand, dismissive, as though brushing away an unexpected bit of fluff. The vision sharpened, honing in as if waiting for acknowledgment. An ice-wrapped towel shimmered into existence at the edge of the coffee table, its energy haloed in a cool, frostlit aura. With unhurried ease, Izayah collected it and passed it off to Zane, who had slumped into a chair identical to Diesel's green velvet one.

"Well, I didn't see him there! Why would I expect some lamp to jump out while I'm walking?" Zane muttered, annoyance threading his voice as he pressed the cold compress to his head. "My stomach's in knots. My head's pounding and I might be sick." Still gripping the trash bin, he leaned awkwardly into the plush cushions, shutting his eyes tightly against the brightness.

Across the room, Nester's light flared with agitation, casting jittery shadows along the walls. His rigid, black-piped frame seemed to puff up slightly, as he climbed methodically from the floor to the coffee table, finally perching on the armrest of Diesel's chair. The sheen of his bulb-like head slid from bright yellow to a faint pinkish orange.

Diesel knit his brows as he rested his hand briefly against Nester's small frame, patting a subtle rhythm against his radiant companion. "Nes," Diesel murmured, his voice steady but carrying a quiet edge of authority, "you've made your point. Stand down." His tone softened slightly as he added, "He's already nursing his wounds—no need to add to the drama."

His bulbous head blinked in response, the pinkish hue reluctantly fading as if conceding to his master's point. Diesel's hand lingered for a moment longer before withdrawing. "You'll both be just fine," his words calm and resolute.

Daxler's guffaw erupted, loud and unrestrained, like a boulder crashing down upon the room's strain, scattering it like shards of shattered rock. "Well, your head did have a spectacular introduction to the kitchen island," he quipped, lounging lazily against the mantle. "Not exactly the softest of surfaces," he added, his grin widening with unapologetic amusement as the firelight flickered behind his relaxed form.

Izayah hunched closer, his elbows pressing against his knees. His focus landed on the edge of Zane's boot. Faint crimson smudges stood out— streaks left by the tread, each groove releasing beads of dirt that stubbornly clung to the wooden floorboards. The air tightened, wrapping the room in a stifling silence. He tilted his head slightly, locking eyes with Zane, a glint of unspoken understanding sparking between them.

Daxler turned toward the mantle, as though seeking refuge in the warmth of Missy. The light rolled across his features in languid waves, tempering the edges of his grin into something that bordered on reflective.

He exhaled sharply, as though trying to shed the weight pressing down on his chest. His attention drifted toward the dancing flames, his thoughts seeming to flicker and dissolve within the light, like ephemeral images forming and fading. "Well," he began, his voice strained. "What are we working with? What do we know? Let's start there." His brow tightened, one hand pressing against his temple, massaging away the tension.

Missy dimmed the lights in response, the fire's radiance softening with a quiet, soothing purpose that cradled the frayed nerves of those within her care.

A faint smile tugged at the corner of Daxler's lips. He lifted his glass, his fingers brushing the mantle in a silent gesture of acknowledgment. The floorboards beneath him creaked, a contented hum like the purr of a cat nestling close. He bowed his head toward the mantle, a small gesture of gratitude to the ever-attentive home.

Diesel's rough tone cut through the quiet, subdued yet burdened with distrust. "The High Priestess has her own agenda. She revolves around herself, and *herself alone.*" The words carried a foreboding gravity, heavy as a storm cloud brewing overhead. His tone darkened further, anger simmering beneath the surface. "We need to scrutinize her every move, question every word she utters. Her role in the deaths of Father Ezekiel and High Lady Nadine is still more presumed than proven."

Diesel sat motionless, one large hand cradling his face, fingers pressing firmly against his temple. His focus lingered on the table's surface, his words falling with a dull *thud*, a weighty burden long unspoken. "I won't go into the full story—most of it's irrelevant now. But after Ezekiel discovered the twins, Nadine stepped in to become a surrogate, offering to carry Runa."

Izayah's head jerked up as he surged to his feet, his movements sharp, almost violent. "What the hell are you talking about?" The words snapped out, venomous, carrying the full weight of his shock. Around him, coils of darkness surged, unfurling from his clenched hands with a life of their own. They twisted and writhed, warping between solid and vapor, snaking outward as though searching for something to consume.

The dim firelight wavered, struggling against the spreading gloom that expanded across the walls and ceiling. The dark streams mounted, casting jagged, fractured patterns over the wooden beams. A low vibration resonated through the space, not quite a sound, but a presence that pressed into the chest like an unspoken warning.

The force of Izayah's quintessence grew heavier, dense as a storm rolling in from a distant sea. The coils—now ribbons of shadow—lashed against the furniture, curling around the legs of the coffee table and brushing the edges of the walls. The air turned cold, laced with the tang of damp earth and midnight, amplifying the strain that hung over the group like a suffocating veil.

Izayah's knuckles turned white as he fought to rein in the storm within. His breath came ragged, the dark streams retreating slightly only to surge outward again, responding to his turmoil. The distorted shadows hissed faintly, a sound like wind whispering through unseen corridors, echoing his struggle.

The oppressive charge bore down on everyone, the space itself seeming to shrink beneath the weight of his rage. His words, when they finally broke free, were edged with fury. "My mother was Runa's mother! That's what killed her!" he snarled, his tone daring anyone to deny him. His head lowered, shoulders tight with the weight of it. "Runa was the reason she died..." The words bled out, each syllable laced with venom that left the truth hanging in the air—heavy and stinging.

"Told ya," Daxler interjected, turning toward Diesel with a knowing look and wagging his finger, as if referring to a conversation they'd already had. His casual ease belied the raw underbelly of tension lurking just beneath. "Take it down a notch, Dark Dynamo. Don't make me start handing out candlesticks just to see through this fog."

"Maybe," he continued, "instead of wrecking the room and undoing everything we've built, you sit your ass down, and we actually figure this out." A faint smirk tugged at his lips, though his voice carried an unmistakable warning. "You know—like adults."

Izayah exhaled sharply as he turned back toward the couch, his steps measured, both hands dragging through his hair before clamping down on the crown of his head. He halted beside Zane's chair, his chest rising and falling with the strain of holding it together. "This makes no goddamn sense," he said.

Daxler's smirk widened, his confidence unwavering as he gestured toward the now-clearing room. "See? That wasn't so hard. Pull the storm back, sit down, and—what's the phrase?—oh yeah, wade through the shit to find the treasure." He stepped back toward the mantle, brushing his fingers against it, as if signaling a truce.

In response, the study settled into an uneasy quiet, the remaining shadows flickering faintly at the periphery, their edges pulsing softly, like a storm waiting for its cue.

"Are you kidding me? You truly didn't know?" Diesel ground out, dragging a hand over his face as if to wipe away the stain of Visha's manipulations. His fingers pressed against his temples, attempting to force clarity through the chaotic revelations. "Fuck—I'll never get used to the stench of her lies," he muttered, his words coated in a thick film of frustration that clung to him like smoke.

"Come on, are you serious?" Zane paused mid-thought, gripping the edge of the bin as his body shuddered with an almost inaudible retch. He fought it back, swallowing down the nausea clawing at his throat. His voice came raw and uneven as he rasped, "Runa's always been Visha's and Ezekiel's daughter."

A ragged exhale followed as Zane lifted his head from the bin, his hands unsteady as he wiped his mouth with the back of his sleeve. His chest heaved once, like he was trying to reset himself, to find a center that kept slipping away. "Tabytha has a twin—Layla. That's its own disaster," he added hoarsely. "I assume…that's why both leaders were ousted." His explanation trailed off, unfinished, like a thread snapping under too much strain.

He tried to rise, but his knees buckled, forcing him back onto the cushions. One hand clamped around the armrest to steady himself as he shoved the bin aside with a shaky push, setting it near his feet with reluctant care, as if still wary of needing it. "Why…would you even think Runa was our sister? I know Ma carried her—but Runa has never been blood." His voice cracked, disbelief seizing him. "Father's done plenty I don't agree with, but he would've never allowed that. And Ma…" He swallowed hard, squinting at his younger brother as though the words themselves hurt to form. "She would've never crossed that line. Not her." His features pulled taut, confusion and horror battling beneath his skin. "Are you really suggesting something like that…of her?"

Zane exhaled, pulling himself upright just enough to slump back into the green velvet, his arms bracing against the armrests to steady himself. "You know," he said, his tone softer now, the words strained by the sting of rawness, yet tempered by reluctant acceptance, "if you'd just brought this up—if you hadn't gone at it alone—Rayanna might've already cut through the crap before you left." He hesitated, his brows knitting. "Wait…" The single word hung, tentative, over the uneasy stillness gathering in the space.

"What difference would it have made if I had told anyone?" Izayah snapped, the shadows around him twisting outward again, alive with the anger pouring from him, their movements erratic and barely restrained. He shook his head suddenly, as if trying to dislodge years of ruminated frustration tearing through him. The thoughts were old, jagged, relentless—their weight grinding against him like stone against stone. He muttered, slipping into fragmented phrases as he began pacing again, disgust and disbelief twisting his features. His jaw tightened as if chewing through the thick, unyielding leather of thoughts battering him. "None of this..." he muttered, dragging a hand roughly through his hair, his steps uneven. "*Fuck.* None of this. *None of this* makes any sense. None of this *ever made* any sense." His movements grew harsher, his fingers locking behind his neck as he paced, his elbows jutting outward with each stuttering intake. "*Do you know* how many times *I've tried* to put these *fuckin'* puzzle pieces together?" he burst out, his voice cracking under the strain. "And every *goddamn time* I look at it—it just looks like *a fucking mess.*"

"We were doing so well." Daxler's mocking chuff cut through the room, biting and unrestrained as he pushed off the mantel and made his way to the couch. With a careless drop, he flopped into the soft leather cushions, the worn material giving way beneath his weight. Picking at his teeth with a nail, he lounged deeper into the seat, his posture loose and unbothered. "Seriously, Zay? We're burning daylight so your shadows can put on a melodramatic puppet show because you couldn't be bothered to speak up?" His grin slashed through the tightness with wicked precision. "Next time, maybe trust the people who actually *give a damn.* Wild idea, *huh?*"

"He's not wrong," Diesel stated. "Stick to what you know, not the shit you've been fed. You've spent years building a truth around Visha, and now it's crumbling. That's what's tearing you up." His voice hardened, precise as a blade. "You're pissed because you're finally seeing her for what she is—and hating yourself for taking so damn long to come to terms with it all."

"So, again," Daxler said, lifting his chin with a casual flick, "what do we actually know about Runa? Now that we're all finally in the same room, having...whatever the hell this is." Folding his arms over his chest, he reclined back into the leather with a weary exhale.

"What I know so far," Daxler continued, a snort of derision punctuating his words, "is that Visha's greatest skill seems to be making people choke on her crap—or run screaming from whatever mess she's peddling. Hell of a talent, right?" His smirk widened, the glint in his eyes hardening. "So, Zay, what exactly did High Priestess Nutcase tell you? Nutcase—yeah, that feels about right." He clicked his tongue, his smirk tilting into a full, unapologetic grin. "We're overdue for answers."

Diesel straightened in his seat, his smirk fading into a sharp line. "Izayah, stop pacing!" The words carried a clipped authority. "You're gonna wear a hole in my floor—and I'm not entirely sure I want to see what's under there."

Izayah's footfalls eased, each step heavier than the last as he crossed the room. The lingering wisps of quintessence curled faintly around him, drawn in as he inhaled deeply, bottling the energy back into himself. Without a word, he dropped onto the couch beside Daxler, the worn leather groaning softly under his weight.

Zane's voice, steady but edged with weariness, picked up where Diesel left off. "Listen, man—she's not our sister. Not even close." His tone softened slightly, though an undercurrent of urgency threaded through it. "I get it—you've been kicking yourself over this for years. But here's the thing: you didn't screw up. You didn't know what you didn't know. And that's exactly how she operates. She's the queen of manipulation. Point blank. Nobody else was willing to say it out loud. *Now we can.* I mean, look at it—after Father Ezekiel passed, everything changed. The families stopped getting together. Pa kept his distance. We all did. Visha *made sure* Runa stayed out of sight unless it was some formal event—and even then, she *wasn't allowed* to stick around and interact." He adjusted his position in the green velvet chair, the fatigue in his posture unmistakable. "She's *good at what she does.* But that *doesn't mean* we can't start undoing it. Let's stop spinning our wheels and start dealing with this the *right* way."

Still pale and visibly drained, Zane let out a low groan, stirring the air with circles of his hand. "Alright, let's get this train back on track," he muttered, his voice flat, as if he'd rather be anywhere else. He jerked his chin toward Izayah. "Let's just find an onramp while this one calms himself down." Pulling his attention to Diesel, he added, "Where's Ray with her studies lately? Rayanna's got this Truth Teller thing, right? Pretty sure she's like a damn cat chasing fireflies—bonus points and all—always darting after those threads of truth.

"Truth Tellers—especially the females—they're something else entirely.

It's like they're tuned into a frequency the rest of us can't hear." Diesel stated, his expression turning thoughtful. "Damn near scared me a few times with how fast Rayanna caught on." As he spoke, Nester sprang from the armrest with the effortless grace of a cat, landing soundlessly before bounding up the spiral staircase. A soft scuffle of tiny feet echoed briefly before he leapt onto the desk, snagging Diesel's well-worn pipe—Old Faithful—with a deft motion. The small figure darted back, delivering it into his waiting hand without a word, landing neatly on the armrest with a soft whir of satisfaction. With a quick flick of his wrist, Diesel lit the pipe with practiced ease, the embers casting faint halos as smoke curled upward in elegant, languid trails. Drawing a steady pull from it, he exhaled, the smoke slipping from the corner of his mouth in a lazy curl. He huffed out a chuckle, his amusement understated but genuine. "She's gonna outshine me someday." He drew another careful intake from the pipe, coaxing the embers into a soft flare; a faint crackle answered, and the smoke unfurled from his mouth in leisurely streams. His voice dropped lower, thoughtful. "Shadow binding will slow her down a bit—but it's just a delay, not a full stop. And who knows…maybe that second Dawning Day will help her along when the time comes." He paused, the admiration in his cadence unmistakable. "Hell, she already figured out the Runa connection before I did. Not that I'm salty about it or anything." His smirk widened briefly as he leaned back into his chair, letting the pipe hang loosely between his fingers. "That's why Rayanna had to be part of Starlight. She started her Dawning Day before most—showing her quintessence around thirteen." His tone turned reflective, the smoke coiling gently from the pipe like threads of thought. "Lord Brannon specifically spoke about the topic, even after you boys did." His gaze darted between Izayah and Zane. "He knew what she was becoming. And I'd bet he had an inkling about what Visha really was. As much as you might not see eye to eye, your father—well, he does have a strong background in strategy." Diesel exhaled, the smoke tumbling upward in thin, deliberate barrels. "And Nadine…" His voice trailed off, his expression darkening slightly. "There's more to her story than meets the eye. I'd wager Brannon knew that too."

Zane leaned forward, bracing his hand against his knee. "What kind of progress are we talking about? Because when I asked her, she never went into specifics—which isn't like her." He scrubbed a hand over the back of his neck, the motion rough. "I just figured it wasn't anything grand if she hadn't been going on about it."

"Truth Tellers—are like bloodhounds for bullshit. And Rayanna? She's on a whole different wavelength. You ever watch her work a room? It's like she's weaving an invisible web, tugging threads until something snaps loose." He drew from the pipe again, smoke wisping from the corner of his mouth as he continued, his voice dipping into a more reflective cadence. "It's also not something you can turn off. It's like a constant buzz in the background. You've got to learn how to sift through the sand, figure out which grains matter, or you'll drown in the noise." He exhaled through his nose, the smoke streaming outward in thin threads. "That was my last lesson with Ray. She adapts fast, and she's tough as hell under pressure. I wouldn't call her studies warm and fuzzy, but she gets it." A smirk tugged at the corner of his mouth as he tapped the side of the pipe lightly with his thumb, keeping the ember alive. "Give her time, and she'll be sniffing out lies like a bloodhound on a fresh scent trail—won't even let the stench of deceit cling to her shoes. And when she's done, she'll unravel it so clean, most people will be left flat on their asses."

Izayah let out a rough bark of laughter, his mood lifting for the first time. "Oh, her and her damn shoes." He scrubbed along his jaw, grinning back at Diesel as he gestured toward the ancient sapling twining up the bookcases. "You said before the Tree of Life might help her...How's that supposed to work?"

Diesel exhaled, the smoke rising in lazy, rolling columns before he answered. "Nester's already got her lined up for heavy training once she's out of the shadow binding. He thinks the Tree will pick up on her energy— how it evolves after all this—but we'll see. Might surprise us both."

Nester's bulbous head warmed to a soft amber, a conspiratorial wink of color that gleamed with silent mischief. Diesel's chuckle rumbled low in his chest, his grin turning wicked. "The guy's sharp as a tack—always working on something clever. Hell, he's even plotting a way to bypass the Seers altogether. Little genius, he is, like a walking bag of tricks." He glanced toward Nester with a glint in his eye. "Keeps life interesting, doesn't it, my old friend?" Drawing another pull from his pipe, he exhaled, the smoke rising in lazy, rolling columns as he nodded. "When the time's right, Ray will stay with us, and we'll hand over the book. I've got no doubt she and Runa will click. Rayanna's going to protect her like it's etched into her bones. And once Ray starts unraveling Runa's story…" Diesel's smirk turned sharp, his voice dropping to a dangerous edge. "Visha's going to wish she'd stayed in whatever pit she crawled out of." The soft hum of Nester's frame sharpened, urging the conversation forward. Diesel caught the hint, leaning back slightly with a knowing glance and patting his small companion. "Alright," he muttered dryly, "Nester's dying to hear it—what kind of half-baked theory made you think you're Runa's brother, huh?"

"I bet it was some twisted bedtime story, handed down on a chipped plate by good ol' Nutcase," Daxler interjected, brushing an invisible speck from his sleeve, his grin turning sharp. "Let me guess—someone passed you the wrong family tree at a reunion?"

Izayah froze, the room tightening around the sudden quiet. It hit him like an old wound tearing open—years of questions, doubts, and half-truths crashing in at once. "That's what I was told before…" His voice faltered, the next words catching uselessly in his throat. For a moment, it looked like he might say more, but the effort collapsed under the hollow weight of it all. The words that slipped free were raw, brittle—the punchline to a joke that had never been funny.

Daxler's smirk faded, replaced by a thoughtful frown, his posture growing sharper. "Is this why you showed up early to our Shadow Guard selections?" His voice dropped. "The drill instructors tore into you like wolves on fresh prey—no mercy, no favors. Just hell, plain and simple. And you took it, like every other poor bastard out there. *But you…you were* paying for something more."

Izayah rose stiffly from the couch, his movements tight, as if the words had shoved him upright. He crossed halfway between the wet bar and the study door before crouching down, elbows braced on his knees, his gaze locked onto the floorboards.

Daxler leaned forward slightly, his voice hardening. "You pulled strings, didn't you?" He scrubbed a hand over his head, the pieces clicking together. "You knew exactly what you were signing up for. Fuckin' hell—your enlistment wasn't even scheduled for months." He bobbed his head once, sharp and certain. "I always figured it was because of your family connections—being Lord Brannon's son and all. Well," he shrugged, "so did everyone else." His gaze swept over Izayah, then landed on Zane. "People talk, you know. They say he's a ruthless *bastard*."

"You're barely scratching the surface," Zane muttered, low and biting. His gaze snapped briefly to Izayah, then dropped away. His hands curled loosely in front of him. "I'm the one who pulled the strings. Got him into training early. Could see he needed out." He cleared his throat, pressing on. "Nobody really saw Runa after Ezekiel's rites. Not properly. Not for years. Sanctuary didn't shut down officially, but it might as well have. Everything got…tight. Careful." He rubbed at the back of his neck, his movements sluggish, the lingering nausea clear in the set of his jaw. "*Shit*— years blur together after a while, don't they?" He hesitated, ticking the numbers off on his fingers. "She must've been two, maybe three, when Ezekiel passed. And her Dawning Day didn't hit until she was twenty-one. About the norm nowadays, I guess." He shook his head, the memory weighing heavy. "All that time gone. Eighteen, nineteen years where we barely glimpsed her. And even then, it was staged—paraded out when required, no real interactions." His mouth twisted into a grim line. "Limited. And that's putting it kindly. Our families just…stopped crossing paths. Stopped trying. Maybe five years after Ezekiel, everything just faded out. Ru would've been seven or eight. You, Zay—probably ten or eleven."

He dragged a hand down his face, the exhaustion bleeding through. "I don't know exactly what happened during her Dawning Day. But whatever it was, it changed everything. His whole demeanor regarding Runa— different. And considering everyone knew how he felt about her ever since they were young—back when they were both still just younglings…" Zane shook his head again, his throat working against a surge of old frustration. "It was stark. Night and day." He pressed his palms against his knees, grounding himself. "Like I said—I'm the one who pulled the strings. He needed out, and I did what I could. He never really opened up to me about it, but man…when he came back, I heard whispers. Possibilities. Assumptions. People talked. Nobody wanted to say it outright. And the few accusations that did surface? They sounded so outlandish, none of it made sense—well, not until now." He looked up at Izayah, his voice steady but low. "You know how I hate hearsay, Zay. So I guess this time's as good as any. You ready to talk? Because I'd love to hear what actually happened."

Izayah's shoulders sagged, his eyes fixed on the floor, refusing to meet anyone else's.

"So, let me get this straight—it was all because you wanted to court Runa?" Daxler asked, his brows pulling together in confusion, his tone tinged with disbelief. "Why was that such a problem? You're both from royal lines. A union like that would've sealed the alliance between Sanctuary and Shadow City. Win-win, right?" He gave a half-hearted shrug. *"What's not to like?"*

"I honestly *don't know—couldn't tell you* why," Izayah muttered, rubbing the back of his neck, the heat of shame creeping up his spine. "I was told— *flat out*—it was *her* decision." His hand dropped to the floorboards to steady himself. *"Apparently,* I didn't measure up. I *wasn't* what she wanted." His voice cracked at the admission.

Daxler frowned, confusion splintering through his usual bluntness. "So how the hell did it get to the point where you thought she was your sister?"

Diesel tapped the bowl of his pipe lightly against the side of his boot, the last embers flickering weakly as he cleared his throat. "Just show us what happened. Give us the quintessence of the memory." He passed the pipe over without a glance, and Nester whisked it away with a faint whir, darting back toward the desk without breaking the quiet hum of the room.

Izayah's voice wavered, caught between barely contained anger and humiliation. He stood, flushed, his gaze darting toward the corner of the room—as if he could feel the girls lingering there. Nonetheless, he drew in a sharp breath, dipped his head briefly, and turned back toward the others.

Zane tracked his brother's movements, his brows furrowing as he glanced toward the empty corner that had caught Izayah's attention. A few beats later, Nester returned, resuming his perch on the armrest beside Diesel. The small motion seemed to pull the group's focus back in, the pivot almost reflexive—turning in near-unison, a chain reaction that didn't go unnoticed.

Ashla cleared her throat. "This part's a little disorienting, Auntie Ru," she said, her inflection weaving through the tension like a stream slipping between stones. "Just remember—it's his perspective of what he believed once." Her gaze tilted toward Rayanna, calm and faraway. "Make note of this, Auntie Ray," she added. "I was told this snippet will be used for

training later." She tossed her chin upward, a small, assured gesture—
Proceed.

As if answering the summons, Izayah's wrist snapped forward, releasing a low, resonant *hauuuu* that rippled outward. The effect hurled a wrenching gravity into the space, pulling at the marrow of his being—a raw fragment of his soul cast onto the table's waiting surface. The sound hissed—*shhhhhhhwwwpp*—a sharp, haunting echo, like molten iron searing into cold steel, the tension bleeding outward through the room.

"It was Runa's Dawning Day," Izayah said, his voice roughened, as the memory began to surface—pulling not just himself, but the entire room, into the jagged current of his experience.

He rubbed his hands together with a forceful, grinding pressure, his fingers digging into the heels of his palms as if he could shove the tension straight out of his skin. His shoulders tightened as he turned his back on the materializing scene. The table behind him began to cloud, a smoky haze twisting and writhing across its surface like something trapped between worlds. His head sank lower into his hands, his palms pressing hard against his brow—not soothing, but bracing—drawing strength, barely, from the burning friction of flesh against flesh.

Without thinking, he crouched down, hunching over—not just waiting for the moment he knew was coming, but confronting the one he had carried silently for years. A moment he had dreaded yet somehow always known would be dragged into the light. His body curled tighter, instinctive, as if trying to shield himself from what was already unfolding.

Behind him, the shroud thickened, bubbling like molten glass before spilling outward in slow, tremoring waves. A faint hum charged the air—subtle but insistent—the way the first breath of an orchestra stills a theater before the conductor's hand falls. The tabletop pulsed once, then unfurled, beginning to unveil the memory, piece by inevitable piece.

Sanctuary rose from the mist—its grand, polished halls materializing with breathtaking clarity. The marble floors gleamed like liquid light, so reflective that every tiny step left faint ripples across the surface, as though the space itself rejected intrusion.The court stood in formation, figures composed in elegant restraint, each gesture performed with the poised precision of ritual. Clusters formed instinctively, alliances revealed in the subtle tilt of heads and the conspiratorial glint of jeweled masks. Resplendent attire shimmered beneath the towering candelabras, whose commanding glow unveiled every meticulous detail of their self-proclaimed superiority.

Columns stretched toward the vaulted ceilings, their surfaces veined with milky quartz and streaks of blue lapis lazuli that shimmered like frozen starlight. The room carried an aura of pristine sterility—an overwhelming sense of perfection that bordered on oppressive. No corner lingered in shadow; no imperfection dared exist within Sanctuary's walls.

Rising to full height, Izayah's leathers flexed faintly—like old parchment creasing under a familiar hand. A giving of someone taught to perform, even when splintered inside. Tension bled from his frame, the motion betraying the pain laced in the effort. He turned toward the table in a fluid, sweeping gesture, his shadows standing at attention, hushed at his heels. "The court of noble men and women," he stated with sardonic grit, dipping into a shallow bow—measured and formal. No mockery. Just tradition. Expectation. The kind beaten into him since boyhood. The kind you never really forget. As he straightened, his gaze lingered on the floor a beat too long, regally braced in the posture of war. "They were all there for...*the grand presentation. An elegant showing* of mates." His voice struck harder the second time—like gravel beneath silk. And still, he didn't look up.

Turning his back to the projection, Izayah brought a hand to his mouth, thumb grazing his bottom lip in quiet thought. His fingers drummed restlessly against his chest, the uneven rhythm betraying his attempt to beat the unwelcome notions into submission. "Each suitor was required to present themselves before the High Priestess—to declare their intentions, to offer something of value to Sanctuary in exchange for the honor of courting Runa." His tone was measured, but the fracture beneath it was clear. "It *wasn't* a private moment. It *wasn't* intimate. *It was* a spectacle. A *grand* performance." His gaze lifted—drifting to the corner of the room where no one stood, at least not in this time. The line of his jaw flexed slightly, as though willing himself to keep going.

With a low exhale, Izayah's hand slipped from his mouth and lifted—not in flourish, but in a numb, effortless sweep through the air, as if brushing away smoke. The projection on the coffee table hummed in response, its edges warping slightly beneath the strain of his quintessence.

He didn't turn. He didn't need to. The memory was too well-worn, carved into him with relentless scrutiny. The manifestation wavered under the gravitas of power as the prospective suitors advanced one by one, arranging themselves into a presentational line at the center of the hall, like a rehearsed dance. A muted tapping of dress shoes and the faint clink of metal reverberated through the space, a ghostly reminder of the reverence demanded by Sanctuary. Each carried an offering—gilded boxes, artifacts, scrolls—objects of wealth, power, or knowledge, their steps rigid and measured. Izayah's figure among them wore the dark, formal military attire of his station, a plain black box cradled steadily in his hands—unadorned, severe, and silent.

The crystallized noblemen reached the raised dais at the heart of the hall, placing their offerings with meticulous care at its base. Above them, a throne-like chair loomed—simple in form, yet unyielding in presence—carved from the same bluish, star-speckled stone that veined the surrounding columns. A figure could almost be imagined seated there, but the memory left the throne conspicuously empty—its vacancy a quiet, potent reminder of the one who held dominion over the court.

Izayah's hand dropped, and the projection stilled—its images freezing mid-motion, suspended in breathless pause. His gaze fell with it, dipping deeper into the well of bitterness that had long since settled in his chest. "This wasn't about love—it never was." His intonation frayed at the edges. "It was a show. All for Visha. From what I see now, it was her presentation…*her opportunity*—her chance to destroy a soul."

Izayah lifted his hand again with a weary push, as though sliding aside something that refused to move. His quintessence flared, and the projection stirred in response. From the vision, a swell of live orchestration began —a delicate lull at first, strings drifting like mist through the air, then tightening into sharp, needling tones that could have pierced skin. The music carried an edge of something wicked, something unknowable, looping through the room like a whisper too close to the ear. Beneath the dais, beneath her elevated chin, the sound lingered — a command that demanded submission to the order of things. And when the final chords unraveled, they left behind an atmosphere so heavy it felt hollowed out—emptied by the resonance.

The crowd pivoted like puppets, forming a semicircle along the sides and curling around the back of their showcased space. They stood rigid, silent, their bodies locked in postures too perfect to be natural. Eyes forward. Expressionless. Tethered to her presence, as if some invisible thread held them in place. *Hypnotized.*

With every gaze fixed on the ceremonial dais—those within the memory and those watching from the study—the High Priestess's form began to materialize. Blurred and indistinct at first, like a figure glimpsed through frosted glass, her presence drew the room taut. Energy coalesced, her outline crystallizing into something mesmerizing—harsh, striking, and undeniable. Perched atop with a languid indifference—legs crossed, arm draped loosely over the side, a glass of red wine dangling from her fingertips—she radiated a sharpness more cutting than diamond on glass.

Izayah's teeth ground together, rage swelling beneath the surface as he stood with his fingers interlocked behind the base of his skull—elbows angled out, his stance rigid. Though his back remained turned to the projection, he knew exactly what was unfolding. Disgust emanated from him like a palpable force, shadow pooling at the heels of his boots—darkening, but unmoving.

The neckline of her gown emerged first, plunging dramatically to her navel. Crystallized silk, so fine it could have been spun by spiders, clung to her curves—a marvel of delicacy and control. The bodice, threaded with black and gold, wove an intricate lattice, constructed with such meticulous precision it bordered on divine intervention. Below, the skirt cascaded into creamy white—soft and pristine—a tantalizing dance at the edges of light and shadow.

She wasn't simply wearing the gown; she was its purpose, a living embodiment of dominance and allure, impossible to ignore.

The crown followed, its antique gold finish gleaming faintly with age, a massive blue jewel atop scattering shards of light like ice shattering across a frozen lake. Her hair unspooled in cascading waves, dark and lustrous, each strand falling into place with flawless, almost unnerving grace. High cheekbones caught the light, intense and sculpted, framing a face so perfect, so exact. A beauty crafted to be worshipped from afar, yet so cold it defied and repelled all warmth.

"Well, if that doesn't arouse body parts…I don't know what does," Daxler muttered, his voice spilling like liquid through the fractures of splintering wood. He dragged a hand to the back of his neck, adjusting his fighting leathers as the rising heat caught him off guard.

Zane's glare cut sharply in his direction, his posture loose, unfocused, as if the motion had to catch up to the nausea still threading beneath his skin.

"Hey, man, I can't always control my physical response," Daxler added, throwing up his hands in defense. "Come on…you know we're all thinking the same thing."

"That's her allure," Diesel interjected, his tone calm but weighted. "It's part of her quintessence. Ezekiel and I always felt there was something… off about it."

"Keep going, Zay," Zane said, his hand rotating lazily in the air—more sway than command—as he urged the continuation of the story.

Speaking to the floor, Izayah projected his voice. "As you can see, I was third in line, yet she called me up first."

As he spoke, the High Priestess's head inclined—just enough to mark her notice. Her gaze, cool and hollow, swept toward him as though drawing a blade with a honed certainty. She did not stir further; her stillness was more commanding than motion.

"It's a fuckin' draw," Zane murmured, dragging a hand to his forehead, massaging at its center.

Diesel's voice clung to the walls. "Think of her like a siren—pulling ships from the sea—but *something else entirely.* Otherworldly. *Unfounded. Unbalanced.*" He rubbed at the bottom of his chin, exhaling deeply. "It's definitely a thread she'll use." His cheeks caved slightly as he sucked them in, the click of his tongue breaking the silence. "She isn't going to hold back on you going into this next phase of the mission, Izayah."

Izayah bobbed his head in acknowledgment. "I'm more aware of that than ever before," he uttered. He stared toward the far corner of the room —where, to everyone else, there was nothing. But the girls were there now, and his eyes, shadowed beneath a furrowed brow, remained fixed in their direction. His fingers pressed firmly into his biceps, as if bracing himself against the tide of memory rising within. A long sigh slipped from between clenched teeth, a disciplined containment. Then, with composed control, one arm lifted—a finger rotating in a slow circle near his chest, a silent cue only he could give. The gesture, restrained but unmistakable, set the projection in motion once more.

Mist curled upward in thick ribbons, spreading outward in heavy, undulating vines. It unspooled from the left side of Visha's elevated image, spilling across the scene and settling before the gathered crowd. Within the deepening field of memory, new forms began to surface—emerging not as fragments, but as additions, rendered with eerie clarity as the next sequence locked into place.

At the center of the hall, beyond the line of suitors, in a space where shadows dared not linger, a light bloomed. From its glare emerged a figure —lanky, skeletal—a man barely held together by skin and bone. He stood utterly motionless, head bowed, exuding a wrongness so profound it rippled through the throne room. A blindfold of deep crimson wrapped across his eyeline, stark against his pallid skin. The nobles stood frozen, their disbelief spreading through the room like a tide too heavy to resist.

Daxler adjusted his posture in the seat, uttering, "Is that a fuckin' projector? There's not supposed to be any quintessence like that left." His gaze flicked to Diesel, seeking confirmation.

Diesel, already perched on the edge of his seat, elbows braced on his knees. "Well, I'll be fuckin' damned to hell," he murmured. "Now that changes things."

The man remained unnervingly still—like a statue poised to spring to life the moment you looked away. The deep crimson fabric across his face concealed his eyelids, which had been cut away, leaving only exposed, unblinking orbs resting in hollow sockets. One of the guards stepped forward, hesitant, as though afraid to disturb the fragile balance of something sacred—*or cursed.* His fingers trembled as he grasped the cloth and pulled it free. The moment it slipped away, the projection plunged into darkness, huffing out all illumination within the ballroom. Shadows surged, collapsing inward like breath drawn too deep.

In the study, Izayah's quintessence responded—fast and unthinking. A muscle-deep reaction. His shadows spilled outward, swallowing every trace of light. The hearth wavered and sputtered out. Nester's filament dimmed, silenced mid-tilt. Darkness extended along the walls. The candelabras drew cold, snuffing out Missy's warmth—until even that vanished into the swell of him.

It was an all-consuming safeguard—his instinct to contain, to compartmentalize, to lock it all down before the memory could spread too far. And yet, he was the one forcing it to surface. Pulling old threads forward. Knots of pain catching on heartstrings, lodging themselves in the hesitation of sharing. This instantaneous beat of restraint fractured the memory's rhythm—a brief rupture in the rope of quintessence he'd dared to unravel. His body held still, but his breath did not: drawn in short, audible bursts, then forced out through clenched teeth in a low, guttural exhale. This was more than a retelling. It was a transmission. A full-body echo. A truth pulled from marrow. The darkness might have been his armor, but it could not hold everything.

The silence that followed held for just a beat too long—deep, absolute, and untouched by even a flicker of light. The room was still, as though holding its own breath, unsure of how to follow what had just been felt.

And then, gently, Missy responded.

The hearth cracked softly—just one pop of ember, like a thought breaking the surface. A second followed, then a thin curl of flame reappeared, measured and steady. The candelabras whispered back to life, their glow diffused and low, casting a muted warmth that softened the edges of the space. Nester tapped his bulbous head, reigniting a gentle gleam—a smolder that pulsed low and steady. The study held him in this exhaled space—quiet, warm, and sure. Understanding threaded through every beam as Missy *plip-plopped* the floorboards beneath Izayah's booted feet, a quiet nudge from within. Not pushing. Not pulling. Just reminding. *You don't have to disappear into it. You don't have to carry this alone.*

Izayah's hands dropped from the back of his head, arms extending outward in a wide, mindful sweep, as if surrendering something invisible. Then, with a quiet pull, he drew them back in—hands crossing over his chest, pressing into the place where the memory lived deepest. His shadows responded, withdrawing from the edges of the room, shrinking inward until only a faint trace clung at the heels of his boots. The darkness didn't vanish—it settled. And in that stillness, he gave in to the reminder Missy had whispered through the bones of the house.

The projection stirred—soft at first—a giving back, a movement renewed, a continuation of raw release.

Light did not flash. It didn't suddenly reveal. *It crept,* flowing from the crystallized floor at the base of the dais and sliding outward across the marble—like moonlight poured through water. It drifted toward the figure of skin and bone at the center, brushing against his feet before climbing. Up gaunt ankles. Along hollowed legs. Crawling past the jagged rise of ribs until it reached his face—nothing to veil it now. Just the pale orbs of his eyes, fogged and unfocused, as if sight had long since unraveled. From that deadened gaze, strands of living quintessence began to rise—hazed and spectral, like smoke drawn from a wound too deep to close.

As if stirred by the same spectral current, the High Priestess's arm lifted —disturbingly elegant, beautifully wrong—guiding the room's attention toward the portrait frame beside her throne. Its surface, inky and lightless, began to alter. Not with color, but a hushed bleed, like ink through parchment—moonlight and memory seeping outward in soft saturation. Runa's image whispered into flesh, not all at once, but in increments. A shoulder. The curve of her cheek. The sweep of her neck. Each detail softened into existence as though the frame itself exhaled her into the room.

There she stood—petite, as she'd always been. But nothing about her read as gentle. She was sharpened now, like a rough-cut diamond forged under pressure—still the same shape, yet edged in something more brittle, more dangerous. Shards of glass, barely contained. The space around her bent in unnatural ways, as if even the light wasn't sure how to land. A paradox made flesh—what once was softness now carried the quiet precision of threat. She was a war between light and dark in the shape of a woman. And her gown—the way it breathed with shadow—left no doubt which side was winning. Jeweled with intricacy, its threads looked spun from despair itself—an enigmatic weave that distorted the projection's moonlit incandescence. The fabric toyed with the quintessence around her, ebbing like the final shimmer of a dying star. The blackness of her garment consumed every glint that dared come near, swallowing it whole and leaving behind an oppressive absence.

Her hair, pulled back into severe, unforgiving braids, evoked the poised threat of a whip—precise and methodical. Once luminous, Runa's skin had dulled to a chalky pallor, like weathered stone stripped of its brilliance.

"Well fuckin' hell…that's a different look," Daxler muttered. "If that's not death dipped in diamonds, I don't know what is."

Izayah didn't move. Arms still crossed, shoulders taut, he held the silence for a beat too long. Then came the exhale—slow, pressed through grit teeth—as his hands dragged down his face, fingers pausing at his eyes. He breathed into his palms. Then lowered them, rubbed them together once—twice—before his voice found its way out, frayed and cracking. "Her eyes..." The words barely landed. "No light. No reflection. Just... nothing. They weren't tired, or distant. Just hollow. Empty in a way that felt infinite—like staring into a void that could pull you under and never let go."

He turned at last. His hands met at the heels, pressing and circling with a steady rhythm, as if friction alone could pull the right words free. A muscle-deep reminder to keep letting go. To not compartmentalize. Not this time. His steps moved forward, slow and grounded—but his gaze never truly lifted. Fixed at a low angle in front of him, he stared past the room, past the table, anchoring his vision just enough to function, but not enough to feel. "Visha never took her eyes off me," Izayah said, his voice held steady by force of will. "Every move I made, every breath I took—the High Priestess studied me. Not the court. Not the spectacle. *Me.*" His tone sharpened, scraping raw. The bitterness didn't just bleed—it spread, smeared across the table like a bruised confession. "I believe the High Priestess was waiting to see what would break me first—Visha, herself, or the weapon she came loaded with." He stopped at the table, gaze narrowing. "At the time, I assumed it was contempt. For the decision I made...for walking away from Shadow City's throne."

He cleared his throat, forcing the words forward. "I didn't challenge Zane to the death. I didn't fight for the right to lead Shadow City. I stepped aside. I chose the Shadow Guard Elite—the military, the battlefield—over the throne. I chose to be a protector, *not a ruler.*" His voice dropped, thicker now, heavier. "*To them...to her...*that wasn't strength. It wasn't honor. It was weakness. *A coward's choice.* A decision that turned me into something despicable in their eyes. Someone to loathe—for walking away from what they believed *I should've been.* A leader who could unify Sanctuary and Shadow City."

He crouched down, reaching for the edge of the coffee table. "I just stared at her," he said, fingers curling along the cusp so tightly the blood drained from his knuckles. "It was as if the space that once held light now held only ash." Across from him, Runa's illusion hovered—weightless, unmoved. "I kept searching for the part of her that used to radiate…that childlike gleam." His voice tightened, cracking at the edges. "It was like someone flipped a switch and took everything with them. No matter how many times I tried to piece it together, it just felt off." He swallowed hard. "Then Sienna saw it for what it really was. And Rayanna, the moment she stepped into Sanctuary, perceived something else entirely. Both were true. Both were different." A pause. His mouth opened, then closed again. When he finally spoke, his voice was quieter—almost reluctant. "It all feels like a jumble of notions pressed too tightly together."

"That's how memory operates—fractured and out of order." Diesel inhaled slowly, then exhaled with the weight of hard-earned experience. "With a Seer or a Truth Seeker, you don't just watch it—you sort it. The timeline's the first thing we fix—and we'll get there." Nester, silent until now, hopped down from his perch and promptly bounced back up to the armrest, a tiny clipboard in hand. As he began scribbling with brisk, efficient strokes, the filament in his bulbous head chattered with a rhythmic pulse—flaring and dimming in a conversation only Diesel could follow. The general gave a nod. "Nester reports we've got sharp eyes covering every angle—for you, for Runa, and for the girls. From what I've seen, that holds." He leaned back into his chair, elbows pressed into the armrests, hands splayed, palms skyward. Then, with a subtle dip of his head—a motion somewhere between reverence and promise—he added, "And when they rise fully from being bound…" His voice trailed off, the rest unspoken but understood: a salute to the strength still forming, to the ones not yet returned.

Izayah nodded once—tight, precise—before continuing, "This Dawning Day wasn't…for Runa. Or maybe it was. I'm still struggling with that part of it all," his voice dipped back into the well of bitterness. "It was a public form of shame for me, and at the time…it's what broke me." His gaze remained locked on the figure of Runa, now fully formed, poised in unnerving stillness. A subtle twist of his wrist brought her image to the forefront of the display. Angular features sharpened, the hollowed shadows in her cheeks amplifying the severity of her presence. Every detail—every motion—felt intentional, a chillingly vivid recreation of that moment, branded into his mind. "I see it now…a testament to the depth of Visha's calculated cruelty." His shoulders tensed, knuckles digging deeper into the wood as he crouched lower, shadows clinging to him like an extension of his fraying control. He pushed the frame back outward. "This is the part that I got lost in," he uttered. "The part that felt—and still feels—more like spider webbing than anything else."

Runa's figure rose more fully within the rendering, stiff and unnatural, like a marionette pulled by invisible strings. Her hollow gaze swept the room, sharp and unforgiving, daring every soul to meet her eyes before settling on Izayah's small form within the projection. When she spoke, her tone was ice—calculated and dripping with disgust. "I simply pity you," her image spat. "You have chosen to be a weapon. Nothing more." She scoffed. *"Tethering to you?* Now that's a *fucking insult.* What a...vile, tragic...*fucking joke."* She leaned forward, propping her chin in her hand. "Look at you—pathetic. *Silent.* Of course *you are,"* she sneered, lifting her chin higher. "Nothing to offer? What could you possibly utter that... really...would matter *now?"*

"This one?" Visha purred, syrup-sweet and suffocating. A languid hand glided up the length of her throat, fingertips brushing beneath her chin before her lips curved into a sinister knowing smile. Her attention never left Izayah, not for a second, yet her presence swelled, bleeding outward like spilled wine, staining every corner of the room with cruel intent. The laugh died on her lips. Her fingers curled near her mouth like a serpent tightening around prey, dragging the silence with them—long and disciplined, like nails raking over wood. "He also happens to *be...*" she paused, hand slithering downward as if discarding the thought entirely, her voice sinking into a velvety hush, *"your* half-brother."

The words sat there, thick as tar, oppressive in their gradual descent. A faint gasp stirred through the blurred ranks of assembled spectators, their collective shock shivering like wind across a dying flame. The High Priestess hummed softly—predatory satisfaction dripping as she eased back into her seat, movement fluid and feline. *"Hmm.* But that's a story *for another day,"* she mused, a quiet breath hissing past her lips, "How utterly...*mortifying."* The final word slithered from her tongue and coiled around the dais like smoke, deliberate and damning. *"Tsk.* All that potential...wasted on conscience. What a bore." She waved a hand, lazy and dismissive, as if shooing away a nuisance. *"You've played your part.* There's *nothing left* here for you but *shame."*

Runa's expression twitched—an erosion of hollow indifference giving way to something darker. Yet beneath it, a flicker of confusion pulsed: her chin lifted, lips parting as if to speak, but no words came—only the tremor of breath.

The study seemed to absorb the silence, the moment pulled taut as if the room, the crowd, and the memory itself were holding a single, collective inhale.

Then, as if on cue, she recoiled—as though the notion had finally hit, sudden and jarring. *"My, what?"* she hissed.

Visha's laugh was haunting, and died as quickly as it began. "A weapon that weeps *is not worth my time*—it is rotting flesh. It's, *failure incarnate.* Something to be *discarded, forgotten, and burned."* Her voice dropped lower, colder—each word a cruel whisper laced with the chill of utter finality. "You are *nothing.* You are less than nothing. *Garbage. Filth.* The kind that stains even the hands that touch it. And yet *here you* stand, clinging to scraps as if they'll make you whole. *How pitiable. How laughable."*

"Fuckin' A," Izayah's voice broke. "In front of everyone. Nothing but scraps for them to feed on—*to mock."* He drew in a sharp, labored breath, letting it out in shallow pieces as he got up and pushed away. "I just stood there. Couldn't make sense of it. This wasn't the Runa we grew up knowing—" He stalled, voice catching. "...the one who ran through fields, laughing, spinning stories." He raised a hand, dragging it down his jaw, pressing into the tight muscle like he could knead the tension free. His head tilted back, eyes fixed on the ceiling as if the beams might hold an answer. "That wasn't her, *was it?"* His shoulders sagged, tugging at the fraying edges of his sanity. "The laughter started gradually. At first, just a few snickers—like no one knew what the hell to do with it. But then it spread, swelling until it felt like the entire hall was overjoyed with whatever the fuck that moment was. Their faces don't really matter. *But that sound*...that sound never left."

Within the study's space, the exposed beams dimmed, grayness pooling above like the first whispers of a storm. Tiny droplets began to form—soft, shimmering sprinkles that never quite touched down. Their gentle patter filled the room like a quiet rhythm of grief made visible. Missy's tears hissed as they touched the flames in the hearth, sending up faint, curling wisps of steam, absorbing it all, aching in tune with him. And then, as if to offer comfort in the language she knew best, mugs of cocoa appeared on the table—each one perfectly warm, crowned with a dollop of whipped cream teetering like a cloud, ready to be caught before it floated away.

Diesel reached for the mug that had settled near the edge of the coffee table, drawing it toward him without breaking his gaze. The other hand lifted, fingers moving through the air as if plucking a thought from the fog —catching something fragile, then tucking it away, a silent gesture of respect. He didn't speak at first. Just sat with the heaviness, letting it land. Then, he wrapped his hands around the mug, the warmth grounding him. "Memory's personal. Truth isn't—and it doesn't usually land softly," he said, voice low. "Truth Seekers don't dig to soothe. We dig to understand. To clarify. And more often than not, what we uncover looks nothing like the memory."

The projection zoomed out, trailing his miniaturized figure as it wove through a sea of faceless bodies. He moved with rigid grace—head held high, shoulders squared, every step exact. Not pride. Not defiance. *Just discipline.*

In the study, Izayah's voice cut through the murmur of hazed droplets. "I didn't look back," he said, steady as steel. "If I had, I would've broken. So I kept my chin up. I kept walking. Because that was all I had left." He paused, jaw tightening. "I mean...*fuck*. What was I supposed to do?" The projection tracked his smaller form as it slipped between blurred silhouettes like a ghost severed from its own name. "My mind went blank," he murmured. *"Just...blank."* The memory that he cast, clung to him— haunted, restrained, directionless. "The laughter followed. Chased me down the hall, echoing off the walls—haunting the place I'd just left behind." His voice dropped. "Whether it was real...or carefully orchestrated...it didn't matter. Still doesn't, really."

The recollection began to disintegrate, its spectral fibers thinning as the tabletop wavered. A soft quail of light swept across the surface—fast, exact —rotating a full circle with the cold precision of a blade locking into place. A new scene bloomed: the horse's quarters. His miniaturized figure stood near the entryway, posture rigid, as stablehands approached with his mount. The city's royal advisors materialized in the doorway—silent and sudden—as if they'd been waiting there all along, an ornate scroll in hand. Izayah blinked hard across both timelines. "And then...their proof." His voice thinned. "A royal-declared birth certificate. Pristine. Sealed with Sanctuary's crest." He turned his back to the younger version of himself, and his next words strained at the seams. "I stared straight at the top. Ezekiel. Nadine. Not Visha. Their names. Zane, our mother's name was there. Clear as day. No confusion. No mistake."

His pacing resumed boots brushing faintly against the floor. "They called it *evidence*. Said it explained her rejection. Justified *everything*." He came to a halt in the same quiet spot—his gaze distant, heavy, cutting straight through the space where the girls stood now, unseen. "That was it. Their grand answer. Why I didn't deserve her—their words, not mine." His jaw flexed. "And let's be honest…I mean, *I'm her—was—*" He faltered, the words collapsing on his tongue. "I was told I was her *fucking* half-brother." His voice cracked—bitter, hollow. "And at the time…nothing. No words. I—" He exhaled. "I just stood there, holding a piece of paper. Gutted. Raw. *Utterly lost.*" He blinked hard once more. "For the first time in my life, the one thing I hoped for—" A sharp breath snagged in his throat. "The one person I thought would get me." He shook his head, sharp. "But that didn't even matter anymore. She couldn't get me. *She's my half-sister.*" His voice broke again, more disbelief than rage. "*What? Well, I—I—I—I* couldn't stay. Not after that."

The projection shuttered back at him—seamless and unrelenting—as the image of a miniaturized Izayah blinked into view on horseback, tearing across the winding path beneath the canopy of the Dark Forest. His cloak snapped with each stride, the horse's hooves kicking up damp soil as light struggled to reach through the overgrown tangle above. The trees here had long since swallowed what remained of fire scars—thick roots curling over blackened stone, trunks rebuilt around ruin. Towns emerged and fell away in a blur—some carved directly into the ancient trees, doorways and windows flickering past like watching eyes; others nestled at the base, wrapped in moss and root, while a few climbed impossibly high into the canopy, their bridges stretched tight between swaying limbs like veins pulsing through the forest's skin. None of them slowed him. The wind rolled with him, carrying the scent of loam and smoke and distant fires never fully extinguished. Lanternlight shimmered in pockets, momentary warmth swallowed by the forest's breath. He didn't turn. Didn't pause. The trees thinned only at the final stretch, giving way to a massive archway of stone and blackened wood—gothic, towering, carved with faces worn smooth by centuries of rain. The royal gates of Shadow City loomed ahead, already beginning to part, languid and groaning, as if sensing what approached. Guards stood at attention, expressionless, but the weight of what he carried was already pressing ahead of him—announcing itself long before he crossed the threshold.

As he passed through the gates, the fog surged upon the display—thick, unnatural—curling into hoofprints that had long since faded. The projection dimmed, warped, and then dropped out the bottom of the table like a floor giving way, revealing a new space: stone walls, iron hooks, and the unmistakable scent of damp leather—gothic stable stead. "So I packed my things," he said, his voice steady, "right after Zane caught up with me." The projection showed his miniature self moving with practiced efficiency —changing clothes, tossing a satchel aside, descending the stone steps into the lower levels of the keep. "We talked. Briefly. Then I went down to saddle my horse. Got ready to leave." He exhaled, gaze flicking back to the display. "By the time I reached the stables of Shadow City, my own guards were already whispering. No one said anything—not directly—but the hush when I passed? The glances?" He looked up. "They knew." Izayah's shoulders sagged, his hands within the projection working furiously to tighten the saddle straps, as his voice sharpened in the room around them. "They tried to act like they didn't care. Like it was just another day. Just another task. But the questions were there—in their eyes, in the way they avoided mine. I was their lord. And now…I was something else. Something they didn't understand. Something they pitied." He paused, his voice slipping into a whisper, tight and raw. "And as I mounted that horse, with every hoofbeat that carried me farther from Sanctuary, the laughter followed. It wasn't just laughter—it was hunger. Dark. Alive. It bit into me —sharp, unrelenting—tearing away pieces I didn't even know I could lose. Even when I passed back through the gates, it stayed with me. Not just in my ears…but deeper. Buried. Waiting. *Festering*."

He exhaled sharply, bitterness slicing through his words like shards of broken glass splintering in his hands. "And like a *fuckin' fool*, I left. She just *baited* the *fuckin' trap* and watched me walk straight into it. What a fucking deception. For years I believed it. *FUCKIN'* owned it. Let it shape me— define me—and worse, I let it define *our mother's memory*." He shook his head, voice unraveling. "God, this is stupid. I thought she was my sister. Like…I really believed that. But this is the thing—deep down, it never sat right. In my gut, it just felt *off*. And I can't believe I'm still talking about this. I didn't want to have this conversation. Never did. I'm glad I did—but I didn't want to. Not really." His voice thinned. "Through my eyes. Through my own damn *fuckin' perceptions*…she used me." His jaw clenched. *"FUCK!"*

The projection stuttered, the image warping in brief pulses as if the memory itself resisted letting go. Izayah had already turned away from the vision before it fractured, his breath still uneven, but the tightness in his shoulders had begun to loosen—just barely. Not ease. Not comfort. Something quieter. Resignation, maybe. The kind that settles in the bones once the words have finally been spoken. He blinked once, hard, as if to clear the last remnants of what still clung to him, his jaw working in silence. The air in the room altered, no longer caught in the pull of the past, but hovering on the edge of whatever might come next.

"I had this gut feeling it wasn't gone," Izayah said plainly. "What you saw today, Dax—that's the version I thought I'd lost. But Ray…our *amazing* ray of sunshine saw her differently. She got Runa to the cabin—don't know how, but she did." A faint smile tugged at the corner of his mouth. "Leave it to our little Ray…*huh.*"

Zane bobbed his head, "Leave it to *that* mastermind."

Izayah's smile faded, silence curling back into the space between them. The fire crackled. Mist veiled the windows, descending in a reverent stream—Missy's way of quietly listening. The echo of heartbreak held steady as he pressed on. "Those letters…" He exhaled through his nose. "Every…*every fucking letter.*" He let his eyes fall shut for a beat, one hand bracing his chin as he stood there—staring into the corner, speaking as if it were the only place that might understand. "I never wrote her back. All those letters she sent…" He swallowed hard, eyes dropping to the floorboards as tears began to well. "Every one of them broke my heart. Because how the hell do you write her back? What do I say—'I'm your half-brother'? How do I talk to her? *How am I not despicable? Why the fuck* does she keep reaching out?" His voice sharpened, brittle. "Hell if I could figure it out. And still, I wasn't writing her. Everybody was already talking. And she…she denied me. Or so I fucking thought." His jaw tightened. "Yet I still clung to them. I reread every single word a thousand times." His hand swiped across his face. "I cherished them, but what did I have to give back? NOTHING. I had *simply* nothing. I—" He faltered, then flung a hand out. "And then Sienna…" The words snagged in his throat. "Then Sienna, on top of everything else, tells us what was really there. Tells us *why* they were written in red—**FUCKING ink.**" His breath came shallow now, like each gasp punched him from the inside. "They were written in *Runa's own fucking blood.*" He flung his hands out to either side. *"How do I fucking miss that? What is wrong with me?"* The scream cut through the quiet. "How do I fucking MISS that?" His voice climbed, ragged with fury, as he spun back toward the heart of the study. "How is it that I can run drills, lead field missions, do the dirtiest shit in the military—and *miss BLOOD* on a *fucking letter I've read a thousand fucking times?"* His voice broke again, quieter now. "How do I miss that?" He drew in a breath. "Because I fucking chose to." His next words fell low and raw. "I was so wrapped up in *my own fucking ego…*I missed it. *Fuck me."* He rubbed one eye with the back of his hand. *"Fuck me and my nonsense."* His chest rose, then fell—long and hard—as if the final intake was a blade drawn from his own back.

Izayah looked to each grim face. There was a sadness in their eyes—one he didn't have the strength to name. Then he froze—dropped into a crouch as if the weight of it all had finally pulled him down. The anguish surged, raw and uncontainable, as he roared, *"IN HER OWN FUCKING BLOOD!"* The words didn't just echo—they detonated. They cracked through the study like lightning through bone, sharp enough to rattle the walls, violent enough to tear the air from the room. A wound laid bare, bleeding heat and fury, too big for language and too brutal for silence. The whole fucking sky inside him split open, and the pain came roaring out—ugly, raw, volcanic. Even Missy stilled. The mist recoiled mid-air, droplets suspended as if the house itself flinched from the force of it, backing away from the violence now loose in the room. "I am such a *FUCKING asshole,*" he spat, "falling for Visha's illusions!" His hands loosened slightly, but tension rippled through him, vibrating through the space like an uncoiled spring. "And now, knowing it was all a game—she crafted this entire farce…*for what?"* His jaw clenched, his voice dipping into something raw and fractured. "It feels worse. *So much worse."* The fight drained from his voice, leaving only ash behind. "Day in and day out, reading and rereading each note." His body sank lower, shoulders caving. "Sitting at the North Star," he uttered, "a cup of coffee in hand…not thinking anything of it." He whispered, "This town was built on sacrifice—and hers is buried in its bones, right beside mine." A low hum rumbled from his chest, guttural and spent. "That's humbling. And I don't have the right to say that—not really—because I don't know." He swallowed. "What I do know is…every stone, every step, was shaped by what we gave together. Just differently." His head dropped, completely bowed, as if the notions themselves had taken what little strength he had left. "*Gods.* What she's been through." Silence wrapped the room. "I had no clue. I had no—*fucking clue.*" He inhaled, deep and trembling, then let it go —long and low. "But I'm ready to find out."

Chapter Twenty-Six

The weight of Izayah's outburst clung to the room like smoke that refused to dissipate. Faces hardened—stone still, jaws slack—scrutinizing, yet silent. A stillness settled that no one dared disturb. Izayah remained crouched, gaze locked to the floorboards, shoulders sunken, his body the brittle remains of a bridge long buckling under the burden of everything left unsaid. The fracture hadn't just opened—it had poured out of him, unstoppable, staining the air with grief too vast to name.

"I missed it—all of it. I took the damn bait. Truth was right there, and I walked straight past it. I let myself go deliberately deaf—and got blind-sided. Should've felt it. Should've known." A harsh, jagged breath tore free as his hands dragged from temple to jaw in a punishing sweep. Rising, he traced the strain like a map, reorienting himself to the space between him and the wet bar.

Missy responded not with warmth, but with a tentative nudge, guiding Izayah one step closer to the others. Quiet. Intentional. A friend urging him to lean, just a little, on those holding space for the rawness of it all.

"Damn near rewrote who I was. Not overnight, but close," Izayah said, the words dragging as if each one cost something to admit. "Holding on to those letters…it wasn't about hope. It was just…*all I had.* I didn't even know when they started arriving. Thought they were delayed. Thought maybe they were just catching up with me. I didn't ask questions—*I didn't want to ask* questions. I just read them. Over and over." He moved across the room, his breath catching under the ache of it all as he came to Zane's chair, resting his forearm across the back, elbow bent, body leaning into it like the words themselves had nowhere else to land. "And I know we have to get the timeline right—But in my head, the timeline's a fucking disaster. Nothing makes sense. And I guess that's what I've been doing—just trying to pull threads, find patterns, some version of the truth that feels like it could be right. Even when none of it lines up." His gaze flicked upward, but his focus was elsewhere—distant, like he was speaking to the memory of her more than to anyone in the room. "At the time, my headspace took to her words, her dreams…and carved them into every stone in this place. It's what I could do. I figured, if I could build her hopes into the bones of this town—*this haven*—then maybe, somehow, it would help. Maybe her. Maybe me. I don't know." A bitter sigh escaped, half a laugh and half a fracture. "I'm not trying to sound like I've figured anything out. I haven't. I'm just…" He dragged a hand down his face. "Fuck, man. I'm just trying to navigate."

"Well, for starters," Daxler downed the rest of his cocoa and set the mug on the edge of the coffee table, bracing his elbows onto his knees. "*Professional Nutcase* told you Runa was your sister?" His stare honed in, razor-sharp. "I'd have bailed too. That's a low blow, even for Visha. Hell, even a saint would've bolted. Only move you had left was to walk." He huffed, trying to shake the sheer absurdity of it loose. "Shit—man." He tossed a pointed question in Izayah's direction, his tone edged with curiosity and lingering outrage. "Those Treefall perimeter drills—they flagged you because of this shit?"

"Yeah. Something like that." Izayah clicked his tongue against his cheek, his jaw tightening. "You got caught in the crossfire. You were collateral because someone told them I was chasing my own damn sister. I never understood why you didn't do the same."

"Well, because I'm not an asshole," Daxler said, throwing a hand toward Diesel. "Now, have I heard the whispers among units? Sure.

There's a reason I had that conversation with the General. But I saw you for who you are. And you think I give a damn about any of that?" His voice sharpened. "No regrets, Zay. None. But for fuck's sake…" He exhaled, a grim smile sliding in. "At least you're not boring, huh? 'Almost courted your own sister'—definitely not a story for the grandkids, but shit, it's one hell of a conversation starter." He massaged the nape of his neck as he made his way to the spiral staircase to the left of the hearth. His jaw adjusted, tight and silent, before a low utterance escaped him: "Fuck…" Head in his hands, debating a thousand silent points he wouldn't speak aloud.

Izayah turned his back on the group, striding toward the far corner where the females observed. Their translucent forms shimmered as he passed through them. Ashla giggled softly. "It never fails to feel like a thousand fireflies dancing under my skin."

"This is fucking brutal," he muttered, voice tight with frustration as he crossed to the nearest shelf, fingers trailing along the book bindings as if searching for something specific—or simply something to anchor him. "I should've listened, Zane." His voice cracked, the edges frayed and uneven. "I should've *fucking* listened." Izayah's obsidian boots scuffed across the floor. He shoved a fist deep into his pocket, tension coiling through his frame like a wire drawn too tight. "Might as well get it all out now," he spat. "Truth is, I never gave much thought to the union between the cities —at least not until Zane brought it up so long ago." He hesitated. "It still feels so surreal. Are *you sure* she isn't our sister?" Izayah glanced between his older brother and Daxler, anguish carved deep across his features.

Zane exhaled. "I tried to get you to stay," he said, his voice calm but weighted. As he clasped his hands loosely in front of him, the leather vest he wore flexed faintly, layered over a forest-green shirt open at the collar— its fabric flexing faintly with the movement, like even his clothes were carrying the weight of memory. "I get why you didn't want me involved," he continued, the clean lines of his shaved scalp framing the dark braid that ran back from the crown of his head. His eyes fixed on his knuckles. "But yeah…I'm certain she isn't our sister. Ma and I talked about it before she passed." He ran a hand along the side of his head. "It wasn't like her to share something like that, but I think she was wrestling with it. I must've been…I don't know, fifteen? Seventeen? It was before my Dawning Day.

We were sitting at the table—just a normal breakfast—and out of nowhere, she starts talking about The Lands, the quintessence, how things were changing. And then she tells me about Runa. About being a surrogate. She said Father had his reservations, but once Ma set her mind to something…" His voice softened, almost reverent. "Nothing could stop her. She believed it would help Ezekiel. That it would mend the rift between Sanctuary and Shadow City. That something better could come from it—for the people, for the Land. You know that's Ma in a nutshell." He pulled back slightly, running his thumb along the seam of his vest. "*Gods*, I wish you could hear it from her. But I promise you, brother—Runa is very much not our sister."

"Listen, Zay—you didn't miss out on anything, because High Priestess Nutcase is full of shit," Daxler stated. "Simply put, the truth always surfaces. And lucky for us, we've got one of the last Truth Seekers still kicking." He tipped his chin toward Diesel. "But what really puts the frosting on the cake?" Leaning back with a smirk, he stretched his arms wide, claiming the space like he owned it. "The General's officially on babysitting duty for your sister, who'll probably dig up half the planet once she's back on her feet. 'Cause if she's anything like you lot"—he gestured around the room with exaggerated flair—"she's gonna be itching to get shit done."

"Izayah, sit." Diesel cleared his throat as Izayah's hand stilled on the worn spine. "I believe I can shed some light on High Lady Nadine and the surrogacy," he stated. "Let me lay out exactly how we got here." He ran a hand through his peppered hair. "You need to understand this part. It's not just about clearing up your confusion, Izayah—though that's valid and important. You don't move on a target without clarity first and I have that for you. It'll help you focus your drive. Your fury." He raised a finger. "And for the record, she is not your sister. This'll clear some of that fog." He lifted the empty cocoa mug gingerly, holding it aloft just long enough for Missy to whisk it away without a sound. Then he steepled his fingertips with quiet readiness, expectant of follow-through.

Izayah moved across the space and took a seat on the leathered couch, throwing one ankle over his knee, pressing into the conversation. Diesel bobbed his head; his emerald eyes darkened as he continued, "But more than that, this ties directly to what's coming. Sanctuary isn't just a place—

it's a web of secrets and deceptions. Untangling this is the first step, I believe, to unraveling everything else waiting for us." He paused, his expression hardening like armor being fastened into place—a silent declaration of resolve. "Visha's last pregnancy—Tabytha and Layla—was carefully monitored. Watched around the clock. Myself, Ezekiel, even a chambermaid—we rotated shifts, ensuring someone was always present. I'm certain that vigilance is the only reason the twins survived her."

Diesel rose from the deep green velvet chair with quiet intention, crossing to the wet bar tucked along the far wall. He reached for a glass, poured a modest stream of whiskey, and shaved in a sliver of cinnamon bark—his movements, ritualistic, as if honoring something heavier than thirst. With the drink in hand, he made his way to the hearth, settling into the narrow crevice between the mantel and the nearest bookcase. One bicep rested along the carved wood, the other hand cradling the glass, its amber contents catching the firelight. He crossed one ankle over the other —relaxed in form, but not in spirit. "As you know," he began, "Father Ezekiel and I shared a bond similar to the one you have with Dax. But ours was forged in childhood—something different, something deeper in its own way. He wasn't just a leader. Ezekiel was my mentor, my guide, my brother in all but blood. He faced problems head-on, his judgment clear and unclouded by ego. Ezekiel believed in unity and the strength that comes from trust. After the Great War, when the territories were divided, that trust became a cornerstone of his role. Sanctuary and the revered 'Tree of Life' became his charge—a responsibility laced with its own shadows, its own web of secrets—and dangers."

Diesel stared into the fire, the flames licking at the grate with restless hunger, their light glinting in his eyes like a storm brewing on the horizon —the fire twisting and writhing like the memories he didn't want to touch but couldn't avoid. "After King Moros fell, there was a moment—a crucial one—when a committee was formed. Their task was monumental: to unite the fractured territories, give survivors a path forward, and rebuild even a fragment of what had been lost." He paused, "They weren't just rebuilding; they were reshaping. The mission wasn't just about giving people back their lives—it was about deciding who would lead them. Who could be trusted to make the hard decisions, the right ones. It was about finding leaders who could carry the burden without breaking beneath it."

Diesel cleared his throat, the sound gritty—like gravel grinding in the pit of a dry well. He pushed away from the mantel, needing to settle deeper into the information, and lowered himself back into the hefty velvet cushions. "We'd talk late into the night," he said, his voice roughened by thought. "And every time Visha's name came up, it was like someone cracked open a window in the dead of winter. The warmth in the room disappeared, leaving only the chill—and the quiet that said too much." He pitched forward, elbows resting on his knees, fingers locked tight as though bracing against something vast and formless. "Ezekiel felt it too. He didn't say much—it was all in his posture. The way he'd sit back, his eyes tracking the corners of every space she occupied, like he was waiting for something to emerge from the shadows." A muscle flickered at his jaw. "Her name didn't just linger—it moved. It crept." Diesel's knuckles paled against the crystal as he tightened his grip around the whiskey glass. The silence that followed was heavy and raw, until he finally looked up. "Izayah," he said, his voice low and steady, "back then, I was still finding my way as General—just like you are now. And I missed things. Crucial things. I've had to carry that ever since."

On the edge of the vision, Ashla's translucent form gleamed with a liquid, holographic sheen as she tugged on the tether linking the group of female observers. "Come on, sit with me!" she whispered, her voice hushed yet brimming with childlike excitement. She looked to each of them before lowering herself gracefully to the floor, folding into a cross-legged seat. The others followed with reluctant hesitation, their descent marked by stiff motions and quiet huffs of frustration."This is getting so good," she added, casting an expectant look at the group.

Layla, seated directly beside her, shot Ashla a sharp glance. "It's not exactly a bedtime story," she said dryly. "This isn't a cozy read—it's a goddamn mess."

Ashla shrugged, airy and unbothered—bright-eyed and bushy-tailed as the tale spun on. "You'll see. It's one of those stories that twists first, settles later—and the sideways parts?" Her voice dropped to a conspiratorial whisper. "Always the best."

She *kerplunked* her chin on her free hand and added, "Besides, it's like watching an epic tale unfold. Doesn't mean I'm rooting for the bad guys."

Layla sighed heavily, slurped at her blueberry fizz, then muttered, "Just try not to enjoy the trainwreck too much, okay?" Her expression tightened, bracing for more.

Diesel stared into the fire, his gaze distant and fixed. He took a pull of whiskey, letting the burn settle as though it were a part of him. "Visha has her ways," he said quietly, "and she's good at what she does. Even as a Truth Teller, there wasn't much I could see through her hazed shadow."

Ashla leaned in slightly, despite Layla's protests. *"See? This is where it gets twisted,"* she whispered.

Layla frowned. "Great. Let me know when the doom parade ends," she muttered.

Diesel's fingers pressed against his temple, moving in slow rhythm as if coaxing the pressure from becoming a full-blown ache. "Back then, information wasn't just scarce—it was guarded. Knowledge was a treasure, and books were the map. And there weren't many maps left." His attention pulled toward the scorched coffee table. He leaned in, tracing the burnt edge with a finger—drawn by the familiarity of pain made permanent. "Visha knew how to twist that scarcity—how to turn it into her weapon. And by the time we saw it for what it was…what was done, was done." He paused. "Ezekiel had a gut feeling about her—something he couldn't shake." The rasp in his voice deepened, like steel scraping against stone. "Before the Great War, tethers were common. Not an everyday occurrence —but not rare either. Quintessence back then didn't have the same fractures, the same…distortions. When two energies aligned, it just happened —like a lock snapping shut." He sank back and drained the rest of his glass, setting it down beside him like a period at the end of an idea. "But after the Great War?" He exhaled through his nose, sharp and controlled. "Everything changed. The balance of energy across The Lands shattered. The binding of the Tree of Shadows didn't just alter the flow of quintessence—it fractured it. Made it volatile. What was once natural became almost impossible. And when a tether did happen…" He let the words hang, his lips thinning into a grim line. "It was like lightning striking twice. Undeniable. Powerful."

Diesel's hand curled around the armrest, knuckles paling as the leather creaked beneath his grip. Though his posture remained upright—disciplined—a tautness wound through him, evident in the way his boots pressed firm against the floorboards. "The seers believed these rare tethers were the answer to everything. They thought the bonds would bring back what was lost—that they could restore quintessence to the way it was. Leaders were meant to forge these connections, rebuild what had been broken. But Ezekiel's tether to Visha?" He shook his head. "It wasn't just rare. It felt wrong. And Ezekiel...he felt it, too."

He gestured toward the chair where Zane sat, angled slightly within the group but still parallel to his own. Its darkened cushions, stretched taut from years of use, bore the memory of countless nights spent carving out space for hard conversations —deliberating over decisions too heavy for one man to carry alone. "The last night Ezekiel sat there, he told me something I've never been able to forget. The union between them shouldn't have happened. But their powers aligned perfectly—like two blades forged from the same molten steel. And still, he questioned it. Said her quintessence felt...off. Twisted. Like it had been tampered with." Diesel paused, the fingers of his free hand drumming once against the armrest before going still. "I couldn't prove it. I followed every lead, pulled every thread. But the answers stayed buried. And with most of the Truth Tellers executed after the war, there was no one left to help untangle it."

His shoulders sagged slightly. "Ezekiel believed in my ability to seek truths, yet he always encouraged me to keep it quiet. He'd say, 'I just have this weird feeling.'" Diesel rubbed the back of his neck, stalling. "When I was a youngling, a seer from the Valley of Visions stopped me in the Shadow City marketplace. She pulled me into a side street. At first, I thought she was a beggar." His voice lowered, flattening as if he were reading from an old report. "She didn't look like anyone you'd stop to notice at first. She was tall, willowy—but there was a sharpness to her. A resolute way she moved, like she floated just slightly above the ground. Her hair wasn't dulled silver—it was molten moonlight, shimmering as if it had a life of its own, spilling out from beneath a deep blue hood that veiled most of her face."

He drew forward, elbows braced on his knees, while Nester scuttled up to collect the glass—whether out of boredom or timing, it was hard to tell. Diesel didn't acknowledge the interruption. "The seer's robes were patchwork—layers of fabric that didn't match, but somehow felt intentional. Like they didn't belong to any one place or time. It was as if she wore pieces of forgotten history, and it weighed on her." His gaze dropped, firelight guttering across his features as though he were seeing her again through the flames. "Then she looked right at me. It wasn't something I was ready for." He expelled a harsh breath. "Her eyes…they were enormous. Silver. But not like her hair—no, they moved. Like smoke caught in a jar. Always shifting. Always watching. And they didn't just look at you— they dug in. Found the places you didn't even realize were there."

His fingers drummed an uneven rhythm against the armrest, the sound faint—like raindrops on windowpanes. His posture remained rigid, back straight against the chair as though bracing for impact—or perhaps holding himself in check. *The war will never truly end*, she had said. And the seer's voice—it hadn't belonged to her. It was too large for her frame, deep and full of something that wasn't entirely human. *Not while shadows walk among us. You are bound by truth, but if you reveal your gift, you will draw attention you cannot survive.*

Diesel slowly extended his palm, fingers loose and upright. Nester, who had been circling quietly on the floor, bounded into the offered hand, then leapt nimbly to the armrest and folded into a cross-legged perch. With a soft hum of purpose, he retrieved the clipboard nestled in the chair's crevice. Diesel didn't glance his way, but his shoulders eased—just slightly —grounded by his presence. Pushing forward, he said, "She grabbed my wrist like she meant to root me in place." His voice had dropped, pitched low. "Her touch didn't feel human—it was ironclad, unrelenting. Like she could've crushed the marrow from my bones if she'd wanted." The chair gave a muted groan as his boots adjusted against the floorboards, a strained exhale slipping free. "*Keep your abilities hidden,*" she told me. "*Until the time comes when it cannot be blanketed anymore. The Lands will need you— but not yet.* And then…she vanished. No sound. No trace. Just gone—like she'd always been made of smoke."

His voice rose slightly. "I didn't speak of it. Not to Ezekiel. Not to anyone. But years later, he told me the same damn thing—said I had to keep my gift hidden, train in secret. Back then, I thought it was about survival. *Now…*" His voice trailed off as he stared into the fire, the flames flickering in his eyes like something alive—something ravenous. "That moment stayed with me," he continued, softer now—almost reverent. "I always wondered about the seer. *Ezekiel knew.* Visha was always a step ahead, weaving her web before any of us realized we were caught.

Twisting reality into truths the world could believe...threading lies so seamlessly they became impossible to untangle." His grip curled around the armrest again, the leather groaning under the strain. He grimaced, dragging a palm across the bristly line of his jaw. "Looking back, I'm not sure about much of anything anymore. But I'm certain of one thing—she'd already started the game, and the rest of us were too blind to see it."

A breath caught in the memory's weave, stuttering it into silence—just for a moment—before a wisp of a titter stirred and tugged at the heartstrings tethering the females. "How can you not feel it?" Ashla's tone carried a lilting excitement, like a bird chirping at dawn. "It's exhilarating —don't you see? The twists, the webs, the why of it all—it's like standing on the edge of something magnificent. Don't you feel it?"

Layla groaned. "Magnificent?" Her voice edged with exasperation. "Ashla, this isn't some grand adventure in a storybook. This is real. It's not exhilarating—it's a disaster waiting to happen. And trust me, it's already half-happened."

Ashla's smile didn't falter. If anything, it grew softer—almost serene. "Oh, Layla," she said with a gentle shake of her head, as though Layla were the one missing something vital. "Even disasters can be beautiful, in their own way. It's all part of the tapestry." She turned her gaze back toward Diesel, her expression rapt. "And this one? This one is particularly...dazzling."

Layla's mouth twitched, caught between rolling her eyes and outright glaring. "Dazzling? Tapestry? You sound like a poet with a head injury," she said flatly. "This isn't dazzling, Ashla. It's chaos. Dangerous chaos."

Ashla shrugged lightly, still watching Diesel with an almost dreamlike expression. "Chaos has its place too, you know," she murmured. "Sometimes it's the best place to start something extraordinary."

Runa released a long-steeped breath, her cadence snapping through the rising hum of Ashla and Layla's exchange with a calm firmness that didn't need volume to command attention. "Enough," she said—firm yet tender, like the steady current of a river urging everything in its path to follow. "This isn't the time for debates, poetic or otherwise. If we're going to make sense of this, we need to listen."

Ashla's wide eyes blinked, her excitement dimming by the barest shade, as though gently nudged out of a dream. She glanced down, her free hand fiddling absently with the hem of her translucent skirt. "I just meant—"

"I know," Runa interrupted softly, a small, understanding smile tugging at her lips. "But let's save the meaning for later. Right now, we need to focus."

Layla huffed, "Finally, someone with a sense of priority," though she didn't bother hiding the faint smirk at the edge of her mouth.

Runa's smile widened briefly. Her fingers gave a reassuring squeeze to the orb binding them together. The vibration skimmed along their linked connection, and the tiny sphere swirled in response—brushing green and gold against Runa's chest like a cat's purr. *Appreciation?* she wondered fleetingly, before turning forward. Her attention sharpened as Diesel's voice resumed, pulling them back into the heft of his words—and the moment unfolding before them.

"With the resurgence of the Tree of Life and the guidance of the High Seer, the Valley of Visions began to regenerate," he said. "Slowly, The Lands began to awaken with new life—though it came with hesitation." He went quiet for a beat. "That's when the tether happened. During our visits to the Valley, and Sienna—Daxler's mother…"

Daxler's brow tightened as his gaze snapped to Diesel, a mix of caution and disbelief pulling at the set of his jaw.

"Sienna tried to reach Ezekiel and me. To warn us. But her message got lost in the chaos of reconstruction." His jaw locked, as though trying to suppress the memory. "The knowledge she carried was critical—but by the time she understood the tether, the union…" He fell silent for a moment before speaking. "It was too late. The bond was already forged—set in stone."

"Wait—what?" Daxler jerked upright, his voice cutting through the stillness. He didn't move beyond that—his body frozen, disbelief anchoring him in place. "How the hell does that even happen? Ezekiel's ordained in quintessence, and Visha's…" His words trailed off for a second before snapping back, sharp. "A glorified manipulator?"

Diesel's lips pressed into a hard line, his gaze falling to the flames. For a long moment, he said nothing—the room brimming with an uncomfortable silence that didn't break, only stretched. When he finally spoke, his voice carried a grim certainty. "She has her ways," he said. "There's *more to her* than meets the eye. The High Priestess *isn't just anyone.* She is one of *King Moros' daughters.*"

"You've got to be *shittin'* me," Daxler muttered through his fingers.

"Sienna knew better than most what Visha could become," Diesel said, turning to Daxler. "That's why she raised you in the Valley of Visions—to shield you from her influence."

Daxler's brow furrowed, as though trying to piece together a puzzle with missing edges. "My mother mentioned bits and pieces of her childhood, but she never outright stated her sibling's identity."

"Would you?" Izayah's voice cut in, blunt yet calm.

Daxler hesitated, his jaw tightening barely before he nodded. "Fair enough." His eyeline went skyward, as though searching the ceiling might unearth some long-buried truth. "She told me once that she thought about claiming the title of High Seer within the Valley," he mused, the edges of his words mellowing. "But she chose my father instead. She called it a more humble, rewarding, and honorable life." A fragile smile tugged at the corner of his mouth, but it faded almost as quickly as it came—like a shadow retreating in the fog. "What I don't get," he said, rubbing at his eyes as though trying to clear away the confusion clouding his thoughts, "is Visha's endgame here. She's already running the show as High Priestess, so why the hell does she care if Izayah's courting Runa? What's her angle? Does she really need a new hobby?"

Diesel met Daxler's question with a faint smirk, the corners of his mouth pulling tight as though he were chewing on a notion too bitter to swallow.

Daxler's voice lightened, though it was no less pointed. "Wouldn't you want your daughter tied down to someone who's got the guts to kick his own ass when needed?" He paused, letting the words hang, before adding with a faint chuckle, "Might be off my rocker, but there's got to be a chunk of this story we're still missing." He snorted. "She's sitting on top of the world—she's got it all: power, control. So what's her deal? What's she playing at? Is she just stirring the pot for fun, or is there a nasty surprise waiting that we haven't figured out yet?" His boot tapped a steady rhythm against the floor, each thud underscoring his growing irritation.

"That's Visha," Diesel said flatly. "Questions worth asking. That's what this phase of the mission is meant to clarify. There's more coming—we'll address it when operational timing aligns. One thing's certain: The High Priestess is a master of deception. That's why you have to take the fall for what happened at the cabin. The Elite Guards will face their consequences. Your task is to identify her endgame. And for your awareness—I've already spoken with Lord Brannon. The matter is understood."

Daxler's voice cut in, steady and hard-edged. "Yeah, well—last thing we need is a scenic route. Staying on track's critical," he said firmly, his expression unwavering. "The females need time to reach their first phase of renewal—and that won't happen until Runa's Dawning Day. She's the youngest. We don't have the luxury of veering off course now."

Diesel puffed out his cheeks briefly before exhaling. "Sienna mentioned something crucial," he began. "Once Visha thinks she's won, she gets cocky. That's when the fractures start to show—she leaks pieces of the truth. Not to confess. To gloat. It feeds her ego, but it exposes her. That's the weakness. And we use it. When you return to Starlight, Rayanna will be fully unbound. Her Truth Telling will be active—sharpened by training and shaped by everything she's survived. That gives us an edge we haven't had. Truth Seeking was never meant to be solitary. One person can only see so far. Doesn't matter if it's instinct or logic, empathy or analysis— every mind brings a different facet to the table. That's how we catch what's buried. What one person misses, another feels. And Rayanna—she brings something I can't. Intuition. Emotional read. That quiet knowing women carry into a room before anything's said. You don't teach that—it's just there. Add to that the fact she's crossed through two Dawning Days…we don't know how that'll alter her quintessence. Could be it heightens her perception beyond what any of us have seen before. All I know is—she's not coming back the same. And with her at the table, we've finally got a fighting chance at pulling the whole web apart."

Izayah's jaw tightened, his gaze dropping to his boots as he mulled it over. "I don't doubt Ray's abilities," he said. He glanced briefly at Zane before continuing. "That's why we put her with you and Mama D. But what's this all have to do with Runa?" Curiosity, concern, and frustration all balled up into the question. "What truth did Visha twist to make such a believable lie? I need to get inside her head." His hands moved restlessly over his mouth, as though trying to physically sort the chaos of thoughts swirling in his mind.

"There's a lot of backstory to this." A somberness crept into Diesel's features, drawing his brows together. "But I'll give you the abbreviated version."

"Aw, I always hate the short version of anything," Ashla groaned, her shoulders slumping dramatically.

"Shh," Rayanna hissed, pressing a finger firmly to her lips.

"I wouldn't have minded if popcorn was involved," Runa said, her lips curving into a mischievous smile. As if on cue, the faint aroma of buttery popcorn wafted through the air, teasing their senses with an unexpected warmth.

"I see we've officially moved into scent-based telepathy. Neat," Layla muttered with dry amusement, nudging Runa lightly and stifling a chuckle as she lifted her shoulders in a small shrug. "I'm not complaining," she added, her grin lingering as the group's focus pivoted back to Diesel.

"When Ezekiel and Visha formed their bond, it wasn't just rare—it was unprecedented. Like I stated earlier, tethering had become almost unheard of after the Great War, and their connection sparked hope. The expectation was clear: their union would restore balance, reestablish the strength of quintessence, and build a lineage powerful enough to stabilize The Lands." Diesel's voice was deep, as though searching for a memory that had grown distant and faint.

"But every time Visha conceived, the child never survived. Each loss didn't just wound Ezekiel's hope—it carved at his soul, a relentless ache that gnawed at the core of who he was. I watched my brother break—baring it all, each heartbreak deeper than the last. It stripped him down to nothing, but he kept going, clinging to the belief that they were meant to save the future, even as that future slipped further from reach." His grip tightened around the armrest, the leather creaking under the strain.

"Visha, though…she didn't mourn. She didn't grieve. After each loss, she carried on like nothing had happened—cold, detached. There was no sorrow in her. To the High Priestess, such losses were mere inconveniences—disruptions to be managed, not tragedies to be mourned. There was no sorrow in her eyes, no crack in the stillness where grief should've lived—just a frigid focus on her next move, as if each loss were nothing more than a minor setback."

Nester tilted his head, his glow drawing inward, then expanding again

—soft, rhythmic. The subtle rise and fall cast delicate waves across the walls and floor that never quite settled. Diesel exhaled roughly, the sound grating like stone against stone. "Nester wonders if she ever truly mourned," he muttered, bitterness infiltrating his words. "Or if that's just what people wanted to believe. Ezekiel gave her everything he had—tried to be the bond she needed in those moments. Moments that should have broken them both." His breath caught, chest tightening as though the words got lost in his throat.

"I just..." His voice faltered, snagging on knots of buried sorrow. "Back then, the loss of children was a grim inevitability in the rebirth of The Lands. It wasn't uncommon, but that didn't make it any less cruel. It wove itself into daily life like tendrils of darkness that refused to fade—always lurking, always waiting."

Nester extended a hand, patting Diesel's wrist gently. Diesel pressed on, clearing the gravel from his throat. "It wasn't just the first loss that broke him. It was the second. The third. How do you even begin to explain that kind of pain? Watching those small lives slip away, one after the other...It was unbearable. Far too soon, far too often."

His gaze lifted to the exposed beams above, as though searching for solace among the weathered fibers—something solid to anchor the ache clawing at his chest. A silent prayer passed through him, a plea to the Blessed Father to make the retelling bearable.

"It wasn't just the losses—it was the pattern. The relentless, soul-crushing repetition. It hollowed him out, scraped him clean until there was nothing left but despair." His voice tightened, every syllable dragging as if wrestled free from a weight too heavy to lift.

"That's when I was summoned to Sanctuary—to dig deeper, to try and understand what couldn't be understood." His words fell like stones into still water, rippling outward, stirring something dark and restless. "Quintessence was weak then," he went on, his voice rough, unsteady, like gravel grinding underfoot. "The Tree of Life was barely holding on, struggling to take root again. The Lands were fragile, split wide open and bleeding out. Sanctuary felt like a place waiting to die."

"What happened when Ezekiel found out about Tabytha and Layla?" Izayah's voice cut through, low and sharp.

Diesel's hand bounced rhythmically on his thigh as he answered.

"When Ezekiel found out there was a chance for twin girls, it was like seeing a lifeline thrown to a drowning man. He thought he could pull himself out of the nightmare, claw his way back to something good. They weren't just his daughters—they became more than that. They were twin beacons for Sanctuary, glimmers of hope in a place where hope had no right to grow. Fragile lights trying to fight the dark. They were the foundations of Starlight. A reason to keep moving forward."

The silence that followed was taut—sharp as a blade slicing through the space between them. Diesel's jaw clenched, the muscles flexing as though holding back a torrent of words too heavy to spill.

"That's when it became clear—nothing could be left to chance. Every move had to be calculated, every step fortified." His voice dropped lower, a raw edge bleeding into each word. "With Lord Brannon's approval, I was tasked with leading Sanctuary's training. The Guard needed to be stronger. The alliance, tighter. And more than that, I needed answers. Answers to why Sanctuary was failing to cultivate its next generation—the ones meant to rebuild the bonds, the families, The Lands themselves. Shadow City's survival depended on the Tree of Life." He paused, his emerald eyes darkening. "Because our Tree of Shadows was bound...with no way to unbind the quintessence."

Ashla's voice chimed in, soft like sunlight breaking through storm clouds. "I've done plenty of unbinding in my time," she said, her expression dreamy, head tilting as though she were studying the problem from a hundred angles at once. "Knots and threads, webs and walls—but unbinding an entire tree?" She tapped a finger thoughtfully to her lips. "I've never tried that before. I wonder...could I?"

"You act like you're a bazillion years old," Layla groaned. "Ashla, this isn't about figuring out your next party trick. We're talking about the Tree of Shadows—not some ribbon you're untangling."

Ashla glanced at her, unbothered by the sharpness in her voice. Her golden hair carried a pearlescent sheen as she swayed, as if imagining herself standing before the bound tree. "I didn't say it was simple. General Liam's body is still bound to it, isn't it?" Her gaze gleamed with something close to reverence, though her tone remained curious. "Solidified to its roots, like the anchor of a chain too heavy to break." She blinked, her voice dropping to a murmur. "I suppose that makes sense. It had to hold against the demon's pressure, after all. Chains forged in desperation don't come off easily, do they?"

Her words lingered. Though laced with the same whimsical air, the weight of her insight was undeniable. For a moment, even Layla looked uncertain—caught between scolding her and trying to understand the strange connections Ashla always seemed to see.

Runa glanced her way, a slight furrow forming between her brows. "Are you saying unbinding the tree would mean undoing all of that— Liam's sacrifice, the demon's hold?"

Ashla's eyes widened, almost childlike in their clarity, though her voice grew uncharacteristically solemn. "I think the chains were meant to keep the shadows contained, yes. But chains like that…" She frowned slightly, as if the notion unsettled her. "They don't just hold the shadows in—they start holding everything out. The light. The quintessence. Maybe even the truth." Her gaze slid back to Diesel, her tone lifting with a gentle brightness. "But who knows? Maybe we just need the right pair of hands." She smiled, almost playfully. "Or someone brave enough to unbind what's already been broken."

Diesel cleared his throat—rough and dry, like forcing grit out of a wound. "In short, Ezekiel devised a plan—a desperate, last-ditch attempt to protect them. To uncover why so much had been taken in so little time." His gaze slipped past the room, far away, to a place no one else could follow. "He thought he'd found it. A sliver of safety—or the closest thing to it. Just enough to keep the darkness at bay. Ezekiel let Visha believe her own lie about what happened to Tabytha." His voice cracked, splintering under the weight of the name. "But we knew the truth. Layla's story…it twisted into something else entirely. Something darker. A thread I still can't fully unravel." The room seemed to shrink, the shadows pooling deeper around the vein of memory weaving through the fibers of the floorboards.

"I don't want to be the asshole here, but someone's gotta ask," Daxler said, rolling his neck with a dull pop. A half-grimace pulled at his mouth. "You sure she even wanted any of this? The bond, the younglings—all of it?"

Diesel's gaze lifted, sharp as the edge of a blade dulled by overuse. "It was part of the tethering," he said finally, his voice firm but hollow. "Ezekiel wouldn't have bonded with anyone who didn't want it. He was insistent—he needed someone ready to take that on. Someone willing to walk that road with him." The words lingered in the air, heavy as lead, as Diesel's face lost its color. "Fuck—I wish Ezekiel were here," he murmured, shaking his head like he could scatter the thought, but it clung to him, unyielding. "There's so much more to this story. To both their stories. And the more I think about it, the less sense it makes."

"Oh, good. Feelings. My favorite," Daxler muttered. "If that doesn't pull at your heartstrings, I don't know what would. The whole situation— it's a goddamn nightmare." He twisted his neck sharply; the loud crack reverberated in the quiet. "I try to keep an open mind, you know? Makes the bullshit easier to stomach. But hell—this is bleak. Bleak even for me. It's like trying to read a map while the world's on fire—and someone stole the compass."

Diesel gave a solemn, curt nod—accepting the comments before steering the conversation back. "Ezekiel forbade Visha from conceiving any more younglings after Tabytha and Layla," he began, his voice easing into the space like the first rays of twilight breaking through a heavy storm. "From what surfaced, his reasons were clear, though the tales surrounding those decisions…well, they're for another time." His voice grew steadier, gaining a faint edge of clarity. "This," he said, "is why Runa was placed under Nadine's care. This is where the lie begins to weave its threads. Nadine became Visha's surrogate, making it easy for her to spread the story that Nadine and Ezekiel had made 'a time of it.'" He paused, his words settling heavily over the room. Then his gaze locked onto Izayah, sharp and unyielding.

"Your mother, Izayah," Diesel said, his voice carrying a quiet but devastating force, "put herself between pure evil and a youngling destined to change everything." He drew in a breath—deep and measured—before advancing. "Let me make this clear—your mother, Nadine, shielded Runa from the High Priestess, her biological mother. And with her strength— and her unwavering devotion—she safeguarded Layla and Tabytha too. So if anything, she gave of her life in the most meaningful way possible."

Missy's walls trembled with an energy—raw and grieving—the sconces wept radiance, their shimmer quivering like tears suspended mid-fall, draping the space in a wavering wash of sorrow. Diesel's expression thinned as he acknowledged the silent ache. And then, as though drawing from some hidden reservoir of resolve, the luminance gathered itself—rising, anchoring—until it burned with hushed determination, like the first gleam cresting the ridgeline, ready to face what was to come.

"But again," Diesel rasped, "that's a story for another day." He sank into the velvet, silence reclaiming him.

Layla flung a hand—quick, brittle, burning—just as the remaining fizz sloshed from her glass, splattering across the floorboards. "What? That's it? You're stopping there?" Her glare snapped downward as the Lumis Bloom responded—the droplets sank in with a delighted sizzle, a faint sparkle of sugar-crystals dancing along the grain, as if the memory itself were savoring the spill. She looked up again, incredulous. "I'm invested now! You can't just drop a cliffhanger like that."

Ashla bent forward, blinking slowly. "Well, that's new." Her cadence eased into thoughtfulness, half-speaking to herself. "Then again, I've never shared a drink with a memory before. It's kind of like…" She trailed off, her eyes tracking the wash of iridescence left behind. "*Next time,* let's try honey. See if it smiles." She glanced toward Layla with a light shrug. "Maybe the Lumis are more like us—some of them crave sweet things. Especially when the truth's been bitter for so long." Ashla tilted her head. "I did tell you, didn't I?" Her grin turned impish. "*Ohhh, Lala*—that's what I'll call you now. It's the name someone earns when they pretend not to care, but their heart's already in the story. It sounds like laughter, like lightness—like someone who's already too far in to back out."

"Please don't," Layla deadpanned.

Ashla teetered her head before continuing, "Stories have a way of pulling you in when you least expect it." She gave a whimsical wink. "It's like fishing for stars—sometimes the brightest ones take the longest to catch."

Layla groaned. "Seriously? What the hell does that even mean?" She shot Ashla a side-eye, though the corner of her mouth betrayed the faintest smirk. "Fine. Whatever. Just someone finish the damn story already."

"Oh, you'll see," Ashla replied, wide eyes sparkling with mischief.

"You're impossible." Layla dropped her head back, as if pleading with the ceiling for patience.

"And yet, Lala," Ashla said, her grin widening like the crescent of a moon, "here we are—both wanting to know what happens next." She turned toward Diesel. "Go on," she urged, as if inviting him to tell a bedtime story. "I'm sure there's a very thrilling reason you're keeping us in suspense."

"You know," Diesel said, breaking the study's stillness, "I always thought retirement would look different. Fewer ancient betrayals. More fishing at a cabin by a lake. Quiet." His chuckle was dry. "Some ass-kicking now and then—just to keep the edge. Train the new blood. Simple stuff."

The smile dissolved as his attention drifted toward the fire, his voice dropping a shade deeper—like a front rolling in over calm waters. "But here we are." His waterline hazed. He wiped it without ceremony, like batting at a gnat. "Didn't think I'd be the one digging this deep into the past."

Izayah folded forward, tapping a finger to the cusp of the coffee table's seared edge. "Did Visha catch a fit over your arrival? I mean, you were Shadow City Guard Guild—a Truth Teller. Wouldn't she have been wary of you?"

Diesel nodded. "You're asking the right questions, Lieutenant," he said. "Visha wasn't stupid. She knew exactly who I was—and that's where it got…complicated. Truth Seeking was more assumed than confirmed, like I mentioned before. I worked hard to keep it under wraps."

He exhaled. "She allowed my presence because of my ties to Lord Brannon, the alliance between Shadow City and Sanctuary, and my bond with Ezekiel. That trifecta bought me time. I played the role of an 'unknowing male,' and to my surprise…" He let out a hollow breath, a bitter laugh escaping him. "She bought it. Again, after the Great War, all the other Truth Seekers disappeared. That could've been part of it. We're more of a communal bunch when it comes to our quintessence."

His tone turned to steel, dragging like a blade over stone. "Her deceit was—and is—masterful. Even then, she knew how to bend reality to her will. But the Elite Guard's training and my time with the Truth Seekers gave me just enough to keep up the charade. It's the only reason I sanctioned your assignment behind enemy lines." His voice dropped, heavy with what couldn't be undone. "The Moons and Shadows mission is no ordinary task—it's designed to fracture anyone who isn't prepared."

"This isn't just a test of endurance. She'll put you through trials that'll make the Elite Selections look like a warm-up. It's not for the faint of heart

—it's a dismantling of everything you think you are. You'll be dragged through devastation, forced to confront parts of yourself that shouldn't see daylight. She'll unravel you, twist you inside out until you don't recognize the person staring back. And she'll do it all with one purpose: to see what's left of you when the breaking's done, and then break that."

"With all due respect, sir," Izayah began, straightening slightly, "I've prepared for this. I understand the risks, and I'm ready to do what's necessary. Runa has endured more than anyone should ever have to. And yet, she still finds a way to smile, to play with the younglings in the fields. She carries so much, and she does it with a grace I don't fully understand." He chewed on a notion before continuing. "But I don't know what I saw on her Dawning Day. That projection of her…" He trailed off, his jaw tightening for a moment.

"In my assessment," Diesel said flatly, his voice carrying the clipped precision of a seasoned commander, "that wasn't Runa. Whatever you saw —it wasn't her essence. That projection will be woven into Rayanna's Truth Seeking training. The threads she pulls from it could reveal more than any of us anticipated." He exhaled once, measured. "We suspect Visha's a shifter. We know she's a manipulator. Which means she doesn't just distort events—she hijacks identities. Faces. Voices. Movements. She wears people like uniforms, sends them in to probe for weaknesses. To test the edges of awareness. To see who's paying attention. Who sees past the surface. Who tracks the truth."

"A test," Izayah echoed. "To see if I had the instincts of a Truth Seeker… *like my sister.*"

Diesel nodded once. "Appears you passed, Lieutenant. But don't mistake that for safety. Visha exploits every flicker of doubt, every inch of hesitation. She'll press until she finds the fault line—and rip it wide open."

Izayah remained silent, a single nod his only response—confirmation that silence would be his tactic.

"Exactly what I expect from my second." Diesel's gaze narrowed, voice dropping into a low growl. "This isn't just pressure—it's a full-spectrum stress test. Slip once, and she'll drive the knife in."

"Acknowledged." Izayah nodded sharply.

"Then let's hope you're ready for what's waiting." Diesel raised his chin—a silent order given and returned.

A beat passed before Izayah turned his hand in a subtle gesture of encouragement. "Continue the account, Sir. "What followed, involving Ezekiel?"

Diesel's eyes flared wide—just for a moment—then he pressed on. "Before Tabytha and Layla—Ezekiel's joy was like sunlight swallowed by storm clouds. Every loss, every youngling that didn't survive, pulled him deeper into a darkness that devoured everything."

He rubbed his temple—an absent motion, as though his fingers might smooth away fragments of memory too jagged to handle. "And Visha..." His voice trailed off, drifting into the flames, letting their flicker dance like restless spirits. "She'd vanish, slipping off into the Dark Forest beyond Shadow City—a place so twisted, even the trees looked like they wanted to reach out and choke the life from you." His attention pulled to Zane. "It's where you'll take your girls when all this is over. We've secured a place— safe, hidden. No one will think to look there, and there's no record of it. Lord Brannon approved it, but even he's been kept in the dark on the finer details."

Zane rolled his neck, a bitter chuckle escaping. "Of course he would," he muttered.

Diesel gave a nod—barely there—then pressed on. "When she came back, there was always something missing. Like the forest had leeched part of her soul. She moved differently. Colder. Hollow. Ezekiel saw it too. Every time, it got worse—but she never gave him answers. The forest didn't just take from her...it gave something back. And whatever it was, it clung to her like frost on a chilled glass. Got into the air between them. Made it hard to breathe. Whatever tether they had—it couldn't hold under that kind of weight. And truth be told, I don't think she cared. She had the power she wanted. The power she needed." He dropped his gaze, calloused fingers curling slightly before he looked back up, eyes darker now, shadowed by the weight of memory. "That's when the cracks started. Small, at first. Then deeper. Until there was nothing left but loss. And in the end...there just wasn't enough warmth left to hold back what came next."

Daxler let out a dry laugh, harsh and brittle. "Just another cheerful fuckin' day in paradise," he belted, slouching against the stairwell. A glass of apple butter bourbon appeared beside him—Missy's silent offering. He raised it in a toast, the amber catching the dance of firelight. "Here's to the sunshine we'll never see," he muttered, then tossed it back. The empty glass landed with a firm *thud* on the step beside him.

"Seriously?" Zane snapped. "You're not helping."

Daxler shrugged, unapologetic. "Hey, between you blasting through Tabytha and whatever the hell happened back at the cabin, I'd say I've earned a little wiggle room." He shot a crooked half-smirk at Zane, then tipped his chin toward Diesel. Twirling a hand in a loop of impatience, he added, "Let's keep the story time rolling."

Diesel propped an ankle over one knee and spoke sharply. "Visha's actions were like brushstrokes on a chaotic canvas—each one vivid, demanding Ezekiel's attention. Every loss? Another streak of madness. Painted in blood. There were whispers. Chambermaids talked—but only in hushed tones. One of them came to me once, said the timeline never changed. Every loss hit the same beat. Same rhythm. Like some fucked-up choreography no one dared call out. And every time, Visha came back the same. Cold. Emotionless. Like grief never touched her. In Sanctuary? No one spoke of it. Not out loud." He tilted his head back, eyes tracing the ceiling beams like they might offer something solid. "Those who did… *disappeared*. Sanctuary was built to heal—but it couldn't heal what was festering within its own walls."

Zane's brow furrowed as he flared his hands wide, then drew them back together—fingers interlacing tight, like stitching shut something unraveling. "So let me get this straight," he said, voice edged with disbelief. "She was losing younglings before she ever went into the forest? Or was it after? Because I'm trying to lock in the timeline here, and it's not tracking." He glanced toward Diesel. "I've met her. Spent time with her. Visha's detachment now is ruthless. Cold like steel. So I can only imagine what it was like back then."

"At the start, it was early—just a couple weeks into the pregnancy. Then it shifted. Sometimes a couple months out from the birthing date. The last one before the twins…that loss came barely a month before." Diesel's voice sharpened. "The only constant? The Dark Forest. She always went in. And every time she came back, the same cycle played out. She lost another young soul. Then came the public mourning—one week exactly, sometimes two, but never more. Just enough to plant the seed of sorrow in everyone's minds. But after that?" He shook his head. "It was like watching a spark catch on dry kindling. Ruthless. Glaring. It burned through every room she walked into, consuming any pretense of grief." He cleared his throat, the sound rasping like gravel underfoot. "In short, Sienna discovered that Visha was tapping into the younglings' power—in its purest form." The words dropped like stones, heavy and jagged. His hands dragged across his face, then rubbed together like he could scrub the truth from his skin before shaking them out—anger crackling off him like static. "So many little ones lost. To what end? That…I still don't know." He uncrossed his ankle from his knee, boot thudding heavy against the floor, as his fingers tapped against the armrest—uneven, restless. His gaze lifted to the ceiling's blank expanse, searching for solace where none existed. "But there was more."

"There's more? What do you mean, there's more?" Daxler spat, shaking his head. "How much more can there be? This is like a storm that doesn't know when to quit spinning." A bark of laughter escaped him—dry and jagged as shattered glass. "I keep thinking—this can't possibly get worse." His hands flared wide. "What's next? A wicked witch in the forest building a candy house? Hell—why not toss in a dragon while we're at it?"

Diesel's sharp inhale snapped the room to attention. He exhaled hard. "What I was told—later, by the chambermaid—was that she followed the caravan into the forest. Hid in the reeds off the lane. And she was the one who saw them…Layla and Tabytha. Alive."

"*Still alive?!*" Daxler lurched forward. The manic humor drained from his face, replaced by a sharp, burning curiosity. "*Why would they have been dead?*" He blinked, then muttered, "Okay, yeah—that sounds like a dumb question, now that I hear it out loud. But considering High Priestess Nutcase's track record? *Maybe not.*"

Layla's eyes widened. "Still alive?" she echoed. "Oh, now we're getting somewhere."

"What do you mean, *now* we're getting somewhere?" Rayanna scoffed. "You're alive, Lala."

Layla shrugged, grinning. "Doesn't mean I don't wanna hear *how.*"

Rayanna rolled her eyes. "It's like being surprised by the ending of a book you already read first."

"Cool it, Ms. Sassypants. I am trying—to listen." Layla shot back.

"The chambermaid took one of them," Diesel stated dryly.

Layla's excitement faltered, her voice dropping to a stunned whisper. "Took one." She exchanged a quick glance with Ashla, who offered a dreamy, knowing smile, as if to say, *Told you this was worth it.*

"What do you mean—she took one of them?" Daxler leaned back, folding his arms with a mocking grin. "Why didn't she take both? Why only one? When did we start stealing younglings?" He threw a hand in the air. "At this point, I wouldn't be surprised if the universe just decided to kick me in the balls for good measure. You know—for the *complete experience.* And because clearly, things haven't gotten ridiculous enough yet!"

Izayah shot Daxler an irritated glare, but Daxler merely threw up his hands in feigned distress. "Hey man—I'm not the one stealing younglings, lurking in some creepy lair, or plotting to off her own kids for whatever twisted reason this *Highness Nutcase* has."

"YET—" Diesel's voice swelled, then softened into a deeper, more measured cadence. "Upon our return to Sanctuary with the Lumis Bloom to collect and sift through the memory, it was as if the chambermaid had never existed." He blinked rapidly, shaking his head, the weight of it still pressing on him. "The others acted like she'd never been there. Their faces? *Blank.* Like someone wiped their minds clean—as if she simply didn't *ever* exist."

"Only took one of us?" Layla stiffened, perched atop a prickle of irritated confusion. "I don't know *this* side of the story."

"You're catching on." Her tone danced like bells tangled in a breeze, playful and sure. "This is why we're here. It's much grander than Runa alone."

"Gods help me, but I think Ashla's actually right," Rayanna said, the words rough in her throat but steady. "This isn't just about one of us. It's about all of us. Runa might be the key—but you and Tabytha…*you're part of the foundation.*"

Layla opened her mouth, then snapped it shut. The quick, sarcastic retorts she usually had on hand was replaced by a stunned silence. Finally, she muttered, "This just keeps getting stranger and stranger."

Ashla hovered forward by a breath, the mischievous glint returning as her earlier clarity tugged back into its well-worn playfulness. "Well, we did say this *wasn't just* bedtime stories," she teased, her smile faint and full of secrets. "But you're listening *now*, aren't you?"

"So that we're all on the same page—and circling back to my previous question about what information we actually have—let's recap." Daxler threw up a hand, his tone sharp. "High Priestess? A fuckin' fabulous nutcase doing something unhinged in the Dark Forest, twisting perception until you question your own sanity. Runa is not Izayah's sister. And The Lands? They're just sitting and waiting for a war that never ended to finally crawl out of its lull." He let out a breathless laugh—dry, bitter. "What's next, huh? She gonna pull the moon from the sky?" Rising suddenly, fervor unchecked, Daxler began pacing in front of the fireplace— energy turbulent, spilling off him in waves. "Wouldn't that be something?" he muttered, more to himself than to anyone. "Can you imagine—Shadow City's Elite lion emblem yanking at the moon's edge? Raw energy pouring down like a waterfall, sending High Priestess Nutcase a damn good reminder of who she's really screwing with." He rubbed his chin thoughtfully, a crooked smile twisting across his face. "Huh. That'd be quite the show, wouldn't it? Now that would be a fuck-freakin'-marvelous calling card, wouldn't it?"

Nester scribbled furiously on his tiny clipboard. Then, pausing, he tapped Diesel's forearm and pointed toward the leather sofa—his etherlight spasming in rapid succession, as if he could already hear Izayah's next words forming before they were spoken.

"General," Izayah began, "ensure that whatever happens, the truth of these memories reaches our girls. It's crucial they know—no matter the cost."

"Truth will be our foundation," Diesel answered. "And from it, trust will be reborn. Our path forward must be paved with transparency— reconstructed from the ashes of the deceit we're here to burn."

"Noted, sir," Zane breathed, a slight dip of his chin—not formality, but out of respect for the souls in the room. "Transparency and trust," he repeated quietly. "Built from the ashes of every lie we're burning."

"We dismantle her illusions," Izayah stated firmly. "We blow the *shit out* of what she's built and rebuild from the wreckage."

Daxler scoffed, his voice dry and frayed. "Ashes, huh? Let's just hope she doesn't decide to burn us all at the stake first." He resumed pacing, restless as a caged predator. A dark half-smile tugged at the corner of his mouth. "We're walking straight into *her* playground."

"I know," Izayah cut in. "And we treat it like any hostile terrain—controlled entry, eyes on every angle, no room for assumption. We're not walking in blind. We're walking in prepared. We have to reforge trust—especially considering the girls' shadow binding. This time apart has to serve as both distraction and reconnaissance. When we return, it'll be an introduction—and it needs to be rooted in full disclosure. That's non-negotiable. They need every raw detail. We can't afford to bury this anymore. I'm not proud of what's come to pass. But it's essential they understand. And Runa...she needs to hear it directly from me." He paused, gaze steady. "General, can we make sure this happens?"

"Consider it done," Diesel said, dipping his chin as his voice rumbled low and gritty.

As the Lumis Bloom vision frayed at the edges, shadows bled across the walls, cloaking the chamber in a creeping gloom. Words flared to life within the darkness, glowing like hot coals:

'To hell if the Elite fail...'

The phrase drifted in the void, each letter burning with urgency. What rose next was the truth laid bare—a vow unlike any before it.

If the old world must burn for healing to begin, let the Elite be the spark. We will kindle the flames that consume the past—and from its embers, behold: a world reborn. Like a phoenix rising, watch as she ascends from the ashes.

The proclamation carved itself into the dark, lingering in the shadows, casting a quiet promise over what was to come.

Out of the darkness, a spectral lion emerged—majestic as an omen and haunting in its ghostlit splendor. Its roar—guttural, primordial, resounding—rolled across the chamber like a tremor through the earth. The vision quivered, dimmed, and then dissolved, as though swallowed back into the void that birthed it.

As the vision receded, the contours of the environment blurred. The figures of the males faltered—projections nearing their end—until even they faded. The scene retracted, as if being pulled through a narrow aperture, drawing them back toward the stark, inescapable reality of the dark lavatory.

The mirror caught a final image: sealed in stillness, reflecting only the afterglow of what had passed. Then—darkness. Complete. Heavy. It wasn't just the absence of light; it was a presence. One dense with foreboding. A silence that pulsed with the secrets yet to be uncovered...and the war waiting just beyond the veil.

As the scene settled, it was as if Papa D's pipe emitted one final puff of smoke, the tendrils weaving through the now-still air, intertwining with the last traces of the vision. The lingering smoke blurred the line between the ephemeral and the real, between memory and the present, leaving the observers in a liminal space where past and future were intricately—and inextricably—linked.

The females stood in the dimly lit lavatory, their reflections stark and hauntingly vivid against the mirror. As the last whispers of the Lumis Bloom dissolved into the shadows, only fragmented echoes of their revelations remained. Silence enveloped them, heavy and poignant, broken only by their soft, uneven breaths and the occasional muffled sniffle. Tears shimmered in their eyes, restrained by sheer will, as they grappled with the raw truths they had just witnessed.

Runa sheltered the glowing sphere in her hands, mesmerized as the tiny light within pulsed and flickered, acknowledging her presence with a respectful bow. Her movements were gentle, almost reverent, as she raised the orb towards the waiting vine. The leaves, sensing her approach, parted gracefully, forming a cradle of greenery.

With utmost care, she placed the orb into this natural nest. The leaves then curled around it, embracing the sphere like a mother enfolds a newborn. The light within the orb shimmered a final time, casting a brief, radiant glow that bathed Runa's face in soft, dappled light. Then, as if exhaling a long-held sigh, the vibrant luminescence ebbed away, leaving the orb to transform into a translucent, gelatinous droplet, encased within a cocoon of leaves like a dewdrop at dawn.

Exhaustion weighed heavily upon them as their hands reluctantly parted and the threading of light dissipated. Slowly, the group emerged from the dim confines of the lavatory, stepping into the communal area now bathed in the gentle glow of morning sunbeams streaming through the windows. Long, comforting shafts of light stretched across the floor, casting soft, migrating patterns—quiet signals of a fresh start and the fragile promise of new possibilities.

"When the light calls, you rise with it. Are you ready?" Nadine asked, stepping just beyond the back side of the couch. "It's time for you to rest. You've been through so much, and it'll take space to sort through it all." Her focus settled on Runa, her tone warm and encouraging. "Three months to bind and weave your thoughts, and three months to unbind. Just as before, you will not be alone."

Runa nodded with weary silence.

Nadine's attention turned to Ashla, arms extending as the dark golden strands of her hair caught the light like threads of bronze. She leaned in gently, placing a kiss on Ashla's forehead. "And you, my sweet—ask before doing."

With a gentle smile, she stepped back, turning toward Runa and Layla. "Come in close, ladies," she said, her arms unfurling with grace to draw them near. Their bodies aligned, heads easing into the warmth like a soothing lull, and around them, a golden sphere unfurled—its radiance bathing their faces in a feather-light sheen. The air carried the scent of newness, like dew on untouched earth, filled with quiet promise. "Moonlight awaits."

Within the orb, Nadine's cadence suspended itself in a melodic undertone—graceful, poised, and unmistakably royal. "Some are born of moonlight, destined to spread radiance amidst shadows, mist, and fog. Rest now, my lovelies, and remember—even in darkness, your light can lead the way." Her words circled them like a lullaby, and as they exhaled a shared, quiet breath, the fabric of the moment seemed to gather and fold around them, drawing their forms into a gentle spiral. They began to fade, outlines softening, gilded with light, as they slipped into the veil between memory and becoming. With a delicate whoosh—like a page turning in a silent room—they vanished, leaving behind only the trace of their presence and Nadine's vow suspended in the hush: a quiet current of hope, lingering like breath caught in golden light.

Chapter Twenty-Seven

Present Day

The golden haze rolled, coiling delicately around Nadine as she cradled the sleeping forms of Layla and Runa. Their heads rested against her chest, their breathing easy and unbroken, as though the mist itself held them aloft. The dawning sheen, enveloped the trio in a protective cocoon that rippled with the rhythm of their shared exhales.

Nadine inclined her head toward Mama D in a small, graceful bow as their figures began to dissolve. The luminous drift ascended, drawing their forms inward as though through the eye of a whirlpool. The air wavered, the fabric of time stretched and bent like silk teased by a breeze. A huffed *whoosh* jolted through the room as the protective shield over the cottage unraveled in a radiant cascade, shattering with a delicate *chhhhshh*.

For a moment, everything stilled—time suspended in a fragile, golden balance. Then, with a final breath-like release, the shield collapsed along the property line. The world hummed with life once more, the chaos of the past hours receding. A sea breeze swept through, pulling the forgotten scent of saltwater and nature into the space the three women had left behind.

"Really? That's it?" Rayanna spun around, her words catching like splinters in her throat. She swayed a touch, as if the lingering thinning of time hadn't quite settled beneath her feet. "I didn't expect them to leave for Moonlight so quickly." Her focus darted between Mama D and Ashla, "Yes, and I could hear the whispering…so don't ask."

"I wasn't going to ask," Ashla said, her tone lilting as an inquisitive blink fluttered across her features. "But that's good. It means you're coming back into your Truth Seeking abilities. You'll get used to the voices." She tilted her head, gaze drifting out of focus as if listening to a conversation only she could hear, then swatted absently at the air—batting away unspoken words like a bird in no hurry to land.

"You say that like it's supposed to be comforting." Rayanna's scowl drifted into place like a passing cloud. "Perfect. I got stuck with the loony one who's treating voices like background music," she muttered. "Totally normal. Like tea at sunrise. No big deal. Who needs silence anyway? Not I…obviously."

Ashla, seemingly unfazed, tugged at a stray thought, her fingers tapping gently against her cheek as if testing its weight. "The shadow binding—it's like a wedge," she said, miming the act of prying something apart with a graceful sweep of her hands. "Imagine an artist without paint…or a weaver without thread. You've always been good at pulling out bits of truth, haven't you?" A serene, knowing smile rose to her lips. "But right now, you can't do much of anything. That would make anyone a bit…well, cranky."

She didn't answer. Just a breath—low and weary—gone before it landed.

"It'll get better soon." Ashla drifted an inch closer, swaying like a blossom responding to a hovering hummingbird, her eyes slipping closed as she tuned into a far-off current of sound. "Maybe some tea would help calm your nerves," she added, her voice lilting, as if the thought alone might be the remedy.

"Where the hell is she going now?" Rayanna snapped, exhaling sharply as she flung her hands in the air. Her footsteps thudded as she stomped into the kitchen, the cupboard creaking loudly as she yanked it open. A mug clattered onto the counter, and the steady pour of coffee punctuated the silence that followed. "Seriously, what the hell are we supposed to do with all this?" she muttered, gripping the edge of the counter as if to steady herself. "It's been one shitstorm after another." She lifted the mug to her lips, sipping leisurely as steam curled around her face, her gaze shot to Ashla. Pulling the cup back and cradling it to her chest, she snapped, "Let me guess—you're just going to sit there and hum your way through it all?"

With one arm slung over the back of the couch, Ashla's chin rested at a peculiar, dreamlike angle as she listened intently to chatter that dipped just beyond everyone else's reality. Her fingers settled into the crook of her hip, posture light and untroubled. "She's probably blood reaching with Nester," she said, her voice soft and lilting, like leaves brushing against one another in a breeze. "You know, Diesel doesn't like those kinds of things here in Starlight. It has something to do with the ley lines. The oaks still speak of the last time. It went rather poorly. Oh, dreadfully so—not even a little bit well. But then again, with Nadine gone, she might not need to blood reach at all. The hold on the cottage has been released, after all. Though, I suppose it might take time for the rest of Starlight to relinquish such a connection. These things don't just…vanish, you know. They may unravel slowly, in phases." She punctuated the thought with a quiet *humph*, as though mildly disgruntled by the complexity of it all. "I'm *still* learning, but if she *does* blood reach, she'll definitely catch him before he leaves. The cabin is simply lovely this time of year, you know." Her eyes squished up in a playful smile that spread across her face.

"I'm pretty sure there's something wrong with you." Rayanna took another swig of coffee, eyeing Ashla over the rim of her mug.

Ashla's expression brightened as her focus pivoted fully to Rayanna, one finger lifting gracefully, as if to emphasize a point. "Did you know Moonlight bears a striking resemblance to Starlight? Of course, the buildings are a touch larger, and the names are different, but the layout is nearly identical. Quite symmetrical, really." She skimmed a hair closer, her cadence slipping into a conspiratorial, singsong murmur. "And their cottages? Thatched, you know. So much more charming than ours." Her lips curved into a delighted smile as she added, "Oh, and Mishka—you'll meet her one day. She's simply marvelous. Truly marvelous." Ashla dipped her head, tapping her fingers together lightly, as though revealing the most delightful secret imaginable.

"What the…?" Rayanna whispered, the thought slipping out unbidden as she stared at Ashla. Her lips parted, but no other words came, absurdity hanging between them like a feather tumbling from a nest of confusion. "Where do these things even come from? Is that what you're constantly plucking from the air?" Her fingers flexed against the counter, gripping the edge as if it might tether her to reality. "Not trying to be mean, but do you even hear yourself?" she finally managed, her tone sharp with incredulity. "It's like you're living in your own little…tea party or something. Don't get me wrong—it's entertaining watching how you navigate the world. I'm just…struggling to keep up with you." She let out a short laugh, more exhale than humor.

"Well, thank you. It's perfectly fine," Ashla said, her head lolling to the side, her high blonde ponytail bouncing as if it had a mind of its own, batting away any hint of worry. "It will be easier after you're unbound. It's the little things, really." She inhaled deeply, her expression serene, as if they were discussing something as mundane as the weather. "You know, I don't think he's the only one," she mused.

"What *are* you talking about?" Rayanna knit her brows, her mug hovering just below her lips. *"Who isn't* the only one?" she asked, taking another sip of coffee.

"Nester, silly," Ashla said plainly, a dreamy smile tugging at her lips. "He's very real, you know." She turned casually, leaning her backside against the couch, her posture loose and unhurried, as if she had all the time in the world. "I think you're going to like him—and he, you." Her arms folded loosely over her chest.

"The house—Missy," she began, her tone careful, "seems to have a weird obsession with Daxler, doesn't she?" Rayanna lips twitching upward a fraction, resisting the urge to smile as her expression landed on something more inquisitive.

"Oh, she'll come around eventually," Ashla said with a soft pop of her lips and an absentminded wink. "Good luck with that." With fluid ease, she pushed herself off the couch and glided around the room before settling back into the plush cushions. She peered up at Rayanna and patted the seat beside her. "You know, Ray, some things just have their own way of being—like Missy. She's attached to Daxler for reasons probably wrapped up in moonlight and whispers," she mused, her attention coasting toward the balcony. "But isn't it more fun to let some secrets stay tucked away, like a surprise waiting to be found? Understanding always arrives when it wants to. Try to chase it, and it just floats further off—like a dandelion seed on the breeze."

"Sometimes I think you live to be cryptic," Rayanna said, brushing past Ashla and dropping onto the seat across from her. "Tell me more about Moonlight."

Ashla's lips brushed into a wandering, curious smile. "Oh, Ray, Mama D doesn't miss a single thread. If Nadine's taking them, it's because she already saw where it leads. Heartstrings don't vanish with space, Ray. They hum quieter—but they're still there." Her nose scrunched haphazardly to the side. "Well, maybe she doesn't have the exact map in her pocket, but Nadine does. And, of course, I do too." She gave a casual shrug, her attention sweeping from the balcony back toward Rayanna. "It's quite charming, really." She tapped her chin lightly, then added in a whisper, "I could tell you all about it later…though you'll have your book soon enough."

"What's with this book, anyway?" Rayanna asked with a huff, crossing her arms tightly over her chest as though trying to rein in her irritation. "Sounds like you know Moonlight quite well, my little muse."

"Over the years, we moved quite often. Orders, really," Ashla said, her head swaying gently from side to side. "Beyond the misted wall, there is much to share with you."

"What misted wall?" Rayanna grumbled. "I assume Mama and Papa D know all this," she added, her gaze flicking downward for a beat before returning with intention.

Ashla snorted, a flicker of amusement crossing her face as Rayanna grabbed a billowy pillow from the corner of the couch and smashed it between her arm and head, curling in on herself. "So how is it that you know so much about all this?" she asked, the words muffled by the pillow.

"I'm surprised you haven't figured it out by now," Ashla said, tenderly, as if speaking to a tiny creature perched nearby. "But then, you've had a lot to absorb lately." She cleared her throat before continuing. "Since my father is your older brother, that makes you my aunt." She gave a shrug, her shoulders bouncing lightly. "He never kept any of this from Nissa and me. But Pa never did anything without a good reason." Her lips curved into a small, reflective smile. "It's quite the story, if I say so myself, really." She briefly closed her eyes, wiping away the faint moisture gathering on her waterline. A quiet sniffle escaped as her fingers fluttered, batting away an invisible thread. "But that's for another time, I suppose," she said, her tone lifting gently, the moment of seriousness drifting away like a passing cloud. "Stories like that need their own perfect moment, you know? They're like little seeds—they only grow when you're ready to hear them."

In a sudden snap of clarity, like sunlight catching glass, a notion dawned on her. "You know…" Ashla bounced a finger thoughtfully against her lips. "We do have a bit of time. Would you like me to release the rest of the shadow binding on you while we wait?" Like a child peering eagerly into the window of Dagny's Seaside Sweets Shoppe, Ashla wiggled in her seat, her excitement barely contained. "There isn't much left—it's not as intricate as Runa's, you know. Nadine or Sienna will have to handle that. They're much better at undoing delicate bindings. But yours?" She bit her bottom lip, a mischievous grin spreading as her gaze sparkled with delight. "Yours is simpler. I can see the little threads that remain."

Rayanna's head snapped up. "What do you mean you can see the 'little threads that remain'? Wait—how much more complicated is Runa's? And what about Layla?"

"As Layla stated, she was bound a bit differently." Ashla's smile spread, pensive, as though she were floating in a pleasant reverie. "She didn't need her memories contained. She needed more information added in—and her quintessence held back while in Starlight." Her cadence brightened. "Your curiosity is…a charming indulgence," she mused, patting at the wandering dustlets as if congratulating them simply for showing up. "Shadow binding looks like a grayish fog that wraps around certain parts of your body—mostly your head. It just kind of hovers there. But don't worry, only Unbinders and very well-trained Seers can perceive it." A wistful sigh escaped her. "There aren't many of us Unbinders left, you know?" Ashla drifted closer. "Truly, there is no need to fret. Runa will be in a very deep, restful state through most of it—in fact, she might not even notice anything at all. That will help with the pain, of course."

"What kind of pain are we talking about? Burns and bruises?" Rayanna hunched forward slightly, curiosity piquing.

"Burns and bruises?" Ashla echoed, her brows lifting in faint amusement. She raised her other hand, palm up, in a way that made it seem like she was catching something invisible floating just out of reach. "Oh no, it's nothing like that. It will be more of a mental journey…visions of sorts that she'll need to navigate." Then, with great care, she brought her hand to her chest, cradling the unseen notion as if it were something precious. "She'll definitely need time to recover," Ashla continued, her lashes fluttering in absent drifts. "Maybe even sleep for weeks—like a bear in winter, tucked away…and dreamy."

"Weeks?" Rayanna exclaimed, sitting up straighter and pulling the pillow into her lap, attention spiking.

Ashla fell into a hush for a moment before continuing. "Based on what I've studied, the visions she'll have will be…welcomed," she said gently. "That's why Sienna has to ensure no one interferes. Opening doors before they're ready could be detrimental—to her well-being and to the mission. It's really all about timing," she added with a singsong lilt. "It's another reason you needed to stay in Starlight. You have to give her a moment— and Layla will be more capable of such things." She fluttered her lashes with an innocent grin. "She's a bit more patient than you are, Auntie."

"You can't be serious. I *am* patient!" Rayanna's voice shot out, sharp and incredulous, each word punctuated with defiance as she hugged the pillow to her chest. "Patient," she repeated, almost daring Ashla to challenge her again. "I've put up with more than enough, if I say so myself."

"Oh, Auntie Ray," Ashla giggled softly, the sound light and tittering. "You are hilarious."

"Okay…I've been meaning to say this, but let's go ahead and rein in those horses with the *Auntie* stuff. I am not there yet."

Ashla's grin widened, curling into playful mischief as she reached out to give Rayanna's knee a light, teasing pat. "Come to think of it, it took her three months to complete the binding." She hummed. "It could very well take just as long for this first phase to unravel."

"*First phase?*" Rayanna's voice jumped again. "How many phases are there?"

"No one can really be sure how many phases. What *is* known is that each one will look very different." Ashla's lips crooked to the side, amusement flickering as she sank back into the cushions with a wistful sigh. "Sienna mentioned to Nadine that releasing it might be even more intricate…something about the shadows taking root." She made a soft popping sound—almost like a kiss to the air—before continuing, "Back when all this started, when shadows were first woven for you all, there weren't enough Unbinders to carry out the work. Actually, there haven't been for a long time. The Seers had to step in and take over the process instead. Nissa and I were too young then to help, and now, even with Nadine, unbinding has become more difficult—so few of us can still see the threads." She scrunched up her mouth, shaking her head slightly, a flicker of frustration crossing her otherwise serene demeanor. "Runa's is just so much more complicated. Think of it like a journey," she said, her fingers tracing invisible paths in the air. Pulling her legs beneath her, she curled into a ball and wrapped a black knitted blanket snugly around her body, the yarn whispering against her skin. "Like stepping from shadow into light. She has to find her own way—there will be guides, yes, but in the end, it has to be her journey alone."

"Fine," Rayanna said, forcing a tight smile as she shrugged off the moment, too tired from the rollercoaster of emotions to press further. "So, do you want to get on with this unbinding? Apparently, we've got time. Will it take long?"

"Oh no! Not much time at all." Ashla's grin spread wide as she threw off the blanket, then rubbed her palms together. As her hands parted, intricate threads of obsidian ink blossomed between them, glimmering as they morphed into a blackish-golden hue. The threads were dappled with an iridescent radiance—thick and tactile, carrying their own weight and warmth.

As Ashla continued weaving the glowing strands of quintessence between her fingers, the cottage stirred to life. A single cupboard door eased open with a curious creak, its hinges groaning before closing with a quiet *thunk*, as though testing its strength. Another cupboard followed, trembling on its hinges, pots within rustling awake. The activity gained momentum—a drawer slid out halfway before snapping back, and a mismatched stack of dishes rattled on the counter, wobbling precariously before settling.

Rayanna's focus darted toward the kitchen, alarm flashing across her face. She reached for the pillow she'd discarded earlier, pulling it into her lap and hugging it tightly, her fingers curling into the fabric as though it might shield her from the unseen mischief. "Uh, what was that?" she asked, her voice low but edged with unease. Her attention bobbed nervously between Ashla and the sounds. "I swear, this just gets weirder every second."

Ashla, her hands still weaving, gave her hair a tentative tousle before snapping back. "Not now," her tone soothing but firm, as though chiding an impatient child. The rattling subsided, though a single cupboard door gave a final, creak of protest before closing with an audible *humph*.

"Okay, I'm just going to say it—and I don't even expect a straightforward response from you." Rayanna blinked, her brow furrowing as a fork wobbled on the counter before lying perfectly still, as though appeased by Ashla's command. "What the hell is happening?" she demanded.

"It's just the cottage," Ashla remarked, as though explaining something obvious. "She doesn't think I should be doing this right now." Her fingers never faltered, weaving the gleaming fibers with measured exactness. "But I know what I'm doing." A pot lid hopped noisily on the stovetop, as if crossing its arms in defiance, before clattering still. The doors and drawers flung open and slammed shut before abruptly quieting, though the room seemed to hum with muted disapproval. Ashla's lips twitched into a soft smile. "They mean well," she mused, "but oh, the dramatics."

She turned her focus back to the filaments, the shimmering blackish-gold hues undulating between her fingers, as though the brief interruption had been nothing more than a passing cloud. A small twinkle lit her eyes as she added, "You know, that might be one of the reasons you get along better with them than you'd think." She winked at the strings of light, her tone turning playful. "You've never failed to be one for grandeur and all that silliness." She gazed down at her hands, her smile growing even more radiant. "Isn't the process fascinating?" she pondered aloud, her cadence brimming with awe. "Unbinders are so rare now—each one uniquely different, like singular threads in a vast tapestry. Because there aren't many of us left, we're safeguarded, protected. Father says we are essential." Then, as if the weight of her words hadn't fully settled, she added dreamily, "It's one of the reasons my father had to do what he did…for my Ma."

Rayanna's breath caught, the weight of Ashla's words striking her like a thunderclap. Her throat grew dry, as though the moisture had been drained from the room itself. She blinked, each movement controlled, as if trying to process the enormity of what she'd just heard. Her fingers twitched in her lap. A fiber of gold danced at the edge of her vision—a fleeting radiance that fluttered briefly before vanishing. She squinted, trying to catch the luminescence, but it disappeared as quickly as it had come. Finally, she croaked out hesitantly, "Oh…I feel like I know…this bit."

"You do," Ashla replied. "The key lies between life and knowledge. That's where you'll find her." She moved closer, closing the space between them, her energy humming faintly as she waved her hand in fluid, hypnotic motions, her smile unwavering. She swatted gently at the air in front of Rayanna as she eased to the edge of the couch cushions. "Now… this won't hurt at all!" she declared with an encouraging lilt. "Think of it like loosening the knots in a necktie or a bow. Over time, as you move about, the rest will simply fall away." Her voice softened, taking on an almost melodic rhythm as her fingers mimicked ripples gliding across water. "It's like the ocean. I've been practicing endlessly to make sure it's as comfortable and soothing as possible for you."

She clasped her hands together, her fingertips tapping rapidly, her excitement spilling over in an almost distracted rhythm. Between her fingers, the murmuring threads slackened, their once-taut shimmer loosening into soft arcs of light, swaying gently as though waiting for her focus to return.

"Umm…is it supposed to look like that?" Rayanna blinked slowly. "Well, I'm so thrilled you practiced," she added, her voice dripping with dry sarcasm.

"It was mostly on fruit—" Ashla chirped, her grin lighting up like the morning sun.

"Fruit?!" Rayanna shot upright, her eyes widening in disbelief. "Did you try it on anything that breathes?"

Ashla's grin stretched impossibly wider, her eyes sparkling with mischief. "Oh yes…on unknowing Tiddlywinks—" she paused, a playful twinkle dancing in her gaze, "and it went well for *most* of them." She squished her face in mock seriousness as if weighing her own admission. "Okay, well—lean back and relax."

"…for most of them?" Rayanna's expression deadpanned. "I do not find this comforting by any means," she muttered, her skepticism intensifying as the cupboards in the kitchen began slamming open and shut with growing fervor, the sound reverberating like the house itself was objecting.

Without missing a beat, Ashla flicked her thread-laden hand toward the kitchen. The commotion ceased immediately, the silence so abrupt it was as though the house had been gagged mid-argument. "That's about enough from you," Ashla muttered, her tone firm but still tinged with affection.

"Now, lean back, Auntie—oh, wait." Ashla squinted playfully, one eye narrowing in an almost-wink, a sly little grin tugging at her lips. "Not Auntie." She scooted closer as if to casually brush it off, her palm settling gently on Rayanna's forehead. "Anyway, lean back." Her fingers splayed out like delicate tendrils, each touch specific yet tender.

"Close your eyes," Ashla's voice carried the gentleness of a breeze sweeping through tall grass. "Just listen to my voice—breathe in—breathe out." Her fingers moved in languid circles, massaging Rayanna's scalp with an almost hypnotic rhythm. "That's it," she murmured, her voice dipping to the lapping of waves against a shore. "Just follow—shhhh." The fibers between her fingers sparked feebly, responding to the energy. Their radiance receded in waves—no longer glistening, but anchored, like a thought folded inward.

The binding curled through Ashla's fingertips, winding in fluid motions like smoke writhing through cracks in a wall. The shadowy tendrils clung to Rayanna's mind, dense and tenacious, their fog-like presence refusing to yield. They felt alive, sentient even, resisting Ashla's pull with a stubbornness born of deeply rooted intent. But as her hands moved, deft and patient, the strings began to loosen, their tightly wound knots fraying, bits of twilight giving way to the fragile rays of dawn.

Her fingertips pooled with a dusk-born gleam, an otherworldly brilliance casting ghostly contrasts against the darkened strands she worked to unravel. The fibers seemed almost hesitant, clinging to shadowy veils like a child refusing to part with a favorite blanket, but Ashla coaxed them free. Slowly, they unraveled, their dark shrouds giving way to a dim, dancing sheen—like the hesitant light of a candle guttering in the wind. Each filament, fine as spider silk and twice as stubborn, slipped through her fingers, writhing though resistant to letting go. Her hands lustered with the faint pulse of illumination, seeming to exhale, as though the fibers themselves sighed in reluctant surrender.

"Look," Ashla whispered. "See how they begin to dance? These are the places where your thoughts and memories once nestled—tiny pieces of yourself, waiting to be unbound. The process is about waking up pieces of yourself. One thread at a time." As she pulled each gray-hued wicker strand from its resting place, they ignited with a spark that haloed out delicately with a quiet *fsss*, similar to the strike of a match against its box. "Each strand is like a bookmark for your mind," she murmured.

The once-dull fibers flared into a golden radiance—a light that didn't merely illuminate but seemed to inhabit the air, crawling along the edges of shadow. "As they let go, they create pathways within you—like a dam breaking, forcing all that's been held back to come rushing out." Each release left behind a pale, luminous imprint on her forehead, a ghostly afterglow that quivered paper-thin before fading. The loosened strands drifted, curling through the air like ethereal smoke, twisting lazily before evaporating with the merest sigh—as if surrendering to a hush woven between worlds.

Ashla moved as if time bent around her, each motion chosen like a note in a lullaby. Her fingers pulled and twisted the strings free with an intensity of someone dismantling a fragile spider's web. "Let go—rise, like lanterns into the sky—free to float and find their place," she whispered, her voice almost melodic, though its cadence carried an edge that felt too measured, too intentional, like a tune designed to soothe.

The threads obeyed, their emberbright sheen curling upward like wisps of fire, vanishing into the dim ceiling as if consumed by the cottage's breath.

"You should feel the weight lifting now, Ray," Ashla murmured, her words tender, yet somehow heavy with meaning. She glanced briefly at Rayanna's face, her expression unreadable—equal parts reverence and something almost too knowing.

Rayanna felt the tension seep out like water escaping through cracks, leaving her suspended in a stillness that wasn't entirely comfortable. It was a weightlessness tinged with unease, like being caught in the eye of a storm.

"Keep following my breath," Ashla urged, the words pooling around Rayanna like silk, deceptively soft. The final strands slackened, resisting until the last possible moment before unraveling with a near-imperceptible snap, each one extinguishing with a sharp *pfffffft*. The space around them gleamed faintly as the threads dissolved entirely, leaving behind a stillness strung tight like a drawn bow. Ashla murmured, "Almost there," her voice lilting like a haunting melody that slipped between dreams and waking. The tendrils swayed—not gently, but with calculating grace—as though contemplating defiance. The murk that had clung so fiercely now began to unravel, each strand dissolving with the reluctance of something that knew it was not meant to linger. "It's always the last one," Ashla mused, her fingers moving with eerie specificity, weaving and unwinding in equal measure. "They hold on so desperately, don't they?" She hummed a low, incoherent tune, her eyes half-lidded as though the act itself had lulled her into some private reverie. Without looking up, she added with a faint smirk, "Such drama from something so small."

Then came the *snap*—a sudden, sharp *twang*, like a string breaking under too much tension. The final tendril shot upward, twisting and contorting, uncertain in its release. It danced erratically, a spiral of dark silk caught in a concealed current, before vanishing with a faint puff, as if exhaling one last, reluctant breath. A translucent haze lingered where it had been, a spectral echo that shimmered briefly before dissolving into quiet.

"It's gone now," Ashla whispered, her tone touched with finality. A dreamy smile played on her lips. "They never go quietly, do they?" She tilted her head, strands of her pale hair catching the fading glint. A satisfied sigh escaped her as her fingers flexed once, still echoing the sensation of release. "Always a spectacle."

A soft radiance clung to her fingertips—no longer luminous, but muted, like the embers of a fire banked for the night. Gradually, the sheen diminished, fizzling into a hushed crackle, like warmth giving way to the silence before snowfall. She sighed, her presence settling into a tempered quiet, a resonance humming low in the space they shared. It felt like something pushed back—a breath not her own—followed by the creak of a door opening to an essence long forgotten.

Rayanna blinked, her vision unsteady as she attempted to rise. Her body felt oddly buoyant, limbs sluggish with the pull of whatever lingered. "What just—" she rasped, as Ashla reached out, steadying her with one hand to her shoulder and guiding her gently back to the sofa.

"Not yet," Ashla murmured, moving toward the kitchen island. From a carved wooden plate resting near a folded linen, she selected a small crusted wedge of artisan bread. Returning, she cradled it in both palms with composed tenderness. A warm, sun-blushed hue bloomed from the center—subtle, earthy, and gold-touched, like honey steeped in late afternoon light. The warmth radiated outward in steady waves—not bright, but anchoring. "This will help," Ashla said.

Rayanna hesitated, her fingers hovering above the radiant morsel. Her grip faltered before she finally took it, the warmth seeping into her palms, anchoring her amidst the intangible currents still swirling in the room. Above her head, golden ribbons of light floated lazily, twisting and curling like smoke caught in a breeze.

Ashla leaned closer, her expression tranquil yet intent, a dreamy smile playing at the corners of her mouth. "Everything will settle soon," she murmured. As her hand swept through the atmosphere, the floating tendrils undulated in response. "Don't mind those bits and bobs," she added with a whimsical lilt. "The strings of truth will be waiting when you wake."

Rayanna chewed, a gentle heat blooming through her chest as she swallowed. Her breath grew steadier, her body sinking deeper into the cushions. The luminous current above softened into dusky embers as her eyelids drifted closed—and she sank into a soothing, dream-bound rest.

Mama D alighted softly onto the balcony, the planks beneath her feet humming a quiet, familiar tune. Morning sunlight pooled around her toes, golden and tender, wrapping her in radiant sheen. A breeze nudged her toward the railing's edge with delicate insistence.

Focused, concentrated, yet grounded, a swirling pressure built behind her closed eyelids—colors blooming and unfurling like fireflies, wildflowers dancing upon the canvas of night.

An explosion of shifting shapes—foggy, yet not formless—gradually sharpened into crisp projections: a nook, a safe haven, awash in soft familiarity.

Breathing in—her fingers clasped the cool handrail, grounding her with its reassuring steadiness.

Breathing out—the weight of expectations dissolved, melting into the murmurs of the world.

Breathing in—the light sharpened, steady and constant, a trusted and unwavering beacon.

Breathing out—a flicker of radiance revealed Nester's bulbous calming filament, his petite piped appendage extending in a gesture both ancient and tender.

Breathing in—the air surged with ancestral radiance, imbued with the wisdom of centuries.

Breathing out—she leaned closer, drawn toward the delicate strands of light interwoven in the ether. Blurred shapes crystallized, each edge drawn with quiet intent.

Breathing in—her fingertips traced the faint bluish-tinged veins on her wrist, lazily yet intentional, rooting her in the ritual.

Breathing out—fibrous threads unraveled, releasing luminous strands laced within her network of arteries, a breath of life fluttering outward, reaching, connecting one soul to another.

Breathing in—focus honed sharply, drawing energy from one point to the next.

Breathing out—words formed, carried by the rhythm of her breath, a quiet incantation of binding:

> "By the glow of morning's rise,
> Link our souls beyond the skies.
> Thoughts entwined in silent grace,
> Meet me now in this shared space."

As their minds intertwined, fibers of thought converged at the center, weaving luminous blood bindings into a single, vibrant current. The boundaries of time and space dissolved, leaving only the hum of a soulful bond, alive and thrumming with purpose.

"Nes, where you reside, time remains stalled." D's words dusted like starlight across their shared connection. "The release will come within the hour—or so I've been told. Just hold. This lapse grants access to what must unfold." Her breathing filled the space—a steady, rhythmic cadence, slow to rise and deep to fall, grounding the fragile link between them.

She dove beneath the surface of thought, the cool, otherworldly waters folding around her like velvet. Holding her breath, she let the daze of projection envelop her, the sensation intoxicating, a quiet tide pulling her deeper.

Breathing in—"Listen, Nes." His gasping breaths spiraled upward along their channeled lifeline, jagged and uneven.

Breathing out—"Diesel must listen. He must make contact." Her words resonated with unyielding clarity, cutting through the haze.

Breathing in—"He has to hold the words to read," her voice wavered, tempered by exhaustion, "the encrypted message from the tree." The pause hung heavy, her chest rising sharply as if to steady herself.

Breathing out—"The answers he seeks rest there." Her words coiled around the connection, sinking into the tether like roots into fertile soil. "It can only be him."

A hue of gold slipped from her exhale, shimmering and radiant as it spiraled upward, delicate beads of sunlight caught in an unseen stream. "The pendulum has swung," she murmured, her tone soft but unrelenting, "and the moment is here; it's quite lovely, my dear."

Her eyes fluttered, half-closed, the faintest tremor quivering through her lashes as she shared the vision of the luminous orb drifting now closer to Nester's translucent form. Within its radiant halo, three female figures began to take form, their silhouettes ethereal, like apparitions encased in liquid light.

Quivering with apprehension, Nester's aura wavered, its once steady hush of firelight faltering and trembling at the edges. *Why are you blood reaching?* The words, faint and fragile, carrying the weight of disbelief. *D, you can't be doing this,* his thought expanded, the cusp of his presence fraying, his uncertainty bleeding into the luminous space.

Mama D's head swayed in a measured arc, her neck rolling on its axis. A faint grinding sound, like grains of sand sliding deep within her spine, marked the release of buried tension. The murmuring of captured knowledge followed, a whisper riding the edges of her consciousness. "Runa is gone," she said softly, her voice a fragile echo of the truth she bore.

The air thickened, heavy and expectant, as though holding its breath alongside her. "Layla is known," she declared, each word sharp as a blade.

Her hands gripped the banister tightly, her knuckles bleaching white, fighting back the rising panic that clawed at the edges of her composure. Down the bridge, his filament spiraled—a sigh of conveyed knowledge traveling across the tether. In its wake, shadows gathered, dense and volatile, fuming with a fatherly anger. Darkness clashed with the radiance, a blurred haze of emotion laced with panic. Colors streaked wildly through the room, painting a chaotic dance from one edge to the other, as if the urgency of the moment had seized their reality and refused to let go.

"Nester," her voice cracked, suffused with urgency. She gasped, breath uneven. "Explanations will come—upon my return, accompanied by Ray." Her gaze turned inward, plunging deeper into the wellspring of knowledge. Waves of information cascaded over her, droplets spilling out between her labored breaths. "Your 'Tree of Life' has a twin," she managed, her voice teetering on the brink of collapse as the weight of understanding threatened to pull her under.

"Diesel," she said, gathering herself with effort, "must be the receiver of the message." Her hands tightened their grip on the balcony's ridge, the strain evident in her trembling arms. *"He must stay."* She exhaled the words with finality. "Nester, you aren't alone," her voice softened with an ache of tenderness. A single tear gathered at the corner of her eye, its weight tipping it free to trace a path down her cheek. "Nadine holds life. *Ezekiel breathes. Nadia lives. And his Elite…have been found."*

The bulb pulsed, its light surging with an intensity that sent tendrils of energy crackling and snapping in frantic bursts. The pressure built until, with a resounding flash, the bulb shattered, releasing a cascade of raw, hissing sparks. The brightness swelled, consuming the space for a fleeting moment before plunging into abrupt darkness.

The roped bridge wavered in its final glow, shimmering briefly before dissolving into the stillness, its presence erased as if it had never been.

Mama D's chest heaved as she forced air into her lungs, fingers pressing against the base of her neck, steeling herself against a current that threatened to pull her under. Gradually, the constriction in her ribs loosened—each inhale fuller, more controlled.

A faint smile ghosted across her lips as her gaze lifted, catching the muted glow spilling across the floorboards. It kissed her skin, and the world clicked into sharper focus—clearer, steadier, though still threaded with the remnants of strain. With one final, anchoring breath, she turned and stepped back over the threshold, her movements unhurried, tinged with the sway of lingering unease. Nausea rippled low through her core. She reached back, fingers fumbling before finding the handle and drawing the patio doors shut. The latch caught with a quiet click.

"Ray," she called, her voice frayed at the edges, trembling through the lull like a fiber pulled too tight. "Time to head out."

Chapter Twenty-Eight

Twilight State: Processing

Future: Month two of Unbinding

How I crave this. *Here I am, wrapped in this fleeting moment, a cocoon of plush blankets that hold me like the whisper of a promise kept, indulgent and laced with solace.* Yet now, everything blurs at the edges, reality slipping into a haze where surfacing feels like pushing through the weight of an unseen current. *The unraveling…my process of unbinding…it's nauseatingly endless, like being lost in a storm that never breaks, and yet somehow, it feels as if I only just sank into this softness a heartbeat ago.* The notion clawed at Runa, *It's as though I've tumbled down a queer rabbit hole, where up bled into down and moments slipped away, unanchored.*

A thought fluttered into the room, feather-light and fleeting, like a golden robin trilling an unfamiliar tune. *Or was it a…a bobbing bubble slipping through the cracks of my memory? Nadine?* The question echoed, mocking Runa with its repetition. *Was she here earlier?* Reality splintered, its jagged fragments skittering just out of reach. *Slippery little buggers, really… All this confusion. I'm glad no one else can read my thoughts.*

Curling tighter beneath the blankets, mentally scribbling the notions into the margins of her mind—as if ink could anchor anything. *It's as though I have become lost between the lines of pigment and pages. I want to shout, Get on with it, stupid girl. Hurry up and process.*

But healing is never straightforward, is it? It bleeds and bends, elusive as a flame caught in the wind, moving at its own whim, defying any attempt to hold it steady. They always said we couldn't rush through the hard moments, as if the struggle itself whispered secrets we needed to hear. But does that even matter now? Or was it just another lie we told ourselves to make sense of the chaos?

She nestled deeper as the gauzy, earth-toned linens pressed around her, their folds easing with the whisper of a morning breeze that seemed to speak in riddles. The fabric draped along the length of the bed, gliding over well-oiled railings—its movement both graceful and uncanny, as though drawn by phantom fingertips. The pushing back of the veil had an immediate effect. A mellow, dreamlike golden light spilled into the room, reminiscent of a misty orb shaded within shadows, as if not to disturb the fragile moment. The first light of dawn crept in, softening the vibrant hues outside the window and casting an eerie half-light. *Nadine? Am I really here, or am I still lost in this spiral?* The question lingered as she tugged the comforter tighter, seeking its hold to stave off the flood of splintered memories.

There it was again—that sweet bird. The subtle scent of vanilla and tobacco intermingled with the soft coos. *Shhhh, my child, it will be okay,* the golden-chested bird whispered. *Hush, sweet girl, you're almost through.* A gentle flutter touched down, and it turned its back to where Runa lay. "She is almost there. It seems she is processing the last layer of her first phase of unbinding."

The wee bird popped closer and cooed softly, *This space is yours—cool, calming, an oasis of warmth and silence. Sink in deeper, my dear. Draw on a steady breath and let the outside world blur at the edges.*

Shhh, came the command, subtle yet firm. A dull pressure, like a curtain drawn over her eyes, dimming the gilded veil of light—a thin film that both hid and revealed raw truth. The bird chittered, *He cannot be here,* its small form deepening into a pinkish-red as it quivered with tension.

The one to whom it spoke flared up, their presence cutting through the stillness and quickening Runa's pulse. Heat radiated from the bird. *She is affected by your presence here. You can't have any interaction. Sienna warned you both already.*

Runa's mind surged as a long-sealed portal emerged from the shadows, ancient and formidable. It loomed through a heavy mist, wrapped in claw-like carvings that curled into the top of the frame. *Bam!*

A cataclysmic slam resounded as it flung open, shaking the very core of her consciousness. The threshold, forged of twisted, blackened iron, was etched with jagged runes that pulsed dimly, like the faltering beat of a dying heart. Cracks splintered outward from the hinges, as though whatever lay within had battered against the barrier, leaving deep, dented imprints. Shadows writhed like living tendrils, unfurling with a life of their own and latching onto her, dragging her deeper into the storm of resounding dreams.

The passage burst fully open, unleashing a tempest of dust, shadows, and stench that tore at her throat and clawed into her very soul, scraping against buried memories and long-dormant fears.

I'm drowning, the thought clawed at her, a silent scream as tendrils coiled closer, creeping along the floor in saturated clouds of darkness, thick and ominous, carrying with them whispers of forgotten promises and chilling threats. Her breath faltered, sharp and uneven, under the crushing weight of the storm that pressed against her chest.

The bird's voice simmered with urgency, its feathers darkening as if charged with anger. *No, no, no! That door cannot be opened yet. She isn't ready for this. Out! Out! Out! This will only harm her. You need to leave. NOW!*

A cool draft swept over her, momentarily soothing the searing pain within. "Yes, I know where you will be. It's not your time. Son, *You. Are. Not. Helping.*"

A shiver coursed down her spine as the quintessence of darkness unfurled like a cloak—heavy, ancient, crusted with moons and stardust. *It felt familiar. Almost safe.*

Her hand trembled, stretching out, drawn to an old vow held within the lunar luster—a silent beacon of forgotten…*of what, exactly?*

But from the other side, an insidious force stirred. Born from the iron portal, tendrils of shadow coiled around her ankles—frigid and unforgiving. They slithered with malevolent intent, tugging her toward the passage. The stench of decay seeped out, thick and suffocating. She coughed, choking on a breath steeped in the rot of buried fears. Smothering notions long repressed surged, jagged and desperate, ripping at her soul.

No! She slipped on the slick edge of the word.

The silvery night answered her silent plea. Bathed in stardust and moonlight, it bent toward her, warm and knowing.

An embrace from an old companion who'd witnessed her darkest hours. One who had survived the playgrounds of hell and the silent prisons of torment.

Silvery slivers of light burst forth, cutting clean through the coils that clung to her legs. *Zipp—zipp—zipp*—they recoiled, hissing in retreat, shriveling into the obscured recesses of the gateway's depths. With a final, groaning scream of spectral momentum, the iron door thundered shut—a shockwave shuddering through the landscape of her overwhelm.

The deafening slam echoed like a war drum's final beat, sealing the threshold. Beyond its welded frame, the shadows shrieked and splintered-- sound diminished, but still audible—scraping, raking, battering, and striking against the barrier in a frenzy of fading fury. The tremor of desperation threaded itself into the space, leaving her breathless and raw.

The little yellow bird flittered back into a sheer, veiled view, its golden wings slowing as it descended and nestled against her. Warmth seeped into her skin, draping over her like a nurturing, weighted blanket. *Shhh, sweet Ru*, it whispered, its lullaby wrapped in the soothing notes of vanilla and tobacco, coaxing the tension to unwind from her limbs.

A cusp of feathered dawn, yellow with a chest of white, brushed against her as a tender hum registered through her body—an unspoken promise that stilled the racing of her heart. *Rest in me now, little love. No words, just breath.* What remained was the silent assurance of a guardian standing vigil in the quiet night. *Sleep, my sweet one.*

A soft tune hummed within the room, a melody that cradled her in its tender wrapping. *It all feels so achingly familiar—the kind of warmth that holds one close, like being cradled in the hollow of a heartbeat.* The gentle rhythm surrounded her, a lull that whispered safety and unspoken love. *But those thoughts could wait.*

As drowsiness lowered over her like a soft, second blanket, she pulled the comforter up to the tip of her nose, burrowing into its cocooning hold to stave off the flood of memories. She needed this moment, this space, to simply exist and gently absorb it all.

Chapter Twenty-Nine

The door latched shut behind them with a clicked finality, the cottage's presence lingering like breath at their backs, woven into the fibers of the turquoise patina. Mama D and Rayanna moved in unspoken unison along the whitewashed planks, the wood gently creaking beneath their weight. Without pause, they continued down the rockwork steps—weathered and uneven, shaped more by storms than softened by time. The crisp air met them with the scent of damp earth and the hush of woodsmoke curling through the trees. That same ash-laced trail drifted through the arch of the moongate as they passed beyond it, gravel crunching beneath their footing. Rayanna nudged a loose pebble with the worn edge of her steel-toed boot, watching it skitter and bounce toward the moss-softened base of the low stone wall. Her gaze lingered there a moment longer before drifting upward, squinting into the light filtering through the oaks. She rubbed the back of her hand against one eye—still brushing off the last traces of sleep.

"You sure Ashla's going to be okay putting away all that food?" she asked, blinking through drowsy concern as they stepped past the arch of another moongate, its curved silhouette folding into the wave of stone that flowed along their path.

Mama D's steps didn't falter, but her response came quick, sharper than usual. "She'll be more than okay," she snapped, "She'll manage—on her own. Besides, what we need to tackle—right now—will take time. And focus." She exhaled deeply, the tension in her voice loosening just slightly. "She'll be there when we get back."

Rayanna winced, her gaze drifting upward as they passed by another moongate. The curvature cast heavy shadows, like an arc of silver sharing sunlight. "She just looked really tired after the whole unbinding thing," she murmured, guilt underscoring her words.

"We're all weary," Mama D groaned, adjusting the strap of her bag with a practiced motion. "These things drain us—all of us. But Ashla's stronger than she looks—or lets on." A beat passed before she spoke again, her voice lifting just an octave: "We've been at this a long time, Ray."

"I know, but—" She bit her lip, flinging out her arms, exasperation rising like steam beneath her skin.

"But nothing." Mama D came to a sudden stop.

"Why didn't I ask? When I was a youngling…why didn't it even—" Rayanna stilled mid-inquiry.

"Because you are you, Ray." Mama D pivoted deeper into the conversation, facing the source of her frustration with a sharpness that silenced the younger woman mid-sentence. "Your *before-self*—before shadow binding— questioned that too." Her hands landed on Rayanna's shoulders, firm but not unkind. "We look after our own," she said plainly. "Ashla knows that. You should too." Closing her eyes briefly, surrendering to a tempered exhaustion, she released her grip, letting her hands fall to her sides. "She also knows her limits—and when to ask for help. That's why Ryker will be over sooner rather than later."

"Shouldn't he be running things at the North Star?" Rayanna asked. "They should definitely be open by now, considering it's the morning after Starlight."

"He'll go where he's needed," Mama D bit out, adjusting the brass buttons of her trench coat, the deep green fabric rippling with the motion. "Don't bother yourself with the café. Everything is very much handled." With that, they fell back into steady motion.

"Bit moody, are we…" Rayanna mumbled, barely audible. Her steps eased, and her eyes lifted to one of the towering trees. For a moment, its shadow seemed to stretch unnaturally toward them—dark and deliberate, as though straining to overhear their conversation.

"Don't you start with me!" Mama D snapped, shooting the treeline a look of death as she jerked the strap of her bag higher onto her shoulder with an irritated huff.

A soft sigh escaped Rayanna. "It's just hard not to worry," she uttered, still staring up at the fringe of green.

Mama D stopped abruptly, one hand reaching out to Rayanna as she backtracked, resting it on her shoulder. "It's okay to worry. It shows you care," she said, her tone softening. "And Ashla has felt your absence—more than you realize. These moments? They mean something to her. She needs to feel your concern."

Exhaustion blinked behind Mama D's lashes as she exhaled, tossing her waist-length pale steel hair back—its strands spilling like silk down the back of her trench coat. "But don't let it cloud your judgment. We have too much to prepare, and fretting won't help her—or us." She pivoted sharply to fully face Rayanna, her boots grinding into the gravel. "On top of it all, I don't feel bad for her," she added, her tone biting. "She knew better than to unbind without supervision." One hand rested on her hip, where the strap of her massive bag settled against the gleaming black leather of her pants. "She knew—"

"Well, the cottage did do a lot of protesting," Rayanna's words slipped out as though she hadn't meant to say them aloud. Her gaze dropped to the gravel at her feet, her fingers moving almost instinctively to the silver bangles clasped around her wrists. The metal felt colder than she remembered, carrying a chill that went deeper than temperature—something alive, something aware. The delicate knit of her oversized black sweater slid down her arm as she traced the delicate feather engravings etched into the bands. The designs were impossibly intricate, their grooves impeccably precise, as if they had been carved by hands steadier than any human's. Her thumb paused on one of the grooves, her brow furrowing as she pressed against it, half-expecting the bracelet to shift, to quiver, to acknowledge her touch. It didn't. *Of course it didn't.*

"I still don't understand these," she stated, throwing her hands up in frustration, the bracelets catching the light. For a moment, her fingers hovered in midair, the silver cuffs suspended as she watched how light and shadow played within the crevices of their etched design.

They're not just adornments. The thought struck her like a wave, tightening her chest. *They're binding. Responsive. I can feel it.* Beneath the surface, a faint hum stirred—subtle yet undeniable—like a whisper she wasn't meant to hear. *And whatever force controls them…it's not mine to command. Not yet.*

Ashla had worn that unreadable expression when she fastened them—almost gentle, almost kind. But not the sort of look you trust. It meant: *This is bigger than you. And now, the bracelets sit in waiting—for something, or someone.*

"They will become what is needed," Mama D remarked with wry confidence, her lips curving into a faint smile—sharp, knowing.

Rayanna rolled her eyes, but despite her skepticism, something curious began to unfurl like the first stirring of a butterfly's wings. The lightness was fragile, a quiet rebellion against the suffocating weight she'd carried for far too long. That weight—clinging like an ill-fitting coat—began to unravel. Bit by bit, the sensation teased its way through her, as though phantoms were tugging loose the tightly bound threads buried deep within her core. It wasn't painful, but odd in its suddenness, almost nonsensical—a feathery, insistent pull at the cusp of her awareness that sent a ripple of unease down her spine. Her breath caught. The unexpected freedom in her chest was startling—like a veiled corset had finally been broken open, leaving her diaphragm free to expand with a fullness she hadn't realized she'd been denied. Each inhale felt indulgent, almost too easy, like stepping into a world where the air itself had more to give.

The sensation was peculiar—a quiet rousing, as though it were remembering something long forgotten. *What is all this?* she thought. Each inhale stretched deeper, lungs filling more completely, and the tangled knots within began to fray, strand by delicate strand. Phantom threads, sewn tightly and wrapped around veins for what felt like an eternity, softened with an almost musical rhythm—just like Ashla had promised they would. With the unbinding complete, its effects stretched out in waves, images and feelings clicking into place with steady succession. *You won't notice it all at once*, Ashla's statement hovered like concentric rings, expanding across the shadowlit terrain of her mind.

Warmth seeped into the spaces left behind, unhurried and intent, like roots threading through soil, filling every hollow and crevice as they spread. Her pulse settled into a rhythm—unfamiliar yet grounded, intentional and alive. It moved like honey trailing the grooves of a dipper, viscous and unhurried, each drop suspended before surrendering to gravity.

In the deepest corridors of her consciousness, where shadows wove like cobwebs, something began to rouse. The darkness didn't simply lift—it loosened, peeling away to reveal a faint, melodic hum, steady and persistent, like a whisper reverberating through an abandoned hall. Thoughts long tucked away began to stretch and unfurl, moving with the inertia of a dream—slow to rise, as if they'd forgotten they were meant to wake at all.

Mama D's voice fractured the stillness—intentional, incisive—a spark meeting dry kindling. "This week, your mind might feel like stepping into an old room full of forgotten boxes—dust-laced, untouched, and long overdue to be opened. Even though I'm not thrilled with you girls right now about the unbinding," Mama D continued, her displeasure sharpened to a fine edge, "you must ask questions as they come. It's the only way to unpack what's been stored away—the things buried so deep, they've leaned toward this moment without you even knowing."

Rayanna fell into step beside Mama D once more, their pace contemplative—unrushed, reflective, shaped more by thought than destination. She bobbed her head slightly, as if still wrangling with the gravity of her own misstep. "I didn't realize it was such a big deal," her voice quieter now, edged with retreat. "Ashla made it sound like it would be no more disruptive than lying in ocean water."

Mama D rolled her eyes with practiced restraint, the gesture settling into the faintest crease of amusement across her otherwise composed expression. "Of course she did. Ashla's always been the free spirit—things don't stick to her for long. Nissa's not far behind, though. She's different—focused, anchored, the rational one. They balanced each other, even as younglings, figuring things out mostly on their own. Ashla's always had her head in the clouds—more of a sky-high thinker—while Nissa kept her feet on the ground. It's no surprise Ashla's not the one who nurtures the

Lumis Blooms—her green thumb is a bit more sideways, with beads of hued sparkle. I'd say she's always been a little blurred at the edges, if that makes sense."

Her breath carried the kind of heaviness that came from years of memories she couldn't quite leave behind. Pressing into the beginning of it all, she said, "I stepped in when I could, but Zane…" She paused, her hand lifting to cover her mouth, as though the words had slipped out faster than she'd meant them to. For a moment, silence stretched between them. Then she continued. "After the cabin—and everything with Tabytha—Izayah and the Elite carried the fallout instead of him. During those years, the girls spent most of their time in the Dark Forest and the Valley of Visions. They learned to live away from Shadow City, carving out their own space within The Lands."

"Wouldn't that have been good for both of them?" Rayanna asked, questions searching for something—reassurance, maybe, or clarity that might not quite be there. "Wasn't that why I was given to you and Diesel after my ma's supposed passing?" Her words faltered, her expression cracking under the gravity of her own question. She scratched at her neck —a quick, restless motion betraying her unease.

"Izayah took the heat for everyone without blinking an eye." Mama D cast a sideways glance toward the treeline, her voice lower now, before returning her attention to the path ahead—toward where the ghosts of the past still loitered in shadowed corners. "And yes, for Ashla and Nissa. But you…you were the first person Izayah ever looked out for. Even though he always said, 'Ray doesn't need it; she can handle most anything on her own.'" Her lips tugged into a faint smile, but it never reached her eyes. "I think he always knew you needed more than he could give. *That's why* you came to us."

Around them, the ancient oaks leaned closer, their towering frames stretching beyond property lines like sentinels guarding secrets. "They all know you lot are unbound," Mama D murmured, her eyes following the restless sway of the branches. The faint rustle of leaves carried whispers too soft to make out, but charged with the kind of watchful energy that hinted they'd been listening all along—hungry to catch more than just the tail end of the conversation.

"You don't have to be so muddy about it all. Ray knows at least that much." Her words belted up toward the canopies before drifting back down, her attention settling on Rayanna. Tilting her head closer, her voice dropped to a conspiratorial whisper. "Such gossips. It's all pulled through the root system, like the fabric of the town's sprawling history—just one story bleeding seamlessly into the next. I guarantee the excitement will be bubbling over at town hall. I'll be hearing about this repeatedly by the end of the day." She chuckled to herself. "They do adore you all—and mean well."

Mama D's hand closed around Rayanna's wrist, pulling them to a halt just as Rayanna started to speak. "I know we just went through the Lumis Bloom memory he left for us all," her voice quieter now, "but I feel like I'm remembering him in ways beyond what he chose to show us. I can see it—stepping out onto the deck, watching Runa run through the forest expanse with Tabys, Ashla, and Nissa. I remember how I used to throw such a fit when he couldn't do my hair after Ma's...well, you know." Her gaze dropped briefly. "We'd sit together—him drinking his coffee black, and me with mine watered down—even after I came to live here in Starlight Beach."

A faint twist tugged at the corner of her mouth. "The North Star was his favorite. I still see him sitting out in the square at sunrise, having breakfast. The cobblestone streets would be full of his Elite brothers, yet there he was—completely engrossed in each page. I remember coming up to him once, and he'd just tuck the notes back into the inside pocket of his fighting leathers like they were sacred."

She hesitated, her voice dipping as they resumed their stride. "I didn't realize he *truly believed all that*...though. I had no idea." Her hand lifted to her mouth, fingers brushing her lips before falling away. "I do understand why he left...so abruptly...for the Guard. I mean, he didn't leave me—I was already here. But he cut himself off...*from her. Completely.* I don't think I've ever seen him give up like that."

Rayanna squinted into the weight of her own questions. "How did he even hide the truth? Because if I'm as good as I've been told...how would he have gotten it past me?" Her teeth caught her bottom lip. "Not sure how Izayah does it all...without breaking. As you've said, he purposely threw himself into hell..." The smile faded, her voice thinning, barely holding. "I always knew he adored Runa. I saw the threading, Mama. I saw the

strained heartstrings he holds in the vision," she whispered. "They're tethered, aren't they?"

"Yeah, well," Mama D cut in, "the hell he went through with the
Shadow Elite during basic—and whatever fresh nightmares he's faced
with Visha—probably doesn't compare. Or maybe it's just on par with
what he endured in the Shadow Arena as a youngling. Especially with
Zane." She hesitated, watching Rayanna closely as they walked. "It's good
that you're starting to remember. That's exactly what Izayah hoped for
when he set forth to acquire the Lumis Blooms. They're like tripwires—
meant to help you find the pieces that have been waiting to surface. He
always did have a knack for setting things in motion, even when you
didn't realize it."

"I just...I didn't see it back then. I threw such a fit when he couldn't do
my hair, like it was the end of the world." Rayanna's hum was brittle,
cracking into an undertone of guilt. *"I didn't understand* how much he was
carrying."

Mama D bobbed her head as she hefted the bag higher on her shoulder.
"Oh, I recall. He was stretched thin, that's for sure. But you know something? He treasured those mornings with you—tantrums and all. The
North Star, though—that was his special place. I agree, I can still see him
sitting in the square at sunrise, a plate of food in front of him, cold as ice
because he'd been reading and rereading those notes. He wasn't just
engrossed, Ray. He was pouring over them, as if the words could somehow
hold him together." Mama D tilted her head slightly. "Going back to your
previous question, though—Truth Seekers aren't trained to see the truths
people believe for themselves. It takes a rare skill to untangle something
like that. And back then, most Truth Seekers were hidden away or wiped
out after the Great War, their teachings scattered. You didn't have the guidance to understand everything he carried."

She paused, her eyes narrowing slightly as she glanced up at the oaks
leaning over the path. "But that's why this time is different. You've gone
through your second Dawning Day. It's more than just a rebirth—it's an
intensification of your quintessence. After being unbound, it's assumed
your quintessence comes back stronger, more attuned. Your skills will be
sharper now—a honed craft that will help you step into who you're
becoming." Mama D stopped walking, letting the stillness settle between

them before continuing. "And yes, Ray. He adores Runa. But it's more than that. Your previous query, Diesel also believes they are tethered. It *hasn't* been confirmed—not anointed—but they are equivalents. That kind of bond…it's rare. And it changes everything." Mama D sighed, her breath misting. "We'd best pick up the pace. I imagine there are some who've noticed your absence."

"So, how exactly is this supposed to work between Runa and Izayah? Does he just head to Moonlight and casually reintroduce himself?" Rayanna asked.

Mama D chuckled. "I wish it was that easy. It's not straightforward, Ray. None of this is. Izayah can't just walk back into Runa's life—not in this phase. He's treading with extreme caution because of everything she's been through. Runa has to build trust first. That's the foundation. It's raw, unfiltered truth. You know how Starlight Beach works, right? How certain smells—vanilla, sea salt, citrus—help surface memories? It's the same for Runa. Smells help her find a safe zone—something grounding she can hold onto as she moves forward. I don't think we realized just how much vanilla and tobacco would mean to her."

Rayanna's brow knitted. "Vanilla and tobacco?"

Mama D nodded, her voice softening. "It's biological. Feral, even. Smell and memory are deeply linked. Before Runa was shadow bound, during her thought weaving process, Sienna asked her what smells brought her comfort. Without hesitation, Runa said vanilla and tobacco—because they reminded her of Izayah." Her focus turned distant for a moment, as if picturing the memory herself. "That tether is real, Ray. It's why we use those scents during this phase. They're not just comforting—they help her start the unbinding process from within. They awaken something primal, something she can't always put into words. We just didn't realize the gravity of it all." She inhaled, "Really, what it comes down to is this: there's a military precision to how we handled the process. Before entering thought weaving or shadow binding, you're run through a battery of questions—protocols designed to ensure no one compromises the operation. Izayah was adamant about getting this right. He…" Her voice caught. "Diesel was determined not to fail any of you—not ever." She lifted a hand to cover her mouth briefly, tears shimmering in her eyes, threatening to spill.

"When Runa arrived…why don't I remember seeing her the night of the Starlight Festival? It snowed that night too, didn't it?" Rayanna asked, the question catching somewhere between confusion and certainty.

"We kept Runa from both you and Layla when she first arrived. She was left on our porch, bundled tight. Diesel held her for hours, Ray. Hours." Mama D exhaled through her nose. "We wanted you to grow up loved. To feel safe. That's why we kept you away from the harsher sides of military life during this bound period. Diesel was able to lean more into the softer side of himself because of you. You softened him, Ray. You changed him. This go-around, each one of you did—into the most amazing version of himself." A tear slipped down her cheek. She reached out, taking Rayanna's hand and giving it a squeeze. "What we're about to show you is real," she said. "What you saw in the Lumis Bloom—the immersive —it's raw truth. It's how Izayah wanted it to be. But there's more to it than that. Missy isn't just a house, Ray. She's more than our home. She is our family." She hesitated. "Diesel and I…we've waited a long time to share this piece of our lives with you again. With each of you."

Nearer to the house of their younger years, the atmosphere thickened, as if the air itself remembered her—turning over echoes like pages in a long-forgotten book. The path narrowed slightly, the oaks leaning in, guiding them forward. Rayanna's attention caught on a faint shimmer along the perimeter. It wasn't bright or glaring—just a tender, iridescent sheen encircling the stone wall edges like a living veil.

"What is that?" Rayanna breathed.

"That's Missy's safeguard," Mama D noted. "She wove it into the land itself. It's recall, Ray. Everything this house has held, everything it's protected—Missy tied it to the people who call it home. That halo you see? That's the very foundation, rooted in our ley lines."

Rayanna's eyes lingered on the faint, sunlit haze refracting along the perimeter, its radiance muted yet unyielding. Her breath caught as she reached out instinctively, her fingers hovering just shy of the light's velvet edge. "It's beautiful," she whispered, unable to look away.

"It is," Mama D agreed. "And it's a reminder. Everything we've done— everything Izayah has done—it's been for this. It grounds us in why we've stayed through the hardest moments. When weariness sets in, it's Missy's sheen-woven currents that bring it all back—this is what we've been fighting for all along. For you. For Runa. For Layla. For…" She reached for Rayanna's hand again, giving it a steady squeeze. "This is just the beginning, Ray. There's so much more waiting for you. And it's time you saw it all."

Mischief flickered in Mama D's eyes. "You get to use the keystones again. This time, I'll get to walk you through how to use them."

She extended her hands, palms up, the motion smooth and controlled. Resting across them were two sets of intricately inscribed squares—three in each palm—arranged in a calibrated formation. The patterns mirrored the slate stones of the pathway, gleaming gently with iridescent hues. Each groove was filled with luminous points that rekindled in small waves.

"The left," she explained, "is for departure. The right, for arrival."

"Keystones," Rayanna whispered. Her fingers traced the fluid designs etched into the surface of Mama D's hands, her focus intent, as though committing each pattern to memory. Straightening, she broke into a radiant smile, the earlier wonder giving way to a tender heartiness. "Well, look at us—mystical keymasters!" she declared, lifting her chin and stepping forward.

Mama D's chuckle spilled out like a hum. She kissed the pad of her thumb and pressed it gently to Rayanna's forehead, a featherlit spark snapping like static. "A nudge," she murmured with purpose. "Like lifting a veil."

Rayanna's hands tingled; a faint, prickling warmth spread across her palms. Startled, she glanced down as elaborate linework surfaced on her skin—woven formations that mirrored the delicate scripts etched into Mama D's hands. But the sequence on Rayanna's palms began to shift, forming a unique map that outlined exactly where she needed to step. The hazed markings pulsed tenderly.

"Each square is a placement. The illuminated ones will lead you. Thought weaving will manage the transitions for now—access has already been granted. Your quintessence generates a new code each day; it adapts and responds," Mama D stated matter of factly.

Squinting at the evolving markings, Rayanna adjusted her focus to the pathway below, where the stones remained unmarked—until she advanced.

"Remember though, the keystones aren't just tools. They're pathways—

threads of memory, space, and intent. They don't simply open doors, Ray. They reconnect, weaving what's already within you, pulling threads of the forgotten back into focus. Every journey shapes its own design. It's not just about finding the path—it's about discovering the parts of yourself you thought were lost." She paused, her attention settling upon the doorway ahead. "These particular keystones don't just lead to Missy—our home. They unlock…the classified side of our world. The side we've had to keep from you girls."

Stepping ahead to demonstrate, each placement triggered a surge of energy—a tender, chime-like resonance, like a bell rung from deep within the earth. A subtle vibration followed. Rayanna moved after her.

"Step lightly but with purpose. Command the space," Mama D instructed. "We need to finish correctly, or the door won't open."

Rayanna adjusted her pace. Her exaggerated steps began as playful and theatrical, but gradually gliding into rhythm, her footfalls syncing with the keystones' reply. A subtle *tick, tick, tick* followed their progress, like the house was keeping time. The halo beneath their feet flared brighter with each correctly placed step, accompanied by a thin *whoosh* and the drifting scent of salt and sage.

As they reached the third slate stone, a low *click-thrum* echoed just beyond the threshold, reverberating like a signal sent deep into the heart of the house. The door creaked open—its weathered surface revealing traces of its past. Once whitewashed, the wood had aged into a soft, antique-gray patina, its tones complementing the deep green siding that framed the entrance like a hidden treasure chest tucked into the beachfront.

A bloom of diffusion spilled from within—inviting and familiar. Rayanna froze for a moment, watching as Mama D climbed the steps and crossed the threshold. Then she followed, her attention pulled to the wood along the doorframe, worn smooth from years of touch, thrumming beneath her fingertips. "I think I missed you, dear girl," she whispered. A soothing radiance flowed through the trim—a quiet acknowledgment of her presence, like an old friend whispering, *I remember you too.*

Before her eyes, the doorway's exterior altered, folding in on itself as if responding to her words. The deep green faded into white, the antique gray of the door blending seamlessly into a freshly whitewashed hue, the transition alive with motion. Pencil-etched notches emerged along the casing—names and tick marks, memories carved into Missy's being. Rayanna leaned closer, her fingers brushing lightly over the markings, as the green returned, whispering back, *I didn't forget you, my sweet one.*

Drawn further into the hallway, Rayanna let the space pull her in. Behind her, the door shut on its own with a quiet *click*—not the cold precision of machinery, but something organic, like an exhale, sealing them within.

Her breath trembled as she looked around. "This...this is it," she sighed, wonder and certainty threading through her words. Her fingers lingered on the encasement, gliding over the walls as a mellow light cast a golden luster across the deep forest wallpaper, adorned with intricate threads of winding branches. The steady hum beneath her touch balanced her, each note weaving together a quiet symphony of familiarity.

A quiet undulation moved through the space, subtle and alive, as though Missy herself adjusted to their presence. The walls, unassuming yet wise, held a quiet knowing. An iridescent undertone flickered just out of view but undeniably there. The faint glow of the keystones in Rayanna's hands reflected off the surface before sinking back into her skin. The scent of sage and citrus woven in, delicate, intentional, and chosen with care—*an offering, a welcome.*

Mama D's smile deepened, the weight of her bag settling fully onto the floor as she adjusted her shoulder. "Welcome back," she said softly. She reached out, cradling Rayanna's hands, the faint thread of vanilla and citrus still stitched between them.

Rayanna's focus, however, was already drifting—drawn toward a flare of movement in the hallway. A glint, like sunlight catching on crystal. Squinting against the ambient murmur of diffusion, her breath hitched. Goosebumps rippled across her arms as a jolt of recognition surged through her. "Liam!" she gasped, pulling back from the embrace and darting toward a nearby portrait.

The man in the frame leaned casually on the edge of his painted scene, his gray tweed cap tilted low over his forehead. He grinned at her, eyes sparkling with mischief, and raised a glass of amber liquid in her direction. "Aye, there's my lass!" he declared, his voice brimming with warmth. "Blimey, it's taken ye long enough tae get back here. It's been, what...a handful o' years?"

Rayanna gave a short, sardonic laugh, her fingers brushing the edge of the frame. "It's been a bit," she quipped. "I was a little…tied up." She scrunched her nose at him, daring him to argue—a beat not missed.

He gave a breathy laugh, tipping his glass in her direction. "Aye, bound up or not, yer timing's still impeccable." His smile softened as he moved nearer within the frame, his voice dropping just enough to pull her closer. "It's good tae have ye back, little one." The pet name tapped at her chest like a knock on the door—an old rhythm, beloved and unforgotten, tugging loose another hidden thread of memory.

Her fingers stilled along the paneling. "Good to be back, Liam," she murmured. "Feels like it's been longer than it should have."

"Just a blip on dae fuckin' radar, really." Liam tipped his cap, his grin widening. "Oh, ye know, just sittin' here, watchin' ye grow up all over again. Took all me restraint not tae shout advice at ye through dis blasted frame." His attention drifted to Mama D, who stood with her arms crossed, a knowing smirk tucked at the corner of her mouth. "Dis one," he said, nodding her way, "would've skinned me alive if I'd so much as opened my gob. Said it'd be rude tae meddle." He winked at Rayanna. "But I've been waitin', lass. And I must say—it's a sight fer sore eyes tae see ye here again."

"Oh gods. If that was just a blip, I'd hate to see what *long* looks like." Mama D huffed, rolling her eyes in an exaggerated arc. "Ha—restraint," she drawled. "If endless muttering and grumbling under your breath counts as holding back, then yes, Liam, you were the picture of self-control."

A burst of warmth bloomed in Rayanna's chest. "That's okay," she shot back, "because I seem to not be far behind you, Liam." She winked, then spun in a slow circle with her arms outstretched. "I assume Missy was responsible for all the interior changes while we were around as younglings? If I remember right, she loved to decorate on occasion."

Mama D arced her chin upward, gesturing around them. "And let's not forget how accommodating she was when you lot came to us shadow bound. No hesitation at all—just dove right in and 'redecorated' to suit her quaint little preferences. I'd call it a gift…that keeps giving."

Missy stirred.

Energy coursed through the golden branches etched into the wallpaper, intricate veins flaring to life. Rayanna's chest tightened as the radiance streamed along the walls like sunlit blood rushing through veins—vivid, undeniable.

Then came the *thrum*.

It rose from the floorboards—low and resonant—traveling upward, vibrating through their legs and rooting itself deep within their cores, thrumming with something older than language.

"Well then, m'love," Liam said, raising his glass, "time tae stretch dose walls again—time tae brace them beams—*we've got chaos movin' in.*"

The house answered with a shuddering groan—a sound somewhere between wood creaking and joists bracing for impact. A full-bodied tremor ran through the walls, sending Liam's picture frame into a precarious teeter on its hook. The portrait tilted sharply one way, then the other, as if it couldn't decide which direction to settle. Inside, the glass of amber liquid slid across the polished surface of his painted bar. "Oi! Missy!" he barked, lunging for the glass just as it neared the edge. Before he could reach it, the frame tipped the opposite way, sending the drink careening back across the counter. He darted after it, muttering, "Blimey, lass, yer timing's bloody perfect!" With an exaggerated flourish, he caught the glass, clutching it tightly as he straightened—his roguish grin returning full force. "But fair play," he added, lifting the drink in a toast. "It's a time for celebration, aye? Here's ta our Ray O' Sunshine." His voice was rich with pride. "Da feathers are waitin', lass. Time tae spread yer wings."

The walls began to stretch outward, rumbling deep in anticipation as Missy reconfigured. New paneling slid into place with a low clunk that reverberated through the marrow, the layout pivoting to make space. It wasn't seamless—it was adaptive, responsive, unmistakably sentient.

Rayanna's focus snagged on an old portrait hanging beside Liam's. Its frame tilted subtly before righting itself, settling with quiet insistence as the room adjusted. Three young girls—dirt-scuffed and mid-laughter—spun beneath the outstretched limbs of the great oak. Her breath caught, a throb curling behind her ribs as her gaze narrowed on the figures: herself, Runa, and the girl she'd always remembered as Tabytha. But clarity stripped away the veil. It had been Layla.

The sight unraveled something within her. Their joy—the blur of motion, the way sunlight scattered across their faces—wasn't just recollection. It was revelation. Not merely a glimpse into the past, but an embodied truth that refused to stay buried. And for the first time, she let it in: the astonishment, the ache, and the quiet wonder at what this house—what Missy—had preserved for her. For them.

She moved closer, her breath uneven, as though her lungs had forgotten how to expand beneath the press of emotion. Fingertips grazed the glass. The girls inside the portrait shimmered into motion, their laughter brushing the air like leaves caught in the wind. A tear slipped free. "Now—this feels like the truth," she whispered. Her hand drifted to the edge of the frame, smoothing along wood worn down by time and touch. In the version bound within her, the image had always been frozen. But not now. Now, it breathed. She lingered there, tracing the corners, letting the stillness anchor her.

"You're not the only one feeling it," Mama D said, voice low, threaded with something quiet and certain. "Come on, Ray. There's more to see."

Rayanna's fingers slid from the rim of the frame. One final glance. A smile that didn't press—it simply settled. As she moved deeper down the hall, the floor creaked beneath her step, expanding and welcoming her in. "Now we're getting somewhere," she murmured. *"Fuckin' finally."*

Chapter Thirty

Twilight State: Processing

Future: Month Three of Unbinding

Nestling deeper into the plush fabric, Runa turned onto her side, fingertips grazing the plush fibers as she tucked the blanket beneath her chin. The aroma of nutmeg and spices had embedded itself in her knit white sweater—a cocoon of warmth and comfort. A contented sigh slipped through her lips as she drew her right arm underneath her body. *Just a bit longer,* she told herself.

This space was a barrier to everything beyond—a refuge from the obscurity that had haunted her for years. Beasts had sunk into her muscles, claws taking root, anchoring in memories she could scarcely bear to touch. Her very core was laden with an ache *I've only now begun to understand. No matter, though—the pain doesn't chase me here.*

Allowing the fabric to tuck her into this cushioned pocket, she drifted deeper into the hidden realm behind closed lids, where a gentle pool of obsidian water offered a strange, uneasy comfort. *Have I tiptoed into this fracturing stillness? Or have I been here all along?* She brushed the thought aside, returning her attention to the boundless dark—just as a shooting star whisked past. A curious ribbon of light twined through its hazed, luminous path, looping and swirling with purpose. *Almost there*, it sang. An utterance of glittering, sheer beads called to her.

A promise? A riddle? She strained to catch its meaning, but the feather-like phrase quivered and sputtered, dissipating like the last breath of a dream. And from that same dusky silence, an emerald-green stem sprouted—*Is that what I heard?*, it murmured, each leaf shaped like an inquiry.

She blinked, her musings breaking apart like a startled flock of birds. *What sort of question is that?* she wondered, tilting her head in contemplation.

Above her, the vastness shivered, gave a curious teeter, and tilted sideways—the inky dark rippling like velvet. All at once, the glittering cosmic jewels scattered—a cheeky sprinkling of starlit gems. Tumbling askew and seeking new footing, they glinted down at her in shy acknowledgment. Each flare wasn't merely a glimmer, but a wink that clearly said, *I see you.*

Her heart swelled at this silent nod of approval, yet a seed of uncertainty took root within her. *So, this is the tail end of the unbinding, is it?*

With a knowing look, she cast her line into the void—a mere pebble of a voice plopping into fathomless depths. *I wonder*, she mused, *will my reply come now? Later? Or perhaps, not at all? But one thing*, she supposed, *is clear as crystal: If I don't fish for answers, how can I expect to catch a single one? After all, no one snags clarity without a tempting morsel of curiosity on the hook.*

Moments later, at the very tip of the stem, a blossom of the most extravagant kind began to uncoil, its petals spiraling outward in a dizzying dance, each one veiling itself in a blush of pink before easing open—slow, wondrous, and strange. It bloomed not in haste, but as if the very fabric of this realm were entertaining the notion of revelation, coaxing wonder into form. *At least I'm heading somewhere*, Runa mused. *Perhaps this is a waypoint —an elaborate overture toward whatever comes next.*

And with the barest silvered threads, the cusp of the bloom shone—delicate as spun sugar—giving a tender nod, an utterance whispered across the folds of light: *Questions, dear girl, always lead one to peculiar places.* The flower opened little by little, each silken leaflet revealing a golden core that bled light outward in gentle pulses. *A portal, perhaps?* she wondered, curiosity tugging at her like an ghostlit cord. And so, she let herself sink into the heart of the velvet bloom, into its spun-cloud cradle and impossible glow.

She sank into surrender as the wispy ribbons curled and wrapped around her—a comforting cocoon of color and quiet, swaddling her in shadowed calm. *I've seen these before, haven't I?* A spark flickered—Mama D's voice, her smile, the flowers she always chose for the Starlight Festival. *Yes. Yes, of course.* She knew them now. And as if the blossom itself could hear her recognition, the soft shades began to fade—not pink, but the color of *dawn before it knows it's morning*—dimming in gentle waves, drawing her deeper. Farther inward still.

She reclined into the silk-lined hollow as the vision bloomed ahead. Tendrils of smoke coiled and twisted, gathering at a single point before solidifying into a trembling surface. It wobbled like a mirage, flickering to life with peculiar shadows that stretched and swayed, as if caught between greeting her and slipping away. The cusp of the screen blurred, rippling like the edge of a dream, casting silhouettes that felt both familiar and unplaceable.

This was a setting she had stumbled into before—a threshold where past and present tangled together in a chaotic waltz. One side held the snarls and knots that had once bound her in place; the other unraveled in an elegant spiral, each recollection brushing past her like sea breeze and quiet wholeness. She blinked again, and there it was—the cottage, stitching itself together from the golden thread of remembrance. *Snapping—Popping—Plinking.*

With the audible traces came an almost palpable taste of laughter, mingling with nutmeg and ginger apple snaps from Dagny's Seaside Sweets—the flavors darting across her tongue and tumbling down her throat.

In an instant, with a muffled *whoosh*, Runa materialized within the warm, golden glow of the cottage. Her present self had folded into time, as they called it—shooting forward, bending reality through a precious, fragile veil. Now, she sat atop her spun-sugared Starlit bloom, just beyond her younger self, who gazed wide-eyed with wonder as each dish floated past in a giddy procession—clattering, clanging, bobbing, and twirling, each one delighted by the richness of its own aroma.

Up, up drifted the voices. They slipped into the crevices of the exposed beams, the recollection so vivid it practically sparkled. Nadine's hands were a blur, a graceful flurry of quintessence as she channeled energy to summon a medley of marvels. Beneath their towering, grumpy guardian—dishes lifted off the long wooden tables, jostling and bowing in a cheerful parade. Bits of sauce and morsels skittered across their platters, floating and twirling like pebbles in a lively stream, each one seeming to dance to its own rhythm.

Ignoring the wobbling and pirouetting dishes, her seat eased deeper into the breathlit brilliance, drifting through the glow to settle among the group. *Here we are again,* she acknowledged, noting her own translucent, ghostly form against the cottage's mellow, candlelit hues. *I'm not sure I'll ever get used to this,* she thought, settling into her role as a silent observer. *Still, I need to pay attention—there must be something I missed the first billion times I watched this scene unfold.*

Her gaze drifted back to the dishes jostling merrily through the turquoise-patina door, journeying deeper into the heart of the cottage. Pots and platters waltzed toward the expansive kitchen island, each one settling with a soft, contented *thunk.*

For the first time, she became aware of the bookshelves lining the walls, swaying ever so slightly, as though listening to a silent, joyous melody. *How have I never seen this until now?* she wondered, feeling the subtle energy of the room anew, as if it had been waiting all along to reveal itself. *And yet,* she mused with a smile, *how very odd that I've overlooked this little dance.* The cottage itself seemed to *wink* back at her, pleased to finally reveal one of its quiet little secrets.

In a repetition grown thin with time, she observed as Nadine, guided her past self to the plush, L-shaped couches. There had been something about the quintessence, the delicate nature of unbinding, and the uncertainty of how Runa's core essence might respond: *My dear girl, we just don't know what could possibly set off another pull of shadow binding. We can't chance it.* Nadine had patted the younger Runa on the shoulder, then slipped back toward the bustling clatter of the awaiting buffet.

In this moment, for the first time, she was no longer content to simply sit beside her past self, as she had on so many occasions before. Now, she was ready—to move, to absorb, to see every detail from every angle. With quiet resolve, she hovered closer to the diffused luminescence radiating from Nadine's hands.

Curiosity is sometimes the only way forward, Mama D had said once. *It's uncomfortable, letting go of our self-imposed notions,* she'd warned. And now, a new kind of curiosity surged within Runa like a spark igniting—too intense to brush aside. Despite all the times she had watched and rewatched this moment, this was the first instance she truly wanted to understand it—to discern how each intricate piece functioned in tandem.

She leaned in, captivated by the threads of energy spiraling from Nadine's fingertips, casting hues of yellow, white, and a whisper of orange. Each strand seemed to warm the Golden Guard's hands as she moved, hovering over each dish with a grace and care that left Runa breathless. The pots practically purred beneath her touch, as if they could feel that affection—stirring like contented creatures, nestling in as though ready to finally settle into slumber.

The fragrant garden focaccia—a masterpiece topped with basil stems and ripe tomato blooms—and Mama's cheesy root vegetables, glistening with thyme-infused butter, released a savory richness that radiated outward in whimsical, curling wisps of herb-scented steam. Warmth pooled around them; the air itself softened as the quintessence thrummed delicately, filling the space with a gentle, musical hum that sent the kitchen into a dreamlike lull.

But just as Runa leaned in a breath closer, one of the threads shivered— ever so slightly. The yellow flickered to white, then pulsed again, sharper this time, as if something in the memory had caught. Her gaze drifted toward Nadine's face, expecting the familiar calm, but a furrow had formed between her brows—subtle, restrained, yet unmistakably new. It hadn't been there before.

It felt as if life itself had traveled from one corner of the world to another, settling perfectly on their clattering island haven. Nadine's hands hovered above, gently willing each platter to find its place. Patience radiated from her as they jostled about, dancing with quiet delight.

A sudden burst of sunlight fractured through the balcony doors, scattering gold across the floor. Within the radiant hue, a little yellow bird shimmered into view—bright as citrus, curious as dawn. It dipped once, then twice, its flight so light it barely stirred the air, before landing on the back edge of the couch. *Settle, my sweet,* it tittered, voice like a thought half-formed. *Pay attention to your gut. Where does it pull you?*

She folded herself into quiet, letting the richness of it all tug at something deep within—a bittersweet tenderness—*That I once believed impossible.* Her eyes flitted open as she watched Nadine lower her hands. She had seen this a million times. *Yet this time, I chose a different course of action.*

Her ghostly frame stood there as realization hit. *She sees me. She's actually seeing me.* Runa had always wondered why Nadine seemed to grin at absolutely nothing after lowering her hands from the pots.

Perspective changes everything, doesn't it, dear? the little bird chirped in delight.

Then it struck her: *This was it. Standing here was the catalyst of curiosity I'd overlooked all those other instances.*

The little beaked beauty fluttered near, filling the air with cheerful chattering and whistles—a delightful ruckus of sound and wingbeats. With a sudden shake, it puffed itself into a vibrant cloud of feathers—sun-kissed, with edges tinged in white and a dash of orange. Then, after a single blink in her direction, the winged rascal pivoted gracefully, slingshotting forward and slicing cleanly through the wall that held the bookcase, pantry, and elongated bathroom—as if the structure were nothing more than a veil of smoke.

A faint *poof* of pigment lingered in its wake, drifting like powdered paint and faintly dusting the books on the shelves. Through the space it pierced—a crevice now rippling—plumes of sunlit pollen spiraled outward, a weightless blooming.

For the first time, she stepped away from her floral seat. It drifted behind her as she glided toward the bookshelf, fingers reaching to dabble in the golden powder. She drew her hand back, gently rubbing thumb and forefinger together. Bringing the dust to her nose, she inhaled. The scent was soft and sun-warmed—familiar—like memory itself blooming open. *Simple, yet complex. Was it Nadine who'd said it? It couldn't really be that straightforward...could it?* She paused. *What I do know is this: Nadine's smile had held something—something knowing. And yet this—this golden bird, this moment—it all feels entirely new.*

Her mind perused down a side street of consideration, ideas ricocheting softly within her. *It seems like a signal—a puzzling confirmation that intrigue has unlocked a hidden passageway. Perhaps a door opening—one I couldn't discern until I was ready to step through.*

Her fingers traced along the spines, patting the bookcase as if greeting an old friend. Some of the books almost giggled beneath her touch, like younglings tickled by her wonderment. *Well, isn't that fascinating.*

As her fingertips grazed the crevice where the wee bird had slipped through, a muffled suckling met her skin—a gentle, rhythmic tug, as if the threshold itself were tasting her presence. The sensation deepened, pulling at her fingerpads like a mouth drawing breath—a low siphoning that seemed to echo beneath the surface of the world. The landscape around her warped, bending inward, as though reality had loosened its grip. With effortless strength, the pressure yanked at her soul and slung her forth into the dark—a space where shadows didn't melt away, but settled in, a found place, claiming the folds of this obscurity as home.

She came to a shuddering halt, the jolt knotting her stomach with the epiphany that, for the first time, she was no longer within the familiar bounds of the cottage. She had been drawn out—beyond its rockwork property line.

From the outside looking in, the abode remained visible—encased in a halo of gilded energy, the very protection the Golden Guard had placed around it upon her arrival. *Well, that's curious,* she mused—then, like her, the notion was swallowed up and swept away by the surrounding abyss of obscured unknowing.

With that, the little yellow skylark tittered from the haze as it materialized, then gracefully came to rest on her shoulder. Fresh scents of vanilla and tobacco wrapped around her—a subtle sweetness she hadn't expected. *My heart hurts being here,* she uttered. *It's a pull of loneliness that simply feels familiar.*

As it will. Reliving old pains can have such effects. The songbird's lilt threaded cheerful chatter back into the stillness—a fleeting reminder of words once spoken: "Your binding is much more intense than that of the other girls, necessitating phased releases from the markings. The tattoo, placed on all, is there to prevent the floodgates from drowning everyone."

Observing from the stonewall perimeter, Runa watched as the cottage balcony doors swung open and a glistening version of Nadine stepped out, holding two glasses of sloshing, warmed whiskey, leaning toward Runa's materializing form.

The little fluff of feathers continued, *Your unbinding is like peeling back layers until we reach the core. This process was enacted to ensure that you'll be able, over time, to control what your true nature is meant to become.*

Runa's eyes fluttered as the scene came into focus—Ashla and Nissa strolling the grounds beneath the old guardian oak. The image trembled, softening into a vision of two little girls sprinting through a sunlit clearing, giggling as Runa chased them, growling low with playful menace. Their laughter flared through the void like sparks flickering in obsidian mist. She paused, tilting her head, as the two younglings transformed back into the blonde sisters—now older, supporting the community cleanup after the Starlight Festival.

The bird chittered again, tugging her attention back. *Two decades at Starlight Beach was a gift, my youngling—a time for quiet healing.*

She turned to look at the little yellow fluff beside her. *A pause from what, though? I understand it was a chance to mend the hardships of my past, to prepare for the unbinding I still face...yet there has to be more to it all. It still escapes me—why was I the one folded away like something precious?*

My dear, the bird trilled, *moments like these may seem simple on the surface, but they're full of layered truths yet to be consumed.* With a rustle of plumage, it shuffled lightly along her shoulder, angling toward her ear. *Remember what you were told: 'Your future self is relying on your curiosity.' This is what the unbinding needs from you...an openness to discover who you can become, if you allow it to unfold.*

But what was I? Runa whispered in return. *I don't get it. I've felt every-thing—pain, flashes, fragments—but I have nothing real to hold onto.*

She looked back toward the auric shell of the cottage—the brightness that made her heart ache with a blend of joy and sorrow. This was the embodiment of her final Starlight Night Festival, the evening before she and Nadine would pass through the moongate portal. The image stood as a threshold between what had been and what waited ahead—a parting from the place that had held her in warmth and welcome.

Runa began to pace with intent through the middle of nothingness, her bare feet patting the cool surface as if treading along the edge of her own mind. She ran a hand through the shadows, feeling their weight—yet they yielded like mist around her skin. *Life before Starlight Beach felt like licking love off a knife—sharp, painful, and dangerous. That much is certain,* she murmured, letting her fingers trail through the familiar nether, tracing patterns that dissipated as quickly as they formed.

The cottage is me being handed a spoonful of something soft, safe...and entirely unconditional. Surreal, really—like I'm undeserving of such things unless I've paid for them with my life, she breathed, the words fragile, yet an important side of the coin she knew she needed to flip. Pivoting into the darkness, she searched the misty outlines of where she'd come from. *But this... this heaviness is tangible. Familiar. It's real. Alive. Like staring through a threshold of fogged glass—and yet, if I try to open that door, it feels like the whole thing might fracture beneath my fingertips. It's conditional. Limiting. And it always comes at a price.*

The bird ruffled its plumage, settling more comfortably on her shoulder, as if curling up just to listen. She cooed in return, *My dear Ru, I am limited to offering you only a fragment of what once was.* She bowed her head, a tiny tear trickling down her beak and soaking into the fabric of Runa's sweater. *I know you long for more, but I cannot give you everything; this version of you isn't quite ready to bear the weight of the past.* With a tilt of her head, the tittering, tiny creature leapt into the air, zipping around Runa in playful loops. Her wings stirred the in-between into a tender, dreamlike breeze. Then, darting full force into a distant corner, she tugged at the velvet blackness as though she could peel it back to reveal the information needed.

And just like that, the curtain of gravid darkness fell away—revealing the trio perched on rough boulders by the ocean's edge, their silhouettes framed by starlight, sea water, and conversation.

Above them, the first flare streaked across the heavens—and then the second—each leaving a gleaming trail that glinted against the ink-swept sky. Runa's pulse quickened as the two celestial bodies climbed higher, steady and luminous, casting a resonance that thrummed in time with something deep inside her. She could feel the chill of stone beneath her younger self, the bite of salt on the updraft, the solid press of Rayanna's hand in hers—but here, in this unveiled memory, it was Layla's face that came into view, gently overtaking what she had always assumed to be Tabytha's. Runa's heart twinged with confusion. *How could it have been Layla...when I was certain it was Tabytha?* And then—her eyes. Not the cool, teal-and-violet gaze she'd once associated with Tabytha, but something far more intricate—turquoise lit from within, threaded with cobalt and cocooned in honeyed blossoms of vivid reddish-orange. The colors weren't just saturated—they were luminous, rich with emotion, like living pigments drawn from memory and meaning. They glinted, not just with light, but with a beautiful, breathing vitality. They didn't just belong to Layla...they revealed her. A truth Runa hadn't been willing to see. Until now.

It was like seeing her past through a veil—strange, yet familiar—as if she were being shown a half-forgotten story that was altering before her eyes. The night and the markings on her skin seemed to whisper, threading themselves into the edges of her memory, binding her to this moment and drawing her deeper, as though beckoning her to find what lay hidden within its depths.

A tremor pulsed through her recollection—a surge of force, ancient and potent, crackling from their joined hands and bursting forth in a shock-wave that rippled across the ocean's vast expanse. The essence unfurled like a silent storm, sending curling outward, carrying something raw and untamed within its depths. Even now, Runa could feel the reverberation in her bones—the residue of that first, unknowing encounter with the quintessence that thundered through them.

Yet as she recalled the energy that had rushed outward, something darker seeped in from the edges of her vision, stretching forward like an invasive shadow. The beachfront comfort slipped away, flipping the coin of perspective. The rippling ocean began to twist and writhe, its currents thickening—almost gelatinous—morphing from water into an inky blackness that spread across her sight. The threshold of fogged glass gave way to a haunting chill, crafted of tendrils of gloom that coiled and slithered, winding around her wrists and creeping up her arms like cold, slick vines. Their touch left trails of icy dread, and shadows dipped in a hellish, age-old potency—boundless and disturbingly familiar. She felt them tugging at her, coaxing her toward a place beyond light—a place that felt like home in the most dangerous of ways.

The void surrounding her was not just empty darkness—it was an intrepid, living presence, weighted with an insatiable hunger, as though it held eons of suffering, resentment, and a relentless thirst for dominion. Its essence seeped into her, thick and suffocating, pressing in from all directions. She felt it filling her lungs—a heavy, viscous weight that stole her breath—like sinking into an endless, nightmarish abyss that refused to let her go.

She wavered, teetering at the edge, her body and soul caught in the pull of something that felt both foreign and intimately known. A part of her recoiled, yet the power throbbing beneath her skin carried a grim familiarity—like the echo of an addiction she couldn't fully recall. A force that had once threaded through her veins, a drug she'd been fed without ever knowing the source or the reason.

Tendrils of murk tightened like a noose, their grip absolute, dragging her back toward the hollow where no warmth dared follow. She gasped—a jagged breath that scraped through her—heart hammering as she wrestled against the pull, straining to anchor herself to anything that felt real. Beyond the gloom, her gaze locked onto it: a distant glow, unwavering, like a heartbeat pulsing at the edge of memory. She lunged toward it, not just moving, *but choosing.*

The radiance bloomed inside her, filling her lungs with the comforting scents of Starlight Festival—roasting spices, fresh bread, and the sweetness of honeyed wine. A hush of memory, a whisper of home. It cradled her gently, drawing her from the void with a grace she hadn't known she still deserved.

Then she faltered—a stumble, slight but costly—and the obscurity surged in, seizing its moment. The little yellow skylark burst back into view, wings frantic as they beat against the encroaching bleakness. The bird shimmered with an inner fire, each feather aglow, casting sparks of warmth into the consuming haze. A gust of scented heat followed—rich with marrow, roasted spices, and something heart-achingly familiar. Runa's chest tightened with longing.

The skylark's wings beat more fiercely, conjuring the warmth closer with each motion, as if coaxing her from the abyss back into the haven she'd once tasted. The air filled with the aroma of something simmering— rich, nourishing, and steady. A pot stirred, gently folding time into flavor. Marrow, collagen, and bone softened into golden richness, a metamorphosis of essence into sustenance.

Beside it, a rustic loaf waited, its crust ambered and inviting. One couldn't help but tear into it, dipping the porous bread into the stock, watching it soak in the orange-tinged broth like it was drinking down memory. Each bite rewove something frayed inside her—tender threads weaving across the tongue, unraveling forgotten revelations and unexpected clarity.

The sensory onslaught hurled notions at her—unbidden, but inevitable. *Why does comfort feel more dangerous than pain? Because I want it—desperately —not to be. I want to feel. I want to want. I want and need to accept that something gentle can stay.* Her mind recoiled, as though thrown from a cliff she'd known all too well. A jolt passed through her frame, realigning her senses with the present. Her mouth watered from the ghost of a feast, her whole being still echoing with flavor, texture, and the promise of comfort she could almost—*almost*—taste.

A dissipation of disacceptance—was that a thing? It is now, Runa thought, the realization dawning just as the little yellow skylark reappeared, its feathers now tinged more pink than gold. It fluttered wearily in a looping arc before landing lightly on her shoulder, its presence grounding her in the quiet obsidian space. Both sides of the coin saturated—not into gray, but into something whole.

She smiled at it, letting the delicate weight of her feather friend's talons draw her fully back into herself. With a slow intake, she eased down to sit, tucking her legs beneath her as the skylark hopped gently to her knee, watching her with an almost knowing tilt of its tiny head.

She tried to flutter her eyes open, then narrowed them quickly against the softness of the diffused light. Her hand drifted upward, shielding her face from the glow.

How long have I been asleep? The question floated through her—settling low in her belly, where a gentle hunger stirred. She was tired—her spirit still tangled in the quiet labyrinth of unspooling memories, layered understanding, and phased healing. She hovered between the before and whatever lay just beyond.

As if in response, Runa sank deeper into the plush fabric, the bedding exhaling softly beneath her weight. She tugged the knitted blanket tighter around her shoulders, its loops catching against the ridges of her fingers. A unhurried inhale. The scent of vanilla and something faintly spiced lingered in the fibers, and with it, warmth spread through her chest—quiet, steady.

She pressed her fingerpads to her eyes, holding them there as if the pressure alone might dissolve what still clung beneath. A slow rub—circular and careful. Not to erase, but to soften the ache threaded behind her lids.

The bird shifted upon her thigh, fluffing its feathers with a faint murmur, and she allowed herself to sink into the silence, letting it hold her. A low thrum of readiness began to weave its foundation. Her skin prickled with the weight of what hadn't yet happened—but already felt near.

Just a bit longer, she told herself. *Just a bit longer.*

Chapter Thirty-One

Diesel leaned into his clasped hands, the knuckles scuffed and raw—a silent testament to years spent breaking, building, and, more recently, trembling under the weight of half-truths cloaked as belief.

What was it Ma used to say?

Even now, he could hear her tone slip through the twisted alleys of Shadow City like a blade riding wind—thin, sure, and cutting clean through the riot in his head. *"Diesel, Truth Seeking's a delicate art. When someone believes their own lies wholeheartedly, it's like trying to untangle smoke. It takes practice, patience, and the wisdom of elders. And even then, sometimes the world's tools make it nearly impossible to see clearly—but one day, it'll all make sense."*

If he closed his eyes, he could still see her clear as day: standing in the old stone kitchen, her silhouette carved from flickering lamplight spilling through cracked, leaded windows. Outside, the city had been alive with its own restless rhythm—metalworkers clanging their anvils, hooves clattering on mist-slick cobblestones, and the toll of the bell tower marking hours no one bothered to name.

She'd always been there, unwavering in the gloom, a figure etched into the shadows of that place. Diesel remembered the lavender-and-ash scent of her coat, the way her calloused, ink-stained hands would cradle his face with gentle reverence. *"One day, Diesel, you'll see."*

"But when, Ma?" he'd always ask, crouched by the stove with kindling in one hand and questions in the other.

The storm inside him picked up again, a cyclone dragging wreckage from dark, forgotten corners of his mind. *Shadow City trained me to hunt every kind of darkness, but it never warned me how easily the truth could vanish —dissolving into the light of twisted facts and well-worn lies.* The words circled like an old hymn, worn at the edges but steady in their haunting refrain. His lips brushed the ridges of his knuckles, and for a fleeting moment, he tasted the salt of his skin—earthy, bitter, grounding. Still, the tempest refused to quiet, its winds ripping through memories he'd sealed behind walls of stone and silence. *How the hell did I miss all this?* His thoughts tangled further. *Am I that rusty? Or was my judgment buried under layers of grief?*

The room seemed to breathe around him—a response to his misgivings. The fire crackled and hissed, its embers flaring like fleeting bursts of thought. Shadows slithered across the dark wood-paneled walls—specters that leapt, twisted, and shrank, only to lash forward again.

For the briefest moment, a lick of fire rolled like liquid. Not flickered. Not warped. But swelled—with an intent that didn't belong to heat. His body drew taut with trained instinct. He didn't reach. Didn't breathe. Just held the line against something that had no name. The torrent lapped outward, sweeping low—bowing toward the tome—before stilling mid-arc, held aloft in an unnatural hush, as though *listening*. Then, as if on cue, a notion linked—like a splinter driven beneath a nail: *She is with us, and we will not fail.*

"Fuck Z, and your damn puzzles," Diesel exhaled sharply, an onslaught of considerations pummeling his awareness. *I need to move. To hit something. To shatter through this speechlessness. Or let it all come crashing down. Suspended in dreamlike surrender. Waking up to the actual reality of what was. To be plucked from the depths of Truth Seeking in a pit of smoke—utterly blindsided.*

Instead, his fingers stilled, then resumed their tapping against the armrest, a halting rhythm like Morse code—private, frantic, transmitting some truth only his mind could decipher. A message he wasn't sure he wanted to understand. The uneven beat broke the silence again as he muttered, "All this time…" He swallowed hard, the words scraping like gravel in his throat. "I believed Ezekiel to be dead."

The confession lingered like smoke, curling and seeping into every darkened corner of the room. It settled into the cracks of the worn leather, into the wood grain that had absorbed decades of whispers and silence, into the shadows that moved—too sharp, too deliberate to belong to firelight alone.

His jaw clenched, and the hearthlight danced cruelly across the sharp planes of his face, carving out every doubt, every failure, every goddamned *what if* he'd been too blind to see. His hand drifted to the back of his neck, fingers pressing into the slick, damp heat where tension sat like a heated stone—lodged deep beneath the skin, anchoring the simmering thrum of anger, worry, and doubt that clung to him like smoke. This room wasn't just a witness. It didn't simply hold stories; it buried them, clung to them, and breathed them.

"The plan…" The word slipped out, gritty and worn, tasting bitter in his mouth—*too heavy, too real, too late.* His fingers dropped again, fidgeting compulsively at the fringes of the armrest, plucking at its fabric in tense, measured pulls. The faint rustle—soft, persistent—might have gone unnoticed by anyone else, but to Diesel, it echoed like footsteps in an empty hall. *Move. Act. Now.* But he didn't. He couldn't. And yet, burrowed deep in the soulful marrow of him, a feral need to rise stirred.

The fighting leathers—deep obsidian black, worn smooth with the oils of his skin—hugged him like armor made to forget it was ever needed. The seams, strong and pliant, had molded to every ridge and contour over the years. His body and the material had come to know each other well—a quiet partnership built over time. Yet tonight, the faint creak of leather brushing against itself seemed louder, intrusive, breaking the familiar hush it usually held—*as soft as file folders sliding free from a shelf.*

Etched ghostlike into his arm and blending seamlessly with the leather was the emblem of the Shadow Guard Elite: the silhouette of a lion, poised and still, radiating quiet presence. Behind it, encircling the proud figure, was the crest of the Shadow Guard Guild—a new moon, veiled and watchful, symbolic of the guild's unyielding vigilance in obscurity. Together, they spoke of two distinct yet intertwined purposes: the Elite, silent hunters born of precision and cunning; and the Guild, steadfast guardians who thrived in the shadows, their presence felt even when unseen.

The design wasn't for show. It wasn't meant to gleam or catch the eye—it was meant to dissolve into the night, as much a part of the lightless as the wearer himself. These leathers and their markings were built for invisibility—for slipping unnoticed into the depths of silent dominion. *Predatory. Crouching. Waiting. Calm, yet alert,* Diesel thought. *Its strength, forged in patience, is a force—far more lethal in the waiting.*

The leather embodied that creed, its shrouded texture dissolving into the low light of the room—a testament that he could still disappear without effort. Being alone in the drench of shadow held a power most would never master. But for the Shadow Guard Elite, it wasn't just control.

It was survival.

It was duty.

It was sacrifice.

It was a way of life.

He ran a hand over his face, the rough stubble scraping against his palm like sandpaper, grounding him even as the weight in his chest refused to budge. His gaze fell to the empty green chair across from him, where the fabric sagged ever so slightly—as though it, too, remembered. *How many conversations had we buried there? How many truths had been put to rest or concealed without my knowledge? How and why? Why would Ezekiel keep such things from me, even as the General of the Shadow Guild?* He'd filed those thoughts away long ago—shoved them into the back corners of his mind like relics better left untouched. But now, it felt like he was walking through his own catacombs, trailing his hands along dusted truths, running his fingers over old wonderings and the faint outlines of answers he never found.

His body screamed at him to move. *To rise, to do.* To drown out the demons of doubt, which spun faster, churned louder than the haunting trill of splintering glass. But the silence held him fast. The fire crackled on, and just beneath the soft hiss of wood splitting and snapping, he could hear it—his own quiet exhale. Yet there he sat, jaw tight, hands restless, held by the very thing he hated most: the *waiting.*

Restlessness gnawed at him, a splinter dug so deep it refused to be dislodged. It was the same feeling he'd had as a youngling—a youngling who'd been taught to listen, observe, and learn that silence held as much power as truth. But the silence had always been where his demons danced, their whispers threading doubts so thin they almost went unnoticed. *Almost.*

Missy stirred at the edges of his awareness, the house as much a witness as he was. A low groan rolled through the beams—a sound born deep in the marrow of her frame. It moved like a sigh through the floorboards, reverberating outward until it settled heavy in his chest. *The pressure of presence. An exhale. A friendly reminder.*

The memory seeped in, uninvited, dragging him back to a night years ago. Ezekiel had sat across from him then, boots planted on the old floor, the firelight licking at his profile.

Diesel's own voice cut through the murk of recollection: "What if the war happened because something greater was at hand? What if wiping out the Truth Tellers and the Unbinders wasn't just collateral damage—but the point of it all?" It had been a truth half-formed, a ghost of suspicion plucked from the corners of his mind. But it had landed like a stone in the belly of the room. "You know it's not a coincidence, Z," Diesel had pressed, quieter now, like speaking too loudly might unravel everything. "There has to be a reason all the gifted disappeared—except for myself."

And Ezekiel—steady, stoic Ezekiel—had said nothing. Had only looked at him, a fragment of something unreadable in his expression. The kind of silence that says too much.

Now, in the study, Diesel stared at that same chair, his shoulders tight, his mind walking back through those old halls. The questions were still there, shoved into dusty boxes, like the labyrinth of his mind had grown roots through their very walls—roots he wasn't sure he wanted to pull up. But it was too late. The pondering of such thoughts had them clawing that night back to the surface.

The floorboards near the hearth gave a faint *pitter-patter*—a subtle foot-tap, a nudge she knew he needed. He heard it the way an elder might clear her throat, as though the house was tired of his pacing mind, tired of the way he tore into himself.

"The plan..." The words escaped him once more, barely a murmur—heavy and raw, gravel dragged across stone.

In that moment back then, Ezekiel had nodded—restrained, yet purposeful. "I can see it weighs heavily on you, brother," he had said. His cadence had always been unshakable, like he carried answers he didn't yet want to share. "But remember, not all shadows are born from darkness. Some are cast by the light we seek."

Diesel had chewed on those words for years. It was the kind of truth that didn't offer answers but reshaped the way you saw the space where light met shadow. The systematic disappearance of his kind during the war had always gnawed at him with the relentlessness of a wolf at bone. King Moros had been the villain—an easy name to blame. Yet Diesel's instincts pulled harder, urging him down paths no one else dared to tread. There was something beneath it all—something unchecked, as elusive as breath on frost. *"Do you ever wonder if we're chasing ghosts?"* he asked. He looked to Ezekiel then, searching his brother's face for a reaction. When nothing came, he continued—*"Or worse—if they're leading us?"*

Ezekiel had nodded. *"The ghosts of the past…"* he murmured. *"They could be leading us—and we'd never know."* His tone dropped, almost reverent—like a prayer whispered into the dark. *"I'll admit, the pieces don't line up cleanly. But the pattern's still there—just buried, tucked beyond the edges of where the firelight stops telling the truth."*

The honesty of the words had shattered into jagged edges, scattering through Diesel's mind in sharp, chaotic bursts. They felt close enough to touch—yet whenever he reached for them, they unraveled, slipping through his fingers like mist in motion.

And now, sitting with it alone, Diesel's breath came shallow. A bead of sweat traced a slow path down his temple. He pressed a hand to his sternum, as if he could physically force the knot there to loosen. *"The plan…"* The words escaped him once more. *"The plan was just Starlight."*

"My dear brother," Ezekiel had once said, *"the stars mirror the moon, casting its light into the darkness. But it's not the light that guides us—it's the shadows that reveal what we're meant to see. Don't just chase what shines; look for what the light hides."* He had paused then, choosing his next words with care—words he'd repeated many times before: *"The stars mirror the moon, casting its light into the darkness."*

In this moment, the questions returned—unbidden, but insistent. *What if the answers weren't in the places I'd been looking? What if they rest in the margins? What if they're found in the shadows at the edge of the firelight—the places no one dares to chase?* Diesel's eyes narrowed, goosebumps prickling along his arms as he turned the notions over and over in his mind, heavy and unrelenting. "But *what if* the stars are the one's misleading us? he uttered aloud. *"What if* the light we're following *isn't* the truth...*but a distraction?"*

He looked to the matching velvet cushions, hearing his brother's resolute tone like it had never left: *"Not every light leads to safety. Sometimes, the brightest star is the one that blinds you."* Ezekiel had cleared his throat before continuing, *"Remember that night on the cliff, Diesel? The moon was hidden, and we thought we were lost. But it wasn't the moon that showed us the way—it was the faintest reflection of the stars on the water. Sometimes, the smallest, most unexpected lights guide us through the darkest paths."*

One memory bled into the next—another night, another thread— woven together by the gradual rise of understanding. *"Z, there has to be a reason all the gifted disappeared."* He had pressed, desperate for something— anything—to tether his suspicions.

"Perhaps," Ezekiel finally said, measured and almost reluctant. *"But maybe the answer isn't in the reason they disappeared. Maybe it's in what they left behind. Sometimes, it's the absence that speaks the loudest."*

Now, in the stillness of the present, Diesel felt his chest tighten as he sifted through fragments of meaning—each one jagged and incomplete, like shards of glass scattered across a floor. Every step forward only unstitched him further, but the path behind had long since disappeared. "Why do these questions still haunt me, Nes?" His voice came out dry, tasting of old frustrations and lingering doubts.

Nester's small form hopped up onto the center of the coffee table. Without a word, he nestled his bulbous head into his cupped hands, elbows braced, posture still. His filament lifted into a hue both warm and steady, like a patient flame that didn't push but gently invited. He didn't need to speak. The sheen alone held space, urging Diesel to keep sifting, keep searching—offering quiet companionship in the pause between thoughts.

And in that quiet, something older stirred. Another time whispered through the present, like veins carrying lifeblood to forgotten places. *"Sometimes, the answers we seek are hidden in the dark, waiting for the right moment to reveal themselves."* His brother's voice wasn't just remembered—it permeated, flowing through the cracks like water saturating dry earth, each drop reviving long-dormant questions. The fragments of the past intertwined with his here and now, stitching together something larger than he could yet comprehend.

Missy's candelabras shuddered as a thread of citrus and woodsmoke curled through the rafters—her way of remembering. The scent stretched outward, blooming like sunlight through mist. It was her, coaxing Ezekiel's voice from some dust-covered box Diesel had buried deep in the soil of his remembering.

"You always seem to know when I'm struggling, don't you?" Diesel uttered, the words heavy with gratitude, roughened by the effort it took to admit it.

The floor beneath him gave a weighted creak. The grain of the wood quivered—faint but certain—like breath pulled in and held. A hush folded over the room. The air thickened just enough to brush his skin, tracing the outline of his shoulders before settling, expectant.

A faint smile twitched at the corner of his mouth as a light *tink* sounded nearby and a small saucer materialized. An orange posset, its smooth, creamy surface adorned with a clove star and a cinnamon stick, crested the edge. "You know more than you let on, don't you?" he said aloud as he reached for the saucer. "The secrets, the lies…What am I not seeing here, Missy? What's hiding in the cracks?"

The shadows along the walls shrugged faintly—as if to say, *You're asking the right questions…finally.*

Diesel lifted the spoon, tasting the cool sweetness as Nester's words drifted in—soft and steady: *It's not the blaze, but the ember, that often shows us what we need to see.*

Allowing the flavor to sit on his palate, he considered the statement before asking, "Okay, tell me this. What reality lies hidden in the mist and shadows?" The question pooled around the clove star as he flipped the notion over, checking its underbelly. His thoughts churned, like sifting through pages in an old ledger. *I know the answer is there,* he thought, *a truth submerged in layers of doubt and misdirection.*

Missy and Nester remained silent.

He inhaled deeply, eyelids pulled shut. A focused exhale followed—

then, something gave. His mind cracked open, a door flung wide, scattering fragments in all directions. He stood motionless in that inner wreckage, breathing in the faint tinge of orange, as if the scent alone might draw clarity to the surface. *"Ezekiel didn't lie,"* Diesel said at last, the realization hardening his voice. *"The truth was always there. Hidden in plain sight—waiting for me to look beyond what was comfortable."*

The fireplace snapped, its embered breath the only sound. The room simply waited, patient and composed, knowing the next move was his to make.

"He knew I had to find it on my own," Diesel murmured. "That I had to peel back the layers myself." He lifted the spoon again. The tang of citrus met his tongue, bright enough to slice through the mental clutter sprawling across the table of conclusions. And somewhere, loitering within that chaos, Diesel knew: *this was, and still is, only the beginning.*

Chapter Thirty-Two

Diesel sat back, letting his head tip against the worn velvet as he scraped the last remnants of the posset from its dish. The citrus tang lingered on his tongue, like the heftiness of fractured notions. The slim shards of clarity he thought he had collected over the years fell away, scattering like broken glass across the floorboards.

With eyes still closed, he gave a slight shake of his head, as if trying to dislodge answers that refused to settle. "There wasn't anything that needed to be truth told," he muttered, scrutinizing each syllable. "It's not just the light that guides us—it's the shadows that reveal what we're meant to see."

He exhaled as he ebbed forward setting the bit of china upon the crest of the seared surface, the dish swept away before his hand had fully retreated—an efficiency he appreciated. His chin dipped as his fingers trailed across his temples, feeling the slight thrum of tension building. "Not all shadows are born from darkness. Some are cast by the light we seek." He kept repeating Ezekiel's words softly, almost reverently, testing their edges like a blade in his hand. The truth of it was undeniable now, though it left behind a sting. He was weary of waiting—yet even so, the shadows that once crowded the room's edges no longer felt oppressive.

Not every light leads to safety. Nester's filament hazed a pale gold, like moonlight on water—guiding not by direction, but by invitation. *Even in the darkest corners, there's always a glimmer. It's just there...Sometimes, the brightest star is the one that blinds you.*

"Agreed. Yet..." Diesel pushed back and drummed his fingers once against the armrest. "To take the light secures the darkness."

The study doors creaked shut, the lock sliding into place with a quiet, steadfast click. Missy's candelabras brightened, as if to say: *Location secured. You're cleared to proceed, sir.*

The little lighted figure bobbed his head as he popped back down onto the floorboards. *Confirmed, sir. The premises have been locked down. Keystones have been disengaged.*

In response, Diesel's hands fell to his lap, brushing against the fabric of his leathers before trailing back to his temples. He inhaled to the root of his being, letting the cool air fill his lungs, then released it with effort—sinking into the wellspring of remembrance.

The wooden door creaked open in his mind, the vault beyond biding its summons—an aged sanctuary, weathered but welcoming. The warm scent of leather and timeworn paper drifted up to greet him, anchoring him in the quiet reassurance of this inner refuge. The shelves stretched high above, their spines glinting faintly in the golden light spilling from overhead. It was a library of memory and knowledge, meticulously curated over years of experience—its orderliness a stark contrast to the chaos swirling in his chest moments before.

His boots landed in measured cadence against the smooth stone, a quiet testament to control. A faint *tinging* echoed—like a spoon on glass—out and beyond. He gave no notice as he moved between the aisles, eyes scouring the neatly labeled spines.

Midway down the third lane, just before the carved archway that marked the deeper vault, a spine caught the light. Ezekiel's name met him where he knew it would be—the gilded lettering faintly dulled, like a memory traced to often. His eyes settled on the folder, its worn leather breathing quiet recognition. He didn't move. The moment hadn't called for touch—only acknowledgment. Some truths, he'd learned, didn't come when summoned. They arrived when they were ready.

"Alright, Ezekiel," he muttered to himself. "Let's see what you've left me." His tone reverberated through the vaulted expanse, a sound swallowed by the vast stillness of this mental sanctuary. The dim burn from ornate chandeliers spilled in warm, greyish-blue halos, painting the endless rows of mahogany ledges with an almost ethereal wash.

Each shelf stretched beyond sight, a labyrinth of vestiges and contemplations carved into the darkness. The intricate details of the wood—curved filigrees and imperceptible etchings—whispered of secrets and the undertones of a thousand truths Diesel had once uncovered, each one meticulously filed away like treasures too fragile to hold for long.

"I know it's here. The question is where?" His words sifted beyond dusty fragments of musings and facts dulled by irrelevance. A focus honed in and tugged him onward, Ezekiel's pondering resounding through the stillness: *Not all shadows are born from darkness. Some are cast by the light we seek.*

A calling to reasoning—perceptions and expectations laid bare. Above him, bluish-gray fibers swam high along the aisles, gliding with fluidity, a breathtaking kind of grace. Their faint pulses drifted forth, casting wavering contours along the racks below—each ribbon flowing like a sentient current, intentional yet untamed. They didn't carve new paths, but followed ancient ones—trails so well-worn they seemed to fold back into themselves, an eternal navigational system.

Occasionally, a fluttering filament would dart low, weaving briefly through the stilled air before vanishing into the embrace of a waiting folder or box. The shelves thrummed with a muffled, ever-watchful presence.

Leather-bound bindings stretched and yawned open, their edges curling in anticipation, as though awaiting the arrival of a stray filament. High above, wicker boxes rustled softly, their lids creaking open to absorb drifting fragments. Some envelopes reached out with intent, their motions smooth and practiced, drawing in a passing strand and tucking it away like a parent settling a child into bed. Others remained motionless, their contents guarded, awaiting a confirmed command.

Diesel's gaze followed the gliding lace above, his thoughts momentarily scattered as a golden strand fluttered low. Its sheen blushed, catching his attention as it circled lazily before edging closer—a tempting distraction. "Not now," he grumbled, batting it away dismissively, irritation sharp in his movement. The filament recoiled, its light dimming as it darted toward a wicker crate. The container snapped open with a faint, satisfying sigh, swallowing the errant thread before falling still once more.

Above, a forest-green filament emerged from the shimmering network, its vibrant hue catching Diesel's attention against the muted background. He tracked its controlled arc as it dove between two parcels, then zipped ahead to land inside a polished leather folder on a nearby shelf. A brief shimmer of dust spilled outward like scattered stardust. The cord seemed to wriggle into place, retreating with a faint olive glow trailing behind, vibrating softly as if acknowledging its new position.

Diesel chuckled, the sound filling the space. Ezekiel's words thrummed through the air once more: *Not all shadows are born from darkness. Some are cast by the light we seek.* The folder stirred at the baritone of its owner's voice, awakening as if roused from a deep slumber. Then it leapt free with a graceful flutter. Its descent was elegant—birdlike—and it landed with precision in Diesel's outstretched hand.

"Objective secured," he stated, patting the folder as it settled in his palm. Cool, yet alive with energy, it hummed as he ran a finger along its stitched binding.

Exhaling slowly, the tension he hadn't realized he was holding began to dissipate.

Once settled, the container opened fully on its own, its edges wavering subtly. A deep gray ombre emanated from within, the darker shades at its core blended into lighter hues that fluctuated with a restrained vitality. Threads of memory hovered inside, their vibrant strands weaving together like a suspended tapestry. The green-hued cords stood out among them, their richness bold and unmistakable.

The tome responded—tucking the agitated filament inside. The fibers stilled, their frantic movements gradually calming, retreating deeper within the folds with a sense of quiet submission.

Then, with measured gentleness, he coaxed the other filaments aside as though reaching for something fragile. Carefully, he extracted the green-hued film, cradling it like a small, delicate creature.

It wavered in his palm, warm and assured, as if it knew it was safe—

eager to reveal its truths. It coiled gently around his fingers, like a tiny being finding refuge in his calloused hand.

The folder snapped shut with a sharp yet graceful motion, its task complete. It hovered for a moment, bowing in acknowledgment, before soaring back to its place on the shelf above. Diesel watched it settle, the air around him calm once more—though the weight of the memory in his hand promised anything but peace.

His breath slowed, each inhale and exhale marking the retreat of the labyrinthine corridors within his mind as he steadied himself before returning. With a final, exacting release, his eyelids snapped shut—and a deep, guttural reverberation filled the space. Ancient and resonant, it thrummed through his chest like a heartbeat echoing through the ages. Primitive. Familiar. A sound that seemed capable of tearing open the fabric of time itself, acknowledging his presence.

When the motion subsided, Diesel found himself before the towering gothic panels that marked the threshold between his internal sanctum and the world beyond. Each was adorned with a regal feline visage, encased within a full moon that shimmered with ethereal brilliance—almost like fog. The light didn't glow outward but gathered from within the celestial body itself, a iridescence that glided with the ambient shadows of the space. The lion's eyes, carved with meticulous accuracy, watched him— commanding and eternal.

His gaze dropped instinctively to the polished floor, where the lunar orb and beast were faintly mirrored in rippling reflections—their edges shimmering like light refracted through water. The lion's mouth, mid-roar, moved in the silence—its animation eerily deliberate, as if speaking a language beyond sound.

Diesel tilted his head, his brow creasing at the unexpected display. The muted roar, though soundless, seemed to resonate in the quiet, carrying an intangible weight. The moment inscribing itself in his mind—a fragment of meaning yet to be understood, a thread in a larger, unfinished tapestry. But the present tugged insistently at his focus, demanding his attention for what lay ahead.

The thrumming deepened as Diesel pressed his palm against the smooth surface, the intricate carvings humming barely beneath his touch. The moon's light, nestled behind the lion's head, billowed just barely—a pulse echoing his own heartbeat. With a low groan, the twin slabs began to part, their weighty wood grinding as they grinded outward, granting him passage while safeguarding the truths within.

Beyond the threshold, the study's embrace beckoned—steadfast, familiar. He shot a final glance over his shoulder, the silent roar of the lion lingering at the forefront of his consciousness. It had somehow been threaded into the labyrinth that would always loom within his mind. Too vast to comprehend on his own, it would forever *tap-tap-tap* at his shoulder with every step.

Pressing his palm firmly against the door's surface, the intricate mechanisms stirred to life. Deep in the thick walls, bolts churned and ground, their movements measured and ancient, bearing the weight of centuries. The cool wood whispered against his skin, melding into a recognition woven into its core—a silent communion between the seeker and the gates within his inner vault.

The grayish-gold hinges creaked and groaned, straining under the immense pressure of each slab as the bond sealed everything in. Rolling his neck, the constraints dissolved, granting Diesel the time to fully compartmentalize—tucking away this piece of himself.

Refocused, he turned his gaze upon the surface of the projection, his physical form never having truly left.

Settling in, Missy flared to life. A chuckle pulled at the corner of his mouth—a reminder of unrestrained joy on a holiday morning, anticipation bubbling over and spilling across the floor.

Leaning forward, the emerald filament woven between his fingers glimmered with shared excitement, alive with a subtle sheen. Soft green trails of light spilled over his hand, tracing faint paths against his skin, twisting and curling as though resisting containment. This was no inert fragment of the past—it throbbed, almost imperceptibly. It wasn't merely a memory; it was a presence—patient, yes, but with a growing insistence, as though it had lingered in the shadows for too long and now demanded to be known.

Setting the film on the charred coffee table with care, he listened as its contact was accompanied by a sound so soft it felt like the breath of wind wandering through a rain-soaked forest.

"Let's see what you've been keeping from me, Z," he said, the words edged with the grit of weathered stone. A dull, pervasive weight coiled in his gut, explaining the weariness that had seeped into his bones since the supposed passing of his bonded brother.

Then the realization cut through him like a blade drawn clean, separating what he had carried for so long from what had truly been hidden beneath. *Grief*—real and consuming—had been layered there, yes, but it had been deliberate. A veil. Strategically placed to conceal something far more insidious.

Epiphany struck.

Holding the film in his hand had felt like unsealing a long-buried chest—its contents spilling out and rushing back into the void where they had once belonged.

It wasn't just clarity, though clarity came with it. It was reclamation—the slow, steady return of something essential. A part of himself that had been tied down, shadow bound to this memory. A part he hadn't even realized was missing. The sensation was both startling and disorienting, like blood rushing into a limb that had fallen asleep—bringing with it the sharp, stinging ache of revival.

The hollow pang he'd carried for years began to take shape—and for the first time, it made sense. He had thought it was only grief—the kind that carves itself into your chest and stays there, a permanent void. The loss of Nadine. The loss of Ezekiel. The weight of those absences was genuine, and they burned as they went down. But the shadow binding had twisted that pain, coiling it around him to keep him blind. Now, as the tether unraveled, he could feel the difference. This wasn't just sorrow. It was deprivation—the lack of being fully himself.

"This is why I didn't see it," he muttered, fingers flexed instinctively, tingling with disbelief as he tested the newfound freedom of this truth. *Ezekiel wasn't gone.* That rawness had been buried beneath layers of shadow and pain, distorted by the parts of him that had been locked away. *I hadn't been kept from it by failure—but by design.* And now that the binding had loosened, he could finally feel the full gravity of what had been taken from him.

For so long, every breath had fallen just shy of full—caught between inhale and exhale, leaving him half-filled and aching for more. Now, as his reality unraveled, it felt like his lungs were expanding for the first time in years. The strain of not knowing had been suffocating, but he hadn't even recognized it for what it was. Bitterness had kept it bound—a twinge that settled in his chest, the sharpness of understanding slicing into place like a shard of glass against tender flesh. The grief he had carried wasn't false; it had simply been layered with purpose—a carefully woven barrier meant to shield him from the truth.

"And as always, Ezekiel's train of thought—happens to be—twenty steps ahead," he posed, his tone tinged with something darker. "When you're unable to do what you were made for, the part of you left idle begins to rust, leaving you unprepared—a burden that challenges your control. That strain builds, becoming a thorn in your side, an irritant that rattles the mind. It's why the girls have been running on fumes, and you, of all people, have just shown me why."

His fingers hovered above the surface, the space between them trembling as Diesel stretched his quintessence—something simple, a soft nudge of air. His muscle fibers responded to the gentle motion—almost imperceptible—carrying bits of dormant strength forward, like a shallow breath drawn through ancient lungs, tousling the filament ahead.

Bursts of olive hues flared in rhythm with the strand, like raindrops plinking into stagnant water, causing reflections to ripple across the grain of the wood. There was a patience—timeworn and watchful—heavy with a quiet hunger, as though it had been *tap — tap — tapping* its fingers in restless anticipation, finally exclaiming, *At last, you're ready to listen!*

The table responded—not with waves, but with a slow, predatory grace. Like frost claiming a windowpane, the surface ebbing with methodical exactitude, absorbing the undulating fiber into its chilled core. Diesel remained motionless. This wasn't merely a moment of revelation—it was the burden of clarity: of seeing what had long been veiled, confronting what had been withheld, and recognizing the toll that restricted authorization had exacted.

His fingers tightened along the rim, grounding him as his focus held fast to the illuminated weave. It swelled with expectancy, radiating a muted urgency—alive, insistent. For a fleeting moment, Diesel allowed himself a sliver of belief. Not for ease. But for answers.

The filament stirred gently, its light uncertain yet gathering, a ribbon of thought long dormant but ready now to lift. It curled upward, steady as smoke drawn by a measured pull. As it climbed, the mist thickened, blooming outward in fragile, translucent layers—like petals unraveling from a flower too delicate to touch. Each wisp uncoiled, its olive-green hue morphing with intention, teetering between solid grayish-white and ephemeral, caught between light and shadow.

"This isn't a memory," he muttered, then hesitated. "It's...*a map?*" He faltered, then corrected himself. "Fuck...no. *It can't be,*" his voice darkening. "No...you're fucking debriefing me, you damn bastard." A sharp chuckle escaped him—not sinister, but edged with recognition. "You set this up." He clicked his tongue. "Well, I'll be fuckin' damned. A breadcrumb hidden in a labyrinth of raw truths." He shook his head. *"Fucking brilliant, brother."*

The haze held its shape, confined to the charred borders of the coffee table, as though respecting the limits Diesel himself had established. Yet it throbbed with restrained intent, murmuring of boundaries it might one day breach. Shapes stirred within—indistinct, like candlelight glimpsed through steam-slicked glass. The filament, now alive in its liberation, stretched outward in sweeping arcs, swelling with an expectancy that was beautifully tangible.

"What I don't get just yet is this," Diesel muttered. "How the hell did you work your way into my mental vault without notice?" His focus wavered, gaze lifting to the ceiling as if the answers might be scrawled above. "Smart bastard—*smart*—*fuckin' bastard*, you are." He slammed his fist against the armrest. "Well, Missy...I'm guessing you all know something I don't. Get to it, then."

In response, Missy's light erupted with unrestrained exuberance. Her candelabras tossed jubilant waves of amber and gold across the walls, splashing bursts of brilliance like a painter drunk on joy. The hearth flames surged to life, sputtering embers that twisted into shimmering motes of light, darting and spiraling—tiny, defiant fireworks caught mid-celebration.

Raising his eyebrows, his chin tilting just enough to level his dry tone, Diesel tracked one of the sparks flitting close to his shoulder, erratically beaming with bubbling determination. "So, I was right—you've been sitting on Ezekiel's little secret," he said, puffing out a chuckle. "How about we don't set the place on fire in the process, huh?" His words were clipped, sharp, as his gaze followed the drapes twitching in the corner—almost like Missy was applauding with invisible hands. "I get it. You're thrilled. But let's not blow the roof off, yeah?" He watched as the room reined itself in, energy folding back like an excitable child trying to behave. With that, he returned his focus to the tactical update before him.

The verdant filament paused momentarily, as if waiting for Diesel's full, undivided attention. Once it had been reacquired, its tendrils extended outward, weaving deeper into the projection's veiled depths. They dispersed in intertwining hues of shadowed silver and burnished bronze, the colors merging seamlessly, with the olive threading itself further into the scene's enigmatic heart. The motion held him fast, drawing him forward as the interplay of dark and luminous forms entwined.

Like the fated rise of a sacred tide, the convergence of radiant strands and coiled shadows emerged, their voices an ageless resonance pulled from the marrow of existence. *"Join us,"* it beckoned. Smoke billowed upward, spiraling into transient forms, words blooming within the coils: *"You are right on time, as I always knew you would be, my, dear brother."*

He simply observed, as a ribbon of luminescent silk unfurled into a milky, billowing haze—reaching forward like breath giving shape to thought. *You and your chess games*, he thought, watching a miniature night sky paint itself into existence. A canvas of deep obsidian, speckled with faint celestial brilliance, tugged at something primal, spinning itself into a lone word—*stars*. The compact statement quickly dissolved into haze before bursting into motion. A streak of vaulting light, silver-tailed, gracefully arced and crescented through the miniaturized heavens, scattering trails of mist and stardust in its wake.

"The stars…" Diesel repeated, his tongue clicking against his teeth as he sank deeper into the cushions. "The North Star and Starlight Beach?"

As if in rebuttal, a leisurely rising moon emerged, etched with craters and valleys bathed in muted brass light, shadows clinging stubbornly to its rim.

"Okay. Stars…and a moon," his cadence tightened, voice edged with growing impatience. "Come on, man, I don't need *all this bullshit.*"

The cusp of the moon flickered once, as if blinking back—dumbfounded by his remark. A dull gleam spilled into the thickening fog, taunting him as it languorously wove a curtain of vapor and shadow, rippling across the backdrop. Words rose from the ghostly veil—*'deliberate'* and *'purpose'*—hovering like reprimands delivered from on high.

"I get that it's deliberate and has purpose. I'm saying I don't need the light show."

Diesel's focus tightened. His palm cracked hard against his knee. "Get fuckin' on with it already!" he barked.

The table responded like a creature startled into movement—its pace accelerating. From the hollow space where the star had erupted, another streak surged upward, carving a stardusted arc across the path of the moon's now-muted glow. It dove into the mist with a *ploof*, the fog undulating outward in steady waves.

From that rupture, a single ember lifted—drawn into the orbit of Starlight's lighthouse, its silhouette resolving through the fog like a memory too vivid to forget.

"Perfect," he muttered. "Let's add more layers to the same damn thing."

Across the room, Nester's filament swelled into a friendly reminder: *Foundation is everything, Sir.*

Starlight guides those adrift, a beacon for lost souls. The notion churned through the scene's mist, its acceptance bringing forth a silhouette—standing tall on the fog-drenched shoreline. Diesel leaned into the butt of his palm, eyes narrowing as he tried to make out the outline, hauntingly familiar.

The figure flickered between light and shadow, blurring the boundary between reality and imagination. Ezekiel stood, a delicate thread unraveling downward. Its end effortlessly caught and clasped within his fingers, behaving like an inflatable toy, bobbing slightly with each subtle movement.

Then, as if triggered by some unseen mechanism, Ezekiel's voice reverberated through the space—fluid, strong, and unexpected. "The light and the darkness, Diesel—they are not opposites. They are partners, bound together in a dance as old as time itself."

"It's already known that they are tethered. Like the stars and the moon, guiding each other—shadows and light, night and day," Diesel stated. The words left him as he mulled over the ideas. "I get all that, though. But could it have more to do with what's obscured by this…curtain of mist and shadow?"

Incandescent stars clustered tightly together, as though the very fabric of reality was twisting and reshaping itself along the shoreline in response to the inquiry. Just as Ezekiel's figure had materialized, a second, petite presence stepped into the scene.

As her form came to a standstill, parallel to her father's, she erupted into a blinding brilliance, forcing Diesel to avert his eyes. Through parted fingers, he observed as Runa fluidly balled up, melding into a heated orb of concentrated light and raw quintessence.

Her form whirled like a top caught in a ferocious, gusting storm. The air vibrated with an escalating hum that surged, pressing against him, filling the space with its relentless crescendo. Her outline blurred, fracturing into a cascade of dazzling radiance—a nova teetering on the brink of eruption.

"Is she…" His words stumbled, faltering upon the goosebumps tumbling down his arms and pooling at his wrists. "She is the light…and Izayah is the darkness. Their quintessence—it's of the old world's essence…"

As soon as the last syllable left his mouth, her form shot skyward, a violent motion shattering the fragile stillness, erupting into a cascade of radiant particles. What had once been Runa now rained down like fractured stars, distorting the light into fragmented hues.

"Rainbows of hope…" Diesel's reverence threaded through his tone as the spears of life and light pierced through the air. As each glittering bead touched down, shifting shadows began to emerge—an elegance that defied comprehension. "Her quintessence *heals*…" His voice splintered with disbelief. He watched as the mist rippled outward in gentle, choreographed waves of mossy green, knitting itself into intricate structures within the lighthouse background.

Buildings took shape as cobblestones clicked into place; the sound of stone meeting stone was faint but sharp. The boardwalk stretched ahead, its wooden planks leading toward the central courtyard, framed by pastel storefronts. The facades glowed warmly under lanterns strung between rooftops, a steady line of light.

The courtyard, the heart of the town, was where the cobblestones converged, radiating outward toward the boardwalk and the activity around it. At one corner, the North Star stood—a towering structure, anchored deep in the haven's foundation. Its polished surface reflected the starlit sky above. The courthouse and town hall, with their curved arches and subtle seaside features, provided a sense of permanence—symbols of Starlight's enduring purpose. Stars reignited above, scattered across the night sky, their light sharpening every detail, as if daring Diesel to ignore the truth unfolding before him.

"She brought Izayah back, the one who stitched this place together by leveraging patience, passion, and purpose." His tone softened, a hint of reverence threading through. "She's a beacon; a renewal." A breathy huff escaped him, "Is she the fuckin' answer for the younglings?"

Strings of olive threads bloomed skyward, a nod to his statement, confirmation bleeding into the briefing.

The miniaturized figure of Ezekiel raised his fingertips to his forehead, a sharp gesture of saluted acknowledgment. Redirecting his gaze back to the stringed moon, he tossed a thumb over his shoulder, signaling Diesel to slid his focus to the obscured veil dividing the projection. As the notification registered, the mist thickened, and a dim, oscillating beam revealed the faint contours of another lighthouse and its shoreline, briefly illuminated.

When the rotating beam of light gave way to darkness again, the shadow settled over the coastal edge, revealing only a faint inlet. Lanterns flickered to life, weakly beating like embers on the brink of extinction. Their fragile glow battled against the thickening fog.

Appearances deceive; clarity demands patience, Diesel thought.

Seekers—beaded up within the swirling haze, letters coiling and looping with an ethereal light that cut through the dusted mist.

The unhurried inscription pressed against his thoughts, demanding full attention. "*More* Truth Seekers? Beyond *this* shroud?" His jaw tightened as his boots scuffed along the floorboards, treading through the uprooted possibilities. "They *still* exist." The thought struck, like a battering ram against stone. "Well, I'll be damned. He found a way to conceal them. That's why he needed me shadow bound and kept on this side. Intel without knowing."

As if nodding to the weight of insight, the moon's light shifted—shedding its familiar silver, bleeding into a tarnished relic of time. Brass hues seeped down its sides, pooling beneath Ezekiel's feet like spilled oil. His form, once vibrant, dissolved into the brassy puddle—a presence that had fulfilled its purpose.

He pressed his knuckles to his mouth, jaw tight, speaking through the grip. "Firehearts and quintessence flames still remain." The moon hung steady, continuing to leak thick, glooping blobs of molten light. It wasn't revelation—it was a tactical assessment. An idea forming, tested aloud.

Between the twin beams of sweeping light, a silhouette wavered—haunting and half-formed, flickering between substance and nothingness. Each pass sharpened its outline. The figure took a step forward—just one—and the mist latched onto it, curling around its edges like a jealous tide unwilling to let go. It didn't care. It stood tall, defiant—for just a moment—before sinking into the clouded expanse, dissolving into the gloom like it had never been there at all.

But just as abruptly as it had vanished, the figure reemerged—this time within the radiant bounds of Starlight's side of the projection. It stood tall, unwavering, its form etched against the beam of the lighthouse. The light didn't just expose—it assessed, confirmed, classified. Every line was drawn with intent, its brilliance bordering on reverence. From its outstretched fingers, tendrils of shadow unfurled, deploying in strategic formation. No wasted movement. No uncertainty. Every thread carried a directive.

"Izayah was briefed on both havens?" Diesel snapped—a demand for confirmation.

A low hum rippled through the table and floorboards, vibrating with restrained power as the wall of shadow quivered, restless, pressing at the boundaries like a force testing for weaknesses.

Izayah stood, his presence exacting, unshaken. The Elite's leathers marked him—tailored for functionality, melded perfectly to his form to enable controlled, precise movement beneath the reinforced fabric. His shadow stretched long across Starlight's cobblestone paths, its reach an extension of the power held in reserve.

"The North Star holds the pathways." Izayah's voice carried softly through the air, its low cadence hooking Diesel's attention like a thread pulling taut. "To a greater depth of understanding…it's a beacon for those who seek, for those who question."

He lifted a hand toward the moon as though beckoning it closer. Between his fingertips and the celestial plane, a faint thread of light pulsed, tethering him to its radiance with each measured movement.

"Ryker holds ownership of the North Star. An *Elite guard* with an *Elite purpose.*" His voice thinned as his projection began to dissolve—fading back into the cobblestone haze of Starlight like a shadow retreating to its source.

"Noted," Diesel grunted. "Ryker holds an assignment I'm unaware of."

Before the silence could settle, Nester scuttled down from the desk, his miniature arms sweeping in an animated flourish. *Starlight is only the beginning, Sir.* His bulb-like head flickered between shades of blue and green— uncertainty woven into the declaration. *We were instructed not to say. I'm sorry, Sir.* His luminescence faltered, draining into a dull, sickly green—the color of regret.

"Wait a minute…you knew about this too?" Diesel's gaze hardened, the words clipped and low, tempered with incredulity. "There are other havens. Other sanctuaries." He scoffed, shaking his head. "Between you and Missy…I swear." His tone softened into a weary smirk as he eyed Nester. "*Let me guess,* you were bound by operational security for the mission as well?"

The small bulb atop Nester's head bobbed in a considered affirmation as his tiny form shuffled closer, each articulation tentative. Reaching Diesel's feet, he hesitated. Without a word, Diesel lifted the little figure effortlessly, setting him on the armrest beside him.

"Nes," Diesel began, voice steady. "Sometimes we have to withhold intel from those we care about—if it means securing the bigger picture. Operational outcomes matter."

Nester's small form slumped against the armrest, but the filament inside him flared bright yellow—a quiet surge of relief, of appreciation. Without a word, he reached out, placing a tiny, piped arm against Diesel's forearm. His light steadied, then sparked with renewed focus, drawing Diesel's gaze back to the projected surface.

The display responded with measured grace, rotating through a calculated 180-degree arc and shifting Diesel's vantage. At its center, a thick wall of mist and shadow held firm—an impenetrable divide slicing through the field. A division in motion, where on one side, Starlight Beach faded into obscurity. Its former clarity dissolved into dense haze, its lighthouse—a steadfast beacon just moments ago—now flickered weakly, its beam distant, diminished, like a memory worn thin with time.

Opposite, the concealed terrain surfaced. The moon hung low and heavy, its deep brass hue casting elongated silhouettes across the shoreline, sharpening Moonlight Beach into focus. As the projection continued its steady rotation, the once-shrouded town came into view—its features resolving like figures behind a misted pane of glass.

Like its twin, the beacon of this newly revealed haven seized Diesel's attention—stark, vivid, commanding—the same scrutiny once given to Starlight Beach's guiding light. A beam of radiance threaded through the scene, reaching outward as ocean waves surged and retreated in unbroken cadence. Each measured sweep ignited the coastline: lanterns flared to life with a soft *whoosh* and *shhhh*—honeyed flames swaying with the seaside breeze.

Stone walkways unspooled with steady grace, winding through the streets, weaving between shopfronts that settled into place with weighted finality—*clunk, clunk, clunk*. Their thresholds hinted at life just beyond. Cobbled paths extended outward, their rhythmic *clink-clank-clunk* forming a purposeful cadence as the town exhaled into its own quiet rhythm.

At the heart of the coastal refuge, a steadfast tower stood watch— Southern Star Café, its name carved in elegant script that spiraled along its frame. At its peak, a beacon flared to life, spilling a wash of warmth across the courtyard. Tiny, hand-carved tables nestled into the plaza, their sturdy forms grounding the space as faint strains of music drifted upward. The melody wove through the sweeping arc of light, an undercurrent of intent —the café's walls treasuring every secret, cradling each story, and lingering in handcrafted joy.

Diesel rose, instinct drawing him toward the misted divide of the projection. Curiosity coiled low in his gut—restrained but unmistakable. He paused briefly, repositioning behind the cushioned chair, adjusting for a broader vantage of Moonlight Beach. From this angle, the town stood sharp and resolved—each detail etched with intent. Not just a settlement. A stronghold. Weathered, yet fortified.

Diesel's gaze lingered, absorbing the clarity before breaking focus and stepping forward—crossing the divide. His boots pressed firm against the floorboards as he took position squarely in front of Starlight. Instantly, the display sharpened—brilliance restored. The lighthouse beam cut through the night, unwavering, steady. From this vantage point, the town breathed —vivid, unclouded—each detail laid bare, as if the mist and shadow had never existed.

He took a step back, frown deepening, noting that from his seat, Starlight Beach would once again fade into obscurity, its glow swallowed behind the thick wall of vapor and murk. Moonlight Beach, however, remained uncompromised—stark in its definition.

Sinking back into the velvet, he tilted his head against its billowed edge. The realization snapped into place. *One remains visible. The other fades. It all comes down to positioning.* His jaw tightened. *It's not a barrier—it's a filter. A condition. Shift into the right place, and the truth surfaces. Stand at the wrong angle, and it distorts—deflects.*

"They're only slight contrasts," he murmured into his knitted fingers as the thought skimmed the edge of revelation. "The wall isn't there to separate. It's there to obscure. To protect." Clarity struck with pinpoint force— undeniable, cold. "The wall isn't here for us—it's to conceal them. To keep us in the dark about what's really at play."

He took a moment, cleared his throat, then barreled on. "What we once assumed to be an imminent threat has revealed itself as a carefully planned operation—each element placed with strategic intent. Not the chaotic randomness we believed. This is a barrier—one that keeps us cocooned up and away." His jaw tensed. "So then…what's reinforcing it? What's maintaining operational control?"

The revelation hit with unrelenting weight—raw, unyielding in its depth. "Sanctuary. Shadow City. The Lands…" Diesel's voice was edged now—hard, resolute. "Every ounce of effort, every sacrifice—we gave everything in service, and all the while, we were the ones shadow bound. Kept in the dark." He exhaled, "The war…never ended." The words slipped out, low and bitter, soaked in the weight of a truth long buried. It wasn't just an answer—it was a reckoning. "And yet, this rebellion's *been years in the making.*"

His chest tightened. *When did the planning begin?* He latched onto the thought, desperate to dissect the connections—the star, the moon, the lighthouses. *It's all tied together.*

"How and when did Ezekiel figure all this out? When exactly was I shadow bound?" he demanded, his focus snapping to Nester.

The air cracked in response to his demand. The moon trembled, its surface distorting as if under pressure before spiraling into chaos. Diesel's attention swung toward the projected heavens, drawn to Izayah's shadowed form as it streaked into the obsidian night, trailing ribbons of mist like an unraveling thread.

The gathering dark dispersed like ink in storm-stirred water, coiling and folding in on itself with uncanny intent. Tendrils of black laced through the air, shaping themselves into a single phrase—*Moonlight Beach* —before collapsing back into the thickened haze.

"No surprise there, given the moon and stars," Diesel muttered. "Tell me something I don't know, Lieutenant General."

Tendrils lashed outward once more, relinquishing control to the message that came in low and commanding, each word sharp and unrelenting: *"Beyond this wall, quintessence has the potential to reach full capacity once more. The Tree of Life has a fragmented twin, and the Tree of Shadow has now sprouted."*

Diesel turned his attention to the sapling—a stark contrast of purpose, two opposing forces bound by design. The pieces were aligning. "Moonlight is where they took her in," he said with certainty. "You clever bastard."

His gaze followed the Moonlight beacon as it cut through the mist. Thatched roofs and weathered facades whispered of simplicity—rustic and unassuming, yet unmistakably intentional. The finer details caught and held his focus: enchanted lights swayed, their glow hinting at untold stories; bundles of herbs hung from eaves like silent wards; shop windows framed carvings so intricate they seemed to stir in place.

"It *is* of the old." His finger tapped the space just beneath his nose, the rhythm subtle, habitual. "What I know right now is this: where Starlight guides the lost, Moonlight challenges the seekers—masking everything in uncertainty, forcing them to confront the raw reality of what is."

Izayah's form swooped back down, stepping into the heart of the town. His leathers drank in the dim light, rendering him a shadow against the darkness pooling at his feet. Cool mist wrapped around him —not as a veil, but as an extension of presence. He didn't simply exist in obscurity; he commanded it—an unyielding force carried forward by will.

He moved to the center of the square, just beyond the Southern Star, which stood firm—its dark frame rising above the rooftops, pressing into the brass-hued glow of the moon. The weathered stone foundation bore deep fissures, jagged veins like fault lines—scars left by the relentless hand of the Great War.

Pausing at the base, his gloved hand rose, fingers closing around a string pulled taut. It vibrated with a low *ting* as it stretched skyward—a golden thread linking the café's beacon to the celestial brass orb above. Patient and waiting.

"He's the guardian of the unknowing. Where Runa breathes life and light, Izayah measures it in darkness and shadow. That's why he walked willingly into Visha's hellhole. Two decades in her playground, and she thought she earned the right to break him. All the while, she was building him. He's fuckin' stacking his deck."

The mist around the tower coiled tighter, a silent nod in response. "I can hear the thrumming between the two havens, Nes. Like a taut wire—light and shadow locked in equilibrium."

Nester bobbed his head in reply, leaping from his perch. His piped hands clasped behind his back as he paced the length of the fireplace, listening.

"They're two sides of the same coin," he murmured, the thought clicking into place. "Starlight and Moonlight...Runa and Izayah...they don't just coexist. They're intertwined—essential. That's why the burn mark healed the way it did. It wasn't just a scar—it was a bond." He paused, jaw tightening as the implications rooted deeper. "If their soul weaving runs that deep...what if Runa has the ability to heal Izayah after whatever happened with the Netheron?" His brow furrowed. "I wonder... I wonder if distance factors into it."

His gaze snapped back to Izayah, though his mind veered slightly off course, circling the same truth from another angle. *Shadows don't just obscure; they test. They refine. Darkness forces light to rise—to define itself. Without contrast, light has no meaning. Light doesn't simply fight the dark—it exposes it. Shapes it. Gives it boundary. Gives it purpose. Without radiance, what is darkness but a void? No form. No weight. Just empty.*

"Izayah might be the night and Runa the dawn—they're not adversaries. They're two forces, attunement by equal intensity. The moon doesn't diminish the sun, and the sun doesn't erase the moon. They frame each other. They give context—balance." He lingered in the in-between of thoughts before pressing on. "They're soul woven, not because one compensates for the other, but because *each* amplifies the other's essence. Light shines brighter because darkness sharpens its edges. Darkness gains strength because light defines its boundaries. Separate, they stand in opposition. Together, they close the gap—bringing balance, restoring order."

Diesel threw one ankle over the opposite knee, conclusions fused, looping back, tested, rechecked. "Well, I'll be damned, Z." A small chuckle followed, unbidden, edged with disbelief. "I have to ask—was he behind his own demise?"

Missy's curtains rustled as the planks gave an encouraging creak, as if to say in a singsong voice, *Ohhh…getting warmer.*

"And Nadine…" He trailed off, comprehension and inquiry threading together. "Were the Unbinders and Truth Tellers just all tucked away somewhere?" His eyes locked onto Nester's pacing frame, knuckles paling as he wrestled with the implications. "Did Ezekiel construct the wall of mist and shadow? And if so, how did he manage that?" He held still, considering. "How would it even be possible?"

Nester's piped form paused, then perched cross-legged on the edge of the hearth, bulbous head bobbing with quiet gravity. *It's not my place to say, sir,* he intoned, *but I can tell you this—you're asking the right questions.*

"If the Tree of Shadow and the Tree of Life have siblings…or cousins…or whatever you call them, it all ties back to something like that, doesn't it?" A guttural sound rumbled in his throat—half growl, half sigh.

He's been trying to figure out a way, Sir. Nester's filament dimmed to a grayish-blue, tinged with quiet strain.

"What do you mean, trying to figure out a way?" Diesel's tone sharpened. "We know the wall is there. I've seen it. I see it now." He steadied himself, then pressed forward. "The wall of mist and shadow—it's not just for show. It's protection. It keeps them hidden. Keeps them safe…from Sanctuary, from Visha, from the not knowing." He blinked at the projection, trying to align the fragments, questions piling. "With these twin towns confirmed, are there more? Who else has this intel? How were they built? When did this happen?"

Diesel's fists slammed into the armrests with a crack that reverberated through the room, sending a jolt through the floorboards and into the projection itself. Threads of light wavered, distorting for a breath before snapping back into place. He shoved himself up from the velvet chair, its legs scraping sharply against the hardwood. Nester's filament flared—startled by the sudden shift in energy. "*You couldn't* have left me a damn hint? *A fucking clue?*" His voice cracked—low, ragged, the edge of it splintered with bitterness.

The fire in the hearth dimmed, its emberlight shrinking like a scolded child. Shadows crept across the walls, gathering thick in the corners like a looming threat. Missy pulled back, retreating beneath the weight of his frustration, while the curtains shivered faintly—a hush of reassurance Diesel wasn't ready to accept.

Then, without warning, it came—a sharpened frequency slicing through the tension like a direct transmission, blaring in his ears with the precision of a distant alarm. Diesel froze, body taut as the sound cinched around him. *Unmistakable.* A signal that struck deep, stilling him at the marrow.

"Well, that hasn't happened in…" He trailed off, a bitter laugh slipping free as the ringing deepened. Pressing a finger to his tragus, he gave it a slight wiggle, adjusting the pressure in his ear canal. "…*a fuckin' long time.*" The resonance swelled, clinging to him—thrumming between his ribs before dulling, refusing to fully release.

Then, like the horizon's first light edging into darkness, her scent arrived—radiant and grounded. It was steady, unmistakable, infused with warmth and memory. Not a whisper, but a surge of honey and spice that cut through tension like a blade to fog. The faintest thread, yet it unraveled everything—quieting the alert, tempering his edges, guiding him back into composure.

A dry laugh slipped out as a memory flashed into frame. "Aye, Diesel, you're one lucky bastard, ain't ya?" He could see it—Liam flicking the brim of his tweed cap, that sideways smirk in full effect. "You lucky sod— she's a gem, that one."

"Through all the darkness…after the losses from the Great War—she's the one who carried me through the wreckage. My lighthouse in the chaos." His breath stalled as the signal in his ears finally faded into silence. Notions drifted into place—one after the other—like linens pinned to dry beneath a steady sun.

My darling D. My sweet glass of whiskey—spicy, sweet, or somewhere in between, depending on the day. His hands folded, kneading away the tension, gratitude settling through him, as heat sank into muscle. *And she's all mine. The one person who's kept me sane.*

Her scent landed—clean and fierce—unwinding the mental snarl he hadn't realized had formed. It wasn't just a fragrance. It was tether. Memory. A thread spun through centuries, anchoring him to what mattered. *She was in it—her laugh, her touch, her impossible strength.* The pieces of her he'd carried for over nine hundred years. It calmed him. Drew him back from the storm in his chest. Reminded him who he was— *because of her. Some things don't fade. Some bonds don't fray. Even now, after all this time…She's my anchor. Always.*

Diesel glanced toward Missy, catching the subtle sway of her curtains and the quiet creak of floorboards. The soft pull of fabric suggested presence—Missy nudging him gently, reminding him he wasn't alone.

"Thank you." He bowed his head. "You always remember." He cleared his throat, and pivoted the conversation. "Didn't realize how much I missed having another pair of eyes that see the way I do." His focus slide back to the projection on the scorched coffee table, the illumination holding steady—serene in its stillness. Waiting. Curiosity stirred as he gestured toward the display. "I wonder if Rayanna's presence will change things." A beat passed. "Can't be that easy, can it?"

In response, a hum began to build in his ears again—diffused, but insistent—rising into a low buzz that pressed at the edges of his awareness. Diesel winced. "The alarm shouldn't have triggered twice," he muttered, jaw ticking as the sound swelled. He pressed his thumbs against his tragus and wiggled them slightly, trying to ease the pressure.

The buzz waned, then surged again—deeper now. Its resonance crawled across his skin like a current beneath a tide, ancient and undeniable. His shoulders squared, instincts on alert. "Make note of this, Nes. It could be tied to her unbinding."

Nester gave a quick nod, shuffled toward his journal, tucked it beneath one arm, and plopped back down along the hearth, the timeworn binding splaying open across his lap. With a practiced flick, he unlatched the pen and let the ink trail purposefully across the parchment—his documentation a ritual of contemplative focus.

This sharp ringing—it wasn't new. It had occurred before, though rarely, and never since the girls were shadow bound. It was a reaction, like a hidden tripline springing to life at the arrival of another Truth Teller. Their shared quintessence carried a frequency that struck a nerve—tuning them to one another like matched strings drawn taut by the same breath of wind.

Diesel pressed harder against his ear, willing the sensation to ebb. The buzzing settled into a heavy thrum, but its presence remained—anchored deep in his chest.

"You know, Nes," he said, voice low and edged with something like amusement, "I'll give it to you—I've missed this kind of alignment." He squinted slightly into the ache. "Good to see protocol still kicking in after all this time. Honestly…I wasn't sure the safeguards would hold. Hell, I'll still take it."

He glanced toward Nester, whose small form swayed in rhythm with the notion. The filament within his dome—normally a calm, silvery-blue—adjusted into deep green, then slowly flushed into muted gold, like lamplight softening over aged brass. A silent agreement, reverent in its gleam.

Still recording, Nester tilted his head without looking up—the answer already threading between them. *Affirmative, Sir. Their approach is confirmed. Protocols have begun to respond. I'll finalize verification regarding the resonance trigger—its source remains unclear. The keystones have been reactivated. Access will be granted.* With that, he clicked the pen back into place and gently closed the timeworn tome across his lap, its spine creaking in quiet satisfaction.

From within the walls, a low grind began—deep and deliberate—followed by the diffused clink of internal mechanisms engaging. Missy was already responding. Latches disengaged, ancient safeguards retracting. The study door creaked open, its inner workings humming back to life —welcoming those once locked out, now recognized for return.

Just as the last latch disengaged, Nester sprang into motion, practically bursting upright. His spectral sheen flared to a jubilant amber as he tucked the journal beneath one arm, excitement scattering off him in tiny, kinetic bursts. With swift motion, he darted toward the desk's edge, bounding from step to ledge to the heavy surface above.

"Don't go bursting a bulb now," Diesel smirked, a low chuckle following as the sudden flurry of activity unfolded around him. "I like how we've just decided this is a last-minute party."

As if swept up in Nester's infectious rhythm, Missy sprang into motion. Cabinet doors snapped open and shut in quick succession, each movement crisp and purposeful. Pots shuffled with confident clinks, and the oven groaned before slamming closed with firm finality. Diesel arched a brow.

"Missy," he drawled, "we don't have time to bake cookies at the moment—no matter how good they'd be."

From the bookshelf came a flutter of pages—an eager rustle, like laughter skipping through old paper.

"I appreciate the enthusiasm," he added, as she swept across the floorboards, brushing away dust and tossing the curtains open with a confident flourish. "Why don't you go with a bit of D's vanilla and citrus blend? Should help the process."

Nester tucked his tome into a drawer, then turned his attention to the desk—his tiny piped hands straightening papers with the meticulous care of someone restoring order to a sacred space. He adjusted one, tapped the corner of another, his movements brisk but purposeful. Then, mid-motion, his light flared—a sharp, sudden gleam—as if a forgotten task had just struck him. Without hesitation, he sprang upright, momentum catching like a coiled spring released. In a blur of motion, he zipped toward the spiral staircase, arcs of light trailing behind him as he ascended, his energy scattering along the walls in flickering bursts. Even after he vanished onto the upper floor, the charged air hummed in his wake—alive with intent and urgency.

"Where are you going?" Diesel called, tracking the erratic levity as it darted toward the balcony above. "Giving her space, huh? Smart man. Always thinking ahead." He laughed aloud, rubbing the back of his neck as he pushed to his feet. "You ready for a bit of change, Missy?" he added, with dry amusement.

Her response came instantly—bold and unfiltered. A thick plume of vanilla and citrus erupted upward like a tossed curtain, hitting him full in the face. He recoiled with a bark of laughter, eyes watering as he turned his head. "Stars, woman," he coughed, swatting at the air. "You tryin' to season me alive?" His laughter tumbled out—raw, unguarded—as the floorboards swelled with animation, nudging him with playful insistence, an old friend elbowing him toward something he'd nearly forgotten to want.

His gaze lifted to the exposed rafters, expression softening. The house had always known him better than most. She prodded when he needed a push, waited when he craved stillness, and never missed her chance to remind him: even in uncertainty, there was space to grow. His laughter lingered like smoke suspended in a sunbeam—curling into the crevices, threading through the grain and fibers of the old wood like joy building a nest. *Even she can make room for the unknown…so why can't I?* He smirked, rubbing the back of his neck once more. "Alright, Missy." He gave a sharp clap, the sound bouncing off the beams, then started to work his palms together. "Let's get crackin'—see what secrets you've been sittin' on…and just how deep the shadow binding went."

Chapter Thirty-Three

Present Day

Click—clink—click—clunk.

The keystones activated in rhythmic sequence, each sound ticking through the beams like a timeworn watch resetting itself. Missy exhaled—a low, resonant breath that rippled through her walls, the very frame of the house altering in a graceful sway atop its foundation. The motion sent a muted sheen gliding along her interiors, casting a warm, ethereal luminance. That light coursed like lifeblood through golden patterns of painted branches etched into her structure—like exposed veins extending along the deep green paneling, weaving between portrait frames like a living conduit.

The branches threaded around and through the portraits, brushing light along their perimeters. Within, the inhabitants stirred from their long repose—lids fluttering, gazes sharpening with recognition, as though drawn from a centuries-old slumber. A few lifted languid hands to their temples or raised them to shadow their eyes, silent and watchful—vigilant, composed, unmistakably Elite. Their expressions bore only reverence, bearing witness to the return of something sacred. Their eyes followed the luminance as it swept onward like a migration of butterflies, dawnkissed wings unfurled in quiet succession. And in its wake, it left a hush of breathless awe—like the rustle of plumage rising from the forest floor.

The luminance swept beyond the portrait gallery, bypassing the kitchen as it curved around the study's entrance—just enough to anoint the threshold—before slipping through the inlet and tracing the room's perimeter like a tide seeking its shore.

It reached the hearth. The flames flared—lapping hungrily from the firebox. Then, as if a giant had inhaled too sharply, the blaze collapsed inward, the heat pulled back in a single, forceful breath that nearly snuffed it out.

Shadows surged, bowing low—grazing the floorboards to breathe across the fading embers, coaxing them back to life. Smoldering tongues stirred, curled, then caught—igniting anew in a retrained, rising blaze. A rebirth born not of flame alone, but of refusal to fade.

Diesel fell back toward the wet bar, arms folded firmly across his chest—a quiet command as he observed the light take hold. Yet, beneath hefty boots, the floor groaned—a deep, resonant alteration that rolled like thunder held in marrow. The timber responded, a recalibration as floorboards of deep ebony lifted, tilted, and slid into place with an architect's eye and a soldier's exactitude.

With a low groan and a subtle roll, the walls flanking the hearth began to stir. The bookcases—long anchored beside the stonework—detached with a gentle release and glided outward, making way as panels of hidden shelving extended from within the walls—stretching like ribboned paneling drawn along concealed tracks. Grain by grain, the timber unfurled, broadening the study's reach as though the room were stretching through an expansive yawn.

Bookshelves sprouted from the newly revealed walls with a sharp *shhhink*, their raw, rustic wood carrying the scent of fresh-cut boards. The fragrance mingled with the musk of old paper, crafting a living archive of memory and renewal.

"Guess it's as good a time as any to expand the office space!" Diesel called out, raising his voice over the jubilant chaos.

As the metamorphosis persisted, a muted brilliance filled the room, coaxing the Tree of Life from its long slumber. Its limbs pulling wide, shaking loose like a dog rousing from a tempered nap, bristling with newfound energy. The grain sighed and flexed, ancient wood acclimating like trunks reaching for sun after a centuries-long stillness. From its core, a mossy aroma emerged, laced with leathery undertones—a creamy, earthen fragrance that lingered in the air, warm and inviting. The boughs thickened with life, grazing the edges of the bookcases as the study continued to blossom.

A sharp thud cracked through the commotion as Liam slammed both palms down on the bar counter. The sound cut clean through the chorus of groaning timbers, shifting walls, and creaking shelves. Diesel threw a glance over his shoulder. Contact made.

"Gone a bloody blink, and you've rearranged da whole place like it's a new era. No note. No warning. Classy as eve'a," Liam called out, raising his voice above the din. He narrowed his eyes at the swelling limbs as they nudged the shelves aside, a smirk tugging at his lips. "Oi, Missy—hold up a tick, would ya? If you're fixin' ta change out da framed bits again, I'd like a say in it dis time."

Diesel shook his head, calling back, "And here I thought we were tapped out on shelf space. How wrong I was. Plenty of room left—for all the sap inked pages I didn't ask for." He sidestepped and settled into the doorframe, eyes sharp as another set of bookshelves eased out with a *clunk*, the house itself offering a smug *humph*. "Tell me—was this your idea, or Sir Izayah's genius plan to impress his sister?" His smirk deepened as he ran a hand through his hair, letting out a long, exaggerated sigh. "Who needs a cushy retirement when you've got a house with expensive taste?"

"*You?* Retirin'? Don't be daft. Ask any Elite—dey'd tell ya plain: no bloody deck you ever held had dat card." Liam chuckled, stepping in closer. "But best be grateful, Diesel—she might just save ya from goin' fat, bald, an' slow."

He adjusted his stance, one shoulder nudging the edge of the study's door. The panel swung outward with a soft *whoosh*. Rayanna reacted quickly, catching its edge with one hand before it could slam against the stopper.

"Well, somebody's excited to see us," she said, a crooked smile slipping into place as she threw a thumb over her shoulder. "Mama says these expansions aren't normal—but expected with this phasing. You look utterly thrilled."

"Yeah, well, this one's on you—Ray," Diesel said, throwing his hands up in mock surrender.

Rayanna chortled a laugh. "Nice try. This isn't mine to own. That said…" Her gaze drifted across the expanding room as she angled herself away, making room for Mama D, who swayed into his solid frame for support. "Look at her go—building a masterpiece while the rest of us are still untangling breakfast."

Without hesitation, his arms dropped to steady her fragile frame. "Nothing like blood reaching when you're not supposed to, eh?" he said, the words clipped—a grimace tugging at the corner of his mouth.

Rayanna watched as Diesel reached out, his fingers brushing the intricate braid resting over Mama D's shoulder. The gesture was measured—as if he were forcing himself to stay composed. He caught the end of the braid between his fingers, holding it loosely. His grip was distant, detached. Beneath the surface, frustration simmered, held back with visible effort.

"So, blood reaching wasn't in the game plan, huh?" Rayanna stated, dry and edged with sarcasm—enough to ease tension, but pointed enough to make her stance clear.

Diesel's hand dropped to his side, his movements clipped as his attention slid back to the chaos around them. The noise swelled, but his silence spoke volumes—his jaw tightening as though bracing against the moment. He cleared his throat. "Took a while this time, *didn't it, D?*"

She offered no reply as a faint blush crept back into her pallid cheeks. Instead, she pushed off him—movement firm yet unhurried—steadying herself. Tossing her head in silent acknowledgment, as if to say: *I know— leave it alone—for now.*

Diesel's chin lifted as he released an audible exhale—a stoic response, even for an Elite.

Rayanna leaned parallel to the arch, arms crossing as she observed the pair in silence for a moment. "You know," she said, "it's oddly comforting watching you all fumble like the rest of us. Makes relationship building seem *way more* attainable."

The wood beneath her backside rippled, catching her off guard and causing her to bound forward. "Hey—*lay off!*" she exclaimed at the mischievous wainscoting, as the floor beneath her feet gave a teasing shudder, like a quiet laugh at her expense. "I'm just trying to make a point!

Because between this whole unshadow bound—or whatever the hell you call it—and these two lost in La-La Land arguing about blood reaching, and then Mama looking like she's a dead woman walking, just saying—it's a bit much. And for the record," she continued, her tone taking on a sing-song lilt, "Ashla didn't seem to have a problem with the blood thing. But then again, Ashla doesn't seem to have a problem with anything."

She fluttered her fingers in mock elegance, pretending to pick at the air as her counterpart often did, her expression exaggeratedly serene. "'Oh, she's probably blood reaching or whatever,'" she exclaimed, reeling back as her tone dropped into dry irritation, "and that's it! Then she's off catching imaginary butterflies or whatever else she plucks out of the sky." With a shrug that lifted her shoulders to her ears, she added, "Meanwhile, I get left with a house that's practically shedding its skin, and everything feels serious—but would anyone know that? *Nope.* Not if I had to depend on Ashla for information. Like I said, she's just off running amok and stuffing invisible things in her pockets." She pointed sharply at the wall, where Missy gave another playful flutter through the floorboards. "How did I end up with the loony ones?"

The branch swung suddenly, its leafy arm catching her on the crown of the head, tossing her farther into the room. "Oh, come on!" she yelped, spinning around with an incredulous laugh. "What even is this? It's been, what, 12 hours? Maybe 17? And my entire world is about-faced—yet laced with wonky free spirits. To top it off, now I have a tree reaching out to connect?" She jabbed a finger at the ceiling. "Missy, quit it!" she barked, then pivoted toward the bough. "And you—behave." Then, looking at Diesel: "And yes, *about-faced wonky* is an insane term, but it's *my term.*" Huffing out a frustrated sigh, she trudged back over to the sidelines and plopped down.

Diesel's shoulders eased, the faintest smile breaking through his otherwise stern demeanor. Lifting a hand to cover most of his reaction, he muttered, "Welcome back...to the chaos." His voice carried just enough humor to let the tension in the room dissipate, leaving a rare moment of levity in its wake. "Can you tell they missed you...just a bit?"

The sweet Starlight Beach abode quivered, a subtle shimmer coursing through her walls as if laughter itself had tickled the grain—light and unexpected, stirring from within. Delicate tremors whispered beneath the floorboards, unsettling the foundation just enough to shift the balance of the room.

Mama D faltered, stumbling backward—her footing lost. Diesel moved fast, one arm snapping out to catch her across the back, the other guiding her into his chest. The impact struck true against the solid calm of him— broad and unmoving, encased in the leather of someone always ready. His arms closed around her without hesitation, strong and certain, anchoring her as if nothing in the world could breach that hold.

"*Missy, stop.*" The command was fiercely precise.

The house groaned, its expansion grinding to a reluctant halt—like strained gears faltering under immense pressure. Yet the tension lingered, a faint vibration running through the walls and beams, as though Missy herself were holding back an overwhelming force with sheer will.

Diesel turned his focus to her fragile form, his sharp demeanor soften- ing. One hand slipped to cradle the nape of her neck, his touch grounded and sure as he lifted her chin to meet his gaze. Her eyes—normally a deep, rich brown—had dulled to a hollow gray, shadowed by exhaustion. His thumbs traced along her cheekbones with light pressure, coaxing faint warmth and a hint of color back into her skin. As he held her, she closed her eyes, heavy with a collision of fear, devotion, and hushed reproach. Her voice trembled as she began, "I needed you to know before—"

"D," he whispered, cutting her off as he bowed slightly, bringing her closer.

"*I know...*" she breathed, the words fragile as she inhaled deeply, grasping for a moment outside of time. "Nadine found your Elite...they found them...and the girls."

"I can't lose you." Diesel's tone crumbled under the strain of the words. "Nothing is that important. Nothing. Do you hear me?" He searched her shadowed irises for a spark of clarity. "Whatever you needed to tell me— there are other ways now. Ashla could have..." His sentence dissolved mid-thought. She closed her eyes, allowing his thumbs to brush gently over her lids, warmth radiating from his touch—soothing, healing—as quintessence passed subtly between them. Lowering himself slightly, he pressed his lips to her hairline, lingering as if sealing a vow of devotion. "Your life always comes first, D. *Always.*"

Missy groaned beneath the pressure, her walls shivering as though on the verge of collapse. The floor released a long, warping creak, vibrations spiraling upward through the beams like the faltering thrum of an unsteady heart. Diesel's massive desk trembled—no longer immune to the unrest threading through the room. The tall bookcases lining the walls quaked, their shelves clattering in quiet rebellion, while over at the whiskey bar, the glasses chimed in a sharp, discordant cadence. Dust spilled from the arch above, swirling briefly in the dim light before settling like a held breath, waiting to break.

"Hey, lovebirds!" Rayanna called. "Think you could wrap up your heartfelt moment? Pretty sure Missy's about to blow a gasket." She threw an exaggerated glance at the trembling walls and vibrating furniture, her smirk curling into place—though it couldn't quite disguise the flicker of unease in her eyes.

"Ah," Liam drawled, a wolfish grin rising as he lifted his glass in a mock salute, the whiskey catching the light. "Oh, dat wee ray of charm ya carry around like da weapon. Always so full o' a bit of sunshine, aye?"

Rayanna mirrored his smirk, tilting her head as if to catch radiance along a blade's edge. "Well, you know me, Liam—here to light up your existence." She swept her arm in a flourish toward the trembling walls. "Speaking of charm, any chance you've got an idea how to calm this one down?"

"Och, now, lass, dinnae pin all the blame on Missy. She's just tryin' tae keep up wi' all dis emotion." He leaned forward, crystal glass tilted toward the pair, his grin broadening. "Looks like ye've got da whole house ready tae fall apart o'er yer wee love story."

Mama D's slender figure eased out from behind Diesel's imposing frame to meet Liam's gaze. Her expression drew taut, like steel struck against flint. Liam's grin faltered, dimming for a beat like a candle caught in a draft. With an awkward chuckle, he raised a hand, palm out, in mock surrender. "Ach, steady now! I'm only here tae enjoy the show."

"Enough." Diesel's voice landed with weight—coating the moment in finality as he pivoted back toward her. Tilting her chin up with two fingers, he met her gaze head-on. "We good?" he asked. A faint twitch in his jaw betrayed the strain beneath his composure. "No more blood reaching. Not here. Not while we're in Starlight."

She pulled away from his touch, her focus dropping as a quiet cough broke the silence. "We need a way," she said finally, each word rasping against her inflamed throat.

"With Ray's Truth Seeking door open—and Ashla in Starlight—you shouldn't have any trouble reaching me. Or Nester," Diesel stated.

"Yeah, well, Ashla seems to get along with the trees just fine," Rayanna quipped, her gaze lifting toward the faint quiver of the beams overhead. "Maybe those guardians can pass a message to this sapling that's desperate to sprout here in the study." She paused, eyes narrowing slightly. "Wait a minute…how do Truth Seekers talk to each other at a distance?"

"It'll be part of your training and I am not sure if oaks can communicate with the sapling. Though you've already managed it—with Runa. The communication thing. Not the sapling thing." Diesel replied. "As for the oaks talking to the sapling—" Diesel shrugged. "Can't see why not. The root system could link up—it's something to look into." He paused, looking back toward Rayanna.

"I thought that was more Runa than myself." Rayanna raised a brow at him. "Wait—how do you even know that?" Her look was equal parts curious and suspicious as she shot him a sideways glance. "Seriously, if reaching into people's blood is such a chore, I can whip up some truth plane—or maybe pick up a few construction tips from Missy. Problem solved. But really—are we good? Because this one"—she gestured toward the trembling walls—"is about to implode."

Missy's paneling groaned in response, the deep, resonant sound reverberating through the study like the rumble of a distant storm. The arch above the door shuddered, dislodging a stream of dust that spiraled downward.

"Ah, aye," Liam drawled, brushing at his shoulders as flecks sprinkled across his jacket. "Nothing like a house tryin' tae bury ye alive just for a wee bit o' fun."

Diesel maneuvered around Mama D without a word. He extended one broad hand and delivered a firm *thud* against the wall—solid, purposeful recalibration. The walls gave a stuttering shudder, then stilled. Beneath the surface, Missy responded—with released restraint. What had been braced in her structure began to ease, like a body interrupting a hiccup with sheer will. The tension uncoiled from her beams. Her framework, once locked in resistance, realigned from the inside out. The very marrow of her form reoriented in real time, dust whispering loose from long-held places.

"I'm not sure whacking her was quite what I had in mind," Rayanna quipped, tilting her head slightly as she stood.

"Och, lass, it's like a hard reset," Liam replied. "Tappin' dae rump o' a horse or pup when dey're too fixated. Sometimes ye've got ta remind 'em where ta focus." He shrugged, his wolfish grin widening. "Good tae see the old girl's back in da game."

For a moment, nothing happened.

Then, with a sharp *snap*—like a bowstring finally unleashed—the tension broke.

The study erupted into motion—its walls pressing outward with a fluid, almost reverent grace. A rolling *whoosh* swept through the space, carrying a kinetic tremor that pulsed along Missy's framework like a heartbeat rediscovered. Bookshelves responded with a crisp *shhhink*, resuming their gradual slide as they barged confidently into the outer edges, reclaiming ground with intention.

Above, the ceiling arched in defiance, releasing a resonant *pop-crack* as if shedding centuries of tension. Gilded trim along the edges rippled and gleamed, casting dappled reflections that danced across the room like sunlight refracted on open water.

Then came the *snap-snap-snap*—sharp, rhythmic, and certain—as the perimeter walls unfurled with the conviction of sails catching wind at sea. A deep rumble answered beneath their feet, like thunder rolling back through the skin of the earth. One by one, new planks emerged along the remaining unfloored stretch of the study, each sliding into place with an engineered *ker-thunk*—dark boards, gleaming, as though burnished by artisans working in real time. The ground seemed to inhale, settling each piece with reverent precision.

Above, along the second floor, alcoves bloomed from the widening span— elegant, curved balconies etched themselves into existence with a faint, steady *whir-thrum*, a resonance that moved like thought crystallizing into matter. The very structure hummed with intent, as if Missy herself had chosen not just to rebuild, but to remember what she was made of.

The air densified, saturated with the mingled scent of seasoned timber and fresh varnish, folded into the earthy musk of rain-soaked moss. It was no longer just motion—it was memory, structure, intention made tangible.

"You definitely can't deny that she's a go-getter," Rayanna called out, steadying herself against the doorframe as the deep clunking continued. "That walk-in closet just might be in your future, Ma." Her attention wandered toward the newly forming alcoves. "Yeah, the way things are going? Judging by the pattern here…more furniture's gonna be necessary."

A long sigh slipped from Papa D—part amusement, part dread. His stance loosened into something familiar, something grounded in family. A dash of admiration lit his gaze, drawn to the elegant arches taking shape above them. "Well, if Missy's preparing," he said, voice steady over the clamor, "she's doing it with some serious flair." His nod was subtle but approving, tracking the intricate golden motifs unfurling like ivy across the ceiling. "No one handles the unknown quite like this one."

The exposed rafters grumbled through the grain, a calibration—a measured release of tension held deep within the marrow. The resonance was low and primal, arcing like the ribs of some vast, mythical beast adjusting its spine. The spans of flying buttresses lifted with sculpted elegance, summoned skyward by a phantom architect's hand. Pale green currents of visible quintessence coursed along the ceiling joists, threading like lifeblood through twining, diffused veins—crafting the newly forming superstructure. At the apex, as each buttress crested, the core-sourced energy shimmered downward—illuminating the framework, revealing the grandeur of what she was becoming.

From the heart of the vaulted space, green-blue tendrils of energy spilled into the air—delicate and radiant. They bled outward like strokes of living paint, threading through the rising spans and transforming the ceiling into a canopy of shifting hues—colors that shimmered like sunlight scattered across billowing water.

"She's making room, Ray. Those bracelets aren't just for show." Mama D's gravelly tone threaded itself into the room's evolving current, laced with reverence as her gaze traced the intricate carvings spiraling into existence.

"What's that supposed to mean?" Rayanna called out, absently stroking the metal.

The house inhaled—tightening control, cinching the quintessence inward like breath held between beats.

Then she exhaled.

The energy flowed with intentional grace, sweeping back through every corner of the room—not as a flood, but as reclamation. Strange glyphs cascaded down the grain in silken gradients—faint and fleeting— vanishing as they fell, whispers from a language older than sound.

In the cusped corners, emberlit caches flared to life, beading into a strand of soft golden motes that drifted upward like fireflies summoned by memory. From the ether, the floor along the far wall—once bordered by plain casements—curved upward and reshaped. With a sequence of sharp *shhhinks*, slender panes slid into place, rising into lancet arched windows. Through their seeded starlight-smoked glass, vibrant hues refracted across the room, scattering prismatic patterns in a spectacle worthy of the finest Starlight Festival.

Shelving emerged from the walls above the windows, their lacquered bases marking the first contours of a third level beginning to coalesce. Drawn forward with deliberate force—less torn, more sculpted—they shaped the foundation of high-set alcoves. These recesses extended outward, stabilizing into full balconies fitted with smooth bannisters. From there, walkways spiraled along the study's upper edge, unfolding into passageways lined with uninterrupted tiers of bookcases—set end to end, with only narrow thresholds where one could cross. Above, arches and galleries stretched toward unseen chambers nestled just beyond sight. A hush echoed faintly—tapping like tiny feet—distant, thoughtful, as if the structure itself was still building its memory.

Then the tomes descended in a sweep of emberlit sparks, their spines aglow with quiet vitality. Each *plink, plank, plunk* struck a note in the symphony of transformation—titles inscribed in gilded script, gleaming as if sunlight had been trapped in ink.

Rayanna's eyes roved across the newly revealed expanse. "Well, would you look at that," she drawled. "Guess she's been saving the theatrics for the right moment."

"Or the right person," Papa D quipped, a glint of pride surfacing in his gaze as he muttered, "Atta girl." He turned his chin toward Rayanna, his smirk mirroring hers. "Happy now? Plenty of room for your truth planes—and whatever else you manage to conjure."

"Oh, don't worry," Rayanna said with a wink. "I'll think of something."

He angled himself between the two women, pulling their heads close as if to share a conspiratorial secret. "She's a hoarder! I'm convinced this was her plan all along." With a half-step back and a grin tugging at his lips, he called out to the shelves, "Well now—seems the vault's finally openin'. How big are we going? Is this really necessary?"

Above, a volume flapped loose from the second-level bookcase with unceremonious force, swooping dangerously close to his head. He ducked instinctively. "Hey—easy there, Pages! I prefer my reading material without the threat of a concussion," he quipped, voice light but wary as he tracked the book's erratic flight. "They say books broaden perspectives, but in this case, I'm keeping mine closed."

The manuscript fluttered with indignation before drifting downward. With an air of finality, it landed in the green velvet cushions, its covers snapping shut like a bird ruffling its feathers—as if it had claimed the throne by birthright.

"Ahh…looks like you've made a friend," Rayanna chortled.

"Fantastic," Diesel muttered through a smirk. "Exactly what I needed—sentient literature with attitude."

As the book settled in, the atmosphere within the rafters altered, sending a shimmer of dawnlit haze spiraling through the newly risen skyward spans. A golden dusting followed—radiant skeins of energy unfurling like molten aura, descending with spellbinding grace.

The rafter-born vault darkened, its once-vibrant wood deepening into a moody, celestial sapphire. Shadows bled into the beams, their outlines softening as the architecture dissolved into the illusion of endless twilight. One by one, stars blinked into existence—faint at first, like hesitant fireflies testing the edges of night. Their radiance grew bolder, scattering across the vault in constellations that felt both ancient and impossibly new.

A gentle luminescence spilled from the stars, brushing the tips of the arched supports and illuminating the study's newfound grandeur. The upper spans drew back like heaven's tide, dissolving into a boundless, starlit canvas—as if Missy had peeled open the skin of reality to reveal the universe long hidden beneath.

"Wait a minute..." Diesel flung up a hand. "What was the point of all the elaborate woodwork if you're just gonna cover it with sky?" He grimaced, casting a sideways look at Mama D.

The study's transformation eased, its vitality settling into a hushed hum. It was no longer just a room—it had become a threshold to the cosmos, a liminal space where the tangible and the infinite converged. Rayanna's smirk faded, replaced by a gentler stillness as she tilted her head upward. "Now that," she whispered, "is a hell of a view."

Above, the stars glistened in quiet accord, their winks of brilliance ebbing with a midnight sort of hush—the breath of something ancient and enduring. One bead blinked back, as if to say: *It is done.*

"Oh," Mama D whispered, her voice carrying the fragile gravity of recollection—like a suitcase brimming with moments too delicate to fully unpack. "Do you remember when you and the girls were little? After school, you'd all rush home...and your bedroom ceiling..." As she spoke, the pull of it all drew her in, her hand settling against the velvet backing of Diesel's chair.

Her fingertips lifted, tracing the constellations as if greeting old friends. "It wasn't stars then. Just tiny specks of light—pinpricks that glowed like moonbeam freckles. I still remember the way you'd lie there, staring up, convinced they held the secrets of the universe."

She exhaled, her breath feathering out, catching against the edge of emotion. "Even then...Missy found a way to make it real. She couldn't say it—couldn't show it outright—but you girls...each of you...you're her treasures." Her fingers drifted along the wall, searching for something unseen, something just beyond reach. "I know it must have taken everything in her to stay hidden. To hold back all that she was."

Her voice quivered, thick with feeling. Tears pooled at her lashes, glinting like mirrored starlight. She swallowed hard, then lifted her chin—quiet defiance rising to meet the swell in her chest. One determination met by another, unflinching. A steadiness reclaimed as a single tear slipped free.

"The first time, though...after Nadine..." Her voice dropped, barely more than breath—words so fragile they seemed liable to splinter if spoken too loud. She turned slightly, her gaze finding Rayanna's. "You'd come here—to this very place...this study. Back when Missy didn't have to hide herself. When Liam took over for Izayah, brewing that ridiculous, morning-watery coffee." She cleared her throat, running a finger along the bookshelf, a wistful smile tugging at her lips as the room turned with her—toward where Liam sat, chin propped on a knuckled fist.

He brushed at one eye with the back of his inked hand. "Och, aye. 'Bit o' sunshine time,' I called it, didn't I?" A soft chuckle followed. "Daft name, sure—but it fit. We'd have ourselves dose wee rose cakes an ginger biscuits from Dagny's." His grin widened, though the glint in his eyes betrayed what it cost him to recall it. "You'd flit about like a sparrow, chatterin' a mile a minute, dancin' tae yer own tune afore school."

Mama D stepped back to the soft velvet. "You'd curl up right here," she whispered, "nestling into the corner while Diesel worked late into the night." Her hand pressed gently into the cushions, her body leaning into its familiar sturdiness. For a moment, she paused—lost in the memory. Diesel moved closer, his arms encircling her middle with a kind of ease, the gesture as steady as the man himself. She continued, "He'd carry you—up to bed—every night. Without fail, you'd wake up just to tell him you wanted to come back down…because you didn't want to miss a single moment with him."

In response to that final word, Missy's hum thrummed beneath the floorboards, twining through the hearth's stonework as though coaxing it awake. The fire crackled, arching—its embers twitching like the breath of a slumbering dragon beginning to stir. Then, with a shudder, it stretched incandescent limbs skyward, flames licking upward with sudden, vital force. Amber flared into luminous blues and verdant greens, casting the room in surreal, prismatic hues—where reverie brushed against the sharp immediacy of now.

Mama D's hand stilled mid-air.

Energy gathered in the walls, coiling with quiet force—like a storm poised on the edge of release. A delicate tinkle of crystal echoed from the wet bar. Missy was calling them back.

"Alright. Enough dreaming. Let's move," Diesel said, his voice low and certain. The trio eased back toward the perimeter, giving Missy the space she needed.

"Brace yerself. Dae sky's aboot tae go daft wi' somethin' grand." Liam leaned casually against his painted bar, a sharp grin slicing through the surging quintessence. "Och, thought ye brought a dragon into ta room, Ray? We've got ourselves enough space for it now wi' ta new renovations, aye? Think it's safe?" He nodded toward the stuttering blue blaze. "Maybe ta fire's tired o' sittin' quiet an' wants a turn at ta old stories, sir."

He swirled the amber liquid in his tumbler, shrugging. "Suppose ta beastie's gettin' herself ready ta steal da show." He sloshed the glass in Diesel's direction. "Aye, sir…'fore I forget—rain, coinage, an' a pack o' Elites loungin' at da springs like bloody royalty. Cabin's what we figured. Full debrief once da dragon's done breathin'."

"Why wouldn't I bring in a dragon?" Rayanna arched an eyebrow. "Seems subtle. Though, I doubt dragons are standard issue." A smirk curled at the edge of her voice. "Besides—I'm not lookin' to end up a toasted marshmallow. You can keep the spotlight…and the sparks."

"Nonetheless, let's stay clear of the chaos," Diesel said, a brief chuckle catching in his throat.

Another round of sparks spiraled into the boughs of the tree, the embers flaring like molten radiance as they wove themselves into the canopy—deliberate, gleaming threads etched against shadowed bark.

"Should we…be worried about this?" Rayanna asked, crouching low as the branches creaked, stretching outward like something alive and listening.

"Worried?" Liam's laugh rolled out, warm and amused. "Lass, ye've got a cosmic tree in yer livin' room an' a hearth breathin' new colors—and *dat's* when ye start frettin'? Me, I'm still bettin' on a dragon. Pretty sure Missy'd be just fine wi' it. Maybe we'll end up wi' a basement too, at the rate she's goin'."

Diesel stood behind Mama D, his hands resting firmly on her shoulders, anchoring her as the tree above began to stir. Small blooms unfurled with soft, audible pops. Each petal drank deeply from the glowing, ember-hued wisps. A soft radiance rose, illuminating the intricate, lace-spun patterns stitched across the blossoms themselves.

The elegant tendrils of Memory Vines spilled downward with serpentine fluidity. From each span, budding Lumis pods emerged in slow rhythm. Their translucent sacs gleamed with hushed anticipation—glistening faintly, like breath suspended in moonlight.

"There's more?" Rayanna's eyes widened, her gaze fixed on the glowing orbs. "Hmmm…curious they'd end up here." A slight shake of her head betrayed a question too long unspoken. "Are they all from Izayah?"

"Och, no way in ten hells." Liam's voice cut through. "Ach, I've not seen dose in…" He flicked a finger toward them, disbelief tethered to the edge of comprehension. "How in dae name o' all that's holy did dey get here?" His eyes darted to Diesel, then Mama D—both shaking their heads, equally stunned. His brow furrowed, concern carving itself deeper. "Dose only grow in Treefall. Ye know what dat means, aye? How're dey sproutin' here?" He froze, jaw slack, the impossibility of it hitting like a stone to the chest. A low whistle escaped him. "I'll be damned sideways."

But the Lumis blossoms paid no mind to the astonishment. They continued their hypnotic unfurling, each sac swelling as if drawing from some unseen pool of etherlight. They swayed with uncanny grace, their translucent skins catching and scattering light in soft, prismatic sweeps. The gentle *ploop, ploop* of their settling punctuated the hush, echoing like droplets into an unseen pool. It lent them a quiet mischief, as though they delighted in the mystery of their own arrival.

From their radiant cores, slender threads of arcane sheen began to weave outward—gossamer filaments spiraling and dancing midair. The glow spread like enchantment, dappling the walls and floor in shifting illumination. Shapes emerged and dissolved—constellations forming and fading in a silent celestial rhythm. A language of flicker and pulse. A private dialogue with Missy—unmistakable and ancient.

As the orbs brimmed with luminous vitality, their interiors revealed impossible depths—like miniature galaxies mimicking the star-strewn ceiling above. Each sphere rotated with spectral layers, oceans of colors churning softly within, whispering of secret worlds and uncharted dreams. The air grew lush, perfumed with the scent of rain-drenched moss and the crystalline sweetness of starlight.

The room leaned in with a breath, scenting the depth of quintessence shared. Its edges softened, contours bending as though pulled inward by the blossoms' aquamarine allure. For a suspended beat, the space felt unmoored—adrift in the mesmerizing cadence of their expansion. Overhead, the buttresses swelled with expectancy, poised for the splendor of the next inhale.

"Well, I'll be damned, Papa D," Rayanna murmured, clasping her hands beneath her chin. Her fingertips tapped together, betraying the quiet thrill coursing through her frame. "They say your priorities reveal everything—and if Missy and this tree are the metric, whatever's coming? It's not something we can afford to overlook. I'd wager you might have missed a sign or two."

"Who said I was overlooking anything?" Diesel countered, his voice even, a flicker of challenge in his tone.

Rayanna rolled her eyes with theatrical flair, sweeping one arm in a broad arc to encompass the living tableau around them. "Well, I show up— and in 2.5 seconds flat, we're finally making progress." She tilted her head, her arched brow daring him to disagree, amusement dancing in her eyes.

Mama D's laughter burst forth—unfettered, melodic—like the first bloom cracking through winter frost.

The tree answered her joy, releasing flushes of blush-toned buds that spooled outward from the canopy in fluid, widening arcs. Satin-layered petals in muted, iridescent gradients laced with wisps of indigo and violet fanned outward—laughter made visible in motion and light. One especially striking floret burst forth in a radiant flourish, its chromatic fringe stretching toward Rayanna, as if longing to be seen.

"Well, aren't you a little show-off," Rayanna murmured, her voice brushed with quiet wonder.

"I think it wants you to be proud of it for blossoming," Mama D tittered. "I've never seen the tree respond to anyone like that."

"It's definitely different," Diesel stated as he eyed the blue and violet petals scattered among the more common pink blossoms. The unusual colors were enticing—their velvety texture catching the ambient light like dew glinting across silk. A faint warmth radiated from within, akin to tiny heated stones nestled at their core—a living sensation that tugged at him. Despite the hesitation knitting through his movements, his hand inched forward.

Before his fingers could make contact, the nearest tendril recoiled— snapping back with sharp, animalistic energy. The Lumis Blooms jolted in tandem, yanked backward and folding in on themselves. Their retreat carved arcs of color through the air, light flaring and dimming in erratic pulses across the polished floor. The blossoms collided softly in withdrawal, their luminescence brushing against itself in quiet, echoing impacts—like a shiver threading through the bones of the house. Even their glow faltered, dusting the space in a hesitant rhythm that gripped the room's stillness.

"Interesting," Diesel said, his gaze flicking briefly to Rayanna, then toward the spiral staircase as he drew his hand back. "I haven't seen those since the Great War." A beat passed, and a faint wink curved the corner of his mouth. "They're an ingredient that's…exceptionally valuable."

Liam's voice rang out from his gilded frame with the vigor of a startled stag. "Hell aye, they're valuable! But how in blazes did they end up here?" He leaned out slightly, peering from his portrait at the glowing blooms. "Missy, lass, ye've bin holdin' secrets from us?"

Rayanna turned, curiosity threading bright in her gaze. "Expecting someone, Papa D?" she asked, planting a hand on her hip. With a teasing smirk, she added, "Or is Missy not putting on enough of a show for you, sir?"

Diesel rolled his eyes, the sound that followed a low chuckle laced with fondness—and just enough exasperation. "My little radiant desk nymph has been unusually quiet," his voice dipping into a wary drawl. He stepped carefully away from the backwall, his gaze sweeping the ethereal space. "He's like a pup that's gone too quiet. Never a good sign."

Liam's voice belted across the expanse. "Nester! What ta bloody hell happened tae ya? Did ya get yerself stuck? We need tae make sure one o' these fancy new bookshelves didn't go an flatt'n ya!"

As Diesel crossed to the far side of the expanded room, he ran a hand across his forehead—considering, collecting his thoughts. Just as he reached the undercarriage of the balcony nearest his desk, Missy interrupted with a resonant *tink*—a heavy glass settling onto the coffee table. Amber liquid sloshed against crystal walls, its placement an unspoken invitation—or perhaps a pointed command, as if to say: *We have things to discuss, sir.*

He paused mid-step, sucking in his bottom lip as though weighing his next move.

Behind him, the planks beneath his velvety chair let out a series of impatient *plinks* and *pops*—like fingertips drumming against wood, urging him to quit stalling and take his seat. The cushions gave a dramatic *puffff,* launching the nestled book skyward like a startled bird caught in a gust. It arced across the room before landing with a clean *thud* on a nearby shelf. There, it gave a subtle shuffle—nestling between two ancient tomes as though reclaiming a long-forgotten seat of importance.

At the center of it all, the projection of Starlight and Moonlight swirled in the foggy expanse above the coffee table. Within the display, a dense wall of mist and shadow loomed—batting at the holographed quintessence as if daring Diesel to step closer.

"Well, it seems Missy's got no qualms about the conversations ahead," Mama D quipped, slipping off her green jacket as she sank into the leather couch. She undid the straps and buckles on her boots, tucking her legs beneath her with practiced ease—her movements fluid despite the fatigue lingering in her frame. Casting a glance toward the doorway, she added, "Where is Nester, anyway?"

"Why would Missy worry about the conversation ahead?" Diesel retorted with a note of playful irritation. "Clearly, she's thrilled about the grandeur of her new décor. Ray's right—at this rate, I'm going to need new furniture again. You remember how well that went last time."

He dropped into the weighty velvet cushions, sprawling comfortably with his elbows braced along the armrests. Narrowing his eyes with mock sternness, he added, "But let me make one thing clear—change everything else, Missy, but leave my green chairs alone. I am *not* going through another round of purple upholstery. That was a low point for both of us."

"But 'til then, we've got some tings tae hash out, don't we?" Liam drawled from his gilded frame, his focus set on Diesel.

Before Diesel could reply, soft footfalls drew their attention. From the newly expanded spiral staircase, a diminutive figure emerged, bounding downward with eager momentum. A subtle aureate gleam radiated from his bulb-like head, catching in the boughs above—where blossoms shimmered in response, refracting faint coronas of light along the stairwell like halos forming in his wake.

Ah, Lady Rayanna, Nester greeted, his voice light and brisk as he descended with the delicate clink of his tiny boots, accompanied by the whisper-soft sweep of his finely stitched leather apron. *A pleasure to see you again.* A small leather-bound book was tucked beneath one arm, and a miniature quilled feather pen sat jauntily where an ear might have been—

perched on the rim of his luminous dome, as though placed there by whim or ritual.

Rayanna's lips parted, but no words came at first. Instead, she shook her head, a breath of laughter slipping free as her hand rose to her brow. "I...I'm sorry," she murmured. "It's all coming back to me—pieces of it, anyway." Lowering her hand, she blinked, as though reaching deeper into the folds of memory. A hesitant smile curved her lips. "If I recall correctly..."

"It's Nester, eh? The brains behind yer trainin', dat ye be havin'. Dae key tae dae next...whatever tis be." Liam laughed, the sound rolling out like a warm tide. "But, lass, don't be too hard on yerself. What's it been? Twelve? Seventeen hours? And only 'bout an hour o' unbindin'? Ye've barely had time tae take a proper breath! Give yerself a break—ye'll manage jest fine!"

Reaching the final step, Nester paused, his glow intensifying for a beat before offering a formal bow in Rayanna's direction. *Indeed, your memory will serve you well. But for now, we'll take what we have—in time, we shall piece the whole together.* With that, he hopped lightly from the last stair, landing on the newly polished floor with a soft *clink*. His gaze swept the space, pausing at the lustrous grain beneath his boots. *Missy, my dear girl—you've outdone even your own flair for the dramatic,* he intoned, crouching briefly as one jointed hand glided across the surface before he straightened again. *But Liam is quite right—we've much to discuss.* He cleared his throat, his cadence easing into a gently admonishing register. *Though...even if I can see you've already taken certain liberties—perhaps several—when it comes to furniture in your excitement over Lady Rayanna's return...I'd still advise holding off on any further "enhancements."* With a pivot, he placed one hand on his hip. *And please—no more purple chairs. Diesel's grievances over that debacle lingered far too long. Let's avoid another disaster—natural palettes only, Missy.*

Liam's laughter rang out again. "Och, dey were these godawful, frilly things—lace trim and all! Made for tea-polties and such—nothin' wrong wi' dat—but I'll tell ya, it was damn near impossible ta keep a straight face watchin' Diesel try ta lay out strategy with all the seriousness of a war council—while sittin' on bloody doilies." He snorted, grinning wide. "Best entertainment I've had in years!"

Diesel groaned, bracing an elbow against the armrest. "Remind me again—why do I keep that old painting up and about when all it does is smart off all the damn time?"

Mama D chuckled, her eyes sparkling as she glanced at the gilded frame. "Well, it *does* offer some good points," she quipped, tossing a playful wink in Liam's direction.

"Saints above! I knew I liked ye better dan that grumpy lump sittin' dere wi' ye!" Liam's laughter rolled out, warm and unrestrained, carrying a lilt of pride and mischief.

Turning her attention to the small, luminescent figure, Mama D gave a thoughtful nod. "I do agree with you, Nester. Let's not get too carried away with furniture and the like just yet. *This time...*" Her voice softened, taking on the unmistakable cadence of authority. "I'd like to have a say in the matter. Especially if you've got plans for my kitchen—or my closet." She clicked her tongue, the sound sharp and final.

As if acknowledging the request, a sweep of translucent, greenish-blue birds darted between the branches above, their ethereal forms weaving through the boughs like living threads in a loom. Nester paused mid-step, tilting his glowing head skyward.

The winged creatures, though? A thoughtful hum accompanied his words as he strolled past the velvet chair, giving its foot a pointed tap with one jointed knuckle. *A charming touch, Missy. But do consider the spatial harmony moving forward—especially if you're thinking of adding more flair.* His glow arced upward again as he took in the arboreal centerpiece now claiming the room. The tree's boughs, burdened with blossoms that gleamed like diffused constellations adrift in ethereal motion, swept outward with sovereign grace. *Now that...is remarkable,* he mused, the admiration sharpening ever so slightly in his tone. *I'll need time to examine it properly. Missy, you've outdone yourself.* A slight shake of his luminous head followed, a gesture of restrained awe giving way to focus. *But I digress. We've matters to attend to. Your skill is needed, yet with the binding in place...*

Rayanna raised a hand, cutting him off with gentle firmness. "Ashla already went through the unbinding with me," she stated.

Liam groaned dramatically, "Oh, fer the love, didn't I jest say dat? I'm standin' here, talkin', but no one's listenin'—chopped liver, eh?" His crystal glass came down with a sharp *crack* against the counter. "Next time,

I'll just leave ya to yer guessin'—see how dat works!" He threw his hands up in the air and walked out of frame.

I can rarely trust his sense of humor to align with the facts—particularly when, to my recollection, he made no mention whatsoever of Lady Rayanna's unbinding, Nester remarked, his filament arching upward as though lifting a brow—a tinge of quiet exasperation bleeding into his cadence. *Always so theatrical.* Turning toward Diesel, the ambient light along his frame stabilized, coalescing in a steady, focused shimmer. *Is this so? Can you confirm Lady Rayanna has been unbound?*

"It appears so." Diesel lounged comfortably in his chair, one knee stretched out, a glass of amber liquid in hand. He raised an eyebrow in acknowledgment, the faintest smirk tugging at his lips. "You know Ashla—she isn't one to follow the script. Most of the time, she tinkers with it, delighting in doing anything but the ordinary."

Nester let out a soundless hum of thought, his radiance shifting as his focus returned to Rayanna. *I see. That changes things slightly. How this session unfolds may yet surprise us all.* Stepping forward to the coffee table, the tiny book beneath his arm made a soft *thwap* as he set it down. With a flick of one small hand, the table gave a low creak as it rotated on its base, the swirling mist above its surface reconfiguring—Starlight and Moonlight bending, crystalizing, drawing into focus.

This, Nester tapped the side of his head, *is where truth resumes its course.*

Chapter Thirty-Four

All attention shifted to Nester, poised at the edge of the projection. With meticulous accuracy, his small arm nudged the surface into a orchestrated rotation, setting the mist above into motion. It quivered with the rhythm of tightening and release, like a dam groaning under the strain of mounting pressure.

Rayanna caught her breath as she sank into the leather couch, watching as silken tides of fog spilled free—tumbling from the seared precipice of the table and unraveling into winding tendrils. The heavy veil draped over the framework in endless, altering layers, each one thrumming with subdued, unwavering intensity. Her eyes tracked the haze as it crept outward in undulating waves, gliding along the polished wood like ground mist curling in languid, preordained currents. An unspoken story-teller—silent words slipping free, desperate to be heard.

Upon the surface, two distinct projections offered fleeting glimpses into contrasting worlds.

In one, Moonlight Beach's amber sheen bathed quaint streets in a diffused richness, where natural wood structures and ancient timbered facades exuded a quiet timelessness. Its inhabitants meandered with casual ease, their gentle laughter weaving through tucked-away corners. Rayanna found herself captivated by the small groups lingering beneath lanterns or near open shopfronts, their rhythms stretched as if the haven itself relaxed into each cobblestone. A comfortable lull settled over the scene, and for a moment, she wondered—*Is this how Ashla sees the world? Drifting, not rooted. Whimsical, but not aimless. Internally guided, even if others couldn't see the path she's on. Ethereal—or just slightly sideways from reality. Maybe that's why, to me, she feels so untethered.*

Across the expanse, Starlight Beach's silver sheen gleamed—reflections dancing across polished surfaces and structured pathways. Its town center moved with focused determination: precise, calculated, bound by an undercurrent of order woven deep into its militaristic fabric. Despite the efficiency, a palpable vitality gathered—a dry-edged blade of humor tucked beneath the discipline—but it was ambition that pulsed at its core. Progress. Purpose. Every movement fed a service-before-self philosophy.

Rayanna studied the sharp lines and measured rhythm of the town, and a notion surfaced unbidden. *Of course, this would be the place he built. It feels like Izayah—driven, exact, always reaching for something more.* The realization settled in her chest, pulling tight like a knot. *I suppose that's why I never felt out of place here. The apple doesn't fall far from the blood-kindred tree, now does it?*

Thoughts unspooled further, threading into speech—a gradual cascade of recognition. "The contrast between them is just…striking." Her eyes followed the rotation, each turn layering new observations, the gentle resonance of its motion anchoring her. "Moonlight looks older. Much older than Starlight. And yet, that doesn't make sense—Ezekiel and you began building Starlight—or at least its foundation—after the Great War. And if I recall correctly, Izayah repurposed the old Shadow Elite outpost and town using whatever remained in military storage—stockpiled remnants from the aftermath of that conflict, right?" She gestured lightly toward the dense mist dividing the two havens. "So if Moonlight is older, how could it have remained hidden without that wall of quintessence fog? And if the cocoon was already in place *when* Moonlight was built…who would've had the means to build it at all?" Her gaze lingered, brow furrowed. "I guess what I'm really struggling with is the timeline." She paused, glancing back toward Diesel and Mama D. "Does any of that make sense?"

Diesel gave a small nod, silent but sure.

"Lord Brannon—I mean—Father was aware Izayah was constructing Starlight, yet he chose not to understand the particulars. Why?" Rayanna exhaled. "The more I examine this, the more it tastes like answers I've already encountered. Salty and sweet. The things I'd rather avoid, tangled with sugar-coated truths I can't help but chase." Her gaze drifted, unfocused, as if the words themselves stirred something long dormant. "Maybe he avoided knowing because awareness demanded responsibility—demanded action." The thought gnawed at her, bitter and cloying all at once. "It's all muddled," her voice lowered, as if saying it aloud might untangle it. "Bitter, sweet…and still, I keep tasting it." She leaned in, pointing toward Moonlight as the town drifted past. "And this is where Runa went?"

"Yes. This is where they've taken Runa," Mama D confirmed.

Rayanna's gaze swept across the two havens, narrowing as it caught on the dense veil of shadow. "And this mist and shadow…it's real?" The question pulled from her throat like a frayed thread unraveling between two halves of the same whole—split, but still bound.

Nester bobbed his emberlit filament in quiet affirmation.

"Very real," Mama D said as her hand traced the thick vertical curtain. "It is the consequence…the shadowed aftermath."

A hiss of static bristled up Rayanna's arms—sharp, biting, as if something concealed gnawed its way through bone-deep certainty. It whispered through her ears and sank, heavy and electric, into a pot of boiling questions. *What if the war was never truly over?* The idea gripped her, latching onto other loose notions winding through her mind. *What if King Moros's reign wasn't the end at all—but the beginning of something worse? Something unfinished?*

Nester's filament dipped in a soft arc—a faint echo of a smile. *It's okay to ask such things, Lady Ray. Truth Seeking takes great courage—because it begins with the questions most are unwilling to voice.*

Papa D and Mama D exchanged a subtle nod—an unspoken gesture of confirmation.

Her stomach tightened. Her jaw locked. She gave a single bob of her head, then hurled the rest of her wonders into the air, daring them to land. "Did Ezekiel know the war hadn't ended? Did he sense what Visha would become? Then why…why would he leave his daughter in the middle of it?" Rayanna drew a long breath, anchoring herself in the one truth that refused to yield. "This is Father Ezekiel's town," she said quietly but with resolve. "So I'm going to assume he, and he alone, created Moonlight. And again, I ask…why?"

Mama D hesitated, her expression unreadable as she lifted her chin slightly—an elegant deflection, volleying the question toward Diesel without a word.

Across the way, Papa D remained settled deep in his chair, arms now loosely crossed over his chest, his posture relaxed but attentive. His gaze didn't waver, fixed on the careful dissection of information unfolding before him.

Rayanna glanced between them, expecting more than their subtle nods —some gesture of reassurance, some thread to pull. Her brows lifted slightly, eyes widening as if to say, *Well?*

"I'm not offering more than listening," Papa D said, his cadence tinged with curiosity. "I want to see where this takes you—where the projection leads, and what answers might surface. You wanted the reins. Here you go."

Rayanna gave a small nod in return before leaning into the deluge of puzzlements—like a thousand fluttering pages disturbed by a single sigh. Simple, and impossible to ignore. "I get the sense this barrier is symbolic. It's always been seen as a divide. But what if it's more than that?" Her tone softened. "A boundary…protecting more than knowledge. Maybe it's guarding something else. The future. Innocence." The thought hung there, suspended for a beat, then drifted into something deeper. "What if this wall is more like us than anyone realized? A shadow bound town, hidden away, waiting for memory—or truth—to surface. Maybe that's what this has all been about." When she spoke again, it was barely above a whisper. "Maybe Father Ezekiel took what rose from the ruins and built something meant to last—a place where people had to relearn how to speak to one another. To rebuild from what was broken."

She rose, slightly nauseated, and drifted toward the opposite velvet chair—standing there, hesitant, yet transfixed. The tension she'd carried since being shadow bound had begun to loosen its grip. It had clung to her like a second skin, distorting her natural instincts—tightening her defenses, sharpening her protectiveness, amplifying an irritability that wasn't entirely hers. It had been her silent companion: ever-present, quietly corrosive. The suppression of her Truth Seeker nature had carved those traits into jagged edges, forcing her to navigate an existence thrown off balance. But now, as the unbinding unraveled what had restrained her, that suffocating tension, began to ebb, leaving behind a lightness—a clarity as crisp and undeniable as morning light breaking over a dark horizon. This was the answer—the root of the strain she hadn't fully grasped until now.

"This feels inevitable." Her breath caught on the words as her grip tightened on the chair back, a massive mental door buried deep inside her pushing forward with a grinding *thunk*. "These truths have been waiting— not just to be found, but to be questioned." The groan of ancient iron followed, dragging across stone. The outline of the door formed behind her eyelids—solid and imposing—its sheer tonnage daring her to open it. But before she could reach for it mentally, the image flung her out—snapping her back into the present with jarring force. She gasped, head whipping around as her reality twisted violently, its rhythm breaking apart mid-thread.

Her eyes locked with Nester's glow. *It's not ready for you yet*, came his voice, calm and steady—a guidance of understanding. *Those answers are still finding their shape.*

"It's them…" Her voice trembled—as if the realization itself had seized her by the throat, cutting off air.

"You're closer than you think. What you're after has a way of surfacing," Papa D said, letting out a low rumble—the sound resonating like distant thunder in his chest.

She blinked, pulling herself from the velvet chair to the edge of the slow-rotating surface of the table. Lowering to the floor, Rayanna settled cross-legged at its base, the quiet motion grounding her. She hesitated, nose-to-nose with the truth rising in her chest—as if it were too vast to speak. But the words came anyway, steady and certain, as though they'd been waiting all along. "Runa and Izayah…They're light and shadow. Starlight and Moonlight…day and night."

Her exhale softened, drifting like a current into the cotton haze. *Maybe this is what Nadine meant about muscle memory*, the notion surfaced—tugging up something sharper, more personal. "It's strange…calling someone your mother when you've spent most of your life thinking she was gone." But that connection could wait. *This—this—I need to figure out first.*

Diesel's lips curved into a fleeting, resolute smile as he observed the metamorphosis—a transformation that felt less like revelation and more like destiny asserting itself.

"But that's not right, is it?" Rayanna uttered into the sheen of fogged light. "The two havens aren't about day. Starlight and Moonlight—they're both nighttime events. How does that even connect?"

The mist's pigments deepened, pooling beneath the projection like eddies of her own consciousness, reverberating with the swirl of unanswered questions. Along the shadowed divide, the vapor began to reweave itself, the opaque formations converging. Gradually, the strands turned from muted grays to argent silvers and smoldering brass-orange, fusing the two towns with uncanny control. The renderings hovered in suspension, their stillness magnetic—waiting for her comprehension.

As she stared into the smoky hues, a quiet discernment stirred. "Light and shadow aren't opposites; they're complements."

Just beyond her nose, a soft rustle—like the brush of silk or the turning of pages—echoed through the mist, as truth itself stirred. Moonlight's amber glow leaned into Starlight's silvery coolness, each tempering the other in perfect equilibrium. The space between the pair thrummed with an unmatched resonance.

"They are…*simply*…two halves of a whole, bound to one another. A connection as vital as the divide that's kept them apart all these years. Just like Runa and Izayah."

Diesel drew his chin into the butt of his palm, remaining silent—listening, letting her breath find its place.

"And the mist seems to guard the balance for both havens." Rayanna's words hung, her tone teetering on the brink of something she couldn't name. "What I'm sensing is that light can't exist without shadow, and shadow finds its purpose in light. The answer isn't about separation, but the harmony born from their constant interplay—two forces intertwined in perpetual motion, neither overtaking the other."

Her gaze drifted between the two manifestations, tracking how Moonlight's radiance tempered Starlight's starkness, and how Starlight's clarity etched Moonlight's haze. A deep thrum tugged sharply in her gut, like a cord pulled taut through her center, as unfiltered truths continued to spill from her lips. "This balance isn't opposition; it's a partnership—creation and destruction, chaos and order—each defining the other's purpose. Runa and Izayah aren't just reflections of this; they're living embodiments of it." She closed her eyes and pressed the heels of her hands into her eyelids— not to block the thoughts out, but to lean into them. "Runa's quiet resilience—her unwavering light—it's not blinding. It's enduring." Her tone slipped into tender resonance. "Like a lighthouse standing against a dark sea. It doesn't shine to dazzle. It stays constant to guide."

Her hands dropped to her sides, fingers brushing against the soft, ashen-gray denim of her jeans. "Even in shadowed spaces, her incandescent presence held steady. Whether she knew it or not, she balanced Izayah's sharp focus and relentless drive. But...his force was never meant to burn like the brilliance of day." She paused, the statements forming carefully. "After what was thought to be the loss of our mother..." Her throat tightened briefly. "It was Runa's letters. The quiet persistence in her words. They shaped him in ways I doubt he ever imagined ink could. Her radiance, written in blood—always there, leading him back to shore."

She hadn't noticed Nester settling quietly beside her. He placed a piped hand gently on her knee, tilting his tiny chin up to hers and dimming his light so as not to blind her. His presence—calm, warm—nudged her to continue.

Scrutiny sharpened, drilling deeper into the slow-turning haze. Somewhere within the mist, notions began to spark—brief, electric flashes bursting like lightning in a cloud. Epiphanies fractured and fused, fragments snapping and shuttering into fleeting moments of clarity.

"Runa's shadow bound past...how deep does it reach? How dark does it go?" She traced her fingers absently across her lips, barely feeling the motion. "What's still locked inside her? And when those pieces—those fractured parts—finally surge to the surface...then what?" Her brows drew tight, each thought stitching deeper lines across her forehead, etching clarity where hesitation once lingered. "Will she still balance Izayah the way she does now? Or will the scales tip? If her light sharpens—becomes more focused...could it tilt everything between them?"

The questions hung for only a moment before she pressed on, certainty crystallizing. "A new angle is what they need," she stated with a defining boldness. "Moonlight...it's the next necessary phase of realization. The kind that only surfaces after you've survived the worst of it. It's not just healing—it's learning how to carry the realignment into the chaos and stay steady. The lesson now is balance. And maybe, for the first time, she's seeing what was—with real clarity. From there...she can finally adjust, within a sanctuary that offers deeper renewal than Starlight."

She paused, gaze distant but sure. "From what I gather, Moonlight Beach's values are rooted in secrecy—knowledge handed only to a select few. Tucked behind mist and shadow, it was never meant to be easily found...or discovered at all. And still, the question won't settle: why did Father Ezekiel stage his own end? I don't think we're meant to understand yet. Not fully. Not without the other side of the story. And that's the work, isn't it?"

Truth Seeking isn't just about waiting in the middle—it's about staying with the tension, sifting through the silence, and refusing to look away. It's the persistence to keep searching between what's seen and what's missing until you catch hold of that one true thread—and once you do, everything else starts to unravel, right down to the heart of it. Nester's filament flared briefly—tender gold, a hue of acknowledgment—then dimmed again as he patted her knee.

She exhaled, her tone slipping into a whisper. "I can see the pieces...but how they come together—that's still unclear." Each syllable strained with a truth she wasn't sure she was ready to face. "It truly is...so simple, yet complex. Just like Ma always phrased it." She faltered, the words catching in her throat. "Or...what she might offer now." Her breath hitched slightly. "That's...a difficult truth to digest."

Nester gave her knee one last gentle pat, his filament gesturing toward the sofa. *Go on, Lady Ray. Even Truth Seekers need a place to land.* With that, he hopped up, reaching for his small journal still resting near the edge and tugged it down. Diesel leaned forward, allowing him to spring into his waiting palm. The little figure then climbed up to settle neatly on the armrest—book in lap, posture upright, already preparing for the next chapter.

Rayanna rose from the floor, crossed to the couch, and sank into the cushions—her voice carrying the group forward. "I just...I can't seem to hold onto the idea that Nadine—I mean...ma—" she shook off the stuttered notion, "I mean…that *she's* still alive." The words felt brittle, but beneath them, something deeper stirred—a trembling reservoir of longing, confusion, and something harder to name. *Hope, maybe. Fear. Or both,* pressing against the edges, ready to spill.

"As her faith bound sister…it was unexpected, to say the least," Mama D remarked. "She understands that, though. It's what we spoke about while the Lumis Bloom shared its story with all of you."

Rayanna huffed out an audible sigh. "I'm not even sure what I'm looking for. Not answers. Not really. More like…piecing myself together—old and new. Maybe that…that clicking-into-place moment that will reshape me into something I'm not even sure I understand yet. It's like trying to solve a puzzle without knowing what the picture is supposed to be." She pulled her gaze from her lap and grimaced, then gently steered the conversation back toward an earlier wondering. "Can I ask…what exactly are faith bound sisters?"

Mama D stilled, the weight of deciding how much truth to share washing over her. She inhaled and when she spoke, her voice was careful —as if handling something fragile. "It's a sacred, chosen connection between two individuals. Forged through shared purpose, fate, and a binding ritual that runs deeper than blood." Her voice grew quieter, but no less certain. "Souls bound by intent. A sisterhood held together by absolute loyalty, devotion, and belief in one another." She paused, the next words pressing forward, heavier than the rest. "For us, that vow meant I would claim you as my own—keep you, guard you—if Nadine could no longer do so." She allowed the explanation to pool before continuing—her final words soft, but unyielding. "But if that belief falters…the bond shatters." Between a heaved breath, she added, "The vow was made without my knowing what would come to pass. But we wanted you to have a place to land—somewhere you could become who you are, not just who your title says you should be. Your father, Lord Brannon, understood that."

Rayanna released a soft *humph,* her fingertips skimming the coarse seam of her jeans—a fleeting gesture, as though grasping for something real. Yet even that small connection felt distant, like she was tilting sideways, untethering from reality. Her attention trailed back to the projection, where wisps of cloud curled and then tremored along the sewn divide, like breath brushing across still water. She blinked, as if staring into sudden glare. "Is this normal? Because it feels like it wants to swallow me whole." The notion slipped out unbidden, winding through the haze fraying at the edges of her mind. Somewhere within it, she caught the subdued low octave of Papa D's voice—but the words didn't reach her. The room thinned at the edges, colors draining to muted silvers and shadowed blues. Everything blurred—until only he remained, steady and whole, like a figure anchored in the mist. "Is this part of my Truth Telling?" she murmured, the words thick, dragging through water.

A sharp *ssssiippp* needled through her eardrums as the room constricted, sending energy crackling—like static clinging to skin. Her focus yanked hard, as if invisible fingers had hooked the bridge of her nose and snapped her head around. *Focus, damn it.* The command surged from somewhere deep within—urgent, relentless. The jolt tore through her, sharp and unforgiving. *Fuckin' A*, she thought, as a wave of nausea coiled tight in her gut. Reflexively, her hand shot up, fingers digging into the back of her neck, kneading the muscles that had seized from the force as she blurted, "Not sure if this Truth Seeking quintessence is a blessing or a curse."

"Hits hard, huh? Close your eyes. Press in…slow circles. Dissolves the sickness." Diesel eased back, arms crossed, observing. It was the stance of a man drawing from experience more times than he cared to count.

Grimacing, Rayanna obeyed, pressing her palms over her eyes, dragging clockwork-sure circles across her lids. The dizziness peeled away in thin layers, releasing the motion and drawing her gaze back to the display —where a miniature Runa now drifted along the storefronts of Moonlight Beach, her figure small but unmistakable.

Without realizing it, she dropped to her knees, folding forward as her fingers clamped around the seared edge of the table, halting its slow rotation. The surface stilled, and Moonlight snapped into razor-sharp resolution. Within the scene, Runa's form lifted a hand and waved—reaching through vision like a ripple through glass.

"Izayah and Runa don't merely coexist." As Rayanna spoke, her fingertips drifted along the rim, tracing a blackened scar within the wood she hadn't noticed until now. The truth didn't simply settle; it embedded itself —deep, solid, unshakable. "What I understand as of this moment…" Her throat tightened, dry. She swallowed hard and pressed on. "…is that they strengthen each other." She paused, holding the thought delicately beneath her fingertips, steadying herself before letting it go. "One cannot stand without the other. They aren't broken by the strain—they're forged in its heat."

She lifted her chin, honing in on the veiled expanse stretched between the two settlements. Like ancient fabric—weathered yet resolute—it shifted and resettled in an unending rhythm, never fracturing. Its seamless weave made the divide between the towns feel intentional. Finished.

The mist shivered, as if attuned to her awareness—an invisible resonance responding in kind. *You're close,* it seemed to murmur. *Keep going.*

"Perhaps the tension isn't meant to be resolved," she stated. "Maybe it's what holds everything in balance. *The ebb. The strain.* It's *not meant to be conquered*—it's what keeps them upright." Comprehension crystallized— undeniably sharp. "They were never meant to weaken one another. Their differences are not barriers—they are bridges."

She tugged at her bottom lip, brows drawing inward as the truth dug in deeper. "The bond between Runa and Izayah isn't about conflict or peace—it's about the necessity of their contrast." Her voice steadied, though each word felt newly unearthed. "Their paths have always been distinct ...but they're two halves of the same narrative. The same force. The same foundation."

Her cadence softened, reaching for something quieter, more grounded. "It's in the honesty. The rawness Izayah's already begun weaving with the Lumis Blooms." The words lingered—weighted now. "He understands she needs to taste it, breathe it, hold it. Because that's what she gave him. Those letters she wrote—years ago—they kept him alive."

Her breath evened. "And what he handed her back...was Starlight Beach. It wasn't just an answer. It was *a vow. His vow. Regardless of how it ends.*"

She paused, her voice falling into a hush. "Runa thinks love has always been meant to be licked off knives instead of spoons. Izayah understands the why. He must *show her.* Not give. Not tell. *Show.*"

Pulling herself back onto the couch, she tilted her head slightly. "He's not trying to change her or soften her edges. He's offering a love that's steady—a love meant to anchor, not wound." Her fingers traced the display's endless tide, its rhythm both familiar and unfathomable. "It's always been a dance. Moving in tandem, yet never touching. A quiet devotion. A faith too sacred for words."

A faint smirk ghosted across her lips, a memory brushing against her like a leaf caught in a breeze. "Their infernal, never-ending interplay—or lack thereof—used to exasperate me," she murmured, her voice thinning into the hush of the room. "I understand now why Izayah never acted. I didn't then. He was always so relentless, like fire chasing meaning. But with Runa...he waited. Watched. Treaded carefully—her first Dawning Day was consecrated ground."

The rotating beams of the lighthouse stilled, pinning each other in a silent cross through the hazed wall. It caught her breath—her thoughts momentarily unspooled— before she found her voice again. "They're like day and night...a balance The Lands can't endure without. That much I see —as clearly as the place where sea meets sky. The cusp of dawn and the hush of dusk—it's not merely where they converge. It's where they belong. Where one relinquishes, and the other begins, as though time itself breathes their names." Her tone drifted in like fog spilling across the tide, rooting itself in silence, then dissolving into the eternal turn of the waves.

Her cadence eased as she traced the weathered grain of the coffee table, as if seeking answers within its quiet resilience. "And Visha *knows this*," she murmured, her voice softer now, turned inward. "But I still can't fathom *how*."

The display faltered, its light flickering—a subtle bow of resignation. *That's enough,* it seemed to whisper, withdrawing with the tenderness of a parent settling a child to sleep, closing the moment with reverent care.

The projection blurred, then seeped slowly into the scorched ridges of the table. Luminous threads drew back, gathering itself within the grooves like silk drawn through open palms—as though the wood inhaled the vision, and tucked it quietly into its grain.

The mist, once draped in soft, layered veils, began its retreat—curling inward like gossamer gently wrapped around invisible hands. It thinned… drifted…*phhhshhh*—dissolving like ash surrendered to the sky. The surface lay bare, yet Missy's floorboards gave a quiet inhale, absorbing the final traces of what had been.

The corner of Rayanna's mouth tensed as frustration gathered behind her eyes. *I guess that's all I'm getting—for now.*

The room blinked tenderly back to life as Missy coaxed warmth into the paneled walls and well-loved furniture, enfolding the space in a familiar embrace—as if to say: *You're right. Time to move forward, love.*

Rayanna sank deeply into the weathered leather, the material cool and burnished with age, velvet-smooth against her skin. It exhaled a low groan as she settled in—the kind of sound furniture makes when it has borne witness to lifetimes of stories but holds them close, never spilling a word. She allowed herself to lounge there, like the weight of a warm, softhearted hand resting gently on her shoulder.

Her gaze drifted toward Papa D. The amber liquid cradled in his glass caught the light with a hushed gleam. He didn't speak. He didn't need to. He sat like a man who knew the world would keep turning whether he moved or not. His eyes weren't sharp, nor soft—just patient, as though waiting for the next piece to find its rightful place.

Considering it's your first time seeking discernment through such a display, Nester mused, *that was handled with remarkable composure. Fatigue is to be expected, of course—though you appear far less so than I anticipated.* A narrow ribbon of light stretched across Diesel's chest—diffused, yet contemplative. *What you've touched is only the surface of understanding. Depth, as you might imagine, takes time.*

"It felt like I was brushing up against something…just enough to sense it, but not enough to hold onto it," Rayanna said, the edges of her voice fraying as exhaustion crept in.

Precisely, Nester replied, the shimmer around him drawing inward before turning skyward. *Understanding favors subtlety. It unfolds in layers, not leaps. That's the nature of truth.* His presence settled—quiet, assured. *It resists being seized. It prefers to be invited.*

Papa D's chuckle rumbled low and unhurried, like gravel shifting beneath old treads. "Spoken like a scholar," he said, flashing Nester a knowing grin before turning back to Rayanna. "But he's right. This is just the beginning. And beginnings…" His voice dipped—steady, warm, and anchored by the weight of hard-earned wisdom. He finished with quiet finality, "They all come with a learning curve. And that's what teaches you how to truly listen."

A steadied breath slipped past her lips, forming breathy words meant to take a stand—but missing their mark. "I don't feel the need to rush." Her eyelids drooped. "At least…not yet."

Rayanna blinked hard, then gave a sluggish shake of her head as she pushed herself upright from the sofa, her body lagging behind the pace of her thoughts. She rubbed her palms together; the dry rasp of skin on skin sent a faint jolt through her limbs. With a few light taps to her cheeks, she nudged the edges of her focus back into place.

A low groan escaped as she stretched, arms rising overhead, fingers fanning wide before falling limp at her sides. "I've been waiting so damn long for these answers," she said, her voice steady now, leveled by quiet conviction. "I'm not letting this go. I *need* to know. I *have* to understand." Her pacing began—one step, then another, as if her thoughts were pulling her forward, churning just beneath the surface.

Diesel chuckled, gravelly—like crushed stone rolling through shallow water. "You remind me of Izayah right now. Two peas in a pod, really."

Rayanna halted mid-step as she turned toward him. "I'm being serious," she said, her eyes narrowing, a flicker of amusement threading through her fatigue.

"I know you are." Diesel's voice gentled. "But this isn't just about Izayah and Runa. Your role as a Truth Seeker is just as vital. Their path? It's easier to see—like standing across the room, looking at a painting. The whole picture comes into focus. But your own path?" He shrugged, fingers drumming softly against the padded arm. "It's like standing nose-to-nose with a mirror, trying to make sense of what's staring back. It's harder. Closer. And it takes a different kind of clarity. It's difficult to stay objective when you're the one inside the frame."

"So what—you expect me to step back and pretend I'm not the one living this?" Rayanna retorted, heat simmering beneath each syllable.

Diesel leaned forward just enough to anchor himself in the space between them. "No. I expect you to learn how to see it from both sides. To find the balance between living your story and understanding it. That's the hard part."

Rayanna drew in a long, weighted breath, her head dipping in a reluctant nod as she turned toward the doorway. Her eyelids sagged—each blink heavier. *Stars, I'm drained,* she thought, the weariness thick and inescapable, settling in her bones like dust in long-forgotten corners. *I could collapse right here. I feel like I've been wrung dry.*

"Let yourself go," Diesel said, clearing his throat—a low, guttural sound rumbling up from deep in his chest. "It's normal, Ray. Give in to rest."

The candelabras exhaled in response, their golden glow dimming into something softer, more forgiving—spilling warmth into the room with the unhurried grace of eyelids surrendering to sleep.

Rayanna didn't need to look at him to know he was shaking his head, already leaning back into the velvet cushions, eyes likely fixed on the ceiling. She could almost picture him dragging the back of his knuckles across his mouth, brushing over the coarse pepper of his beard.

"Missy always knows," he muttered—gruff, but certain.

A muted sheen of light slipped across Rayanna's hair as she gathered it into a high, messy bun. A few strands slipped free, falling around her face with an effortless kind of grace.

Her focus lifted, and as if in response, the dimmed candelabras seemed to dissolve deeper into the quiet. Shadows pooled like a hammock woven of dusk, and a soft amber blush stretched across the walls—curling inward, coaxing her to let go.

Even breathing feels like work. The notion settled with unshakable weight. The space felt hushed and enveloping—a cradle for fatigue and unspoken thoughts. *If I sit down, I might never get up again.* Rayanna rubbed her pointer fingers against her eyelids, stifling a yawn that curled low in her throat.

Her oversized sweater—a weighty knit of obsidian wool—slipped down, bunching at her elbows. There, the bangles Ashla had re-gifted her caught the faintest breath of radiance. The etched feathers glinted as shadows threaded through the inlay of metal, guarding truths tucked deep into their crevices. The delicately forged bands clung to her skin like fingers gripping a cliff's edge—resolute, enduring, silent.

Her hands drifted down, fingertips grazing the cool rim of one bracelet. The carved feathers offered a fleeting comfort. As her touch lingered, something slid—subtle, undeniable. It wasn't sudden or jarring, just a quiet imbalance, like the beads of rain falling into a leaf already heavy with dew. So delicate it might've passed unnoticed—yet it stirred.

The bangles exhaled. Their edges eased and blurred, transforming with the ease of breath. The metal yielded—not melting, but dissolving with fated inevitability, sinking into her skin as if it had always belonged there, even as her thoughts frayed and scattered like windblown ash. *It's not cold or warm...just alive.*

She yanked her sleeve back, vision blurring as dark ink bloomed from wrist to elbow—petal-shaped markings creeping in slow, tender currents. "It's like I can feel them threading along my muscles."

Ahh...now there we go. Nester's tone slid in beside her disbelief—low, reverent, interlaced with quiet certainty. *"I was beginning to wonder if the bond would take."*

"Been a while since I've seen an emergence—can't say I've ever seen it resurface. That's a whole other story," Diesel tossed back. "Wasn't worried the bond would take—just didn't know when it'd decide to show itself."

He glanced toward Mama D, a smirk ghosting across his lips. "I remember how mine materialized." He huffed. "Welcome back to the club, Ray. Welcome back."

Rayanna turned just in time to catch him lifting his glass in a casual salute. But the twisting sensation beneath her skin yanked her focus back— each pull of liquid metal felt like ink stretching through veins, jagged webs branching, evolving. And yet, it was exquisite. Delicate. The dark pigment seeped into fine, feathered veins, threading along the backs of her hands. Black and white wings rose in perfect contrast, the patterns climbing her forearms—each line etched with the precision of a shadowed master artisan, the craftsmanship defying logic.

Papa D edged forward, setting his glass at the corner of the scorched table. "Exquisite, isn't it?" he murmured, his tone tinged with reverence. "Every Truth Seeker's mark...it's never random. Character reveals itself through it."

Rayanna stared—suspended between wonder and disbelief—her breath rising and falling in sync with the faint pulse of the markings.

His gaze held steady. "You crave structure. Control. Answers." His tone remained matter-of-fact. "Yours will have edge—sharp contrasts. It'll question both sides—dark and light."

Slowly, reverently, she lifted her forearms, her fingertips trailing the intricate contours of the design—each line paradoxical: impossibly smooth, yet subtly raised. Her voice slipped out in a hush. "The details...they're so vivid. So textured." She drew in a notion. "It almost feels like the wings could lift—spread wide and fly."

Mama D drifted into the conversation, her presence tender but intentional. "These markings aren't merely inscribed upon your skin. They belong there—threaded through you, waiting to be remembered." She folded inward, as though settling into something ancient and instinctual.

Rayanna's movements remained intentional, unhurried, allowing for precise observation. With each tilt of her wrists and flex of her fingers, the pigment responded with near-liquid precision. She angled her forearms, letting Missy's well-placed light glide across the interplay of black and white—like ink diffusing through water. With every subtle motion, new intricacies came into view.

Plumes of liquid shadow rose with organic finesse, each arc etched with uncanny detail, imprinted with gossamer strands of binding ink. There was no weight in these markings, no burden—only a quiet resonance beneath her skin, like roots tunneling through earth: anchored, patient, and fluid.

She lifted her gaze to Papa D, her cadence hesitant but clear. "Whatever this is attached to...has it been shadow bound too?"

He gave a single nod, his focus steady—an assessment laced with quiet honesty. "Interesting you can see them now," he said, voice low and reflective."Shadow binding lulls part of you into slumber. Memories, abilities, thought weaving—it quiets them, tucks them deep beneath the surface like they never existed. But your mind still knows. It aches against the silence. That's why you've felt the agitation—why it's been pressing at the edges." His tone deepened. "Unbinding, in this sense, isn't about unlocking power. It's about reawakening what has long slept —an emergence both gradual and purposeful, like light cresting the horizon."

Rayanna's eyes dropped again to her arms, the markings rolling faintly —like breath caught just beneath the surface. "So...you have these markings too, then?"

He didn't answer immediately. He held her gaze with the calm steadiness of someone long reconciled to the truths he carried. Then, without a word, he reached out and reclaimed the crystal from the table, taking a contemplative sip to stretch the silence between beats before his voice followed—gruff, low. "Received mine what feels like a lifetime ago."

Nester reached out to take his glass, allowing Papa D to turn his arm over atop the green velvet, exposing the underside of his right forearm. His fingers found the seam running the length of the leather guard and, with practiced care, traced its line. The material stirred in response—awakening beneath his touch—parting with the effortless surrender of a river split by an immovable stone. The worn hide peeled back with fluid assurance, coiling upward toward the curve of his bicep to reveal the skin beneath.

The motion carried a near-sentient grace, the softened leather molding to him as though not merely a garment, but an extension of his will. It moved without resistance, each fold a testament to the quiet bond between form and bearer—a silent allegiance forged through purpose, precision, and time.

Engraved along the inner plane of his forearm, from wrist to elbow, an intricate lion stretched in dark, shadowed lines—the emblem of the Shadow Guard. Rayanna's lips parting as her gaze fixed on the image. A pulse of recognition thrummed through her—a tremor braided with stories unspoken, truths suspended just beyond reach.

She followed the contours of its mane, which unspooled with fierce elegance, each strand engraved with impossible detail, its gaze unrelenting. Encased within a lattice of overlapping triangles, the lion's chest was not confined but shaped—its strength channeled, its presence distilled. The geometry didn't restrain; it refined, sculpting the creature into a sigil of disciplined power, echoing command, clarity, and control. It was more than an emblem. It was a threshold—one she sensed but could not yet cross.

Without a word, Diesel turned his arm again, revealing the wing marked along its upper side. The feathers, broader and darker than hers, bore the weight of time. His ink carried the gravity of experience—etched with the silence of endured storms and the memory of battles survived. The tips were weathered, textured like stone shaped by centuries of wind and rain—unyielding, scarred, and steadfast. Some feathers bore gaps, their edges seared and frayed like the blackened ridges of the coffee table. Marked by fire, but never undone—their imperfections rendered them holy.

A history was inscribed into his markings—an essence forged not just in fire and shadow, but in the crucible of experience, tempered by trials only he could name. Where her ink bore the grace of something newly awakened, his spoke of endurance—of purpose honed by time and sharpened through adversity. Wisps of unspoken truth seemed to rise from his skin—intangible, yet irrefutable—disturbing the air around him with a magnetic pull.

As she stepped closer, a piercing ring fractured the stillness—sharp and sudden, cleaving through her senses. Her hands flew instinctively to her ears, but even as the sound reverberated within her, she couldn't look away. Blinking through the pain, her focus narrowed to the interplay of symmetry and divergence etched into their inked designs.

Clutching her head but anchored by awe, a notion slipped free—soft, but unwavering: "Yours are like ancient stone carved by centuries…" The ringing intensified, clawing at her equilibrium, yet she pressed on, her voice gaining shape through the pressure. "…like shadows stretching across a battlefield at dusk."

"Press into your tragus," Papa instructed, lifting a hand to demonstrate —tapping the small ridge of cartilage just before his ear. "Both sides—it'll ease the pressure. The ringing happens when another Truth Seeker is near," he said, each word paced with intent. "It's a signal—an alert embedded in your quintessence. You're nearing full awakening as a Truth Teller, and this —" he gestured toward her ears, "—is part of that transition." He paused, letting the moment settle before going on. "It's a safeguard—designed after the Great War by the High Seer of the Valley of Visions. I requested it myself. Most were reported lost during the war, but I couldn't give up on those who simply vanished. It was my way of holding onto the possibility —that not all were gone. It's a remnant of that era, encoded into the marrow of what we are." He inhaled deeply, releasing with purpose. "Once your essence acclimates to the presence of another like me, the ringing will fade. It'll only return when someone unfamiliar crosses your path—an echo of recognition. Think of it as a magnetic tether—a resonance that draws you toward those who share your core frequency."

Diesel adjusted his gaze from the markings on his forearm back to Rayanna, his presence steady—like a mountain long-scarred by storms but unmoved by them. He studied her in silence, the edge of his jaw tightening ever so slightly before he spoke, his voice low and coarse, like sand dragged across old wood. "I can see the questions forming. Layer upon layer—stacking themselves inside you."

Without breaking focus, he turned his attention back to his forearm. He raised it deliberately, rotating it beneath the light. Shadows and amber hue flowed across the markings—not merely catching the lines, but moving with their radiance. The motion was tender, like a father brushing soot from a child's face. Blinking, he refocused. "The ink—it isn't just pigment. It's a map. A chronicle of every battle fought. A record of memory, carved into the boundaries of my own body. A history."

His fingers moved again, gliding along the weathered grooves, his touch a quiet echo of reverence. "Each line..." he murmured, then paused. "Each line is a silent witness. Of what I've endured. Of what I've stood against to make it here. It's a catacomb of memory I carry with me. And you'll build your own haven—your own archive of truths. Truths you'll have to see through, filter, survive. They won't arrive all at once."

He leaned forward slightly, his voice softening—gravel giving way to steel. "That's what most people don't understand about Truth Seekers," Diesel continued, his tone sharpening with quiet conviction as he looked back at Rayanna. "They think we're lie detectors. That we can see everything instantly. But it doesn't work that way. We can only discern what's revealed. Truth doesn't always show itself in real time—it unfolds in fragments. And if the one sharing it..." He paused again, his hand brushing once more across the lines etched into his skin, "...is holding something back, we're left with only pieces. Shadows of what's missing. Sometimes, all you can do is wait. Let time do the unraveling."

He leaned back slightly, taking the whiskey glass from Nester, his gaze drifting toward the balcony above. "That's why other Truth Seekers matter. Why we need each other. Picture this glass of whiskey sitting in the center of the room. From where you stand, your view of it is different than mine —and different still from D's if she were looking down from the second floor. The glass doesn't change. But the angle, the light, the reflection? That's what makes the difference. *Perspective matters.*"

His fingers tapped a contemplative rhythm along the armrest. "That's the strength of working alongside others. They see the same threads, but from where they sit, they might catch something you overlook. Each seeker brings their own narratives, their own sacred discernments—insights the collective may never hold on its own. That's how we begin to unravel the architecture of a story—disentangling realities, teasing out falsehoods, learning what truly resides beneath." He exhaled, the memory surfacing. "After the Great War, Father Ezekiel and I traveled across the surviving realms for that very reason. We needed to see the full scope—the living patterns, the undercurrents. And I was curious, too—whether I could sense any others like us still tethered to the truth."

He massaged the back of his neck, rolling the tension from his shoulders. "We'll come back to this." His hand drifted down, fingers brushing the inked contours of his forearm, drawing quiet attention to the designs threaded there.

"What you need to understand now is this: all Truth Seekers are bound to one," Diesel said, his voice steady, tempered by repetition—like words that had carried him across years. "And one to us." His gaze held, unwavering, the weight of that truth settling like stone between them.

"This will make more sense later," he added, shifting his arm to reveal more of the intricate tattoo. The adaptive light slid across the ink—its texture alive, its depth unmistakable. Then, with a practiced motion, he tapped the rolled leather at his elbow, and the material responded—unfolding with silent precision to cloak the skin once more. His mouth curved into the faintest smirk. "But trust me—it's a hell of a lot more comfortable than those damn bracelets."

Rayanna lingered on the markings inked into her skin, her fingertips tracing their paths as if seeing them—truly seeing them—for the first time. Their weight felt different now. Changed. Transfigured. "That makes sense," she said on a breath. "They're pieces of me—a reflection of who I was…who I am, and who I'm becoming." Her gaze lifted, meeting his. "It feels like you just gave something precious back to me. Not a thing…more like someone handing Nester to you after he'd been gone too long. Does that make sense?"

Diesel bobbed his head with quiet understanding. "Sounds about right."

"The mirror you mentioned earlier," she began, her tone thoughtful, weighing the words before releasing them. "It feels like I've finally picked it up—my own reflection—as if the world is finally allowing me to do so."

The aroma of coffee drifted into the room—warm, grounding—wrapping around them with a quiet, familiar ease. Rayanna angled her chin a fraction, catching the scent as though a playful breeze had risen to brush the tip of her nose. A steaming cup appeared on the table with a delicate clink, its sudden arrival a featherlight reminder of routine nestled within the extraordinary. Her brow arched, a smile tugging at the corner of her mouth. "Just like when I was a youngling…though I'm hoping it's a bit stronger this time."

Diesel let out a hearty laugh, the sound low and full. "I told you… Missy remembers. She always knows."

Rayanna crossed the firelit expanse, the tread of her boots thudding gently against the polished floorboards—each step a metronome breaking the lull of revelation. Until now, she hadn't noticed the rhythm of her own movement. A new awareness stirred within her, vast and rising, as though space were being cleared—carved out and reshaped—into a catacomb of knowledge, a sacred haven etched into her soul, designed to hold all that had been, and all that was still to come.

In her mind, a distant *boom* echoed—like ancient doors settling into their hinges. Inevitable. Final. The day had unraveled in a blur of truths and reckonings. Her thoughts spun just beneath the surface, drawn by the gravity of revelations she could no longer outrun…and the soundless weight of questions she'd folded away for later.

The light filtering through the tall windows had eased, mellowing into the golden hush of late afternoon. She glanced toward the dimming rays— amber streaked with shadow—a echo of her own weariness. *Hours…how many have slipped past?* The sun had descended from its blinding zenith to the softened promise of dusk. Each step carried more gravity than the last, not from exertion, but from the sheer magnitude of all her mind had absorbed. *If I just close my eyes for a bit…maybe I'll be able to make sense of it all when I wake.*

Her gaze wandered across the space—the fire burning low, the ink on her arms catching glimmers of light—but none of it quite registered. Everything felt distant, suspended, like a dream hovering just beyond wakefulness. The cadence of her stride tethered her to the present, a quiet anchor against the rising fog of exhaustion. *I've never felt this tired. Not in body…but in here.* Her chest lifted with a deeper sigh, the solemnity of the moment pressing against her ribs. *I need to rest. I need to make sense of this. But there's still so much…*

The hearth's steady warmth saturated the air, a silent offering of comfort against the ache radiating inward—from thought, not muscle. The lingering aroma of coffee hung—earthy, familiar—filtering through her haze, coaxing her focus inward. *Rest isn't surrender. It's preparation. If I don't stop now, I won't see what I need to—when it matters most.*

Reaching the couch, Rayanna lowered herself into the worn leather. The cushions yielded beneath her with a tender sigh, as if recognizing her need for stillness. The coffee table gleamed, its polished surface catching the emberwash of firelight like a warm pool reflecting the silver hush of early evening. She inhaled, sinking deeper into the seat—as though even the room itself had been waiting to hold her.

Missy's aura suffused the room, dissolving the shadows that clung to its edges. Light spilled upward, merging with the mural of the night sky above, where stars shimmered—golden dust suspended mid-fall—folding the space into something both infinite and tender. The fire's measured crackle harmonized with the hum of Missy's luminescence, forming a rhythm that swayed through Rayanna's thoughts. The dwelling itself seemed to transform into a hammock, rocking her into a lull spun from enchantment and memory.

She tilted her head back, her gaze lifting to the ceiling. The constellations altered—almost imperceptibly—like the majestic turning of a distant carousel. The burden of the day's revelations ebbed, eclipsed by the insistence of the present: a flutter of comfort coaxing her toward surrender. *You never forgot how to tuck me in, did you?* Rayanna thought, drowsiness pooling around her like a velvet cocoon. Every sound—the whisper of the fire, the low thrum of Missy's coziness—wove itself over her senses, one layer after another, each gentler than the last, lulling her deeper into the hush of stillness.

A feeble sigh slipped from her lips as her shoulders eased, tension unspooling. "Okay," she murmured, her voice light and dream-threaded. "What do you need of me, Nester?"

Mama D moved with a quietude that spoke of decades spent tending to weary hearts. She undid Rayanna's boots, slipping them off with a tenderness shaped by years of knowing.

"I almost forgot you were here, Ma," Rayanna whispered. The words left her on a breath, her exhaustion settling with a weight that felt older than her body—something earthen, ancestral—holding her in place even as her thoughts drifted. She tucked her legs beneath her, instinctively seeking refuge in the familiar.

Sliding back to the opposite end of the couch, Mama D's cadence pulled at her heartstrings. "I know it's been a lot, Ray. Just rest, my dear." The stillness she offered was woven from practiced comfort, smoothing the edges of the moment like balm drawn over weathered skin.

Rayanna's gaze, languid and unfocused, drifted toward Nester, perched atop Papa D's armrest. His small frame swung his legs over both sides as if riding an oversized horse, a voiceless vitality emanating from him like the first blush of dawn. A quiet, eager kind of waiting.

The gradual tide of fatigue beckoned her inward, coaxing her from the edge of wakefulness. With both hands tucked in, Rayanna sank deeper into the cushions, cocooned in a hush of soft, gray stillness. Across from her, Nester slipped his leather book beside Diesel, climbed down from the old velvet, tapped along the floorboards, and *plipped* himself onto the couch next to her—his ambient glow casting a tender contrast against the waning firelight. He turned away from the flames, watching as their fluctuating dance cast evolving patterns across her body—a subtle rhythm that mirrored the rise and fall of her breath. Each inhale. Each exhale. Slowed. Softened. Until the dreamscape claimed her.

The bulb of his head tilted toward Diesel, who gave a slight nod—its gravity steeped in wordless understanding. "She needs sleep, Nes," Diesel said gently. "I know you're excited to have her back—but this can wait."

Nester's radiance dimmed—his usual vibrance subdued by disappointment. With a hushed shuffle, he slipped from the couch, his tiny leather boots tapping softly against the polished floor. His apron fluttered faintly with each step, and as his hands dropped to his sides, his whole frame seemed to wilt.

Head bowed, he padded toward the hearth, as though Rayanna's retreat into rest had exhaled something vital from him as well. Perching once more on the stone, he folded inward. With a purposeful motion, he kicked off his boots—the gesture carrying the dramatic pout of a child gently denied their turn. His glow flickered once…then stilled. A single bead of condensation trailed down the outside of his bulb, *tinking* tenderly against his piped forearm. Silence followed. Not hollow—but contemplative.

"Hey," Diesel began, his voice steady, reassuring. "I know you don't want to wait, Nes. Especially when you're itching to dive back in. But Rayanna needs time to recover—so she can come back even stronger." A chuckle rumbled from deep in his chest. "I'll admit, though—the vibrato with the leather boots and apron? Pretty damn compelling." The fondness stitched easily into his cadence as he studied the tiny figure. "Sometimes the hardest training is the kind that demands patience."

From her nearby seat, Mama D offered a small, knowing dip of her chin in return.

Nester's head lifted, the ambient shimmer around him dimming as he glanced between the pair—his gaze finally settling on Mama D, who leaned forward, her knuckles pressed lightly beneath her chin.

"Oh, Nes," she murmured, her voice steeped in warmth, "she can't process it all in one day. It's been a lot—for all of us. You've waited this long—what's a little more time?"

Adjusting his miniature apron, Nester puffed out his chest and gave a theatrical bob of his head, as if to say, *I do look rather dashing, don't I?* The radiance surrounding him shimmered in agreement, aligning itself with the room's emotional current.

Rayanna's breathing eased, the last strands of tension loosening as she nestled deeper into the cushions. "I've missed you too, Nes," she whispered. "We'll play later, okay?"

Nester gave a single bounce, then sprang up and retrieved his boots, plopping them back on with a flourish. *Just a little longer, then.* He tossed his legs out in front of him to admire the craftsmanship. *Good thing I moved the sap ink and the jug upstairs. No need to overwhelm her yet. She's going to have questions. So many questions.*

"I was wondering where that lot had gone," Diesel remarked, nodding toward the tree as he watched Mama D lean forward to retrieve Rayanna's coffee, then settle back with effortless poise.

"Sap ink? A jug?" Mama D inquired lightly, curiosity tracing itself through her tone. "That must be what Nadine was referring to. Moonlight holds the other fragment of the Tree of Life."

Diesel's response came clipped, irritation flaring beneath his tone. "Found out right around the time someone decided blood reaching ought to make a comeback."

"Oh, spare me." Mama D's reply was dry, unamused. "Diesel, for the love of the Blessed Father, you know exactly why I couldn't do that with *you*. Blood reaching between two bonded—or tethered—would've carried far more force than I needed. Nes is bound to you...and to the tree." She exhaled. "Nadine was clear. Reaching through Nester"—her voice tightened—"was safer. Everything outside the cottage had been suspended, shielded by the Golden Guard, and sanctioned by the Blessed Father himself. Since the Tree of Life shares its quintessence not only with the fragment but with Nester—who *is* pure quintessence—it would've registered as nothing more than a tremor. A flare. A flicker from the tree. Just another pulse in the living system."

Diesel clenched his jaw, turning his head to rest against the velvet backing as his gaze drifted toward the freshly darkened sky. He let the silence stretch—searching the constellations for the answer he wasn't ready to voice.

It was Mama D who broke the hush, her voice a murmur that shifted the moment with grace. "Do you think she'll remember the doorway when she wakes?" Her eyes followed the hearth's flame, tracing its languid, rhythmic dance. "It's strange...how she doesn't recollect taking the vow of a faith bound sister." A thoughtful pause lingered, her next words chosen with care. "I would've assumed that memory would have arisen first since the solidification happened before shadow binding." Her cadence faded, carried off like embers drifting into the rafters.

"No," Diesel said at last as he leveled his chin, casting a glance toward Rayanna. "Not yet. But it's there...like everything else." He lifted his head a fraction higher. "Revisiting an earlier point—since some of us have chosen not to completely sidestep the conversation," he added, arching a sardonic brow at his partner, "Nes, how well-acquainted are you with the quintessence of the tree...or trees?"

I can only hypothesize, sir, Nester replied, his concentration undisturbed as he continued inscribing meticulous notations into a timeworn ledger. *Nothing has ever been definitively tested, as this is still only a sapling.* Each stroke of the quill carried the gravity of ritual—less transcription than preservation, secrets held in ink. *With Lady Rayanna returned to us, I expect our pace to accelerate. Substantially.* He paused, gesturing toward the outstretched canopy above them. *Given its rapid expansion, I would surmise it's preparing to absorb far more—soon.* Another flicker of hesitation passed through him as he touched the glowing quill to the side of his rounded head. His light dimmed to a contemplative gray before brightening once more as the quill resumed its path. *I believe the next phase will yield meaningful revelation.* His filament brightened briefly, then faded into a more shaded hue. *Though, sir...if I may switch course slightly—I'm quite curious about what Izayah and the Elite have uncovered.*

"I've been wondering the same," Diesel said, leaning back as his arms crossed over his chest. "Ezekiel always said the faith bound didn't need to remember. It wasn't about the memory—it was about the meaning. Vows don't vanish. They wait—until the moment arrives to be reclaimed." He tapped two fingers against his arm, the gesture more meditative than idle.

"Do you know where she left the key?" Mama D inquired.

Diesel exhaled sharply, a dry scoff curling from his lips. "D, this blood reaching's got you ricocheting all over the place. Pick a lane and hold it." He leaned back again, his gaze lowering. "If I had to, I could probably track it down. But that's not the real issue. The real question is whether it would even respond to me—if she's unable to recall where it was placed."

As the conversation ebbed, the firelight continued its quiet labor—crackling in the hearth, casting erratic shadows across the timeworn walls. Missy moved with clockwork grace, her broom murmuring along the baseboards, while the mop echoed faintly from the kitchen like footsteps in a distant hall. Nester's quill rasped in even rhythm, the rustle of parchment folding into the hush like a well-rehearsed refrain—routine and recollection entwined.

Rayanna's breaths rose and fell in gentle cadence, punctuated by the faintest brush of a snore. Mama D, ignoring Diesel's jab, hummed a wordless melody—low, steady, grounding. Diesel remained still, but far from settled—his thoughts shuffled like dry leaves caught in a crosswind.

The air bore a familiar gravity, a warmth steeped in memory that sank deep into the marrow. Yet beneath the tranquil cadence of everyday life, a quiet expectancy laced through the stillness—like a breath caught mid-inhale, suspended. It was an unspoken knowing, weaving itself into the bones of the room, settling like memory steeped in stone.

BOOM—WHABAM—CHHHSHHH!

The stillness ruptured. Tranquility shattered like crystal beneath a hammer's strike. The room—once steeped in domestic grace—fractured into kinetic dissonance. Shockwaves pummeled the foundation, each blast a serrated intent, raking through the structure with unrelenting force.

The broom and mop struck the floor as Missy's candelabras spasmed—flaring between shock and sharp recalibration. Nester jolted, his hand jerking mid-stroke—ink rupturing across the ledger like a wound torn open by memory itself.

Rayanna stirred with a splintered breath—her snore catching, momentarily disrupted, then slipping back into fragile slumber. Mama D's humming fell silent. Her mug remained upright, but her knuckles blanched against the ceramic. Her gaze snapped to the wall behind Diesel's monolithic desk—where metal groaned, a deep, ominous strain, as though something immense had begun to pummel the very skin of the house.

Diesel was already in motion. His chair scraped harshly against the floor as he rose, meandering thoughts dissolving, replaced by honed precision—his gaze sweeping the room, assessing, calculating.

"What the..." Mama D's voice faltered. She moved closer to Rayanna with protective fluidity, positioning herself as a barrier. Her eyes locked on Diesel, waiting for direction.

"Hold steady." His voice didn't rise—but it carried. As he advanced, his hands flexed at his sides, readying for impact.

Missy's light flared violently, a resonant hum surging as her quintessence fractured. No longer the warm, steady glow that softened the room, it splintered—crackling like raw current snapping in jagged arcs. Each burst threw violent shadows against the walls, transforming the hearth into a theatre of smoke and warlight. The darkness didn't tilt—it lunged, clawing through the air with a serrated whine that shredded the silence, wave after wave tearing through breath itself.

A low, prowling rumble arose beneath the floorboards—more than vibration. It clawed its way upward, twisting into a strength that slammed against the framework like a boot grinding down on bone. Overhead, the ceiling's celestial landscape fractured, stuttering once, then snuffed out—as wall panels drove inward, splintering like a beast tearing into its own ribs. Missy's structural reinforcements deployed with tectonic finality, interlocking with the precision of a fortress sealing for siege.

Mama D froze, one hand gripping the back of the couch. The mug she'd set down moments earlier wobbled violently, its contents trembling like a creature cornered and afraid. Her lips parted, but no words came—only silence, devoured by the piercing, high-pitched wail. The walls screamed beneath the pressure, bearing the weight of something vast pressing inward—not merely breaching, but seeking to invade, to consume.

A muscle ticked along Diesel's jawline as his gaze snapped upward, tracking the ceiling as it cinched inward, folding the room into itself like a clenched fist. The house wasn't preparing—it was fortifying. Bracing against unrelenting force.

"Missy." The name landed flat and clipped, a command forged in battlefield instinct as dust rained from the rafters. She flared in defiance against the mounting pressure, emberlit debris hissing to the floor as her light surged—caught in the maelstrom, yet still she held.

Then chaos ripped through the space—*thwack*, then a concussive *boom* that rattled the walls to their marrow. Missy's defenses had sealed in defiance—only to be wrenched open again by massive, phantom hands raking down into timber and stone. Joists fractured with a sickening crack. Support beams groaned, then gave—snapping sharp, like ribs under a heavy tread. The sounds came in waves—a chorus of rupturing architecture and guttural vibration, each note more jagged, more violent, more inevitable than the last.

Diesel's gaze held steady on the wall behind his desk, where the vibrations thickened—reverberating not with chaos, but with intent. This was no accident. This was a siege. And Missy was bracing with all her might.

Diesel's tone rolled out low and lethal: "Nester, be advised—breach confirmed." He barked the words like an order detonated, cleaving through the din like a landslide breaking loose. In one fluid motion, he reached back, fingers grazing the hardened leather of his gear. His hands found the hidden clasps—and with a sharp *shhhhwinkkk*—he drew twin swords of staggering heft. The steel cleaved the air with a predatory hiss, each blade forged with breadth and balance to match the stature of the man who wielded them. Their cold weight settled into his grip with a brutal promise. A growl rumbled low in his chest as he widened his stance—blades in hand, body coiled, every line of him carved in readiness and war-born instinct.

Nester's filament pulsed erratically. *I'm stabilizing what I can,* his voice wavered through the thread, his corelight dimming before flaring again. *But whatever this is—it's not just forcing entry. It's anchoring. It's pulling Missy apart at the seams.*

"Missy, hold the perimeter!" Diesel commanded—but she was already in motion, her quintessence igniting in a radiant surge. Light erupted outward, forging a volatile barrier that seethed with raw force. Sparks fractured violently along its edge as tendrils of the invading force struck in relentless succession. Her radiance faltered—splintered, yet held steadfast.

Sir—it's splitting through the keystones. Dragging them, Nester warned, his light pulsing crimson, urgent and strained. *If those give—if they collapse—the entire structure—*

"I know!" Diesel snapped, cutting him off. He shifted, blades raised, each movement exact, his eyes locking on the heart of the storm—a swirling vortex of gold and silver tearing through the center of the room. It didn't shimmer. It *ripped.*

A brutal surge of light gouged the air, carving through the Tree of Life's bough as if existence itself had thinned to pulp—reality unraveling in sheared layers.

The walls convulsed beneath the strain. Cracks spiderwebbed through the timber, veining outward like frost across brittle glass. Above, the ceiling buckled—groaning beneath a pressure that fell like the hand of a god.

Then—a sound tore through the chamber. A screech, raw and piercing, split bone and thought alike as a beam gave way. Splinters knifed downward, scattering like shrapnel, only to be hurled skyward again in a violent backlash—as if Missy herself had chosen to strike back.

Mama D's voice lashed out, sharp and focused. "Diesel, the center! It's targeting the center!" She moved instinctively, positioning herself between Rayanna and the unseen threat, her body taut with protective resolve, hands raised. "It's ripping through Missy's foundation!"

Diesel's gaze snapped to the heart of the room, where the swirling energy writhed violently. With each churn, its tendrils gnashed outward—tearing toward the inner walls, the ceiling, and the earth beneath their feet. No hesitation. No time.

With a powerful lunge, he folded through space toward the center, his blades cleaving the air with a *sinkkkkggg* of steel. The first strike met resistance—sparks erupted as metal clashed against the storm's thrashing limbs. The force shoved back, nearly staggering him, but Diesel held, muscles locked as he drove the blade deeper.

A roar erupted from the core, rattling beams loose and hurling debris like a scattershot eruption. The walls convulsed under the pressure, the very architecture buckling—as if reality itself had begun to writhe.

Missy faltered. Her shield quaked—on the verge of collapse. Nester's radiance thudded erratically, like a panicked heartbeat. *She can't hold it much longer!* His voice flared, his filament dimming beneath the strain.

"Then don't!" Diesel barked. "Redirect it! Funnel it toward me!" He struck again—blades shrieking with friction, sparks igniting like fire in a gale—quintessence split and scattered as the storm surged, wild and tearing.

Missy didn't hesitate. Her form convulsed, then expanded. The wards fractured—and in the same breath, with a thunderous snap of will, the energy veered, slamming toward Diesel like the wrath of a god unbound. He braced. Blades raised. And the storm struck.

The impact detonated through the chamber, a shockwave distorting the walls outward as if the house itself screamed. He staggered—boots cracking through the floorboards—but he held. The force tore through him. And still, he stood.

With a guttural roar, Diesel lurched forward once more, his swords plunging into the storm's volatile core. Light and shadow buckled around him in violent bursts of gold and silver, each arc of motion leaving reality stuttering in its wake. Every strike landed deeper. Every swing, a command. The onslaught recoiled beneath his assault, driven back by the relentless wail of muscle and memory.

Behind him, Mama D pressed her hand firmly to Rayanna's chest, her voice low and steady—an anchoring thread spun in calm defiance. "Stay with me, Ray," she whispered, eyes locked on Diesel. "He's got this." She leaned in closer, the quiet hum of an ancient lullaby spilling from her lips —its melody steeped in centuries, bearing the weight of forgotten vows. Rayanna curled inward, her breathing softened, drawn deeper into stillness as the song wrapped around her like dusk.

Along the hearth, Nester pressed his piped hands against the roots of the sapling, a greenish radiance flaring beneath his touch. The light surged in stuttering beats, each pulse a lifeline driven into the faltering keystones. His essence funneled downward—threaded into the core—where the foundation groaned beneath the mounting strain. *It's weakening!* his voice rang through the thread, taut with urgency and resolve. *Sir—she's going to collapse if this keeps up!*

But Diesel didn't answer. His focus was singular. Unbroken. Absolute. He moved like flame through oil—blades, a blur of steel and firelight. The storm writhed in fury, its tendrils lashing wild, molten, unmoored. Its resistance faltered—rhythm splintering, chaos unraveling. And then—an ear-splitting shriek, high and final—as the vortex collapsed inward, imploding in a burst of blinding white that swallowed the chamber whole.

Silence fell. Sudden. Absolute. Oppressive.

Diesel stood at the center, chest heaving in controlled intervals, both swords locked in white-knuckled fists. His shadow stretched long across the fractured floor, cast by firelight now guttering—dim and unsteady, like breath caught in the lull that follows fury. "Status," he barked, voice carved from stone, slicing through the hush.

Missy's candelabras stood askew, their glow dim but unbroken.

Nester slumped beside the fireside, the filament at his core casting a diffused sheen, his radiance faded by another shade. *Stable—for now, Sir.*

Mama D exhaled, her palm still resting against Rayanna's chest. Relief unspooled through her limbs, easing the tension coiled deep within her frame. "What the hell," she breathed—words ragged at the edges.

Diesel didn't move. His eyes swept the room, taking in the wreckage— the splintered beams, the scorched floorboards, the shadows clinging to corners like echoes of something unspoken. And there—crumpled on the floor—lay a body, radiant and broken, the source of the storm now stilled. His voice cracked as his gaze locked onto it. "Ashla," he uttered, the name fractured in his throat before his tone hardened. "What the..."

The floorboards, briefly still, began to tremble again—low, ominous vibrations thrumming through the foundation, crawling up their spines. Parchment whipped upward from behind the desk, torn loose by the spiraling force of Ashla's quintessence, curling at the edges like scorched leaves. The windows rattled violently in their frames, glass quivering—uncertain whether to hold or surrender. The storm, lulled but unfinished, clawing its way back in.

Then—*crack*.

A crisp, electric snap split the air.

Ashla unfolded from the ground, her body wrenching upright as time and space convulsed to accommodate her return. Her hair lashed outward, wild and animate, each strand crackling with raw current—a corona of ungoverned power illuminating her fractured silhouette.

She lurched forward, steps uneven, breath ragged—dragged in like air through flame. Her eyes, wide and abyssal, burned with urgency. The golden aura clinging to her stuttered in erratic bursts, convulsing out of sync with the fraying rhythm of her limbs—volatile, uncontained.

The vortex collapsed with a gasp, imploding as the room suspended its breath—caught between aftermath and another oncoming surge. The walls, already strained, cracked along the far edge with a sickening groan. The barrier bowed outward as though Missy herself were trying to reject the force radiating from her depths. Ashla was the epicenter now—unleashed. Unbinding.

"Ashla—you have to stop this—" Mama D called, her voice firm but drawn taut, straining beneath the weight of rising desperation.

The words had barely left her lips before Ashla cut through them. "There's no time!" Her scream tore out—raw and ragged—each syllable serrated with urgency, tumbling in a breathless cascade. Her focus darted wildly, her luminous form trembling with barely contained force, every muscle coiled like a spring moments from release. "You have to let Ryker and Nissa in—now! They tried the other side, but they couldn't get through! I—" She faltered, staggered, buckling beneath the strain. Residual quintessence coiled around her like a noose, tightening with every breath. "I had to unbind...my way through." Her hand snapped out, seizing the arm of a crumpled chair for balance. The fabric hissed and smoked beneath her touch, energy bleeding through her skin like a live wire. "She needs help! Nissa—she has to go back!" Ashla's voice fractured into a desperate plea, rough-edged and trembling, but beneath it, she was unwavering. Resolute.

"Rayanna can't—she's barely—" Mama D's words were thrown back at her in splinters.

"She doesn't have a choice!" Ashla snapped, her voice cracking through the air like a whip. Power surged outward from her core, rattling the windows and groaning the bones of the house. "If she doesn't, none of us make it out of this intact!" The air thickened, choking with the scent of scorched timber and the grinding tension of stone buckling under invisible weight. Fissures webbed across the floorboards, and Missy quaked beneath them—as if the house herself were drawing ragged, final breaths.

Then—Diesel's voice tore through the clamor. "Ashla—*ENOUGH!*" The command struck like thunder, slicing through the haze of her unraveling essence. "You're tearing at Missy's walls. You're unbinding her core. You… have…to…stop." With ingrained discipline, he moved—swords sheathed in a single, fluid motion—*shhhwwwhhh*. The sound of steel sliding into leather rang out, clean and absolute, a rhythm of control in a room unraveling. Ashla's attention jerked to him—feral, skittering, quintessence arcing off her in erratic bursts. Her limbs quaked, electricity skittering across her skin in spasmodic bursts.

"I can't…" she gasped, her voice brittle. "I have to…she needs me!" Each word trembled under the weight of desperation, dragging through the air like thread pulled through a tear.

"ASHLA!" Mama D's voice rang out again—quiet steel slicing through the breathless chaos. "You're pulling too hard—too much. If you don't stop, Starlight will be found!"

The room buckled as if in agreement. Walls shuddered. Plaster split and curled. Missy's strained defenses heaved against the encroaching force, her foundation groaning beneath the pressure.

Ashla's hands trembled, fingers coiling into fists as flares of energy whipped around her. Her quintessence lashed out—a wild, searing current that scorched the very air, leaving breath tight and brittle.

"Ashla—FOCUS!" Diesel's tone was flint. He stepped forward, each thudding bootfall anchoring against the quaking floor, pushing into the storm. "You're stronger than this. *Control IT!*"

Missy's light sputtered, thinning into a bass-deep undertone that coursed through the space. Her quintessence, threadbare, whispered across the telepathic line: *I can't hold it much longer…Ashla…please.*

Ashla let out a guttural cry. Her head snapped back, the energy around her contorting—unstable and furious. The room distorted. Shadows stretched into unnatural lengths. Furniture quaked, suspended at the brink of collapse.

Diesel didn't break stride. He closed the distance between them, his frame steady—a shield forged from grit and history. "Ashla!" His voice dropped to a near-whisper, but it struck like steel. "You don't have to do this alone. Breathe. Listen."

Her luminous line of sight met his breath, hitching as the tempest within her faltered—wavering under his words. For a moment, the current surrounding her stuttered, streams of power hesitating, as if awaiting her command.

Mama D advanced with care, palms lifted in a pacifying gesture. "Ashla, you're not alone in this. Trust us. Trust me…trust…*yourself.*" She closed the distance, her hands settling firmly on Ashla's shoulders. On contact, a violent strain surged through her form—a scream tearing through the room as threads of blue and gray whipped through her pores like unraveling silk. She gritted her teeth, barreling through the agony. "I can't open the house until you settle, Ashla." She gasped between syllables. "You've…got…to…stop pulling, or I can't open it. You're tearing me —*apart.*" Each word landed heavy, breath thick with effort. She held Ashla's focus as the halo around them began to fade, her voice gentling. "*Love*…you're hurting me!"

Diesel grimaced, his mouth tightening into a hard line. "FUCK! Dammit, D! *ASHLA,* FUCKIN' CONTROL YOURSELF!"

And then—with a sudden, jarring stillness—Ashla exhaled. The volatile currents collapsed inward, dissolving into the ether with a final, searing thrum. Her knees buckled, hitting the floor as the full weight of the moment bore down on her. The room seemed to exhale with her, its walls groaning in relief. The cracks remained—a silent testament to how near they'd come to the edge.

Diesel stepped back, shoulders loosening though his posture remained alert. His focus didn't waver, his cadence holding firm. "D, go open the door."

Ashla's head lifted, her luminous eyes dimming as her breath began to steady. "I...I didn't mean to..." Her tone was hoarse, raw with regret, before she collapsed against the floorboards.

Mama D sank down beside her. "We know," she murmured.

"D, get the door," Diesel commanded, his expression carved from granite. "We'll be *conversating* about this—later."

Ashla's breath caught—a ragged exhale tearing loose from her chest. The tension snapped like a frayed wire. Her body crumpled further, folding into the jagged wreckage of broken planks, limp as a discarded marionette, as the last of raw force drained away.

The filaments of light that had once splintered outward from Mama D now recoiled—like silk threads being rewoven into the quiet strength of a tapestry. She inhaled deeply, her quintessence flaring faintly with every draw—seeping back into her skin like moonlight dissolving across still water.

Diesel extended a hand. She met it without hesitation, her fingers wrapping tightly around his—forearm to forearm, a soldier's grip. He steadied her as she rose on trembling legs. She had done it—soothed Ashla, stilled the storm just long enough for Missy to breathe again.

The walls that had held fast now began to ease. Missy's essence—once taut with stress—unwound, diffusing as the room's energy waned. The house exhaled, its very structure sagging inward, like a weary body finally surrendering to rest.

Nester stepped forward on unsteady footing, his light stuttering like a faulty filament—vacillating irregularly between wan gold and silvery blue. The hues trembled through his center. It wasn't just acknowledgment—it was burden, uncertainty, and fragile resolve tousled in and out of coherence.

Diesel met him head-on, voice a firm command. "Nester. Go help Missy." he didn't soften. "You both need each other. Share your quintessence. You'll understand the Tree of Life better than anyone I know. We need Rayanna to wake—and find the door she created."

Nester bowed his head, the light within him dimming to a slate-gray sheen before blooming into a deep, resolute amber. Without a word, he turned toward the spiral staircase. His movements were uneven, legs trembling faintly as he climbed—each footfall clinking against the battered steps that vanished into shadow above.

Diesel remained at the center of the room, surveying the settling quiet, though his attention hung on Ashla. He crouched beside her, his grip steady as he gathered her into his arms. With care honed by years of control, he carried her to the couch, laying her gently beside Rayanna. His focus darted toward her slumbering frame, untouched by the storm. Diesel wasn't surprised. The first bout of Truth Seeking hollowed a person so thoroughly that sleep became both shield and surrender. The leather she rested on stood like a still point in a spinning world—a quiet island of peace amid the aftermath.

Ashla stirred. Her body trembled with effort, limbs sluggish but driven by sheer will. She forced herself upright, gasping as though each dragged breath scraped her lungs raw. Her voice fractured—scattered shards of words spilling out. "Diesel…Nissa…she needs help…needs…you…to open the door…" Another gasp wrenched through her frame. "Her legs…" Her words crumbled, her head bowing between her knees, shoulders folding inward beneath exhaustion's gravitational pull.

"Rest," he said. "You've done enough. Let us carry what remains."

Then came the clunk—deep, resonant. It reverberated down the hallway, followed by a rising metallic timbre, like ancient gears grinding back into alignment. The house had begun to open.

Moments later, the weighted thud of heavy boots echoed through the corridor. The study door lurched open against the rubble, its crooked hinges protesting with a drawn-out groan, as Ryker's lanky frame to form in the threshold. Draped in simple black cotton, his clothing seemed to absorb the surrounding gloom—a seamless extension of the darkness itself. A scar carved a vertical path across his left eye, yet its aqua-blue gleam cut starkly through the dimness, while his right eye, deep brown and unyielding, swept the room with focused intensity. He advanced with measured resolve, cradling Nissa in his arms as though she weighed nothing.

Her body hung limp against him, each inhale hitching—as if her lungs were locked in quiet rebellion. Where legs had once been, a mermaid's tail was taking shape. Scales, fine as morning dew, bloomed like cascading water—tumbling downward in a delicate, iridescent veil that tugged upon the meager light. The pattern continued to climb, ridges blooming and threading across her form like an ancient song made visible, as though the sea itself were reclaiming her. Silver-blue scales, streaked with veins of gold, caught the dim shimmer and scattered it like shards of starlight on dark water, casting ephemeral, otherworldly brilliance across the space.

Ryker hesitated in the doorway, his focus fixed on Nissa's metamorphosis, his entire frame coiled in high alert. "You're going to have to unbind the next level and force Rayanna to remember where the key and the door are," he said, voice low and exacting. "Because Nissa doesn't look like she's got time to wait for Ray to wake."

Ashla pushed herself upright, as if dragging her limbs through molasses, every muscle screaming in protest. Still, she leaned in, pulling back Rayanna's onyx sleeve—her hand settling over the marking etched into her forearm: a moon inked in stark black. The air between them crackled with the static of unfinished work.

A greenish hue wilted in and out—weak at first, like a dying ember—before flaring to life in jagged, uneven bursts. It spread outward in dotted lines, pulsing with erratic rhythm. Then the force surged forward, clawing into Rayanna's mind with all the subtlety of a battering ram. Her head snapped back, a gasp ripping from her lips as memories crashed against her consciousness—each one striking with the violence of waves obliterating a crumbling seawall.

Ashla's breath came in fractured bursts, her vision swimming—but she didn't let go. Couldn't. She held on, driving the energy forward, her will the only force keeping the fragile connection from shattering entirely.

Then, suddenly, Rayanna pitched forward with a strangled gasp, her knees colliding hard with the edge of the coffee table. The impact sent a dull thud jolting through the room. A scream tore from her throat—raw and serrated. "Fuck you, Ashla! That one…*fucking hurts!*"

Chapter Thirty-Five

Present Day

Her hands clutched her kneecaps, the bruising impact against the coffee table radiating down her legs—anchoring her to the chaos surging within. A burst of pain flared along her forearm, radiating from the place where Ashla's touch had lingered. The connection had severed, unleashing a torrent of wild, unrelenting energy—an onslaught of truths cascading like diamond rain. The suffocating wall of disorientation shattered, collapsing like a dam under unbearable weight, awakening parts of her mind long bound.

Rayanna's breath tore through her lungs in ragged bursts. At first, her chest seized beneath the agony, as though a rusted chain—shadowed and corroded—was being dragged free from the depths of her soul. Each link scraped along her spine, rending hidden barriers and prying open locked memories. Her lungs expanded in uneven gulps, coughing through shards of recollection. Fragments crashed into one another, spiraling back to the moment ink surged like tidal waves on Starlight Beach—the reckoning that shattered their perfect world and obliterated every illusion of control. Pieces of who they had been—parts she hadn't known were missing—

clawed their way to the surface. *This isn't the same,* she thought bitterly, *but it's damn close.*

The room lurched, the ground pitching and buckling beneath her like a ship hurled into merciless seas. Her body, unmoored and at war with itself, crumbled beneath the relenting force. Notions erupted into the light—remnants long entombed, jagged and aching. Shadows scattered, fleeing as recollections found one another, locking into place with brutal, irrevocable force—rewriting the very bindings of her mind.

With trembling hands, she gripped the scorched edge of the coffee table and hauled herself upright. Her fingers clung to the solid wood as if scaling a crumbling cliff—its weight the only anchor holding her to reality. The vibrations within her hammered a punishing tempo, propelling her upward even as chaos clawed at the frayed edges of her resolve. The devastating force of unbinding slammed into her core like a gut punch—sudden, raw, and unfiltered. It was a visceral rupture, a severing of shadowed ties, leaving her exposed and teetering on the brink of collapse.

"Fuck you, Ashla! That one...*fucking hurts!*" she spat, fury cracking, a brittle shield against the onslaught of searing sensation. Her knuckles blanched, gripping the table's edge as her glare sliced through the haze of pain. Each word dropped sharp and bitter. "What's next? All this part of some grand cosmic plan?"

Ashla tilted her head into a dreamy stillness, untouched by the venom, her expression softening into a wistful calm. "It will pass soon," she murmured, her tone light and vaporous. "Like I told Runa...it's never the same for everyone, you know. It twists and turns in its own peculiar way. Yours...well..." Her mouth hung slightly open, gaze unfocused—like a sleepy turtle watching a butterfly flutter by on an updraft."Yours has a certain flair."

Rayanna pressed the heel of her palm to her temple, her balance wavering as the room pitched in a nauseating swirl. "Seriously," she growled, "If there's a guide for this mess, toss it my way—before I completely lose my mind with this one"

A glimmer of amusement danced across Ashla's features, her buoyant demeanor seemingly impervious to Rayanna's frustration. "Oh, but answers don't come with handbooks," she mused, her fingers tracing idle, invisible patterns along her thigh. "They arrive like fireflies—fickle and fleeting, if you're lucky enough to catch one." Her eyelids lowered briefly, as if to clear away the lingering fog of contemplation. "Though I imagine yours will be a bit more...structured. Expectantly stubborn in its pursuit of clarity."

Rayanna groaned, dragging her hands down her face as if trying to stitch herself back together. "I don't even know what you're talking about," she muttered. "Your words *make* my brain *hurt*." She pressed her palms over her eyes again, shutting out the world with a strained exhale. "You have got to be winging it from here, *because* I doubt any of this is going according to *any godforsaken plan.*"

Ashla's grin widened. "Winging it, mostly," she replied, as if the chaos swirling around them was nothing more than a passing breeze. "But *I think you're* doing great."

Rayanna blinked, dazed. "You know what...*fuck* this unbinding *bullshit.*" She shook her head, movements sluggish and unfocused as she tried to steady herself. Her socks caught on the jagged floorboards, snagging against splintered edges she barely registered—her mind still reeling from the storm Ashla had plunged her into.

Ashla rose fluidly from the couch and stepped toward her, extending a hand in effortless offering. "I unbound you a little more," she said, voice laced with faint whimsy. "You must remember where the door is, Auntie Ray." Her words were light, yet heavy with intent. "It's tethered to your vow, to all that matters—woven into the now, as it has always been. There's no more time for lingering."

"Wait. Wait, *wait*—" Rayanna stumbled back toward the hearth, her voice sharp with disbelief. "You pushed me further—because *you* need *something?*" She shot the words like sparks, trembling with fury. "I'm done. I am so *fucking* done. What am I now? One of those dandelion *puffs?* I guess...just pluck me up. Blow me out. Make a *fucking* wish, Ashla."

"Ray, take it down a notch," Diesel interjected, stepping between them. "Being done isn't an option. You *will* find the door."

"What door? What vow?" Rayanna snapped, spinning on her heel, arms flung upward in frustration—almost as if pleading with the room itself for answers. She exhaled hard, whirling back around to jab a finger at Ashla. "Can someone else *please,* for the love of the Blessed Father, explain this to me? Instead of *her?* She's giving me a fucking headache."

Mama D stepped from the shadows, her calm presence like the hush of dew on foliage before the first light of dawn. "He's right, Ray," she said, voice level but unyielding. "What lies ahead…walking away isn't something any of us can afford."

"Runa was right," Rayanna bit out. "This *fucking endless* cycle is *bullshit*." Her palms pressed hard into her temples, as if she could hold the spiraling chaos inside at bay. "I can't do this. I *don't* want to do this." The words fell out sharp and frayed, thick with exhaustion.

Diesel's jaw clenched, irritation sharpening his gaze. "You've been stuck in this 'endless cycle' for what—twenty-four hours?" he snapped. "That's enough, Ray. Enough with the excuses."

Rayanna staggered back a step, her shoulders rising and falling as the sagging walls groaned around her—wooden beams creaking, shifting, as though testing their own resilience. Her breath hitched in shallow intervals as the unbinding passed through her again—slow and grinding, like ancient gears awakening, shaking loose decades of dust and buried weight.

Beneath her feet, the essence of Missy had begun to knit itself back together. The walls realigned in subtle increments, the faint creak of mending timber whispering through the space. It was imperceptible at first —more sensed than heard—as though the house had drawn a breath and was now settling its bones. But Rayanna, lost in her inner tumult, remained unaware.

Roots from the Tree of Life arched upward, veins fracturing across the floorboards. Her heel snagged on one, sending her stumbling. She flung her arms out, catching herself against the edge of a chair.

"I'm not sure what you *want* from me!" she shouted, her voice cracking with frustration. "Some miracle worker? Am I supposed to perform on command? What's next—do I…"

"Rayanna. CUT. THE. *FUCKING*. BULLSHIT. *NOW*," Diesel roared— his words sharp, final, cleaving through the storm like a blade.

"Sorry…" she muttered, eyes closing as she exhaled. "Just…frustrated. I know you need me to find this key…door…or vow thing, but I don't have *any fucking clue* where it is."

A dull ache settled behind her eyes. She pressed the heels of her palms into them, rubbing slow circles over her lids before letting go. Darkness swelled, then splintered—bursts of light flaring and fading in rapid succession. The brightness surged all at once—warped and streaking, like after-images burned into her retinas—throwing her balance further off-kilter. She blinked rapidly, trying to orient herself through the onslaught.

Her vision sharpened. Chin lifted.

And then the full weight of the study's ruin struck—like stepping into blinding sunlight after hours in shadow, like colliding with an unmovable wall: jarring, absolute.

The room—once meticulously ordered—had unraveled into disarray. Shelves slumped at precarious angles, their contents strewn in careless heaps. Books lay open, pages curled inward, as if recoiling from the destruction. Overhead, the balcony tilted dangerously, its railing marred by jagged cracks that spread like frozen lightning. Across the floor, papers scattered like discarded secrets, their edges singed and curling inward.

"Umm…" Her mouth hung open, fingers pressing lightly against her cheeks—tapping, searching, as if the motion might somehow coax out the words she couldn't yet find.

From the darkened corners, leaves shimmered faintly, their glow dimming to muted green hues. Scattered among them lay aging Lumis Blooms—silver and blue spheres rolling aimlessly, some folding inward as if suffocating in the absence of the energy they once held.

"What the hell happened?" Rayanna exclaimed, disbelief thickening her voice as her steps faltered. She caught herself on the edge of the same overturned chair, knuckles whitening as her focus swept the wreckage, searching for answers her mind couldn't yet stitch together. "How long was I out?" The words rasped from her throat, raw and frayed, like exposed wire. She jolted, eyes locking onto the lanky yet grounded figure in the doorway. Her breath caught—warmth blooming beneath her skin as her cheeks flushed. "Why is Ryker here?" Her brow furrowed, confusion knitting tightly across her features. "Is that Nissa?"

Diesel scraped a hand down his thigh, fingers dragging up to the back of his neck. "About ten minutes," he said curtly. His palm lingered there, massaging the tension like he could press the frustration straight through his skin. "Ashla doesn't waste time when all sense goes out of her head." His jaw flexed, a muscle ticking in the hollow beneath his cheekbone.

"Holy shit!" Rayanna's voice shot upward, disbelief spilling out of her in a rush. "You have *got* to be kidding me."

"That's what happens when quintessence is unbound without preparation," he muttered, frustration threading through every scuffed step across the debris-strewn floor. "We'll help her clean this up once—" His words cut off, gaze snapping upward.

Nester stood at the top of the spiral staircase, shoulders slumped. The faint, dusky halo around him wavered; his form swayed ever so slightly. His tiny leather boots and apron had been discarded what felt like ages ago, leaving him bare—struggling just to stay upright.

"Nester," Diesel called sharply.

A sluggish dip of the head. A faint flicker of acknowledgment. Then his body sagged further, as if even the effort to respond had cost more than he could spare.

Diesel's jaw ticked, a current of concern flashing beneath the surface as he redirected his attention to Ryker and Nissa—then back to Nester. "We need to sort this out," he muttered, wagging a finger at the forming mermaid. "Nester! You good with that?"

The little figure stirred again, head lifting in a jerky, fractured motion before nodding—subtle and unmistakably weary.

Before Diesel could press further, a sharp *pop* broke the stillness.

"*Weel*, this is a right shite show." His remark landed hard, the tell of a man unflinching in his cool detachment—someone well-acquainted with disaster. "Looks like a bloody storm had itself a fine ol' time in here. This what ye lot call progress?"

Scanning the space, Liam's gaze landed on Nissa—the strained rhythm of her breaths drawing his focus. "Her Dawnin' Day, aye? Quintessence risin' to dae surface. A bit o' sunlight findin' its brilliance." His Adam's apple bobbed as he studied her, quiet intensity tugging at the lines of his face, letting the roughness in his voice breathe. "Dey be not only a mair-maid, but one wit' a knack for unbindin'—aye, dat's a rare sight."

With that, he ducked beneath the bar, lifting a single finger into view—a silent *hold yer britches*. Below, the scrape of shifting objects sounded: glass clinking against crystal, dull chimes filling the hush. He resurfaced with a grunt, elbows braced against the counter, a worn leather-bound book in hand. With practiced ease, he flipped to a marked page—as if he'd done it a thousand times. Without looking up, he slipped a finger into the binding, anchoring the thread. Only then did his gaze rise, locking onto Rayanna.

He tipped the book's spine in her direction. "D'ya ken how rare Unbinders are these days, Ray?" His tone was casual. The weight beneath it was anything but.

She blinked, her shoulders drawing tight beneath the press of his scrutiny. "No," she murmured, a resigned shrug trailing just behind.

"I'll tell ye this much, and ye can take it or lave it," he said with languid grace. With his free hand, he rapped his knuckles twice against the book's worn cloth cover—the sound dull, solid, unhurried. Its edges were frayed, softened from years of handling, but the gravity of its knowledge remained untouched.

Using the spine, he gestured toward the scattered Lumis Blooms. "Them ones there…" His voice dipping into something close to reverence. "If ye ask 'em proper, wi' the right intent, they'll give what's wantin'."

His mouth quirked in a knowing smirk. "I once courted a mairmaid, y'see—sharp as a blade, she was—and she swore by it. Said those blooms would give her just enough breath, if needs be."

His words landed, settling like fresh snowfall—soft, weightless, absolute.

Gradually, attention drifted, drawn across the splintered floorboards. The scattered Lumis Blooms stirred weakly against the wreckage, their dim glow beckoning awareness back to Nissa and Ryker. Her breath rasped thinly, chest rising in shallow, uneven tremors. The transformation held its course—agonizingly unstoppable—as the room remained suspended in reverent awe, watching, absorbing, waiting.

"D'ye plan on makin' a move, or do ye need it spelled out?" Liam scoffed. "The blooms won't be rollin' around all day. Keep twiddlin' yer thumbs, and dey'll be dead before ye blink." He planted a hand on the bar top and dipped forward, sweeping his sightline over the wreckage—taking stock of the scattered orbs, their dim luster stammering weakly against the debris.

"They might even answer her, lass," he added, his brogue gritty but sure, eyes still pinned to Nissa. "Back in the day, we used ta rely on 'em durin' missions, afore the Great War. If one o' us got banged up real bad, sometimes they'd pull us back from the brink. Dependin' on where they are in their life cycle, they can be used for all manner of things." He paused momentarily, giving into the thoughts of old.

"But keep in mind—dey need askin'. Ye can't just grab at 'em. Dinnae work dat way. You think dis room's in rough shape now? Touch da wrong one, and it could blow yer bloody arm off." His mouth curled with dry amusement. "Tink it's bad now? Imagine one of 'em turnin' volatile. Dat'd be a proper mess—moody little buggers, they are." Liam knocked his knuckles twice against the book's worn cover—the sound dull but deliberate.

"Ya ken how Lumis Blooms can hold memories wi' purpose, aye? That's the older ones—the ones that've sat, gathered wisdom, turned temperamental wi' time." His voice rose with enthusiasm, words picking up pace. "The mid-aged ones—they're more willin' to shift, adapt. Fickle, but useful. But da young ones? Ah…them wee things guard their secrets tighter dan a miser hoardin' gold."

He dipped his chin, eyes narrowing. "That storm Ashla kicked up must've knocked 'em loose afore they were ready. Day weren't meant ta fall yet." A breath left him, "But dat might just be what saves her."

His stare bounded from the nearest orb to Nissa. "If any would heed her, it'd be them. Young, unshaped, drawn 'ta what feels like their own. And her?" He huffed, nodding toward her barely conscious form. "A mairmaid and an unbinder? Aye, that's kinship if I ever saw one." Keeping a finger wedged between the binding, gripping the spine as he gave a sharp, expectant tilt of his chin—gesturing Ryker closer. "Weel, get to it, lad." A beat passed before his smirk deepened. "Still, we're nae exactly drownin' in options, are we?"

A deep, resonant tremor moved through the walls—a telling sign the earth itself had drawn breath and begun to alter. The Tree of Life, ancient and ever-knowing, bristled as though waking from a long slumber. Its massive trunk flexed, golden light ascending its spine in a measured, inexorable current—like fire spiraling its way along a whisper-thin wick. Then it shook—not a mere shudder or an idle sway, but a full-bodied convulsion, the kind a great beast gives to rid itself of rain. Leaves sighed and shivered, and branches stretched outward with a groaning creak, their tips flaring with deep, pulsing gold.

The house reacted instantly. A guttural moan rumbled through the foundation as wood bent and swelled, fibers knitting together with unnerving exactitude. Splintered planks lurched back into place, each seam mending with the sound of fabric being stitched—tight, seamless, absolute. Above, the broken balcony steadied, then pressed back into alignment, stone grinding against stone in a methodical restoration. A sheen of luminous amber cascaded through the walls, moving like breath across glass—sealing fissures, smoothing warped beams, restoring the house in one sweeping, undeniable act of will. The very foundation anchored beneath them, exhaling relief.

And yet—the quintessence did not stop at wood and stone. It billowed outward, a rolling force that momentarily stole the breath from their lungs, sinking into their bones like a second heartbeat. For the briefest instant, it felt as though Missy herself had stretched open her ribs, letting the Tree's will flood her entire being—before drawing it all back in, whole once more.

The air recalibrated—stunned into a dense, echoing hush. It wasn't quiet born of peace, but of aftershock, the kind that stretches wide after something ancient finishes speaking.

"Weel, I'll be damned," Liam said, folding his arms across his chest as he surveyed the room. "Looks like clean-up's sorted." His chin tipped toward the staircase, drawing every gaze upward.

Nester remained slumped against the first step of the second floor—marginally steadier, but still hollowed out from the strain.

Yet Ryker's attention held—anchored not to Nester, nor to the murmurs drifting like vapor through the room, but to a single Lumis Bloom nestled near the base of the wet bar. It lay inert, quivering in faint resonance, as if echoing Nissa's own waning strength.

And then—it stirred. Drawn by his focus, the bloom rocked forward, teetering between motion and collapse. A sluggish, uneven lurch followed, its form inching ahead—not fluidly, not with ease—but in a faltering drag, as if its core had buckled, caving inward. Each strained rotation deepened its collapse, its fragile luminescence fluttering—flickering perilously close to extinction.

It wasn't simply moving. It was falling forward—*slowly, painfully*—wilting with every inch as it reached for him.

"Brin' her closer," Liam said with softened insistence. "If dere's even a chance these beauties'll answer, we've nae time da waste."

Ryker exhaled sharply, adjusting his grip on Nissa as he lowered into a crouch. His body tightened, muscles flexing to counterbalance her weight.

Precision was everything. No room for missteps. Years of training under Izayah and Daxler had carved it into him—adjust, stabilize, execute.

Still…this is different. Ryker pulled the notion forward. *I've been through combat drills, assassination protocols, survival exercises in black zones. But negotiating with glowing orbs? If someone had told me a week ago I'd be laying a half-conscious mermaid down like an offering to the world's moodiest light bulbs, I'd have laughed. Maybe cracked a joke. But now?*

His dark eye locked on the bloom—ember to ember. No hesitation. No questions. Just motion. One fluid descent, each step considered, grounded. The hush pressing inward—dense with unspoken hope—though he moved as if the weight of every gaze didn't touch him.

Ashla's voice cut through the quiet, lilting yet certain. "Don't touch them directly. Lay her down gently. The bloom will do the rest."

"Ach, ye movin' through fuckin' molasses, lad?" Liam quipped. "Or is dis yer way o' keepin' us all in suspense?"

Ryker halted mid-stride, easing Nissa from his hold in a smooth, calculated release. A wry smirk tugged at the corner of his mouth as he glanced over his shoulder. "Oh? And here I thought slow was your thing," he fired back, straightening to his full height and rolling his shoulders, stretching out the tension from cradling her weight.

"I have to ask—do you just sit around in that frame dreaming up new ways to screw with everyone? Because right now, I'm internally debating fifty different ways to say 'fuck you' before these blooms start feelin' neglected and pop off." He exhaled sharply, flexing his fingers. "I was approaching this like I'm wading through a damn minefield. Excuse me for moving with purpose." His hand swept outward in a vague gesture. "You just told us they're moody buggers. I've got zero experience with 'em, and frankly, I'd rather not blow up today."

Liam dipped his chin, the motion slight but conceding—an unspoken *touche.* But Ryker had already turned his focus back to Nissa.

He drew a measured step backward, his line of sight fastening onto the pearlescent sheen of her skin as the orb's dim radiance edged closer. Its movements tentative and searching, like a thought not yet decided.

"Ashla," he called, without glancing up. "That work for you?"

She inclined her head in quiet affirmation.

With a pointed glance toward the golden-framed portrait, he added dryly, "I don't know about you, Liam, but it seems to me Ashla's a hell of a lot more informed than you and your book—she just prefers to keep her mouth shut most of the time."

The Lumis Bloom teetered in its unsteady roll—slumped and faltering—yet as it neared Nissa's frail form, something recalibrated. The faint sheen at its core steadied, no longer a flicker but a burgeoning spark—hesitant, yet insistent. Its radiance coalesced, fragile vitality crystallizing into quiet resolve, as though her presence alone had summoned it into purpose.

He noticed the opalescence of her skin echoing the bloom's center—*like calling to like*—a silent resonance that coaxed the sphere forward. It fumbled forward, halting mid-roll in its uneven rhythm, burdened by fatigue. For a breath of time, it hovered, and within the depth, the iridescent fluid began to sway. The closer it drew, the more its stuttering swirl thickened—teal, opalescent, exquisite—like the waters of a far-off lagoon sloshing against gelatinous boundaries, depths long dormant now stirring awake. A gradual resurgence—filling, replenishing—as if the orb had found in her a viable source to survive.

It traced a lopsided path, curving along the contour of her body before nestling into the hollow of Nissa's neck. It shuddered—trembled—then, with a soft *shhhk*, it anchored itself to the delicate ridges forming along her neck.

For a heartbeat—*nothing.*

Then—Nissa's chest seized. Her lips parted in a silent gasp before she inhaled—a singular, desperate breath surging into her lungs like the first inhale of a newborn breaching the surface of water.

A soft, gloopy pressure brushed against Rayanna's foot. She jolted, instinctively flinching back, her heel catching just enough to send a second Lumis Bloom tumbling forward. The gelatinous orb—cool and pliant, a pulse of living jelly—bounced in a clumsy arc before flopping against a chair leg with a wet, blubbering *plop*.

It quivered violently, its edges rippling as though recoiling from the sudden jolt. With a shivering wobble, it pressed itself deeper into the folds of the overturned chair—tucked in tight, uncertain, adopting a protective stance.

"*Weel,* dere ye go. Let's jest boot 'em about, shall we? That oughta help," Liam drawled, scratching lazily at his brow. "Fabulous job."

From his relaxed post at the threshold, Ryker folded his arms, a smirk tugging at one corner of his mouth. "Hold up—you can't give me shit for moving too slow, then gripe when someone else moves too fast. At least Ray still owns her foot. I call that a win."

Rayanna rolled her eyes and pointed. "Pa, would you help me?" She nudged at the chair with her toe, glancing up—expectant.

Together, they righted the twin velvet seat, its plush form thudding softly into place. Freed, the trapped sphere gave an unbalanced wobble— its rhythm disoriented, as if it had lost its sense of gravity.

As it lurched forward, Ryker peeled himself from the doorway, moving on instinct—his hand shooting out toward the orb.

"No, no." Ashla's voice cut clean through the air—gentle, unwavering, a quiet authority glowing across her porcelain frame. "Let it go to her," she murmured. "It knows where it belongs."

Ryker froze mid-reach, fingers curling inward as he withdrew. Reclaiming his post, he leaned back against the frame and re-crossed his arms with the ease of someone who had no intention of intervening again.

The room hushed—watching, waiting—as the sphere tottered forward, its unsteady path mirroring the first. With a intentional purpose, it pressed against the opposite side of Nissa's neck, nestling into place with a soft *shhwip*. The twin orbs paused—teal fluid swirling hypnotically within their translucent shells. Then, in perfect synchrony, they stilled, their aura smoothing into a steady, unified luminescence. At last, they had found their rhythm—an equilibrium forged through instinct and intention.

Nissa's breath leveled, yet Ryker's gaze remained fixed—scanning for any trace of distress. When none appeared, the notion of hope ebbed in, like light breaching the surface of an otherwise guarded expression.

The room held steady, anticipation thickening with the quiet certainty that this attempt would hold. Ashla offered a serene nod—silent, assured. From his golden frame, Liam arched a brow, then gave a curt, near-imperceptible dip of the head—approval glinting, faint but undeniable.

That was all Ryker needed.

Pushing off the doorway at last, he crossed the room in steady strides, gathering Nissa into his arms with instinctive control. She felt insubstantial, weightless—something fragile yet familiar. With exactitude, he lowered her onto the leather couch, arranging her with quiet mastery—

aligning her posture, adjusting the angle of her legs, and bracing her emerging fin against the coffee table's edge.

Where her feet had once been, metamorphosis continued to unfurl—dark teal ink pooling at the base, fusing flesh in gleaming waves. The transformation climbed her skin like a tide rising at dusk, arcing from storm-lit ocean to soft, iridescent teal. Beneath the surface, golden veins glimmered subtly, ribboning through delicate webbing that stretched outward—like butterfly wings touched by salt and light.

Her tail budded—powerful and certain—the edges flexing as if testing unseen currents. The change swept upward, seamless and sure, her human form yielding to something ancient, elemental. Past and present collided, folding into a form written into her marrow long before her first breath.

Only once she was settled did Ryker straighten. His gaze flicked toward the twin orbs—still glowing, their quiet, synchronized rhythm a living testament to the stability they'd gifted her. Awe brushed the edges of his awareness, threatening to root—but he refused to let it anchor. *This wasn't the time to marvel.*

So, his focus shifted to Liam.

He swept the longer strands of hair away from the left side of his face, where they fell in loose, shadowed layers—an unruly veil that grazed his cheekbone and temple. In contrast, the right side was shaved close to the scalp, sharp and unapologetic—a scripted imbalance that framed the cool severity of his expression like a blade against calm. It wasn't just skepticism that tightened his jaw; something more intricate wound beneath—curiosity, calculated and coiled behind the steel.

"What book is that you've got?" Ryker called out, nodding toward the leather bound tome still in Liam's grasp, a finger wedged between the time-worn pages, marking his place. "I mean, sure, you've got your mermaid courting stories—charming, really—but where's all this history coming from? Before the Great War, was it? Or have you been keeping something from us all this time?" His brow arched, a smirk ghosting at the corner of his mouth—though beneath it, genuine curiosity threaded through his tone.

Liam cleared his throat, lifting the book slightly as he thumbed it open. "Aye, lad," he said, "Dis here's no bedtime tale, if dat's what ye're thinkin'. But if ye've got a moment, I'll enlighten ye." He flipped to a worn page, its brittle edges crackling softly—like the book itself resented being disturbed. A quiet chuckle followed. "Ah, ye tink I'm spinnin' a tall tale, do ye?"

Rayanna leaned forward, her fingers curling around the edge of the uprighted chair. "So this book—"

But movement sparked at the edge of her vision. A shimmer—small, syncopated, tenuous. Her words withered as her gaze snapped to Nester. His filament undulated in faint, faltering waves, like the last breath of a candle struggling against extinguishment.

Diesel moved instinctively, taking the spiral staircase two steps at a time, the impact of his boots reverberating through the timbers. Above, Nester's diminutive frame wavered—until his knees buckled. He crumpled forward, the clash of pipe and splintering wood echoing with a hollow, jarring finality.

At the landing's third step, Diesel bent low, his broad frame unfolding into a silent, protective cradle. Nester yielded into the space offered—a moment of fragile convergence, where exhaustion met trust. Without pause, they descended, each footfall a quiet assertion.

When his boots touched the ground floor, Ashla's voice rose—laced with wonder. "He holds all the threads," she murmured, her wide eyes following the final flickers of Nester's light. "I've long suspected…but if he *is* pure quintessence…" Her gaze drifted to the towering silhouette of the Tree of Life, her expression darkening with thought. "The tree's energy flowed through Missy—mending the walls, drawing her back together— but it never reached him. Why?"

Nissa stirred at the question, her voice raw and rasping—barely more than a whisper. "Maybe pure quintessence requires connection." She drew a deeper breath, the cadence uneven, as if testing the thought aloud while it formed. "Missy is connected to the tree—its roots weave through her, entwining with her very being. It's part of her now…maybe they're one and the same."

Ashla tilted her head, her gaze brightening with interest. "*Then*…if he sat at its *base*—" she trailed off, the idea spinning slowly between them like a coin on its final edge. "Wouldn't it replenish him?"

Nissa's fingers curled slightly, as if combing through unseen soil. "If the Tree of Life is willing to share…I'd wager it could sustain him."

Diesel's jaw tightened. "How do you know he's pure quintessence?" he asked, voice low, tempered with skepticism.

"We can see them dance," Ashla answered simply. "They shimmer—you know. Drifting. Connecting. Like spider silk in moonlight."

"He stays hidden for a reason." Diesel's exhale came sharp, his grip around Nester's slight frame unwavering. "This isn't something we're eager to expose—or risk someone tearing through the walls to find." He paused, the weight behind his words grounding the room. "I believed breaching our safeguards was impossible. All knowledge of individuals like you"—he nodded toward Ashla—"especially the *extent* of what you can do, was thought erased. But now? We know what you *can* do...and what we *suspect* Nissa may be capable of, too. That changes things. What you did today was reckless." His tone shifted—still taut, but softened by a trace of understanding. "That said...I'm beginning to see more of the why behind the what. From both of you."

Ashla's posture eased, the weight of his words settling over her like the final note of a fading melody—light, but impossible to ignore. "I didn't know," she said quietly. "I didn't realize..." She rose without thought, drifting toward the nearest bookshelf. Her fingers skimmed the spines, then traced the grain of the wood—absent, restless—until her presence thinned to a whisper: "I'm sorry."

Missy responded with a low, settling groan—walls hunkering down like a massive beast, weary and wholly done with the day. A subtle tremor rippled through the floorboards, exhaling outward before surging up through the hearth. The flames obeyed in a concentrated arc, igniting with purpose, licking along the back of the fireplace like silken ribbons before tapering down. It wasn't just heat. It was an acknowledgment.

Rayanna's head snapped toward the blaze as it twisted—gold and green collapsing inward, folding, reforming. Her brow tightened, the edges of her perception fraying, unraveling like thread pulled too fast. The pieces were there—scattered, disjointed—like rifling through old boxes in a frenzy, pushing aside what no longer fit, what no longer mattered. The unbinding churned through her, a nauseating, relentless tide dredging up fragments she ached to anchor, to make sense of. There, *then* gone. As if she had once known it. As if she'd stepped into the room with the certainty of finding something—only to discover the space hollow, the object missing. The memory of it slipped through her like water.

Damn the fleeting notion. No, it's the certainty—lodged where doubt had once lived. There is nothing left to hold. No ledge to brace against. No field for reason to take root. Only this—this ancient, soundless thunderclap of truth rattling through my chest, searching for its owner and coming up empty. From this a question surfaced—uninvited yet, undeniable: *Does it seek who I once was...or what has quietly endured? Maybe that's the struggle. What I've become is shaped by truths only my past self remembers. The key. The door. Yet, this soul still holds them, shadowed in the deepest of memory—but this version of me...this now... cannot recall where the truth was kept.*

Rayanna squinted, refocusing on the bellydancing light bending and swaying in hypnotic rhythm, flickering at odd angles. For a fleeting moment, it didn't feel like fire at all, but something alive. Something watching.

Mama D took notice. The trance that had overtaken her youngling was more than just distraction—it was potential untethered, drifting. *What could become of such a mind left unchecked?* With a sharp snap of her fingers and a firm slap to her thigh, the sound ricocheted through the room— looping around Rayanna's head like a boomerang, tugging through the air in a coaxing arc that lifted each chin and drew every gaze back to her. "There's quintessence in this room," she announced, low, warm—an ember of consideration. "Energy that hasn't surfaced in a long while—unique to each bearer. A core essence vital to rebalancing The Lands, yet still not fully understood. Not grasped. What we need to recognize—" Her voice paused, the thought turning on her tongue, searching for precision. "No..." She reoriented, firmer now. "*Accept.*" The word struck like flint. "We need to accept that even the quintessence that lingered after the Great War has dulled...scattered."

Drawn forward, she stepped toward the newly stretched bark. Her fingers hovered, then skimmed its surface with featherlight intent. The energy thrummed beneath her touch—not veins, but something deeper— woven into the lifewood's very marrow, an ancient pulse steady and unshaken.

In the narrow crevices, a nearly invisible thread clung to the hardened grain—coarse as weathered earth, yet fused with something finer. *Denser.* It didn't lift away but shifted beneath her fingertips, pliant. Alive. Warm. Tangible. Palpable. Like silk spun from pure light, streaked with earthen golds and browns—a quiet testament to the tree's enduring essence.

"What we're seeing here," she said, smoothing the fine thread back into the tree's ridged surface as though folding a crease into sacred cloth, "is the first true resurgence of such force in its full magnitude. The war fractured it, shifted it, dimmed it to embers. And now…its strength stirs." With that, she drifted to the left of the hearth—an inevitable, gravitational pull closing the space between two tethered souls. She looked up at him from beneath her brows, a knowing glance designed to soften his resolve, to call him back toward reason. There, Diesel stood fixed at the base of the spiral staircase, unmoving, cradling Nester in a hold that radiated quiet guardianship. Her focus landed on the small one—his light pale and stuttering, yet stubborn against the deep leather of the general's uniform. Mama D paused, not just observing, but seeing with reverence—the kind of vision that perceives the stitching beneath sensation. "He'll need that connection if he's going to recover," she murmured, letting the thought root itself, solidifying as new possibilities threaded along its edges—immediate, insistent, pressing.

She exhaled. With it, each idea loosened and bloomed—like soft shoots pushing through damp earth, shedding clumps of resistance like golden streusel falling from a warm pie, inevitable and quietly sweet. Her lips pressed together, rolling slightly as if tasting the thought before giving it form. Awareness settled low in her chest—not burdensome, but certain. Present. Waiting to be held up to the light and turned over, slowly.

"Conceivably, that's what this confirms." The notion stretched—thick as honey—sinking into the warm cup of consideration. "The roots didn't merely restore the house—they accepted an exchange. Freely. Without resistance. One could argue that by giving his quintessence to Missy, Nester opened a door." Her teeth pressed gently into her lower lip, anchoring the thought as another thread surfaced. "A shared bond between two—yielding in tandem, offering without condition, like…"

Emotion gathered at the rim of Mama D's composure, a single tear brimming against her lashes. "Like the girls. We did it because it was right. It made sense. They became part of us, and we answered that call. Even when nothing compelled us to, we stepped forward because…"

Diesel reoriented himself, drawing Nester slightly closer, then completed her thought. "We had the means," he said, voice rough with certainty. "We loved because they simply needed to be loved." He lowered his chin, gaze steady. "And Nes gave what he had to Missy. In turn, the roots gave to her."

Mama D's breath caught, the lone tear slipping down her cheek. "And we *needed* them." Her attention returned to the towering presence of the tree—its roots gripping the foundation as if always belonging there. "I believe it understands. It feels the weight of our hearts...the sincerity of intent."

A moment stretched—not hesitation, but gravity.

A quiet *hmm* rumbled in Rayanna's throat—more reflex than thought. "Simple, yet layered. A layered complexity," she said, rolling the words around like stones in her palm, contemplating their shape. "Maybe Ma was only half right on that one. Depends on the angle, I guess." Her voice faded, a hush drifting outward like stillness over deep water.

Mama D let the silence breathe, then asked outright, "Could that be the key to everything?"

Diesel's awareness pulled toward the expanse of bark and bough where the ancient behemoth had rooted itself into the study. Its limbs stretched outward, pressing into the freshly mended floorboards, its presence anchored—breath for breath. *Missy hadn't merely allowed it. She had welcomed it. Embraced it. Or perhaps...acceptance had always been here. Not forced. Not demanded. Just patiently waiting.* The realization struck him—*trust wasn't granted in a single moment. It was built. Quietly. Deliberately. Layer by layer. Through consistency. Through witness. Through time. It hadn't vanished. It hadn't even been forgotten. It had simply lain dormant, waiting for someone to remember how to see it.*

Adjusting his hold on Nester, Diesel took a step forward. Something in the angle of his shoulders resisted—as if releasing him would mean surrendering the small guardian to a force not yet proven worthy of that trust.

Then, unbidden, a thought surfaced. *Ezekiel's voice.* Quiet, unwavering —winding through his memory like an old truth brushing against a half-open door: *When we sow seeds, the unknown isn't there to prove us wrong. It exists because we must learn to break free and grow for ourselves—to become who we are meant to be.* He shook his head, chasing clarity, hurling questions at the silence like stones into a dark lake— searching for answers he hadn't known he needed until now. *Had it always been this? This connection—quietly forged, already whole? Was this what they'd been seeking all along? Was the tree the key forward? The door Rayanna was always meant to find?*

Nothing responded.

No undeniable pull of recognition.

No filament of truth emerged.

Only the resolute, commanding presence of the tree.

Waiting.

Diesel huffed, frustration tightening his jaw, sinew along his neck pulled taut as he released a quiet warning. "Then we'd better hope it's in a giving mood—because if anything happens to Nes, I'll cut this thing out myself." His voice dropped, firm and unshaken, the cadence of a man who never made threats—only promises.

The moment Nester made contact, the atmosphere recalibrated—no longer saturated with hesitation, but thrumming with raw potential. A crisp plume of wild lavender and palo santo threaded into the room, fine and ephemeral, weaving between them like a silken wisp, subtle but unmistakable. As if Missy herself had leaned close and murmured, *I promise, sir. Everything will be just fine.*

The tree stirred.

Not abruptly.

Not with force.

But with unmistakable intention.

Its limbs drew inward—measured, unhurried—then unfolded again, not as growth, but as awareness. Roots, thick with age yet precise in movement, coiled upward from the base, rising with an ancient grace. They did not seize or entangle but folded inward, layer upon layer, forming a cradle of living wood beneath Nester's slight frame.

The bark, worn and furrowed, adjusted—yielding where it mattered. It didn't enclose but received him. The fibers flexed, reweaving around him, not in possession, but in welcome.

The moss beneath him swelled—rolling in gentle, undulating waves, deepening in texture as it wove itself into plush cushioning over the rigid cradle of roots. It extended further, creeping along the base—an organic tide drawn instinctively toward its source. Beyond the buried nerves of memory, it unfurled across the floorboards, nestling into the bedrock of the hearth—a living tapestry anchoring itself into place, settling where it remembered it belonged.

Diesel had felt quintessence before—woven through battlefields, humming beneath ancient ruins, lingering in the bones of forgotten strongholds. *But this...this is different.* He had never encountered it with such magnitude—never breathed it in and found the very air saturated with its presence. It murmured through him—not violently, not in warning—but with a self-knowing that raised the hairs along his arms. *Have I simply never been still enough to recognize it? Have we all been moving too fast, looking too hard—circling something that's been here all along?* Steady. Unmoving. Just *waiting to be seen.*

His jaw tightened as the realization set in. *This isn't a question of trust. It never was. It's about faith. And being bound by it.*

Bound by faith. A mantra Ezekiel had lived by. A truth Nadine carried in her every step. Bound by faith—that was the key, he thought. *Doubt had been the lock. Grief, the corrosion. Time, the fraying thread. But the tether—the thing that held it all—had never changed. Bound by faith wasn't just legacy. It was the way forward.*

Diesel's chin dipped, gaze drawn to the lush tufts cradling Nester. "Nes...you good?" A pause followed—brief, intentional. "Because I've never seen anything like this. *You?"*

The dew-laced greenery had thickened, curling into the grout and seams of the hearth's stonework with each breath. No longer just a lush underlay—it had become something richer, more intricate. A living bed, not merely spreading, but evolving. Its tide feathered along the base of the towering form, weaving into the gnarled roots—not as a claim, but as recognition. A reunion.

Not...like...this, sir. Nester's voice echoed in Diesel's mind. *The tree...it has...I have—it's just...it feels...natural.* His small shoulders lifted in a faint, uncertain shrug. *I never...really thought about...its healing nature. But I can... hear it. Like I hear you.*

Rayanna's brow furrowed, lips parting as she watched the velvet moss knit itself tighter. "It reminds me of the moss Runa produced," she murmured, fingers brushing the emerald drapery. Her gaze slid to Mama D. "It's how she healed the oak."

Diesel's head snapped up. "Runa's moss healed the oak?" His focus locked onto Rayanna—sharp, unrelenting. "What happened?"

Mama D waved a hand, dismissing the questions with practiced ease. "Not now," she said evenly. "I'll debrief you *later*." A glint of knowing amusement curved at her lips—just enough to say: *You'll get your answers— when I say it's time.*

Diesel grimaced, jaw ticking as his regard tracked between Rayanna and Mama D before he released a breath—resigned, but restrained.

Nissa's laugh spilled outward—rasping, airy, and meandering with something strangely fluid, like warmth stepping out of its cup and wandering off in liquid spirals. "It's...copying your chair," she said, the realization crystallizing even as she spoke it.

"*Oh,*" Ashla replied, inclining forward, posture contemplative—almost regal in its absentminded grace. "I do believe it's paying attention." A grin unfurled, blooming like a thought that had waited patiently to be noticed. "You're right—it's crafting Nester velvet cushions." She tittered, birdlike, her chin tilting upward, eyes gleaming. "How delightful. I adore such a notion." Then, as if the idea had landed gently on her shoulder, she mused aloud, "This piece of the tree...it hums louder than the one beyond the veil, doesn't it, Nissa? *Feels rarer. Wilder.* Like its quintessence never learned to whisper." Her fingers hovered just above the moss, curiosity sharpening her gaze. "It's aware. It listens."

A ripple of murmurs stirred across the room as others took notice—the resemblance too precise to dismiss as chance.

Ashla pressed her fingertips together, bouncing slightly in her seat. "Oh, Missy..." she sighed, laughter tumbling softly from her lips like wind through branches. "I'm almost glad I broke through and unbound you. Otherwise, we might've missed this."

The room filled with the scent of damp greenery—soil and moss warming the air like a living breath.

Diesel cast a flat stare in her direction. "Pretty sure Missy would have a different take," he said dryly. "Considering you tore through her like a storm...and lucky for you, the tree decided to clean up *the* mess."

Ashla blinked, her expression teetering between sheepish and wholly unbothered. "That's a fair statement," she conceded with a shrug—though her gaze had already drifted, following the massive limbs as they stretched outward like a slow revelation. "There's still so much we don't understand about the Tree of Life," she murmured, her voice turning wistful. *"It's as if...we were never meant to come this close. Not to *this* one."* She fluttered her hands lightly, fingertips sketching unseen patterns through the air as she followed the endless lattice of bark and branch. Her head tilted, expression hovering between wonder and bemusement. "Isn't it curious how Missy kept something so vast—so terribly powerful—all folded up inside her?" she mused, her palms lifting slightly, as though weighing the thought itself. "You'd never guess...not in a thousand star-lit nights."

Her attention slid toward Rayanna, chin angling with quiet consideration."She looks a bit lost," she observed, tapping a thoughtful finger to her chin. "And yet...I do believe she's onto something."

Rayanna barely registered the words—still locked on the fire. Something in the way it moved—too fluid, too aware—held her transfixed. The glow pooled at the base of the hearth, curling in queer, almost foreknown contours, like the memory of motion. *Not fleeting. Waiting.*

Ryker's awareness diverted back to Liam, "Not to interrupt insight hour," he said, stepping toward the wet bar and pouring himself a drink, swirling the liquid before raising it toward Liam in a lazy salute. "But I'd like to inquire about that book, sir." His smirk was effortless charm, but the intent behind his eyes was razor-sharp. "Since you seem to be the appointed keeper of all things sacred and secret, care to enlighten us?"

Liam tilted his chin upward, tapping the spine of the weathered tome. "Aye, lad. If ye're after tales o' Treefall Lagoon and da merfolk that call it home, listen weel. Their history's no scribbled in any common journal." He turned the leather-bound volume in his palm, its worn edges catching the light like relic bone. "Dis is da last o' its kind. Passed ta me before the Great War."

A lazy smile curled at the corner of Ryker's mouth. "To be clear," he drawled, lifting a brow, "somebody handed you a centuries-old codex on the merfolk of Treefall Lagoon?" He snagged a toothpick from the dish, tucking it into the corner of his mouth as his legs crossed at the ankles, his weight tilting into a practiced lean. "Explain something to me," he inquired dryly. "Out of all people—*you* were the one they trusted with that kind of intel?"

Liam snorted—rough as boot leather. "As for why meself?" A beat. A breath. "I've my reasons. Dey've theirs. And I've never been one for explainin' what doesnae need explainin'." His fingers tapped once against the book's worn cover, then shifted to drum lightly along the counter's edge. "Now…ye want tae tale, or are ye jest here tae rattle me ribs?" He rolled his shoulders, letting the words settle before continuing. "The merfolk dinnae see themselves bound by land nor sea. Dey're guardians o' balance—deir bond tae da waters is sacred." His voice steadied, into something carved from the marrow of history. "But dose rare Unbinders among 'em…" He exhaled through his nose, shaking his head faintly. "Dey're somethin' else entirely."

"Unbinders among the merfolk?" Ryker straightened, hoisting the question like it wore its own weight. The toothpick rolled idly between his teeth. "What kind of rare are we talkin'? 'Once-in-a-generation,' *or* 'we dare not speak the name unless it's in hushed reverence, bare-assed, and lighting candles on the beach' kinda rare?"

"As in da kind dat outlive legend," Liam returned. "Only a handful across da eons. Dey're said tae be tethered tae dee lagoon's quintessence itself—a livin' bridge between dat's seen an' dat's hidden beneath. Their gift isn't jest in healin', nor in severin' binds—it's da unbinding of essence itself. Of creation. Of destruction. They don't jest undo what is—dey set loose what time locked 'way."

His words carried on, but Liam's brogue thinned, voice fraying at the edges of Rayanna's awareness as her gaze wandered—drawn past Nester, past the velvet-green moss and rooted cradle—to the hearth.

Then—she saw it. Goosebumps scattered across her arms and spine, breath hitching in her throat. The flames—the hearth. All breath, no sound. Just the crackle of wood swallowing the space between.

Something clicked. Not cleanly. Not gently. But jagged and unrelenting. Memory and instinct snapped together with a lurch, misaligned gears grinding behind her ribs. Thoughts jammed, teeth resisted, logic rusted from disuse. She shoved into it, *pushing* against the stubborn, rusted cogs of old logic, willing something—*anything*—to click into place. Frustration ebbed and surged, but she did not retreat.

No, this time, she stepped forward.

Her internal self—the part of her that had spent too long sifting through broken pieces, trying to fit them into the wrong spaces—moved with purpose. No hesitation. No careful dissection. *Just raw certainty.*

She lifted the hammer of instinct and swung.

The old mounts shattered. Gears snapped loose, sending useless mechanisms clattering into oblivion. What had once governed her thoughts—rigid logic, measured caution—lay in pieces at her feet. And in its place, something else rose.

Instinct.

Raw. Unfiltered. Undeniable.

It wasn't smooth. It wasn't easy.

But it was *truth.* Uneven, unshaken, *wholly hers.*

Liam's voice deepened, reeling her back—just enough. "Dey're ain't mere merfolk. Dee maermaid unbinder's existence is said tae be a gift o' the deep waters, a sign dat somethin' monumental is arisin'." The spine of the book rapped against the bar counter—once, twice—the dull thuds a deliberate tap against Rayanna's forehead without ever lifting a finger. A silent punctuation of thought. No need to call her out, no words necessary. Just a pause, a well-placed smirk—assessing whether his audience needed just a bit more showmanship.

Her focus pulled back, the edges of her thoughts ebbing into the rhythm of his storytelling, caught in the undertow of the narrative. "Der elders claim ya presence binds daa lagoon ta dae greater forces o' the realms, uniting what was never meant tae be separate."

What was never meant to be separate? Rayanna repeated the words with a sharp intake of breath, lungs locking as something inside her twisted—caught between reflection and reckoning. *Wait. What was…never meant to be…separate.*

The firelight quivered, casting fleeting shadows across the firebox. For a split second, she swore she could see it—something murmuring at the margins, threading itself between rock and mortar, glimmering on the threshold of perception.

Knuckles raked against the grain of knowing, fingers pressing into the hardened fibers of thought, ghosting along the fringe of comprehension. And then—like a battering ram—it struck again. *What was NEVER meant to be separate.* A force demanding action. *It wasn't just fire. It was its own enigma.* She surged up from the floor, the movement not entirely her own—more like something had grabbed her by the collar and yanked.

"Binding beyond the realms." The words scraped out, rough, half-thought, half-instinct, like a door swinging open too fast, biting its frame. Her mind scrambled to catch up, not in panic, but in demand. *Look. See. Understand. DAMN IT!*

The embers in the hearth popped, flaring—two sparks colliding, flickering like kernels of popcorn in a heated pan, tumbling, reforming, drawn back together by something veiled, something undeniable. And in that moment, she knew.

NEVER meant to be separated!

The tiny sparks moved—too knowing—as if something was breathing into the foundation of the flames, pressing into its very core. The words ricocheted through her mind, bouncing off the wreckage of old logic, the rusted gears of outdated purpose crumbling, disintegrating into dust.

Convergence.

Scattered pieces of perception crackled, snapping into crisp, undeniable understanding—not sudden, not jarring, but inevitable. Like the slow, wrenching release of a knot she hadn't even known she'd been trying to untie.

Her feet carried her forward before realization struck. "The door," she breathed, the words braided with disbelief and certainty—thick with something ancient, something undeniable. "The hearth...the fire—*it's the door.*"

A stir. A shift.

Nestled within the mossy cradle, Nester's radiance had steadied—still faint, but stronger now. He turned slightly, the firelight catching on the dimmed filament, tracing a subtle shimmer along its tender wire. *Hm...I never noticed the...connection.*

"What exactly are you getting at, Ray?" Diesel's tone stayed level, but the furrow in his brow carved deeper. "You're telling me the key to all this —*whatever this is*—sits in the damn fireplace?"

Rayanna swallowed hard, her pulse drumming steady against her ribs. It was absurd. Impossible. And yet, the thought refused to dissipate, clinging like smoke in the rafters. "I don't know how, but...*yes.*" Just a whisper, yet it landed like stone on glass—thin, fragile, and absolute. "It's tied to everything. I can feel it."

Liam snapped the book shut—a stern finality, like a gavel striking stone. "Dee flames, aye?" He leaned in, chin settling into his palm, scrutiny sharp as a whetted edge. "Are ye sayin' we've had da answer burnin' in plain sight dis whole damn time, an' nae a soul had da sense ta see it?"

Unflinching, Rayanna held her ground. "I believe so." The words scraped out—thin, nearly lost—caught between certainty and something keener, pressing against the edges of a reality still tilting beneath her.

The bed of embers lapped upward, taunting—a muted secret poised at the tip of its heated tongue, waiting to be spoken. The inferno didn't just burn; it moved, coiling and unfurling within the cinderscape—not imagined, not illusion, but real. Insistent. Unrelenting. It didn't beckon—it sank in, lodged like a splinter beneath the skin, and aching to be unearthed. The pull cinched through sinew, threading into the marrow, knotted so tightly along her spine that breathing felt like bracing against a locked door.

"But I can't be sure just yet…" A breath caught—her teeth pressed into her lower lip, as if the pressure alone might anchor her to the floor, keep her from spilling forward. "It's there," she whispered. The blaze leaned in. The pull didn't waver. "It's there." Lifting a hand to the tip of her nose, her wrist turned, fingers curling in a fanning motion—not reaching, simply coaxing. The faint aroma drifted closer, warm and familiar. Honing in, testing instinct against the expectation of reason.

Jabbing a finger in Diesel's direction, Liam let out a rough chuckle. "Aye, dis one's got day knack, dat's for damn sure." Amusement scraped up his throat, coarse as weathered stone. "Seems ye've got something sharp there, me little Ray. Now all ye need is da right question ta make it come undone." His chin tipped toward the ceiling, fingers drumming a steady, measured cadence against the underside of his jaw—lazy, contemplative. "So? Ye want me tae keep goin'?"

Rayanna's fingers sank into the ridges of the hearth's rough edge, the uneven surface biting back, rooting her—holding tight. But it wasn't the stone that resonated. *It was the fire.*

The flames surged in acknowledgment, a quivering swell like breath caught between exhale and whisper, color folding over color. Reds and oranges bled into smoky blues, deepening into green-lit plums before plunging further—emerald swallowed by the weight of deep water, bursting into something else entirely. Aqua. Teal. A shade that didn't just flicker but held, like the surface of a gemstone turned liquid, its brilliance wrapped tight, teetering on the edge of poised discovery.

A ragged inhale snagged against the heat. Her palms pressed deeper, the warmth seeping into her skin—not searing, not scalding. A pulse within the hearth's stonework. *Warm. Steady. Rhythmic.*

Rayanna's inhale faltered, her exhale rattling unevenly from her chest. A shift. A pull.

Cords of quintessence rose—streaming from the rugged stone of the hearth before her, ghostly hues curling through hesitation. They reached— not forceful, not demanding, but unavoidable. An ancient whisper. Something elusive. A vow woven into the marrow of the world, sending goosebumps trembling up her neck and cascading down her arms.

A tick.

Not the delicate cadence of a wristwatch, but something vast. A clock buried in the bones of existence, counting down with the weight of inevitability. A measured, mechanical patience.

A gear turned.

Not small. Not simple. Massive. Iron groaned against iron, deep and ponderous, like mountains adjusting—like the earth itself stirring from slumber. The first drag of resistance—sluggish, reluctant—then smoother, faster, a rhythm unspooling, winding up…or winding down.

A boom.

Not an explosion. A release. A latch unfastening as colossal vaulted doors rose. Spirited radiance spilled forth like water rushing over rock— zestful, fervent, desperate to be seen after eons of silence.

Stone against stone—but not in the study. *Not here. Or…was it?*

The question burst inside her mind and vanished just as quickly, flung backward into whatever this moment had become.

The rumbling wrenched her inward—not to the room, but to the vast, unseen depths of her mind. It surged from an ancient foundation she had never touched, never noticed. *Until now.* A structure buried within her, forcing itself into awareness, unearthing what had always been waiting.

The sound rolled through the air, thick with finality—reverberating outward. A summons. A reckoning. A return.

Rayanna's breath caught. Her body remained in the study, fingers braced against the hearth. But her mind—her mind stood elsewhere.

The doors.

Colossal. Immutable. Bound in shadow and mist. Their edges welded shut, darkened threads sealing them in a haze—not seen, but felt. Holding them in place.

A whisper slipped past her lips, uncertain if it lived in thought or breath. *I've seen this before.*

Diesel's voice broke through—whether from memory or something more, she couldn't be sure. *Your safeguard of all truths will find you, for you are bound to one, and one to you.*

The weight of the words settled—a tether in the storm.

The vault. *My vault.*

It rose before her—vast, boundless, an ancient chamber carved from bouldering terrain, stone stacking upon weathered stone, rising within the recesses of her mind. The walls stretched beyond where her thoughts dared reach.

And yet, it was here. Rising from the depths as though it had always existed.

For how long? I don't know. Perhaps forever. No—this has to be part of the unbinding. A release, bit by bit. And if this was only a fraction of what was to come—Holy shit.

Perhaps this had existed since the first breath of the realms. Threads of light danced along the perimeter—quintessence once severed, now weaving anew.

She saw them. Looping. Twisting. Fraying. Unraveling. New filaments of quintessence slipped into place, light replacing darkness, mending what had once been bound. The doors didn't open. Not yet. But beneath her fingertips, beneath the very marrow of the stone itself—The structure shuddered. A deep, belly-clenching *clunk.* A *churn.* A *thud.* A release. Clean air rushed in. A force. A break. Like standing at the precipice of a mountain and feeling the wind slam into her, curling through her, reaching inside— whipping through the chambers of her ribs, slamming into locked spaces, demanding to be known. And just like that—*She knew.*

Chapter Thirty-Six

T*hud.*

The heavy spine of the book slammed against the bar.

Thud. Thud.

A final, foreknown strike—not a warning, but a call back. A tether yanked taut.

Rayanna inhaled sharply—a ragged, hollow sound, like the last pull from the bottom of an empty glass. The kind that rattles and drags at the dregs of something already drained. It sucked her back—ripped her from the expanse of her mind, from the vault, the doors, the quintessence still unraveling in unseen places.

The present rushed in—study, firelight, voices. The denseness of the hearth beneath her fingertips. "I don't...understand," Rayanna breathed, her voice nearly lost beneath the soft crackle and pop of flame. Her fingers curled tighter against the masonry, anchoring herself to something tangible. Her gaze deepened. The colors within the hearth, swelled and morphed—shimmering with the fluidity of water, yet radiating the molten certainty of something forged from a past deliberately obscured.

The contradiction held her captive.

Diesel loomed. Ashla tilted her head, curiosity prickling at the edges. She waved them both off. A sharp, clipped motion—*not now.*

"Liam." Rayanna's voice cut through the room, piercing. Not quite a command, not quite a plea. "Keep talking. I don't care what about—just… keep talking." Her throat bobbed. "Keep the questions coming. Whatever this is—it's pulling something out of me." She remained transfixed, locked onto the restless glow. Its blaze a deep teal braided with vibrant hues of blue, undulating like a living current. "It recognizes me," she murmured, the words drawn from someplace both distant and innate. "I don't fully grasp it yet…but the quintessence—it's bound to this."

A beat of silence.

A pulse.

Then—a chuckle. Low. Dry. Amused. "Aye, well, dat's plain enough, even from up here, lass." From his gilded frame above the wet bar, Liam arched a brow, the golden filigree catching the light as it danced across the room. "Good ta know me tales have such an effect." He dipped into a slight bow, all exaggerated charm. "But if ye insist…ye won't have ta tell me twice." With a casual ease, he flipped open the leather-bound book again, his finger still wedged in the marked page.

"Daa merfolk," he began, his tone settling into the steady cadence of a storyteller, "like I was sayin' before—eey're nae just dwellers o' water. Dey're its guardians. Tae bridge between land an' sea."

The flames wavered. The teal deepened cerulean, undulating like water lapping against her vision. Rayanna's fingers twitched, biting into the stone, determined to press through, to force understanding to the surface. Her breaths came shallow and sharp, her focus narrowing as Liam's brogue rolled through the room like a rising tide.

"Treefall Lagoon," Liam continued, voice dipping into the weight of old knowledge, "is sacred—its waters steeped in quintessence, a blend o' land an' sea energies. Dae merfolk, aye, dey live as part o' that balance. But the rarest among dem…" Deliberately pausing, he lifted the book, rapping its spine once, twice against his palm before turning it toward Ryker like a man knocking on a door. Dramatics—to ensure all were listening. And listening *well.*

"Like I said," he continued, his lilt curling around the theatrics, "tae Unbinders, lad. Aye, dey're a different breed entirely."

Ryker's fingers toyed with the toothpick, pulling it from his teeth, tapping it absently against his bottom lip. A habit. A tell. Curiosity gnawed at him, steady and insistent, yet skepticism lingered—clinging like salt to the rim of a glass, sharp and bracing. "What makes them so rare? Why are there so few of them?"

Liam's grin stretched—the kind of smirk that belonged to someone who thrived on the art of a well-placed pause. A storyteller who knew exactly when to pull a thread and when to let silence do the work. He exhaled through his nose, a low, amused huff, fingers drumming once against the book in his grip."Because, lad," he drawled, voice dipping into something damn near conspiratorial, "dey're *nae* jest merfolk."

A pause—intentional. Weighted. The air practically begged for him to continue. Then, with the ease of someone laying down the final piece in a long, drawn-out game, he tipped his chin, let his words drip intentionally. "Dae Unbinders are da lagoon, right down tae deir marrow. Somethin' ancient—woven straight into da cartilage o' deir bein'. The quintessence disnae just run through dem—it *is* dem. Ye don't walk away from dat. Not truly." A deep breath, stretched thin. "Every step away yanks at 'em like a chain wrapped 'round der ribs," Liam murmured, his thumb idly scraping along the book's spine. His other hand lifted, plucking his tweed cap free, bouncing it absently—like airing out the heat of fanfare—before settling it back into place. "An' deir soul…" The words sat heavy. His usual sharpness dulled just a fraction. "Aye, lad—it comes at a cost. Always does."

Then—sweet like honey, smooth as if poured into a warmed cup of coffee—Mama D's bare feet padded against the floorboards as she made her way toward the couch. A quiet presence. A deliberate one. Lowering herself beside Nissa and Ashla, her focus remained unshaken, fixed solely on Liam as she spoke. "It does lend weight to the assumptions made about Treefall." Her fingers drifted along the arm of the leather, tracing invisible patterns.

"So that's it, then?" Ryker tapped the toothpick against his cheek, a measured rhythm as he turned over Mama D's words, eyes narrowing just a fraction. "That's why Treefall went stagnant after the Great War?"

"From what's been told, everyone within Treefall Lagoon was sealed in. Locked away. Some say they fell into a sleep, their bodies steeped in stone —swallowed by the very earth they once walked. The land stopped moving. Time stopped shifting. It's assumed the place has been weathered down by stillness rather than age." Mama D's attention flicked toward Rayanna. "The oaks outside the cottage speak of it. The way foliage rises, untouched and unfathomable in height. Growth unchecked. The silence that lingers. Nothing comes out."

A pause.

Liam's thumb marked the page once more, his brow furrowing—not in dismissal, but in consideration. A slow nod. A thoughtful lull. "Aye, love." His voice deepened, thick with something contemplative. "Dae unbinding mairmaid would have bin taken out for tea land to go stagnant like it has. Dat kind o' stillness—ney, it's not natural. Ya don't lose dat much hum without somethin' vital bein' ripped clean out."

Diesel planted an arm against the mantel, solid, unmoving. "So," he started, his tone just shy of disbelief—not quite acceptance, just the hard edge of realization settling in,"You're telling me the unbinding merfolk were wiped out right alongside the higher-born seers and Truth Tellers?"

Liam didn't hesitate."Aye, dat's how it would seem." A huff followed—low, edged with old bitterness. "Dat'd be King Moros' way, right nough." He rolled his shoulders, like he could shake loose the weight of history. "Burn ta bridge. Salt ta damn earth. Make sure nae soul ever treads dat path again." The book's spine tapped against his palm. "Todal hold. Snuff out dee ones he couldnae bend. Dat's how ye rule an empire without resistance."

Above Liam's portrait, it appeared—just at the edge of Diesel's sight.

A thread.

Beaded into existence, hovering, weightless. Purple at one end, blurred red at the tail—like a truth unraveling, bleeding at the edges. Spinning, shifting, untethered. Instinct kicked in before thought. He lifted a hand— just a fraction, just enough—and the thread snapped toward him. It sank into his palm like a needle threading through flesh—not painful, but there. Anchored for later dissection. His fingers curled reflexively, jaw ticking. He didn't flinch, didn't move beyond the gradual lowering of his hand. He was unnoticed. Still, his gaze drifted—searching—until it found her again. Rayanna. Shoulders taut, hands pressed to her ears as if silence alone might hold her together. Whatever was happening to her, it wasn't just a reaction. It was recognition.

Liam's voice rolled on, steady as the tide, but Rayanna had stopped listening. Her hands clenched against her earlobes, fingers pressing in. Hard. *Fuck. Maybe all the Truth Seekers just threw in the damn towel after the Great War.* The thought rooted deep, jagged and intrusive. *This couldn't be the great, legendary quintessence of many. No, this was bullshit. Whatever the ideal was supposed to be for a Truth Seeker, this sure as hell wasn't it—not by any stretch.*

The flames surged—eager, unrestrained—as if they had been waiting for her to falter. Their roar unfurled like a chorus pulled from the marrow of the hearth, drowning out the study's voices until even silence felt distant. The room wavered, bending inward—not collapsing, but folding, the way a dream turns in on itself just before waking. The air thickened, not with heat, but with something older—like vapor made from memory. Unspooling, slow and reverent, until space itself felt rethreaded—stitched into a pattern she didn't recognize but somehow remembered. Reality tilted, softened. Then reassembled, unfamiliar and impossibly near.

Then—collapse.

Heat bled into humidity, damp and suffocating as it clung to her lungs. The scent swelled, brined with salt and the sharp decay of something ancient.

Then—a plunge.

Crashing through a hard surface, water swallowed her whole. But she wasn't fully submerged. Her mind pitched forward, dragged down into the depths. It wasn't water in its natural state—it was something denser. A gel-like substance where memory itself latched onto her, seized her by the face, and tore her under.

She didn't choke. Didn't thrash.

She simply sank.

A bubble of awareness wrapped around her, enclosing her in a space separate from time. Her fingers sliced through the current—water thick with silt, dense with a presence older than memory. No true temperature, no edge—only motion. It folded around her, moved with her, molding to her skin like a second pulse.

Recognition thrummed—a tether linking past and present. The Lumis Bloom in the bathhouse, the quiet knowing that had settled there.

A rhythm, unbroken. A truth resurfacing.

Light fractured above, splitting into long ribbons that diffused into deepening shades of green and blue. The surface blurred, slipping further from reach.

Driftwood floated in tangled heaps, caught in the quiet. Waterlogged remnants of something long forgotten. Hollowed-out shells. Coral bleached brittle with time.

Not lifeless. Not gone.

Suspended in waiting. Like what Nadine had done at the cottage—stilling time just beyond the property line. A breath held. A moment stretched. Neither past nor present, only the pause between. *Could it be?* A place once thriving, once sacred—caught in the in-between.

Something beneath her skin stirred—stretched—fanning out from where it had once been buried. A memory long folded into stillness. Hidden. Pocketed away.

The hush of the lagoon exhaled—and with each rise and fall of her chest, it stirred—though she couldn't tell what, or who, was waking. *Is it me? Or the water itself?*

A whisper curled through the recesses of her mind, threading through her ribs, clinging to her marrow, rattling through her bones. *I know this place. I have been here before. Treefall Lagoon.*

She spun, abruptly blinded by the sun's fractured ribbons through the water's surface, throwing her hands up to shield her eyes. And when she lowered them—*Zane.* Emerging from the dense folds of foliage, his arms wrapped tight around Tabytha's frail frame. Dried crimson stained his skin. His jaw locked, tendons pulled tight, but silent tears tracked down his face. He stepped into the shallows, boots sinking into the lagoon's edge. The water—thick, stagnant—shivered. A ripple spread outward, slow at first. Then quicker. Teal. Gold. Light seeped through the depths like something waking from slumber.

The lagoon *breathed.* Beneath them, a resonating life—weak, *but still present.*

Rayanna longed to surge forward, to grasp at whatever *this* was—but something anchored her in place. Silken strands of lagoon kelp coiled around her limbs, binding her to the moment, unwilling to release their hold.

She inhaled sharply. She wasn't here. *Not really.* Yet within feet, a younger version of herself emerged from the dense shrubs, stepping forward.

The inlet was waking—more so as Zane knelt, lowering Tabytha into the shallows with care. No words passed between them. No sound, only the rhythmic slosh of tide as it lapped against her faith bound sister's fragile form.

He stood in silence, gaze sharpening as her past self shuffled through the tall foliage, drawing his focus to the Rayanna now stepping to the water's edge.

The pair met—grasping forearms, an unspoken understanding passing between them. And then, without hesitation, she threw herself into his arms. From where she now stood, unseen, watching from within the depths, tears streamed down her cheeks.

At the edges of the shallows, wildlife stirred, testing the weight of their own voices. A chirp. A splish. A ripple of movement through the reeds.

The thought slammed through her, unrelenting. *They're right. Mama D. All of them.* The world here had stopped breathing. Yet because of Zane and Tabytha—now it inhaled.

Sucking. Spinning. Ripping.

A scream tore through her chest before she even knew she was back. *"Tabytha—!"* The study reformed in a violent snap, her own voice slamming into the space. The force of it shoved her back from the hearth as the cobalt and azure bled away—back to warmth. Back to flickering, regal flames. Everything had recalibrated. And everyone was staring.

Dazed and disoriented, Rayanna's voice tore through the space, raw with shock. "You're right," she shot back, rough, the words tumbling out before she could slow them. "It is stagnant. I mean—it *was* stagnant." She turned sharply, gesturing toward Ashla, thoughts sparking through the air like embers snapping free. "It's suffocating. Or *was* suffocating. The water was the only thing still moving. Zane was in it…holding Tabytha."

Ashla bobbed her head knowingly, extending a hand, as if to fan Rayanna forward. Encouraging. Willing her to *see*.

Rayanna sucked in a breath, realization detonating at the edge of her mind. *"Oh, shit!"* The exclamation barely registered before she lunged, flinging herself forward, landing hard on her knees. Her hands latched onto the hearth's margin, fingers digging in, knuckles whitening.

Hope clawed its way up her chest, tangled in the sharp crest of expectation and the quiet dread of disappointment. *Could it be?*

A beat of nothing.

Then—the flames changed.

No longer fire. No longer light. Thick. Liquid. Gelatinous. A substance slipping between states—pliable yet restrained, alive yet bound.

"The water…" Her fingers curled against the stone, the hearth's warmth radiating through her skin, but she barely felt it. "It's waiting. But it's bound. Like I was. Like *we* were." Her palms pressed harder against the hearth, as though sheer will alone could bridge the gap between worlds. A notion ricocheted through her: *What was…never meant to be… separate.*

Her breath steadied. "The fire—*it's the key.*"

"We knew it was paused," Diesel replied, his voice neither skeptical nor soft—just careful. "No one's been able to enter Treefall since the war. It's like walking into a wall. No way in, no way out." His gaze sharpened, unreadable. "Why would we want a key *in*?"

"Oh, there is definitely a way in," Ashla chimed, her tone light as spun sugar, certain as a dream. "Like Pa says—anything's possible with me. Most of the impossible happens before breakfast…though I suppose that depends on who's setting the table." She nudged Nissa's shoulder, a quiet giggle escaping, as if the idea had amused her into movement.

Nissa's fingers drifted absently along her jawline, then down to the Lumis Blooms nestled at her throat. The tiny flowers sloshed against her skin, nuzzling like small creatures burrowing in for warmth—pressing in, absorbing…a whisper.

Ashla stilled. Her expression was unreadable for only a moment—then, clarity. She nodded once, as though Nissa's words were clear as daylight.

Ryker blinked, rubbing a hand along his jaw, his brow furrowing. "Did anyone else hear that? Or did I just—" He hesitated. Shook his head. "Did I just lose sound for a second?"

"I didn't hear a thing, girls," Mama D frowned. "Come again?"

Ashla giggled. "Sorry…Nissa believes that with her dawning, she'll be what the lagoon needs to revitalize." She bumped her shoulder against Nissa's, lighthearted and easy, as if nothing in the world could weigh them down. "The lagoon holds answers the Great War *thought* it buried." Her brows arched, a beat of mischief danced about. "According to Nissa… someone was *very* wrong to assume."

Rayanna, still crouched by the hearth, tipped her head, voice low but firm. "So, you're telling me the fire—it's tied to the lagoon's quintessence?"

Ashla leaned in, "It's not fire at all…it *just* looks like flames."

Rayanna's hand hovered slightly above the hearth, nostrils flaring. *"Right.* Just your typical underwater bonfire. Totally normal."

Liam thumbed through the brittle pages of his book, gaze shadowed with thought. "Aye, lass, ye're on ta somethin'. Dae merfolk spoke o' a givin'—an offerin' made. Dey called it da Path o' Reflection, a way tae merge ta quintessence o' fire an' water. Ta flames turn tae water, aye, if ta offerin's pure—unitin' what was never meant ta be separate."

Rayanna's eyes snapped to him, sharp with urgency. "But the inferno already smells like water. What other kind of offering can we give?"

She lifted her right hand from the stone, rubbing at her face—and instantly, the right side of the fire reacted. A burst of yellow and orange spit upward, wild and high, as if startled. The room froze. Every movement stilled. Eyes widened in collective confusion.

Rayanna's breath snagged in her throat. She dropped her hand back to the hearth—at once, the flames reeled, bleeding into deep teals and lapping blues, settling like a tide drawn home.

Liam exhaled, "I would say ya are part o' dis offerin'. Yer a piece o' what was taken, lass. Dae unbinder gives what da fire demands, an' it opens da way. But nae everythin' given can be taken back."

"Would it need a scale?" Ryker's voice cut in. "Could Nissa's newly formed scales be the key to the lagoon itself?"

Silence blanketed the room. Every line of sight snapped—stunned— toward the two of them.

Ashla tilted her head, thoughtful. "That would make sense," she murmured, patting her cheek as if sorting through half-formed memories. "As our mama's faith bound sister—"

"Yes…yes, I know this already. Get on with it." Rayanna's hands dropped from the hearth. Instantly, the fire dulled—its hue dimming into a muted reddish-orange. She huffed in exasperation, shaking her head. Then, without hesitation, pressed her palms back against the stone. The flames snapped back—teal-green light lashing out in a wild arc toward her. Anger equaled consequence.

She flinched, laughing. "Hey mister, I like my hair, thank you."

Ashla barely stifled a giggle before continuing. "You are our Ma's faith bound sister. Before you were shadow bound, she tethered us to you. By faith, we are yours, Auntie Ray."

Rayanna blinked. "Wait a minute...I have kids now?" Her eyes widened. "I'm going to need a nap after this."

Ashla and Nissa tittered like birds after a morning rain. "Oh no, not quite, silly," Ashla corrected, drawing out each word like she was savoring the sound. "You see, Nissa and I...we've already passed our Dawning Days. That means we're of age now." She paused, head tilting slightly, as if listening for something just beyond reach. "Father told us to stay back until Nissa was ready—until she could help wake what had gone still. The land beyond the door."

Her fingers hovered near her sister, reverent—like tracing the outline of a legend turning real. "Nissa isn't just ready now," she said softly, a quiet certainty blooming beneath the words. "She's part of the key, Auntie Ray. The piece you need."

Rayanna drew in a long breath, casting a glance over her shoulder. "Alright then...who's doing it? Who's taking a scale from Nissa?"

The room stilled. Eyes shifted. Avoided. Deflected. *Not it*—unspoken but loud.

"Oh, heavens! Well, it can't be me, because I seem to be bound by faith to keep my hands on this *damn* bit of rock." Rayanna motioned toward the hearth with a shrug of her elbow, expression exasperated but amused.

More silence.

Then, in perfect unison, all eyes turned to Diesel.

"Yeah, *no*. My vast existence is already overflowing with unnecessary experiences. I think I'm good." Diesel's focus glided to Mama D. "And while we're at it, I'll go ahead and speak for her too."

She bobbed her head, no hesitation whatsoever.

He exhaled heavily, scrubbing a hand down his face. "She's been through enough today. And since we have no idea how this is gonna shake out, maybe let's not add to the list."

In response, the teal-green flames surged—licking hungrily, a restless tide pressing against its perimeter.

"She can do it," Ashla coaxed.

Nissa drew in a purposeful breath, her attention ticking briefly to Rayanna before lowering—to the iridescent fragments woven into her skin. Her fingers hovered above a single scale—larger than the rest, glistening like light caught in deep teal waters.

Rayanna's knuckles blanched against the stone. She swallowed hard. "The fire..." The words barely scraped past her lips as the flames deepened, sputtering—its base like lungs held past their breaking point.

"Ach, weel, I'll be damned straight tae hell." Liam propped his chin upon his knuckles, watching like a man who'd seen too many stories take a bad turn.

Nissa exhaled—drawn-out and bracing. Her fingers hovered, then anchored at the base of the scale, gripping as best she could before pulling. It resisted. She pulled again—harder. A wet, sinewy crack tore through the hush like a bone snapping beneath pressure. Her breath hitched, shoulders curling inward as pain surged through her frame. A bead of translucent liquid welled at the torn seam—thick, luminous, pooling like liquid mercury as she pressed a trembling palm over it.

"Here." The word barely made it out—strained and frayed—as she thrust the scale forward. "Take it," she rasped.

No one moved.

"*Aye, weel*, if it's anythin' like ta Lumis Blooms," Liam drawled, a smirk twitching at the corners of his mouth, "I'd wager it needs yer word o' approval, me dear. *Lucky them.*"

Nissa's breath steadied, if only slightly. Her attention sliding—until it found Ryker. Still at the wet bar, legs crossed at the shins, posture loose, detached. Like none of this had a damn thing to do with him. The toothpick skimmed lazily between his teeth, his expression unreadable, half-absent.

Without a word, she extended the scale in his direction. The choice hung there —suspended. Waiting.

Liam exhaled sharply and snapped his fingers. "Oi, Ryker, ye plannin' ta stand dere dreamin' all day, or are ye gonna take ta damn thing? Nissa ain't holdin' it out for yer decoration."

Ryker blinked, disoriented, his brow knitting. "Me? Why not—"

"Just take it," Diesel cut in, voice edged and sure. "She entrusted you."

"Aye, lad, seems tae me ye oughta quit yer whinin'—merfolk and Treefall folk alike are dead set on dis bowin' business, whether ye like it or not." He waved a lazy hand from where it rested on the counter. "Really, it's an honor, if ye ask me. I'd do it meself but, well…ye know, the frame and all."

Ryker gave a reluctant nod and stepped forward, plucking the scale from Nissa's outstretched hand. A jolt ran up his spine. The scale throbbed —alive with static, its charge biting into his skin. "Holy fuck, this hurts." He shot a glare toward Liam. "Now what, fuckin' portrait master?"

Liam's smirk deepened. "Git it in dae flames, lad." He nodded toward the fire, now swirling with a viscous, iridescent light.

"Rayanna's one part o' da key, Nissa's da other. Dae flames ken it better'n any o' us. So if her hand goes on the hearth, then aye, ye best be stickin' yers in the fire. Real complicated, eh?"

"Oh, sure. Ray gets to touch a stone, and I get to set my hand on fire? Yeah, that sounds *real* fair." Ryker eyed the blaze. "Tell you what, Liam— how 'bout I just toss this bobble in and skip the whole burning-alive part?" He jerked his chin toward Diesel. "Or—and hear me out—I'm pretty sure the General wouldn't lose sleep chucking you in right after it."

Rayanna glanced up as Ryker leaned closer, his frame casting a shadow over her. "It's not hot," she said quietly. "More like…a lukewarm ocean lapping at a shore."

He side-eyed her, unconvinced—but extended his hand. The teal and green tendrils of fire slithered toward the scale, stretching with longing. As his fingers broke the threshold, the flames wrapped around him—tight, but not searing. Pressing. Probing. A clipped breath slipped out as they tugged, fluid and insistent, coaxing his grip to open.

He let go.

The scale dropped, catching the light as it fell. The instant it struck the azure blaze, the hearth roared to life—color and sound bursting outward like a heartbeat made visible.

From the heart of the hearth, a hiss escaped—*Shhhhhhhhhhh… chuuuup…*

Rayanna's head snapped up. The brilliance spilled out over her skin, raising goosebumps in its wake. *"The door…"* she whispered.

The inferno collapsed inward, folding into a whirl of molten motion. Bricks loosened, then realigned as water traced their seams—thin rivulets of incandescing teal, their light brimming like a mirror caught between worlds. From below, the sound of water coursing through hidden crevices echoed, climbing upward. The threads met. And in one breathless moment, the back of the hearth split open—solid brick bleeding into a pane of rippling glass.

Through its fogged surface, a lagoon took shape.

Still. Waiting. Expectant.

Rayanna turned to the others. Their expressions mirrored her own: wonder, disbelief, silent confirmation.

Ashla's cadence drifted from the couch. "Told you…no more separation. It's all quite unnecessary now, isn't it?"

Nissa flung her half-formed fin off the coffee table with a wet *slap*, arms outstretched toward Ryker in wordless insistence. Her breath came quick, urgency etched in every motion.

"Dis is where dey're a different sort o' folk," Liam announced, clearing his throat as Ryker instinctively scooped Nissa into his arms. "Settin' her down jest dere should do. She needs tae make dae trek tae dae water herself. Somethin' about a rite of passage—from earth tea water." He paused, focus lingering on the reshaping portal. "I'd wager it holds more weight now dan ever before."

Diesel nodded, exhaling through his nose."If she's the last of the merfolk who can undo what's kept this place locked, and that's what it takes to set Treefall loose again—my question is, how long before the rest of the territories notice?"

Liam tapped his lips, eyes narrowing. "Hard tea say. But seein' as Sanctuary's bin festering in its own filth, I'd wager it'll take a bit o' time."

"From what it sounds like," Mama D murmured, "it will reconnect everything within the lagoon." Her gaze gliding back to the liquid threshold, as though glimpsing something just beyond the veil. "And if that's the case…I'd imagine it takes time. Breaking old constraints—especially ones this vast—isn't immediate."

"Well." Diesel cocked his head, considering. "That might just work in our favor, then." He reached for the velvet chair, righted it with a grunt, and turned it toward the hearth. Then he dropped into it with a familiar thud, one ankle crossing over his knee as he settled in to listen.

Nissa inched closer to the firebox, the extra Lumis Blooms she passed rolling forward of their own accord, latching gently onto her—like jeweled waterpods attuning to her pulse. Energy thrummed through her veins. The scales along her frame flared to life, undulating like waves—emerald, sapphire, and gold-edged, catching light with each small movement.

She approached Rayanna, pausing just beside her. The tied-off skirt she wore brushed against the iridescence now creeping across her limbs. Her transformation was almost complete—skin shimmered like sunlit tidewater, each motion leaving trails of refracted light in its wake.

Without hesitation, she fell inward and wrapped Rayanna in a hug—gratitude and reverence braided into the gesture. Her voice dropped to a whisper. "This is the threshold—between life and knowing. Keep that thought. Runa might need it one day." She pulled back just enough to meet Rayanna's gaze, hands resting steady on her shoulders. "After I go through, you'll understand why it had to be you." Their foreheads pressed together—a quiet communion. "Wait until you see the cliff's edge through the doorway."A smile ghosted across her lips before she exhaled —soft and rhythmic—through the fully formed gills at her neck. "Without her, part of the answer will remain hidden," she said, her voice no louder than a whisper of sand. "Remember: not until you see the cliff."

Then, with one fluid motion, she hitched herself forward, lifted her hips, and pivoted around Rayanna. Headfirst, she slid onto her belly and into the hearth—which, at some point, Missy had made immaculate. The walls were swept clean of soot and ash, the space gleaming like a prepared altar.

Nissa slipped through with a *shhhhhhhhhwwwippp*.

The moment her body met the water, a ripple flowed outward—delicate, resonant—as she passed beyond the veil. Beyond the glass, she sank, then rose—spiraling upward, her form trailing light as colors refracted around her like a prism in motion.

The threshold widened, rippling with breath. Sandy banks unfurled beyond. Stony figures stirred—creatures once dormant now stretching, rousing from centuries of stillness. A breeze coiled through the hearth, then into the room itself—salt-laced, ancient, alive.

And then—through the fogged pane, Rayanna saw it.

A rocky precipice jutted out into a vast expanse of stone and wild, tangled foliage—suspended in nothingness, vanishing into mist. The clouds churned above—dense, slow-moving, like whipped cream melting into dark coffee.

And just beyond the edge, the sky parted—only slightly, only for a breath—but it was enough. The impossible revealed itself. And for a moment, everything held still. The image, sharpened into perfect clarity.

Ashla giggled softly.

"It's all right to release it now. Nissa cleared the path for you—to glimpse the first truth, the one long buried at the core of your soul." She tilted her head, reaching out as if tracing the reflection shimmering in Rayanna's gaze yet, the hand drifted to her own chest, fingers splaying across her heart. "That's why it's been restless—why you've felt the pressure, the agitation, building as you drew closer to your unbinding." Her smile curved with quiet certainty. "You're going to need sturdier footing than socks can offer, Auntie Ray" she said with a glint of amusement. "I'll follow your lead."

Just beside the hearth's edge, the air shimmered—and with a soft *thump*, Rayanna's boots appeared where stone met wood. Missy, ever attentive, had answered the unspoken need.

Rayanna let herself fall back slightly, weight braced, as the other reached for the boots. Her fingers moved with swift familiarity, sliding them on, tugging each strap past its catch, and fastening the buckles with a practiced grace. She bit at her lip, cleared her throat, then shoved her feet through the opening at the back of the fireplace.

The pull was immediate—an unseen force, swift and undeniable.

She was through.

Her feet struck solid rock with a sharp, jarring *thud*, the force rattling through her bones. She landed in a crouch, breath coming hard, fingers pressing instinctively into the stone's cool surface before she pushed herself upright.

And then—*she saw it.*

The precipice stretched before her, vast and endless. Jagged walls of red and orange rock flanked either side, standing sentinel over the land, their edges worn but unyielding. Above, the tips of earth were blackened, charred by time's quintessence fires yet, reclaimed below. A forgotten place held in time—not abandoned, but repurposed by the natural world.

But ahead—glistening, untamed, magnificent—a waterfall thundered from impossible heights, its cascade carving through stone before crashing into a basin of lush greenery. Below, the teal waters stirred, lapping at the shore, vibrant, alive.

Behind her, Ashla stepped through, her hand finding Rayanna's shoulder. "Here is where you will find Ma. She's been waiting for you, Auntie Ray."

Rayanna's breath stalled, goosebumps rolling across her skin. "Wait, what?"

Ashla blinked three times. "Here is where you will find Ma."

Rayanna, still lost in the sheer magnitude of what lay before her, blinked back completely dumbfounded by the words, her mind racing.

"Ma is here. She's been waiting." Ashla's voice was gentle, unshaken. "This is where you told Father to put her. You said, *'No one would look here.'*" She smiled softly, sunlight catching in her eyes. *"You were right."*

Rayanna's pulse pounded. She barely registered the way Ashla's hand lifted, pressing lightly over the feathered ink at her arm.

"You knew the truth of what Nissa would become before you were shadow bound. And Ma…she trusted you beyond measure." Ashla leaned in, voice dipping into something reverent. "She is *your* faith bound sister."

The words settled, deeper than bone, deeper than reason.

Ashla's fingers drifted over the inked markings, tracing them like they held a story only she could read. "You'll need different clothes for where we're going," she mused, voice light, as if the thought had just floated into her mind. "So, we'll come back. She has much to tell you."

She swayed inward to gently bump Rayanna's shoulder. "There's much to unravel," she stated matter-of-factly, as if it were the most natural truth in the world. "You've earned that." Ashla offered a playful wink and took a step back, just as Rayanna took a step forward.

There, Rayanna remained—rooted in place, observing all that was possible.

Feet planted. Eyes fixed on the precipice.

The world stretched before her, overwhelming in its beauty, its enormity. Its truth.

And for the first time, she understood—what it truly meant to be bound by faith.

This marks the close of *Moons and Shadows:* Book One—but the journey is far from over.

The unraveling has only just begun, and what lies ahead will take us even deeper.

You're now an official Moonlighter—and with that comes your first glimpse of the *special edition cover,* currently in the works. This edition will feature an exclusive chapter: a bridge between Book One and Book Two. It doesn't quite belong to either…it belongs to *what's coming next.*

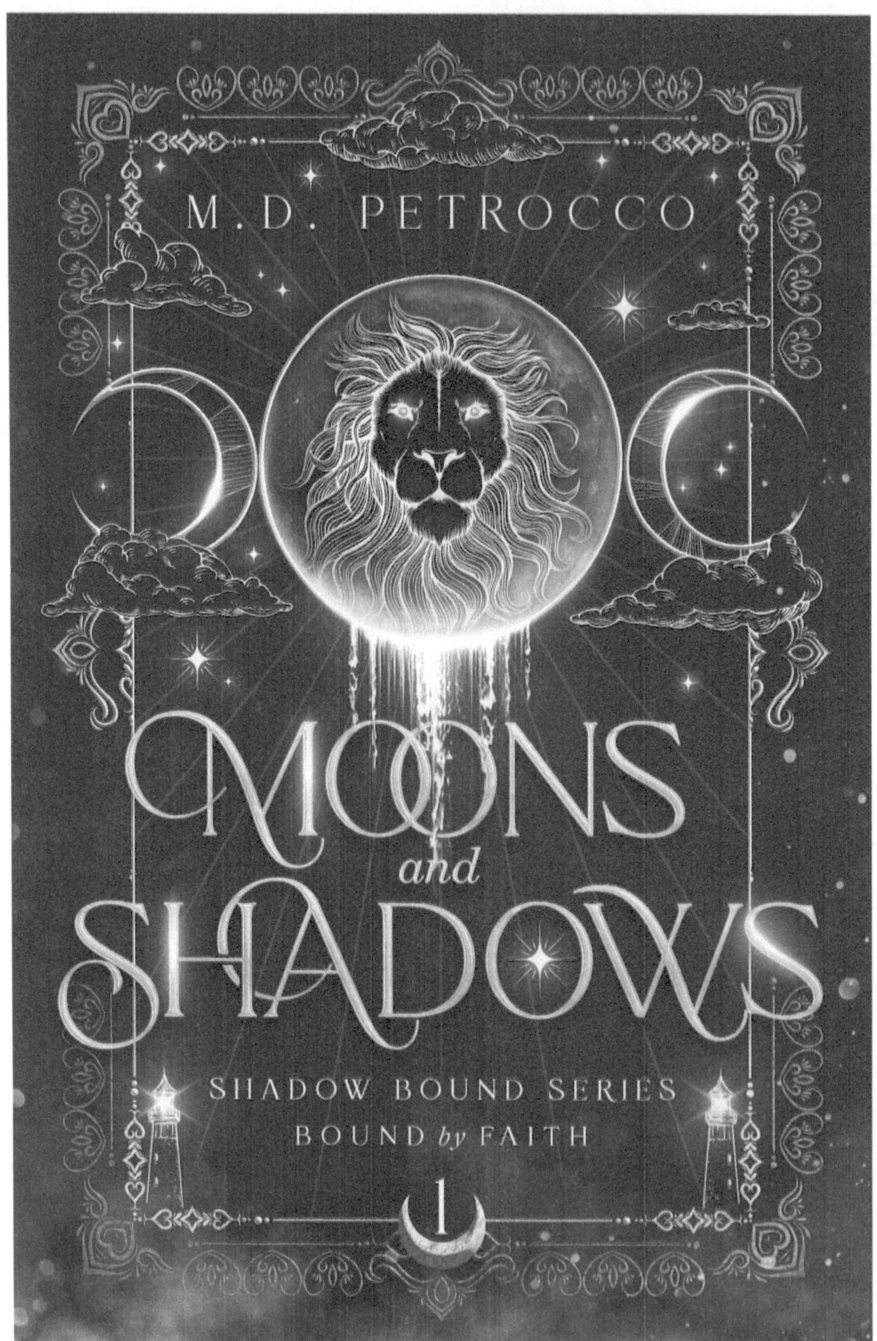

M.D. PETROCCO
MOONS
and
SHADOWS
SHADOW BOUND SERIES
BOUND by FAITH
1

If this story moved you, I'd be honored if you left a review for *Moons and Shadows: Book One*. Reviews are how stories travel—how new readers discover them—and how indie authors like myself, continue to grow this world, one voice at a time.

Amazon Review: Click Here
Goodreads Review: Click Here

What to stay connected?

Join the newsletter, follow **M.D. Petrocco** on socials, and hang out with other Moonlighters like yourself on our Discord.

You'll be the first to know when the special edition drops.

https://www.theshadowboundseries.com/

Sign up. Stay tuned. Let's stay connected!

M.D.Petrocco

About The Author

M.D. Petrocco is a Southern California native, lifelong educator, and passionate storyteller. She currently teaches fourth graders online and writes emotionally rich, cinematic fiction woven with transformation, faith, and quiet power. *Moons and Shadows* is her debut novel and the first in a larger series of interconnected stories.

When she's not writing, she's gaming, going broke with house renovations, or working out—where most of her best plot twists tend to show up. She lives with her husband, a U.S. Air Force Reservist, and their endlessly wiggly co-author pup, Jaxie.

Follow her journey at TheShadowBoundSeries.com

facebook.com/MDPetrocco

x.com/MD_Petrocco

instagram.com/author_m.d.petrocco

threads.com/@author_m.d.petrocco

tiktok.com/@m.d.petrocco

Acknowledgments

When I sit down to write acknowledgements, I go quiet. Not because there are so few to thank—but because there are so many. And the harder I try to name them all, the more I fear I'll forget someone. So, I'm going to do this a bit differently. If you know me…surprise, surprise—right?

To God: For the breath behind every word, the vow I made to honor, and the grace to carry it through.

To my husband, Chris-py-Fish: Thank you for seeing me through all the brokenness—for reminding me that my kinda funny is more than okay, and that questioning reality is not only allowed, but welcome.

To Jaxie—my co-author: Your little wigglybum heard me when my heart broke—and helped me stitch everything back together.

To Hershey—my ultimate truth-seeker and little grunter: The snorts, the dancing, the sideways glances—you always knew when I needed grounding. I'll meet you at the rainbow bridge, forever ever and always.

To my Chief of Operations, D: For your steadfast support, ridiculous research skills, and your ability to answer the phone at all hours of the night—though more often in the early morning. Thank you for helping me laugh when I wanted to cry, and for holding steady when I wanted to crumble. For listening, re-listening, printing, unprinting, and bearing with every moment of unraveling—I'm grateful beyond words.

To Robin—my insanely amazing marketer: Thank you for putting up with my inability to shut up online, for keeping me on brand, navigating my nutcaseness, and delivering those midday chuckles with scarily perfect timing.

To Brandi, my dear friend and editor in arms: Thank you for your sharp eyes, sharper questions, and for laughing through the rewrites, revisions, and chaos. For your faith in the story—and in me—I'll never stop being thankful.

This one is for you, Bill—The bearer of amazing smiles, the best hugs, and the greatest heart of all time. How I will always love you, brother. I say —let's do lunch soon.

To every alpha reader, beta reader, listener, question-asker, challenger, cheerleader, and quiet supporter: Your honesty, your belief, your courage to speak truth—especially when it wasn't easy—shaped these pages.

To the ones who stood in the trenches with me: For the unfiltered thoughts, the late-night cries, the handholding through the hard. For the Mama D/Papa D moments that molded this tale. For the debates over hyphens, the overpriced guacamole, the 'bow moment' and the VLR workout chats that always returned to real life. Thank you for all the read-ings and rereadings (and rereadings…and rereadings). You get the drift. By faith—always.

And to my Moonlighters—those already here, and those still on their way: You are the ones who will make this tale successful. Why? *Because* you took a chance on it. You stumbled into this world—and *chose* to stay. You're the ones who take the time to read this section, who understand that this series is the beginning of an awakening. A realization that—no matter where this story lands—your voices, your courage, your belief… they are the threads pulling at the seams of someone else's darkness, tugging at the heartstrings of those around you, drawing our community toward something brighter.

This—right here—is the return of wonder. Not manufactured, but real. The kind that dares you to dream before breakfast, whispers questions to the wind, and offers a cup of quiet curiosity to someone you've only just met.

I'm so grateful to have found you in Starlight Beach.

This is just the beginning—of remembering how to dream…with me.